Y0-BZN-790

Books by Ken MacLeod

THE FALL REVOLUTION

The Star Fraction
The Stone Canal
The Cassini Division
The Sky Road

THE ENGINES OF LIGHT

Cosmonaut Keep
Dark Light
Engine City

Th

The Engines of Light

Cosmonaut Keep
Dark Light
Engine City

KEN MACLEOD

50 YEARS SFBC SCIENCE FICTION

This is a work of fiction. All the characters and events portrayed in this novel are either products of the author's imagination or are used fictitiously.

COSMONAUT KEEP   Copyright © 2001 by
                    Ken MacLeod
    Publication History: Tor hardcover, May 2001
                         Tor paperback, January 2002

DARK LIGHT   Copyright © 2002 by Ken MacLeod
    Publication History: Tor hardcover, January 2002
                         Tor paperback, January 2003

ENGINE CITY   Copyright © 2003 by Ken MacLeod
    Publication History: Tor hardcover, February 2003

First SFBC Science Fiction Printing: April 2003

All rights reserved, including the right to reproduce this book, or portions thereof, in any form.

Published by arrangement with:
Tor Books
Tom Doherty Associates, LLC
175 Fifth Avenue
New York, NY 10010

Visit the SFBC online at *http://www.sfbc.com*

Visit Tor online at *http://www.tor.com*

Tor® is a registered trademark of Tom Doherty Associates, LLC.

ISBN 0-7394-3298-2

PRINTED IN THE UNITED STATES OF AMERICA

Contents

Cosmonaut Keep

For Iain

and one of the chiefe trees or posts at the right side of the entrance had the barke taken off, and 5 foote from the ground in fayre Capitall letters was graven CROATOAN without any crosse or signe of distresse

Contents

0

Prologue

Y OU'RE NOT HERE. Try to remember this.
Try not to remember where you really are.

You are in a twisty maze of dark corridors, all alike. You slide down the last of them as smoothly as a piston in a syringe, and are then ejected into the suddenly overwhelming open space of the interior. Minutes ago, you saw outer space, the universe, and the whole shebang itself didn't look bigger than this. Outer space is, fundamentally, familiar. It's only the night sky, without the earth beneath your feet.

This place is fundamentally unfamiliar. It's twenty miles long and five high and it's bigger than anything you've ever seen. It's a room with a world inside it.

To them, it's a bright world. To us it's a dark, cold cavern. To them, our most delicate probes would be like some gigantic spaceship hovering on rocket jets over one of our cities, playing searchlights of intolerable brightness across everything. That's why we're seeing it through their eyes, with their instruments, in their colors. The translation of the colors has more to do with emotional tone than the electromagnetic spectrum; a lot of thought, ours and theirs, has gone into this interpretation.

So what you see is a warm, rich green background, speckled with countless tiny, lively shapes in far more colors than you have names for. You think of jewels and hummingbirds and tropical fish. In fact the comparison with rainforest or coral reef is close to the mark. This is an ecosytem more complex than that of the whole Earth. As the viewpoint drifts closer to the surface you recall pictures of cities from the air, or the patterns of silicon circuitry. This, too, is apt: here, the distinction between natural and artificial is meaningless.

The viewpoint zooms in and out: from fractal snowflakes, rainbow-hued, in kaleidoscopic motion, to the vast violet-hazed distances and perspectives of the habitat, making clear the multiplicity and diversity of the place, the absence of repetition. Everything here is unique; there are similarities, but no species.

You can't shut it off; silently, relentlessly, the viewpoint keeps showing you more and more, until the inhuman but irresistible beauty of the alien garden or city or machine or mind harrows your heart. It will not let you go, unless you bless it; then, just as you fall into helpless love with it, it expels you, returning you to your humanity, and the dark.

I

Ship Coming In

A GOD STOOD in the sky high above the sunset horizon, his long white hair streaming in the solar wind. Later, when the sky's color had shifted from green to black, the white glow would reach almost to the zenith, its light outshining the Foamy Wake, the broad band of the Galaxy. At least, it would if the squall-clouds scudding in off the land to the east had cleared by then. Gregor Cairns turned his back on the *C. M. Yonge*'s own foamy wake, and looked past the masts and sheets at the sky ahead. The clouds were blacker and closer than they'd been the last time he'd looked, a few minutes earlier. Two of the lugger's five-man crew were already swinging the big sail around, preparing to tack into the freshening wind.

Much as he'd have liked to help, he knew from experience that he'd only get in the way. He turned his attention back to the tanks and nets in which the day's haul snapped, slapped, or writhed. Trilobites and ostracoderms, mostly, with a silvery smattering of teleostean fish, a slimy slither of sea-slugs, and crusty clusters of shelled molluscs and calcichordates. To Gregor this kind of assemblage was beginning to look incongruous and anachronistic; he grinned at the thought, reflecting that he now knew more about the marine life of Earth's oceans than he did of the planet whose first human settlers had long ago named Mingulay.

His wry smile was caught by his two colleagues, one of whom smiled back. Elizabeth Harkness was a big-boned, strong-featured young woman, about his own age and with a centimeter or two of advantage in height. Under a big leather hat her rough-cut black hair was blown forward over her ruddy cheeks. Like Gregor, she wore a heavy sweater, oilskins, rubber boots, and gauntlets. She squatted a couple of meters away on the laden afterdeck, probing tangles of holdfast with a rusty old knife, expertly slinging the separated molluscs, calcichordates, and float-wrack into their appropriate tanks.

"Come on," she said, "back to work."

"Aye," said Gregor, stooping to cautiously heave a ten-kilogram trilobite, scrabbling and snapping, into a water-filled wooden trough. "The faster we get this lot sorted, the more time for drinks back at the port."

"Yeah, so don't stick with the easy stuff." She flung some surplus mussels to the seabats that screamed and wheeled around the boat.

"Huh." Gregor grunted and left the relatively rugged trilobites to fend for themselves in the netting and creels while he pitched in to deal with the small shelly fauna. The vessel rolled, slopping salt water from the troughs and tanks, and then freshwater from the sky hissed onto the deck as they met the squall. He and Elizabeth worked on through it, yelling and laughing as their sorting became less and less discriminatory in their haste.

"As long as they don't *eat* each other. . . ."

The third student on the boat squatted opposite the two humans, knees on a level with his broad cheekbones, oblivious to the rain pelting his hairless head, and to the rivulets that trickled down his neck then over the seamless collar of his dull gray insulation-suit. The nictitating membranes of his large black eyes, and an occasional snort from his small nostrils or spit from his thin-lipped, inch-wide mouth were the only indications that the downpour affected him at all. His hands each had three long fingers and one long thumb; each digit came equipped with a claw that made a knife, for this task at least, quite unnecessary.

Gregor eyed him covertly, admiring the machinelike ease with which the long fingers sorted through the heaps; tangles ahead of them, neatly separated columns behind; the butchering strength and surgical skill and clinical gentleness of thumb and claw and palm. Then, answering some accurate intuition, the saur rocked back on his heels, washed his hands in the last of the rain, and stood up with his part of the task complete.

Elizabeth and Gregor looked at each other across a diminished area of decking on which nothing but stains and shreds of wrack remained. Elizabeth blinked wet lashes.

"Done," she said, standing up and shaking rain off her hat.

"Great." Gregor heaved himself upright and did likewise, joining the other two at the stern rail. They leaned on it, gazing out at the reddening sky in which the god glowed brighter. The highest clouds in the sky—far higher than the squall-clouds—shone with a peculiar mother-of-pearl rainbow effect, a rare phenomenon that had even the sailors murmuring in amazed appreciation.

Behind them the big sail came rattling down, and the engine coughed into life as the steersman took them in toward the harbor. The cliffs of a hundred-meter-high headland, crowned with a craggy castle, the Keep of Aird, rose on the port side; lower green hills and fields spread out to starboard. Ahead the lights were coming on in Kyohvic, the main port of the straggling seaboard republic known as the Heresiarchy of Tain.

"Good work, Salasso," Gregor said. The saur turned and nodded gravely, his nostrils and lips minutely twitching in his species' equivalent of a smile. Then the great black eyes—their sides easily visible in profile—returned to scanning the sea.

Salasso's long arm and long forefinger pointed.

"*Teuthys,*" he hissed.

"Where?" Elizabeth cried, delighted. Gregor shaded his eyes and stared along the white wake and across the dark waves, so much of it there was, until he saw a darker silhouette rise, humping out of the water about a mile away. For a moment, so it remained, an islet in the deep.

"Could be just a whale—" he murmured.

"*Teuthys,*" the saur insisted.

The hump sank back and then a vast shape shot out of the surface, rising in an apparently impossible arc on a brief white jet; a glimpse of splayed tentacles behind the black wedge of the thing, then a huge splash as it planed back into the water. It did it again, and this time it wasn't black—in its airborne second it glowed and flashed with flickering color. And it wasn't alone—another kraken had joined it. They leaped together, again and then again, twisting and sporting. With a final synchronized leap that lasted two seconds, and a multicolored flare that lit the water like fireworks, the display ended.

"Oh, gods above," Elizabeth breathed. The saur's mouth was a little black O, and his body trembled. Gregor stared at where the krakens had played, awed but wondering. That they were playing he was certain, without knowing why. There were theories that such gratuitous expenditures of energy by krakens were some kind of mating display, or even ritual, but like most biologists Gregor regarded such hypotheses as beneath consideration.

"Architeuthys extraterrestris sapiens," he said slowly. "Masters of the galaxy. Having fun."

The saur's black tongue flickered, then his lips once more became a thin line.

"We do not know," he said, his words perhaps weightier, to Gregor, than he intended. But the man chose to treat them lightly, leaning out and sharing an aching, helpless grin with the woman.

"We don't know," he agreed, "but one day we'll find out." He jerked his face upward at the flare of white spreading up the sky. "Even the gods play, I'm sure of that. Why else would they leave their . . . endless peace between the stars, and plunge between our worlds and swing around the sun?"

Salasso's neck seemed to contract a little; he averted his eyes from the sky, shivering again. Elizabeth laughed, not noticing or perhaps not reading the saur's subtle body-language. "Gods above, you can talk, man!" she said. "You think we'll ever know?"

"Aye, I do," said Gregor. "That's *our* play."

"Speak for yourself, Cairns, I know what mine is after a long hard day, and I'm"—she glanced over her shoulder—"about ten minutes from starting it with a long hard drink!"

Gregor shrugged and smiled, and they all relaxed, gazing at the sea and chatting. Then, as the first houses of the harbor town slipped by, one of the crewmen startled them with a loud, ringing cry:

"Ship coming in!"

Everybody on the boat looked up at the sky.

James Cairns stood, huddled in a fur cloak, on the castle's ancient battlement and gazed at the ship as it slid across the sky from the east, a glowing zeppelin at least three hundred meters long. Down the dark miles of the long valley—lighting the flanks of the hill—and over the clustered houses of the town it came, its course as steady and constant as a monorail bus. As it passed almost directly overhead at a thousand meters, Cairns was briefly amused to see that among the patterns picked out in lights on its sides were the squiggly signature-scribble of Coca-Cola; the double-arched golden *M;* the brave checkered banner of Microsoft; the Stars and Stripes; and the thirteen stars—twelve small yellow stars and one central red star on a blue field—of the European Union.

He presumed the display was supposed to provide some kind of reassurance. What it gave him—and, he did not doubt, scores of other observers—was a pang of pride and longing so acute that the shining shape blurred for a second. The old man blinked and sniffed, staring after the craft as its path sloped implacably seaward. When it was a kilometer or so out to sea, and a hundred meters above the water, a succession of silver lens-shaped objects scooted away from its sides, spinning clear and then heading back the way the ship had come. They came sailing in toward the port as the long ship's hull kissed the waves and settled, its flashing lights turning the black water to a rainbow kaleidoscope. Other lights, underwater and much smaller but hardly less bright, joined it in a colorful flurry.

Cairns turned his attention from the ship to its gravity skiffs; some swung down to land on the docks below, most skittered overhead and floated down, rocking like falling leaves, to the grassy ridge of the long hill that sloped down from the landward face of the castle. James strolled to the other side of the roof to watch. Somewhere beneath his feet, a relief generator hummed. Floodlights flared, lighting up the approach and glinting off the steely sides of the skiffs.

Almost banally after such a bravura arrival, the dozen or so skiffs had extended and come to rest on spindly telescoped legs; in their undersides hatches opened and stairladders emerged, down which saurs and humans trooped as casually as passengers off an airship. Each skiff gave forth two or three saurs, twice or thrice that number of humans; about a hundred in all walked slowly up the slope and onto the smoother grass of the castle lawns, tramping across it to be greeted by, and to mingle with, the castle's occupants. The gray-suited saurs looked more spruce than the humans, most of whom were in sea-boots and oilskins, dripping wet. The humans toward the rear were hauling little wheeled carts behind them, laden with luggage.

He felt a warm arm slide through the side-slit of his cloak and clasp his waist.

"Aren't you going down?" Margaret asked.

Cairns turned and looked down at his wife's eyes, which shone within a crinkle of crow's-feet as she smiled, and laid his right arm, suddenly heavy, across her shoulders.

"In a minute," he said. He sighed. "You know, even after all this time, that's still the sight that leaves me most dizzy."

Margaret chuckled darkly. "Yeah, I know. It gets me that way too."

Cairns knew that if he dwelt on the strangeness of the sight, the feeling of unreality could make him physically nauseous: *la nausée,* Sartre's old existential insecurity—Cairns wondered, not for the first time, how the philosopher would have coped with a situation as meta-physically disturbing as this.

L'enfer, c'est les autres.

He turned around resolutely, taking Margaret along with him, and together they set off down from the castle's heights to meet the bourgeois with a smile. Under his left elbow he held the furled and folded flag, the star-circled banner which he'd lowered, as was his custom, at sunset. Behind him the steel rope clanged on the mast, bare against the windy night.

They descended the spiral stair, down steps a meter and a half wide and about thirty centimeters high, each of whose treads had been worn down over millenia into a terrifyingly deep normal distribution curve, as though the stone itself were sagging. The iron handrail around the central well was only centuries old, and at the right height for human hands; the electric lighting, though dim, was tuned for human eyes.

James and Margaret kept close to the wall as they descended. Margaret went first, clattering and chatting merrily; James followed, half listening, the rest of his attention devoted to the many fossils embedded in the stones of the wall's interior cladding, some of which generations of curious or reverent fingertips of successive species of the castle's occupants had polished to a mahogany sheen. He trailed his own fingers across the fragmentary remains of fish and dragons and sea-monsters and other organisms in a bizarrely Noachic, diluvial conglomerate whose ordering had little to do with their evolutionary succession; as always when he climbed up or down these steps, the line he'd used on his children and grandchildren came to mind: this castle had been built by giants, mined by dwarfs, stormed by goblins, and left to ghosts long before people on Earth had laid so much as one stone upon another.

Sounds and smells echoing or wafting from below intensified as the old couple descended. The arrival of the merchant ship might or might not have been expected, but the keep's staff planned routinely for such a contingency. For this first evening nothing much was expected but hot water, hot food, and a lot of drinking and some kind of bed to stagger off to afterward: merchants just off a ship were usually in no condition for formal negotiations or celebrations. The saurs would require even less.

The exits from the spiral stair went past, their numbers as fixed in James's mind as the numerals on a lift's display. He and Margaret stepped out on the ground floor—the stair still had many levels to go, down into the rock—and made their way around several zigzag turns of narrow defensive corridor. Antique space-suits stood in artfully placed ambuscade niches.

The corridor opened to the castle's main hall, a cavernous space hung with retrofitted electric lights, its fifteen-meter-high walls covered with carpets and tapestries, oil-paintings of members of the Cosmonaut Families, heads and hides of dinosaurs, and decoratively arranged displays of the light artillery with which these gigantic quarry had been sportingly slain.

The wide doors stood open; the hall's blazing fire and more practical electric radiators did little to repel the chill inward swirl of evening air. The merchants, their saur companions, and their servants were already mingled with the welcoming crowd that had gathered from all quarters of the castle. Mingled, but easily distinguishable: for this evening at least, the castle's occupants—Cosmonauts and stewards and seneschals and servants—outdid the merchants in the style and spectacle of their attire. In days to come, the most senior of the Cosmonauts and the richest merchants in Kyohvic would be easily outshone by their visitors' youngest child or lowliest page; their present plebeian appearance, though partly dictated by the necessities of interstellar travel, was for all its apparent casualness part of a protocol—setting themselves conspicuously below their hosts—whose invariance James Cairns had observed many times before.

Right now the new arrivals had discarded their protective clothing in a careless heap in the doorway's broad vestibule, and were padding around in woollen socks and likewise warm gear, shaking or kissing hands with all and sundry, smiling and laughing and slapping shoulders. Children scampered and scooted, chased by their own servants, tactfully redirected from the big room's many exits by swiftly posted stewards. Through it all the saurs drifted, their domed heads bobbing in the throng like stray balloons.

Hal Driver, the Security Man, was in the center of the pressing crowd, already deep in hearty converse with a mature, burly man who had "merchant prince" written all over him, albeit he was dressed like a trawlerman. Red hair sprang in a great shock from his head; freckles spattered his broad-cheeked, flat-nosed face; his rich voice boomed above the babble, his asides to Driver now and again dropping to a confidential murmur.

Margaret nudged James with a confidential murmur of her own.

"Didn't take them long to figure out who's in charge here."

·　　·　　·

"Aren't you going up to the keep?" Elizabeth asked.

Gregor finished hosing the scales and slime off his oilskins and hung them in the locker. "Nah," he said, pulling his boots off. "Time enough for that when they have the big bash. Won't be for a day or two yet." He sat on the low fold-down bench, tugging off his thick socks and stuffing them in the boots, then carefully eased his feet into his leather shoes. "Fancy coming along yourself?"

Elizabeth reddened. "Oh, that's nice of you—thanks, but I just don't know if I can."

"Well, the invitation's open," Gregor said, oblivious to her momentary embarrassment, and turned to the saur. "How about you?"

The slow-swinging electric light's reflection made tiny arcs in Salasso's black eyes as the saur waited patiently in the converted hold's low narrow doorway. His clothing needed no cleaning or adjustment. Nor, Gregor suddenly realized with a blush of his own, would it need any possibly expensive alternative for social occasions.

He ducked to lace up his shoes as Salasso said he would certainly come along.

"Don't worry about, uh, dressing up," he called after Elizabeth as she stepped up to the deck. "You know what the merchants are like, they wouldn't know what the fashion is here anyway."

"I'll think about it," she told him, not looking back.

Up on deck the three students thanked Renwick, the skipper, who was making the last check of the boat before leaving it for the night. The specimens, safe in their various containers, would keep until the morning, when they'd be hauled off to the Marine Biology Station.

"Pint at the Bailie's?" Elizabeth asked Renwick.

The skipper shook his head. "Nah, I'll have a short with the crew. Last seen heading for the Shipwright, I think. See you tomorrow, folks."

The harbor was so old it might have been natural, but it was merely pre-human. The quarter-mile–long mole was built of the same hard metamorphic rock as the castle's exterior walls, and was reckoned to have been blasted and lifted from the harbor basin in ancient times, either by the brute force and primitive ingenuity of multitudes, or by the laser lances and gravity sleds of visitors from outer space. It formed one curved arm of the harbor's embrace, the other being provided by the headland's cliffs. Beyond it, the rocky outcrops gave way to a long, white sandy beach, which broke up in the distance to tussocked dunes.

Gregor scrambled up the rusty rungs of the ladder and out onto the mole. A few hundred meters across the water, on the harbor's central docks, a small knot of humans and saurs had gathered around the landed skiffs. Gregor glanced at them incuriously and turned to gazing again at the sky as he waited for the others to join him.

The rainbow clouds had dispersed. Gabriel, the evening and morning star, burned like a lamp low in the west, its light outshone by the god standing higher in the sky, and by the auroral flicker of the starship floating on the sea beneath it. High above them all hung the icy gleam of Raphael and the tiny spark of Ariel, its moon; and—following the ecliptic around to the east—the bright sickle of the new moon, beyond which Gog and Magog, the ringed gas giants of the outer system, glowered like a monster's eyes.

Crossing the sky from north to south, alone in its polar orbit, deserted for two hundred years, went the old ship from home. To Gregor, tracking it with a rapidly blinking eye, the *Bright Star* seemed a stranger and more evocative sight than all the familiar constellations—the Musketeer, the Squid, the Angel's Wing, and the rest—that straddled the sky on either side of the Foamy Wake.

And, ironically, more difficult for humans to reach.

The two humans and the saur walked briskly along the mole and into the waterfront streets of Kyohvic, turning right along a bright-lit, cobbled esplanade to the Bailie's Bar, its sign a jolly, pint-quaffing grandee in plumed hat and lace cravat. Inside, it was long, low-ceilinged, its plastered walls decorated with naive murals and shelves and brackets supporting harpoons and stuffed ichthyosaurs; its tables and bar counters half filled with men just off the boats and ships. It was that kind of place, at this time of the evening; later, the sawdust would be swept up, the tables wiped, and a cleaner crowd would pour in from the shows or the eating-houses; but for now it reeked of sweat and fish, yeast and baccy and hemp, its dim light glinting with the glitter of glasses and pots and the glazed, lidded gaze of men relaxing thoughtfully over their long pipes. The regulars recognized the students with a nod and a smile; others, seamen in from another port, frowned at the saur. As Gregor waved Elizabeth and Salasso to a seat and strode to the bar, he heard hissed mutterings about "snakes." He ignored it; the saur himself turned a black, blank glare in that direction; and, out of the corner of his eye, Gregor noticed the most vocal objector getting an urgent word in his ear from one of the barmaids.

Gregor ordered pints for himself and Elizabeth, and a tall billican of hot fish-stock for Salasso. As he waited for the stout to settle and the thin soup to be brought back to the boil, he found himself worrying again about the unerring aim that so often connected his foot with his mouth. The awkwardness, he was sure, came not from the difference between the sexes but from the perhaps greater communicative gulf of class. Elizabeth Harkness was of predominantly local descent, albeit of good family, some of whose members were prominent in the Scoffer heresiarchy; his own ancestry, give or take a good deal of exogamy with the locals, came from the *Bright Star*'s crew.

From the bar's mirror behind the bottles his own face scrutinized him: the same thin nose and grim mouth and long black hair swept back from a high hairline that he'd seen in generations of portraits. He felt their presence like a weight on his back.

"That'll be five shillings, Greg."

"Oh!" He blinked and shook his head; with that slight start recognizing the barmaid as Andrea Peden, one of the undergraduate students whose work he'd occasionally supervised. Her rippling auburn hair was loose on her shoulders rather than tied back, and he'd only ever seen her in a lab overall, but still. "Uh, thanks, Peden. And, let's see, an ounce of hemp as well, please." Alcohol was not a saur vice—it was a physiological difference; they assimilated it without intoxication—but hemp had definitely taken with the species, centuries ago.

"Another sixpence, then," the girl said. She glanced around. "And we're off-study, so first names, okay, Greg?"

"Ah, sure, Andrea, thanks."

He just knew that if he commented on her working here it would come across as yet another clumsy reminder of the difference between his economic status and that of most other students, so he forbore.

Back at the table he raised his glass soberly to Elizabeth as Salasso nodded almost imperceptibly at both of them and took from a thigh pocket a thin aluminum tube and a long-stemmed bone pipe, its bowl elaborately carved. The saur sucked up fish-stock through the tube and began filling the pipe from the paper twist.

"Hah!" he sighed after a minute, his mouth opening, snakelike, suprisingly wide and showing little fangs. Gregor winced slightly at the momentary waft of carnivore breath. A thin brass rectangle appeared between Salasso's long fingers like a conjuring trick, and he applied its faint flame to the tamped hemp and puffed. "Hah! That's better!"

"Any idea where the ship's from?" Elizabeth asked, as though Gregor might know. But it was Salasso who answered.

"Nova Babylonia," he said, and inhaled on the pipe. His lashless eyelids made a rare blink, and his third eyelid—the nictitating membrane—was flickering more rapidly than usual. "Of the fleet of the family Tenebre." His voice was reedy and harsh. He passed the pipe to Elizabeth.

"Recognize it, do you?" she asked, puffing for politeness' sake.

Gregor was a little disappointed by her seizing on this point. To hell with how the saur knew about it, the ship's origin was what mattered. Ships from Nova Babylonia were rare. From his twenty years, he could recall two such visits.

"Yesss," said Salasso, leaning his narrow shoulders against the seat's tall back. He drew on the metal straw again, hot colors briefly flowing in the gray-green skin of his cheeks. "I have seen that ship . . . many times."

Elizabeth gave Gregor a skeptical look as she handed over the pipe. Gregor returned her a warning glance and just nodded at Salasso, keeping his face carefully expressionless as he sucked the last vile embers of the hemp. He tapped them out on the floor and began refilling the pipe.

"So you might know some of the shore crew?" he asked.

Salasso's shoulders lifted. "It is very possible. If so, I'll find out when I go to the reception at the castle." His great eyes closed for a moment. "Of the family Tenebre, perhaps a few. The human generations pass."

Gregor struck a match on his boot and relit, the cannabis rush roaring in his ears like a burn in spate. He heard Elizabeth's light laugh.

"This I have to see!" she said. "For this, I would come to your party as I am, rags and holes and boots and all!"

"Yeah, you do that," he said warmly. "Come as a scientist."

"Oh, thanks," said Elizabeth indignantly, then giggled. Gregor returned the pipe to the saur, who smoked the rest of it but said no more, his body still, his mind gliding into a typically saurian trance. The two humans watched in silence for a couple of minutes, supping at their pints until the pipe clattered from Salasso's fingers onto the table.

Gregor leaned across and stroked the dry, warm skin of the saur's face. No response was forthcoming.

"He's offline," he remarked.

"Another pint while we wait?" Elizabeth asked.

"Aye, thanks."

No time, or a long time, seemed to pass before she returned.

"Do you think he meant that literally?" she asked, as he settled in again. The saur's head, its great eyes still open, suddenly lolled sideways

23

against her shoulder. She patted it. "Well, that's me here for the duration!"

"About twenty minutes, I reckon," Gregor said abstractedly. "Um, how could he not have meant it literally?"

Elizabeth leaned forward on one elbow, careful not to disturb Salasso, gazing with what seemed like half-stoned fixity into Gregor's eyes. "You know. Metaphorically. Might be that their families, or lines, or whatever, know each other from way back." She laughed. "Do you really think our friend here is that old? He doesn't *act* like it."

"We all know the saurs live a long time."

"Supposedly."

Gregor looked straight back at her, narrow-eyed. "The saurs say it, and I've no reason to doubt it."

Elizabeth nodded slowly. "Aye, well, sometimes I wonder if the saurs are . . . ancient people. That they are what people become, if they live long enough."

Gregor laughed. "It's a nice idea. But the saurs, they're obviously reptilian—or saurian, if you want to be exact!"

"And so? The reptilian genes could still be in us, and only expressed much later in life than people normally live."

"You might have a point there," Gregor conceded, not entertaining the idea for a second. "Nobody's ever seen a saur dissected, after all, or even a picture of a saur skeleton."

He shook the last of the crumbled leaf into Salasso's ornate pipe. That moment when saurs got well and truly whacked by the hemp was the only time they'd open up for a few seconds, and they'd let slip weird things then. But that might just be the drug talking.

"Has anyone ever asked for one?" Elizabeth wondered aloud.

Gregor shook his head. "And I'll lay good money Salasso won't answer any questions we ask him when he comes back to the land of the living."

"Hmm, I wouldn't even try. He'd be touchy about it."

"There you go."

This was an old subject. The saurs' individualism and prickly sense of privacy made humans look like some kind of garrulous, gossiping animal that hunted in packs. They might all look the same to a casual or hostile eye—though here, Gregor had found, familiarity made their distinctions apparent—but their personalities were unpredictably diverse. The few traits they shared included a ravenous thirst for knowledge and a great reluctance to divulge any. Their language, their sexuality, their social relationships, their politics and philosophies—if any—were as mysterious as they must have been to the first terrified savage they'd encountered, many millennia back in humanity's history.

"Well," Gregor said, lighting up, "the least we can do is smoke the last of his weed. He sure won't be needing it."

"Hmm." Elizabeth puffed quickly and returned the pipe. "No more for me, thanks. I want to keep my head clear to write up some notes."

Gods in orbit, his colleague was beginning to look attractive as her merry eyes stared with fathomless pupils into his mind, even though her face and frame were a little more . . . angular than he usually took to in a woman. . . . That girl Peden at the bar—now, she was quite something. . . .

Elizabeth laughed, and Gregor had a sudden suspicion, sobering as a cold wave over the deck, that he'd actually said what he'd just been thinking . . . but no, his dry lips were still stuck to the stem of the pipe.

He licked his lips, overcome by another effect of the weed: sudden hunger. "What?"

"The way you look, Gregor, I wouldn't advise you to bother writing any notes tonight. They won't make much sense in the morning."

Her voice, or the vibration of her laughter, made Salasso stir and sit abruptly upright, blinking hard and looking around. Elizabeth stroked his hand, lightly grasped Gregor's for a moment of what he took to be stoned affection, and rose.

"Good night, chaps," she said, and was gone before Gregor could ask her if she had any plans to *eat.*

2

Resident Alien

I WAKE WITH my ears ringing and a light flashing in my right eye. It takes a licked forefinger to ungum my eyelid enough for the two deliberate blinks that put the incoming video on hold. Then I tug at my left earlobe to take the audio call.

"Yes?" I say testily, sitting up. It's some ungodly hour like eleven in the morning. The bed's a mess and the whisky I incautiously drank while listening to music after coming home from the pub last night is making my head ache.

As soon as I hear the coins drop I know it's trouble. England is the only place outside of sub-Saharan Africa that still has coin-operated payphones. My friends use them not because they aren't bugged—they bloody are—but to signal an unspoken message: Yes, trouble.

"Hi, Matt?" says a familiar American voice. "It's Jadey. Can you meet me at the Market? Say around five?"

Jadey's our local Yank. She has resident-alien status as an exchange student, or something, but spends most of her time running ops for the resistance down south. I've never been sure quite who she really works for, but I've always been happy to modify the software for the hardware fixes she takes with her on visits to London. My little hack for the face-recognition neural net was a rush job, but, like Jadey said, it beats balaclavas.

"Yeah, sure," I say, trying to sound casual. I have a bit of a thing about Jadey; hopeless, given who she probably is and what she probably does, and anyway she's away a lot.

"See you there," she says. The money runs out in a dribble of *bleep*s.

I blink my eye again and patch the other call over to the wallscreen.

26

I peel the phone from my cheek, annoyed that I fell asleep with it on, throw it in the trash and look at the screen. It's an offer from one of the agencies, and I check it out while scratching absently at the weal the phone left.

It looks like another quick and dirty contract job for the European Space Agency; it'll involve digging down several levels of emulation running on top of each other to find a bug in the underlying operating system; which, knowing my luck, will probably turn out to be MS-DOS. I'll have to rope in an old programmer for that, preferably one who hasn't been a paid-up lifelong member of the Linux jihad.

I put in a bid—costing and schedule—making sure to allocate myself about double the time the job should take to do properly. The agency bounces back instantly with a schedule that'll give me about half the time I'd need to do the job properly. But the fee should cover the code-geek subcontract on top of my other expenses and my own day rate, so I take it.

Software project management has always been like herding cats. So I've been told, anyway, by old managers, between snorts of coke in the trendy snow-bars where they blow their well-hedged pension funds. In their day, though, the cats were human, or at least the kind of guys who are now code-geeks. These days, the *programmers* are programs, as are the systems analysts. My job as a project manager is to assemble a convincing suite of AIs—not untried, but not too far behind the curve, either—then let loose marketing strategy webcrawlers to parade their skills before the endless bored beauty-contest of the agencies' business 'bots, take the contracts and ride herd on the whole squabbling mob when a deal comes in.

You need something almost like people skills to do it, but you need to be practically borderline Asperger's syndrome to develop these skills with AI. And when you need code-geeks for the bottom-level stuff, you need to be something of a sociable animal after all. It's a sufficiently rare combination to be worth more than the average wage. I'm an artist, not a technician. It pays the bills.

This contract is for a manufacturing control interface for ESA's asteroid mining project. The asteroid in question is 10049 Lora, a stray piece of junk between the orbits of Earth and Mars, about thirty kilometers long, with a low albedo—currently, I vaguely remember seeing, swinging by within a few million miles of Earth; detected in the 2020s, reached by an ESA probe about ten years later, and found to be a carbonaceous chondrite. A potential source of immensely useful organics for space settlement, if that ever comes up. ESA's experimental mining station, built around a ship called the *Marshall Titov*, has been running for years, with notoriously poor returns: Think groundnut scheme, think *Mir*, think bottomless pit.

I stare at it for a few minutes, flicking my thumb to tab down the pages, and down: The background info seems excessive, but (I check) it's indexed and searchable. The actual spec is large but manageable. I can handle it, but not before breakfast.

My flat is on the twenty-fifth floor of one of the new Housing Authority high-rises at the top of Leith Walk. The fabric of the place is showing its age—five years, about the expected half-life of new-tech constructions—but for four rooms it's cheap. I traverse all of them, ambling from the bedroom through the living-room to the kitchen via the bathroom. It's in the bathroom that I conclude that I look like shit.

In the kitchen I chew a brace of aspirins and drink coffee and crunch my way through a bowl of cereal. I scroll through the morning's news without much attention, skipping channels. I gaze unseeing through the south-facing kitchen window at the castle and the tall towers of the South Bridge. The sky is blue and the clouds are white, whipping across from left to right, east to west. Their steady procession cools my mind.

The project keeps me busy all afternoon. Whenever I need a patch from outside the E.U.—and let's face it, you do—the connections turn bumpy. At four-thirty, bug-eyed and sore-jointed from jollying the AIs along, I save the story-so-far to a satellite uplink and hit the street.

Waverley Market was a posh bijou shopping-center until the third week of the Ural-Caspian Oil War, by which time Edinburgh was irretrievably enemy territory. A U.S. cruise missile missed the railhead and took out the eastern end of Princes Street, and with it the Scottish government offices which had probably been the real target all along. These days it's a fine example of the role of the flea market in a Socialist Democracy. I browse the electronics and biotech stalls in the late-afternoon, late-summer sunlight, shoulders hunched in a parka—Scottish Augusts have been a bit chilly since the Gulf Stream downshifted—and elbows on guard against the crowds of tourists jostling for the bootleg foreign tech. The Edinburgh Festival is still the biggest in the world, and pulls in tourists from all over the E.U.: I see a Siberian woman pounce on a sliver of nerve-driver memory from Brazil, an Italian couple arguing over whether they can afford a Raytheon eyepatch—months obsolete in America, years ahead of our stuff.

Our stuff . . . I can smell it on the wind. New tech, wet tech: bioelectronic manufacture, with its whiff of acetone and alcohol, Edinburgh's familiar technology of brewery and distillery and refinery expanded to produce a whole new range of hardware kit, as cheap and disposable and recyclable as paper. All very nice and sustainable, but the old hard tech of America's fossil/metal economy still has the technical edge.

Jadey finds me with her usual alarming ease. I look up and there she is, leaning over the stall. Cropped blonde hair, blue eyes, heat-exchanger tank top, arm-warmers, and a mil-green nylon pod-skirt. She has one of those girlie versions of a rucksack on her back. Her tired smile matches her London-train drained look.

"Border hassles?" I ask.

She shakes her head as she catches my elbow and begins steering me toward a coffee stall. "Nah, but man, I've had hassles." Talking's safe enough, here; the buzz from the gadgetry on sale jams all but the most dedicated surveillance. Most of the street-cameras and other sensors in Scotland and the rest of the E.U. get regularly fucked over by hackers anyway. The arms race between surveillance and sabotage is Darwinian, a Red Queen's Race in which the hackers are usually a whisker ahead. It's a bit tougher down south, where the authorities use heavier, harder apps and hacking is more effectively suppressed by reverse social engineering. Hence my specialist devices for Jadey.

She says, "The gear didn't work—"

"What?"

"Not your fault. Something's changed. Most of the cells down there got the old dawn-knock this morning. It's like, shit, all our codes are being cracked or something. I think they're even on to me—the cops at King's Cross just waved me through with that knowing smile they have."

Jadey lives in the cracks between jurisdictions: U.S.A. and E.U., the Scottish Republic and the Former United Kingdom; within the F.U.K. she plays off the jealousies and incompetences of the contending post-war authorities—the English, the Russkis, and the blue helmets.

I buy two paper thimbles of espresso and we sit on a bit of broken wall, sipping.

"You mean the resistance is getting smashed as we speak?"

She stares down, fiddles with the drawstring at her skirt's hem, looks up sadly. "That's about the size of it, Matt. I gotta get out."

"Okay," I say, with a pang. "What do you need?"

"New ID. Oh, not a retinal job or anything, just a new passport and history. If they're going for bio checks I'll be picked up before I've had time to fiddle a DNA hack anyway."

"Hey, don't sound so fatalistic. You're depressing me." I jump up. "Tell you what. Let me get you something to eat, then we can hit the Darwin and see what's on offer. I've got a job of my own to check out there, anyway."

"Great," she says. "McDonald's."

"What?"

She glances back, already heading up the path to the street.

"Last place the cops'll come looking for an American."

As we edge through the crowd in the Darwin's Arms I check the nasal readout in my left eye. Thank God for smokeless cigarettes—they make pheromone analysis a breeze. You try pulling that trick in Turkey, or Azerbaijan, and you get botanical data, not psychological. The atmosphere's oddly tense, with an undercurrent of brittle hilarity. Now that I notice it on the air, I can pick it up in the sound as well. Jadey, walking behind me and leaving a spreading wake of lust (I can see the little red line humping up on the readout), must have caught it too.

"Edgy tonight, huh?"

Her American accent is making me weak in the knees.

"No kidding." I plant my elbows on the bar and finger out a card. "What you having?"

"Cally Eighty."

I grin my appreciation of her good taste, and order two pints. "Let's take it easy," I say. "Play it cool. We're safe here anyway, but . . ."

She eyes me across the rim of her raised glass. "Okay, cheers."

We lean against the bar and scan the room as though looking for seats.

"Bit crowded, too," says Jadey.

"Uh-huh," I reply. "Odd. It's only six o'clock, and the place doesn't usually get jammed until about eleven, our time. That's when the eastern U.S. hits five P.M."

"Yes. And?"

"Well, U.S. office hours are peak time for legacy system problems. Keeps our old guys busy most of the afternoon and evening."

"Thought programming was a young man's game," Jadey says wryly.

"That was in the old days," I say, still idly examining the pub's clientele. I hope that's how it looks, anyway. The old crowd are in far earlier than usual, and so are the new crowd, the young managers; and more of each than I've ever seen in the place at the same time. "Still is, in a way, for the sort of stuff I do. But programming as such is so tied up with legacy systems that it's practically a branch of archaeology. Even the new stuff is something you can keep pace with past your twenties. You've heard of Moore's Law?"

She shakes her head, outstaring some geezer who's looking at her a bit too long.

"Not surprised," I say. "It was the projection that processing power got twice as fast for half the price every eighteen months. That curve went flat a long time ago." I laugh briefly, taking in the sights. "Just as well, or this lot would be as gods."

"Scary thought," Jadey agrees. She looks into her pint, looks up. "Can we talk?"

"Hmm," I haw. The pub's secure, that's its selling point—they put electronic countermeasures in the dust—but I'm not feeling very secure myself.

"You got some reason to be here? Apart from what I want, that is."

"Yeah, sure," I say, realizing she isn't being paranoid. Tradecraft: Always have a legit cover story. I idly ramble on for a bit about the ESA contract, then—

"Wait a minute," I tell her. I've finally caught the eye of the guy I seek, and beckon him. Jason, long and lean, black-clad, hottest card-sharp in the city, picks up his drink and sidles over. "Let's get inside a game."

The three of us amble over to the only vacant games-table and pull on gloves and glasses. The table tunes in and suddenly becomes much broader and a faint, undecided gray. The rest of the pub becomes abruptly remote.

"What game d'you want?" Jadey asks, fingertips poised over the keypad.

"Quantum Pool," says Jason.

Jadey clicks the choice, and the table shimmers to green. The air becomes smoky, layered thick under a low ceiling. Slow light illuminates the pool-table's green baize and colored balls. Outside that light, close by, in a bar that doesn't much resemble the one in the Darwin's

Arms, the barmaid is chatting to one of the men who leans or perches at the counter. Somewhere a games-machine jangles, and on a jukebox Jagger sings "Sympathy for the Devil." A little farther away—if you look along certain angles between gaps in the walls and partitions—is another bar, another pool-table, other machines and women and men: the place goes on, repeated as though in mirrors. No windows; but there are doors. Beyond one of them, as though through the wrong end of a telescope, is the real bar we're in. Beyond the rest are bars which I hope are fake, but they add to the authentic Old World atmosphere.

I reach under the table and pull out the Schrödinger box, within which a virtual cat's virtual life is at the mercy of a randomizer linked to a decaying isotope somewhere out there in the real world.

"Dead or alive?"

"Dead," says Jason.

The cat is definitely dead.

"Your break," I say, closing the box. I slide it into its slot under the table. Jason chalks his cue, leans across, sights along it, makes the break. A couple of greens and pinks collide, and each scatters into six blues.

Jadey laughs. She's leaning on something, probably the back of a chair, which the virtuality software has painted up as a garish, brassy bar counter. Jason straightens his back and looks over at her.

"So," he says. "What's your problem?"

She rubs her hand around the back of her neck. "I need a new passport, and new ID and an exit visa. Like, fast."

"Ah." His eyes narrow. "You CIA?"

"If I was," she says, "do you think I would tell you? Or need you to work for me?"

He shrugs. "A deniable non-denial. That'll do me."

It won't do me; in fact this whole question bothers me a lot, but I keep my mouth shut for the moment.

They dicker over the deal's details and the spec while I set up my first shot. I move the cue too fast—almost as fast as the slow light. The Fitzgerald-Lorentz contraction shortens the tip by a foot and I miss completely.

"Damn."

Jason swoops over the baize, leaving me in a tricky position, but not quite irretrievable.

"Why's everyone in so early?" I ask.

Jason grunts. "All the transatlantic connections have been very choppy today."

"Yeah, tell me about it," I say sourly.

"And not much bloody work coming in."

"Aha," I say, chalking the cue. "Interesting."

I pull off a neat relativistic shot: allowing for the contraction, slamming the cue ball hard, cannoning one of the small, light ultraviolets so fast that its mass increases enough to shift one of the greens, which does a slingshot around one of the corner-pocket black holes and sets up a few other balls it collides with to snooker Jason's next. . . .

But he manages a comeback and clears me off completely.

"Again?" I reach for the Schrödinger box.

"Nah." He shakes his head. "Gotta work. Mind if we stay in here for a bit?"

"No problem."

Jadey ducks out into the real world for another round. Jason flexes his fingers. A long, low table trundles through one of the virtual doorways and comes to a halt beside us just as Jadey returns with our pints.

"Don't put them down there," Jason reminds her, just in time. The big table, conjured from his own softwear, can stop his datagloved hand, but ours—and any other real-world object, of course—would just pass through it. Jadey places the drinks on the real games-table and we watch Jason work. He turns for a moment, frames Jadey's face with his fingers, then places the resulting portrait on the flat and begins morphing it: from passport photo back through employment ID, graduation pic, prom, grade-school group picture, baby . . . Other cards and pictures pop up on the surface of the big table, and he shuffles and slides them around with expert speed. Before our eyes a whole new biography of Jadey comes together, from maternity ward to tourist ticket. He sweeps them up into one stack, taps the edges on the table, and makes them vanish up his sleeve.

Dismisses the table and turns to me, with a broad wink at Jadey.

"Time to make it real," he says. "One for the code-geeks."

Old programmers never die. They just move over to legacy systems.

They even look that way. Early adopters to the last, they don't pop telomere tabs and mitochondrial mixers like the rest of us—no, they have to try out untried biotech, so they tend to look a bit patchy: gray skins–and–smooth beards sort of thing. Jadey, Jason, and I circle cautiously around the edge of a raucous, twenty-strong clot of the old villains, all quaffing beer and talking at the tops of their voices.

"What's with the fucking news?" someone's saying, shaking his head and blinking hard. "I can't get CNN, can't even get Slashdot . . ."

This particular clique aren't all programmers. Sometime half a century ago, back in the nineties, their social circle overlapped that of the Scottish literary intelligentsia. Neither group's fashion sense has exactly moved with the times. The writers wear variously distressed jackets in fake-prolo denim or fake-macho leather; the coders go more for multipocketed waistcoats laden with the hardware for hardware fixes—Gerber and Leatherman multitools, Victorinox Swiss Army knives, Maglite torches, and over-faded trade-fair T-shirts: Sun, Bull, SCO, Oracle, Microsoft . . . This isn't irony, this is advertising—not of the products or the companies (most of them long gone), but of the skills, not at all redundant, of hacking their legacy code.

I try to look respectful, like some fanboy at a con, but I don't respect this lot at all. The ruling Party considers them unreliable, but as far as I'm concerned this is just the CPEU being its usual stuffed-shirt self. Vaguely left-wing, precisely cynical, they affect a laid-back, ca'canny approval of the so-called "imported revolution" that followed our defeat in the war. It was their kind of crap attitude to quality control that let the Russkis past NATO's automated defenses in the first place.

On the other hand, if you want to hack Unix-based filing systems in dusty metal boxes in schools and hospitals and personnel departments all over the continental U.S., they'll get on your case without asking questions, especially if you pay in dollars. I zero in on Alasdair Curran, a tall nonagenarian with long white hair and boastfully black sideburns.

"The guy who trained me worked on LEO," he brags loudly, "and he was trained by a some spook who'd been at Bletchley Park, so I reckon—"

"Yeah, Alec, and you're still shite!" someone else shouts.

As he rocks back in the general laughter Jadey catches his eye, and I take the opportunity to catch his ear. "Got a minute?"

"Oh, sure, Matt. What you after?"

"Well, I need an MS-DOS subbie—"

Curran scowls, then jerks his thumb at one of his mates. "Tony's your man."

"—and Jason needs somebody with a bit of early-dialect Oracle."

"Ah!" Curran brightens. "That, I can manage."

"We need it, like, now," Jadey tells him.

"Now?" He looks regretfully at his pint, then back at Jadey. She hits him with her best smile, and he has no defense. Hey, it makes my face warm, and I'm not even in the main beam.

Back to the quantum pool-room, but this time we don't even pretend to be playing. Curran boots up some clunky VR database manipulator, Jason sets up his card-table again, and I call up some of my software agents to handle the interface protocols and break the American fire-walls.

I get the uncanniest sensation of pushing at an open door. Within moments Curran's up to his elbows in U.S. admin databases, Jason's slipping unlogged updates on Jadey's life story, and I'm keeping the one and only record of the changes and my AIs are booking the new ID an airline ticket.

We back out.

Jason passes Jadey a plastic card.

"That's the lot," he says. "Take it to any copyshop, they'll print and bind it for you. It'll even have the right bloodgroup stains."

I'm shaking my head. "Too bloody easy. It's like all the U.S. codes had been cracked. . . ."

"Shee-it," says Jadey.

Then I remember too. The English resistance network, unraveling. "Uh-oh."

Curran's looking at us sharply as we move back to his lot's side of the room. "What's up?"

"Oh, nothing," I say hastily.

Then I notice that the whole place has gone quiet and everybody's watching the telly wall. There's that little jazzed-up flourish from "Ode to Joy" that precedes official announcements, and Big Uncle's face appears. CPEU General Secretary Gennady Yefrimovich normally looks appropriately avuncular, jovial, with an underlying solemnity. Right now he just looks insufferably smug.

"Comrades and friends," he begins, the translation and lip-synch software maxing his street-cred as usual in all the languages of the Community. For this particular nation and region, he comes across speaking English with a gravely Central Belt Scottish accent, which I know for a fact has been swiped from old tapes of the Communist trade-union leader and authentic working-class hero Mick MacGahey. "I have an historic announcement to make. The exploration station of the Eu-

35

ropean Space Agency, *Marshall Titov,* has made contact with extraterrestrial intelligent life within the asteroid 10049 Lora."

He pauses for a moment to let that sink in. As if from a great distance, I hear a dozen dropped glasses break, in various places in the pub. He smiles.

"Let me first assure you all that this is no cause for alarm. The alien intelligence is no threat to humanity. These organisms are extremely delicate, and would be vulnerable to attack or exploitation. It is fortunate for themselves and for us that their first encounter with humanity should be the peaceful explorers of the Socialist Democracies, and not commercial companies or military forces."

Something about the ironic slant of his bushy eyebrows gives the message that he's carefully not saying anything that might give offense to the imperialist exploiters, but that we all know whose companies and forces he has in mind.

"Needless to say, we warmly invite the closest cooperation with the scientific agencies of the entire world, including the United States. Great vistas of cooperation are opened up by this astonishing discovery. I now turn you over to the regular news for further details, and wish you well on this historic evening."

Sign-off, with another flourish of trumpets.

Fade to black, with *something* in the middle of the screen . . . and then I recognize some of it and the scale of the rest of it hits me.

I've got chills like water's running down my back; every hair on my body is standing up, and I'm thinking this is the biggest news in human history, this day will be remembered forever. I'm staring at the wallscreen, transfixed like everybody else by the images from space; 10049 Lora looks like a lump of clinker, the space station a tiny filigree on its side. I manfully resist the rising impulse to give a nervous giggle.

"Aliens?" I hear myself squeak. Jadey turns around, almost spilling her pint, as everybody starts yelling at once. She drags me bodily away to a table, past old code-geeks whooping and cheering or, in some cases, just staring slack-mouthed with tears welling in their eyes.

"What?"

She's jammed in beside me in a corner bench, and she looks like it's only our mutually awkward position that's stopping her from slapping me. "Yeah, yeah," she says impatiently, "giant leap and all that, but—"

In one section of screen the Russkis' prettiest newscaster is twittering brightly about "our heroic ESA cosmonauts" and "brilliant scientists"; in another, much smaller window, a reporter outside the European Parliament drones on about a new scandal, some Trot MEP exposed as taking a bigger wage from Washington, or possibly Langley. Any other time, it'd be the hottest item; now it just seems trivial and tawdry, literally mundane. Why are they running it at all?

"Will you fucking *listen* to me?" Jadey hisses. I blink and shake my gaze loose from the screen's hypnotic virtual grip, and focus on her face, tense and pale in the warm light.

"Okay. Sorry." Jesus. I can feel the urge to look back at the screen, like gravity.

"Matt, that ESA station, it's the one you got a job from today."

"Yes!" I say. "That's what's got me so gobsmacked, apart from the . . . uh,"—I replay her cynical words—" '*giant leap*' stuff."

" 'Comrades, this is no accident,' " she flips back. She gives a quick, disdainful glance at the screen; I take this as permission to do the same. In the bottom corner there's a mug shot of Weber, then a clip of him being bundled into a black maria in Brussels, then a quick vox-pop with a shocked constituent on some street where sunshine glares on tin shacks and high-rises and palm trees.

"Where's that?" Jadey asks.

"French Guiana," I answer, unthinking.

"As in, famous for Kourou? That place where they have the *other* ESA launch-site?"

"Yeah, he had a big constituency with the space workers—"

I stare at her, with a wild surmise.

"Another non-coincidence," she says.

We both gaze soberly at the follow-up, an interview with an understandably defensive cadre of Weber's party, the *Ligue Prolétarienne Révolutionnaire*. It's almost drowned out by one of the old programmers.

"Think low-temperature physics, think Bose-Einstein condensates, think quantum computing," he explains at the top of his voice. "Say good-bye to crypto, say hello to the panoptic society. Shake hands with America's missile launch-codes and open the door to the Fourth World War. And that's not the end of it. That's just what the *Russkis* could be doing. What are the *aliens* up to?"

He's a solidly-built man perched on a stool and sprouting curly black hair all over like a burst mattress. He sees us, and a widening circle of others, listening, waves his hands and continues enthusiastically: "That ESA station is a node on the Internet, guys! Who knows what they might have hacked into by now? Hey, if they've been here that long, we can't even trust ourselves, they could've put trapdoors in our fucking DNA back in the Pre-Cambrian . . ."

And somebody else says, "Karl H. Marx on a bicycle, Charlie, aren't aliens *enough?*" and everybody laughs again.

I'll say this for those guys, they adapt to the end of the world we've always known faster than I do. They've seen a lot in their time: the Fall of the Wall, the Millennium Slump, the Century Boom, the Unix roll-over, the War, the revolution . . . By the time Jadey and I have got ready to leave they're talking about how aliens that old must have some *really* old legacy systems, and that they must be needing contractors, and wondering what their day rate would be. . . .

Bastards.

3

Bat Songs

E SIAS DE TENEBRE, Magnate and Registered Member of the Electorate of the Republic of Nova Babylonia, exhaled the smoke from his joint and gave a modest and not entirely coincidental cough as he passed the rather insalubrious object to the lady at his left.

"My own small knowledge of terrestriology," he said to the high lord at his right, "is of course"—he waved a hand, as much to clear the resinous air in front of his mouth as to emphasize his point—"strictly that of a dilettante." (This was, strictly, a lie. His interest in news from the home planet was obsessive, and profitable.) "However, I can assure you that as of approximately one hundred years ago—or earlier today, as far as I'm concerned . . ." (Great Zeus, this stuff was making him verbose; he'd have to watch that!) ". . . no travelers or indeed, ah, involuntary arrivals have turned up claiming a later departure date than your own."

He wondered if this information would have been worth holding back. Probably not—and difficult to do in any case, if he wanted to trade information at all. This local lord was shrewd; a stocky, tough-looking man with a battered Roman nose, every plane of his face and neck converging to the flat, brush-cut top of his bullet head. His native speech was a dialect of English, grammatically degenerate compared to those Tenebre had heard before, on Croatan. Even the unfamiliar scientific words in its vocabulary could often be interpreted by deduction from the classical roots. But for this occasion he, like most people present, was speaking in Trade Latin, the de facto lingua franca of the Second Sphere.

Hal Driver's broad shoulders slumped slightly, and his features hardened after a passing moment of what Tenebre interpreted as sadness, perhaps disappointment.

"None after 2049, eh? Oh well, I suppose there are two ways of looking at that." He pushed his blue silk shirtsleeves back, planted his bare elbows on the drink-slopped surface of the long hardwood table, cupped his hands to his mouth and shouted for more brandy. Some girl got up from the table and hurried to a distant cupboard.

"Either we've blown ourselves to hell back there," he continued, fixing Tenebre with a blearily jovial gaze, "or we're expanding into a different sphere—a Second Sphere of our own, a *First* Sphere!—closer to the home sun."

"That could well be," said the merchant. He diplomatically did not point out that there were several other possibilities, none of them particularly cheering even compared to *all-out nuclear war,* a procedure which he'd gathered was a faint approximation to the much worse disasters that might by now have been visited upon the Earth.

"But for the present," Tenebre went on, "there's no doubt that you're the most recent representatives of Earth to have arrived in the Second Sphere. So, naturally, we're very interested in doing business with you."

He sounded too eager, but he didn't care. The right strategy for this particular opportunity wasn't to dicker down the locals, play it cool, keep his cards to his chest—it was to get his hands on as much technology and knowledge as possible before any of his competitors turned up.

One of the lord Driver's advisers, the one they called the Navigator—the lord Cairns, a pushy character who'd tried his patience earlier with persistent and barely comprehensible questions about, of all things, *calculating-machines*—leaned into the conversation from a couple of spaces to the high lord's right, vulgarly waving a fork on which a morsel of scallop was impaled. Though evidently old, his cheeks frosted with white stubble, he was vigorous and alert; a lean, muscular man with a bald pate, behind which white hair hung down to his back.

"What I'm still not too clear about," he said, in heavily accented English, "is where you would place Nova Babylonia compared with what you now know of Earth as it was when our ancestors left it. In terms of, you know, knowledge and technology and so forth. Standards of living of the masses, and all that." He popped the fork in his mouth, closed his eyes ecstatically, chewed and swallowed, then brandished the fork again. "According to our records and reminiscences, your dozen or

so predecessors over the last couple of hundred years have *babbled*"—
he giggled momentarily at the feeble pun—"about great shining cities,
beautiful parks, spectacular wildernesses, and, you know, moon-
drenched seas . . ." Another self-amused chuckle. ". . . and so on and so
forth, and the justice and stability of the mighty and ancient Republic.
All very well and good, but they've been as closemouthed as any saur
about stuff like, well, what machinery you command, the standard of
living of the masses and so forth."

He apparently realized he was beginning to sound repetitive, because at this point he mercifully shut up. But he still looked steadfastly
at Tenebre, eyebrows raised in polite inquiry, while absently spearing
another marine organism and devouring it with lascivious relish.

"Ah," said Tenebre, feeling that he was on firmer ground, "I can
explain that." He glanced around, gratefully accepting the distraction of
a refill of brandy and a cigar, which he devoutly hoped was pure tobacco—he needed a clear head. This particular hastily prepared dinner
was being held not in the castle's banqueting-hall, but in the servants'
refectory, and the servants were joining in eating the various dishes as
soon as they'd finished serving them. The table at which he sat held
about a score of placings and, like the others, was occupied by a mixture
of men and women, masters and servants, guests and hosts. The whole
room held a couple hundred people, counting the saurs, most of whom
were well out of it by now, gazing vacantly into whatever mental spaces
the hemp opened for them. The din of conversation, what with the crowd
and the acoustics of the low, raftered ceiling and all the pots and pans
still hooked to the walls, was tremendous.

At the table across the aisle he could see a gaggle of women including his first and third wives, a few servant women, and two of the
castle's ladies, one of them Margaret Cairns, who was apparently the
lord Cairns's number one and only wife. They all seemed to be talking
at the same time except when they all screamed together with laughter.
This kind of information interchange was one of which Tenebre did not
entirely approve, but could hardly prevent. And sometimes, by talking
freely, his wives found out things he could never have discovered for
himself.

He nodded his thanks to the girl who'd brought the brandy. She
handed on the bottle casually to Driver and pulled up a stool, looking
at Tenebre all agog. He had an uneasy suspicion that at any moment
she might, like some ignorant peasant child, reach out and touch his
hair.

"You were saying?" Driver prompted.

"Ah yes, our predecessors. It's very simple. They didn't know about your presence here, weren't expecting it at all, and naturally enough were privately somewhat perturbed by it. A human-crewed ship from Earth is quite unprecedented, and could have foreshadowed all kinds of trouble."

"It could have been the spearhead of an invasion from Earth, you mean," said Driver. The thought evidently amused him.

Tenebre nodded sharply. "That's it, in so many words."

"Now, wait a minute," said James Cairns, scratching a diagram on the table with the tip of a short knife. "We've had ships in from Nova Babylonia via nearer colonies who definitely *had* heard of us, and they were just as closemouthed as . . . Oh, right." He stabbed the knife into the table. "I see now. The point is that Nova Babylonia hadn't yet heard of us when they set out, and whatever response it had come up with in the meantime hadn't had time to reach them. . . ."

"Precisely," said Tenebre. "And therefore the Electorate had not had a chance to discuss it. Now that we have, I'll be quite happy to answer your questions. . . ."

It was a folding lock-knife, the words *Opinel* and *France* still legible on its blade, but long since abraded from its plastic imitationwood handle. James Cairns fiddled with its locking ring and doodled gloomily with the tip of the blade. Did France still exist? Even as a physical place? How much of French culture could a sufficiently advanced intelligence reconstruct from contemplation of this simple tool's elegant design?

Cairns wrenched his attention away from this futile but seductive line of thought and back to the present. With one part of his mind he began to keep track of the magnate's answers to the questions that flew at him from all sides of the table; with another, he examined the long-sided triangles he'd scored on the table, matching years past to light-years away.

Nova Babylonia, on the planet Nova Terra around the predictably named Nova Sol, was about a hundred light-years distant from Mingulay. The *Bright Star* had arrived off Mingulay around two centuries ago, and the first merchant starship to drop by had been a couple of years after that, so . . .

News of the *Bright Star*'s arrival had undoubtedly reached Croatan, five light-years away, within less than six years, and the more-distant colonies with a proportionate delay. But a ship en route couldn't receive or transmit information—traveling at lightspeed, a starship participated in the timeless, massless eternity of the photon, making the journey subjectively instantaneous. So ships originally from Nova Babylonia, but visiting various ports of call along their trade-route, would come to know of Mingulay's new settlers long before Nova Babylonia—or any ships sent from it directly—did.

This family Tenebre were thus the first merchants from Nova Babylonia to have some idea of what to expect when they arrived on Mingulay. Interesting. He wondered what they wanted, and what they had to offer in return.

Cairns sometimes felt that, deep down in the most adolescent recesses of his seventy-year-old brain, he harbored a personal grudge against the universe for not having turned out the way his ancestors had expected. He could have *lived with* a universe whose interstellar gulfs could be crossed only with generation ships, cold-sleep, or ramscoops. He'd have been absolutely fucking *delighted* with one that could be traversed with some kind of warp-drive or jump-gates or wormholes or similar fanciful mechanism. In much the same way, he could have been quite metaphysically satisfied with a godless universe; or, if he'd ever come across a convincing apologetic, happy to affirm that this one was the work of God.

Instead he'd found himself in a universe where gods swarmed by the trillion, a regular Oort Crowd of them around every star—most of the gods, as far as anyone knew, being convinced atheists. The only thing the gods had ever created for anyone else's benefit was the stardrive. The stardrive could get you to the stars, in an instant of subjective time. At the speed of light.

There were times when he felt like saying to the gods, *Thanks a bunch.*

". . . purchase a great deal of our staple foodstuffs and machinery from the saurs, naturally enough," Tenebre was saying. "Most of our wealth, as you might expect, comes from the profits of trade. Much of the commerce between the elder species is handled by Babylonian business families, who are thus able to support many of the populace through the purchase of various services. The manufacturing and farming classes sensu stricto tend to specialize in luxury production for the saur market. Among the saurs there is quite a fashion for human handicraft products, a taste for certain fruits and vegetables, spices, and, er, herbs . . ."

Everyone laughed.

The merchant leaned back, patting his belly complacently. "All indications are that the popular masses are quite satisfied with their lot; those who aren't, are free to take ship to the younger colonies, and for several centuries such emigration has been at a low trickle."

James grinned to himself, noticing Driver's slow, sober nod. Nova Babylonia didn't exactly sound like a technologically dynamic society. They'd always suspected as much, but it was encouraging, in a way, to have it confirmed. *We could already walk all over them,* he thought, wondering if Driver—to say nothing of Tenebre—was thinking the same. Not that the elder species would allow them to actually do it, but still. . . .

"So," said Driver, "although this is no time for serious bargaining, I find myself wondering just what you could possibly want from our . . . somewhat isolated and backward society." He shrugged, spreading his hands. "Your predecessors have for the most part traded with the other species here, buying little but our poor local copies of gadgets and trinkets originally manufactured in the Solar System. I hardly think our technology is much of a match for that of the saurs."

Cairns noticed frowns around the table, from their own side's more business-oriented types, obviously thinking that Driver wasn't much of a salesman. He wished there was some secret signal meaning, *Give the man credit for being a bit devious,* then realized that these discomfited faces might at some level be a part of Driver's devious design.

"Oh, when we've had a chance to examine what my family and your traders each have to offer, I think we'll all be pleasantly surprised," said Tenebre smoothly. "Products for human use are best devised—if not necessarily manufactured—by human beings. And we have, as usual, much business to do with the saurs and with our cousins of the mines and the forests: pharmaceuticals, certain rare minerals, hardwoods, and so forth." He waved a hand. "Routine trade. But I will tell you frankly that our strongest interest is in what you have brought from Earth. Art, science, technology, history, philosophy—all the knowledge of the home world. Nova Babylonia thirsts for them all!"

"But that's *information!*" Matt said. "And, as we say, information wants—"

Driver's head turned like a striking snake. His swift glare made Cairns pause.

"Information wants to be paid?" said Tenebre. He smiled around at his interlocutors. "We," he told them proudly, "have such a saying ourselves."

The guests had retired, the servants and younger family members had cleared away most of the evening's detritus and gone to their own beds. The few old members of the Cosmonaut Families who still lived in the castle had made their way through to the front hall, and set themselves down in armchairs in a loose arc around the fireplace. One saur accompanied them, old Tharovar, who had welcomed their ancestors, the original crew, on their first arrival. In his long acquaintance with humans he'd acquired a better head for the hemp than most of his kind, and was now relaxed, rather than comatose in the servants' hall like the others.

Cairns nursed his brandy and cigar, in the chair nearest the dying fire. Margaret sat on the floor, resting against the chair's arm, basking in the embers' heat. Tharovar squatted at his other hand. The others gazed unseeing into the fire for a while: Driver, and Andrei Volkov, and Larisa Telesnikova, and Jean-Pierre Lemieux. Those all had partners or lovers who were from outside the notional, hereditary crew—the cosmonaut cadre—and who had tactfully left them to their private thoughts and conversation.

Driver looked around the depleted company and cleared his throat, spat into the fire. Sputum sizzled horribly for a second or two.

"Well," he said, "I got an interesting offer from Tenebre."

"A different one from the ones he was making at the table?" asked Volkov.

Driver nodded. "He picked a quieter moment. . . . What he offered was to pay us well—for shipping. He could make it very advantageous for us to go into the carrying trade."

Low and bitter laughter greeted this statement.

Cairns felt Margaret grip his ankle, and relaxed his own grip, unconsciously fastened on her shoulder.

"So what did you say to that?"

Driver shrugged, a movement exaggerated by the padded shoulders of his loosened doublet. "I . . . temporized, but gave him to understand we'd be interested."

"*What?*" Cairns almost shouted. The others sat up in their seats, equally agitated. Driver regarded them all with a sardonic smile.

"We always knew it would come to this sometime," he said mildly. "We've prepared for it." He fixed Cairns with a reproving look. "After a fashion. So—what progress do *you* have to report, Navigator?"

James waited for a second or two; Margaret was urgently stroking his foot, and the gentle touch calmed him a little, not much. Tharovar sat tense and rigid beside him; the tendons in the saur's thin neck were like taut wires, and his mouth was, if possible, thinner than usual.

"Come off it, Hal," Cairns said. "For decades now it's been little more than a gods-damned *hobby,* as you well know. It's not easy to interest the younger members of the family in the"—his lips curled—"Great Work, and it gets more tedious with every computer that breaks down and can't be repaired. Every so often somebody shamefacedly turns in a few pages of logic or math. Christ Almighty, I could sometimes swear the paper has had *tears* fall on it, like some kid's exercise book. I put them together in order, I file them, I pass out a few more problems, and they take even longer to come back. People have other priorities, other opportunities, and more as time goes on."

Only the knowledge of how pathetic, how feeble it would sound, made him refrain from adding, *What else can I do?* He hated hearing himself make excuses; it wasn't his manner, not his style at all, not part of the program. *Not done, old chap.* But it was true, and Driver knew it was true, and Cairns knew that he knew.

So he concluded by saying, confidently and aggressively, his oldest excuse of all, a Navigator family joke:

"I'm an artist, not a technician."

That got a laugh—even Driver had to smile—and the tension eased. Larisa Telesnikova took the opportunity to lean forward and speak diplomatically.

"Okay, comrades," she began, as she usually did when talking seriously to any gathering larger than two, "what this means is that we *don't know* what progress may have been made by now. Why don't we use the formal reception for the merchants to invite as many as possible of the Navigator's family, and ask them to bring their latest results, even their latest workings?"

"Better than nothing," agreed Driver.

"That's all very well," said Cairns, "but I don't hold out much hope." He glared at Driver. "As you well know. And what will you tell your new friend Tenebre when it becomes obvious that we can't come up with the goods?"

Driver chuckled darkly, scratching his belly through the bunched cambric of his shirt.

"That's the beauty of it," he said. "I tell him we have technical difficulties, demand a substantial retainer, swear blind we won't cut a deal with any other merchants who may come hurrying to the scene, and ask him to call back on his next trip. For him, that means a wait of a couple of months, maybe a year. For us . . . well, one way or another, it won't be our problem."

Cairns guffawed; the others laughed too, less heartily. Their ages were all in the seventies or eighties, and—even with the medical knowledge that the saurs had long shared with the hominid genera—none of them expected to live more than another few decades. Unless, of course, the secrets of the ancient Cosmonauts could be rediscovered in the meantime—but that was a hope, not an expectation.

Tharovar stood up and strolled over to the fireplace and stood in front of it on the hearth. His silhouette gave Cairns an atavistic pang of unease, like a childish reaction to a familiar person in a frightening mask.

"Have you considered," the saur said in his low, hissing voice, "*accompanying* the family Tenebre to Nova Babylonia and back? You could use their starship as a time machine into the future of this colony, a future in which, perhaps, your mathematical problems will be solved—and your lives could be extended further."

"Yeah, I've considered it," Driver said, surprising Cairns, who hadn't. "I have *no* fucking intention of tearing myself away from my life, my descendants, and my ability to keep up, in order to turn myself into a stranger in a strange time."

Cairns joined in the murmur of agreement.

"Then you could go to Croatan," the saur persisted, "and shuttle back and forth, returning here every ten years. That would surely be sufficient."

Margaret spoke up. "You really don't have much of a handle on this 'progress' thing, do you, Tharovar?"

The smile in her voice belied the criticism in her words, and the saur replied with some humor of his own.

"Perhaps not," he said. "I am only an egg."

Gregor hauled himself a meter off the edge of his futon, elbowed his way across the carpet, and slammed down the button to shut off the loud ringing of his alarm clock. Early sunlight rampaged through the narrow window of his room. He lay half in and half out of bed for minute or two, cheek pressed on the rough fibers by the planet's merciless one-gravity pull, while he made a cautious all-systems check. Thankfully, the various aches in his limbs and back were all accounted for by the previous day's work on the boat; minute movements of his head did not result in any explosion. The feeling in his stomach came from an empty belly and a full bladder; no nausea was detectable. His erection, to which one hand had reflexively returned, was comfortingly hard. His mouth was dry, but tasted no worse than neutral.

It followed that he didn't have a hangover and hadn't drunk too much last night. Memory reported in, shamefacedly admitting to a few gaps in the record, but everything seemed consistent with his having shared one more pipe with Salasso, then walked back to his room, fallen asleep fully dressed, woken around midnight from colorful dreams, read for an hour or so, and then gone to bed properly, a mere five hours or so earlier.

Still moving slowly—in part because of the legitimate (as it were) aches in his muscles, and in part because of the remaining possibility of a stealth hangover, the kind that lurked just outside awareness and then sprang on you like a cat from a tree at the first sudden movement—Gregor rolled over and stood up. Everything still being fine, he wrapped himself in a bathrobe and padded down the corridor to the shared toilet to relieve himself. On returning to his room he bent and stretched his way through the calisthenics of the Salute to the Sun, and finished them invigorated. That done, he switched on the electric kettle and made himself a small pot of tea.

The room was just big enough to contain the futon, a table and chair, hundreds of pages of notes, and several hundred books. It wasn't much of a gesture of independence, considering that his father gave him the money he needed for rent, university fees, and subsistence, but it was better than living at home. At the top of a building in Kyohvic's old town, built before his ancestors' ship had arrived, the room gave him peace and privacy and, if he needed it, the easy company of the other students and older eccentrics who lived in its other twenty or so single rooms and shared its decrepit facilities.

As was his habit, he opened the weighty leatherbound volume—a gift from his father—of the Good Books, the words of the philosophers: the Fragments of Heraclitus, the Sayings of Epictetus, the Teachings of Epicurus, the Poems of Lucretius. Their English paraphrases were among the best-loved works of Mingulayan literature; some said they were better than the originals. His glance fell on one of the Fragments:

This world, which is the same for all,
no god or man has made.

An ever-living fire it is
whose flames forever flare and fade.

The book fell open again at another familiar page, from the Teachings:

Around the world goes friendship's dancing call,
Join hands in happiness for one and all.

That would do, he thought, as a devotion for the day. He drained his cup, dressed, and set off to work, picking up his breakfast on the way.

Elizabeth jumped off the clanging tram at Harbor Halt and walked briskly to the quay. The parked skiffs glowed orange in the early light, their spindly legs and lenticular bodies casting long shadows out over the water like tall, striding tripedal machines. The traders' ship squatting in the sound still struck her eye as a startling sight, intrusive, visibly alien, massively out-of-place. High above, an airship from the skyport on the hill behind Kyohvic wallowed upward to meet a southerly air current, and tiny buzzing airplanes made sightseeing circles around the harbor and its gigantic visitor. For a moment, airship and aircraft looked like pathetic, primitive imitations of the starship and the skiffs.

Along the quay baffled seabats squabbled around the well-protected tanks that Renwick and his crew were already lifting off the deck with a creaking crane and screeching winch. Elizabeth mucked in as best she could, helping to maneuver the tanks and crates onto the department's flatbed truck parked alongside. After a while she glimpsed Gregor hurrying up, and her heart jumped like a fish.

"Good morning," he said. "Sorry I'm late."

"You're hardly that," Elizabeth said. "We were early."

She smiled at him, staring and trying not to, trying not to look too long, hoping that he'd notice that she was looking too long. But he just grinned and nodded and grabbed the rope. His hand brushed hers accidentally as they hauled together; she almost jerked it away.

Things might have been different if he hadn't *grown* on her, if they'd met at some student bash instead of in the lab, if they hadn't worked together and become colleagues and good mates before she'd realized what she really felt for him, and had felt from the beginning. Now she felt completely entangled in that easy friendship and close

49

collaboration, frozen by the fear of losing it in a welter of embarrassment and misunderstanding.

He rode beside her as she drove the flatbed, its electric engine whining under the strain, along the coast road to the marine-biology department on the town's westward and seaward edge. There they turned them over to the keeper of the saltwater aquaria, and headed in to the laboratories to begin another day of the research they shared. The frequent fishing-trips for new specimens were almost a holiday; this was their real work.

Gregor, Elizabeth, and Salasso were cooperating on mapping the nervous system of the squid. Its simple structure, relatively large neurons, and—to be blunt—its absence of a hard skeleton made it an ideal laboratory animal for investigating neurophysiology in general, but it was the peculiarities of cephalopod neural morphology that they were concentrating on. The walls were almost papered-over with drawings, diagrams, and readings of pH levels and electrical potentials.

Salasso, as usual, was already there, crouched over a deep glass dish within which a small squid hovered, oblivious to the fine-needle electrode which the saur was slowly bringing to bear.

"Come here, little one," he crooned through barely opened lips. "This is your lucky day."

Tenebre woke beside his number three wife to the dawn's light and the morning chorus of the bats. Somewhere in the roof-space above the ceiling, birds chirruped and scratched as they settled in for their day of roosting sleep. For a few minutes he, like them, huddled in shared warmth, watching his breath fog. The Keep of Aird, like castles everywhere in the known universe, lacked central heating.

Tenebre grunted and rolled out of the low bed, wrapped himself in one of the quilted robes which his hosts had thoughtfully provided, and dragged on the woollen socks he'd discarded the previous night. Thus fortified, he made his way over to the south-facing window—at least it was glazed, even if not double-glazed—leaned on the sill, and looked out across the harbor to the town.

Seeing Kyohvic from the skiff had been his first shock here. The daylight did not diminish the surprise it afforded. He stared for a long time at the buildings, sharp in the long shadows and pink light of the autumn dawn. When he'd last seen it, four centuries in its past and five months in his, it had been a straggle of low houses along the shore, a harbor busy with fishing-smacks, and a scatter of farms beyond. The castle itself had been empty, superstitiously avoided. Now the buildings had climbed to five or six stories and spread miles along the sides of the valley; the fishing-boats still crowded the harbor, but they were dwarfed by much-larger seaships, tall masts bristling; the fields were laid out in a dense patchwork—some plowed black, some brown with stubble, others green with the shoots of this spring's winter wheat. At the brow of the hill, airships nudged and bobbed among mooring-pylons, and flying-machines (frighteningly rickety aerial vehicles; to his eyes, little more than motor-powered kites) took off on frivolous or fateful missions.

Tenebre was used to seeing change speeded-up, compressed; it was one of the benefits of life as a merchant—it gave one a long view of history, the closest, perhaps, that a human mind could come to the millennial perspective of the saur. In forty years of life and five centuries of objective time he'd seen Mingulay's parent colony, Croatan, surge upward and expand from unpromising beginnings; he'd seen Nova Babylonia fallen in flames, and risen from the ashes . . . but this was different—this was something new under the suns.

These people whose hospitality (socially warm, however physically chilly) he was enjoying and enduring, were descended from independent human space explorers—"Cosmonauts," they called themselves. He relished the word, with a sort of rebellious vainglory in the human species which he'd never before imagined he could feel. In the great chain of being, humanity had a respected but restricted place: restricted not by force but by circumstance.

The gods wheeled in their million-year orbits, indifferent and inviolate in the spaces between the worlds, much as the terrestrial philosopher Epicurus had supposed, and as the poet Lucretius had sung. The krakens plied their trade between the stars, navigating the lightspeed ships. The saurs steered a shorter course, piloting their gravity skiffs and working in their tropical and subtropical biological factories, their *manufacturing plant*.

The humans . . . ah yes, the humans had a place: inventing and manufacturing, trucking and bartering, farming and fishing, all of it on the surface of land or sea, or as passengers in the older races' craft. The only sentient species with a humbler role were humanity's cousins, the small hominidae digging in the mines and the tall hominidae tending the temperate forests. So it was, in variant proportions, on all the worlds of the Second Sphere, the hundred-light-year radius around Nova Sol. This was the generous limit of the journeys on which the krakens' starships were willing to take humans.

Generous, but still a limit.

Matters were managed very differently on Earth, the home planet; and perhaps on this one, Mingulay, to which humans had come from Earth on their own initiative, and their own ship.

Just before he'd gone to bed, one of his saur crew, Bishlayan, had passed on a piece of information she'd picked up from one of the local saurs. Some of the first crew, the original cosmonauts, were believed to be still alive, somewhere out in the wilds. That ship had brought the secret of long life, as well as of long journeys. *A bright star indeed,* Tenebre thought, turning with a smile to greet the waking mumbles and hungover groans of his third wife. The other two were still asleep beside her.

4

Legacy Systems

OUTSIDE, PRINCES STREET was heaving with the usual Festival crowd, but they weren't behaving in the usual Festival way. A surprising number of people were actually looking up, like they expected some shining mothership to arrive at any moment. Others stood about talking, or grabbing passersby and spreading the news: the number of people discussing it or watching the skies was increasing by the minute. I hadn't seen anything like this since the revolution, when I was a little kid, when we emerged blinking from the shelters and basements and ruins to greet the Russki troops on the street. I remembered the noise of the jubilant car horns. Now, the susurrus of human voices, of feet and bicycle wheels and trolleybuses, seemed eerily quiet by comparison.

Jadey grabbed my elbow as I poised to cross the street.

"Where you going?"

I jerked my head rightward, indicating. "Waverley—run your stuff through the station copyshop, then get a shuttle train to the airport?"

"Na-na-na-nah. We gotta think this through. No rush, it's an open ticket, right?"

"Yeah, sure, but the faster you get out—"

She looked at me sharply. "Hey, who's the expert here? Do I give you programming tips? So, shut up and come with me."

Not much I could say to that. She turned left and we headed down Leith Walk, past the new-tech buildings in the bombed area where I lived and on down to the older part of the street. The crowds were thinner here, the bicycles fewer. Trolleybuses glided down the middle of the carriageway. To the north, the direction we were more or less heading, the sky remained noticeably light: a mere few hundred kilometers poleward, the sun still shone.

After a few minutes' silent hurrying past the software stores and delis and restaurants, Jadey took another left, into one of the side streets in the Broughton area, a canyon of sandstone tenements. Stopped at a door beside a tacky boutique shopfront.

"Won't this place be watched, if you're—?"

Another glare. "Like I said."

She thumbed the keypad, peered into the retinal scanner, and the door swung open. I sidled after her, past tangled bicycles and stacked mail and up a stone stairway. On the third floor she unlocked the door of a flat, using metal keys. Hardware.

Inside, it was chilly and dark. She strolled in, flicking light-switches. The windows—I saw when we stepped into the main room—were covered by aluminum venetian blinds. There was a sofa, a screen, and a table, and not much else; the wall-posters were tuned to the previous year's bands. Looked like an empty student pad, and probably was.

"Coffee?"

"Thanks. Black, no sugar."

"Just as well," Jadey said.

By the time she came back from the kitchen I had the screen working, with the sound off. Most of the news channels had moved on to talking heads. Jadey sat down at the other end of the sofa, nodded at the screen.

"Countermeasures," she said. "Built in. We can talk."

"So . . . are you really CIA?" I asked. Not the most tactful of opening lines, but it had been on my mind.

"No, of course I'm not bloody CIA!" she answered, almost spilling her coffee. "Statist sons of bitches! They're almost as bad as the goddamn commies, when they're not doing deals with them."

"All right. I only asked. So what *are* you?"

She gave me a serious frown. "You really want to know?"

"Well, yeah. Call it idle curiosity."

"Hah! All right. I'm working for a political organization that does what we think the CIA *should* be doing: stirring up a bit of subversion in the E.U."

"I'd figured that," I said slowly. "It's the bit that came before it that kind of has me baffled. How does it work? Counterrevolution for fun and profit?"

"Neither," she said. "The money comes from . . . well, basically

54

from legacies and trust funds set up by Net entrepreneurs who got rich in the Century Boom, and who thought it might be a good idea to, ah, invest in the future of the free market. As for the fun—"

She put down the cup. Her hands were shaking. "It was fun for a while, down in old England. Making contacts, setting things up, basic agitprop. But the scene's got a lot heavier lately. You know, like, pseudo-gangs?"

"What?"

"Resistance groups set up by . . . whoever—the Russkis, I guess, maybe even the Brits—to discredit the real opposition with the odd terrorist outrage; black propaganda that makes us smell like fascists; spreading rumors that the *real* resistance groups are pseudo-gangs, that the best activists are police agents." She waved a hand. "You know the score."

"The trusting trust problem?" I asked, translating into geek-speak.

"Exactly!"

She frowned again, looked at her nails. One of her thumbnails was bitten right down. "Shit, I thought I'd *broken* that habit. . . ." Looked up. "Let me tell you about last night."

There's a scene in *Battle of Algiers* where the Muslim women of the FLN are preparing to go out and plant bombs in the European quarter, and they're tarting themselves up in immodest European clothes and applying makeup for the first time in their lives, and as they preen solemnly in front of mirrors the soundtrack becomes a relentless martial drumbeat.

Jadey hears that beat as she gets herself ready for the work of the night. She's always liked her complexion, with its natural-blonde creamy smoothness matching her fair brows and pale lips, but now she's covering it all up with blusher and tint, mascara and eyeshadow and bloody-red lipstick. Dye gel turns her hair black and spiky, stains the swirling water as she rinses her hands under the tap.

Her preparations complete, she waits for a few minutes, watching her watch. Time is of the essence. Two minutes until contact. Time to go.

She checks herself in the mirror: lacy white blouse, small black vinyl skirt, fishnet tights, high heels. Subtlety is not the name of her game. She grins at her own unfamiliar features, and jauntily hoists the red leather shoulderbag. She's already checked the gun inside it.

"You go, girl," she tells herself. "Go out there and slay them!"

The air is damp and the light is yellow. It's a dead pre-dawn hour, but not too late for the tarts to ply their trade. Jadey avoids their eyes, outglares the raised brows of lurking pimps and johns. Up ahead, she sees the back of the man she's after, in Russian military uniform. The hardware is soft and warm through her glove, like a wee lump of that stuff kids play with; or maybe plastique, and just as dangerous: Silly Semtex. She slaps it onto a lamppost and walks briskly up York Way, about thirty meters behind the man. A slow, silently counted ten seconds later, the Russki turns off the main drag and into an alley. Jadey follows him without looking back.

Ten seconds is ample time for the hardware to work: for the lump to fasten and flow like a sinister, fast-moving slime-mold, extending its tendrils into the cable of the street camera on the lamppost, and to insinuate its programs into the datastream. By now it should have subtly degraded the image quality to the point where every face on York Way might as well have a balaclava mask over it. With luck, it'll be burrowing into and editing storage as well as input, scrambling the recognition software, but none of that can be counted on. The input masking, however, can—but still she doesn't look around, doesn't give them even that flicker of a chance.

She walks straight past the Russki, who's pretending to examine a window display of dusty plumbing. Her gaze meets the reflection of his for a fraction of a second, then she's past him. He looks smart in that uniform, though he's less a soldier than she is; all the civil servants of the occupation wear military uniform. It's one of those Russki things.

He waits until her heels have metronomically ticked off five seconds, then whistles after her. She turns, swiveling shoulders and hips, clasping the soft leather of her handbag. She grins at him and glances over at a still-narrower alleyway. He nods imperceptibly and strides over and turns sharply into it; she follows, her gait now businesslike rather than professional.

She looks at Josif with a certain warmth and recognition that no caution can prevent. Over the months she has come to quite like the man. Even so, she is surprised when instead of their usual minute of pretended bargaining he catches her by the waist and draws her toward him. His mouth descends on hers. There's a moment of lip and tongue contact and then she hears, as much as feels, a small metallic object being pushed gently against her teeth. She almost swallows, which might not have been a bad idea, if messy in its long-run implications.

Then she manages to tongue it between molars and cheek. It's about the size and shape of a small coin, with a rounded rim.

Josif moves his head back with a hushing breath. Jadey nods, almost as imperceptibly. Then his chest slams into hers and she hears a thump, feels an impact, and there's a horrible grating noise. As she takes a forced backward step Josif becomes deadweight in her arms and she has to let go of him. His mouth opens as if to scream. Only blood comes out, and then he's down on the wet paving, head and heels hammering, blood pooling and spurting, bowels voiding.

And she's two more steps back and in the firing position, the one-shot plastic Liberator in her locked hands in front of her.

There's a young man facing her, looking shocked, with a big bloody knife clutched in his right hand. Zip jerkin and jeans and gloves, enclosed from neck to sole in filmy isolation polymer: medical or murder gear.

She could have done with some of that herself. There's blood all down her blouse.

The young man's expression turns to annoyance and puzzlement. "You're not—"

"What you expected?" Her mouth is dry; she tries not to bite the thing in her mouth, or her tongue.

"Not expecting me."

She doesn't look away from his eyes, or from the blade. Josif is terminal; not necessarily dead, yet, but it would take a crash medical team here in the next couple of minutes to save him, and she doubts that she can make this happen.

"Back off," she warns. He flinches, and she strains to keep her voice low. "No, I was bloody well not expecting you. Why should I have been?"

Then she realizes what the guy thinks has been going on.

"Oh, Christ, you thought I was on your team?"

The guy nods. In the dim light she can just about make out his buzz-cut hair, hooded eyes, thin face. She doubts if he's out of his teens. Exactly the sort of kid who gets involved in nationalist terrorist cells that think luring Russian soldiers into dark alleyways then killing them is a good way to build an arsenal for the Great Day. Kids like that are the bane of her fucking life.

"Thought it was all set up," he mumbles. His London accent is so thick she can barely follow it. "Shit."

She'll let the implications of that pass, for now.

"Run," she says, gesturing with the pistol.

"And then what did you do?"

"Ran in the opposite direction, down another alley. Just a minute later I'd circled back and crossed York Way again, farther up, and the cops were like flies on shit around the junction I'd been at. That's why I reckon your hardware's fucked. Decided not to go back to my place, headed for a safe house and found it wasn't. Door was getting the heavy boot just as I turned the corner, so I turned the other way pretty sharp. Back in the red-light area, I had a few stashes of spare clothes and ID and shit. Sealed containers spot-glued inside dump bins, places like that. So I used one of them to get changed and ditch the tarty gear. Went into my cover job—it's deliberately a suspicious-looking job, American book import company—phoned you at coffee break and got the midday train. And, like I said, the busies were giving me funny looks."

I stared at her, somewhat shaken by this account—for its implied sex as much as its explicit violence. How long had I known her? A couple of years, at the outside. She'd wandered into a codeshop down Leith Walk, where I was working between contracts—this was before I'd achieved my current high rep as a manager, I hasten to add—dropped a set of Calvin Klein eyewear on the counter and asked for a few interesting modifications. *Serious* warranty-voiding and copyright-violating stuff, and the kind of thing that there really was no legitimate use for: as blatant and illegal as sawing off a shotgun. I took it on, without asking questions, and gave her back the kit a day later. Repeat business was assured, and she'd started turning up in the sort of places I hung out in. We'd chat, maybe have a coffee or do some drugs, but nothing more came of it than that. I wasn't too sure, now, when I'd first become aware that she was involved in the English resistance; she must have told me explicitly at some point, but I couldn't remember when. We'd never actually discussed it.

"Do you still have the thing the Russian guy passed to you?"

"Of course." An object appeared in her uncurling palm like a conjuring effect. I picked it up and turned it over.

"It's a datadisk," I said, not surprised but vaguely disappointed, as though I'd been subconsciously expecting it to be a new secret weapon.

"Tell me something I don't know!"

"Maybe I can," I said. "I can tell you what's *on* it."

She shook her head. "I ran it in my reader on the train. It's garbage, or encrypted."

"Feh." I took my own reader from my pocket, patched it to my phone, and slid the disk in. "It's probably not one of the commercial codes, but I doubt it's the latest mil-spec or there wouldn't have been much point in passing it on, would there?"

"You got a point there." Her voice sounded sad. "Josif wouldn't have had access to real hard secrets anyway—this must be important more because it's current than because it's restricted."

I called up my file of thousands of keys and set them to work throwing themselves at it. This wasn't code-breaking as such, just matching the code to keys which, legally speaking, I had no business having, which is why I kept them stashed on a server far away. On the side of the screen a little red line shrank slowly as the program ran.

"Doesn't seem like enough to die for."

"He didn't know he was risking that," she said.

"Or to kill for."

"You think he was set up?" She made a sour mouth. "It's possible."

Ding, went the reader.

"Wah-hey!"

I started paging through the decoded text. Jadey leaned in to look, murmuring interest and appreciation. I paged faster, suddenly suspecting that it all looked familiar. It was.

"This is an ESA spec. Remember—the space station stuff?"

"Can you check it out?"

"Yeah, sure. Can't *do* very much with it on this thing, but . . ." I patched it over to the big screen so we could both follow it comfortably, and resumed clicking through the pages, more or less at random. Some of them were text, with the elaborate numbering system of tech spec— some individual lines within paragraphs had their own version numbers—and some, which took just a fraction of a second longer to resolve onscreen, were deep three-dimensional diagrams and schematics optimized for looking at, and through, with VR glasses or contacts. Most of these were matched either to a photograph or an indistinguishably hyperrealististic rendering of the final object.

"Y'know," Jadey pondered aloud, "I can't claim to be an expert on asteroid mining, let alone whatever equipment you'd need to talk to an alien hive-mind or whatever, but that sure doesn't look like mining equipment, or a scientific research establishment either."

I snorted. "You're right, there. You do need something like a refinery for asteroid mining, but this is more than that. Looks to me like some kind of automated factory cannibalized out of parts that might have passed muster for either that or a research station. They're *building* something out there, or planning to."

"Any indication what it might be?"

"Could be in there," I said with a shrug, "but it would be a devil of a job to find it. There's more data here than in the *Encyclopædia Britannica.*"

"Well." She gave me a funny look. "I don't think it's for us to try and figure this out." Scratched her head. "Like, I don't think we should even be looking at it."

"Oh." I clicked it off. "Especially not me, huh?"

"Especially not you. For your own peace of mind."

"That is one way of looking at it." I somewhat resented the idea that I had less business rummaging through possible state secrets than she had, but I realized this was irrational—the E.U. was no more "my" state than it was hers, and I was in my own way as much its enemy. Just not as well-trained an enemy. Not that we had torture to worry about—this was Scotland, a happy little Socialist Democracy, after all, not some Third World client-state of either side—but we both knew what the Federal Security Bureau's truth-drugs could do, and the less we knew, the less trouble we were likely to be in if we were caught.

Jadey fetched more coffee and we sat for a few moments warming our hands on the mugs and not saying anything.

"So," I said at last, "what do we do now? You still want to go to America?"

Jadey stroked her lower lip with the upper teeth, put down the mug and shoved her hands under her armpits, rocking back and forth a little. "Oh shit, I don't know," she said. "If it wasn't for the suspicion that all our codes are crackable in real time now, I'd just zap that lot through on the fast pipe and make my way home clean. Hell, if they pulled me at the airport or wherever I'd still be out in a few weeks."

"A spy-swap? But you're not—"

"Ah, some kinda analogous deal. The private sector has its ways too, okay? But as it is, I have to get that thing back physically, and it has to go separately from me. And you know what? I don't think we can rely on the mail."

"Take it to the U.S. consulate?" I suggested brightly. "Diplomatic bag?"

"I don't know if I want the statists to have it either," she said gloomily. "I don't think my friends in the Russki apparat down south wanted that. They wanted this sent to the people in the U.S. who could make the most use of it. And that means *our* people, not the spooks."

I refrained from asking further who "our people" were, and not just for security reasons. Not having been born yesterday, I already had a shrewd suspicion. One of the arguable advantages of living under the Right-Wing Communist variant of state capitalism was that the official media carried quite sensible materialist analyses, of other countries' affairs, anyway. The split in the U.S. capitalist class was a staple of *Europa Pravda* punditry. At the bottom of it, beneath all the talk about Yankees and Cowboys, Globalists and Isolationists, Old Money and New, lay a material interest that was almost embarrassingly crude—oil.

The U.S. domestic oil producers fueled the New Money forces, and the overseas oil investors lubricated the Old. The latter had taken a bloody nose in the Ural-Caspian Oil War, and the Isolationists had enjoyed a brief triumph with the hasty troop withdrawal and an opportunistic settling of old scores in the "who lost Europe?" / "Greens in the machine" witch-hunts of the early 2030s, but it hadn't taken long for Old Money to rise again to the top. Long-festering hatreds and fresh grievances were now being fought out in a low-level civil war—an assassination here, a bombing there, an angry demo against the posthumous rehabilitation of Janet Reno somewhere else.

Jadey had as much as admitted she was a New Money girl, but probably had no more idea than I had of who—behind multiple facades of funds, fronts, and foundations—was ultimately pulling her strings.

She stood up, as if having come to some decision.

"Okay," she said. "Let's do the job right here."

"What, *'here'*?" I looked around the bare room, baffled.

"Here in *Scotland*. You've got the kit and the connections to suss out that thing, whatever it is, right?"

"Well, maybe," I said, dubiously. "I'd have to bring some other people in on it. . . ."

"What I said—'connections.' I suspect part of what's going on is a faction fight somewhere high up in the apparat, which means that one side is giving covering fire to our side, at least tactically. Moves and countermoves, you know? Don't know if whoever is behind it knows we're connected, or if someone's just stringing us along in the hope of pulling in bigger fish. But I get the feeling that to panic and run would just land us, or me, and the data, in the hands of the FSB, which in the way of things is likely to be on the wrong side, from my point of view."

"And how do you know that *my* connections aren't the bigger fish they're trolling for?"

She laughed. "I don't. But, come on. You guys. They could just raid the Darwin's Arms if they wanted your connections."

"Hah!" I said. "That's just the old geeks and a few cardsharps. *I'm* talking about Webblies."

"Guns?" she asked, sounding alarmed.

"No, the union. Information Workers of the World Wide Web—the IWWWW."

She looked dubious. "I've heard about that. It was big in the twenties."

"The Global Strike, yeah, glory days. Twenty twenty-six and all that. You should hear the old bros-and-sis talk about how they nearly brought down Big Iron." I chuckled. "And you will."

"You're telling me it's still around?"

"Not as big as it used to be, but yeah. Down to a hard core of aging anarchos and impossibilists and a few young head-cases. Like me."

"Oh!" She gave me another funny look. "So *that's* where you're coming from!"

"What did you think I was, a patriot?"

"That or a totally amoral criminal."

"Thanks a lot."

She grinned, looking happier than I'd seen her in a long while. "Both of them were looking a bit more unlikely as time went on, but I didn't want to pry, just in case."

I leaned back on the sofa, looking up at her. "You should trust me even less now, you know. There's no love lost between us Webblies and your so-called libertarian capitalists."

She waved a hand. "Oh, that." She laughed. "I don't trust you an inch, actually, but trust doesn't come into it—prediction does. I know now which way you're likely to jump."

"We'll see about that."

I jumped up, surprising her and myself by giving her an awkward, one-arm hug around the shoulders, and walked out to the main door. The drama of this was marred by my being unable to actually open the door, Jadey having locked it from the inside. I stepped aside and let her unlock it.

She looked up at me just before the door swung open.

"So where are we going now?"

"Somewhere safer, warmer, and pleasanter," I told her. "The union office."

"Wow," she said. "You sure know how to show a girl a good time."

"You'll be surprised," I told her.

The IWWWW building in Picardie Place, opposite the Playhouse at the top of Leith Walk, was slightly decrepit but still imposing: seven stories of concrete and glass, post-war but not new-tech. I had no doubt it was watched, but I didn't think the surveillance would be more than routine. Officially classified as "hostile and slanderous toward the state and social system of Socialist Democracy," the IWWWW was officially tolerated as a textbook (and, more importantly, *newscast*) example of how tolerant and pluralist Socialist Democracy really was.

As I swiped my union card through the lock, Jadey eyed the slogan chiseled in neat roman capitals above the doorway: THE WORKING CLASS AND THE EMPLOYING CLASS HAVE NOTHING IN COMMON.

"Hmm," she said as the door swung back for us. "What about common humanity?"

"After three world wars? Don't make me laugh."

The entrance lobby was empty except for the guy at the reception desk, who glanced up then returned to his book. I inhaled deeply of the familiar smell of the place—the rubber flooring, the faint waft of sweat and chlorine from the gym and swimming-pool downstairs; the tang of alcohol and herbal smoke from the bar on the first floor alongside the warmer, steamier cafeteria odors; and underlying it all the sharp notes of wire and plastic and fresh cement from the ongoing overhaul of the electronics.

Jadey, too, was sniffing, watching a middle-aged man and a couple of young women, all carrying towels and soft drinks, stroll past and pad down the steps.

"Not what I expected," she admitted as we headed for the lift. "Reminds me of a youth hostel—or the YMCA." She grinned as the lift arrived. " 'Young Militants' Class-War Association,' anybody?"

"Near enough," I allowed, jabbing the fourth-floor button. "We're a sociable lot. You can even stay the night here."

She smiled, distantly, at some point behind my shoulder. The lift doors *thunk*ed shut. We stood for a moment in infinite reflections and varying g-forces, then stepped out. The fourth floor was not as benign and casual-looking as the ones we'd seen. Long, carpeted corridors, heavy doors, everything beaded with cameras. The electric smell was strong.

I ambled down the corridor, Jadey pacing cautiously after me, until I reached the door marked 413. Another card-swipe and we were in. The room was about ten meters by five, windowless, strip-lit, filled with half a dozen long tables with swivel seats, keyboards, and screens. It had the look of a classroom or learning-lab. Nobody else was there, which was a relief. I stepped over to the wall-mounted keypad and hastily booked the room until midnight: greedy, but unlikely to be challenged.

"Right," I said, sitting down and inviting Jadey, with a suitably expansive gesture, to do the same. She did, curling her legs under the swivel chair's seat and giving it a spin.

"God, what a tedious place," she remarked. "Even the walls are bare. No pictures, no screens."

"Yeah, well, there's a reason," I said. "They're *firewalls*." I smirked at my own feeble joke.

I took out my reader and uncoiled some cable, and connected it to the back of the nearest screen. "Could I have your disk again please?" She spun it over.

I slotted it into the reader, powered up the screen and board, and keyed in a password. The familiar Microsoft Windows 2045 image floated up, to be instantly replaced by a demonically laughing penguin which left the words BUT SERIOUSLY . . . fading on the screen before cutting to the primary interface. I patched through a quick call to the satellite server, asking for an immediate downlink download. That took about a minute—the office, naturally, had roof antennae and bandwidth to burn—after which I leaned back, hands behind my head, legs as close as my precarious balance would permit to putting my feet up.

"That's a load off my mind," I said.

"Great," said Jadey. "Care to explain what I should be feeling relieved about?"

"Depends how much you want to hear about computers," I said, swinging my feet to the floor, my elbows to my knees, and leaning forward earnestly. As usual I felt a little awkward talking about this subject; if I wasn't careful I could easily end up sounding like an old geek.

Jadey waved a hand, generously. "I'll tell you when to fast-forward."

"Fine. . . . Well, basically, we—that is, the biz—have become fairly reliant on what we call the empty-hand model." I waved my reader. "Like this thing. It's a wireless terminal, pretty dumb by the standards of the systems it's accessing, which are usually on hardware a long way away. Makes you overdependent on encryption, for one thing, and on the goodwill of the server owners, for another. That's exactly the kind of thing us Webblies like to avoid. It tends to, shall we say, weaken your negotiating position. We've always been big on the workers controlling the means of production. Result: This building has so much computing power packed in it that you need never go outside it for any program that can be feasibly run at all." I scratched my head. "Apart from ones that need dedicated distributed processors, anyway. What it means is that I've just copied everything I've got, and everything you got, onto the machines in here. And the great thing about them is, they're not accessible from the outside. That download had to go through the equivalent of a series of airlocks and showers before it was stored. Nobody can hack in to them."

"Like, this place is a data haven?" She glanced around, looking more respectful.

"Not quite," I said. "Physically, it's not terribly secure against serious reverse social engineering, but apart from that, yeah—it's pretty safe. We can now work on the data with a fair certainty that nobody's snooping on us."

She cocked her head. "Except from inside?"

"Hey," I said. "This is the union. We have rules against that sort of thing."

"Okay," she said. "What next?"

"I pull together a small company to investigate this thing." I turned back to the screen. "I have a lot of good contacts for this."

"Maybe you do," she said, "but not tonight."

"What?"

She stared at me, then reached out and caught my hand. "Come on. I've had a *murderously* long day. Let's go down to the bar, then I'll take you up on the offer of a bed for the night."

First I knew of the offer, but I didn't refuse.

5

Cosmonaut Keep

ELIZABETH HARKNESS SOUGHT the dress she needed in the back of Ancient Finery, an old shop in the old town, popular with students but hitherto not one of her haunts. Kyohvic, and Tain, and indeed Mingulay in general, had a textile-and-garment industry, but nothing like a self-sustaining fashion industry. Left to themselves, there was little doubt that styles would have changed as slowly in the towns as they did in the villages along the coast: Fashion would have become costume, with mere individual and local variants of cut and decoration. The starships changed all that, their irregular but frequent arrivals imposing a jerky punctuation on that tendency to equilibrium. Fads and fancies, years or decades dead in their places and planets of origin, freakishly flourished in this backwater, until the next arrival of new notions from the sky. The whole relationship, she was pleased to realize, was the precise opposite of what Gregor had thought it was: If the merchants didn't know what the fashion was in Kyohvic, it was because they set (or reset) it with their every arrival.

This wasn't the only relationship Gregor was getting wrong. Elizabeth wasn't sure if he was arrogant or just *blind* or if he just plain found her unattractive or (more hopefully) that he misinterpreted every one of her looks and gestures as part of their relationship as friends and colleagues.

But she had no more idea than he of what would be the Next Big Thing at the merchants' ball, and no way of affording what the better-off ladies of the town would wear to it while they eyed up whatever the ladies of the latest ship were showing off; so the best she could do was to go for something so out-of-date that it wasn't *un*fashionable.

Ancient Finery, the best of several such by-products of Mingulay's externally driven style-cycle, was the place to look.

Thus, a couple of days after the ship had arrived, Elizabeth left the lab early—it was a Saturday anyway—hurried to her parents' home in the new town, and hastily changed and showered to remove the lingering taint of dead marine life from her hair and, especially, her hands, and took the electric bus down to the cobblestoned streets of old Kyohvic below the university's fastness.

A pair of chipped shop-window dummies guarded the shop's doorway. The male figure was resplendent in a generations-old braided guard's uniform from a minor estate on Croatan, the female slightly risqué in a chinoiserie chemise off the last-but-one starship from somewhere farther in. Elizabeth considered it for a reckless moment, then smiled at herself and pressed on into the shop's cavernous, brightly-lit interior. The ceiling was at least two stories high, hung at intervals with clumps of long dresses; the walls accommodated two rows, one above the other, of dresses and coats; smaller and shorter garments were shelved or hung on portable rails standing on the floor. The air of the place was a marvelous mélange of the smell of old but clean clothes, cleaning-fluid, phantom scents, patchouli potpourri, joss-sticks permanently burning, and the occasional cigarette surreptitiously smoked by the girl at the till.

Elizabeth took a deep breath and plunged happily in. An hour passed without her noticing. Apart from the—for her—rarely indulged frivolously feminine fun of it all, something about the layered antiquity of the shop's stock appealed to her scientific spirit. There was history here, even astronomy, an almost inconceivably minute particular of the kind of evidence you could find in the fossil record or the shock-shell of an exploded star. Wisps of fabric and echoes of ideas that had moved at the speed of light. . . . She thought about it with one part of her mind, while another part guided her rummaging and considering and discarding.

Nothing here dated back to the *Bright Star*'s arrival, or even to the cultural explosion that had followed hard upon it. Anything that historic was in the museums, not the secondhand clothes shops. But some of the stuff showed traces of influences, radiated out from Mingulay and bounced back—voyages later, decades later—of fashions from twenty-first-century Earth: silly little details that she recognized from the ship's picture files, such as the drawstring hem and the duffel button, these trivial impracticalities betraying their origins like junk DNA.

History, like fashion, was a necessarily disjointed process in the Second Sphere. New arrivals from Earth were rare, migrations between planets within the Sphere relatively frequent. Any of them could jolt society forward, or at least out of its previous course, as the *Bright Star* had done to Mingulay's.

Approximately six hundred and fifty years ago, Elizabeth's ancestors had arrived on Croatan. About a thousand people: some English, some Indians, a shipload of Africans, and not all from the same place or even (from what later historians had deduced from fragmentary records and traditions) the same time. Others—fishermen, sailors, and slaves rescued from the wild Atlantic by beings that some of them saw as angels, others as demons—arrived in small, bewildered consignments as time went on. The dates of their origin were not necessarily in the same order as the dates of their arrival. Out of two centuries and half of living on this world—newer than the New World from which most of their ancestors had come—and of trying to make some sense of it and of the other worlds with which they gradually came into contact, a sect had emerged that the majority of Croatan's human community called the Scoffers—a name which they eventually claimed proudly for themselves. Their prophetess, Joanna Tain, had preached that the greater universe revealed to them by their displacement, and the strange nature of its other inhabitants, left the Scriptures at best irrelevant ("a Revelation solely to the People of the Earth, as the Law of Moses was unto the people of Israel, and not Universall, as even the Scripture itselfe saith")—at worst, false. The influence of the Stoic and Epicurean philosophies of Nova Babylonia was evident in her doctrines, and deplored.

Blood had been shed, and after urgent appeals from both sides the gray folk had moved in swiftly to evacuate Tain's few thousand followers and to set them down on another planet, which they named Mingulay. They had been there two centuries when the *Bright Star* had risen in their sky, and had brought heresies beyond the wildest rantings of Joanna, and evidence that the universe was even stranger than she had supposed. The ship's library had become the foundation of the university and of most science and technology, and a good deal of the culture and art, in the hands of humans on Mingulay—and on an expanding radius of other worlds.

And hence, Elizabeth supposed, the dress she eventually decided on. She found it in the back of the shop, on the inside of a bundle of frocks on wire hangers suspended from the same wall-hook. She disengaged them carefully, took one look at the last dress, and put the rest less carefully back.

It had a bodice of embroidered leaves, in satin silk and autumn colors; its long, wide skirts of organza over net a darker shade and stiffer texture, fading and fraying to cobweb consistency toward the hems; and to go with it, a long-sleeved short jacket of gold-colored lace. She carried them triumphantly behind the curtain of the changing-alcove, stepped out a few minutes later to do a twirl in front of a freestanding mirror. She liked the outfit so much that she had to make a conscious decision not wear it home on the bus.

If the tall servant just inside the doorway of the Cosmonauts' keep thought her hooded oilskin cape amusing in its practicality and contrast with her dress, his expression as he took it gave no sign. She smiled at him, thanked him, and walked quickly on into the entrance hall. There was no more formal greeting, no announcement or introductions. It wasn't that kind of party; it was assumed, at least as a polite fiction, that anyone turning up already knew enough people present to make such a protocol redundant.

Elizabeth wasn't too sure about that. She felt very much on her own, she would have very much liked some welcoming person to show her in, as she passed from the shadows of the passage to the bright light of the main hall. She felt unsteady on her feet, and not just because the heels of her shoes (borrowed for the occasion from her sister) were higher than she was used to. The only sound that seemed louder than the thumping of her heart was the rustle of her dress, like the sound of walking through a heap of dry leaves.

The great room was laid out for a cold buffet and for dancing, with long tables, chairs, and benches along two of the walls, and tables laden with food and drink along the third, with the musicians—at the moment tuning up their instruments—in the corner formed by that wall and the wall which contained the fireplace. For a couple of seconds, Elizabeth paused just inside the doorway, gawping at the gigantic decorations on the walls; the scale of everything—walls, carpets, animal heads—was about twice what a human scale should have been. Even the portraits were large, and high up. Then she walked firmly onward, relieved to see that about a hundred people had already arrived, so that she wasn't embarrassingly early or late. Several of them—the old Cosmonaut Cairns, the university's Chancellor, the owner of Mueller's Mill—she recognized as from a distance, and one or two she knew personally. Gregor, so far, wasn't among them, which was also a relief, in a way.

"Oh, hello, Harkness." Mark Garnet, the head of the marine-biology department, hailed her and beckoned her over to the huddle of academics at the drinks table. A small, rather fat man with slicked-back dark hair—he'd always irresistibly reminded her of a seal—Garnet was probably her best friend in the staff hierarchy, always helpful with a knotty statistical problem or an obscure reference.

"What's your pleasure?" he asked.

She glanced over the array of glasses. "Ah, white wine for now, I think."

"Very good, very good." He passed her a glass and waved at a slender, almost skinny woman by his side. "Now, Harkness, this is my wife, Judith."

"Pleased to meet you." The two women bobbed politely at each other. Judith's dress was slim-fitted and elegant, not new but not secondhand either, her hair coiled and stacked.

"I should warn you," Garnet went on, "that she has absolutely no interest in biology, so let's not talk shop."

They took their glasses and sat down at the corner of one of the tables, gossiping idly about the department's office politics while watching the growing throng. More people were arriving: guildmasters and journeymen, industrialists and engineers, heresiarchs in tall black hats and Scoffers in black suits with broad white collars, their swords on their belts. The interstellar merchant and his family and retinue made a particularly grand entrance. The men wore long linen coats with embroidered waistcoats over shirts and knee-breeches, the women loose gowns in various jewel or pastel shades of satin. The dresses' construction was simple, their decoration elaborate, with signifiers of age and status suggested by variations in the length, and presence and absence, of collars and sleeves.

"Not bad," Judith remarked, sotto voce. "Looks like Nova Babylonia is still setting its own styles. For now, at least. Our ancestors really shouldn't have let those costume-history picture books out in the universe. Heaven only knows what concoctions are being contrived right now out of Earth's old dressing-up box."

Elizabeth grinned at her. "Funny, I was thinking along those lines myself, when I was looking for a party dress today."

"Hmm, I don't know," Mark said. "I don't think Nova Babylonia has had time to be influenced. I mean, what's the turnaround time?"

"Shorter than a craze, back there," Judith said. She sounded slightly disapproving. Nova Babylonia had a fantasy reputation, going all the way back to the first contacts with Croatan, as a land of luxury, almost of decadence—an image intensified by the relative rarity of actual contact and reliable information. Hundred-year-old news would be eagerly seized upon at this party, and at trade negotiations, and talked about for years, or until the next ship came along. There was little doubt that the frequency would increase, now that Nova Babylonia's merchants were actively responding to the new developments in the colony, rather than discovering them for the first time. But no matter how frequently it arrived, the news would always be a hundred years old. . . .

"Anyway," said Judith, "you pulled a good dress out of the box yourself. So tell me, where did you find it?"

Elizabeth smiled sideways at Mark. "Now *we're* talking shop," she said. Mark gave them both an ironic wave and wandered off to pick up some food and information.

As he strolled into the hall Gregor felt slightly self-conscious in an heirloom outfit of black velvet jacket, white shirt, and narrow black trousers, but nobody looked at him twice. In the jacket's inside pocket, rather spoiling its drape, was a sheaf of folded-up papers over which he'd sweated all that day and most of the previous night. His grandfather, James, had included the demand, as imperative as a tax return, with his invitation.

He knew the hall, and the castle, from holiday memories of childhood and, more rarely, of adolescence. These days, though still fond of his grandparents, he visited it more often in dreams. His father had—wisely, Gregor thought—done what most descendants of the original crew had done, and moved out and struck out on his own in his teens, several years before Gregor was born. Now the owner of a substantial fishing-fleet, Frederick Cairns was pleased that his first son shared his enthusiasm for the business, and brusquely tolerant of his second son's more academic interest in marine life. Of his father James's far more abstract interests and motivations, Frederick affected nothing but contempt.

Over at the buffet table, Gregor selected a small stack of mollusca and crustacea, a pinch of herbs, a clump of vegetables and a spoonful of rice, picked up a glass of red wine on the sound theory that it was the faster route to intoxication, and looked around rather vaguely for anyone he knew or somewhere to sit. Some of the local children, looking stiffer and more awkward in their formal clothes than Gregor, were staring and nudging each other in response to the saurs. It was rare, in Kyohvic, to see as many as thirty of them in one place, and the opportunity to gawp and murmur was also being taken, more discreetly, by the adults.

Gregor turned away, embarrassed by this rustic behavior, and found himself face-to-face with a young woman whom he instantly evaluated as the most beautiful he'd ever seen in his life. Her skin was the color of amber, her long and wavy hair of jet, her large dark eyes of bright mahogany, all of it set off by the glowing pink of the straight, soft dress which gently skimmed and subtly showed the contours of her body. Hands full, like his, with plate and glass and carefully balanced cutlery, she looked at him with a charmingly helpless but somehow self-mocking appeal. She looked as though about to say something, but hesitating to speak. Gregor felt the same way himself. Something—his heart, presumably—was jumping about inside him.

He smiled (a terrifying rictus, he was sure) and took a quick sip of wine to stop his mouth from going completely dry. "Good evening," he said. "Are you wondering where to sit?"

"Yes, thank you," she said. "Actually"—she laughed lightly, and took a sip of her own wine, white—"I have been most firmly told to mingle with the—the natives?—and practice the language and I'm not sure whom to speak to first."

"Well," Gregor said, "perhaps you might like to sit and speak with me, for a while?"

"Oh yes," she said, suddenly sounding confident. "That would be very utilitarian."

Gregor indicated with his eyes an empty space at a table across the hall, and followed her to it, amazed that everyone in the whole place wasn't attending to her every shimmy and shimmer as much as he was. But then—as some gibbering, scientific, detached part of his mind, the monkey on his back, pointed out—he wasn't actually *seeing* the rest of the party, so the issue was moot.

They sat down, half facing each other on a bench. Another moment of not knowing what to say. Gregor pointed a thumb at his chest. "Gregor Cairns."

"My name is Lydia de Tenebre," the girl said gravely; and then, more casually, "the merchant Esias de Tenebre's seventh daughter, third child of his second wife. I am nineteen years old and I was born"—she waved a hand—"oh, hundreds and hundreds of years ago."

"I must say you don't look it." As soon as he'd said it Gregor was certain he'd just made a stupid remark, the first thing which had popped into his head, but Lydia laughed. She flicked her hair back and at that moment Gregor belatedly realized he was smitten, "stabbed by the arrow of Eros" as the poet had said, and that her objective age was not only the strangest but also the most significant thing about her: the one that hung over everything that might happen between them.

"Now, can you tell me about yourself, and your family?" she asked, as though it were the next item on a protocol.

"I'm training to be a marine biologist," he said. "My father is a fisherman, my mother teaches children. My grandfather—over there—has the more or less hereditary post of Navigator."

"What do those old people do, the ones who call themselves the Cosmonauts? How do they live?" She looked around, at the walls and ceiling. "How do they afford . . . all this? They are not merchants. Are they rulers?"

Gregor rubbed the back of his neck, with a sense of being defensive. "No, not exactly, the real rulers here are the Heresiarchy, although Driver—that's the big guy talking to my grandfather—is a very powerful man. The Security Man."

He scratched his head as she frowned over this. "He runs the police business here. It used to be for the castle and the university, but now it's for the whole town."

"All right," she said, as though comprehending, but probably not, "and what about the rest?"

"They're some of the descendants of the crew of the old starship. Every generation there have been a few people who nominally took the posts that their ancestors in the original crew had held." He shrugged. "It's a tradition. The first crew took over this castle because the local people had left it empty, and because it was, well, a castle! Easily defended. When they came here they were able to sell knowledge and technology to the existing population, and indeed to the saurs and later to merchants from other worlds. Eventually they established the university, which became a research center for local industry and agriculture and fisheries. And not just local industry—we get students and scientists from the nearer worlds, particularly Croatan. The nominal crew still get an income from it, and from other investments, and they oversee it. A hereditary sinecure. Not a very demanding job, but they do it to maintain a continuity with the ship, and with Earth."

"A continuity which is now being lost, then?"

A shrewd question, and not one it would be politic to fully answer. "Yes, it's being lost. My father has no intention of becoming the Navigator, and nor do I. But my grandfather, I hope, has many years to live, and if I have sons one of them may wish to take his place."

"Or daughters?"

Gregor's cheeks burned. "Of course, yes."

Lydia's dark eyes sparkled, perhaps in amusement at his evident discomfiture. "And what would it involve, being the Navigator?"

"Oh, I'll show you," said Gregor. He fished the folded papers from his pocket and spread them on the table. The papers were covered with crabbed symbols and labored diagrams.

"A few months ago James, my grandfather, sent me this problem. It involves logic and mathematics, neither of which I'm very good at. But I worked at it, on and off, until yesterday evening, when James sent me a message asking me to deliver the solution tonight." He looked down at the paper ruefully. "I've wasted all day on it, but at least it's done."

She poked at the edge of the papers with a perfectly oval fingernail. "You have no calculating-machines to do this?"

Careful now, careful! "We do, of course, have calculating-machines. But not all calculation can be left to machines." It was an ethical platitude throughout the Second Sphere.

"Indeed not," she said solemnly. "But if you are not talented for this, why not give the problem to people who are?"

You've put your pretty little fingernail right on the problem, he thought. "Ah, well, the point of doing this is to keep certain skills alive within the family."

Which was true, though with a different emphasis to the one he gave it. The explanation seemed to satisfy her, and she peered at the pages for a moment and was on the point of reaching to pick them up when James Cairns hurried over. Gregor stood up and embraced him.

"Don't flash that stuff around!" James hissed in Gregor's ear.

"I wasn't!" Gregor protested, into his grandfather's shoulder. He turned to Lydia.

"Lydia, this is James Cairns, the Navigator, my grandfather."

As Gregor introduced him the old man bowed and kissed the young woman's hand, and groped out over the table with his free hand and stuffed the calculations into his pocket. Lydia, looking straight at Gregor over James's head, observed this maneuver with a wry smile. Gregor covered his embarrassment with a wink.

James sat down, one space down from Lydia. At least he wasn't sitting between them.

"So, Gregor, how's it going for you out on the wild ocean?"

"Oh, fine, thanks." Gregor launched into an account of his recent adventures, and minor though they were they had Lydia gazing at him with her lips parted and her eyebrows occasionally twitching up. James listened, and watched with a more quizzical eye.

"Any new information on the squids?" he asked, when Gregor had concluded with an account of the recent evening when the ship— Lydia's family's ship—had come in.

Gregor shrugged. "Nothing but observations, like that one. I'll write it up—well, one of us who were there will. For what it's worth."

"Indeed." James contemplated the small glass of spirit he'd brought with him, and lit up a joint. Lydia's eyes widened as he passed it to her. She sipped at, rather than inhaled, the smoke and passed it on hastily to Gregor. He drew on it deeply and passed it back to his grandfather.

"Actually," James smiled, "I was inquiring about your research on the little fellas. Not the krakens! As old Matt used to say, they are still a fucking fortean phenomenon."

Gregor glared at him, and the old man turned apologetically to Lydia. "Excuse my language." He passed her the joint again, and again she took the smoke into her mouth, puffed it out, and passed to Gregor.

"I understand 'fucking' and 'phenomenon,' " she said. "But what is 'fortean'?"

"I was about to ask that myself," said Gregor, the lift of the high raising him above his annoyance at the old man's vulgarity.

"Ah," said James complacently, swaying back and forth as he finished off the now diminished roach. "According to the records from our starship, the *Bright Star,* the people back on Earth experienced many phenomena which they could not explain—for which they could not, one might say, account—which were catalogued by a man named Charles Fort, and such phenomena came to be called 'fortean.' These phenomena included, I may add, our friends the saurs, and their gravity skiffs, and for all I know to the contrary, the flaming starships. Sorry, Lydia. And strange monsters in the sea. Now, as far as we are concerned, the goddamn kraken or squids or *Archi*-frigging-*teuthys* are still strange monsters in the sea. But perhaps they're more familiar to you and your family, eh?"

Lydia cradled her chin on her interlaced fingers and looked from

James to Gregor and back again. The only effect that the weed had had on her seemed to be that she saw the funny side of this blatant attempt to pump her for information.

"Oh yes," she said. "We have . . . communion with them. The saurs are with us to translate, of course, but we believe we are talking to the kraken." She smiled mischievously at James. "They are our real 'navigators.' My father is impressed that you have managed to equal their accomplishment."

"If not their feet!" James's pun was lost on her, to Gregor's relief, and at that moment the band struck up at last. Gregor rose and reached out a hand to Lydia.

"May I have the honor?"

"Of course, thank you." She stood up, stepped over the bench in a pink flutter and curtseyed, a gesture with which he was not familiar but which he found charming.

"Have a good time," said James, with woozy benevolence. He shot Gregor a sharp look, not stoned or drunk at all. "I'll talk to you later."

The first dance was measured and formal, more typical of this kind of reception than of Mingulay's native traditions, and Gregor found himself taking the wrong steps. But if Lydia noticed she didn't seem to mind, and after a few minutes the dance's sedate pace allowed them to carry on their conversation.

"Do you and your family actually live on the ship?"

"Oh no." Twirl. "We rent a villa in Nova Babylonia." Two steps back. "On other worlds we rely on hospitality, or on commercial guesthouses." Step forward, half-turn, raise hand, take hand, turn about. "The ship is designed for the krakens, not for us. Much of the interior is permanently awash." Smile, wrinkle nose. "And it smells." Let go, step back two paces. Hold out both hands, step forward twice. "Of fish." Catch.

Warm caught hands, delicate and bony and fluttery and alarming as little songbats. The music stopped. She curtseyed, he bowed.

"So where in the ship," said Gregor, in a voice which to him sounded rather strained, "do you actually travel?"

"In the skiffs, of course. We ride them out to the ship—which may be on the sea or in space, depending on the locality—and off again, as you saw the other night. Sometimes we have to wade around within the ship to check and secure the cargo. So for the journeys we dress rough, not like this." She plucked at her skirt, smiled. "But that's all before and after. The journey itself takes no time." She snapped her fingers. "Like that."

They sat down again, beside their neglected plates. James had wandered back into the crowd, perhaps tactfully leaving them alone. Gregor was uncomfortably aware that he'd be back, or that he'd corner him somewhere and impart some urgent family message. Lydia began to eat, quickly and deftly, interspersed with chat. Gregor munched more slowly; less used to this kind of socializing, he was for most of the time reduced to gestures and nods and grunts, as he listened to Lydia talking about the other worlds of the Sphere. It had never struck him quite so forcibly before how much similarity underlay their diversity, all their different words written in the same alphabet of DNA. They were no more different, ultimately, than continents on a single planet—or rather, their differences were an extension of that kind of reproductive isolation, as though all their continents and oceans were features of a single enormous world. Their model, and the common origin of their organisms, was distant, unreachable Earth.

Wherever he ate seafood, which was often, the thought that there was something subtly wrong with eating squid—even such as now lay on his plate; tiny, non-sentient relatives or ancestors of the kraken— swam to the surface of his mind. It was almost as bad as eating monkeys. But in the warmer climes and worlds, people did eat monkeys. Lizards, too, for that matter. He decided that this was a thought it would be unkind to share.

Lydia dabbed her lips with a napkin and glanced at her empty glass. "More?"

"Yes, please. White."

Gregor made his way through the now much-denser crowd and past the now livelier dancing, on the fringes of which earnest discussions were going on between the visiting traders and their local counterparts. He felt a tremor permanently radiating outward from his solar plexus, the arrow's target. Dizzily he contemplated that he had fallen in love, a most unfortunate experience, but one which like any other illness could only be lived through, or died from. So taught the Scoffers, but at this moment—and this itself was a symptom—Gregor was unable to conceive of ever again being anything but a believer.

As he passed one of the tables he caught sight of a third cousin, Clarissa, who sat there unself-consciously suckling her newest baby, and he paused to greet and congratulate her. They talked for a few moments, exchanging family gossip, while Gregor admired the infant.

"What lovely tiny toes she has," he said, tickling them under a lacy hem.

"Why do men always say that?" Clarissa asked, smiling. "And it's a boy. Owen. That's his moistening-gown." She looked up hopefully. "The ceremony's tomorrow, in the North Street Meeting-House. Would you like to come along?"

"I'll do my best, Clarissa," he said, and after some more chat continued on his way to the drinks table.

He'd picked up a couple of filled glasses when his elbow was gripped.

"A moment, Gregor."

"Oh, hello again, Grandpa."

The old man smiled. "Don't go making me feel old. You're old enough now to call me James."

Gregor dipped his head. "I'll remember."

"I see you're in a hurry," the Navigator said, still holding Gregor's elbow like the Ancient Mariner. "So I'll make it quick."

Just as he'd expected, Gregor found himself backed into a corner.

"Yes, go ahead," he said, holding up the two glasses and pointedly not drinking.

"That girl you're talking to—for gods' sakes don't give her any hint about the family business, about what the Great Work actually is."

"I haven't." He thought for a moment. "And I don't know, anyway."

"Good." James grinned slyly. "I've glanced over what you handed me, Gregor, and I have to say it's good work. Damn sight better than anything your uncles and cousins have come up with. Now, we need to get on with it a bit urgently. I know you have research and responsibilities of your own, but is there any chance you could spare some time to help me out?"

"Ah, I suppose so," Gregor said cautiously. James evidently took his assent as much firmer than it was.

"Thank you," he said. "Let's make it tomorrow." Gregor's involuntary look of dismay was met with another sly grin. "And it would give you a reason to come up to the castle."

"Well, seeing you put it that way . . ." Gregor frowned for a moment. "Tell you what. I'll arrange to meet Lydia, if she wants to see me, at some time and then arrive a couple of hours before that to see you. Probably late morning—I'm going to Clarissa's latest offspring's wetting first, if I'm up to it."

"Excellent!" James finally let go of his arm, and Gregor made his escape.

Elizabeth, after tactfully and politely extricating herself from, in succession, the company of the Garnets, a deep conversation with Tharovar and Salasso, and a dance with one of Gregor's cousins whom she'd two years ago had a fling with, finally caught sight of Gregor's progress around the side of the room. She pressed after him, but by the time she saw him again he was back at the table and talking with Lydia, and it did not take more than a few seconds' observation of both their faces for her to realize that she was altogether too late.

She turned away before either of them could see her. Not that there was much risk of that. Seeing no more of the rest of the crowd than they did, she walked out, at first slowly, then with increasing speed after she'd grabbed her coat from the steward at the door. There was no rain and it was not a cold night, for spring, but she shrugged the oilskin on, buttoning it and wrapping her arms about herself as she walked away from the light and music, the coat's heavy length crushing the fragile skirts underneath it, and she didn't care. Her feet hurt in the shoes as she clattered along the castle's long driveway, and she didn't care. The hell with all that, her boots and breeks would be comfortable enough; she wouldn't meet Gregor again in anything else.

The starship shone on the water like a misshapen moon. She didn't hate the girl—too elegant and delicate and innocent a creature to dislike. No, it was Gregor, the unseeing, unfeeling bastard, with her own attention in his face every day, and who responded to it with friendly familiarity, as though she were one of the lads; she hated him.

6

Trusted Third Parties

Y OU KNOW," JASON said, munching fried slice and looking around
the union cafeteria, "this place is not terribly secure. As in, physically." He waved his hands at the wide windows, one of which was
propped slightly open.

"Tell me about it," Jadey grouched. "Back home, a union office—
or anything kinda oppositional like that—would be a lot more *defen-
sible*."

We'd set the business meeting up as a working breakfast for eleven
A.M., to which I'd invited Jason, Tony, and Alec Curran, all of whom
had useful skills, were unlikely to betray us, and were Webblies themselves. Not that there was any necessary correlation between these three
facts, mind you. I had discussed the two old programmers with Jason
first—guardedly, on the phone—and he'd assured me that they were
sound.

The cafeteria was pretty busy at this time in the morning, mostly
with the support staff and Webbly volunteers—the union was proud to
have not a single full-timer or paid official. Those who weren't en-
grossed in their own conversations were watching the video wall, where
some daytime TV host had set up a discussion between the Pope, from
his home in Rome, and the Moderator of the General Assembly of the
Church of Scotland, from her home in Harare, Zimbabwe. The host's
attempts to pry open some theological differences on the question of
alien life were bouncing off a commendably firm Christian united front.
The Church, one gathered, had always believed that superhuman, but
not divine, intelligences lived in the heavens above us.

Curran made dangerous gestures with his fork, to hold our attention
until he succeeded in swallowing. He turned to Jadey. "It's like this,"

he said, in a maddening tone of patient explanation. "We *could* turn this place into a fortress, but what good would it do? If the state ever decided to crack down on us, it could bring overwhelming force to bear. There's no way we could beat the state at the violence game. Violence is what it's good for. What it's not so good at is spreading ideas around, and it's ultimately ideas in people's heads that make them decide whether or not to use the guns in their hands. The state is good at applying force, but not at legitimizing force. So as long as most people believe we're not doing any harm and should be left alone, we have a good chance of being left alone. Turning ourselves into an armed camp would cut against that, even assuming they'd let us do it."

"I was thinking more about physical infiltration," Jason replied mildly. "Smart dust and stuff."

"Positive pressure," I said. "The windows blow, they don't suck. Besides, the place does not have ECM. Not state-of-the-art, but not bad." I smiled at Jadey. Her toes were exploring the top of my foot, under the table. "Good enough for government work. No, seriously, I think our only problem is reverse social engineering, and as Alec says, that's a political problem, not a physical one. We're as safe here as anywhere."

Jadey looked dubious. "Surely there are places where you can have a bit more privacy? Up in the Highlands, maybe?"

Curran nearly choked; the rest of us just smiled. "The Highlands are the worst," Curran said when he'd got his breath back. "The land reform really bought the Party a lot of support up there."

"Oh well." Jadey dismissed the matter. "I guess that computer room looks safe enough. We're doing it from there, right?"

"Right."

"So what are we doing there, anyway?" Tony asked.

"Basically," I said, very carefully, "We're doing some work on a contract I got yesterday. I need a bit of help from you three, and you're all subcontracted at the standard rate if you want." I waved a hand. "We'll sort out the screenwork later. Okay so far?"

Nods all round.

"Fine," I went on. "However, Jadey here has come across a set of files from ESA. And you all know how important that's suddenly become, and how . . . Well, you remember what Charlie was going on about last night."

I really had their attention.

"I'd like to know what it is. You all warm with that?"

The two old code-geeks responded with piratical grins; Jason nodded soberly.

I looked around. "Okay. Everybody ready?"

We gathered up our final coffees and trooped off up the stairs to what Jadey had called the computer room. Alec remarked how funny that was, how it took him back . . . but it was a thoroughly modern toolkit of readers and VR goggles and contacts that we all deployed as we clustered around the old-fashioned keyboards and screens. I'd already roped in my suite of AIs, had copies of all of them and of my usual software libraries safely corralled in the building's own cores; I'd double-checked with the agency first thing in the morning (over Jadey's mumbled protests; over Jadey's legs . . .) and confirmed that the ESA contract was still valid, even after last night's surprising and historic announcement.

I'd brought in the two code-geeks, Tony and Alec, in case we needed to deal directly with the antiquated underlying software of the ESA system. Jason's specialities, honed in his various ID-forgery sidelines, were in VR work and security systems. VR work looks easy, but without a good grip on indexing and shortcuts and search methodologies it becomes like a physical search for a small object in a large space— not so much a needle in a haystack as a needle on a prairie.

I paused, the goggles on the bridge of my nose. Jadey was sitting on the next workbench along, swinging her legs like a bored kid and doing something delicate to her fingernails with a disproportionately large lock-knife.

"Want to join us?"

She shook her head. "I'll keep lookout."

Hardly necessary, I thought, but if that was how she wanted to play it—

"Fine by me," I said. "Okay, guys, just follow me in."

I slid the goggles up the final quarter-inch and fitted them snugly over my eyes. A blink, and I was in, my viewpoint floating in front of an abstract rendering of the project as a monolithic closed book. The others hung behind my shoulders; I could feel them on the back of my neck, though if I looked behind, I couldn't see them—an odd, uncanny sensation, like being watched by a ghost. My AIs swooped around us like excited birds as I opened the book. Cascading dominoes of indexes unfolded across the virtual space.

The real information necessary for a material-requirement planning system was a barely detectable fraction of what was available here. What I most urgently wanted to find out was whether the end product of the process was defined or described anywhere, and if so, what it was. Fortunately, this was the sort of thing that project-management software and skills were ready-made for, so I led my troops into the jungle with a mental shout of *Banzai*!

The refinery-complex arrangements that Jadey and I had seen earlier were the obvious place to start, so I did. Meanwhile I sent the AIs on a trawl of the documentation, using conceptual search criteria to look for any references to output or completion.

The first thing I realized, now that I had time to look properly, was that I had been quite mistaken about the scale—the "refinery" was in fact only a roomful of incredibly fine machinery. I immediately began thinking in terms of the machinery and supplies required to make such machinery—to bore pipes of that diameter to the necessary tolerances, the expense of supplying even a few molecules of transplutonic stable isotopes—rare artificial atoms from the "island of stability" with atomic weights well into the low hundreds—and set up a production process, or at least a supply schedule, whose product would be this machine, whose own product I didn't know. Close up, the machinery looked almost organic—it had that evolved complexity, unplanned and seren-dipitous, that you can see in electron micrographs of cells and in flow-charts of mitochondria.

"Looks like the fucking Kerbs cycle," Alec muttered, somewhere far behind my right ear. At the same time a flurry of agitation from one of the AIs caught my attention. I zoomed in on it; my companions and the other AIs followed. The excited AI did the equivalent of brandishing a sheaf of papers, and I grabbed them.

The title page read: *Construction Projects 1 and 2—Overview and Recommendations*. It was overstamped with ESA EYES ALPHA and a date: 24 July 2048.

"Bingo!" I said. "Have a look at this on the screen, Jadey."

"Okay." Her voice came from a long way off.

I started paging through it; before long I felt an ache in my chest and a tightness in my throat, and my hands were shaking. The plan for the refinery, or fabrication unit, or whatever it was, had come from the alien intelligences within the asteroid. How this had been accomplished was left unexplained. Two final products were mentioned.

The outcome of Construction Project 1 was referred to as *the engine,* and that of Project 2 as *the craft*. The first instances of the words were highlighted and hyperlinked. I touched them, and the references expanded out into pictures that shone like devices seen in a dream.

The engine—it looked like a model of a jet or rocket engine turned out on a lathe, its fluted surfaces smooth and flowing, but with no visible inlet or outflow, just a peculiar inturning of the surface, unbroken but—as I rotated the view—somehow giving the eye-deceiving impression that there was an unseen opening somewhere inside it, like a Klein bottle.

The craft—this was, in a crazy, eerie way, recognizable. It was a shining lens of metal, with—just inward from the rim—tiny rounded protuberances that in a bad light might have been mistaken for rivets. The exploded view showed the ulterior hatch, the telescopic legs, the internal controls, and the seats curving around the inside, and at the core something like the machine called *the engine* but differently proportioned and integrated into what superficially might be called the hull of *the craft*. It was blatantly, embarrassingly, unmistakably, a flying saucer.

We all backed out of VR and sat or stood looking at each other and talking in a confused, vehement babble. Alec Curran stopped it by banging his fist on the table.

"This is *it*," he said. "The Rosetta Stone. The Holy Grail. It's like the Majestic Twelve documents."

To my surprise Jadey laughed at this and said: "Remember, MJ-12 was disinformation!"

They bickered rapidly for a minute, slinging references at each other; I had no idea what they were talking about. The idea that flying saucers had been built by aliens, rather than by Americans, belonged as much to the twentieth century as sea-serpents did to the nineteenth. Over the past few decades even sightings had fallen off, the whole UFO cult relegated to white-trash backwoods and the waste, howling wildernesses of the Web.

"Isn't it funny," Alec concluded heavily, "that we get the first proof of secret government contact with aliens the day after the government announces it?"

"Well, we got it the day *before*," Jadey pointed out, reasonably enough but without making much impression on Alec. They weren't really debating, I realized—they were both so excited at what we'd found that they each wanted to test to destruction the almost unbearably amazing possibility that it was real. Both of them evidently took the

UFO mythos more seriously than I did—something I unkindly attributed to Alec's age and Jadey's probable background. The popular base of the New Money faction—the white-trash backwoods, to be blunt—was notoriously prone to conspiracy theories, enthusiastic religions, and such-like eccentricities, according to *Europa Pravda*.

"Guys, guys," Jason said finally, reaching out as though to knock their heads together, "this isn't getting us very far, is it? I mean, the disc shape is kind of logical, in a way, for some kinds of flying machine. Hell, they were used in the war. Doesn't mean anything about the old UFO crap, one way or the other. If this stuff has turned up in a genuine ESA work-docket, I reckon we assume it's there for a reason."

"It could still be disinformation, even if the project is genuine," Jadey insisted. "But you know, I don't think that matters. If the *cover-up* is that it's an alien blueprint for some kind of spaceship technology, whatever it *really* is must be pretty important."

I could see some problems with that theory, but discussing them would be a waste of time. One can twist the cable of paranoia only so many times before something gives way, and not necessarily the cable.

Tony, the other old code-geek—the one I'd pulled in for his MS-DOS experience—was chewing gum with his mouth half-open, his yellow fingers wending through his strands of white beard and his nails making unpleasant rasping noises on his chin. I got the impression that he was a little tense.

He wiped his lips on his wrist.

"So—what you planning to do with this?" he asked, looking back and forth between me and Jadey and then glancing at Alec. "Sell it to the Yanks?"

"No, of course not," I said, indignantly and perhaps too quickly. "We're just thinking of . . . spreading it around."

"Presumably you don't think the E.U. should be the only people with access to this tech, whatever it is." Jadey said.

Tony shook his head. "No, no, but you don't know it will be. Yefrimovich said last night that they wanted scientific cooperation. How do you know that doesn't include this thing?"

"We don't." Jadey shrugged. "But some of the circumstances around how we got hold of it suggest otherwise."

"Hmm," said Alec. "That sounds fair enough, I suppose. Information wants to be free, and all that." He stood up and grinned at us rather sheepishly. "Excuse me a moment, folks. Nature calls. Back in a few minutes, okay?"

"Sure," I said. "See you then."

He ducked out. It was twelve-thirty, rather to my surprise—time flies when you're in VR. We went on talking for a bit. After ten minutes, Jadey looked around.

"How long does it *take* to take a leak, anyway?"

My phone rang. I tapped the receiver.

"Hello?"

"Alec here. Uh, Matt, I'm in the bar, and from here it looks like the cops are having a very serious argument with Reception. I'd expect them up in the lift in about a minute."

He rang off.

"Alec says the cops will be here in a minute!"

Jason calmly leaned forward and hit the emergency DELETE. Every trace of our morning's work, and the data I'd downloaded the previous night, would be wiped from the cores. Tony's face showed a flurry of conflicting expressions, then he shrugged.

"I won't run," he said.

Jadey jumped up. "They're here for me," she said. She caught my hand and dragged me to my feet. "You go." She slapped the datadisk into my hand. Her lips brushed mine, for a fraction of a second. "Go now! I'll be fine."

Jason was already at the door, looking back at me impatiently. I joined him on the instant, then looked back myself.

"See you in America," Jadey said.

"Where?"

"The Dreamland gate," she said.

Jason hauled me out bodily.

Jason knew the building better than I did. He darted along the corridor, opened what looked like a cupboard door and jumped in. I followed, and found myself in a sort of dumbwaiter lift which immediately began dropping with alarming speed. I braced my hands against the ceiling of the thing just before it came to a jaw-jarring stop that almost buckled my knees.

I was still checking my neck for whiplash as we stepped out into a low-ceilinged, concrete-floored basement. Sagging fluorescent tubes fizzed and flickered. The damp air smelled faintly of motor oil and cement.

"Used to be the car park," Jason said wryly. "Also an emergency exit."

We sprinted across to a ramp which swung us down and around to a wide metal door, apparently sealed shut. Jason slid back a bolt and a smaller door—or vertical hatch—opened, and we stepped through to find ourselves in Leith Walk, under a showery sky. Half a minute later we were sitting at the rear of a trolleybus going down the road toward Leith.

"*Don't* look back," Jason said.

I flushed and hunched my shoulders, then fished out my reader and jiggled my thumbs on its knurled controls. Most of the channels were snow. Jason glanced at it, then his arms seemed to stiffen. He took out his phone, looked at it, then stooped and placed it on the floor between his boot. He straightened up. I heard a crunch and some scuffing.

"Right," he said. He stared ahead with a look of frantic calm.

"What?"

"Look outside the bus, man. It's like the fucking *Invasion of the Body Snatchers*." His voice was quiet, although the only other people on the bus were a couple of old women sitting up at the front.

I swiveled my gaze sideways, scanning the street. The trolleybus had reached about halfway down the mile-long street; rows of shopfronts alternated with rows of residential tenements. The pavements were busy, but not crowded.

"Everything looks normal," I said.

"That's the trouble," Jason said. "This is Leith, not fucking Morningside. Look again."

And suddenly the way he saw it came into focus for me. There were no idlers on the street, no strollers or beggars or hawkers. Everyone walked as though they might at any moment have to explain why their journey was really necessary. A pair of policemen strode along as though they didn't have to worry about their backs. As the trolleybus lurched and jangled from stop to stop the whole thing became even more incongruous—Constitution Street looked as if its notorious squares and boulevards had been cleaned up by some particularly puritanical local authority (which Leith Council, brazenly on the take itself, wasn't).

Even then I wasn't sure that we weren't being paranoid. Perhaps it was just a quiet time of day. I glanced at my watch. It was 13:10.

Only 13:10. Lunchtime. But still. . . .

I had been through so many shocks in the past twenty-six or so hours—Christ, was that all?—that I could be excused for feeling paranoid. So could Jason. Indeed the same applied to the people in the street, who were quite as capable of drawing troubling conclusions from government announcements as any clued-up geek in the Darwin's Arms. Discovering that the superpower in whose comfortably corrupt embrace we lived had an apparently friendly relationship with *aliens from outer space* would be quite enough to get people more than usually anxious not to get on its wrong side. Perhaps they were jumping at shadows, and so were we—but we were jumping more violently, because we knew more.

And because we had already been betrayed. I strongly suspected that Curran had had a fit of patriotic funk at the thought of our discovery's going to the Yanks, or at least at his being mixed up in such a thing, and had taken his chance of nipping out for a slash to call the cops on us. That he would immediately afterward give us a chance to get away was entirely in character.

"We never should have trusted the old geeks," I said under my breath.

"Too fucking right," said Jason. "Now shut the fuck up about it."

The trolleybus jerked and sparked left into Great Junction Road, and clanged to a halt at a stop.

"Go," said Jason.

Rain was falling. I sealed my jacket and followed Jason again as he crossed carefully at the lights and walked briskly but casually along the southern side of the street, a long way down some backstreets and finally ducked into a waterfront pub, the Deil and Exciseman. The place was crowded, as though all the unrespectable people who were no longer to be seen on the street had congregated here. Doubtless every dive in Leith was similarly packed. This was the sort of place where eyes and lenses turned toward the door whenever someone came in—but, apparently recognizing Jason, everyone turned away again. We made our way through the steam and smell of wet coats in the warm, smoky fug to the bar.

"What's yours?" Jason asked.

"Belhaven Export, thanks."

Suddenly hungry, I ordered us a couple of pasties. The microwave *ping*ed at the same time as the beer settled.

"God, that's welcome," I said.

We shifted away from the bar and stood in a corner, where there was a shelf for our elbows and pints. The music was loud enough to make conversation difficult, and eavesdropping very difficult. Still I, leaned in and spoke quietly.

"Is this place safe?"

Jason chuckled darkly. "It's safe for us."

I wasn't quite as sure of Jason's assurances as I'd been in the morning, but I still had nothing else on which to rely.

"What can we do now?"

Jason shrugged. "Get you to America, I guess."

"What?" I forgot to speak quietly.

"Sure. Isn't that what the lady said?"

"Yeah, but I thought that meant as a last resort. Come on. We can do something—I can get a lawyer, go to the media and the embassies, see if they'll get her out, make sure that if I'm pulled I don't just disappear off the street. I might not even be, uh, wanted."

He stared at me. "You don't get it, do you? Jadey can look after herself. It's endgame. This *is* the fucking last resort."

7

The Great Work

S OME SECTS OF the Scoffers still clung to the old ways—to the Bible, at least as Joanna had interpreted it, and to her early-industrial materialism, complete with such sacraments as the anointing with oil, to symbolize the belief that man was a machine built by the Creator. Others had adopted the dialectical materialism of Engels and Haldane (and had duly, dialectically, split into further fractious factions). Most, including the sect in which Gregor had been brought up, took what they considered a moderate position, venerating the ancient materialists more than the modern prophets of religious or political messianism, while of course acknowledging their contributions (as the tolerant cliché went).

The interior of the North Street Meeting-House was dark with wood, bright with colored glass. Walking as though balancing books on his head, Gregor made his way down the aisle to his family's pew and edged in beside Anthony, his younger brother. His parents leaned forward—his mother with her usual anxious smile, his father with his customary curt nod—then settled back. No doubt they were both grateful to see him; his visits to the house of philosophy were becoming rarer as he got older.

In fact he had come along out of a mixture of motives, in which the desire for material enlightenment was the least. He'd vaguely promised Clarissa, who now sat at the front, her husband on one side, and on the other a comically regular series of successively older and taller children. He still had his good suit, relatively unwrinkled. And his hangover was too delicately poised for him to even think about breakfast. So here he was, instead of in bed, at ten o'clock on a Sunday morning.

The Scoffer stepped up to the lectern and smiled at the larger-than-usual congregation; it was probably doubled by the younger members

of the Cairns family and their more distant relatives. He raised his arms
and in a resonant voice intoned the evocation:

" *'Self-moving matter,*
mother-maker of all,
move my small self!

" *'Lend weight to my words,*
vigor to my voice,
impetus to my instruction!' "

Stepping down, he stood by the font of seawater and waited while
Clarissa carried her baby forward. Gently he took the child in his arms
and asked:
"Who names this child?"
"I, Clarissa Louise Cairns, his mother."
"What name do you give him?"
"Owen John James Matthew Cairns."
The Scoffer dipped his index finger in the salt water, tested on his
tongue that it was indeed salty, wet his middle finger with saliva from
his mouth, then dipped his index finger again and with the two waters
of life drew a circle on the baby's forehead.
"Welcome," he said.
He raised the baby up for all to see: the small, fortunately sleeping
head looking even smaller above the white moistening-gown whose
trailing train symbolized the child's kinship with the gods. Then he
returned the child to Clarissa, who sat back down and listened to the
blessing, formally addressed to the new arrival.
"Owen, you have come to us from the death of stars, and to their
birth you shall return. Nothing you knew before, and nothing shall you
know after. For a moment between, you will enjoy the gift of life. Your
life is now defended by us all." Briefly he drew his sword, swiftly he
sheathed it again. "Your blood is our blood. Your life is your own.
Enjoy it all your days, and when you must, leave it without fear. Your
needs are few and easily satisfied. Understand this, and your life will
be a happy one, worthy of the gods. Long may you live, joyous may
you live, happy may you live!"
The benediction complete, the Scoffer stepped back to the lectern,
opened the Good Books and began his speech. It was an entirely inof-
fensive and banal homily on the good life, the ethics illustrated with

some stretched metaphors from physics and biology, enlivened by brief tales for the children—and, no doubt, all the better for all of that. After about five minutes Gregor's attention wandered to the high stained-glass windows, in which flowers blooming, leaves twining, dinosaurs striding, bats flying, martyrs burning, couples coupling, scientists investigating, and other edifying phenomena of nature, society, and thought, sported in fecund profusion. It was perhaps his bad luck that one panel, for the-gods-knew-what reason, depicted a dark-haired maiden in a pink gown. The pang in his heart brought back the pain in his head, and he was immensely grateful when the discourse ended.

Under cover of the final hymn he made his escape, ducking out of any conversation with his family. The day was fine and blustery; the warm sunshine and cool gusts began to soothe Gregor's hangover as he walked down North Street and up the High Street, on the road out of town and around to the castle. On the way he bought a news-sheet. As he handed over the change and exchanged greetings, he noticed consciously for the first time the romantic novels discreetly displayed in plain covers on the bottom rack at the back of the stall, beneath the eyeline of innocent children and much lower than the racks of books and chapbooks of erotic pictures and fantasies, whose colorful covers were as vivid and public, and as cheerfully explicit, as the stained-glass windows of the meeting-house.

He briefly considered buying one of those under-the-counter love stories, then decided it would be too embarrassing for words.

"Good to see you, Greg. Come on in."

James stepped back, swinging the massive door open, and Gregor entered the study. Dust danced in the sunlight beaming in through the window that occupied most of one wall of the wide, high-ceilinged room. Gregor had known where to find it, from childhood memory. Even childhood memory did not exaggerate the number of stairs to be climbed, or the length and dimness of the corridors to be traversed to reach this room, high in a barely occupied wing of the keep.

But now, the shelves seemed lower, the table broader, the stacks of paper higher and more disorderly, the calculating-machines more eccentric and obsolete. The air was peppery with dust. Suppressing sneezes, Gregor accepted a welcome cup of coffee that the Navigator poured from a vacuum-flask, and sat down on the cleanest-looking chair available. His grandfather relaxed into an old leather sofa from which springs and horsehair sprouted, and waved a hand at the surrounding clutter.

"Well, here it is," he said. "The Great Work, so far. I'd like you to help me . . . finish it."

Gregor's consternation must have shown on his face. The Great Work had been going on for so long that finishing it had never even crossed his mind as a realistic prospect. The task James proposed seemed to loom in front of him like an impossible cliff.

"Oh, don't worry," James hastened to add. "It won't demand much of your time. I just need someone younger and sharper than myself, frankly, to integrate the top level of what we've got, and see if it all makes sense."

"Okay," said Gregor. He sipped at the now cooling coffee. "Just one question. Can you tell me, in confidence if necessary, just what the Great Work actually *is*?"

"Sure," said James. "In confidence, yes—strictest confidence. We're trying to plot a course to take the *Bright Star* to Croatan."

Gregor almost dropped the cup. He had honestly thought that the whole object of the exercise *was* the exercise, a prolonged and ultimately unavailing struggle to keep programming skills alive and within the family.

"All this time we've been doing this *by hand*?"

James nodded.

"Why in the name of the gods haven't we been using calculating-machines, or even . . . computers?"

"The computers the first crew brought down with them from the ship," James said, "were partly organic—'wet tech,' they called them—and have mostly decayed or become unreliable. As to the calculating-machines, mechanical or electronic, well—"

He balanced his cup on the arm of the sofa, spread his hands and smiled disarmingly; then waved vaguely and dismissively at the machines, gleaming or rusty, thick with oil and dust. "You can use them to crunch the numbers, but you can't program a computer *with* a computer."

"You most certainly can!" Gregor protested. "Even I know that."

"So you've looked at the Comp Sci books in the family library," James said, approval and mockery both in his tone. "Well, I've looked at a lot more of them than you have, and I've worked with the old wet-tech computers—oh yes!—and I can assure you that these handy short-

THE ENGINES OF LIGHT

cuts are among the facilities we have largely lost. In the early days, two or three generations ago, my predecessors *were* able to do that, and the work went a lot faster. These days, with the work farmed out to all the country cousins of the clan . . ." He shrugged. "It's as you see. Not that we're entirely degenerating. There's good work being done at the university. Someday we'll build our own computers, ones that can handle this kind of task, right here in Kyohvic. But not soon, and certainly not soon enough."

"Soon enough for what?"

"Think about it," said James. He sprang up and strode to the window and stood gazing out, hands clasped behind his back.

"You've seen the beginnings of it," he went on, not turning around. "Out there is the first ship from a Nova Babylonia which is aware of our presence here. In a few years, when their journey carries them to Croatan and other nearby worlds, they'll see our influence on all of them. Compared with Nova Babylonia, we are a new thing in the Second Sphere. All the people in this sector were . . . delivered . . . from Earth or the Solar System after the rise of capitalism. Most of the ancestors of the peoples of the Nova Terra sector come from the ancient world, lifted from lost legions, dying cities choked in the jungle or the desert, wandering tribes. They have become a great imperial republic, a very advanced and enlightened place by all accounts, but we are not like them. We are new."

He turned around sharply, vehement. "And we are weak. If we don't establish some *decisive* advantage, we'll be assimilated into Nova Babylonia's benevolent sway. Our writings will fill their libraries, our thoughts will fascinate their philosophers, our arts will add new colors to their palette. Some might call that a victory of a sort. But *they will not change,* and we will. What makes us unique, what makes us ourselves, will be lost."

"What is it," Gregor frowned, "that makes us 'unique'?"

The old man smiled.

"Instability," he said. "Nova Babylonia has been absorbing new ideas and peoples, as well as generating its own, for hundreds if not thousands of years, and it's a very stable place. We absorb ideas from them, some of which they took with them from Earth, but look what we make of them! The Scoffers' secular christianity is a very different thing from the rather passive philosophy proclaimed by the ancient materialists in the Good Books, for all that it's hard to make the heresiarchs see that. We change all the time, and I don't want us to change into more of them, and then stop changing. Which, as I say, will happen, as more and more of their ships come in, year after year, maybe month after month. Unless we do something about it."

"What *can* we do?"

"We can build ships of our own," James said. "Ships that don't depend on the krakens and the saurs. We can become *the* trading people of the Second Sphere and beyond. With that power, we will maintain our independence."

Gregor looked up at him, astonished. "Now that," he said at last, "is a *great* work."

"Then let's get to it," James said. He stepped forward and held out his hand. "Welcome to the Cosmonaut cadre."

Gregor was shaken by the casually bestowed honor. The cadre was the core of the Families, the fraction which—by membership in the notional crew of the *Bright Star*—maintained the mystique of a continuity with Earth; with, indeed, its mightiest and most glorious empire, the European Union. Some of the Families had grown wealthy on Mingulay, others poor; but the poorest fisherman or smallholder descended from the original crew felt at least a touch of inherited superiority over his or her native neighbor, and which only the continuity of the cadre with the great union of socialist republics did anything to justify. In the opinion of Family members who'd made it on their own merits, such as Gregor's father, the whole cachet was a hollow tradition.

James ran his fingers through his lanky white hair and tied it back in a ponytail with an elastic band. Then he stalked over to a shelf, tugged out a bundle of papers and spread them on the table.

"Right," he said, leaning on his hands and peering down at them, "this is where we start. The setting of the problem."

The oldest papers, where the task began, were even physically difficult to understand, faded and yellowed, their script sufficiently antique to make reading them an effort.

"It begins here," the Navigator told him, stabbing a ridged fingernail on a row of scrawled numbers, "with these stellar parallax observations. They had to work out the distance to Croatan first, obviously. The stellar drift in the intervening centuries is, uh, within the margin of error. *However*. The drive's working is sensitively dependent on mass distribution in the surrounding volume of space, out to several light-years—say, ten, to be on the safe side. So the process had to be repeated for dozens of nearby stars."

He tapped at another page.

"Next, there are readings from the *Bright Star*'s instruments. That's just the top cover, by the way. The rest are over there."

His hand wave alarmingly took in a couple of sets of shelving, all wooden and all bowed under the weight of stacked paper.

"These two sets of information are, fundamentally, the input. The root of the program, the 'algorithm' as it's called, for calculating from them a setting for the drive which will take the ship to Croatan and not to, let us say, the fucking middle of some fucking inter-meta-galactic gulf a billion light-years across is, *we think,* this set of equations here. Deriving a practical program from it to crunch the numbers is a formidable task in itself, which . . ."

And so it went. James spent the next hour or so showing Gregor the barest outline of the task of integration and interpretation he would be assisting with. It still seemed overwhelming, as though he had been appointed an executor of some terrible cumulative will, landed with the job of sorting out the affairs of generations of procrastinators. When the explanation was, as far as it went, complete, it was Gregor's turn to stand by the window and look moodily out.

"Why can't we just *buy* computers?" he said at last. "The saurs sell us instruments and automation for manufactories. Why not for this?"

"The saurs are very careful about what they sell us," James said, still looking down at the papers spread on the table. "They haven't sold us any general-purpose computers. I mean, we've tried cannibalizing and reverse-engineering the stuff they do sell us, but it's like trying to do the same with living organisms before you even have a clue about genetics, let alone genetic engineering. Fucking impossible. Something hard and shiny turns into a smelly puddle."

"Why don't they sell us computers?"

James sighed. "From what old Tharovar deigns to say on the subject, and even he is a bit cagey, it seems that the gods would not approve. And the saurs are gods-fearing, in a way that we are not. The gods may have been involved in some disaster in their past. . . . We can speculate about its being remembered in tradition, even 'race memory,' something in the genes—but that's all. They don't want to talk about it."

"I've noticed something like that," said Gregor. "With Salasso."

"Anyway, relying for our navigation on computers from the saurs would be . . . missing the point, don't you think?" James abandoned the task and joined him at the window.

"Yes," Gregor said. "I see that."

"Good!" James grinned at him and slapped his back. "Now go and see your girl."

He walked slowly along the dark corridors, and slowly down the long—straight or spiral—stairs. The anachronistic fossil assemblages in the walls' sedimentary-rock cladding held a mirror to the confusion in his mind. Still in upheaval over the immensity of the task his ancestors and living relatives had accomplished, still appalled at the scale and complexity of the task to come, he was already trembling at the thought of meeting Lydia again.

This was not the normal and natural passion of sexual desire, or the easy affection that came from its mutual satisfaction—even, at times, from its friendly mutual recognition. This was the madness of infatuation, capable of suspending reason, of destroying lives. His sudden involuntary obsession with Lydia was only made more intense by the improbability of its ever being fulfilled without unhappy consequences. If they were to be together for more than the ship's few brief weeks on Mingulay, one or the other of them would be separated by light-years and lifetimes from all they had hitherto held dear.

Fleeting sexual liaisons between unattached starfarers and locals were to be expected and were, indeed, welcomed on both sides for the new genes thus exchanged. Every visit resulted in a small flurry of pregnancies, and even temporarily broken hearts. The real heartbreaker, the exclusive passion, the mad desire for the one and only—that was neither encouraged nor frequent. But it was what he felt.

Last night he had not told Lydia how he felt. But she must know! They had talked and talked and talked, until they'd noticed how their quiet voices echoed, and they'd looked around and found themselves among the last few people in the hall. And, just before she turned to leave, she'd placed her hands in his, as she had done during the dance; then danced away.

She sat on a bench against the seaward wall of one of the lower levels of the castle, which faced onto a walled garden: a green lawn surrounded by beds in which rhododendron, hydrangea, and dwarf pine ran riot. Honeysuckle and ivy had long since struck their tiny pitons in that wall of the castle and clawed their way to near its summit. Her eyes half-closed against the distant dazzle and persistent breeze, she gazed out at the early-afternoon sea in whose choppy water her family's starship did not float, but hovered, the humming energies of its engines sending visible patterns of distortion across the surrounding surface. Lighters on the sea, gravity skiffs in the air, hurried to and fro, loading or unloading; invisible from this angle and distance, larger submarine vehicles would be doing the same, transacting the starship's real business, which was between the krakens—the trade of saurs and humans being in every sense superficial by comparison.

Gregor approached her from the side, across the grass, enjoying the unguarded moment before she noticed him. Her hair was blown about her face in a breeze to which her knee-length dress, pleated and folded to a sculpted shell of dark-blue fabric, was apparently impervious. As he came into her peripheral vision she turned her head sharply, saw him and stood up, smiling. He stopped a few feet away, not wanting to stop; wanting to walk right into her.

"Good afternoon," she said.

"Good afternoon," said Gregor.

They stood regarding each other for a moment.

"Would you like to take me for a walk?" she asked.

"Good idea," he said, mentally cursing the banality of his words.

They strolled across the grass, toward the far right corner of the garden where a gate opened on empty air. In the sunlight her hair, so wavy it was slightly frizzy, looked different, as did her skin, in endless fascinating ways. The scent that drifted from within the wide high fold of her dress's collar competed with that of the garden's flora: there was something of the animal as well as of the plant in it.

At the top of the stairway she stopped in front of him, looking down at the rough grass of the headland twenty meters below. The steps were of narrow stone, worn and wet, and they descended in one long, steady flight down the outer wall. She put a hand on the handrail and tested it gingerly.

"It's safe," Gregor assured her.

"It looks like an afterthought."

"It is. Bolted on thousands of years after the stairs." He shrugged. "Which themselves are an addition to the original structure. When they were built, safety wasn't a feature." He gestured at the wall's overhang, now a little above their line of sight. "See the slots along there, where the light comes through? For oil. The steps must have been convenient, maybe, for whoever was in the castle, and a death-trap for any attacker who was tempted to use them."

"That's encouraging."

"I'll go first," he said. He stepped forward and held out one hand. She took it, and blushed and looked down.

One hand on the rail and one holding hers behind him, he began the descent. Her shoes were flat and flexible, made of something that wasn't leather and that gripped—as a few quick backward glances showed—better than his did.

About halfway down, something huge and white hurtled hooting out of the wall a meter in front of his face. His involuntary backward jerk slammed the back of his head into Lydia's belly. Their yells and grabbing and stumbling were simultaneous.

The perilous moment passed. He looked up at Lydia's pale face. His own was burning. They each let go of the parts of the other's body they had grabbed.

"Are you all right?" he asked.

"Yes . . ." she said. Her voice shook a little. "What the hells was that?"

He pointed. A few tens of meters out on the air, a white shape with a meter-long wingspan and trailing black claws circled on the up-draughts. As it turned, its big binocular eyes seemed to be looking at him.

"Nightbat," he said. "They hunt small nocturnal mammals."

He turned, noticing the dark hollow between blocks from which it had emerged. Faint, indignant noises came from within.

"Wow," he said, awed despite everything. "A nest."

"Could we look at it?"

He stared up at her, impressed, and shook his head.

"No, sorry. The parent might get *really* annoyed. And we don't want that."

She looked over at the wheeling, watchful predator, then back at him with what seemed genuine regret. "No," she said, "I suppose it would be unwise."

She held his hand more tightly until they reached the ground. He didn't let go of it as he turned to face her; he reached out his other hand, and she took it.

"That was exciting," she said with a laugh. "Let's not do it again."

"Sorry about—"

"No, that's all right. You couldn't have known about the nest."

"I didn't. It's years since I've been down these stairs."

Lydia grinned and let go of his hands, shaded her eyes and looked up at the wall looming above them. The nightbat had returned to its nest; around the walls flocks of much smaller bats, with long, sharp wings, swooped and soared with twittering cries, catching insects on the fly.

"They're called swallers," Gregor said. Passing clouds gave him the sensation that the wall was toppling. He looked away, at her still up-turned face and the tender flutter in her throat.

"It's an amazing thing," she said. "This castle." She leaned forward and stretched up a hand to the upper edge of the lowest row of blocks. "So huge, so . . . pre-human. But so human too."

"Built by giants," Gregor agreed.

He and Lydia, by unspoken consent, started walking along the path that led up the headland a few hundred meters to skirt the clifftops. "Do you have such keeps on Nova Babylonia?"

"Nova Terra," she corrected him. "Yes, some, on wild shores like this. The city—some of the old temples are like this, but we know they were built by human beings who wanted to feel small."

"Oh." He hadn't thought of that. "What are the gods in the old temples like?"

She shivered suddenly. "I was taken to one, when I was a child, for education. A great empty space, gloomy, lit by oil-lamps with a heavy scent. Sandstone statues in niches, as high as that wall—twenty, thirty meters. But these were of great kings and winged cherubim, not gods. The statue of the god was at the north end of the temple, and it was quite small, like a boulder about as high as a man. It was carved—carved!—from an iron meteorite. It's hard to remember the shape but it was very, very ugly and it seemed to be full of eyes. Not human or animal eyes. It's hard to explain why, but I knew they were eyes. And what looked like rust on it was ancient tracks of blood."

She laughed, and waved a hand as though to dispel the darkness of her words. "I got out of that temple as fast as my little legs would carry me!"

"And ever since have thanked the gods for Epicurus?"

"Yes!" She threw out an arm in a rhetorical gesture, and recited:

> " 'Who stormed the flaming ramparts of the world,
> and superstition down in ruin hurled.' "

He looked sidelong at her, surprised and pleased. "You know the Good Books?"

"Oh yes, we use the Mingulayan paraphrases to learn the English."

"No wonder you sometimes sound quaint," he teased; then relented. "No, really, your English is astonishingly good."

"Oh, I know," she said. "I hope to use it a lot."

"You already are."

She took this as the compliment it was intended to be. Gregor was glad she didn't notice the pain that lay beneath it.

They walked on up the headland until they reached its point, which rose like a prow higher even than the castle. The path turned around a few meters from the very forward edge of the cliff. They looked at the edge, then at each other, and both laughed.

"I can't," said Gregor.

"Me neither."

She dropped to her hands and knees and crawled forward; after a moment's hesitation he did the same. There was something ludicrously reassuring about the ground's still-upward slope. Rationally he knew it was safe: the cliff was of solid metamorphic rock, not given to crumbling. Irrationally, he vividly imagined it splitting away.

They arrived at the edge by inching forward with their toes and elbows, and peered over—black rocks, white water, and in the stupendous volume of intervening air, the backs of the seabats and diving-bats lofting on the upward rush. Gregor's fingertips were digging into the thin soil. With a deliberate effort of will he unlocked one hooked hand and laid it across the small of Lydia's back. Her body's heat rushed at him through the dry, papery texture of the fabric; he heard its whisper, and found that he was stroking her, higher and lower. She closed her eyes; he felt the muscles in her back relax.

"Mmm," she said, "that's nice."

She opened her eyes, still looking down, and shifted so that her side pressed against his. "To feel in danger, and at the same time to feel held, and safe."

His whole arm was right across her now, his hand in the hollow between her upper arm and her breast. Their shoulders were on the very edge of the cliff, their faces looking down at the sea. They lay like that for what seemed a long time, the roar of blood in his ears and the beat of his heart drowning the sound of the surf and the waves and the high cries of the bats.

They turned to each other. Their faces, now inches apart, were drawn inexorably together as if by gravity. Her eyes closed and her mouth opened to his. They kissed above the void for a long minute, then she pulled away.

"This is not safe," she said; then, in answer to his smile, added: "We might not stop at a kiss, and we might be seen. It would be embarrassing to our families."

She rolled onto her back, sat up, and stood in one continuous fluid movement. A few quick strokes of her hands restored her dress to its ideal shape, leaving not a trace of grass or damp or any wrinkle.

He followed her back to the path, and they walked together back to the keep.

On Sunday evenings the Bailie's Bar was relatively clean and quiet. Its usual clientele of maritime and longshore workers, having an early start on the Monday, left it to the students and the former students who'd settled into casual employment and a student lifestyle before—in most cases—finding their real profession.

Gregor drank and smoked with Salasso and Elizabeth and with his brother Anthony and two of Anthony's friends, Muir and Gunn. Ruefully he told them a discreetly edited version of his misadventure.

"I can't bear to be away from her," he concluded.

"So why aren't you with her now?" Gunn asked. She was a bright undergraduate with curly red hair.

"She has to help with the family business," Gregor explained miserably. "I might see her tomorrow. She and her father are interested in our work at the marine station."

"Is that allowed?" Anthony asked.

"Of course it's bloody allowed. We're not researching anything secret."

Not at the marine station, anyway.

"I didn't mean sharing the research," said Anthony, smirking wickedly. "I meant you and her spooning about at work. All these pheromones in the air, it'll probably wreck your experiments."

"Oh, shut the fuck up!"

His brother regarded him with unabashed amusement. Anthony had not seen Gregor making such a fool of himself since he'd broken a leg falling out of a tree at the age of eight, and he was making the most of it.

"You've got it bad," he said.

"He sure has," said Elizabeth. She stared at Gregor.

"Come on," she said. "You know what to do. Lucretius, Book Four, lines 1065–1066:

" *'Oh, ease the pain of love's urgent need!*
On other men or women spend your seed!' "

This helpful quotation from the Good Books was usually offered in a friendly, soothing manner to the lovesick, but Elizabeth spoke them in a bitter tone, for which Gregor could not account.

8

The Dreamland Gate

W ALKING IN RAIN across wet tarmac, I felt exposed. My heels lifted with difficulty, and the back of my head felt a backward tug like sleep. Far ahead of me, nearly twenty meters away, a huge rectangular box loomed through the hissing drops. Much farther away, more than two hundred meters, the cranes and container ship bulked like a space station. Jason had got me a travel agent—or "people-smuggler," in *Pravda*-speak—and that entrepreneur had taken four thousand euros cash to put me on a barge at Leith Docks. It had taken the rest of that day and all that night for the barge to make its way up the Firth of Forth, past the busy site of the Grangemouth oil refinery and the abandoned site of the Longannet power station, through the Forth and Clyde Canal, and down the Clyde. We'd reached Greenock, and the Atlantic container terminal.

I walked up to the big box and walked around it, acutely conscious of a Harbor Patrol blimp hanging just below the cloud cover, a few hundred meters out over the Firth of Clyde. In the far end of the container, which just happened to be turned away from the waterfront and to face the other containers so that it could not be seen from a distance, was an iron door. I turned the handle. From inside came a shuffling, scuttling noise. As the door opened, a little light fell on the interior and reflected momentarily off the eyes of a huddle of perhaps a dozen people at the back of the otherwise empty container. Not quite empty; their small bundles of possessions lay at random on the floor. I could think of nothing to say, so I raised my palms to them and stepped inside, closing the door behind me. The darkness settled around me like a hood of felt. Feet moved stealthily. I slipped the goggles on and tuned them to infrared: The people at the back had begun to spread themselves out along the sides, bracing their feet on the floor and their backs to the wall. They moved as though they couldn't see, with much groping and stumbling. I settled myself down the same way that they had.

About half an hour passed. Once or twice a child whispered, and an adult hissed them to silence. Somebody muttered something about a cigarette. Then came the sound of an engine and of fat tires on a wet surface, the jangle and rattle of chains and the thumps and scrapes as some connection was made to the outside of the box. After a moment of increasing strain, the container was lifted off the ground and carried along. More jolting and clanging, shouts—and then it swung, to the now unsilenced cries of the children. I could feel it going up like a lift, and tried not to imagine the height. Down again it dropped, and was eased—at last, gently—into its place.

After so much motion this felt at first like stillness, but after a minute of silent attention it was obvious that the surface on which the container now lay was itself moving, in slight and subtle rhythm. We were on the ship. After a few minutes we could feel the throb of the engine underfoot, and the sway of the floor steepened a little.

We stayed there, in the dark, for another six hours in which the only entertainment was the long buildup of increasingly agitated whispering before one of the kids took a leak. The glow of the puddle's warmth slowly faded. This cycle was repeated more than once.

Somebody knocked on the door, not too hard. The sound still rang out and made us all jump.

"All right," said a man's voice from outside, "you can come out now. I'm gonna open the door real slow, okay?"

A fan of light gradually widened from the door, giving eyes time to adjust. I pocketed the goggles and hung back, letting the others—the "illegals," as I kept thinking of them, patronizingly *not* including myself in their number—go ahead of me onto the deck. They all walked forward. A family—a man, a woman, two small children—and five teenagers and one man who looked a bit older than me. I fell in behind him.

The vessel was so fucking vast that when I stepped out somewhere near the midline of the deck I hardly felt I was on a ship at all. Beyond the ship, as far as I could see, was nothing but whitecapped steel-gray to the horizon. The horizon moved up and down a little, that was all. The deck was a low, open area between the bow and stern superstructures, and a maze of close-packed and lashed-down containers.

The man who'd opened the door for us was a short, stout Black-American wearing jeans and a T-shirt and an impressive collection of flashy hardware around his fingers, wrists, and neck. The single obsidian curved band of his wraparound goggles suddenly became transparent, and so non-reflective it was almost invisible. He grinned at us as we stood blinking in the noon sun and breathing the fresh air.

"Hi," he said, "welcome to the free world, and all. You're outside the commies' territorial waters, so you can now do whatever the hell you please." He jerked a thumb backward. "So long as you don't get in the way and the captain don't mind, of course."

People crowded around him, hugging, kissing, crying. The older guy actually kissed the deck. I looked on, bemused. I was relieved, sure, to be safe—safe from the state, and not fallen into worse hands—but my companions' behavior struck me as excessive and unwarm.

Over the next couple of days I realized I'd been mistaken about that. Their reaction wasn't excessive at all. For one thing, the crewman was, literally, right—we had effectively already made it to the U.S., there being no immigration controls whatsoever on entrants from the E.U.

The crew of this huge ship was about the same in number as that of the barge that had taken me across Scotland; the men were more like technicians than sailors. I don't remember their names, and their faces are confused in my memory, but their quick unguarded expressions and loud unironic voices still shine and shout in my mind. Even the way they moved was expansive, uninhibited. On duty and off, their attention flitted and flicked between the real and the virtual worlds so fast their goggles seemed sometimes to strobe between dark and clear. Their hands, when not otherwise occupied, flexed in the flow of the five-finger chording alphabets of the virtual keyboards, and their lips synched in silent conversations.

Not all of them were tall, but each of them seemed to be always at his full height. It wasn't so much (I reflected, as I, too, began to stretch) that we'd had a weight on our backs, as that we had lived all our lives under a low ceiling.

Even my handheld reader and wet-tech goggles seemed to brighten up, and access to U.S. sources to become easier, but that may have been just an illusion. I used my comms and comp gear intensely. Prices on the ship—for food and berths, because our thousands had merely paid for the passage, we were told—made our cash evaporate rapidly. I was luckier than my fellow travelers in that I could start my new work in the brave New World right there on the ship, whereas they had to pile up debts. My serious accounts had always been offshore, and were still valid. I plunged into the New York labor market, holding my nose for the descent into legacy systems. The old code-geeks seemed to be out of the running, and I was in demand. A corner of the ship's canteen made an adequate office, with a convenient bottomless cup of coffee.

I phoned my mother. Her image popped up in the dataspace. She was thirty-five at the time and could have passed for younger than me, except for the wary, weary look she had.

"Yi've got yirsel into some trouble now," she said, in a tone of gloomy satisfaction. "Where are yi?"

"On my way to America."

She looked a bit shocked. She was the most conservative person I knew. She believed in the revolution.

"I always told yi, yi'd get nothing but trouble wi' they anarchists and that Yank spy."

After a moment she relented. "You look after yirsel, son."

"Yeah, I'll do that, Mum."

I'd been looking after myself, I reflected after she'd rung off, for quite some time.

In the minutes between hours-long contract jobs, I dived into the mail and the news, trying to find out what had happened to Jadey, and what was going on back home, and about Dreamland. The answers, not to my surprise, were linked.

I still had the trace of Jadey's original records, which Jason and Curran had so expertly distorted; working back through them, I hit—

"What the fuck are you up to, mister?"

The woman shoved her face into my field, making me recoil slightly. The resolution wasn't good enough to tell if she were real or a repro 'bot, but she certainly looked indignant enough, her otherwise kindly, fortyish features blazing like the henna in her unstylish hair.

"I'm looking for information about Jadey Ericson," I mumbled into the throat-mike. The woman retreated a bit and consulted something out-of-field.

"So what do *you* know about her?" she demanded.

"Last I saw of her, she was about to be pulled in by the commies."

"Oh!" She stared at me. Sheets of data shimmered between us like a heat haze. "You're saying you were *there*?"

"Yeah, in Edinburgh," I told her. "What's it to you?"

Her eyes narrowed, and her expression became calmer. "I'm going to ping you," she said. "And you just better be who I think you are, else I'll lock you out."

I could feel my kit being interrogated; the sensation was disagreeably creepy. A faint line of light scanned my eyes before I had a chance to blink. Not that a retinal scan was worth much, these days, but it would have been remiss of her not to do it. Meanwhile I sent a crowd of AI agents burrowing past the connection she'd made by opening communications with me. They returned in seconds, flashing up organizational data. A rapid glance before stashing them left me with an afterimage of an organization called the Human Rights Federation, with a stack of letterhead sponsors, each with a string of impressive-looking letters after his or her name: businesspeople, a few token trade-unionists, academics, engineers—your standard-issue New Money think-tank front.

"Man," the woman said, looking a lot more relaxed, "that biodegradable commie gear is the pits."

"Don't underestimate it," I said smugly, scratching the front of my neck. The throat-mike was days old and giving me a rash like a blunt razor. "So was it the HRF sent Jadey to Europe?"

"Huh, smart," the woman replied grudgingly. "Yeah, we're her backers. And you, Mr. Cairns, must be Thin Red. Her hardware source."

"Isn't this," I asked, "getting a bit beyond need-to-know, at this stage?"

She shrugged. "Ah, the goddamn commies have it all laid open like a book now. But yeah, you might have a point. Just gimme a location, and we'll meet up for some serious talk."

"The Dreamland gate," I said.

"Ah-hah. Nice one. Okay, see you there."

"Where is it?"

"You'll find it."

She blinked out, leaving me gazing at a data structure that my AIs had patiently slotted together in the meantime. It was almost too simple to be paranoid, almost simple enough for a professional paranoid like a security apparatchik to ignore, and it went like this:

The ESA launch-site at Kourou in French Guiana had, a couple of years back, been the locus of a minor scandal, much played-up by the protectionist wing of the Party in Europe. One of the fabricators at Kourou had been buying in launch-vehicle components, not from a duly subsidized plant in some godforsaken corner of Angola or wherever, but from an American company. That company, Nevada Orbital Dynamics, had a vice president on the HRF's letterhead and a production facility at Groom Lake, Nevada.

A place also known as Area 51, and as Dreamland.

Kourou's MEP, Weber, had staunchly defended the fabricators, and after the relevant balance-sheets and quality records had been introduced into the parliamentary debate the deal's critics had made a muttering retreat.

Surely, I thought, Weber's suborning—if that was what had happened—couldn't have been as simple and obvious as that. It could hardly be held against him—he and the fabricators were doing what they were supposed to be doing, both commercially and, in the context of peaceful coexistence (the Party line du jour), politically—and he might even be able to use it as a defense against any trumped-up charges of "wrecking," as unprofitable deals tended to be called if any recrimination happened to be required retrospectively.

Another part of my mind thought, *Bingo!*

I turned with renewed hope to tracking down other information about Jadey. She was in the news, in a carefully obscure way: buried in a bottom corner of an inside page of the online edition of *Europe Pravda,* and blazed on the front pages of utterly unofficial American newsfeeds. WHY, they demanded, was OUR SO-CALLED GOVERNMENT doing NOTHING to free this INNOCENT AMERICAN?

The U.S. government, via small paragraphs in the *New York Times* and *Washington Post,* was making obscure and oblique noises about using "the proper channels." Whether this meant they were making frenzied diplomatic representations at the highest level, or passing token queries from the consulate to the constabulary in Edinburgh, was anyone's guess.

The whole issue of Jadey—which in other times could easily have been inflated into a cause célèbre—was completely overshadowed by the fuss over Weber's arrest (the U.S. government's tone on the allegations against him resounded with injured innocence) and the far greater fuss over ESA's alien contact. Over that, the world was collectively and predictably losing its head. Scrolling through the news from the past few days it seemed that every scientist, philosopher, cleric, general, politician, and standup comedian on the planet—and off it— had been canvassed for their response. I left the resulting cacophony for a batch of freshly hatched AIs to turn into some kind of digest format, and turned away in some relief to the next contract to bubble up my list.

The soothing relief of routine hackwork didn't last. Twenty-five minutes into the job, the AIs started flashing urgently and the ship's cook, Mr. Nguyen, hurried out of the galley and banged the table. I saved-to-server and switched my attention to both interruptions, the human first.

"Big news for you," he told me. "For us all. Check CNN."

"Thanks," I said. The AIs were urging me to do the same. I followed their advice. The global newsfeed had no doubt what was the most important piece of global news, shoving the alien-contact debate unceremoniously down the stack:

REVOLT ON ESA STATION

Scientists and cosmonauts on the ESA scientific station *Titov* today appealed to the world community to prevent the "militarization" of their historic contact with an alien intelligence. An apparently bloodless struggle has ousted the five military representatives from the station's governing committee. Former station security chief Colin Driver, hitherto regarded as a totally reliable Communist FSB commissar, has spearheaded the move.

In a personal statement, Driver announced:

Tab to a clip.

Driver filled the view. To me, it was as though he were sitting across the table. Behind him, in the back of the field, a half dozen or so people clung at all angles to stanchions and grinned wildly at the camera. They looked like scientists, all right. Driver was a thickset, muscular man in a much-bemedaled uniform. His face could have been Slavic, but his voice and accent (in the undubbed version I was getting) were unmistakably Southern English.

"I'm not much given to public speaking, so I'll keep this short. Three days ago, General Secretary Yefrimovich made an announcement which shook the world. The timing of that announcement, after what many have rightly deduced must have been years of secrecy, has given rise to widespread and alarming speculation. My friends, I have to tell you that some of this speculation is partly justified. Almost certainly unknown to the General Secretary and to the leading Party of the fraternal countries, sinister and reactionary elements in . . ."

Driver paused, and then said, "Oh, the hell with this commie crap!" He convulsively tore the ribbons and badge from his jacket, and took a deep breath.

"Okay," he went on. "Folks, I'll give it to you straight. Some of the hard-line generals in the European People's Army think they can use what we've learned from the aliens to hit the Americans hard—to win the Fourth World War and complete the world revolution at what they consider the acceptable cost of a few million lives. Sooner or later, and better sooner. You do the math—they have. But let me assure you, they don't yet have all the information they need. They've got some—most of your crypto's washed-up, as you've guessed. But they can't yet break the American launch-codes. The announcement was, from their point of view, premature, but that may not stop them from some precipitate action.

"So we—the scientists, cosmonauts, and security staff of the *Marshall Titov*—have decided to do what we can to prevent this. We've put our own militarists in protective custody, and we urge the government, armed forces, Party, and peoples of the E.U. to do the same. Until that is done, not a byte of data leaves this station without going instantly to the public nets.

"We're willing to release the military reps on one condition—that all charges against Henri Weber are dropped, that he is released unconditionally and given the chance to mediate between us and the E.U. government."

Driver smiled thinly. "After all, he *is* the MEP representing this station, via the launch-site at Kourou. As an officer—a *former* officer—of the Federal Security Bureau, I'm absolutely certain that he's innocent of the charges. He's not a CIA agent. This charge has been trumped-up to discredit him, and us, and quite possibly the FSB as well. I know this perfectly well, because . . ."

Another pause, another deep breath.

". . . for the past five years he and I have cooperated closely in feeding disinformation to the CIA and in isolating the real CIA agent on this station, Major Ivan Sukhanov, who is now with his colleagues in the brig."

• • •

New York's traffic astonished me. I took a cab from the harbor to JFK and sat back in terrified wonder as it hurtled or idled between and among the biggest, noisiest, shiniest, and smelliest vehicles I'd ever seen in my life. The whole significance of the oil wars suddenly came to life, as well as the difference between the U.S. and the E.U. In the U.S. the internal combustion engine was still dominant; in the E.U., the burning of petroleum fractions was more or less restricted to aviation and the military. The rest of it went straight into new tech. Most civil aircraft in Europe were airships or hybrid vehicles. In the U.S. they were jets. It made air travel faster, but much less comfortable, in ways that you really do not want to know about.

Las Vegas was an exercise in proving that real-life architectural and behavioral excess could still compete with virtual reality; but my strangest moment didn't come from looking out through the vast plate-glass windows of the terminal at McCarran Airport at the vaster plate-glass–and–plastic edifices beyond. I already knew that Dreamland was a place. Standing in the Janet Airlines terminal and looking at the departure board, I felt a sense of untoward excitement and unreality the first time I saw its name spelled out as a DESTINATION.

I walked down the gangway from the little fifty-seater passenger airplane and looked about me with some apprehension as I strolled toward the terminal building, the Base's regular workers striding briskly ahead of me. The flight from McCarran Airport at Las Vegas had taken half an hour. In the early-morning sun Groom Lake's dry lakebed made the airfield's twin runways a blur of dazzling light and dark shadows. A hasty thumbing of the virtuals for my new American-made goggles—spex, they were called here—turned the brightness down and the color and contrast up. The place still looked weird. A flat plain surrounded by mountains, on which the products of human technology stood out like just-dropped alien artifacts.

The former Air Force Base was ground zero for an entire fallout zone of myth and secrecy and suspicion. Between the Second and Third World Wars the region had been used for secret testing—of atomic bombs, missiles, the fabled NERVA nuclear rocket engine, and the U.S.A.'s most advanced and secret aircraft: black projects, from the U-2 through the Blackbird and a series of stealth fighters culminating in the infamous EDSF. The Electro-Dynamic Stealth Fighter had been immensely successful at flying high and fast, at avoiding radar detection, at evading smart missiles, and at generating waves of excited UFO reports. As the Eastern European theater had demonstrated, however, it wasn't at all invulnerable to old-fashioned visual detection and anti-aircraft fire from anyone with the nerve to turn off the aiming computer, look, and trust the force.

After the disasters of the war and the recriminations of the witch-hunts, the whole thing had been shut down—projects canceled, secrets carted off to deep and distant storage—and the remaining facilities turned over to a plethora of private enterprises.

These had included what were, to be kind, nutcase cults— organizations that had wasted years scouring the deserts and the deserted buildings for alloys not of this Earth, for scraps of documentation, for evidence that the pickled corpses of the Roswell aliens had once been here. By now I had stacks of this sort of shit on my reader. It made me wonder—how stupid could people *get*? If unidentified flying objects were seen around secret military aircraft development bases, the obvious inference was that they were secret military aircraft. *But the secret aircraft were secretly reverse-engineered from secretly recovered alien spacecraft.* . . . No, one would think, this particular rescue hypothesis was not going to fly. William of Ockham had shot it down centuries ago—but still it flew, piloted by alien entities unnecessarily multiplied. . . .

More significant, and in the long run more enduring, had been the space companies, some of whose successes were at that very moment making extraordinary maneuvers overhead. Flying triangles and flying discs slid across the sky, shot up and vanished in the heavens.

I entered the terminal past the casual visual and, no doubt, invisible scanning of the camo-clad dudes on the door, and stepped into the air-conditioned coolness. Just across the concourse I saw my immediate destination—an open-fronted airport bar, with its name spelled in flickering, ironic neon:

The Dreamland Gate.

The postmodern tack persisted inside; the walls were papered with ufological and science-fictional posters, and further decorated with battered, rusted metal signs from various sectors of the old perimeter, most of whose legends concluded with the words, USE OF DEADLY FORCE AUTHORIZED. A model of a Gray alien stood in the corner, and obsessively detailed polystyrene hobby-kit flying saucers hung on black invisible threads from the ceiling, swaying erratically in the ventilator breeze. The girl at the bar wore an aluminum fake space-suit and the

113

THE ENGINES OF LIGHT

lad had a Wackenhut Security ID tag pinned to his camos. Behind them, various flavors and colors of vodka were shelved in large flasks within which nauseatingly realistic Gray fetuses floated as though in formaldehyde.

I sat down at a corner table with a Budweiser and a bagel for breakfast, shaded my spex and checked out the scene. About half the crowd that packed out the place seemed to be workers gobbling hasty, preoccupied breakfasts over goggled visions; the more leisurely eaters, chatting loudly or quietly and conspiratorially, were apparently tourists and aging obsessives, with a sprinkle of journalists who had arrived for cheap laughs at their expense. The real alien contact had blown the dust off all the old stories of imaginary ones, freshened them up and revived them to lurch once more through the media landscape like zombies doused with deodorant, and Dreamland was becoming again a mecca for the sad and the mad and—to be fair—the inconveniently inquiring.

"Mind if I sit down?"

A woman loomed over me with a tray and a fixed smile. She was the woman who'd intercepted me in Jadey's records, looking exactly the same, in a most unbecoming fractal-paisley blouse with a floppy neck-bow. I hadn't seen her coming in. She sat down beside me, edging me along the bench and neatly trapping me against the corner wall. Further territorial encroachments were provided by her substantial selection of foodstuffs. Her male companion, tall and heavy in a dark suit and white shirt and darkened spex, sat down opposite, placing an insultingly token cup of Coke carefully in front of him.

"Well, hi," the woman said. She stuck her right hand across to me, for a shake so awkward it must have looked Masonic. "Name's Mary-Jo Greenberg." An eyebrow twitch. "And this is Al."

The big man inclined his head slightly. "From Nevada Orbital Dynamics."

"Matt Cairns," I said. "Pleased to meet you."

"I assume we've checked out each other's credentials," Mary-Jo said. "We know who you are, and you know who we are."

I nodded and glanced around; the inevitable question occurred to me. "Is this place safe to talk?"

Mary-Jo laughed. "Safe enough, Thin Red. Safer than you're used to. Besides our privacy laws and such, there's so much crap being talked here it'd take a damn dedicated processor to sort the wheat from the chaff."

"I'll take your word for it," I shrugged.

"Any news of Jadey?"

"We're working on it," Mary-Jo said. "I mean, we've had a bit of direct contact. The U.S. consulate in Edinburg's on the job, for what that's worth. She's fine. Basically all that has to be done is dicker over the deal. Should be out in a few days, no problem."

"Oh, that's great," I said. This good news combined with an overpowering burst of relief and pleasure at having someone to talk to at last.

"So," I went on, "how much do you want for a flying saucer?"

"Ah," said Al. "I don't think this place is quite safe enough to talk about *that*."

The offices of Nevada Orbital Dynamics were in a long, low, and—most importantly—air-conditioned building. The short walk there had left me somewhat drained. Sweat evaporated before it had time to wet my skin; then, as soon as I'd stepped into the interior, it went all clammy and cold. I sat in a leather-and-aluminum sling chair, gulped a Bud to replace lost fluids, and sipped a coffee to warm up.

The office we were in seemed to be Al's—the name ALAN ARMSTRONG was on the door, and he was familiar with everything within, but he'd not expanded on his introduction. He sat with his feet on the desk, leaning back and sucking a smokeless cigarette. Mary-Jo stood by the window. The painted concrete walls were bare except for a few discreet posters showing cutaway diagrams of obscure machinery and components, cycling through their incomprehensible activities in a distractingly attention-grabbing way.

I told them my story; they acted less impressed than my code-geeks had been. Maybe they'd heard this sort of thing before. When I'd finished, I placed the little datadisk on Alan's desk; they gathered around, looking down at it. For a moment neither of them spoke.

"Do you have something that can *read* this thing?" Alan asked.

"Yeah, sure," I said, amused. I hadn't expected hardware-incompatibility problems, though I should have. I took out my reader, slotted the disk in, peeled out a connection and reached for Alan's desk viewplate, then glanced up at him.

"Do you mind?"

He pulled a plug somewhere—smart guy—then waved.

"Go ahead."

I patched it across, handed him the reader, and stepped back.

"Check it out."

For the next hour or so Alan burrowed through the documentation; as his suspicions eased he added his spex to the interface, keying air and murmuring. Mary-Jo followed him in, but broke off occasionally to give me a reassuring smile or urge me to another coffee. At last Alan came out of it, and pushed the kit away, took his spex off and looked at me. His eyes were blue and mild; the skin around them betrayed tiredness beyond that from examining the specification.

I plucked off the connection, picked up the reader and stashed it.

"Well?" I asked.

Alan nodded slowly, thin-lipped.

"Whatever this is," he said, "it looks damn authentic. The bits I can understand are sound, and the bits I can't are . . . well, *alien* in a way that'd be hard to fake." He laughed briefly. "I've *seen* fake alien flying-saucer specs that were really good—old disinformation, pre-war. They were nothing like this. You always hit some kind of bullshit and hand-waving when you got in deep enough."

"Boron," Mary-Jo said. For some reason they both found this funny.

"Yeah, boron." Alan sighed. "A lot of talk about boron and mag-netism and Tesla. Mind you, they didn't have the transplutonics to waf-fle about back then, maybe that's the equivalent here. There's no 'unobtanium' involved, but the only way this thing can fly is if we are deeply ignorant of the properties of island-of-stability elements. Which, as it happens, we are, so—" He spread his hands.

"Are we talking AG?" Mary-Jo asked.

"Something like that," Alan replied. He rubbed his nose. "I mean, what's a flying saucer without anti-gravity?" He jerked his head back, vaguely indicating the window. "Apart from the ones flying above us, right? *And,* the thing the spec calls 'the engine' looks to me like a space drive."

"Are we talking FTL?" I asked, mimicking Mary-Jo.

Alan shook his head. "No. But fast."

"Could we build it?" Mary-Jo asked.

"Yes, but only in space. That process requires a micro-gravity en-vironment. As for the transplutonics—shit, they're only made in space anyway. By ESA, to be exact. I suppose we could ask nicely."

I stood up, feeling restless; stretched my arms and rubbed my shoul-ders. "I wonder," I said idly, "if they've already built it, out there."

Mary-Jo and Alan looked at each other. Alan's shrug was not quite imperceptible. Mary-Jo turned to me.

"No," she said. "They haven't."

"How do you—? Oh. You're in touch with them."

"Since the mutiny. Yeah. It's no secret. They're doing everything in the open. Unless they're playing some kind of real elaborate double-bluff, which, given the history of commie intrigues, can't be ruled out; they've given us a general picture of what they've learned. Have you seen any of that, by the way?"

"No, I've been kind of preoccupied with worrying about Jadey, and the politics back home."

"Tell me about it," Mary-Jo grinned. "Looks like all hell's breaking loose in Red Europe, huh? *Anyway*—check out the science data, some-time soon—it's fascinating. Man, they are talking to *gods*. But the *Titov* crew have said nothing about this. Alien space-drives—my God, you'd think they'd mention it."

"Oh." I felt a cold wash of disappointment as the obvious inference struck home. "Do you think this stuff could be some of the 'disinformation' that guy Driver talked about in his broadcast?"

Alan shook his head. "I doubt it," he said. "Look at the time-stamp—last year. Whatever this is, it's been kicking around somewhere inside ESA for a while, and if the U.S. government or even the CIA had its hands on something like this, I'd have heard about it. I've been cultivating contacts very busily for the past few days, and if I'm sure of anything it's that nobody on our side knew about the alien minds at all. They were getting stacks of what they thought were bits of valuable scientific information, mainly in Comp Sci and low-temp physics, and all of it true as far as it went, but nothing—I mean *nothing*—of a hint about the full truth. Jesus, these guys did their job well."

"Driver and Weber?"

"Yeah." He rubbed the back of his neck. "Beats me how they stopped the real CIA agent—Major, uh, Sukhanov—from blowing the gaff whenever he was off the station. He managed at least two furloughs on Earth in the past ten years, and he must've had *some* contact on the ground."

"Oh, that," I said. "My guess is Sukhanov's totally innocent, and Driver accused him to stir up trouble in the Army and take the flak off the FSB."

"So who *was* the CIA's—?" He stared at me. "You're kidding."

"Driver," I said. "It must have been. Or that's what the CIA thought! He and Weber were double agents. That's why there was real evidence against Weber."

"If 'evidence' means anything in this context," said Mary-Jo. She sat down on the edge of the desk. "What I wonder about, though, is how the information you've got comes to be on Earth and not on the *Titov*."

"Because it was developed on Earth?" I suggested. "Maybe the design information got passed through without ever having been analyzed, and all the subsequent work was done on the ground, with the intention of not letting anyone on the station know about it until they were sure enough of the security situation, perhaps, to go ahead and build the thing."

"Need-to-know? Yeah, I guess that's plausible." Alan jumped up. "In that case the best thing we can do is get this out to the station. Get that disk, or a copy of it, out there physically."

"Why not just transmit it?"

"Because we don't want the E.U. to know what we're up to," Mary-Jo said. "We need someone who understands the system and the programs. Like, that manufacturing-control program? Someone who can handle the interfaces between hard tech and wet tech, and who's physically fit and politically savvy and politically reliable."

She grinned at me. "Like, for example, you."

9

Light-Years Gone

E LIZABETH SAT ON a stool by a lab bench, sipping the day's first coffee, and stared at the diagrams on the wall. The annotated and revised and scribbled-on tracings of the squid nervous system looked as meaningless as a clump of roots in a random clod. Around her the saline aquaria made a continuous hiss as bubbles oozed from the pumice blocks at the ends of the aerator tubes; the little electric pump that powered them all hummed away in a corner of the lab, reliable as a heart.

Getting up had felt like an act of bravery; dressing, like donning armor; boarding the tram like riding to battle. The wise Stoic saws were little comfort when pleasure and pain were what you wanted to feel: anything but this numb sadness. The only comfort, and it was a cold one, was that Gregor would soon feel this way himself. She couldn't see Lydia staying, or Gregor leaving with her—both had too many attachments. Each would tacitly assess that to tear themselves away from their homes would be more painful than to part from each other; but that parting would be painful enough. She was a little shocked to find herself wishing the pain on Gregor, and hoping that he'd turn to her on the rebound.

More likely, the fool would mope for months. The utter perniciousness of romantic love couldn't be more obvious in his case. Or in hers. Gods-only-knew how many opportunities of a good one-night stand or a healthy, fulfilling, longer-term relationship she'd passed up in the time she'd wasted obsessing over this son of a bitch. And because nobody even knew about it, she'd be insidiously acquiring a reputation as a rather cold character, not really interested in sex. There were such people, whose interest in some intellectual pursuit or physical skill or even in business or politics left no time or energy for human intimacy. It was a respectable, if not respected, way of life—not admired so much as wondered at.

She had no desire to be one of them, but there were times when she feared she was. Surely if she were normal, and her desires as urgent as most people's seemed to be, she'd have broken through the awkwardness of the situation, risked rejection and embarrassment and even their existing friendship, just for the sake of grabbing him for once, of surprising him with one hot honest word or thirsty kiss.

She heard Salasso's quick, light step in the corridor and hurriedly composed her expression, looking up with a smile as the saur came in.

"Good morning," he said. He fingered his lab coat from the hook and put it on, oblivious as always to how comical it looked: too long for his height, too short for his arms, too loose for his torso. He reached for the kettle and set it to boil, crumbling a fish bouillon cube into a mug. "You're in early."

"I wanted to think over what we've been doing."

It was hard to make out where he was looking, the corners of his eyes went around so far. He poured the water and stirred.

"Hmm. Ahh, that's better." Salasso sipped the stock and visibly relaxed. His species had a taste for fish, and a distaste for fishing. The arrival of humans on Mingulay had moved fish and fish products from a rare shore-caught luxury to a staple in the saur diet. Nothing could shift their dislike of the sea and fear of deepwater fishing. As far as Elizabeth knew, Salasso was the first saur anyone had ever heard of who so much as set foot on a boat. It didn't seem to bother him at all.

"Yes, we may expect visitors today," he went on. "Is that why you have dressed differently?"

Under her lab coat she was wearing a white high-necked silk blouse and a black linen skirt to midcalf, with dark stockings and light leather shoes. Salasso had never before given the slightest indication of noticing anyone's clothes.

"Yes, that's it," she said. "To look smart for the trader." *And in front of his daughter.* "You never know, he could be thinking of investing."

"Or be willing to share knowledge," said the saur, rather primly. "We have much to learn about the oceans of the other worlds."

"There is that," she said listlessly.

Salasso's head rocked a little. He might have been insensitive to the nuances of human facial expressions but he was quick to pick up tones of voice.

"You are troubled," he said.

"It's nothing I can explain."

"You mean you would not expect me to understand. I think I would." The saur's huge eyes looked down at the floor for a moment, then back at her. "We have such troubles ourselves. But they are more long-lasting."

She stared. This was the closest the saur had ever come to a statement about his personal life, or about relationships within his species.

Then his narrow shoulders shrugged, and he added, "Perhaps that makes it too different to discuss with profit."

Before she could think of anything more to say, the outside door banged open and voices, then footsteps, approached. Gregor opened the lab's spring-loaded door and held it while the trader and his daughter walked in past him. They wore jackets and jumpers and jeans, as though just off a boat. The sight of how Lydia carried this off made Elizabeth feel simultaneously dowdy and overdressed.

De Tenebre's broad freckled face smiled, his voice boomed.

"Good morning," he said, sticking out a hand. "I believe we met at the party."

"How do you do."

"And this is my daughter, Lydia. I don't believe you've been introduced. Elizabeth Harkness."

Good memory for names. She shook Lydia's hand as lightly as possible. At the same time de Tenebre said, or sang, something that made Salasso almost bound forward and bow over his hand, with a response that sounded like the same word/tones, but faster. After a further such exchange, Salasso nodded and said, "I'm honored to meet you."

"And I you."

Looking pleased with himself at his polyglot tour de force, the trader stepped back a little and looked up at the drawings on the walls and around at the tanks and trays and equipment.

"Interesting," he said. "Fascinating. I've seen something like this back home. . . ." He sucked a lip and snapped his fingers a few times. "Ah yes, the Maritime Museum! Remember it, Lydia?"

"Oh yes," she said. "You took me there when I was small. There was this huge glass case, and inside it was a copy of the brain and nervous system of a kraken, done in black glass. It *did* look like that drawing, but bigger."

"Gods above," said Salasso, "somebody had dissected a *Teuthys*?"

"I believe it was a dead one, washed up on a beach," said de Tenebre, still gazing around. "The scientists managed to preserve it before it had time to decay, and later dissolved it in some fluid that left the nerves and brain intact, and dyed them, and made a resin cast, and then drew out a model in glass. Most ingenious technique. That was a few hundred years ago even then, of course."

"Of course," Elizabeth echoed, unimpressed. "And what did they learn from it?"

"Oh, nothing much, dear lady. Very much a natural-history approach back then. Observation and speculation. The experimental method hadn't yet quite caught on. Still . . ."

His smile traveled from Elizabeth to Lydia. "It gave my little girl an interest in natural history which she still keeps up."

I bet she does, Elizabeth thought. *I bet she collects* butterflies, *and* flowers, *and* feathers!

"It *was* interesting," said Lydia. "That enormous, complicated brain, so different from our own, with its nerve-trunks thick as ropes, like roots sprouting from a bole. Of course the museum was absolutely stacked with interesting creatures, but," she laughed, "it was the brain that made me think."

"What did it make you think about?" It was all she could do to keep the poison out of her voice.

"Languages," said Lydia. "Is the cephalopod mode of communication via chromatophore display something intrinsic to their neural anatomy? Does it vary within the species like human languages? Is it abstractly symbolic or is it fundamentally ideographic and quasi-pictorial? How is translation possible between it and the verbal and gestural languages of hominids and saurs? That sort of thing."

"Ah." This minimally communicative noise was all Elizabeth could come out with.

"Profound questions," said Salasso. "Our approach to such problems is modest and, as your father suggests, experimental."

"Surely *you're* not cutting up krakens?" de Tenebre asked.

"Gods, no," said Gregor, touching Lydia's elbow and urging her in the direction of a lab bench. "We cut up innocent little squids."

"Aha!" said de Tenebre. "On the hypothesis of common descent! Well, you could say it's a start."

"You could," said Salasso. There was some taut vibration in his tone. "But . . . common descent is not a *hypothesis*. It is an observation."

De Tenebre had started to amble along the side of the room, looking up at the diagrams like a visitor in an art gallery who knows what he likes.

"To your species, perhaps, Salasso," he bantered. "To mine, however, it will remain a hypothesis until we start living as long as you do."

Salasso gave a tinny peal of saur laughter—whether out of genuine amusement or obsequiousness, Elizabeth couldn't tell. Amusement, she guessed. Flattery was not a saur vice. Salasso joined the trader and began earnestly pointing out salient or problematic features of the neural mapping. Gregor and Lydia were already leaning over a preparation on the bench, heads almost touching, talking quietly.

Elizabeth was reminded of how she and Gregor had met. In an undergraduate laboratory demonstration, where the students were randomly assigned in pairs to carry out a classic exercise: the dogfish cranial dissection. The fish stank dreadfully, you had to use great dollops of skin cream and wear rubber gloves if you didn't want to smell of dead shark for a week. The guy beside her had gallantly volunteered to do the actual cutting, letting her concentrate on sketching the brain and optic nerves and eyeballs which were the object of the exercise. She remembered his big fingers gripping the scalpel, the precise and confident way he'd slit through the cartilaginous skull and laid it open, his knowledgeable comments. This wasn't the first dogfish he'd had a good look at: he'd cut them up—for bait, and for curiosity—on the deck of his father's boat.

They'd barely looked at each other—well, he'd barely looked at her, and, after the first few sidelong glances, she'd hardly dared look at him—and that apparent, outward-directed, easy camaraderie had set the tone for their relationship ever since.

She walked briskly to another bench and set to work recalibrating an electrode reader, a tedious, finicky job that had to be repeated every morning, because of overnight changes in temperature and humidity. It absorbed her, letting her tune out Gregor and Lydia's lighthearted chat. The saur and the trader continued their sightseeing stroll around the lab; she could overhear their conversation slide back and forth between English and Trade Latin, and fragments of the saurian speech. She wasn't offended that de Tenebre had chosen Salasso to speak for the team's work; the saur's superior intelligence and honesty would make him, as any trader as experienced as this one was sure to know, unlikely to bullshit. (Salasso had once explained to her, with perfect aplomb, that the qualities of intelligence and honesty were linked: with sufficient intelligence one could see the ramifying consequences of a lie, the sheer cost in mental processing-power of sustaining it, and draw back from it. "Perhaps this relationship does not hold for the hominidae," he'd added, with wounding tact.)

A silence made her look up. The trader stood on his own at the front like a lecturer, Salasso off to one side, Lydia and Gregor still sitting together.

"Well, my friends," de Tenebre began, "this has been most interesting. Fascinating. I have to say it's the most advanced biological research I've come across. I'm sure your ancestors surpassed it, but mine never did. Nor have my contemporaries." He smiled disarmingly. "Unless the academies of Nova Babylonia have shaken up their approach in the past century, of course!"

He stalked to a table and propped himself on the edge of it, leaning forward confidentially.

"Now, I'm a practical man, and I have no idea what practical use this research might serve. But I have no doubt that by the time I return here, some useful applications—in medicine, in industry, in the gods-know-what—will have come out of it. Possibly even in calculating—I understand that the Cosmonaut the lord Cairns is interested in something he calls 'neural nets,' and has been encouraging your work to that end."

Gregor glanced back over his shoulder at Elizabeth, raising his eyebrows for half a second. She allowed herself an almost imperceptible shrug and shake of the head. Salasso, she noticed, had chosen this moment to gaze out of the window.

If de Tenebre observed this brief byplay he gave no sign of it, continuing: "It doesn't matter. What matters is that there'll be money to be made from it, and I'd be delighted to put some money into it now for some share in the returns later."

"Thank you," Elizabeth said, before anyone else could speak. "We would be very interested in that. I believe the next step would be to discuss your proposed investment with the syndics."

Salasso nodded vigorously; Gregor turned around again, still looking puzzled, but pleased. Then he turned back and thanked the trader for his confidence.

"Good," said de Tenebre. "Naturally there are details to be worked out, questions of intellectual property—information wants to be paid,

and so forth. And you'll want to ensure that you and your successors don't have their hands tied, about what lines of research to pursue." He held up his hands, palms open. "None of that should be a problem—I really want and expect both sides to benefit. My legal adviser has a standard contract, and we've never had any complaints."

"That's all absolutely fine by us," Gregor said, sounding cautious. "We'd like to be involved in any discussion, as well."

"Of course. But, seriously, if we draw it up properly none of this will affect what you do—you'll just have more resources to do it with, and in a hundred years you or your successors will be paying me a very reasonable portion of whatever gains may be made from it."

Gregor stood up and shook de Tenebre's hand; Salasso and, after a moment, Elizabeth did the same.

"Great, great," said the trader. He took a watch from his pocket and glanced at it. "Well, I'm sure you have work to do—and so have I. Some of my servants are busy up at the university, buying large quantities of books and instruments. We're moving on the day after tomorrow, down to New Lisbon—turns out the meat market's earlier than usual this year. I'll see my adviser this evening, and—"

Lydia sprang up from her seat at the bench, with a loud sob and a sniff, and ran from the room.

"Excuse me," said Gregor, and disappeared after her.

De Tenebre stood looking at the swinging door for a few seconds. Then, flushed and frowning, he stalked out.

Gregor found her outside the main door, facing into a niche in the rough-cast wall, her arm across her eyes.

He put his arm around her shoulder and turned her around. She buried her tear-streaked face in his shoulder and shook for a minute.

"I knew we didn't have much time," she said, muffled and sniffling, "but this isn't *fair*."

He heard the door open, and her father's heavy, hurrying footsteps stop behind him.

"Oh, in the name of Zeus!" said de Tenebre. "Please. Lydia. Stop crying and come and sit down and let's talk about . . . whatever this is about."

Outside the lab-blocks was an area of bolted-down wooden tables and benches, facing the shore, buffeted by swirls of air where the prevailing wind hit the walls and so barely used for its intended purpose of open-air eating. They made their way to a table, Gregor and Lydia

sitting at one side and de Tenebre diagonally across from them. At length the girl's shoulders stopped shuddering and she leaned forward, elbows on the table, propping her face and staring at her father.

"We *can't* just leave in two days!" she said.

He scratched the back of his neck.

"I'm sorry," he said. "I can see what's happened. I can't say I really blame either of you. I'm a reasonable man, and I do have your interests at heart. Especially you, Lydia, you're my daughter. I wouldn't do anything to hurt you, you know that." He gave Gregor a dark look. "And I won't *let* anyone hurt you either. I hope this man has not been giving— or taking—any promises."

"No!" they both said, in indignant unison.

The merchant let out a long sigh. "Well, that's not so bad. Hearts mend but words don't, eh?"

The flippant, philistine saying shocked Gregor. He tried to hold back his temper, which he knew would do nobody any good. By this time Lydia had an arm around him, too, and was holding tight. It emboldened him to speak.

"I love her," he said. "I could love her forever."

Lydia's arm tightened around him, and she smiled at him.

"No doubt you feel that way," said de Tenebre, with a sort of cool sympathy. "And believe me, I understand. But—I can't let that affect my actions. We *must* leave." He sighed. "And I have other appointments today."

The early sun slanted across them, the breeze off the sea tugged at them. Not far across the water, the great ship's fields crackled and hummed. Lydia looked down, flicked flakes of pebble-dash from her sleeve, scowled and sniffed.

"Couldn't I stay for a while?" she said. "I could join you in New Lisbon. They have air transport here, after all!"

"Oh, Lydia," said her father, with a mixture of impatience and tenderness. "I wouldn't trust one of these gasbags or kites with a servant, let alone with you. Leaving aside accidents, they're unreliable and unpunctual."

It was true, and Gregor knew he couldn't object.

"I'll come with you," he said.

De Tenebre rocked back and snorted. "For three weeks of trailing around after us? I can think of no better way of prolonging your pain— and Lydia's."

"No," said Gregor, suddenly dizzy with decision. "I meant—"

De Tenebre raised a hand, shook his head.

"No!" he barked. "I will not hear of it. I will not let you say it. Traveling is no life for someone not born to it, and certainly not for you. You have another calling, man. Do not disdain the gifts the gods have given you. And they have not given you my daughter ..."

He paused, frowning in thought.

"... or if they have," he continued, "it will be through your own work and your own gifts that you will win her."

Gregor squeezed his eyes shut for a few seconds. He was afraid that at any moment he might start weeping worse than Lydia had. Gradually the trader's words sank in. He looked up at him.

"What do you mean by that?" he asked.

De Tenebre stood up and leaned forward on his knuckles.

"We intend to stay on Croatan for half a year. I can leave you a schedule of our route thereafter, every port of call all the way back to Nova Terra. Your chief, the lord Driver, has told me about your family's Great Work. The lord Cairns your grandfather has confirmed it. They have high hopes in you. If you fulfill them, you can come after us yourself, and meet Lydia again within a few months or a few years of your life and even less time in hers. Bring me a ship. If you do that, Gregor Cairns, you can take my daughter, and I will be forever in your debt."

Gregor felt Lydia's arm fall away. The world became, for a moment, black-and-white and filled with white noise. He took some deep breaths. His first thought was outrage at this challenge, this offer to *trade* Lydia for a ship, or for shipping. Then—

Thoughts tumbled, *click-click-click,* like logic gates. If Hal Driver and James Cairns had told the merchant the Great Work could be completed in some feasible time—then that explained James's new urgency about it, and at the same time made it difficult to dismiss de Tenebre's suggestion as unreasonable. And if James was interested in the team's research as having something to contribute to calculation, something to do with neural nets, then there was some connection between what they'd been doing and the Great Work—

A chill went through him as he realized what that connection might be. It unfolded before his eyes, the map of the squid nervous system overlaying the data structures of the navigation problem. He understood the architecture of the mind that could understand the problem, and in so doing he understood it himself. He could see, in principle, how the problem could be solved.

He blinked, and the world came back, in full color and high resolution. Lydia and her father were looking at him very oddly.

"I'm surprised to see you look so pleased," said de Tenebre. He straightened up and took a step back. "And encouraged. I was afraid your seniors were bluffing to drive a bargain."

A bargain—Gregor was struck by a further consequence of his train of thought. The deal the merchant had offered to the team would give him a share in all its future outcomes and applications—and if their research was connected to the Great Work, it would give him a share in the grand starship enterprises that James had outlined. A permanent say in all their futures, and in the future of Mingulay, which would thenceforth be tied to Nova Babylonia.

He swung his legs over the bench and stood up, facing the merchant.

"I'm not pleased at all," he said. "I make you no promises, and I don't accept your offer of your daughter because that's for her to decide." He moved behind Lydia, and laid the tips of his fingers gently on her shoulders. "She may be your daughter but her life is her own, not something to be traded between families. I love her too much for that. I knew from the beginning it was hopeless, but it's possible to love without hope."

Lydia reached a hand up and gripped his.

"You're right," Gregor went on, "that I can't and won't come with you. If Lydia feels about me as I feel about her, she'll stay here. If not . . . I'll do my best to come after you. But what Lydia does then, or now, is her choice. What *I'm* going to do now is go back to the lab and urge my colleagues to make sure that your offer to fund our team is politely turned down."

Lydia's grip on his fingers was beginning to hurt.

Then she let go, and scrambled up from the table and stood looking at him, her eyes wet.

"No!" she said. "You don't understand! Coming for me in a ship of your own is how it should be! When my father said that, I felt for the first time some hope for us! You must do it! You must achieve something of your own to win a woman, that's how it is with us. I wouldn't feel traded at all! If you love me, you'll do it!"

How different our worlds are, he thought. *And how alike.* She could have had his. She still could.

"I do love you," he said, and turned and walked away. He didn't look back, but he hoped with every step—across the yielding grass, and

the crunching pebbles, and down the echoing tiled corridor to the lab—
that Lydia would come running after him.

She didn't.

"It's going," said Elizabeth, from the lab window.

Gregor looked up from a table covered with sheets of paper. White
paper and black ink, scrawled with shapes, speckled with numbers. He
felt utterly dull, as he had for the past forty-eight hours. Unable to
explain the reasons for his objection to the merchant's funding to anyone
except James—who approved of it, and had hastily seen the syndics to
confirm the objection—he was in bad favor with his team, and with the
department. Everyone thought there was something of a scandal behind
it, some offense given or taken, something of a cloud.

But still, lured by the primitive primate urge for visual stimulation,
he made himself stand up and walk to the window. Another sunny,
blustery day. The last of the skiffs were swooping and darting into the
bays in the starship's hull, like seabats to their roosts on a cliff. The
lighters and sightseeing craft, and the little humming airplanes, were
standing or circling well off.

The ship's sides ran with colored lights that scribed names and
logos, flags and symbols. The bays and hatches sealed without leaving
a seam. Around it, the water bent away from beneath it, until it was
obviously not floating but hanging a little above a vast, shallow depression. It began to rise slowly. St. Elmo's fire crackled on masts a
mile away. The meniscus of water rose up beneath it, until the sea
bulged a fathom above sea level.

Then the water slumped back, setting a swell racing out to rock the
distant boats, and the ship rose faster as though released. It began to
move forward as it continued to accelerate up, and within a minute was
lost from sight in the shining unfathomable blue of the sky.

Gregor realized he was craning to watch, his cheek pressed to the
pane. He came down off his toes and took a step backward and turned
his back on the horizon. Elizabeth and Salasso faced him, the saur with
no discernible expression, the woman with a tentative smile.

"Well, that's it," he said. "They're gone."

At that moment emotion returned to him, flooding his veins and
nerves with singing relief. The pain of parting from Lydia, and the pain
of not knowing for sure what that parting meant, broke the grip of his
anhedonic depression. He felt so much the better for it that he smiled.

Lydia was gone, but he still had friends, and he still had work, and it was suddenly obvious how his friends and his work could yet let him see Lydia again.

"Yes, well . . ." Elizabeth was saying. Gregor stepped forward and caught her by the shoulders, grinning. She almost recoiled, but her smile broadened.

"I have something to tell you," he said. Her shoulders, under the rough wool of the jersey, were quivering in a way that reminded him painfully of how Lydia's shoulders had felt. He let go with one hand and clapped the saur's shoulder too. "It's about starship navigation."

"Oh," said Elizabeth. Her face fell for a fleeting moment, and then she looked away and looked back at him, interested. "So, don't keep us in suspense."

But keep them in suspense he did, all the long walk to the castle and through its corridors and stairs. Carrying the papers he'd been working on rolled up under his arm, he marched to the Navigator's room. It was unoccupied.

He waved a hand at the sofa. "Make yourselves comfortable—uh, not on that bit, some coffee got spilt."

Elizabeth perched on an arm of the couch, Salasso found some space that was neither stained nor loaded with books and files, then put his hands behind his head and leaned back with his legs stretched out—a human posture he'd picked up, but one which his height, or lack of it, didn't help to carry off.

"So tell us," he said.

"Our family has over the generations been working on a navigational problem," Gregor said. "That much, I'm sure you know. It's no secret. What I've realized is that the actual solution to this problem requires a non-human mind, specifically a squid mind, and that our research in cephalopod neurology can contribute to simulating such a mind—in its barest outlines, of course, but it's the outline, the structure, the *architecture,* if you will, that counts."

Salasso had jerked out of his laid-back pose and now leaned forward, tense.

"I see, I see," he said. "The electrical potentials, the gross and fine anatomy, yes! Yes! But how would you simulate it?"

"In a calculating-machine, of course," said Gregor. "The brain is a computer, and any computer can simulate any other computer."

Elizabeth looked around at the calculating-machines.

"In *these* heaps of mechanical junk?"

"If necessary," Gregor said. "Yes. But I hope, with them and many more, working in parallel."

"It would still take forever."

Gregor's eyes narrowed. "Oh, you know that?"

"Well, I can give you an educated guess!"

Gregor jumped up. "I can see it all in my head, I can see how it could be done. The structure of the problem and the structure of the brain match so exactly it's uncanny, it's like they were made for each other."

He realized what he'd just said, and added:

"Perhaps they were."

Salasso said nothing, but it seemed his lips became, if that were possible, thinner.

"But you're right," Gregor went on. "In theory, yes, one computer can simulate another. But it's just not possible to do it quickly, without far better computers than we've got." His fists clenched. "Now, if we still had the computers the first crew brought from the ship . . ."

"That might be possible," said Salasso.

10

Launch on Warning

S OMEBODY WAS SHAKING my shoulder. I struggled up from a deep midday doze to find myself sitting on the sofa in Alan's office. Alan was looking down at me with a concerned expression.

"Sorry," I said. "Didn't mean to—"

"That's all right, you've just had a few tough days catch up with you," Alan said. "We'd've let you sleep, only—"

He gestured at the wall, and with that wave of his hand the posters cleared and reconfigured to a patchwork of news-screens. Most of them showed the same face: Jadey's. I jolted into wakefulness.

The picture was recent—no, it was live, the camera tracking her grim face as she was escorted by two women police officers from the Sheriff Court in Edinburgh to a police van. I caught passing phrases. "Remanded in custody." "Extradition hearing."

"Extradition?"

"To the F-U-K," said Mary-Jo, spelling it out viciously. "Down there she's been charged with the murder of a Russki officer they say she was having an affair with."

"That's a fucking lie!"

"One would assume so," Alan said, "from first principles. But how do you know?"

I told them. Mary-Jo's finger's tapped on air all the while.

"Right, right," she said when I'd finished. "Assuming she told you the truth, and I think she did; it explains why they have a sample of clothing with that poor son of bitch's blood and her skin cells. And a bloody knife with no goddamn prints or anything. And even if your ware didn't work, and the whole thing was taped, there could still be evidence that there'd been a hack-attack on the street cameras, which

would make any record showing what *actually* happened inadmissible. Shit."

"It gets worse," Alan said in a flat tone. He dug a couple of layers deeper in the news, to the detail behind the headlines. At this level it was practically raw court transcript—nobody'd bothered to summarize this uninteresting minor detail about a mere Brit—and all that leapt out at me was my name and a lot of pictures of me, mostly grainy surveillance grabs but recognizable enough.

"They want you," Mary-Jo translated from the legalese. "They're not sure yet whether they want to subpoena you as a witness or extradite you as an accomplice after the fact. Whichever—the U.S. government is quite likely to cooperate, and even if it doesn't stand up in the courts you're looking at a long legal hassle at best. At worst the INS will have your ass on a plane back to the commies before you can say 'refugee.' "

"Wait a minute," I said, trying to stop a pebble in the landslide of bad news, "I thought people from Europe had automatic refugee status, or something."

"Nah." She shook her head. "It's all de facto. They turn a blind eye, and that's, you know, policy—to waive the immigration controls—but the laws are still on the books. It's a privilege, not a right, and it can be withdrawn at any time and only challenged in court after the fact. Legally you're still an illegal immigrant."

"All right." I sank back in the sofa, feeling drained. "I can handle that. What about Jadey?"

"Excuse me," Mary-Jo said, "but you *can't* handle that. Jadey's situation, we *can* handle. It's what we *do*. No matter what charges they stick on her, it's still political, we can still do deals. It's not like you guys have an independent judiciary or shit. Whereas over here, we do, more or less. Your problem *here* is a bunch of extralegal—official and freelance—people who might come after you. Hell, any of the camo dudes on the gate here might decide to make a bit on the side by turning you in. You don't want to be either administratively dealt with *or* stuck in the courts, believe me."

She stood up and strolled to the window, as though watching out for the camo dudes or the black helicopters. "Y'know," she said, "your credibility as an E.U. citizen who's an oppositionist has just gone off the scale. You could really talk to the mutineers out there. And you are in deep shit here on Earth."

She turned to with me a speculative grin. "Still think going into space is a crazy idea?"

"Yes," I said. I had given them a lengthy piece of my mind on this subject as soon as the suggestion had come up. "But—"

"Good man!" said Alan. "I knew you'd come around."

"That's a *spaceship*?"

I was used to seeing launch pictures from Baikonur, from Kourou, and for that matter from Canaveral. Even with single-stage–to–orbit, flea-on-a-griddle liftoff they resembled everything back to the V2 in their vertical ascent. This black object, out in the glare of the sun on the bitter flat ground, resembled nothing. It looked more alien than any real or imagined flying saucer. It was like a sculpture of some animal native to the vacuum. Just trying to get a perspective on the thing, to form an image of it as a whole, was making my eyes water and my head hurt.

"Nevada Orbital Dynamics SSTA," said Alan Armstrong. (That was his name, he'd finally admitted. He was only the chief engineer—notoriously modest, according to the info my spex were pulling down.) "Single Stage to Anywhere. It's a refinement of the old USAF Electro-Dynamic Stealth Fighter. Our famous flying saucer that the Russkis chewed up so many of in the war. This one can ionize the surrounding air and electromagnetically pulse it to reach escape velocity *in the atmosphere,* then generate its plasma sail and accelerate further. You could go to Pluto with it. I mean, you'd starve first, but your body could get there."

Plasma sail—I checked the ref, found screeds about the system, a vast electromagnetic field enclosing a spheroid of ionized gas that interacted with the solar photon flux like a lightsail. It could take us to the *Marshall Titov* in days, more than half of which time would be spent tacking and decelerating. Final course-corrections by fusion rocket.

"*Fusion?* So why don't you—"

"Use it for everything? It's expensive, that's why. That ship is worth billions of dollars."

I stared at him. "How do you expect to make that kind of money back?"

He shrugged. "The U.S. military is a bit burned-off with flying saucers," he admitted, "and the commercial space operators don't need anything like this—yet. We might flog it to NASA someday, if they ever get their act together, but for now this is blue-sky, foundation-

funded stuff for the space exploration which we are certain will revive. More certain now than ever, come to think of it."

"Makes me wonder why we need to bother with alien tech," I said.

"Anti-gravity would be worth having," Armstrong said mildly. "Anyway, you're soon going to find out."

"Jeez." I felt cold inside. Already, trucks were rolling up, in a haze of dust and leaks of pressurized gases, to prep the thing for launch in a few hours.

"Bear in mind that it can get you back just as fast," Alan said. "It's not like you're leaving Earth for months, or anything."

I should have known what to expect when the medical included a few minutes of squirming through a long, narrow, dark pipe, with sensors checking my signs to make very sure I didn't suffer from claustrophobia. It was never something I'd thought about before. The mission psychologist said I would have made a very good cave-diver. I told him I'd bear it in mind if I ever wanted to take up safer hobbies.

The gel-packed g-suit was state-of-the-art. What one wore underneath was a sort of skintight, soft combination garment, and what one wore under that—

"Why the diaper?" I asked indignantly.

"In case this pill doesn't work."

"Can I take two?"

I was told to keep my spex on, and provided with a new, American-made palm computer onto which all my AIs and systems-management programs had been downloaded. It, along with the wet-tech reader and the datadisk, went into pockets on my thigh.

The pilot was called Camila Hernandez. She was several inches shorter and years younger than myself, and I hesitate to estimate how many kilos lighter. Her face might have been pretty if it hadn't been so thin, almost anorexic, and if her hair hadn't been buzz-cut to a five-millimeter fuzz. She shook my hand as we sat facing each other on the back of a trailer that trundled us out to the ship. Beyond that she didn't have much to say. She had a look of fierce concentration and I guessed she was fingering some rosary of flight-checks in her mind, so I kept quiet.

The ship, *Blasphemous Geometries,* was about two meters deep in the center. The entrance hatch was at the center. The cockpit wasn't. Camila climbed in and I followed, to find myself squirming along a long, dark, narrow tube. I emerged in a space less than a meter deep and two meters long and a little under two meters wide. Camila was already lying prone on the couch on the right. I pulled myself up on the one beside her, and at the far end stuck my head into a bubble helmet, which sealed itself around my neck. Behind me, I could hear hoses and nozzles snake out and snick onto my suit.

In front of the bubble helmet, curving around in front of and above and below the two of us, was what looked like a bubble window. There definitely hadn't been a window visible from the outside, so this had to be some scaled-up version of spex, but the illusion of having my head up at the leading edge of the craft was perfect. Above, the blue sky; below, the dusty ground, the technicians going about their final tasks; ahead, the shimmering heat haze and mirage of Groom Lake, the craft's shadow stretching ahead of us in the late-afternoon sun.

Camila's hands rested in front of her head on a control panel. The control panel in front of me was covered with a plastic lid, sealed down; I rested my forearms on it and looked ahead. I absurdly thought of Superman's flying pose, and stifled a nervous chuckle.

"You all right?"

"Yeah, I'm fine."

"Good. Shock-gel deploying."

Camila slid back a bolt. With a loud hiss the space around our legs and torsos filled with some kind of foam which set instantly to a rubbery texture that yielded just enough to make it possible to breathe. It pressed hard against my feet and legs and around my midriff.

"Deployed," she said. Then, in a different tone: "*Blasphemous Geometries,* ready to roll!"

The sound of something disengaging, and a siren outside that brayed for a good two minutes. The air in front of us began to crackle and warp; a deep hum came through the soles of my feet and up through my legs, setting each bone and then each tooth resonating at a separate frequency. With it rose a feeling of tension and oppression and the uncanny sensation that my arms and legs were being tugged and stretched.

The ship began to move, slowly at first, dust and glowing flecks streaming around the curved viewplate, the ground flicking past beneath us, faster and faster until it was a blur of straight lines. I looked up. The mountains surrounding the salt-pan approached in a terrible rush, and then—

—dropped away.

The view around us reddened, then cleared—I guessed the view-plate was correcting innumerable wild distortions and refractions. Despite the gel-suit and the shock-gel, I felt as though my weight were increasing so fast that my bones would crack. Every joint ached. Below, the landscape passed like a panning shot, then it became as blurred as the runway had been, only slowing a little as we climbed. In a shockingly short time we were above the Atlantic; and shortly thereafter, above the atmosphere.

I didn't have much time to appreciate the blue view of Earth. The acceleration dropped, ended, and then, just as my bones were creeping back to their full length, returned, milder but more insistent. Around the craft something bloomed like neon, then faded from view as the correction software reacted like an iris adjustment. Earth's horizon, too, rushed upon us and dropped away.

I stared at space and stars in a sky that went all around.

"That's it for now," said Camila, in a more relaxed voice than I'd heard from her before. "Want to see how we looked from the ground?"

"Sure," I said, reluctant to disengage my view of the stars.

She tabbed a few keys and part of the viewplate right in front of us opaqued and showed, somewhat disorientingly, a band of blue sky. Along that band hurtled an accelerating red fireball; and then, in jerky succession, the view cut to ever-briefer glimpses of our ever-tinier bolide streak across increasingly dark skies.

"Twenty-seven missile station alert-status upgrades," she read off from somewhere, "and two hundred and eighty UFO incident reports logged to date. Not bad."

"What do we look like now?" I asked.

She gave me a sideways glance, doubly distorted by our two goldfish bowls. "Um," she said, "didn't want to worry you, you know? But since you ask, because we have thousands of cubic kilometers of ionized gas around us we're, uh, naked-eye–visible. . . ."

A nighttime view, looking up. According to the Cyrillics scrolling along the bottom it was a patch from a local station in Minsk doing an outside broadcast follow-up of a UFO report or war scare. Above a ragged horizon of new-tech housing-pylons we shone plainly, a bright star.

I never heard the proximity alarm, which was for the pilot's ear. The first I knew was when Camila turned to me and asked urgently: "Matt— are you religious?"

"No," I said, baffled by the question.

"Okay," she said. "Holy Mary, Mother of God, pray for us sinners now and at the hour of our death. Amen." Then, in a different tone: "Right, this is where it gets tedious."

Her fingers played over the control board faster than touch-typing. I immediately, with a mercifully apt reflex, clasped my hands across the back of the helmet and pressed it down as hard as I could into the yielding surface of the gel-couch. The viewplate went black. A moment later we were slammed sideways. It was the first of many such buffetings, giddy moments of free fall followed by brutal bursts of acceleration in unpredictable directions. It actually did get tedious, like a roller-coaster ride that goes on far too long, repeating its thrills to the point where they merge into a continuous dull fear and a wish that you could get *off*.

After what seemed like a long time but, according to my clock in the spex, was only about an hour, the violent motions stopped. All the time the forward acceleration had built up—still nowhere near one gravity, but very noticeable.

"We've outrun them," Camila said. "Every nearby burst gives us more gas and more flux, and lets us run faster. Real neat." She grinned across at me, sweat drying on her face. "Really *soaks up* laser strikes too," she added, worryingly.

I felt absurdly apologetic.

"I had no idea the EPAF would try to shoot us down."

She laughed. "That was friendly fire, bro. Our side. USAF Orbital Defense."

"What?"

"Not surprising. Unauthorized launch, overflying E.U. territory— they had to do *something* to convince the commies we weren't about to nuke 'em. Other politics as well, I guess. The Feds are really worried about freelancers taking advantage of the shake-ups in the E.U. defense and security apparats to start something." Her grin became feral. "Bring down the whole stinking commie edifice."

"God, you sound like Jadey," I said. The thought of her returned like an injury that hadn't hurt as long as the fight continued.

"Jadey Ericson? You mean you *know* her? Wow! Tell me all about it!"

"Shouldn't you be flying this thing?"

"For the next couple of days it flies itself, until I have to start tacking." She frowned. "Now, *that* gets tedious. In the meantime there's nothing to do. We can take our helmets off now, by the way. Twist it *so*—right, then left."

We both breathed deeply, in air that was indistinguishable from what we'd had in the helmets, except perhaps for the faint reassurance of each other's human smell.

"Well, here we are. We can suck glop out of these tubes, water out of that. We can piss, but we can't shit. We can sleep." She jerked a thumb. "That stuff stays around us until we dock. Might as well be in a fucking plaster cast. Best not think about it, huh?" She brightened. "But we can talk. And we can follow the news—we're getting a laser feed, if you want to check your spex you'll see it all." She sucked water. "Talk to me or I'll go bugfuck crazy."

"Or I will." I wanted to see the breaking news, but I knew what she meant.

I told her my adventures, leaving out only the nature of the information I was carrying.

"What I don't get," she said when I'd finished, staring out at the unchanging view of the stars—no speed of ours could change them visibly—"is how you guys *live* with it. All that corruption and controls and shit."

"It's not so bad," I said. "The state's a bit heavier than in America, sure, but let's face it, it does get more things done. More education, less pollution, no beggars . . ." I laughed. "And space exploration—let's not forget space exploration!"

"But the *Party*!" she said. "How can you stand that? I mean, nobody believes in Communism anymore, not even the commies."

"Oh yes they do," I said. "They just don't call it that. They call it 'the sustainable society.' What economists used to call the stationary state. And they think they're getting us there, and that everybody will get there in the end, even the Americans."

"Never!" Camila said. "Maybe the East Coast liberals might go for that, but not the rest of us."

I sighed. "It's got nothing to do with what anybody *believes* in. The falling rate of profit will get you in the end. You can evade it for a while by exporting capital, and follow that falling rate like a star sinking on the horizon, which by following fast enough you can raise for a while, but all that gets you is a fully capitalist—and fully capitalized—world, with low profit rates everywhere, and then there's nowhere else to go but the steady state, an economy just quietly ticking over rather

than expanding. In the steady state it's easy for workers to end up employing capital—socialism, near as makes no difference."
She shot me a suspicious look.
"This is Marx, right?"
"Wrong," I said. "It's John Stuart Mill."
"Same difference," she said. "Bloody liberals." Moody silence, then: "Anyway, that's all rubbish because we have space to expand into, forever!"
"*What* expansion? There's no *profit* in space. Nobody's desperate enough to want to *live* there. That gang of libertarians who tried it couldn't stand it, couldn't stand each other—"
"Yeah, yeah," she said. "I know about Hell-Five. But in the long run—"
" 'In the long run,' " I said, quoting another suspect and defunct economist, " 'we are all *dead*.' "

Conversation kept us going for long stretches—we ended up knowing a lot about each other, like pillow-talking lovers—and between that, and sleep, and staring at the stars, there was the newsfeed.
Mary-Jo had exaggerated when she'd said that all hell was breaking loose in Red Europe. But there was no doubt that Driver's message had thrown a spanner in the works of the workers' states. The Party, the Federal Security Bureau, and the European Peoples' Army were maneuvering against each other in an unprecedentedly overt manner: military budgets queried, more MEPs and Party officials under suspicion or arrest, inquiries launched into FSB illegalities, rapid promotions and demotions and cashierings, military exercises proceeding without authorization, unscheduled call-ups of reservists (which, I guessed, added draft-evasion to my crimes).
At this rate it was only a matter of time before the populations, too, would have their say. Whether all hell really would break loose at that point was difficult to predict. Across Europe the peace movement, hitherto a moribund adjunct of official foreign policy, was already organizing mass demonstrations at which Webbly banners were well to the fore. That, at least, was something to count against the (also growing) "patriotic" anti-American demonstrations, which were, with brazen illegality, backed by factions of the Army. The ostensible occasion of these demonstrations was the constant drip of "discoveries" about U.S. links to the "English fascist terrorists" who'd been swept up after the

codes had been cracked. Cameras tracked across incriminating caches of weapons.

"That's you guys' problem," Camila informed me confidently. "You're not allowed to have guns. That's why the Russkis walked all over you, and that's why you can't throw them out."

I stared at her, openmouthed.

"Where do you get that from?" I asked at last. "*Everybody* in Europe has guns. Since the revolution, anyway. The Russkis were shocked at the lack of preparedness when they came in, and they set about making damn sure it wouldn't happen again. Unless you're a conscientious objector—you know, a Quaker or something—it's *compulsory* to have a Markov and an AK and ammo at home. I was top of my class team in pistol shooting in *primary* school, I'll have you know. I did my one year's military service from the day after my eighteenth birthday. I could have kept up my training if I'd joined the CDR—Civil Defense and Resistance—but I never bothered. I'm still in the reserves, though."

It was her turn to stare. "So why don't you all just rise up and overthrow the commies?"

"Because hardly anybody bloody *wants* to, that's why! Look, the Party really does get elected! All we have to do is vote them out!"

Camila remained convinced it was all some kind of scam; that guns issued by the government didn't really count, and that elections with bans on rich people buying politicians couldn't be free.

Of Jadey there was no news at all.

"Oh-*kay*," said Camila, fifty hours after launch, "helmets on. Time to start work." She sounded much more eager than her earlier talk of tedium might have suggested. We were already far beyond the asteroid's orbital position, and about to start tacking—sunward again—to intersect it.

The viewplate went from black to white, with the sun—I swear—represented as an asterisk in the middle, the asteroid as a constantly changing string of numbers. It looked like one of those primitive ASCII games you find squirreled away, a programmers' in-joke, in the most obscure address-spaces of operating systems.

If the display was like a game, the actual approach it registered was another white-knuckle ride, more violent than the missile evasions. Camila exchanged clipped voice-only transmissions with the station between each abrupt change of course. It went on for hours and ended in free fall. With a flourish Camila toggled the viewplate control, and the asteroid sprang into full-color 3-D view, just as we'd all first seen it, as real as television. The station expanded in the view, its appearance changing from something tiny and intricate, like circuitry, to something huge and intricate, like a factory. At the same time, the general view shifted from traveling toward the asteroid to flying over it. The final fine adjustments became increasingly gentle, from the sensation of a jostling crowd, through a beggar's tug, to the suspicion of a pickpocket's pass.

With a last puff of the retro the *Blasphemous Geometries* settled into a clutch of grapples that clicked around the ship's edges. Banging and crunching noises followed.

"What's that?"

"Airlock connecting." She smiled. "Don't I get any thanks?"

I gave her a high-five. "Yeah, thanks!"

"Keep your helmet on for now," she said. She reached up for a switch. "Clearing shock-gel."

A bluish liquid sprayed in from nozzles at the sides of the viewplate, hosing our shoulders and—as the space cleared—other jets hissed on down our backs and sides. Camila pushed herself up, opening a space between herself and the couch, and I did likewise. The liquid shriveled the shock-gel to dry, rubbery strips, then evaporated in a flush of warm air.

"Wow." I waggled my legs, swiveled my pelvis. "That feels good."

The sudden physical freedom made me all the more anxious to escape the remaining restrictions. For the first time I actually did feel something like claustrophobia: the space around me was too small, and the air didn't satisfy my lungs.

We both looked as though covered with ragged bandages—the robot from the mummy's tomb. Camila brushed at the sticky rags of dried shock-gel. They hung annoyingly in the air, drifting.

"Extractor fan in the next model!"

Something clunked and made grinding noises. Camila cocked her head, listening to the voice in her ear.

"That's it," she reported. "Airlock sealed." She waved me past her. "You go first. I get to turn off the lights."

With fingertips and toes I propelled myself backward along the narrow tube to the hatch. Just before my feet touched it, its cover plate slid smoothly aside. Even in the suit and helmet, I could feel the change in pressure, and the draft. Light shone up from beneath, or behind, my feet. I continued on in a direction that now felt like "down," though not from any effect of the asteroid's microgravity, of which I felt nothing. Down, then: down past the locking rings and down another long but wider tube, and then out.

For a moment I hung there, hands braced in the exit of the tube, feet just above the metal mesh floor. The receiving-bay with which the ship had docked was large, about three meters high below the airlock tube, twenty long, and ten wide. Crates and bits of equipment were tethered or taped to stanchions and I-beams. Fluorescent lighting flickered over the garish color-coding. Across from me was a heavy door in front of which a small, crop-haired man in multiple-mission–patched cotton fatigues floated, holding on to a crossbeam with one hand, the other resting on the butt of a standard-issue 9-millimeter Aerospatiale Officier stuck in a webbed waistband.

He let go of the pistol and gestured to me to remove my helmet. I let go of the airlock rim and did so, beginning to tumble over in the air. Camila emerged from the shaft, and did the same with more grace.

The place stank: rank, organic stenches of human and plant and animal combined with the harsher reek of hot metal, burnt plastic, old machine-oil. I almost gagged; Camila just wrinkled her nose. The man favored us with a wry smile.

"You'll get used to it," he said. He stuck out his right hand, empty. "My name is Paul Lemieux. Welcome to the Revolution."

Even looking up at him, one hand holding the mesh of the floor where I'd drifted, I could grasp his meaning—if not, at that moment, his hand—and think:

Oh shit!

II

Manufacturing Plant

Here, at the top of the hill, the wind off the sea was unavoidable and constant. It gave airplanes a little extra lift as they bounded and jolted down the runway taking off, and permitted a lower approach speed as they landed—also bounding and jolting. If the pilot cut too close to stalling speed, when the wind dropped so did the plane.

The wind moaned in the tall bamboo pylons, and made them flex, and made the airships sway at their moorings like bait on a trolling hook. Others, released from the moorings but tethered to the ground, strained and rippled. Gangs of workers used ropes and windlasses and main force to haul and steady the craft for the passengers and crew to get in or out. Tankers of water for ballast and kerosene for fuel (the former conveniently doubling as fire engines) hurried back and forth.

Gregor sat in the glassed-in waiting area and watched, fascinated by everything he saw. He hadn't visited the airport since he was a small boy, and it was somehow galling that all the exciting activity he remembered from childhood had ever since been within such easy reach.

Beside him sat Salasso, then Elizabeth—each, like him, with a traveling-bag at their feet. Salasso's was small and made of something that looked like flexible aluminum; Gregor's was bulkier but not much heavier, of dinosaur hide. Elizabeth's was a laminated suitcase just within the weight limit. She had dressed rather well for the flight, in blouse and skirt and long leather coat. Gregor and the saur were in their usual working clothes, though in Gregor's case, at his mother's insistence, freshly cleaned.

Elizabeth saw him looking, and smiled.

"This is just great!" she said. "What an amazing place, and so close."

"Just what I was thinking myself," he said. He grinned. "Maybe the people who work here never visit the port."

Salasso said nothing. His thin mouth was turned down at the corners, and his shoulders sagged. His eyelids blinked and his nictitating membrane flickered more than usual. His long fingers dug into his bony knees.

"Will somebody please fill me a pipe?" he said.

"You don't want to fall . . . asleep just now," Elizabeth chided.

"I do," said Salasso. "I wish I could. I wish you could *carry* me on board, unconscious. But I realize that would be undignified for all concerned. So please, fill me a pipe. I don't trust my own hands to do it, and I want to at least have it ready as soon as we board."

"Is smoking allowed? I wonder." Gregor asked, as Salasso passed him the pipe and pouch with a visibly shaking hand.

"Yes," said Salasso. "I checked that most carefully. Nothing but potent drugs could keep me calm through a journey on one of these devices."

"Ah, we should have hired a gravity skiff," said Gregor. "Now, why didn't I think of that?"

Salasso's eyes swiveled around, the pupil a deeper black within the black iris.

"*I* thought of that," he said. "But we couldn't afford the expense."

"To tell you the truth," said Gregor, "I never even imagined it was an option. Where can you hire them?"

"Oh, some saurs will do it, if you know who to ask. But usually only to other saurs. It is, as I said, expensive at the best of times, and at the moment it's completely out of the question because all the skiff owners on the planet are making a fortune down south, driving dinosaurs to the meat market."

"That must be quite a sight," Elizabeth said.

"It is. If a little distressing."

"They're just cattle," said Gregor. "*Big* cattle, yes."

Salasso shook his head. "I am not what your people would call sentimental," he said. "Few of my people are! But we all feel . . . some respect, some kinship, with the noble if ignorant beasts on which we prey. Needs must—We are a carnivorous kind, far more than you. But still—we were hunters before we were herders, and before that, we were hunted. We retain some of our past nature."

"And you're saying we retain less?"

Salasso leaned back. "I am not saying that."

145

A warning frown from Elizabeth stopped Gregor's impulse to pursue the matter further. It didn't stop him from turning it over in his mind. It was generally accepted—on what evidence, he wasn't sure—that the saurs had been civilized for millions if not tens of millions of years. Even allowing for their longer lives, and greater intelligence, there was something anomalous and disturbing in the suggestion that they retained some traditions from the savage state.

And for humans, Nova Babylonia represented continuity and antiquity! Even the Keep and the harbor, pre-human though they were, stood shallow in the depth of evolutionary time which for the saurs was *history*.

He finished filling the pipe and passed it back.

A bell sounded and a message flashed on the projection screen announcing the imminent departure of their flight. They picked up their bags and trekked out onto the field with the other fifty or so passengers, into the shadow of the hundred-meter-long semi-rigid dirigible. Salasso ascended the stairladder to the gondola without further demur, headed for the smoking section at the back, and had passed out before the craft had taken off.

"Well, so much for the supercivilized," Gregor remarked, after he and Elizabeth had stowed their bags and sat down on opposite sides of a window table a couple of rows forward of where Salasso sat slumped.

"I suppose to him it's like—I don't know—going out on the ocean on some ramshackle raft would be to us. And some humans have a fear of flying as well, you know."

The airship lurched and the floor tilted upward as the cable at the bow was released a second before that at the stern. Gregor grabbed the edge of the table, Elizabeth threw her arms across it. The engines roared to bring the craft to a level keel.

"Fear of flying, eh? Who'd have thought it?"

She laughed, and they both turned their attention to the view as the airship ascended. How broad the sprawl, how small the ships.

"Wow," said Elizabeth, "you can see our shadow."

"Where? . . . Oh, right." There it was, rippling across street and field and river like a black fluke, paced by the flashing glint of the sun on pool or mire. Then the coastline like a map; clouds from the side and from above.

But after the airship had reached its cruising altitude and had followed the coast southward for a while, even this fascination palled.

Gregor and Elizabeth turned away from the window and settled down like seasoned travelers. Salasso was still sleeping off the effects of smoking an entire pipe by himself.

"Still keen?" Gregor asked.

"Oh yes. Should be interesting even if we don't find any of them. I mean, I know that would be disappointing for you, but . . ."

"Aye, I know what you mean." Gregor sighed, looking around the cabin. Most of the passengers seemed to be on business, and either drinking spirits in a rather forced attempt to relax, or toiling over sheets of paper and hand calculators.

"You know what this world needs?" he said. "A *Beagle* voyage. Somebody to sponsor some long-range travel just for exploration and sampling."

"And to come back with a theory of evolution?"

She smiled, he laughed.

"An account of it," Gregor said. "We already have the theory; what we need is a better idea of how it's gone, here. The planet's story."

Elizabeth looked down at the crawling coastline for a moment, then back at him.

"It would be difficult," she said. "How many incursions have there been? We can't even guess at the number of major deliberate introductions of species, let alone the accidents. I swear it must happen every time a starship comes in—"

She laughed suddenly.

"What?"

"I just remembered. Talking to a lighter skipper down in the Bailie's. He said that if you get to one of the ships up close you can see *barnacles* on them."

"Tough little critters, barnacles."

"Uh-huh. But these must be able to survive at least hours, sometimes days, in *space*."

"Vacuum barnacles!"

She nodded. "There you go, that's one new species right there. And I bet they've spread here."

"Okay," he said. "We'll call the ship the *Barnacle,* and get it sponsored by a manufacturer of anti-fouling paint."

She rubbed an eye. "I think that's a saur product, actually. But, yeah, something like that. Shipowners. Fishermen."

"Hey, don't look at me. My father isn't much of a one for pure research."

"How about the castle?"

"They've got enough on their plate with the Great Work."

They'd continued the conversation without taking it seriously up to this point.

"What?"

"If we succeed," Gregor said, "the Great Work will be done. Over. And the castle, the crew, and the families will be rich. So they might well have more money to throw into research."

He looked out, and down. The coastline had swung inward, and they were now crossing the east-west leg of the L-shaped stretch of ocean, Cargill's Sound, that divided the northwestern subcontinent from its larger neighbor. Mainland was saur country, dinosaur country.

"You know, I could get excited about that," he said. "To sail around the world just to *find out more* about the place."

"That would be wonderful," Elizabeth said, in an uncharacteristically dreamy tone.

"Even if we never did get the planet's story straight?"

"Yeah, even then."

She didn't seem to want to talk any further, hauling down a book from her coat pocket. Gregor looked out of the window for another while, then decided to emulate the business travelers by doing some work.

Paper was the heaviest part of his luggage. He tugged out a double handful of notes, fingered a pen from an inside pocket and began going over them again. They represented the best part of a week's work by him and his companions. How much previous work lay behind it, he hardly dared to fathom. Even then, it was probably inadequate. *If* they tracked down one or more of the original crew, and *if* they still had their hands on some still-functioning hard-tech (as Salasso had claimed), and *if* they were willing to share and cooperate—then *maybe* the figures and data structures summarized here might be the basis for the outline of the model he'd imagined. And even then, the navigation problem itself would have to be formulated and formatted appropriately before it could be entered.

If, indeed, it could. His ideas of the capability of these ancient machines were based on little more than family legend. Even if the most enthusiastic and incredible accounts were true, very likely the machinery had deteriorated over time.

Enough. He could only do what he could. He worked steadily for a couple of hours, pausing only for a coffee brought around by the air-steward, and then noticed that Salasso was stirring. He got up and joined him, leaving Elizabeth nodding off over her book.

"Feeling better?"

"Yes," said Salasso. He looked out of the window and blinked. "One gets used to the most astonishing things. I think I can fill my pipe myself now."

That he did, lit up and toked and passed it to Gregor. After they'd shared two pipes and the saur had passed out once more, Gregor returned to his seat and found that the figures no longer made much sense. Or rather, they made a completely different kind of sense. They'd begun to resemble the physical structure of the squid brain which they mathematically modeled.

Some time after that, he woke to find himself leaning forward over the table and sideways against the window, and Elizabeth having done the same. They each had a forearm across the table, and Elizabeth's hand rested on top of his. He eased his head back gently, wary of cricking his neck. His hair and Elizabeth's had become entangled. As he was easing the strands apart she woke up. She blinked and looked at him, bewildered but beginning to smile. Then she woke up fully and pulled away.

"Ouch! Sorry." She combed with her fingers, freeing their hair finally, and sat up straight. "You fell asleep stoned then I fell asleep reading. Right on top of you!"

"Ah, it's all right," Gregor said. "What are friends for?"

"Good night," said Elizabeth.

Gregor looked up from his stack of paper and cup of coffee. "Good night."

She tugged her overnight satchel from her bag, picked up her book and walked to the end of the cabin where a small stair coiled up to the interior of the hull. Salasso turned from gazing at the night, or at the reflections, and raised a floppy hand. Most of the rest of the passengers had already gone to bed.

Up the stair, two turns. Did gravity *increase* as you rose above the surface? It seemed so. Inside the creaking, tough fabric hull was a warren of narrow, low-lit passages between the translucent plastic bulges of the gasbags. She used a tiny washroom and made her way to a cabin—little more than an enclosed bunk—of laminated wood. Balsa for the walls, aluminum for the bed; thin foam mattress and down covering. There was room to stand, and undress, and hang her clothes. The top of the bunk was too low to sit hugging her knees. She lay on her side, hugging her knees.

Gregor had seemed a little surprised, and pleased, that she wanted to come at all. Really, he'd insisted, it wasn't necessary. Salasso had to come because they had to track down saur rumors—rumors so obscure that even old Tharovar had never heard them. Gregor had to come because they'd then have to track down people, maybe in tough places. She didn't need to put herself to this trouble and possible hazard. Why not continue the labwork while they were away?

She'd told him she had no intention whatsoever of staying behind. She wouldn't miss this for anything. She'd pay her fare herself if she had to. James had assured her that the castle would pay her way, no problem. Research expenses.

So here she was: huddled in a narrow bunk, a few meters away from Gregor, on a journey to find what just might help Gregor catch up with—and catch—Lydia. Her only consolation was that its success was unlikely.

Wonderful.

The thousand-mile journey took two more days and nights. They spent the days much as they had the first one; the nights in their separate cabins in the hull, between the plastic spheres of the gasbags.

On the third morning, at breakfast, Salasso called across to Elizabeth and Gregor.

"Look down," he said.

The ship had descended to what seemed to Gregor like a couple of thousand feet. Beneath them, in a glaring low sun, lay the northern fringes of the manufacturing plant. Here, it was still sparse, but startling nonetheless. Clumps and stands of trees, their green branches angled out then straight up like those of decision trees or clade diagrams, cast long shadows. Some had leaves in the shape of inverted umbrellas; others, diamond-shaped.

"Like giant cactuses," said Elizabeth.

The saur had wandered over and leaned in beside them, his breath smelling of kippers.

"Correct," he said. "The cactus plant was one of the sources of the original genes. Of course, much has been edited in since."

"Such as the pipelines between them," said Gregor. He'd just begun to grasp the scale of what he was seeing. Some of these things were a hundred meters tall. The airship was still descending, and he could see dots moving on the ground. At first he'd thought they were saurs, but now he could see they were vehicles.

He swallowed to ease the pressure on his eardrums. The scale jumped again—the vehicles were chemical tankers. He saw a road and his gaze followed it south . . . to even taller structures, well over the horizon now and rapidly approaching.

"Docking at Saur City One in twenty minutes," the steward announced.

Salasso said something.

"What?"

The saur's lips twitched. "Its real name," he said. "Some of the syllables are outside the range of human hearing."

"Ah," said Gregor, who had been mentally trying to pronounce it. "Fine. Saur City One it is."

As they drifted closer it became obvious that the city was of the same stuff and shapes as the manufacturing plant, but expanded and contorted into towers and gantries, platforms and plazas, aerial roadways and walkways. These structures were clothed and foliated with dense, decorative overgrowths of smaller and more colorful, more vegetation-like versions of the plant.

One tall tower loomed, a helical twist of three trunks supporting a platform that bristled with masts.

"Docking in two minutes," said the steward. "Please return to your seats."

Gregor followed the others down a ladder, made—almost reassuringly—of something like mutated bamboo. The platform, too, was wooden, but without planks or other divisions, and it swayed slightly. Two saurs sat in a saddle out from the edge of the platform, operating levers which seemed to control the snaking vines of the airship's tethers. A steady breath of oxygenated and cooled air from stomata in the wall at the far end of the platform did little to relieve the heat and humidity.

"Over here," said Salasso. The other passengers, disembarking or just stretching their legs before the next part of the journey south, had trooped off through a double-glass doorway. Gregor and Elizabeth lugged their bags after Salasso, through an arched doorway off to the left. Inside, they found themselves in a green, smooth-sided corridor which expanded to a circular room, its walls dotted with yellow-green lights and broken by further doorways. A ring of low seating, like some fungoid growth of cork, occupied the hub of the room.

"We wait here," said Salasso.

"At least it's cooler," said Elizabeth, sitting down. "What are we waiting for?"

"A lift," said Salasso.

Other saurs passed in and out, most busy and incurious, a few exchanging words and gestures with Salasso.

"Why here and not with the other passengers?" Gregor asked.

Salasso shrugged. "They'll be here to make deals, in the human quarter. More comfortable accommodations. We are going deep into the city. Perhaps deeper." He hesitated. "Forgive me. You may wish to stay with the other humans? I can very well go on alone."

"Not a chance," Elizabeth and Gregor told him.

"Good," he said. "You can, however, leave your luggage here."

In one of the apertures something settled with a thud, filling the space behind it. Then it, too, opened up, revealing a small, bright chamber just large enough for a few people to stand in.

Salasso stood and walked toward it; they hurried after him and joined him inside it.

"What's this?"

"Like I said," Salasso explained. "A lift."

A section of the wall slid across the opening. Then, quite without warning, they dropped. Gregor felt his body become lighter for a few seconds, then briefly heavier. The sliding door opened again, to the open air.

They stepped out, onto grass, and then Gregor and Elizabeth stopped and stared. At the foot of all the towers and silos they were as mice in a forest. Sunlight, shining down between the trunks and reflected off their polished-looking surfaces, fell shadowless, filtered to green. Across all the grassy space that they could see, saurs strolled between towers or sat or ran about on the grass. Most of the saurs here looked quite unlike those Gregor had seen before. They wore a diversity of clothing and ornament: loose, flapping trousers and jackets, robes and gowns, cloaks and daggers, in colors vivid and various. Their height, too, varied from taller than Salasso to so short they had to be infants. High-pitched, fluting cries filled the air like batsong.

Salasso looked back from a few meters ahead, and returned a couple of steps.

"I had forgotten," he said. "No human has been here before."

He beckoned, and they followed him to where three saurs sat on a low hillock a little way off the path. Two were of normal height, one in black pajamas, the other in a loose robe. The third, the two-foot-high one kneeling on the grass gazing intently at a wheeled wooden box it pushed along with both hands, was covered in what Gregor at first took to be a fluffy yellow one-piece outfit.

Then he saw how the covering became sparser at the nape, and realized that it was all the infant's own downy feathers. Elizabeth saw it at the same moment and immediately squatted down a couple of meters away from the infant, looking at it intently. Salasso was talking to the adults; Gregor hung back, not wanting to scare anyone. His own knees were shaking. No human had seen a saur infant before, not even in a photograph. He'd heard half-joking, edgy speculations that saur infants hatched from eggs in hot sand and lived like beasts, unparented until they proved their capacity to survive; that saurs didn't even have offspring, that they were as sterile as they were ancient; that they were all constructed like robots by the manufacturing plant . . .

He wished he'd thought to bring a camera, to document the evidence of this close encounter.

The child turned to look at Elizabeth, then stood up. The head was more disproportionately large than that of a human baby. Upon some reassuring sounds from the adults, the young saur ran across the grass and tumbled into Elizabeth's arms and lap. She crooned over it, tickling and stroking; it reached up its clawed fingers to her hair and whistled.

"Her name is Blathora," said Salasso. "She is two years old."

"She's just so cute," said Elizabeth. "Super cute. Such big eyes. Aren't you just the sweetest thing. Wow. What a tiny mouth."

"Sharp teeth," warned Salasso, as Elizabeth's fingers teased around the high cheekbones. "And a taste for mammal blood."

"Oh." She drew back a little. "Gregor? Do you want to hold her?"

"Oh yes."

Dandling the saurian child, drowning in black pools deep as the past of her species, Gregor had one of those moments when time stops. The rarity of the moment, the privilege, stunned him. How many human parents would trust their baby to the hands of even another hominid, to one of the tall hairy men of the high snows? He found himself responding to the saurs' trust, in a rush of affection and protective feeling toward this small but significant life.

He returned Blathora to the adults, and found that she'd left a spot of snotty, chalky guano on his thigh.

. . .

"Where are we going?" Gregor asked, after half an hour of walking on the floor of the city.

Salasso looked back.

"This a very safe area, outside the industrial processes. Like a park, but safer. It's used for relaxation, play, and teaching. I expect to meet one of my old teachers."

"Teachers!"

"Why do you laugh?"

"It's funny to think of saurs having teachers."

"Did you think we hatch knowing everything?"

"Some people do think that," said Elizabeth. "Seriously."

"No, it isn't that, it's just—" Gregor shrugged. "I suppose I imagined you taught by machines, or something."

"Machines!" Salasso hooted. He paused to let them both walk beside him, and continued in a lower tone:

"We have a policy, an agreement. It is not enforced, but . . . nearly all of us see the wisdom of it—not to share much information with you, and especially not about ourselves. We are a very private people, and cautious. But when I hear things like this, I wish we could be more forthcoming."

He hissed through his teeth, a sigh. "But we cannot. Our societies would become less distinct, and the stronger one would absorb the weaker."

Gregor looked around and upward yet again at the biotechnological complex, shining and alien. Spectacular though it was, it held no attraction for him.

"I don't think you need worry about us being absorbed," he said.

"That," said Salasso, "is not what we worry about."

Oh.

"How many people are here?" Elizabeth asked.

"Saurs?"

"Yes. In Saur City One."

Salasso shrugged and waved his arms. He was walking ahead of them again, pressing on, eager. The shadows had shortened, and the light and heat become more intense.

"A million or so. At a guess. We do not number each other."

"Hm," said Elizabeth. She glanced from side to side as she walked, her lips moving, her thumbs moving along the tips of her fingers.

"What are you doing?" Gregor asked, in a low voice.

"Population stats." She looked sidelong at him. "There seem to be a lot of kids . . ." She laughed. "Whatever—chicks? squabs?—anyway . . . young saurs about. But if you actually count them, as in per hectare, and see how each of them is getting serious adult attention . . . it looks like a very low reproduction rate. High K/R strategy."

"Goes with the long life," said Gregor lightly.

Elizabeth shook her head firmly. "No! Not necessarily. They're limiting their population, maybe keeping it just ticking over. No growth."

"While we—"

She smiled crookedly. "Us humans. Yes. How many cousins do you have?"

He waggled his fingers in front of her. "I'd have to take my boots off to count them, unless you have a clicker."

Salasso stopped walking and looked back. His mouth stretched to the sides.

"There she is!" he cried, pointing. Fifty meters away, a saur in a long blue coat was sitting on a cork chair in front of a dozen smaller and younger people, in the shade of a metallic umbrella.

Then he did something they'd never seen him do before. He ran to the adult saur, who stood up and embraced him.

"Gods above," said Gregor. "The little bugger has feelings."

"I knew *that*," said Elizabeth.

Something in her tone made Gregor turn to her, but she was looking away. Salasso waved to them and they joined him.

Up close, neither the greater age nor different sex of the other saur were apparent, at least to them. The features were as smooth as Salasso's, the body—naked where the coat fell open—as neutral and neuter in its external anatomy as that of the male, whom they had once or twice seen swimming, very badly.

"My friends, meet Athranal, my venerable teacher," said Salasso.

They introduced themselves.

"Good day to you," she said, in a stilted, sibilant Trade Latin. "We welcome you here."

"We are honored to meet you."

She laughed, wheezily, for the first time sounding old.

"Indeed you are. I was young when this tongue was new."

Gregor felt his nape hairs prickle. They suddenly felt as stiff as the pinfeathers of the infant saur he'd played with. He preferred to think he'd misunderstood, or that her grasp of the language was rusty. He nodded politely.

"We seek our own . . . old folk."

"So my best pupil has told me," she said. She laid a hand on Salasso's shoulder. "Salasso, Salasso! How good to see you again!"

Turning to the younger saurs—adolescent, Gregor guessed—who were standing politely back, she launched into a declamation in the saurian speech which had the pupils sinking to their haunches and staring at Salasso, who after a time squirmed his shoulders and looked down. Had he learned the body language of embarrassment from humanity? Gregor wondered.

After about five minutes, Athranal stopped. Her pupils thumped the ground with their feet.

"And so we say good-bye," she concluded, clapping Salasso's back and turning to the others.

"Good-bye, and good fortune," said Salasso.

Gregor and Elizabeth stumbled the same salutation.

"We must go," said Salasso.

He almost grabbed them, almost swept them up in his arms as he shot past them, then sprinted to the base of the nearest shaft without a backward glance. With one hurried look over his shoulder at the old teacher, now placidly returning to her seat, Gregor raced after the saur, with Elizabeth's footsteps thudding on the turf behind him.

They tumbled over each other into a lift. The door slithered shut. Their knees buckled as it ascended, then they were pulled sideways as it accelerated horizontally.

"What's going on?" Elizabeth asked. "Why didn't you wait for her to tell you?"

"She told me," said Salasso. His breathing had become deep and rapid. "Into that . . . oration, she worked an account of where they are. The old crew. Not so that the young ones would understand, but I understood."

"How?"

"A code." The lift swung around some corner, and shot upward again. "Something like what you would call an acrostic."

"A what?"

"Initials of words, spelling out a word," Elizabeth explained.

"Many words," said Salasso.

"You did all that in your head?" asked Gregor. "And she must have—"

"Improvised it on the spot. She is clever."

"Why not just tell you straight-out?"

Salasso passed a forearm across his forehead, in a curiously inhuman gesture, like a fly cleaning its eyes.

"If the children understood it, they might tell their parents, and some might think that the gods would not approve."

Well, that clears that up, thought Gregor.

"And where are they?" he asked.

"In and around New Lisbon," said Salasso. "At the dinosaur drive and the meat market. We must catch the flight. There is not another for days, and by then it will be over."

The lift slammed and buffeted them and spat them out into the circular hall. They raced through, barely remembering to snatch up their bags, and out onto the platform just in time to see the airship vanish behind the most distant of the city's towers.

12

Orbital Commie Hell

T HE STATION, LEMIEUX gleefully informed us as he led us through its crowded, cluttered spaces, was no longer called the *Marshall Titov*. It was called (deep breath) *The Darker the Night the Brighter the Star;* after a volume of some obscure biography of Trotsky, I gathered. I wanted to suggest that *The Prophet Stoned* would have been snappier as well as more apt—the people we passed were certainly high on something, maybe the pervasive acetone and alcohol vapors of degrading wet-tech—but I forbore.

I began to get the hang of moving in microgravity, with the occasional shove from Camila to correct my mistakes. Beyond the heavy rubber-sealed door of the receiving area the smells of the place were stronger and more various. The air-circulation system made a lot of white noise but didn't seem to make the air any fresher. Hardly a light source was without its huddle of hydroponics. Rabbits and chickens—the mammals better pre-adapted to free fall than the birds, oddly—floated or dived in airy spaces fenced off with fine plastic netting that contained their droppings but not their odor. People in grubby fatigues or quirky, scant selections of clothing and tools worked at all angles in every available cranny. As they glanced up—or down, or across—at us, they looked pleased enough to see us but returned without reluctance to their work.

At a corner of two corridors Camila took advantage of a momentary collision and entanglement to ask me, sharply under her breath, "Why aren't they *saying* anything to us?"

Lemieux glanced back. "Because they don't know who's listening."

"That's us told," Camila muttered, as she pushed me on.

I didn't believe Lemieux's explanation for a moment. These people didn't look as though they were worried about saying something that might be held against them by whoever came out on top of the power struggle. They looked like people who had something better to think about than that.

Driver looked much as I'd seen him in his announcement, but thinner, with a few days' growth of stubble; eyes bloodshot and sleepless. Patches of his cheeks had been scratched almost raw from the itch of overused wet-tech. He'd angled himself in between a work surface and a wall as though sitting at a desk. A net bag tethered to the surface bulged with crushed smokeless filters and crumpled sets of waste goggles and phones. Shelves of transparent containers, tool-racks, computing equipment, and surveillance gear covered the walls behind him and the ceiling. Postcards of landscapes and seascapes—almost pornographic in the circumstances—decorated them.

Lemieux crouched in an upper corner of the inadequate space, watching us at a disconcerting angle. Camila and I looped our arms through some webbing opposite Driver's desk and relaxed in the air.

"Well," Driver said, "I got a warning from Area 51 that a flying saucer was on the way. Kind of amusing. Didn't say why you were coming, though, or who you were." He grimaced. "We've been announcing you as the first American researchers to accept Big Uncle's kind invitation to join us. So who are you really?"

Camila came close to standing to attention.

"Camila Hernandez, test pilot for Nevada Orbital Dynamics. This is Matt Cairns, a systems manager from Scotland who has some information for you. That's all I know."

Colin Driver's attention switched over to me. "Hey, I've seen you on the news somewhere. The defector, right?"

"You could say that."

"Well, what have you got?"

"I've brought back some information you downloaded to ESA," I said. "It's been ramped up into project designs. It'll drop out a complete manufacturing spec, once I've done some more work on it."

"A spec for what?"

I glanced at Camila and Lemieux and then thought, the hell with it, this was something that everybody needed to know.

"You know, for the anti-gravity vehicle and the space-drive."

Camila turned and stared at me.

"The *what*?"

159

Lemieux guffawed, from his simian perch. Driver contained his amusement not much better.

"First, I've heard of it," he said. "You're telling me it came from *here*?"

I nodded. "Via the ESA planning-system, yeah."

"Well, it *can't* have," Driver insisted. "Everything—the legit info to ESA, the disinfo to the, ah, other side—all went through my desk." He thumped it, in ringing emphasis.

"Perhaps," Camila suggested, "some of the scientists transmitted it independently?"

Driver held up and swirled his hands. "It's possible, sure. Nothing to stop somebody setting up a pirate rig somewhere. But there's no way they could have hacked the ESA planning-system, or my desk, come to that."

"Not even with that alien code-cracking math you got?" I hazarded.

"Uh-huh," he said. "The math came from here, all right, but the resources for applying it are way beyond anything anyone here has, or has access to. They had to grow honest-to-god *forests* of new tech to generate the computing capacity on Earth. Besides, we aren't relying just on encryption. Basic security measures—" Driver shrugged. "You should know."

I nodded. "Okay. You know Alan Armstrong?"

"Nope."

"Heard of him," Lemieux said.

"Check him out any time," I said. "Call him up, if you like. No need to go into details. Just ask him if he thinks what I've brought is gen."

Driver's fingernail worried at his earhole. "All right," he said. "Let's see what you've got."

"Are you the right person to evaluate it?" Camila asked.

"No, but Paul here is. And if any of it really came from here, I can find it in my audit trail."

"That'll take awhile," I said. "We're exhausted, we need some proper food and sleep and a wash."

Driver glowered. "And we don't? We're *all* exhausted here." He slid his fingertips across his closed eyelids. "Oh, the hell with it. You're right. Whatever it is, it can wait another few hours. Okay, Paul, you take them out and I'll catch some kip right here."

Lemieux unfolded himself from his corner of the ceiling, drifted past us and opened the door. "Come on. Let me show you some hospitality."

Chicken, mashed potatoes, runner beans, all stuck to the paper plate with a glutinous gravy; and a squeezable plastic bulb of orange juice. It was the best meal I could remember having. When I'd eaten enough to start thinking again I slowed down and looked around. The servery was a narrow room with one long aluminum table at which the diners could approximate sitting by hooking their knees around the railing half a meter down from each edge of the table. A slow queue shunted past the hatch at the far end of the room. The illusion of being in a normal gravity field must have been important to the room's designers and users—nobody left the table by floating over it, though it wouldn't have inconvenienced anyone.

People ate fast, and talked, and kept their spex on and often shaded. Hardly anyone wore new-tech goggles. At any given time there'd be about twenty people around the table.

"How many people are there on the station?" I asked.

Lemieux looked up from a sticky apple-pie–and–treacle dessert. "Twenty-one with cosmonaut training, including ten science or technical officers—that's me—the five security staff and three military liaison officers—two of whom are currently in the brig, guarded by the third—plus fifteen civilian administrators and two hundred and seventy-two scientists and technicians."

"That's *a lot*," said Camila.

"There's a lot to do," Lemieux said. "As you should know, if you've looked at the science data we've already released."

Camila shook her head. "Seen some stuff on the news, that's all."

"Nor me," I admitted. "I've been too busy running."

"Well," said Lemieux. "We have been in contact for over five years. There is much work. The scientists"—he waved a hand at the oblivious company—"are totally obsessed with it, now that they have freedom to investigate and share and publicize. It was very difficult when it was a big secret."

"Difficult to keep secret," I said, "with that many people here, and I suppose hundreds more on the ground, knowing it."

Camila and Lemieux both laughed.

"Your friend here is laughing," said Lemieux. "She is right. Big secrets can be kept for a long time by many people, and the bigger the secret, the easier it is. As your Area 51 showed, and the Manhattan Project, and our Operation Liberation."

"What are the aliens like?" I asked, smiling to show I recognized how stupid a question it was.

Lemieux leaned forward, elbows on the table, letting his fork float from one hand to the other, catching and releasing it precisely with finger and thumb.

"They are *like* the microorganisms that produce the calcareous mats which build up to stromatolites," he said. "Except that what they build are not stacks of stone, but something between a larger organism and a computer, to put it crudely. To put it delicately, they build quasi-organic mechanisms of incredible beauty and diversity. The basic unit, the builder, is something *like* an extremophile nanobacterium. Obviously these are not the seats of consciousness, any more than our neurones are. Collectively, though, they build something greater than themselves." He smiled, and added: "As our clever English comrade Haldane mistakenly said of the ants, they are 'the smallest communists.' "

Camila made a snorting noise. "Communism sounds just fine for *germs,*" she said witheringly.

"You would not think it so funny when you see what they have achieved. They are not a collective mind as a whole—there are more separate minds in this asteroid than there would be in, let us say, a human Galactic Empire, if such a thing could be."

"And you're in communication with them?" I asked, anxious to avoid any political argument.

Lemieux's eyes narrowed and his lips thinned, as though in momentary pain. "We are," he said. "It is a theoretical scandal, but it is the case."

"What's the scandal?" I asked. "That you can . . . translate? Or that they can?"

"It is worse," said Lemieux. He scratched his head. "There was no need. They know our languages."

"Like, they learned them from television?" Camila asked.

"Impossible," said Lemieux. It sounded more definite like that, in French. "It is simply not theoretically possible for a genuine alien to learn a language from television broadcasts. A language cannot be learned without the . . . interaction."

I had scant respect for linguistic theory, particularly when delivered in a French accent.

"Can you be sure of that?" I asked. "Perhaps, I don't know, something in their code-cracking, something we don't understand yet, some mathematical underlying structure, Chomskyan deep grammar—"

Lemieux caught the fork at both ends and began to bend it.

"That is conceivable," he said. "Barely. We may be all wrong about the theory. That is not the scandal. The scandal is that they understand languages that not only have never been televised or transmitted, but that have had no living speakers since before the invention of writing. *That* is the scandal."

The fork snapped.

We've washed ourselves with wet sponges in cylindrical stalls through which air flows and water flies. We've dried in the same stalls, with hot air. We've been given much-laundered underwear and stiff, fresh blue fatigues and soft plastic boots. Lemieux has left us together in a cubbyhole behind a clipped-on curtain, with a shrugged apology that it's the best he can do. The walls of the little space are hung, like many walls in this place, with loose webbing. We look at each other and laugh. I have three days' worth of stubble and our faces are flushed and puffy with blood that's no longer pulled toward our feet. We hook elbows and ankles through appropriate holes in the webbing and fall asleep against the upper and lower partitions, facing each other a half-meter apart.

I dream. Lemieux's words and worries combine with scraps of pictures I've glimpsed of the interior spaces of the asteroid, the alien city or computer or garden, fractal and crystalline and florally organic. I'm falling on it from a great height, like in an airliner descending on a lighted city, like a parachutist's view of onrushing grass, and every dandelion is a clock. Inside it, tiny green men the size of ants are watching television, laughing in thin high voices, and scribbling notes to each other in cuneiform and Linear B.

I fall onto something and wake to realize I've drifted and been snagged by the webbing. Camila's snoring, openmouthed, a few inches in front of my face. I shrug back into the webbing and sleep again.

And fall again, but this time more gently, onto a bed. Jadey's face, troubled, as in the last shot I saw of her, looms above me. Then she smiles, like she did the last time she was in this position, and our faces and lips meet.

Sometime after that I hear a voice telling me to wake up, and I feel—for a few dozy seconds—happy and comfortable, before I wake to find that Camila and I have worked our limbs out of the webbing and are now huddled and cuddled like frightened monkeys, and that I have a quite obvious erection pressing against her.

She disengages and smiles at me in a friendly, *We're all adults here* kind of way, and rattles the curtain back and pushes herself out. Bending over awkwardly, I follow.

Back in Driver's office we all took the places we'd had before. He didn't look more than marginally refreshed.

"Right," he said. "You ready to show me what you've brought?"

It was easier to walk Driver and Lemieux through the material than it had been with the Americans. The tech was compatible, the protocols familiar to both of them—the ESA-specific ones more familiar, indeed, to them than to me. They tabbed about in it, finding links and paths I'd missed, taking it all in quickly, with rapid-fire, cryptic remarks to each other. Camila hung out on the edge of our shared dataspace, not commenting apart from the occasional murmur of "Holy shit!"

We backed out and looked at each other, blinking.

"Hmm," said Driver. He looked at Lemieux, eyebrows raised.

"Interesting," said Lemieux.

Driver fiddled with the datadisk then slotted it in his desk. "Let me run that past the audit trail."

He put his goggles back on and sucked at a smokeless. Lemieux relaxed into a meditative posture; we fidgeted.

"Shit," said Driver. He peeled off the goggles and flicked his filter into the net bag. "Shit." He looked at Lemieux, then at us.

"It's there," he said. "All spelled out. No way could I have missed it, not back then. Last year, hell, Paul, you remember. We double-checked everything. You and me."

"I didn't double-check the disinfo," said Lemieux. "Obviously."

"Yeah," said Driver, in a dangerously calm voice. "But I'd have known about any disinfo, because anything that wasn't totally innocuous, bland, censored shit about low-temperature chemistry and so forth, *I fucking made up myself.* Not from the whole cloth, sure, but you can bet I read every bloody line of the real stuff that went into it. And I did *not* send disinfo to ESA! You'd have seen it, mate."

"That," said Lemieux, "is not in question."

The two men looked at each other; some unspoken understanding was reaffirmed.

"Okay," said Driver. "So what *is* in question?"

"Who, and how," said Lemieux. "Which of the civilians managed to hack this datastream, and how did they do it?"

"I don't believe it for a minute," said Driver. "They don't have the skills, and they don't have the balls." He considered this for a moment. "More to the point," he added, "they don't have the motivation. I mean, anyone who'd found this would have been all too keen to tell us. And why send it to ESA, if they weren't loyal? Why not send it to the other side—they knew about the controlled datastream going to the West, and it would have been easier, if anything, to slip it in that."

He closed his eyes and scratched his eyebrows. "Or maybe not. Maybe I do need more sleep."

"You do, Colin," said Lemieux, with an odd, affectionate, personal note I hadn't heard in his voice before. "But you are right. It makes no sense."

"What about your CIA spy?" Camila asked.

Driver dismissed this with a wave of his hand.

"That was all bullshit. Sorry." He looked at us fiercely. "I've apologized to Sukhanov about the slander. It was necessary."

Aha! I thought. "So the CIA must have—"

He glared at me, glanced at Camila. "Leave it."

"All right," I said. "You're all making one assumption, which is that someone on this station hacked the datastream and downloaded the 'flying saucer' stuff to ESA."

"Well, no," said Driver. "I've just found the *evidence* that someone—" He blinked, then gave me a sick-looking smile. "Nah! Come on."

"What's so unlikely about it?"

"About *what*?" asked Camila, sounding exasperated.

Enough dramatics, I thought, and said flatly: "The datastream was hacked by the aliens."

Everybody tried to reply at once. Driver banged the desk. "Paul? What do you think?"

"It's possible. That is to say, it is not theoretically impossible and it is not simply improbable, like the scientists' doing it would be. So, yes, we should consider it."

Driver sat silent for a moment.

"Hell," he said. "If they've done it, it's something that has never happened before." He scratched his cheek. "Intervention."

The word hung in the air like the pieces of Lemieux's broken fork.

"Like all the information they've been feeding you *isn't?*" Camila asked.

"I don't think the scientists would call it 'feeding,' " Driver said. "The aliens are pretty selective about what questions they'll answer."

"Oh? And what *do* you call giving the E.U. a massive military intelligence advantage?"

"They didn't necessarily know that," Driver protested. He looked at Paul Lemieux, as though for support. "There's no evidence the aliens even understand the politics of Earth, let alone take sides in it. Nor is there any evidence that our presence is being dealt with at any kind of high level in the alien . . . community. For all we know, we may be in contact with nothing more than their equivalent of the *Encyclopædia Britannica*—and the children's version, at that."

Lemieux was shaking his head. "I know that's what you'd like to think, Colin," he said, "but you know it would be disputed by every scientist on this station, and by me too." He moved his teeth as though nibbling at his lower lip. "Is it not time we—explained the situation?"

"Ah, I guess so," said Driver, and suddenly looked much more cheerful. "It's that or stick them in the brig, and I don't want to do that. The publicity might be bad." He grinned at us. " 'U.S. hostages in orbital commie hell,' sort of thing."

We laughed, with nervous politeness.

"Wait a minute," I said. "Have you any idea about, you know, whether we're going to *build* this thing? Because that's why we came here."

Driver disengaged himself from the desk and reached for the door. "First things first," he said. "Time to meet the aliens."

"He means, the scientists," said Lemieux, on the way out. Driver heard him.

"Same thing," he grunted.

The scientist took off his spex and blinked at us. In a literally laid-back position—and pose—he hung across the end of a small corridor or long cubbyhole, surrounded by more cables than an intensive-care patient. Some of them were fiber-optic, others insulated metal; most, however, had the fibrous, quasi-organic look of new tech. None of them, as far as I could see, actually went into his body, but many of them terminated in the equipment slung around it. His faded sweatpants and baggy T-shirt barely contained his beer gut, and his hair and beard looked as wild and coiled as the cabling.

He waved, in an airy, notional handshake all around.

"Hi, guys. My name's Armen Avakian. And your names have been all around the ship's intranet. Welcome aboard. Have our two politicos here clued you in yet?"

"We decided to let you do that," said Driver. "Including about the *politics*. So far we've only discussed security issues."

"So I'm not on the hook, whatever they were," said Avakian. He let out a laugh that made me want to cover my ears. "Great! So—you got spex? Right, sure, okay. Now just a moment while I tune in to them and call up a consensus space. . . ."

Blankness surrounded us, a shadowless, pearly light. Avakian's voice murmured, somewhere behind us:

"Ready?"

It was somehow obvious, and disturbing, that the question was not addressed to any of us.

The bright monochrome bubble burst, throwing us into color and complexity. More color, more complexity than I'd ever seen or imagined or dreamed. The pictures shown of it in the newsfeeds were a quite inadequate preparation for the real thing. We hung in a vast interior space. Distance and perspective were impossible to judge, the shapes difficult to cohere in the eye. At one moment it made sense as the interior of a vastly magnified, non-human brain; the next, as the view of a city from a height; or a cathedral, made entirely of stained glass; then again, as some multifarious botanic garden in whose gargantuan greenhouse we were as fruit flies.

For a long time the only possible response was silence. The place filled the mind, and the eye, and the mind's eye.

My entranced, meditative moment was shattered by Avakian's laugh. The view collapsed, back into white light, like waking to a dash of freezing water after some warm and vivid dream.

"So much for the big picture," he said. "The actual interface has a bit less bandwidth."

I hung in the air, shivering, blinking away tears behind the spex.

"Just as well," Avakian went on, "because the interface is addictive enough as it is. If we were working in the big picture we'd do nothing but hang around with our mouths open."

He laughed again, the sound even more manic and hideous than before, and even as I resented it and shrank—no, *cringed* from it—I realized that he was doing it deliberately, and in our interests: Without that iconoclasm we would be lost in idolatry. Or worse—our adoration of this celestial city might be the closest any of us would ever come to devotion to real gods.

With an audible *click* the interface appeared—a wide, wraparound screen this time rather than a full-immersion view. If we hadn't seen the latter we'd have been almost as stunned by the former, crowded as it was with still and moving images, depth, and *text*.

"It's what you might call 'feature-rich,' " Avakian said dryly. "This is what all of us—the scientists—are hanging out in, every moment we can."

The image vanished and we became again four people hanging in the recycled air of a smelly, confined, and cluttered space.

"So," he said, "what can I do for you?"

I was about to tell him when Lemieux interrupted.

"No, no!" he said. "First, you will please tell them what you and the other scientists have found, and what your consensus is as to what is to be done—the politics, if you will."

"Oh, yeah, that," said Avakian. He ran his hands through his springy hair, making no discernible difference to its condition. "Well, this place here is unique, right, but it's not *alone*. You know, when Big Uncle made the announcement? That was a bit of an understatement, comrades and friends; old Yefrimovich was a tad economical with the truth."

His fingers rampaged across his head again.

"The truth is there are *billions* of the fuckers. In the asteroid belt and the Kuiper and the Oort. There are more . . . communities . . . like this around the Solar System than there are people on Earth. And each of them contains more separate minds than, than—"

"—a Galactic Empire," said Lemieux.

"Yes! Yes! Exactly!" Avakian beamed.

"How do you know this?" Camila asked.

Avakian hand-waved behind his shoulder.

"The aliens told us, and told us where to look for their communications. Their EM emissions are very faint, but they're there, all right, and the sources fill the sky like the cosmic microwave background, the echo of the Big Bang."

"Sure it ain't just part of that?"

"Nah, it's comms, all right." Avakian sucked at his lower lip. "The point to bear in mind is that our cometary cloud's outer shells intersect those of the Centauran System, and, well—"

"They're everywhere?"

He shrugged. "Around a lot of stars, yeah, quite possibly. Trafficking, communicating, maybe even traveling. They have conscious control over their own outgassings, they have computing power to die for, and it only takes a nudge to change their orbits. It might take millions of years between stars, sure, but these guys have a *long* attention span."

"And what do they actually do?"

"From the point of view of us busy little primates, they don't do much. Hang out and take in the view. Travel around the sun every few million years. Maybe travel to another sun and go around that a few times. *Bo*-ring." He put on a whining, childish voice. " 'Are we *there* yet? He's *hitting* me. I want to go to the *toilet*.' "

He laughed, a genuine and humorous laugh this time, and continued briskly: "But from their point of view, they are having fun. Endless, absorbing, ecstatic, and for all I know, *orgasmic* fun. Discourse, intercourse—at their level it's probably the same fucking thing." He underlined the obvious with a giggle. "They're like gods, man, and they're literally in heaven. And in all their infinite—well, okay, *unbounded*— diversity they have, we understand, a pretty much unanimous view on one thing. They don't like spam."

He looked at three puzzled faces, and at mine.

"Spam," he said. "Tell these good people about spam."

I flailed, literally and metaphorically. It was an obscure issue, difficult to explain to people outside the biz. But I tried.

"Spam is, um, sort of mindlessly repeated advertisements and shit. Junk mail. Some of it comes from start-ups and scams, some of it's generated by programs called spambots, which got loose in the system about fifty years ago and which have been beavering away ever since. You hardly notice it, because so little gets through that you might think it's just a legit advertisement. But that's because way down at the bottom level, we have programs to clean out the junk, and they work away at it too." I shrugged. "Spam and anti-spam waste resources, it's the ultimate zero-sum game, but what can you do? You gotta live with it. Anti-spam's like an immune system. You don't have to know about it, but you'd die without it. There's a whole war going on that's totally irrelevant to what you really want to do."

"*Exactamundo*," said Avakian. "That's how the ETs feel about it too. And as far as they're concerned, we are great lumbering spambots, corrupted servers, liable at any moment or any megayear to start turning out millions of pointless, slightly varied replicas of ourselves. Most of what we're likely to want to do if we expanded seriously into space is spam. Space industries—spam. Moravec uploads—spam on a plate.

Von Neumann machines—spam and chips. Space settlements—spam, spam, spam, eggs, and spam. "

"How about asteroid mining and comet farming?" I couldn't keep my face straight, but Avakian looked grim.

"Don't even *think* about it," he said. "Um . . . Where this all gets political is that it didn't take long for us to realize that the ultimate engine of spam is capitalism. Endless expansion is the great capitalist wet dream, and it's totally incompatible with the way the universe really is. It's certainly incompatible with what the overwhelmingly dominant form of intelligent life in the universe is willing to accept. Quite frankly, I'm no Party hack myself but the fact of the matter is that the Party's aim of a steady-state society with a bit of sustainable, careful, non-invasive space exploration is the only kind of society that the aliens are likely to be happy with." He made an ironically sad face at Camila. "The dream you guys have of treating the Solar System as raw material for orbital mobile homes, guns, and beer cans is *right out.*"

"And what," Camila asked, "are they going to do about it?"

Avakian's thick eyebrows twitched. "With control over cometary and asteroid orbits, you can, oh, engineer mass-extinction events." He spread his hands. "Just a thought."

"Now wait a minute!" Camila exclaimed. "With that kind of threat from outer space, hell, we could all pull together. There'd be real backing for the big stuff—lasers, nukes, battle stations, a proper space-defense system at last! Hey, we could even pull in the commies, once they understood what we're really up against. And with the political will, we could get the heavy stuff in orbit real fast! These aliens of yours couldn't react in time to stop us. And if they tried, they'd find a few extinction level events coming *their* way. Shit—did these guys ever pick on the wrong species to keep cooped up in a keg."

Avakian looked away from her and at me and Lemieux and Driver, who were listening to this little rant with expressions of amusement and disbelief.

"Ah," he said. "You begin to see the problem."

"Don't patronize *me,*" Camila said, shoving her face in front of his and forcing his attention back to her. "Anyway, if the aliens don't want us to go into space, why the hell have they given us the plans for a flying saucer and a space-drive?"

Avakian blinked slowly. "Tell me more," he said.

13

Gravity Skiff

GREGOR GLARED AFTER the departing airship, his fists clenched in acute frustration and annoyance. He turned to Elizabeth and Salasso, who like him were leaning dangerously out over the platform's parapet, as though that would help.

"Can't we ask the tower to call it back?"

"No chance."

"So why the hell didn't you—"

"Listen," said Salasso patiently, "I did not at all expect the people we are looking for to be in New Lisbon. The last I heard, they were rumored to be somewhere else." He waved up at other airships drifting in to dock. "Somewhere reachable by one of those flights. I only sought out my old teacher for confirmation, and for more detail as to the location. If I had thought for a moment they might be in New Lisbon, we would not have walked."

Their stroll along the city floor and their encounter with the saur child now seemed like a futile waste of time, something to recall with regret instead of delight. At the same moment, the mention of New Lisbon made Gregor's heart jump. Lydia would be there.

"Wait a minute," said Elizabeth. "You said New Lisbon's where the gravity skiffs are right now? They can't be working *all* the time. Why not call in and see if any pilot is willing to nip up here and nip straight back, with us?"

"That is a—" The saur's tongue flickered along his lips. "That is a very good idea. I should have thought of it myself."

Gregor dropped his bag and flung an arm around Elizabeth's shoulders.

"Yes!" he shouted. "Brilliant!"

"You anticipate," said Salasso. "Let us see."

They followed him again into the circular room. He marched up to a flat gray plate on the wall and started poking at some small rectangles outlined along its lower border. After a moment the plate glowed dimly, and Salasso began an animated, gesticulating conversation. Gregor watched from one side with a feeling of vague resentment. Television, or the lack of it, was something of a sore point.

Saur display-screens worked outside the human visual spectrum, and even when corrected for that, they didn't make much sense, most of the picture being lost in a blizzard of additional information which the saur optical system filtered quite differently from the human brain. Mingulay's industrial capacity didn't extend to mass production of cathode-ray tube monitors—let alone anything more advanced—and this deficiency was one which the saurs seemed in no hurry to supply from their manufacturing plant.

What made this a sore point was the distinct impression their traders gave that this was entirely to the humans' benefit.

The dim glow faded. Salasso stepped back.

"I have arranged it," he said. "The skiff will be here in an hour."

Two automatic glass doors *thunk*ed open as they walked toward the entrance. Looking from one side to the other rather warily, Gregor and Elizabeth stepped through. Salasso hesitated for a moment, the doors began to close, then opened again as he jumped through. He glanced back at it suspiciously.

The room was quite large, with a counter along one side, fluorescent tubes suspended from the high ceiling. CRT monitors displaying flight information were mounted on the walls, as were long vertical loudspeakers playing indistinct and undistinguished music. Varieties of padded plastic seating and laminated plastic tables were scattered and clumped on the broad floor, some of which was polished wood, the rest carpeted. A few businessmen were sitting about, some still negotiating with saurs, others sipping drinks and looking blank.

"This is bizarre," said Gregor. "Like something from outer space."

Salasso climbed onto a seat by a small table. "Luxurious, anyway," he said, swinging his legs. "Much better than our facilities."

"Speaking of facilities . . ." said Elizabeth.

Salasso pointed. Elizabeth looked at the sign and shook her head.

"Just as well I'm not wearing trousers. . . . By the way, is anyone else hungry?"

The girl at the refreshment counter wore a pink-and-white-striped dress that didn't seem to fit properly, and an apron over it that looked prettier and more valuable than the dress it was supposed to protect, and a similarly frilled band on her head that didn't actually keep her hair out of her eyes. Gregor was troubled by a vague puzzlement about all this, the uneasy feeling that everything here was a copy of something that was itself not the original and not quite right in the first place. He paid for the coffee, sandwiches, and fish-stock in Kyohvic coin, reluctantly accepted change in a handful of New Lisbon hole-punched lira, and returned with the tray.

"Didn't realize humans worked here," he remarked. "Must be boring as hell."

Salasso's mouth twitched.

"They tend not to stay long."

"Hmm," said Elizabeth. "I'd find it interesting. Fascinating. Working in Saur City!"

"The novelty palls," said Salasso.

As Gregor drank his coffee the stimulant rush made him vividly aware of the queasy, fluttery feeling in the pit of his stomach. He realized he was actually nervous and excited at the prospect of traveling in a gravity skiff. In truth, more nervous than excited.

"Salasso," he said. "Would you mind, perhaps, sharing a pipe?"

"You're welcome."

Elizabeth drained her coffee and stood up, taking her half-eaten sandwich with her.

"Excuse me, chaps," she said. "I'd rather not partake, right now. I'll just go and watch the airships."

"Fine," said Gregor, squinting at her around the lighter flame. "See you."

She walked off briskly.

"What's eating *her*?" Gregor asked.

Salasso shrugged. The man and the saur smoked in companionable silence for a while, the saur taking far less than half the puffs. He accepted the final toke. Then he put down the pipe and fixed Gregor with his gaze.

"Perhaps I should not say this," he said in a barely audible voice, leaning forward. "The hemp makes one relaxed and emotionally expressive. Elizabeth wishes to keep very close rein on what emotions she expresses."

"Oh. I see." Gregor frowned. "Is she worried about something?"

Disturbing possibilities flashed through his mind—an ill parent or grandparent, an injured sibling, student debt, some medical trouble of her own—

"Is it something I can help with?"

Of course she wouldn't want to *ask*. Her prickly dignity would get in the way.

The doors banged open as another lot of passengers came in. Salasso fiddled with the pipe, tapping the ash into an ornamental glass dish on the table before Gregor could remind him to use the floor.

"I don't know if you could help," he said. "But—"

He closed his eyes for a second, then looked up at Gregor.

"You must know this. Elizabeth is in love with you and is distressed that you are in love with someone else."

Gregor felt a chill go through his belly like a cold blade. The fuzzy cloud of the hemp dispersed instantly, letting everything else crash in. Never had he felt so surprised, so embarrassed, so wrong-footed; and at the same time, so painfully pleased, and so satisfied—as everything that Elizabeth had said or done in his presence was seen in its true, and now obvious, significance.

But it was his dismay that told in his voice.

"Oh, gods above. I never knew."

"I am sorry I had to tell you," said Salasso, the double edge of his words as polite as ever. "But it may be important for our expedition that you know this. It would be good if you were considerate of what she feels, and if you took great care not to give her any opportunity, in a moment of danger, for recklessness on your behalf." Some humor returned to his expression. "Or against you, come to that."

"Oh, gods, yes," said Gregor. It came out as a groan. "I think I need another coffee to pull myself together."

"Bring two," said Salasso, gazing out through the glass doors. "Elizabeth is heading back."

Fetching the drinks served as a small distraction for Gregor's mind and enabled him to face Elizabeth with some restored equanimity when he returned to the table.

"Oh, thanks," she said.

"How did you find the airships? Or has the skiff arrived?"

"We have about ten minutes," said Salasso.

"I wasn't watching the airships much," said Elizabeth. "The city itself is actually more interesting. More going on, all the time. And I kept getting the scale wrong, it's—"

"Fractal?"

"Yes. Like the waves when we were above the sea. You can't tell how high you are, just by looking down."

"I can," said Salasso. He rolled his eyes from side to side, and they all laughed, and drained their cups, and went out to wait for the skiff.

Salasso spotted it first, and pointed southward, upward, and tracking. Gregor could see nothing but blue sky for half a minute, and then he saw a tiny point of light racing to the zenith, where it stopped. The silvery fleck enlarged above them until it became obviously a descending disc. Other people began looking and pointing, gathering in a small, excited crowd. At a thousand feet above them the disc went into a bravura display of falling-leaf motion, finally swooping around the platform until it came to rest a few meters above and a meter out from the safety rail. Close up, the silvery surface was streaked and splashed with brown muck that looked like dried mud, dung, and blood. Bits flaked off as the hatch opened and the stairladder extended to the platform.

Salasso hefted his case.

"Let's not keep them waiting."

Gregor gestured to Elizabeth. "Let me take your bag. After you."

"Oh, thanks!"

She ascended the ladder rather grandly, raising the hem of her skirt, wrinkling her nose at the faint farmyard pong. Gregor followed, clutching their bags and trying not to look down where the stairladder passed beyond the edge of the platform. As soon as he'd stepped inside, the stair folded in and the hatch closed.

The interior was in apparent daylight, from a window that went all around and which had been invisible from the outside—a screen, he guessed. Around a central fairing was a circular seat, at the far end of which a single saur was sitting in front of a panel, looking back at them over his shoulder, his hands resting on a sloping panel under the window-screen.

He exchanged greetings with Salasso then said in English, "Hi, grab a seat. Doesn't matter where you sit. Or stand if you like."

But, moved by the impulse to avoid being thrown about by acceleration, Elizabeth, then Gregor, crowded up to sit alongside Salasso who had taken the place beside the pilot.

"I've turned the view to your vision," said the pilot. "Hope I got the colors right."

Gregor looked around. Where the screen wrapped behind him he could see people waving from the platform, standing back.

"Looks perfect," he said.

"Okay," said the pilot.

He turned to face forward, and his fingers rippled on the panel. The view tilted away from the tops of the city's towers to the sky and clouds. For a moment it seemed stationary, then the clouds began to grow visibly larger. Gregor looked around to the back, and saw the city tipped at a crazy angle, dwindling behind them. There was absolutely no sense of motion or that the craft was anything but horizontal. He felt Elizabeth clutch his arm as she leaned around him. They shot through a cloud in a white blink and then the view tilted again, revealing nothing but a very dark-blue sky.

Still unable to make his reflexes believe what he saw, Gregor stood up. Elizabeth, hanging on to his arm, rose too. Looking down from the upper side of the screen they could see the ground—or rather, the surface of the planet, the horizon discernibly curving away on either side.

"Oh, gods above!" breathed Elizabeth, letting go of his arm and leaning on the yielding material of the screen's sill, peering downward, then tilting her head sideways and looking up. "You can see *stars*! We're practically in *space*!"

"Welcome to the stratosphere," said the pilot. He leaned back and took his hands off the panel, revealing what looked like shallow imprints of his palms. "Makes a pleasant break for me too, I must say. I've been dodging sauropod shit for weeks."

"Not always dodging," said Elizabeth.

"Nothing a good tropical rainstorm won't wash off. It's their tails you have to watch out for, even in this crate."

He clasped his hands behind his head and stretched out his legs. Gregor guessed that, like Salasso, he'd been around humans for a while.

"Why do you get close to their tails in the first place?" Gregor asked, returning to the seat.

The pilot laughed. "I might have to give you a demo, on the way in to New Lisbon. Don't worry—never lost a skiff yet."

On the area around the palm-prints, tiny rectangles of dim light appeared, flickering back and forth. The pilot leaned forward and scrutinized them.

"Oh good, Coriolis storm ahead. Time for a wash."

He laid his hands on the panel again and the view swung down to a blue ocean surface and, some way ahead of them, a roiling mass of cloud. Within seconds the craft had plunged into it, swooping out of its dive and into level flight. Rain-lashed darkness, a glimpse of blue sky, a rollover in another wet and dark space, then out the other side and up to the stratosphere again.

"If you pull something like that again," Elizabeth said, "you're going to have some cleaning to do on the *inside*."

"If I have to do that again I'll ask you to close your eyes first," retorted the pilot. "It's the dissonance between eye and inner ear that—"

Salasso hissed something and the pilot shut up.

Gregor, now that everyone understood that no motion of the craft could throw them about, was careful to sit clear of Elizabeth. He edged around the seat until he was looking directly behind, to the north and east. The seatback and the faintly vibrating, quietly humming, dimly glowing truncated cone of the engine-faring was between him and Elizabeth, a far more dangerous body. The hurricane, typical of the band of equatorial ocean between Mainland and Southland, receded over the horizon.

As this flight in its turn passed from the magical to the familiar, what Salasso had told him returned in all its novelty and force. He remained at once flattered and appalled. As he reviewed and reevaluated their three years' acquaintance and friendship, he found himself wishing heartily that Elizabeth had made her true feelings known from the start. He couldn't know if he'd have reciprocated, but at least things would have been resolved. He had never thought of her in a sexual context, apart from an undercurrent of approbation of her as a good-looking, healthy woman, hardly more erotic than the sort of admiration he'd feel for a fit and handsome and intelligent man. It was possible, he supposed, that in their work relationship—inevitably close and sometimes physical, when they sweated together on the boat—he'd unconsciously masked off any such thoughts as no more appropriate for fellow scientists than for fellow soldiers.

Now—breaking through that screen—the knowledge that she was in love with him was in itself enough to make her suddenly enormously attractive and exciting, in a way that was both natural and perverse.

Lydia still shone in his mind in a way that made him feel guilty about even enjoying the thought of Elizabeth . . . and yet Lydia had turned back from throwing in her lot with him; instead making it conditional on his meeting her father's extravagant requirement. His own requirement of her, he knew, was perhaps more exorbitant. The fact remained that Elizabeth had chosen to accompany him, and Lydia had not.

He wished that Elizabeth and not the saur had told him of her feelings, but he could not blame Salasso for doing it. The thought of what infelicities and blunders—even perils—his ignorance of the situation could have brought about, made his sweat run cold.

The sea behind them gave way to the long white beaches of the northern coast of Southland, then a broad fringe of manufacturing-plant which in its turn merged almost imperceptibly into the natural rainforest. Gregor stood up and moved around again to the front. When Elizabeth looked up as he sat down, he returned her a smile more gentle, more inquiring, than he perhaps intended.

Again the landscape below tilted upward, almost filling the screen, and they hurtled down to where the rainforest thinned out to grassland. Interrupted only by outcrops and mountain ranges, the sea of grass stretched all the way to the permafrost below the ice cap. Vast herds of gigantic beasts browsed the prairie; from this height, they appeared as stains on the land, irregular patches the size of counties. Untroubled by anything except the packs of predators and hordes of parasites that harassed their every moment, the dinosaurs of the northern reaches paid the high-skimming skiff less attention than they would a fly.

Someday, they might learn a different response.

With a gleeful yelp the pilot took the skiff upward again, skipping over a ten-thousand-meter mountain range like a saucer sent spinning across water. And down again, to the southern plain.

Here, the herds were not patches but rivers, flowing north in their annual autumnal migration away from the oncoming snows to the approaching rains and lush growth. Most of the streams were moving in the direction of gaps in, and passes through, the mountain range. Others had been diverted onto a path that would take them parallel to and south of the mountains, toward the western coast.

A saur voice, distinct from that of the two in the craft, sounded in the air. The pilot made a long, low noise in reply, lifted the craft again and sent it yet farther south, and then down in another swoop until it was skimming along at a hundred meters. Gregor felt his fingers dig into the screen's sill—the forward rush was terrifying at this height, the grass a green-and-brown blur beneath them.

A blemish on the horizon resolved in seconds into a great tide of animals moving along in a cloud of dust and a haze of insects and bats. The craft flew straight toward the herd and then, five hundred meters in front of its leading edge, stopped.

And dropped until it hung a meter above the grass. The herd advanced like a striding forest, the swaying necks of the adults reaching fifteen meters into the air. Gregor could see the ground in front of them actually shake, dust particles jumping above the tough stalks of rough grass. He could see the dappled patterns of their hides, brown-on-green for the most part, their undersides yellow and white. The younger and smaller animals seemed almost to dance along, dodging around the mighty legs of their elders. And darting between them, the dark slinking shapes of the bolder predators. When the compact leading group was a few steps, a few seconds away, the pilot took the craft up and at them. A head that looked bigger than the craft itself loomed in the screen, sending Gregor and Elizabeth into a futile instinctive backward lurch.

At the last moment the pilot veered to the left, jinked about and took them in again at the herd's leaders, from the side this time. They dived directly at a huge rolling eye, then up and over the tossing head's flailing wattles; swung up and away, much farther to the left, to the east, and paced that edge of the herd, setting beasts shying and rearing, shit flying by the steaming ton as they lurched sideways, shouldering their fellows.

Then again in at the group at the front, this time coming at them from behind and to the left. And around at the flank again, and then to the front again, until—the fourth time they approached—the leading bulls and cows broke into a run, veering off on a course that now leaned to the west. At that the pilot pulled the skiff back, zooming skyward and halting at a few thousand meters, surveying the success of his deflection of that whole miles-long torrent. Slight though it was, he seemed satisfied.

"That's enough for now," he said. "I'll be back. I've staked my claim on this lot."

With that he leaned on the indented panel and set a course straight to the west. In the next few minutes they passed to the south of several herds now trudging in the same direction that the craft flew. Other skiffs attended these, chivying them on, blocking any breaks toward the north. Such attempted breaks became more frequent as the mountain range ran down into isolated peaks and foothills. Long-necked carrion-bats, circling on thermals, were thrown into screaming downward spirals by the skiff's wake. Predators and scavengers feasted on the bodies of beasts that had refused to turn back, and had been—as the pilot explained—decapitated by skiffs flown straight through their necks.

"Isn't that dangerous?" Elizabeth's face was white, her hands tight, her lips thin as a saur's.

"Oh no," the pilot said. "Edge-on, it's no contest. It's the tails whacking you from above or below that you have to watch out for. Or getting crushed underfoot, for that matter. You have to be gods-cursed stupid or unlucky to do that, but it happens."

Ahead of them the western sea appeared on the horizon, and as they flew toward it they could see the herding become more intense, skiffs buzzing the great beasts like bees, to the point where entire herds were being panicked into stampeding for the final few kilometers and minutes of their lives.

To the slaughter cliffs.

The skiff hovered, hanging in the air a hundred meters above the level of the top of the cliffs and a few hundred meters out from the beach. The cliffs themselves at this part of Southland's western coast, the reach called by the humans Gadara, rose about two hundred meters above the beaches.

Any sauropod that shied at the edge was pushed implacably forward by those behind. So by the dozen, by the score, the huge animals plunged to their deaths. Any that survived for a moment, their impact softened by the bodies already fallen, were swiftly crushed by the next to fall.

The bodies were given no time to pile up further. For miles around this primitive mass slaughter an industrial process of butchery and preservation went on. Specialized vehicles waded in the bloody surf, dragging and cutting, pumping and hosing. The sea close to the shore thronged with great iron ships, from which hooks and cables and cranes were deployed to haul the hacked meat away. Half a mile to the south an installation the size of a small town stood on stilts in the sea. Clouds of steam and smoke drifted above it.

Above everything, above the beach and the inshore fleet and the processing-plant, the air was filled with the white-and-gray wings of seabats, the surface broken by their diving in a million places like raindrops on a lake.

Gregor found himself gazing at the process with a kind of nauseated fascination. He was very glad that he could not smell any of it. All he could bring himself to say was:

"Isn't this a bit inefficient? Doesn't it contaminate the meat?"

"And," added Elizabeth, likewise transfixed, "isn't it *cruel*?"

"Good gods, no," said Salasso. "Death is swift, perhaps swifter than any other method of killing such large beasts would be. As to efficiency, we use every part of the animal. Contamination, well—it is actually not difficult to hose away the excreta."

"Anyway," said the pilot, "It's traditional. We did it on a bigger scale in ancient times, and less efficiently."

Another unfelt jump took them farther back and higher up, to show a wider view of the coast's black cliffs and miles of white sand.

"See the beaches we no longer use," he said. "Their sand is splintered bone."

The craft spun about again and flew a few more miles to the south. The cliffs sloped away to shingle shores bordering the grassy plain, and a straight road and railway line crossing the prairie and terminating in a kilometer-long causeway came into view. At the causeway's end, New Lisbon hunched in the sea, a rocky island crusted with streets and fringed with quays. Its harbors were crowded with ships and boats. A mile out to sea, attended by the usual fleet of small vessels, the starship hung on the water.

The pilot set them down at the end of one of the quays, and flew off, back to the dinosaur drive. Gregor stood on the boardwalk watching it disappear, and took a deep breath. The breeze carried no taint of the gruesome work being done beneath the cliffs. The meat handled here, being transferred from the shuttling factory ships to the refrigeration tankers for the long haul, was already processed and packaged for freezing, or salted and smoked, boiled and canned. Some of it would be due for a longer haul than an ocean crossing. What delicacies, Gregor idly wondered (eyeballs? tongues? sweetbreads?), would be worth shipping to the stars?

He turned to the island town and to his friends. New Lisbon loomed before them on its volcanic plug, its buildings dense and high, its streets narrow and steep, a haystack of needles.

"So where do we go now?" he asked.

Salasso lifted his case and set off along the echoing boards with dauntless step. Gregor and Elizabeth hurried after him.

"We find a lodging," the saur said. "Then we split, and search. I have a list of places. Simple."

14

Revolutionary Platform

T HE DELEGATES BRANDISH their weapons."
We were sitting on the edge of a rickety stage. Driver and Lemieux—their avatars shabby-suited like Bukharin and Zinoviev—sat behind the table, frowning over data in its illusory depths. Camila, her head seamlessly edited to the body of a bandy-legged horsewoman, propped her cutlass on the shoulder of her yak-hide coat and looked at the gathering throng with nervous amusement.

"What's this based on?"

Avakian, robed as a mullah, looked up from a grubby notebook, his virtual visual display.

"Baku Congress of the Peoples of the East," he said. "Nineteen nineteen, I think. Swiped the details from an old film about John Reed, to tell you the truth. Last week we did the Petrograd Soviet, but there's only so much fun to be had with muddy trenchcoats and Lenin's trousers."

Remember the Twenty-six Commissars of Baku, I thought grimly, as my virtual leather jacket and trousers—Bolshevik chic—creaked around me. My hand tightened on the realistically rusty Afghan-workshop copy of a Lee Enfield which represented my say in decisions. Pathans and Mongols, Turks and Armenians, Kazakhs and Kalmyks and many other nationalities—all in traditional costumes with swords and rifles and fierce expressions—were filing in and taking their seats in a semicircular auditorium under a flapping marquee. The scene and our accoutrements might be testimony to Avakian's warped sense of humor but the meeting was as seditious, and as fraught with consequence, as its original.

Even if none of us ended up shot by the British.

It was the day after our arrival, the day after we'd shown the project data to Avakian. *He* hadn't needed any walk-through from me. After zapping through the whole thing faster even than Driver, he'd come out raving and raring to go, hand-waving wild speculative explanations of the implied AG physics, from which all I could extract was that the density of the transplutonic nuclei generated a quark-gluon plasma at the nuclear core which, when set in cyclical motion, interacted directly with the quantum foam of the space-time manifold, after which matters got complicated and arcane. He also had a few ideas about "the engine," about which he was even more excited and less comprehensible.

"Think fusion bombs compared to atomic bombs," he said. "It's the same physics, but ramped up several orders of magnitude to something that has *no practical limit.* You don't just *control mass.* You *become light.*"

And then his frightening laugh.

Driver had told him to spread the word around the station's intranet, and while he was off doing that, Driver and Lemieux had explained the mutinous crew's brilliant plan for the Revolution.

They were busy releasing the alien mathematics, the basis for completely ripping open any kind of prime-number–based encryption, to as many nodes on the Internet as the station's powerful and highly directional transmitters could reach. With this, it would not take long for the distributed processing-power and collaborative ingenuity of the world's hackers and geeks to pry open the secrets of every military and security establishment on Earth. The people would shortly thereafter have the goods on all the deceptions practiced by the powers of both sides, and . . .

And in this way, we will build the Revolution!

It struck me as the kind of program that could only have been dreamt up by scientists, disillusioned security men, and code-geeks, and exactly the sort of naive, apolitical suggestion that got laughed out of enthusiastic young information-techs at their first IWWWW meeting. Knowledge is one thing, and power is something else.

But I didn't tell them I thought that. Their program wouldn't bring down any states—maybe a few governments—but I couldn't see it doing any harm.

Driver stood up and addressed the assembly.

"Comrades and friends," he said, with only a little irony in his voice, "I know you're all very busy and I know you all know what this meeting's about, so I won't waste time. We've already decided on our revolutionary strategy—"

He was interrupted by a murmur of approval and a shuffle of opposition, both of which Avakian's VR software, getting into the spirit of the thing, translated into a pounding of rifle-butts and a tumult of cries of *"Allah-hu Akbar!"* He smiled and continued:

"—so all we have to do now is decide whether to incorporate the Nevada Projects—as we're calling them—into the program. I can see arguments for and against it. One obvious argument for it is that if the devices perform as some of us seem to think, we'll have an extraordinarily effective means of defense. Against it, there's the obvious point that developing the machines might be a diversion of time and resources from more-urgent tasks. I don't consider myself in any way competent to decide this at present—it's partly a technical question. Over to you."

He sat down, to a jangling quiet. One of the scientists immediately stood up. Her name was Aleksandra Chumakova—a small woman with an intense gaze. She must have hacked her avatar, because she appeared as wearing ordinary uniform fatigues.

"This is a farce!" she said. "Let's stop playing at being revolutionaries: we're scientists. You uncovered some illegal actions by Major Sukhanov and his connections on the ground—well and good. You moved decisively, appealed to the people and the proper authorities, action is being taken. . . . Excellent! And then you went and ruined our moral position by starting this campaign of subversion—"

About two-thirds of the assembly flourished their weapons and flashed their teeth. Chumakova glared at them and continued:

"—which many of us deplore, and which could easily destabilize the military balance on Earth—"

Driver raised a hand.

"We had this discussion last week," he said. "We've taken our decision and reconsidering it is *not* on the agenda of this meeting."

"Very well," Chumakova said. "Let's look at what is on the agenda. You now suggest building obviously dangerous devices, the plans for which have been brought here by an American agent and a renegade! Why not just blow us all up and be done with it?"

The one in three who seemed to agree with her probably just nodded and "hear, hear!"ed in real life, but the VR translated their response as before.

"This could get old real fast," Camila said under her breath. Avakian glanced at her and frowned, but thereafter the responses were less tumultuous.

A man called Angel Pestaña stood up, leaning on the butt of his long rifle. His avatar's black burnoose looked North African.

"I think my colleague Chumakova exaggerates a little. Comrade Driver is not urging us to build the machines, he is asking us to discuss it. Very well, then, let us discuss it! First, the issue of safety is a diversion, as is the notion that this is some kind of American sabotage operation. Those of us who've taken the trouble to check have confirmed that the science data did indeed originate in the interface with the aliens. I can give you the references, Aleksandra!

"What's far more important is for us to understand why the aliens gave out this information, and why they bypassed us to do it. Once we understand that, we can decide whether or not to prioritize building the machines."

"That might delay the construction for a few million years," said Driver. "I take it that's not what you propose?"

Pestaña shook his head. "I suggest asking them."

Laughter.

"Hmm, yes, there's always that," said Driver. He looked around for someone else waiting to speak. Louis Sembat rose next.

"I've been running some calc overnight," he announced, waving what looked to everyone else like a scroll covered with curlicued calligraphy but was probably a hand reader, "based on the work begun by Mr. Cairns here. It looks feasible—we aren't making much use of the fabs for the information campaign, after all. The basic inputs and materials are available. We have enough transplutonics in the labs to build at least prototypes of the craft and the engine. It really is not a big deal. I say go for it. Going by the Cairns documentation the first construction should only take a couple of weeks. The engine might take a bit longer, but the experience gained in building the craft could even speed it up."

I signaled frantically to Avakian, who gave me the floor. A few hastily keyed macro commands got my avatar clunking over in its tall riding-boots to stand in front of the table.

"I just want to make one point following the last speaker. I'm not a scientist or technician, I'm a systems manager, and I know for a fact that any time-estimate you may have found in the documentation will be worthless. So please don't count on getting this thing flying in a fortnight."

My avatar delivered this modest contribution as though addressing troops from an armored train. As it strode or staggered back I told Avakian to stop messing around. He just grinned.

More arguments followed, some of them quite technical, and by the end the two obvious groups in the meeting were themselves divided: Some of those who'd supported Chumakova were in favor of going ahead, perhaps because it was at least something to do other than the information war; some of Driver's supporters opposed it explicitly, for that same reason. The division was looking very close indeed when Driver beckoned Camila. She shot me a surprised glance and strolled over to stand behind the table, looking skinny and vulnerable and fierce.

"Friends," she said, "I'm just a commercial test pilot. I don't know much about politics but I do know about aircraft. If these machines do what Mr. Avakian thinks they do, then you can change the world from right here. You can make it available to anyone you choose, or no one. Above all, you can win a lot of respect if you're visibly handling the most advanced technology we've ever seen. This could break a lot of logjams; it could make space an attractive prospect again—even the stars! You could hold out the promise of the stars! Okay, okay, maybe the cometary minds already own most of the real estate, but we can work something out. I mean, come on, guys, you're scientists! You can do it, and you . . . you know . . . I think you should."

She returned to the edge of the stage in an eerie silence. Avakian, master manipulator, was letting this response take its course.

"God," Camila whispered, "I blew that one, I just let it run into the sand."

"You were great," I told her.

The vote went three-to-one in favor.

"God is great," said Camila.

The delegates brandished their weapons.

As soon as they'd dispersed into the heat haze Avakian shut the display down, and once more I was hooking a leg around an angle-bracket in Driver's crowded office. He, Lemieux, Avakian and Camila and I all looked at each other, blinking and shaking our heads—the usual uncertain moment after coming out of full-immersion VR.

"That went well," said Driver. "No thanks to you, Armen. I'm surprised there wasn't a complete walkout by Aleksandra's mob about the way you were stacking the deck."

"Hey, I cooled it later on, and I'll tread lightly in future, okay?"

"Fine. Matt, how much more work do you need before you can turn the project plan over to production?"

I tried to give an honest estimate. "Couple of days at the most. But I can't promise there won't be bugs cropping up when we actually try it."

"Yeah, sure, no plan ever survives . . . et cetera. Okay. Go for it. Get a material-requirements list—even crude aggregates—together as fast as you can. If we're missing any actual *elements,* we're buggered, but components can be cobbled up in the fabs and there's still a fair bit of raw stuff, from volatiles on up to iron, that we can dig up and refine if we have to. I don't want to find a bottleneck after we've started. If there are any, I want to know about them ASAP."

He turned to Lemieux. "Paul, you get a team together, liaise with Matt and the scientists, pull in Sembat, keep Chumakova's lot on board, get Volkov and Telesnikov to keep the cosmonauts up to speed, and make sure you get their input—the craft won't be much bloody use if the controls are for, I dunno, *tentacles* or something."

Avakian laughed, and interjected: "It's okay, I've seen the panels, they're for hands. Maybe not *our*—Ah, forget it. But definitely, no tentacles."

"All right," said Driver, as though thinking his joke had been taken too literally. "Maybe you could help Matt with systems integration and science data, okay?"

"Yup."

"You square with all that, Paul?"

Lemieux nodded.

"Fine. Camila . . ." Driver studied her for a moment, frowning. "Can you keep us in touch with Nevada, and maybe work with our engineers on your own, uh, flying saucer? I'm sure it needs a bit of turnaround maintenance. No security problems there?"

"It's open tech," Camila said. "Yeah, that's warm."

"Great!" Driver gave a most uncharacteristic wide grin and a clenched-fist salute. "*Per ardua ad astra,* then. Latin for 'Get off your arse.' "

We did.

My first task was the mundane and tedious one of porting most of my software from storage in American hard tech to implementation in European wet tech, and integrating the lot with my reader and the American spex. Fortunately, the station's intranet had an entire library of hacks and kludges for doing just that, but I could have done with an old geek at my elbow. When the crossover had been completed, my sense of triumph was muted by the thought that already half a day's slippage had thus been added to our notional schedule. But worrying about that would only lose more minutes, so—

I sucked a coffee, keyed the spex, and got busy on the real job.

In Avakian's Baku Congress scenario my reflexes, already adapting to microgravity, had been thrown off balance by an environment where virtual objects behaved as though they had weight and my real body didn't. It was a pleasure to get back into my own VR, where everything meshed. I'd never thought of it before, but the dataspace in which I usually worked had zero-g virtual physics. My viewpoint darted about in it like a minnow, now that it wasn't subconsciously contending with my inner ear.

Furthermore, the entire project was now embedded in its original context, from which the ESA documentation sent to me had been abstracted. Concepts and details and reasons that had been leaden and flat the first time, now twanged with resonance. Understanding far more of what I was doing, I did it faster. The AIs also brightened, their suggested solutions often surprising me, going beyond the bounds of their conceptual thesauri. Didn't make some of their suggestions any less stupid, of course, but weeding these out was where I came in, and I was doing it better. You can do a lot with a good dataset, but there's nothing to beat on-site, hands-on problem-solving.

After I'd got the first-cut list of raw material inputs completed and zapped off to the relevant departments I called up Avakian, who merged his workspace with mine and then, increasingly, with the scientists who'd taken an interest in the project. Hours passed, fast—it was like my earlier experience of moving from the hobbled environment of E.U. dataspaces to the U.S., but with even greater freedom because everybody was free to share. It was a style of collaborative work I'd not encountered before, and it was as addictive as a well-designed game.

Eventually Avakian noticed that our rate of errors, misunderstandings, and frictions was creeping up.

"Knock off," he said. "Call it a day shift. See you all in eight hours."

After we'd dropped out of the shared space I hung in the VR for a while, channel-hopping the station's news-servers. In Europe the crisis seemed to be easing off a little, the street demonstrations hanging fire while assorted commissions and committees attempted to hammer out compromises. At the same time, high-level scandals and low-level protests had erupted in the United States. The governments of India and China had lodged with the U.N. some unspecified complaints about allegedly unfraternal dealings by the E.U., putting some strain on the great anti-imperialist alliance. In the background to it all, in both blocs and in the independents, leaks and rumors and speculation about the scale of the alien presence in the Solar System was spreading.

Of Jadey's plight there was no news at all. I sent her a message, care of the Sheriff Court, but without much hope that she'd see it anytime soon. Then I went to the refectory and ate mashed potatoes, grilled carrots, and curried rabbit.

Yum.

I rattled back the curtain of the place where we'd slept, to meet Camila's glare as she wiped her naked body with a damp cloth.

"Jeez! What *is* this, Privacy Central?"

"Sorry," I said, moving to slide the curtain back.

She beckoned. "Hey 's warm, come on in."

I looped in and hung opposite her as she hung herself out to dry. She didn't look as skinny in microgravity as she had in the space-suit, her breasts full above the bony cage of her ribs. She looked back at me in that shamelessly direct American way that, like the accent, had always excited me.

"Do you want me to find somewhere else?"

She shook her head. "It's as bad everywhere. I'd still have to share with someone, and I'd rather share with you than with one of the commies. Especially the women."

"They're not commies."

"Yeah, yeah, I know. Russkis, French—same thing. Weird. Wacko. Not like us."

"Us Anglos, Ms. Hernandez?"

"Like I said. You know what I mean." She dismissed the question. "You look tired."

"Knackered. But we're making progress." I told her about it, briefly. "What have you been doing yourself?"

"Oh, talking to engineers. Wandering about in the real world. Checking over the old *Blasphemous*. Raiding the commissary."

She rummaged in a bundle of clutter behind her.

"Managed to score some dope," she said. "Want to try some?"

"How do you get *that* on a space station?"

"All that hydroponics, someone's gotta put it to good use. And it's hardly like there's a fire risk."

She busied herself with a ten-centimeter roll of plastic and a battery-powered steam-pipe.

"Oh, all right, thanks. My head's buzzing anyway."

She sucked in the fragrant steam and passed me the apparatus. I inhaled gratefully and passed it back, riding the rush. Her dark eyes shone.

"Buzzing with what?"

"When I shut my eyes," I said, shutting them, "I can still see the data structures, the critical paths, the exploded views, the lot, and the craft and the engine at the end of it all, sort of glowing in the dark."

My eyes snapped open. "And the news from home."

"Ah." She pumped the steamer until it hissed and bubbled again. "Jadey. No news of her?"

"Nope."

"Sorry about that." Her pupils widened, her eyelids narrowed. "Really. You and her. Shit. Bad luck for—"

She laughed and passed me the pipe. The air-conditioning roared in my ears.

"Bad luck for who?"

"Ah, for her." She closed her eyes, drifting. "No, to be honest, I meant for you and me both."

I could see where this was going, I hadn't been born yesterday.

"Why?" I asked, as though I didn't know.

She stared at me, drifting closer, her breasts and eyes looming like approaching ships.

"We were real close on the flight," she said. "Talked about everything. Never talked to anybody like that."

I dizzily recalled our conversations. They hadn't seemed so intimate to me—more like . . . I didn't know . . . finding a friend you could talk to about anything that took your fancy. She'd talked about childhood, her grandparents' voyage from Cuba on an inner tube, her education, her training. She had talked about guys, with nostalgia, even sentimentality, sometimes crudity. With both of us clad in shock-gel, it had seemed like time-out from sexuality.

The loneliness of her rare talent and reckless courage hit me.

"I never knew," I said.

"Ah shit, you did—you were listening. Hell, when you were asleep it was all I could do not to kiss you."

"I *love* Jadey," I said. "Christ, I *miss* her."

"I got no problem with that," she said. "And I don't think you have."

Our mouths docked before I could answer.

"Christ, man, you were supposed to get some sleep," Avakian said. "What the fuck you been doing, steaming dope all night?"

"Something like that," I mumbled. I rubbed my bleary eyelids and slid on my spex. "Hard to sleep after all this."

"Yes, isn't it just!" he agreed, as one by one the rest of the team clocked in.

We ran a match on the lists of available and required materials. It took awhile—the trees of acceptable substitutions were multibranched, intertwined, close to a combinatorial explosion, challenging even for the AIs.

"Chug-chug-chug," Avakian muttered.

The display flared into green.

"Yee-hah!"

"Okay, now for the Leontiev matrices . . ."

A program capable of running the economy of a minor socialist republic or a major multinational corporation clunked through its iterations and punched out the complete production plan. We hung there for a moment, just looking at it. For that moment it seemed accomplishment enough. If I'd done this back home I'd have taken the team out for Chinese.

"That's it," said Mikhail Telesnikov, the cosmonaut. His phantom presence radiated impatience. "Let's run the sim."

The simulated production run uncovered enough glitches to keep us busy for hours, tweaking and rerunning it. Eventually the VR models of the fabricators did their spidery work, and spun out the disc.

It floated in the center of our dataspace, a silvery lens that focused all our attention. Doubly unreal, a simulation which we could not in our hearts believe; an original too cheapened by endless fake reproductions and false reports to produce the effect it must have had on its first viewers, or the intent of its craftsman.

"Numinous Geometries," I thought, mentally christening the device. Telesnikov switched to a full-immersion avatar and stood in front of it, looking back at our—to him—invisible viewpoints.

"Well, come on," he said. "It's only a *ship*."

Avakian, silent for once, flipped us all in and we walked up just as Telesnikov reached up and touched the shining rounded edge of the thing. I had a flash of recollection of a Festival preacher in Princes Street Gardens going on about some biblical widget—the arc of the covenant, I think it was called—that could strike you dead if you touched it.

But all that happened was that from the seamless structure a tripod of legs extended, a hatch opened, and stairladder of child-sized steps unfolded. Telesnikov boldly ascended, then Avakian; I cheated my way to the front and followed. The others, not quite so quick off the mark, made do by switching back to non-immersive viewpoints and tabbing straight through the hull.

Inside, the craft was almost familiar—at first disappointingly so, then uncannily. A smooth central casing over the engine formed the back of a circular bench, facing the viewscreen which likewise ran all around the craft. Beneath the viewscreen was a sloping shelf, one section of which consisted of an incomprehensible display of unreadable instruments and a panel in which the shapes of two small, long hands were recessed, as though someone with three fingers and one long thumb had pressed their palms into the material before it had set.

I'd seen very similar arrangements in documents and accounts in the decades' worth of rubbish I had scanned from Dreamland. Just about everyone who'd ever claimed to have been taken inside a UFO, or to have reverse-engineered one from crashed specimens had come up with something like this.

"Devil take this," said Telesnikov. "They're laughing at us."

"Maybe they aren't too clear on the concept of *fingers*," said Avakian.

"No, that is not what I mean. This is ridiculous! This is copied from some shoddy piece of USAF disinformation."

His words set off an agitated babble from our colleagues, swirling around the cockpit like invisible but angry bees. Telesnikov and I seemed to be the only persons present who had more than the vaguest notion of the details of the UFO mythos. The others inclined to Avakian's more charitable interpretation, that it was a simple error in the aliens' grasp of human anatomy, a suggestion which those with the longest experience of interfacing with them seemed to find a lot more believable than I did.

"They think and see on a different scale from ours," Louis Sembat insisted. "There are gaps in their knowledge, blind spots. Imagine us conversing with bacteria! How could we know that certain cilia were significant?"

Avakian brought the discussion to an unceremonious halt by dumping us all back to an abstract workspace where we faced each other around a table.

"Enough already," he said. "Whatever the reasons for this glitch, we know our friends are perfectly capable of providing us with a suitable interface because they've already done it once. It's just a matter of getting into the restricted view and letting them know our requirements."

From the comments and laughs that greeted this I gathered it wasn't likely to be as straightforward as he made it sound.

"We could also have a crack," he continued, unperturbed, "at hacking out some kind of control interface ourselves. We've got some way to understanding the physics of the thing; the controls shouldn't be beyond us. Meanwhile we bash ahead with building it and running the project analysis and so on for device number two—the space-drive."

"Hang on," I said, "if we're looking at a different outcome, even if it's just the controls and the displays, the changes could be feedback to anywhere along the production pathway."

Avakian looked at me. "Yes," he said. "They could indeed. But that's the sort of thing you and your AI menagerie are supposed to be good at finding out."

"Oh, thanks," I said sarcastically. "I thought I might have time on my hands over the next few days."

"Don't worry," he said. "I'll help you, and we can call on a lot of other help." He waved a hand at the others around the table. "If we can't, I seriously doubt if anyone else can, except—Hey!"

He theatrically smote his forehead.

"*And* we're in touch with the only other place that could maybe do better, on the practical side. Your Mr. Armstrong's engineers in Nevada. Make this a *real* Nevada project, huh? I guess that means we'll have to get non-Comrade Hernandez in on the team. Maybe you could persuade her."

His horrible laugh was echoed by enough sniggers for me to realize that in a place without privacy, some news traveled fast.

At the end of the evening shift Driver called me to his office. I saved-to-date and arrived to find Lemieux, Camila, and Avakian with him. We still seemed to be the self-appointed project committee.

"Not bad work today," said Driver. He'd been scanning reports skimmed off by our VR activities. "I seem to remember you saying something yesterday about *hands,* Armen. Why didn't you raise it as a problem?"

Avakian shrugged. "I had only a suspicion, from a few obscure diagrams that might not have been definitive. Besides, I wanted to see what would eventually come out the other side rather than get bogged down in arguments first."

"Fair enough, I suppose," Driver allowed. "Still—anything else like this turns up, and you let me know absolutely clearly, okay?"

"Now that you mention it," Avakian said, "there doesn't seem to be any control interface *at all* for 'the engine.' The big engine. The space-drive."

"Hmm." Driver's eyes almost lidded over. "That could be a problem. We should add that to the list of things we want the aliens to clarify. If we can; or they can."

"What's this problem with getting answers from the aliens?" Camila asked. "I thought you guys had got a lot."

"Yeah, we have," said Avakian. "Trouble is, it's mostly high-level stuff: mathematics, quantum computing algorithms, and so on. Not so much on the concrete, as we'd see it. Nothing on Earth or Solar System history, though we have asked."

"There were some things that Man was not meant to know," I said.

"Not so much that," Driver said. "My own impression from outside the science circus here is that there are some things that Man was bloody well meant to find out for himself."

He reclined in silence for a moment. "Speaking of which . . . When you think it necessary, Armen, I think the people to make the first inquiries should be you and Matt."

"Me?" I said. "But I've no experience—"

"Experience with the interface is valuable," Lemieux said. "But it is not necessarily of value in formulating queries, and in understanding answers. You at least know what kind of answer would be useful. And it is something you should become familiar with anyway. You are very good at cross-platform integration, and this is perhaps the ultimate in that."

"I can't wait," I said.

I suspected that they just wanted me to do it because they feared exposing themselves more than necessary to the seductive, addictive effect of the alien interface, and they didn't entirely trust the scientists who already had done so to come back with anything meaningful.

We dealt with some of the more mundane details of tomorrow's team deployment and then prepared to leave.

"Before we go—"

Lemieux, up in his corner perch, drew something on a physical notepad, tore off a sheet and let it flutter in the air among us. I caught a glimpse: It was an oval, with a single horizontal line a little above the sharp end, and two tilted ellipses on its small axis; the iconic, ironic ideograph of the mythic Gray alien.

"I hardly dare say it," he said. "But as a solution to the problem of how they know our languages, and of the strange design of the craft's controls—I wonder, Camila: Is there anything you might know, even a rumor about . . . the old rumors?"

But Camila was already laughing, giggling an explanation to the still-baffled Avakian. She reached out and grabbed the sketch and balled it up and stuffed it in Driver's trashbag.

She shook her head. "Sorry to disappoint you, guys, but I've been through all that; I've spoken to people who'd know if anyone would. The only Dreamland the little Gray folk have ever been to or come from is the one in our heads."

She smiled around at us. "Come on," she said. For a moment she looked puzzled, as though startled by a sudden thought, then she shook her head even more firmly.

"Nah."

15

The Space Shore

THIS PLACE WAS smaller than Kyohvic, but it felt like a city—or how she imagined, from what she had heard and read, that a city felt. Kyohvic, for all its half a million inhabitants, its university and houses of philosophy, its ships and trade, had "small town" written in its genes. New Lisbon might have but a tenth the population of her hometown, but the people were so much more diverse. It was on the shore, not just of the sea, but of space: Other worlds were in the air, in the smells, in the surprises around every corner; in the attitude that everybody knew everything, but didn't know everybody.

She walked briskly but carefully down a sloping cobbled street, if you could call something three meters wide a street. Gregor walked beside her, having firmly rejected Salasso's argument that it would be more effective for them to search separately. It felt strange to be alone with him. She hadn't realized the extent to which she'd become used to Salasso's presence when they were together. Not that it had ever bothered her. Any inhibition she felt had been entirely her own doing. But still.

Buildings rose to three or four stories on either side, black and narrow as dominoes, and as dependent on each other's support. Overhead, a cable car fizzed and sparked, laboring up the incline at just the right height to barely avoid knocking a tall hat off a man on horseback. (Municipal regulation, she'd been told.) A gaggle of small blue-and-red-mottled dinosaurs which shared the size, shape, gait, and probable fate of geese, slithered and skittered past them, honking in protest at their casual herding by a ragged little girl with a big stick. The street was so steep that Elizabeth could see the ocean when she looked straight ahead.

Which was not advisable, because of the dinosaurs, because the cobbles were uneven, and because out there on the sea squatted the starship.

Yes, it was the de Tenebre ship. Everybody knew that. She had cherished a faint hope that it wasn't. Gregor had said very little about the prospect of perhaps seeing Lydia again; she had rather expected him to prattle on about it, but he seemed to be focusing his attention and excitement on the possibility of tracking down some of the old crew. Which was, she supposed, all to the good.

Salasso had scribbled a list of thirteen waterfront dives ("for a start"), and drawn an elegant and precise street map of the relevant district.

"You got all this from your old teacher?"

Salasso had looked at Gregor as if he were being stupid.

"Of course not," he'd said. "This is my own deduction, from what I know of this place. I have been here before, and it doesn't change much."

Salasso himself had set out to prowl the saur hangouts, from the skiff pilots' bars to the more refined haunts of entrepreneurs in the butchery business. Listening for rumors, he'd explained; he was reluctant to actually ask around, and advised them, too, to be cautious, and to dress rough. And to remember that they were marine biologists, here to scout out possible lines of research, maybe hire a boat to watch kraken, something like that. Near enough the truth.

"You know," Elizabeth said, as the small dinosaurs waddled off down a side alley, "our cover story might turn out to be the only thing we get out of this trip. It's actually a *good idea*. This is a far better place to study the kraken than out of Mingulay."

"You don't hold out much hope of nabbing one of the old buggers, then?"

"We don't even know what they *look* like!"

"I do," Gregor said. "Or I bloody should—I've seen their portraits often enough. Cairns, Lemieux, Volkov, Telesnikov, Driver . . ."

A hairy gigant lurched around a corner and up the street, almost blocking it as he swayed back and forth, singing in a basso profundo whose sweetness made her shiver, drunk though he was. They pressed their backs to a wall, ducked under his arm as he passed.

"But will they still look the same?"

Gregor glanced at her sidelong.

"So the story goes."

. . .

At the foot of the street they turned left, past the cable-car terminus and on to the main drag, the street which ran all the way around the island and debouched to the causeway at the shoreward end. Built along a thirty-meter-wide shelf, it sometimes passed behind the pillars of elegant esplanades, sometimes dived behind outcrops of rock, sometimes overhung the sea. Every couple of hundred meters a jetty fingered out from it, on stilts or stones.

Much of the traffic consisted of carts laden with meat or fish, being hauled toward the railhead by petrol-engined tractors or by massive, plodding quadrupeds. Their drivers, and the pedestrians who crowded the sidewalks, were a roughly equal distribution of saurs and the three most widespread hominid species: humans, gigants, and pithkies. Elizabeth had seen few members of the last two before, and it was hard at first not to stare. The gigants stood about three meters tall, naked but for their shaggy reddish body hair and their belts of tools and weapons. The pithkies, slim and lithe at a meter and a half, wore human styles of clothing over the silver or golden fur that covered all but their sharp faces.

"I thought the pithkies were kind of stockier than that," she remarked in an undertone to Gregor. "All the ones I've seen before were, you know, heavily muscled."

"That's because they were all *miners,*" he said. "But mining's just as unnatural to them as it is to us."

"So how come it's their specialty, huh?"

"Maybe the saurs gave them the mineral rights," he said. "Or the gods did." His glance indicated the god, clearly visible in the early evening sky. "Who knows?"

"But one day we'll find out?"

He turned a warm smile on her.

"Yes!"

His arm moved up and sideways, as though to fling around her shoulders; fell back. Awkwardly breaking stride, he fished in his pocket for Salasso's list, quite unnecessarily she thought; she and he both knew at least the first few names by heart.

"There it is," he said, pointing at a tavern sign ten meters away. "The Headless Chickadino."

"*Bad* taste," she said.

"No, no," he said. "Tastes like chicken."

Her yelp and skelp followed him through the door.

• • •

The tavern was high-ceilinged, bright and airy, with tall windows, sea-faring scenes in their stained glass. Perhaps it once had been a house of philosophy, and later desecularized. The landlord was a gigant, the barmaids pithkies, the crowd mostly human and taking a break. For many people work here went on through the evening; at this time of year, through the night.

"What do you want to drink?" Gregor asked.

"Maybe guava juice, for now."

"Aye, I guess so," he grudgingly allowed.

They sat on stools at the bar, sipping the iced drinks and chatting idly as Gregor eyed the crowd. Most of them were local: sun-darkened men in workclothes, still grubby from cart or quay; a few sailors from Kyohvic, identifiable by their lighter skin and softer accents—one or two of them nodded to him. He presumed they recognized him no more than he did them.

But there was one man, sitting by the window talking to some old seamen or dockworkers, who did look familiar. Gregor couldn't place him at all. Red-haired, pale and freckled like a northerner, very relaxed. Very openhanded—after a few minutes Gregor saw him wave and nod for another round, and pay for a tray laden with tall and short glasses.

"What are you doing?" Elizabeth asked. "Ogling pithkies?"

"They do look a bit sexy," Gregor admitted, grinning. "Foxy ladies . . ."

Elizabeth kicked his shin, not very hard.

"Don't look around," said Gregor, stoically ignoring the sharp pain. "Count to thirty in your head and look in the bar mirror at the young bloke with the old men at the window."

When she turned to the mirror she rather cleverly faced straight ahead, as though at herself, flicking at a stray strand of hair.

"I've seen him before," Elizabeth said, turning back.

"Me too, but where?"

Elizabeth shrugged. "Some guy we see every day without noticing— a docker, someone at the university . . ."

Gregor was shaking his head. "Nah, I'd remember that. We must have both seen him once—"

"The party!" Elizabeth said. "At the castle. Remember?"

Gregor did remember him, in a very similar pose but splendidly dressed, listening to some Kyohvic merchants.

"Oh, right. Yeah, that's it. He's a trader. So much for that mystery." He looked at her, puzzled. "You were at the party after all?"

As soon as he'd said it, he realized he shouldn't have. He could all too clearly imagine how the party had gone for Elizabeth. He also realized that he couldn't let Elizabeth know that he did realize, because she didn't know that he knew.

She looked away, her cheek reddening, sharp and sudden as though slapped. Then she looked back at him with a forced cheerful smile that raked his heart.

"Yes, I was!" she said. "I guess we just missed each other in the crowd. I doubt you'd have noticed me anyway—that was where you met Lydia, wasn't it?"

"Yes," he said. He drained his glass and stood up.

"Time to wander on? And we could get something to eat at the next one if the name's anything to go by."

"The Hot Squid? Yeah, okay, I'm starving."

Out on the street the crowd had thickened. The next place was a few tens of meters on, its sign a lurid scene of cephalopodan coupling, the artist's interpretation of the relevant anatomy owing nothing to marine biology. It was, however, genuinely a bar and grill, much smokier and noisier than the Chick. And larger, with more than one room, impossible to take in from a single vantage.

Stuffed swordfish and sea reptiles hung among the lamps on low rafters. Seafood sizzled on a broad hotplate; mussels, squids, scallops, and fillets of fish were flipped and turned, doused with sauce and sprinkled with herbs in seconds or minutes by a gigant whose long, strong arms made him seem preadapted to the job. Very little grease was involved in the cooking, so the air was fragrant rather than heavy—the smoke came from hemp, not burnt oil, and the whole combination made Gregor's mouth water and belly ache with hunger. Pithkie waiters and waitresses yelled orders in rapid contralto Trade Latin or English; the short-order cook rumbled his responses and grumbles back. In a raised alcove at the back the saur manager or owner, clad improbably in a black business-suit and white shirt, clattered and fretted over a calculator, looking as though he'd be tearing his hair if he'd had any. The crowd was likewise mixed, saurs and hominidae rubbing shoulders, drinking and talking loudly, some half listening to a pithkie soprano at a microphone, her silver satin shift flowing over her silvery fur, her Latin torch-song keening above the babble.

"Bet *she* incites a few cases of hopeless love," Elizabeth said, with a kind of vehement flippancy. Gregor, swinging into a seat at a small table covered with sticky plastic, chose to take her literally.

"Gods, do you really think—" He shook his head with an exaggerated shudder.

"It's no crazier than what people really get besotted with," said Elizabeth, facing him boldly, then turning to wave at a waitress.

"Think we can risk a beer or two with this?" asked Gregor.

"Wouldn't dream of drinking anything else."

"How about white wine?"

She brightened. "Yes, thanks. A small one."

There was a moment of awkward silence after they'd placed their orders. The waitress returned with a brace of beer bottles.

"Do you think we have much of a chance?" Elizabeth asked. "Of finding them."

Gregor scratched at his beer bottle's damp label, then stopped as though catching himself doing something obsessive.

"Salasso seems very confident, and I think—"

"What?"

"He's not just blundered into this. Our squid research, for example. I'll have to check through the university's admin when we get back, but I suspect he had something to do with initiating the project in the first place. And he's a bit odd, for a saur."

Elizabeth laughed. "They're all odd."

"Yes, but he's a lot more open to humans than most. Maybe the ones on the ships, and old Tharovar in the castle, are as friendly. But not many."

"Hmm," said Elizabeth. "He seemed to know a lot about the First Crew, how they went to the saurs to help them hide."

"Maybe he was there at the time," said Gregor. "Why not?"

The waitress arrived with a tray of food and a bottle of wine. Elizabeth put down her half-finished beer as the glasses were filled.

"Speculation," she said. "Let's eat."

They ate and drank for a while, too hungry to talk much.

"Why," Elizabeth asked, "did the old crew go off to live incognito in the first place?"

"I don't know. My guess is that they didn't want to hang around and become a focus of resentment or undue respect. Not much fun being ageless if everybody envies or worships you."

"Or if you have to watch your children growing old and dying . . . but why couldn't they have used whatever it is they had on the rest of us?"

"Perhaps they didn't have the technology to reproduce it for anyone else."

"They could have left us some lines of research!"

Gregor shrugged. "Maybe they did. We're on the way to developing a worldwide biotech industry, eventually."

"Yes, eventually! And the saurs have one already! Why not get them to work on it?"

"Ah," said Gregor. "That's a different question: What the saurs are and are not willing to do for us, and share with us. I'm sure if the saurs wanted to, they could have given us everything they have, from a cure for aging—if they have it—to gravity skiffs. But they don't."

"It might have something to do with what Salasso said; that they don't want to merge our societies."

Speculation seemed fruitless, and Gregor had no wish to take the conversation further in that direction, well aware that he as much as Elizabeth was evading what they really wanted to talk about.

"Finished?"

"Yes." Elizabeth sighed contentedly and wiped her lips. "Let's circulate."

They stood up.

"Together, or separately?" she asked.

"Oh, together," Gregor said. "People are more likely to talk to us that way."

Elizabeth smiled at him defiantly. "We could pretend we're a couple."

"I'm sure everyone will assume we are anyway."

They had reached the third room in the place, and talked to a few men off the boats about their idea for scientific expeditions, without attracting much interest.

"It's like fishing without getting a nibble," Gregor was grumbling, when somebody slapped his back.

"Hi, Matt, what are you up to?"

Gregor turned to see a tall man in seaman's garb, a grin slowly fading from his ruddy face.

"Sorry, mate," the man said. "Mistook you for someone else." He frowned, shook his head, smiled apologetically and walked off through the crowd to the next bar counter.

Elizabeth caught Gregor's arm. "Let's ask him!"

Gregor shook his head. "Wait a minute. Don't want to warn them off."

He took a minute or two to finish his half-pint, and raised the empty glass to Elizabeth.

"Same again please?"

"Okay."

"Back in a tick." She turned back to order the round, her mouth narrowing.

Gregor edged his way between swaying bodies and balanced, brimming drinks, and walked blinking into the brighter light and thicker smoke of the next lounge. The man who'd accosted him was back at a table with some pals, evidently fellow seamen, with three young women wedged in between them. All were talking loudly, and being listened to by the trader Gregor had recognized earlier.

It wasn't that recognition, however, which made Gregor stop and turn away to lean his forearms on the bar and gaze into the mirror under the thin pretense of eyeing the inverted bottles of spirits racked above it. He'd recognized one of the seamen.

Unless he was making the same mistake as the back-slapping chap had done, he was looking sidelong at the mirrored image of the crewman and Cosmonaut Grigory Volkov. The broad features might be a family resemblance, but the blond buzz-cut seemed a little too distinctive for that. The man's face had acquired a few creases and many faint scars, but otherwise was just as it appeared in the paintings, and in photographs in old books.

Gregor felt as though he needed a stiff drink from one of those racked bottles. His knees were rubbery. Taking a deep breath, he steadied himself and returned to Elizabeth. She regarded him quizzically, a little sourly, and shoved the half-pint along to him as he sat up beside her.

"Found one," he said. "One of the crew."

"Seems to have shaken you up a bit."

"Yes." He put down the glass, more carefully, and smooched a splash of beer from the back of his hand. "Grigory Volkov. I was named after him. Famous cosmonaut in his own right. There were *books* written about him."

"Never heard of him, myself."

"Ah, well." Gregor smiled. "Being the first man on Venus probably didn't seem such a big deal after he got here. Anyway, there he is, talking to the trader we saw earlier."

"Any bright ideas about what to do next?"

"No. I can't think of a way to approach him while pretending not to recognize him."

"Well, I can! Come on."

She picked up her drink and slid off the stool. Gregor decided that he might as well take his turn at following. Again the drinkers' walk, threaded with subtle moves and etiquette, like an elaborate dance. As soon as Elizabeth was in fair view of their targets' table, she waved with her free hand and called out a bright hello. Gregor sidled and dodged after her, as all the people at the table turned to look at them.

Elizabeth made straight for the trader and leaned over the table and shook his hand, grinning into his baffled face.

"Well, *hi!*" she said. "I'm *so* pleased to see you again! I didn't get a chance to speak to any of you before."

The trader blinked and half rose, half bowed over her hand. His expression of confusion was swiftly replaced by a puzzled but polite smile.

"Your pardon?"

"The party in the castle at Kyohvic, remember?"

"Ah, of course." He nodded briskly, sweeping his hand to indicate that they should sit and everyone else had better make room for them. "Your dress and hair, so elegant then, I didn't recognize you. Forgive me."

Gregor wasn't sure if this claimed memory was genuine, but as he perched on the end of a bench he had to admire the man's quick thinking and aplomb as much as he did Elizabeth's. She was sitting down beside the trader on the end of the opposite bench, patting her hair and smoothing her grubby jeans.

"Marcus de Tenebre," said the trader. "And now you have the advantage of me."

"Elizabeth Harkness. And this is Gregor Cairns, my . . . um . . . friend. We're marine biologists."

The man he'd recognized as Volkov was jammed up in the corner of Marcus's side of the table, and had been looking at Gregor with a slight frown all the while. On hearing Gregor's name he flinched away, facing one of the women opposite him and initiating or resuming some quiet conversation.

Gregor hoped that his own reaction to the trader's name wasn't as obvious. That man had given no sign of recognizing his; perhaps he was a sufficiently distant, or preoccupied, relative of Lydia's not to have heard any family gossip.

"You've arrived here very quickly," said Marcus.

"Oh yes, we took a skiff," said Elizabeth, as though it were quite the done thing. "We wanted to visit while the meat market was on."

"Why, if I may ask?"

"Oh, it's to do with science," said Elizabeth. "We're wondering how all the meat processing, the factory ships, and so on affect the local sea-life, and maybe in setting up some possible future research. Have a look at the kraken in their home waters, stuff like that."

She glanced around the table. "Anyone interested in some off-season boat hire?"

A lot of head-shakes and shrugs.

"There's no off-season," one of the men said. "The meat processing keeps us busy in the autumn, the meat shipping keeps us through the winter, there's whaling in the spring when the pack ice breaks down south, and the rest of the time it's the fishing. Doesn't mean you couldn't squeeze something in, mind, or maybe get a berth on a trawler or a whaler. You'd have to speak to a skipper down at the docks, or the company offices."

"Plenty of kraken to be seen on the whaling," someone else put in.

Elizabeth smiled tentatively. "You never hit them by mistake?"

That raised some laughs.

"Not a chance," the first man explained. "Clever buggers, they are. Smart, you know?"

"Smart enough to fly starships," Gregor said.

"Aye, but that might not be enough to keep them out of the way of harpoons. Krakens can hunt whales. I've seen ones that got away. Sucker-marks this size on their flanks."

He spread his hands a meter apart and everyone laughed except Gregor and Elizabeth, and Marcus and the man who might have been Volkov.

Gregor asked Marcus: "What are you doing here yourself?"

The trader smiled disarmingly at everyone. "Oh, just relaxing, enjoying the company. I've had a long day. And to be honest, it's beneficial to us to get to know folk."

He turned to Elizabeth. "And your kind interest in me was . . . ?"

"Oh! Well, traders are always interesting! But I just have a quick question, just wondering if you've ever noticed. Do the ships ever . . . change pilots, when they're on a planet's ocean?"

"Ah." Marcus looked puzzled by the question. "I believe they do, though not very often. We understand that the pilot takes some recreation off-ship. We presume it's the same one that swims back! To be honest, it would be hard to tell."

Gregor noticed the recurrence of the phrase, and wondered if the trader *was* being entirely honest. He also noticed that most of the glasses at the table were depleted, and stood up to offer a round. Marcus demurred, Gregor insisted. He left as Elizabeth launched into a detailed query about vacuum barnacles.

At the bar he was joined by someone else from the table.

"I'll help you carry them," the man said. His accent was hard to place.

"Thanks . . . Ah, I didn't catch your name."

They looked at each other sidelong, while the pithkie barmaid met the order with more-than-human efficiency.

"Grigory," the man said. His voice dropped, barely audible above the music. "And between you and me, Gregor Cairns, my surname is what you think it is, but Antonov's the one I wear now. What are you after?"

Gregor fumbled the unfamiliar coins and notes, hesitated to lift any glasses for fear of dropping them.

"We're looking for members of the old crew," he said. "Especially Matt."

"So's our friend Marcus," said Volkov gruffly. "Just pricking up his ears, making idle-sounding inquiries. He suspects, but I don't think he's sussed me out yet, so watch your mouth."

"I will," Gregor promised.

"What do you want from us?"

Gregor hoped their talk could pass for light barside banter. He accepted a tray and began loading it, passing the lighter drinks to Volkov, to have something to do.

"Nav tech," he said. "Comp."

"Ah." Volkov's eyebrows twitched. "Interesting."

They returned to the table and distributed the drinks. The people sitting on Elizabeth's side had crowded the space where Volkov had sat; he took the seat where Gregor had been, and Gregor squeezed in by Elizabeth, suddenly acutely conscious of her warm body pressed against him. Her conversation about barnacles had spread into a free-for-all about invading species, about which everybody had a loud opinion.

Gregor met Volkov's sardonic gaze.

"You a fisherman yourself, Grigory?"

Volkov shook his head. "Engineer on the factory ships, most of the time. I come and go."

Marcus leaned past Elizabeth, his face curiously intent.

"Grigory Antonov—before it slips my mind—perhaps we could have a private word tomorrow? We're interested in marine engines; we have some supplies and techniques that you may find worth a look. Fine lubricants and such."

"Sure, sure," said Volkov. "You can drop by the company office—third block, Quay Four. Ask for Ferman and Sons. Opens at nine. I'll be there."

The conversation moved on; people came and went with drinks, changing places until after about half an hour Elizabeth and Gregor found themselves together against the wall. The place had become more packed, the music louder. A gigant was singing now, in a voice deep but definitely female—strange. Elizabeth began to worry about all the other places they were supposed to visit.

"Think we're doing all right, or would you like to move on?"

Gregor considered this for a moment.

"I think we've found . . . the people we're looking for," he said. The phrase stabbed her. Gregor indicated Volkov with a glance. "Confirmed, by the way."

"Oh. Good."

She looked down at her glass. "But we should move on, because we still haven't found anyone to hire us a boat."

"We can do that in the morning," said Gregor. "Company offices or down at the docks, the man said—talk to a skipper, remember?"

"Oh. Sure. But I'd still like to move on."

She turned to him. His face was close to hers, flushed with the drink and the heat, his eyes a little glazed from the smoke they'd shared. His swept-back hair was rough and stringy after several days without a proper wash. Their hips were jammed together. As she turned, her arm slid behind him and she brought it up around his waist in a sudden

16

Cool Stuff

R EADY?"
       "Yes," I said; but—as before—the question was not addressed
to me. Avakian flicked a datagloved finger and the screen encircled us.
We could see ourselves, and each other, and the interface, and nothing
else. With spex and gloves I could see and touch the screen at a comfortable arm's length; it tracked my glances, its features brightening and
magnifying wherever I looked.

"We reckon it's indexed," said Avakian. "In an unknown alphabet,
alas. Use the search engine. That's it—the slot on the left."

I grabbed the schematics, highlighted the control system, tabbed in
a complex Boolean query we'd sweated over for the previous couple of
hours, and stuffed the lot in the slot. The surrounding screen instantly
shimmered. All the streaming pictures and words which were its icons
vanished, to be replaced by a black background on which the flying
saucers shone. Arrays of discs stretched to infinity in every direction. I
stared at them, fascinated by their endless subtle variations. By focusing
on a column, I could glide along it, exploring the possibilities of a
design path to its limits and beyond. . . .

"It's like being in the middle of an invasion fleet," Avakian said.
"Opening scene of *Mars Attacks!*, with facing mirrors."

His cackle jolted me out of my trance.

"Huh?"

"Forget it. Look at the thing *critically,* dammit! To me that looks
like the least-helpful reply I've seen since my first inadvertent outer
join."

"Maybe that's what we've done."

It's a common and easy mistake to set up a query which returns vastly more than you're interested in, which in fact returns everything *except* what you really want. If you're clever or stupid enough, you can fire off a query whose reply links everything in the database to everything else, and eats every system resource you've got while doing so. Lights going out is a clue.

"Nah," said Avakian. "The syntax is sound, I checked that first."

Of course he had, as had I.

"Well, this sure isn't a response to the question we asked."

"Or we aren't looking at it the right way. . . . Look, can you restore it to how it was before you went off on your little expedition?"

"What?"

Avakian gave me a spex-masked stare.

"You were out of it for *ten minutes,* man. I thought you had *found* something, but I gave up on that when the drooling and heavy breathing kicked in."

"Shit."

I looked around in the array, realized I'd got hopelessly lost.

"Let's just launch it again," I said.

I pulled the schematics and the query out of the search-engine slot like clogged hair from a plughole, and shoved them back in. This time I took great care not to move, and not to look at anything but the nearest disc, the one right in front of my eyes. I reached out and touched it. The tactile feedback was chill and smooth. That disc expanded, the rest blinked away.

"That's better," said Avakian. "Let's tab in."

We looked around.

"This is getting almost familiar," I said.

"Better rendering," said Avakian. "But lookee here."

The control panel had been ripped out, as though for hot-wiring, and the hundreds of sprouting cables labeled. I peered at the tags, then pulled in a few aerospace-engineering handbooks off Camila's palmtop.

"Shit," I said. "They've done it to U.S. military spec."

"By now," said Avakian, "I could believe they wrote it in the first place."

"Dreamland, huh?"

We laughed and saved the ship to our own systems and backed out.

"Let me get this clear," said Driver. "You're telling me we can just rip off the panel and patch in a joystick?"

"Um, no," I said. "The whole control system on this disc is different from the one we have the production plan for. It's not at all obvious how to merge the two."

"Anyone had a look at the control system in the first one?"

"Yeah," said Camila. "I have. It's solid-state all the way down from about a millimeter below the palm-print thingie. I've lowered a viewpoint through that millimeter thickness under high-res, and my best guess is it's some kind of pressure-sensitive pad combined with something that responds to changes in the upper surface's conductivity. For all I know it could be tuned to patterns of heat and sweat."

"Sweaty-palmed aliens," said Avakian. "What a creepy thought."

"And from there," Camila went on, spreading her arms out and upward, "it branches all over the craft, especially to the engine. Nothing as crude as wires, either. It's completely different from the one Matt and Armen have pulled out."

"But you could put a joystick and a viewscreen on that one?"

"Oh, sure." Camila nodded vigorously. "No sweat."

She looked puzzled when we laughed, then joined in.

"The only problem with that is we don't have a plan to build *that* ship."

"Would it be possible to reverse-engineer one?" asked Lemieux.

"Give me a few years," I said. "Mind you, merging the plans would probably take longer."

"Which inclines me to wonder," said Driver, "why they didn't give us the plans for one with human-compatible controls in the first place."

"We could always ask for one," said Avakian.

"Worth a try," I said.

Driver glowered at us.

"Don't hang about," he said.

We ducked out of the office and dived into Avakian's cubbyhole. After ten minutes of discussing the details of the query we dropped into the interface, fired it off, and got nothing but a blank screen for our pains.

"Hmm," said Driver, when we reported back. "Why does this not surprise me?"

"You mean it's some kind of initiative test?" said Camila.

"No," said Driver. "They ain't playing games. They must think they've given us the answer."

Camila poked about in the air in front of her spex, examining our results.

"Something's bothering me here," she said. "The conventions are U.S. mil-spec."

"So?"

She flicked her fingers and looked up.

"You guys—I mean, you can tell me, right? They're not exactly secret, they're in the goddamn public domain. So was it you that passed them on to the aliens?"

Driver and Lemieux frowned at each other.

"Nobody passed anything on," said Lemieux. "We have not been *entering* information in the alien interface. Well, we can, but there isn't much point."

"So how the hell do they know it?"

"That seems an awfully trivial question," I said. "Seeing as we don't even have a clue how they know our languages."

"It is not trivial," said Lemieux. He rubbed his stubble. "And it is not something they merely tapped from our own communications, because we use ESA conventions and we have had no occasion to refer to yours."

"I'm willing to bet," said Camila, "that the only place on this station that spells out U.S. mil-spec conventions is in the handbooks stored right here."

She held up her palmtop.

"And the only thing built to them," she went on, "is the *Blasphemous Geometries*' onboard systems."

"What about our spex?" I asked. "I mean, face it, everybody here uses them."

Driver shook his head.

"All civilian," he said. "Commercial."

"The U.S. military uses them!"

"That," Camila explained patiently, "is because the kind of spex you can buy in any American hardware store or military-base PBX, for that matter, is better than the fucking clunkers that the Army uses. Even your commie biodegradables are better than—"

"What are you getting at?" I said, not patiently.

"What I'm getting at," she told us, "is that the aliens can read every bit and byte of data on every computer on this station."

"Ah," said Lemieux. "Since we identified the earlier datastream hack, that has been our default assumption."

"Well, that's that little mystery cleared up," said Driver. "Now, as we were saying—"

"No!" said Camila. "Wait a minute."

"I'm waiting," said Driver.

Camila, Armen, and I all started saying much the same thing at once. Driver held up a hand.

"Camila."

"You were right a minute ago," she said. "They think they've given us the answer, and they have—they're telling us to build the controls and the engine into the *Blasphemous Geometries.*"

There was a moment of silence.

"All right," said Driver. "Nice idea. But if the thing is modular enough to do that, why isn't it modular enough for a merge of the two alien discs?"

I shook my head. "No, no, it's a totally different problem. Just a minute. Camila, could you zap me through to a spec of the *Blasphemous?*"

She tugged a cable from her palmtop and plugged it in the port of my spex.

"All yours. Remember not to share this information with anyone from a Communist country."

"I'll keep that in mind," I said, diving in.

First, I checked that the controls on the new disc were compatible with those of our own ship. They were, as was the instrumentation. Then I overlaid the two disc renderings and set tracers on the cables in the new one. They did indeed match up with clearly defined nodes on the engine of the first. When I isolated that engine and backtracked it through the production plan, I found that the plan had a concealed modularity—it was possible to build the craft's engine independently. It meant a lot more work, but I could see how to do it.

When I'd tried to do something similar with the two craft themselves, I'd bogged down with the problem of not knowing which parts were redundant—the solid-state control system—and which weren't. This one, however, slotted together perfectly.

"So, let's go for it," said Driver.

The only problem that bugged me, as I checked off at the end of that long day shift, was the question Driver had raised earlier: why the aliens had first given us a plan for a craft we couldn't fly; a craft designed for another species. Was it their answer, I wondered, to a question we hadn't asked?

•   •   •

"Do you think those two are queer for each other?"

"Who?"

Camila looked at me as though from a much longer distance than the half-meter between our faces, as we hung, each with our heels crooked around the other's buttocks, in our companionable cubbyhole. Then she put her elbows on my knees and leaned forward to speak quietly.

"Driver and Lemieux."

"What?" I laughed. "Can't say I've noticed any flamboyant mannerisms from either of them."

"Lemieux—"

"—is French. They all talk like that, except gay men, and *they* sound like Americans. *Très, très* fashionable, I'm told."

"Well," she persisted, "these two have something going on. I'm sure of it."

"Well, what if they are?" I said. "It's not like it's a big deal. Not in sophisticated Socialist Europe, anyway."

"Okay, okay," she said, sounding a little defensive. "What I mean is, if they're not, what are they up to?"

"Now, that is a good question. But come on. They're conspirators, who may have been at it for years. They've just carried out a coup here, one which isn't one-hundred-percent popular on the station. Chumakova's lot are no doubt plotting against them as we speak. When things settle down back home, one way or another they're gonna have a lot of explaining to do. Driver was regarded by the CIA as an asset, and he now claims to have been a double agent all along, but the book's always open on these situations."

"Yeah, tell me about it," she said gloomily. "What are we?"

"In what context?"

She kissed the tip of my nose. "Politically."

"Oh." I thought about it, rubbing my chin, almost surprised at its smoothness; Camila had brought me an electric razor from the commissary, and had been quite insistent that I use it.

"Well, I'm a good European and you're a good American, but not everyone back home might see it that way."

"You said it. I can't begin to list all the laws I've broken just by being here—technology export and trading with the enemy and shit—and you're being called a defector. So—"

She let out a long sigh, and reached sideways for the steam-pipe and the packet of grass.

"So?"

"So it's time we started looking out for ourselves. Making sure we don't get shafted when all this is sorted out. Offered up as a sacrifice to the powers that be, you know."

I shivered in the humid warmth: the phrase "powers that be" seemed strangely inapposite for governments, now that we knew what other powers there were. But I knew this wasn't what she meant.

"I don't see Driver as likely to shaft us," I said. "And not your bosses either."

"It might not be up to them, by then."

She bubbled up the pipe, sucked it, and passed it to me. I inhaled, looking around our den with a sudden surge of paranoia.

"Is it safe to talk here?"

"Sure." She shrugged, reached behind her, and waved a small device like a torch. "There were the usual bugs when we came in, but I've swept them."

"What's that thing?"

"Classified," she grinned, stashing it again. "Take it from me, though, it frazzles millimeter-scale wet tech."

"All right," I said. "What do you suggest we do?"

"Some real spying. Get some information that we can trade with, something that either side might find useful. For a start, find out what Driver and Lemieux are really up to."

"Oh, great." I returned her the pipe. "And how do you propose to do that?"

She grinned ferally at me.

"We listen to them," she said. "Through the alien interface."

I woke and found it was morning in the station's day cycle—not just from my watch, looped by its strap to the webbing a few inches away—but by the increased light around the edges of the curtain and the increased sounds of busyness from the corridor. Listening further, I guessed it might even have been a cock-crow that had wakened me. Someone was filling the food-hoppers at the nearest chicken run.

Camila was still asleep, and we were still wrapped around each other. One advantage of microgravity is that you can sleep in a cuddle without waking to find that one of your arms is trapped under your lover and has itself gone to sleep. I nuzzled her shoulder with my chin, now scratchy again, and stroked her short black hair, which had lengthened by a millimeter or two since launch and now had a very pleasant, furry nap to it. She stirred and mumbled and snuggled closer. We'd had more sleep this night than the night before, though not from any loss of interest in each other, having had sex before and after our conversation and having wakened up to some kind of dozy mutual stimulation in the middle of the night. Right now, if her sleepy strokings were anything to go by, Camila was warming up for another session before breakfast.

As I floated there in her arms, all of that erotic intimacy stood vivid and real in my memory, and only our conversation seemed like a dream. But later, after we'd stickily separated, and gone to wash and dry and dress, it all crashed in on me again like a cold shower. Her assessment of our situation was more realistic—or at any rate further thought-through—than mine had been, caught up as I was in the fascination of the work.

Camila was showing herself to be cool and clearheaded, like not many other people I knew—Charlie, maybe, among the old geeks; Jason; one or two Webblies; and Jadey. The thought of Jadey brought a pang, but not guilt. Basically I was working my way back to her, the fastest way I could. Much as I loved her—and I did—I had no illusions that she wouldn't do the same sort of thing; whatever was necessary to get her through.

And to get through here, and back to Earth, and Jadey free, I needed Camila. And I needed to think like her, to think like a spy. As I pulled on my jumpsuit I felt the familiar shape of the hand reader in my pocket, and beside it, the datadisk.

It was at that point that I did my first bit of thinking like a spy, and what I thought was: *There's something wrong here.* I unzipped the pocket and ran my fingers around the edge of the datadisk, and as I made for Driver's office I pulled it out and looked at it, and realized that it was the piece of the puzzle that didn't fit. There was no place for it in the picture I'd been shown.

I almost shouted, as around that anomalous object the pieces of a quite different picture clicked into place.

"Ready?" I said.

A word floated across my spex:

Yes.

The interface surrounded me.

I'd spent most of that day finishing the modified production plan and handing it over to the people running the fabs, and liaising with Camila, who was working with the engineers—Volkov and the rest—

on the *Blasphemous Geometries.* In one slack period I'd jaunted into Armen's workspace and asked him for access to the interface. As though surprised I didn't have it already, he zapped the key-code to my spex. Betweentimes, I'd checked the news channels, forced myself to ignore them, and worked on a query.

Now, my day's work complete half an hour before the usual late-evening debriefing in Driver's office, I had time for a little experiment.

Fighting off the interface's hypnotic distractions, I slotted the query into the search engine. It was a very simple query, for a set of data I knew to be unique to my own handheld reader because I had made it up myself, very laboriously: Test data for a job I'd done several months ago. The sort of low-level programming that really should have been beneath me, and I'd cursed the limited budget that had made me do it myself at the time. "An artist, not a technician," et cetera.

But I was glad of it now. I had to restrain a whoop when the screen returned a blank, almost the instant my thumb left the virtual switch that fired off the query.

Next I scanned around for a data-input port, and found one—eccentrically but appropriately—at 180 degrees around from the search-engine slot. I zapped the test data in, rotated my viewpoint, and repeated the query.

The data I'd just entered scrolled before me, like another boring chapter in the Book of Numbers.

The sight of it sent chills down my back.

With a sense of satisfaction alloyed with a certain sadness, I said: "Finished?" and the interface said yes and went away.

I joined Camila on the way to Driver's office. Her hand brushed mine, like a wing in flight.

"Hi, Matt." Warm smile. "Did you have time to—?"

"Yes," I said, quite truthfully. "Didn't find anything though."

"Ah. Shit. Worth a try though, anyway. Guess they're being real cautious. Smart guys."

"Yes," I said. "They'd have to be."

But not as smart as you, Camila, I didn't say.

"So that's it," said Driver, after taking the reports. "We can start production tomorrow."

"Hell, we can start it now," said Avakian. "For this job I'd be happy to pull an all-nighter."

This meeting was bigger than our unofficial cabal; the various team leaders were patched in through their spex and ours, filling the cramped room with an unreal crowd and forcing the graphics into surrealism. Driver, probably unwilling to let Avakian show off his skills in yet another frivolous and manipulative manner, had declined the offer of a full-immersion conference space.

The overlapping phantom shapes of Sembat, Telesnikov, and Chumakova all became simultaneously agitated at Avakian's remark.

"We can't do it," Sembat said. "Be realistic. The team is exhausted, we've been prepping the fabs all day—"

"And we've been on EVA hauling materials," said Telesnikov, on behalf of the cosmonauts. "Anything more, and we'll start having accidents. Out there, that means possible fatalities."

Driver took the last point with the bored skepticism of a manager listening to a union rep, but he raised his hand and nodded, glaring for a moment at Avakian.

"Okay, okay, Mikhail, there's no question of working further tonight. It's hardly a matter of urgency. Paul."

Lemieux, shaved and spruce again, smiled down at us.

"However," he began. "There is a growing urgency to the entire project, which I'd like to impress upon you and urge you to communicate to your teams. You've all heard the news today, unless you have been even more dedicated than you appear to have been."

Solemn nods all round. Chumakova looked as though she were about to say something, then thought better of it.

"I must thank all of you for your discipline in continuing to work, regardless of the . . . distraction and anxiety and indeed indignation which the news has doubtless provoked. We must hope that our political intervention will help toward a political solution, and in the meantime we must work harder to demonstrate that much of the political and military conflict is now obsolete, as Camila said."

This seemed to soothe and impress most of the people present and telepresent, but it only made me wonder further just what game he was playing. The day's events were a savage reminder that we weren't playing games; that the strategy of releasing the code-crackers and flooding the world with secrets was not without consequence. People no longer knew what to believe, and a lamentably large number were ready to believe anything.

The news reports I'd put firmly from my mind throughout the day replayed themselves in flashback. Only yesterday it had seemed that the political crisis in the E.U. was easing off into negotiation. Despite—or perhaps because of—this, a rash of riots had broken out across Western Europe. Mostly in the poorer areas, the ones where the mafias had more influence than the Party. (Parts of Leith, I'd noticed, were literally in flames.) Apolitical, apocalyptic slogans accompanied the trashing and looting; a lot of people seemed convinced that the governments, all governments, were somehow in league with the aliens. Not just our aliens, but the aliens of popular nightmare, the sinister, satanic Grays.

"Matt? You with us?"

Avakian's nudge brought me back to the moment. The others had gone, and we were back to the small cabal. I took off my spex and rubbed my eyes, looking around at Armen, Camila, Driver, and Lemieux. We didn't seem such a cozy little clique anymore, now that I knew a bit more about what was going on.

"You're very tired," said Driver.

"Yeah," I said. "And worried. I know a lot of people in the area of the rioting in Edinburgh, and Jadey's still in a jail just a couple of kilometers away from it."

Driver nodded. "We all have worries, we all have people back home. There's nothing we can do, except get on with the job."

I considered confronting him then and there, but decided against it. There was Camila to consider, and I didn't quite have her angle figured out yet.

"Okay," I said. "Let's get some sleep."

Sleep was not on my mind, though it was on my brain. As soon as we'd secured the curtain Camila started climbing out of her clothes, and I did likewise. We bumped and rolled, laughing. She caught me and held me.

"I need this," she said. "I need you. Otherwise I'd get very tense."

"Well, thank you," I mumbled. "So would I."

For a while I forgot about whatever reasons she might have for being tense. Then, as we hung in a contented, conjoined orbit of our own around the sun, the question came back.

"Have you swept up?" I whispered.

"I do that as regular as brushing my teeth," she said. "Why?"

I pulled my face away from her shoulder.

"Could you put some music on?"

She fished out a player, and I adjusted the volume carefully so that it would cover our voices against direct eavesdropping.

"You took a risk," I said, "playing that little game with the milspec stuff."

Her arms tightened, her legs clenched for a moment, then she re-laxed again. She frowned at me.

"What 'little game'?"

"You ported the specs across yourself, zapped your handbooks into the interface, right?"

She screwed up her eyes and shook her head.

"What makes you think that?"

"I found out today that the interface doesn't actually have access to all the data held on this station."

She pushed me away, herself back. We fetched up on opposite par-titions of the space, facing each other.

"Shit," she said. "This is serious. Don't you trust me?"

"Yeah, I *trust* you," I said. "But I don't expect you to always tell me everything. I'm just letting you know that I've figured out what you're doing, and to warn you—because I do trust you, see—that at least one of our friends will have figured out the same thing. Driver or Lemieux knows it."

She closed her eyes again, then stared at me.

"Let's take it from the top, okay?" she said. "How did you find that the interface can't access every computer here?"

I told her about my little experiment.

"And you concluded for that, that I must've zapped in the mil-spec data myself?"

"Uh-huh."

"Well, I didn't! I really don't believe in lying, Matt. Not like this. Why would I do that, anyway?"

"To get first dibs on testing the AG engine, and maybe . . . taking it home?"

She laughed. "It's a neat idea. Wish I'd thought of it."

"All right, so how d'you explain how the interface knew U.S. mil-itary conventions for labeling diagrams?"

"No idea at all," she said. "I'm as baffled as you are. What made you wonder about that, anyway? Was it because you found you couldn't eavesdrop through the interface?"

"No." I omitted telling her I hadn't even tried out her suggestion. "No, it's because I realized that Driver or Lemieux or both of them were bullshitting us the day we arrived. They told us there was no way the project data could have got to ESA without them knowing, and I thought this meant that the aliens had hacked the datastream. But I wasn't thinking properly. There was something I hadn't taken into account."

"What?"

I fumbled behind the webbing and in the pocket of my fatigues, and pulled out the datadisk that the Russian officer had given to Jadey.

"This," I said. "It was passed to Jadey in very dangerous circumstances. Now, I can just about believe that was the result of information being inserted in the data outflow from this station, with an ESA address attached, and that it just sort of rattled around in various automated systems. But getting this thing out would have required deliberation, decision, organization. This was no accident—as the commie saying goes."

"Okay," she said. "Go on."

"Which does rather strongly suggest that it was released deliberately from here, and not by aliens either. By Driver, Lemieux, or both of them, in liaison with whatever organization on the ground they're working with—probably the same one that got the disk to Jadey."

I grinned at her, across that five-foot gulf.

"And Jadey is connected to an organization financed by—among others—Nevada Orbital Dynamics. Your employer's company. Which means you and I, my dear, have been connected all along. Now, isn't that sweet?"

Camila smiled back at that.

"And of course the company sent us here," she said. She described a circle with her finger. "It's all a big chain, and it's all come back to here."

"Yes," I said. "And we know what's at your end of it, the American end, but we don't know what's at the European end—this end. We don't know who's pulling it. We don't know who's hauling it in."

The following morning the news was slightly better, if shots of gutted buildings and talk of firefighting and arrests and casualties counts as "good." The damage ran into billions. The rioters were duly denounced, or carefully *not* denounced, and analysis of the nuances of such pronouncements kept a lot of heads talking. Camila and I were called to Driver's office for a pre-work meeting.

"Just stand by," he told me, "and keep channels open to the fabs. No doubt there'll be glitches when it comes to actually running it. Just keep out of the way the rest of the time, maybe get started on the big 'engine' plan when you have a chance. And Camila, you hang out with the crew working on your ship, make sure they know what to take out and what to leave. Armen, stick close to the production teams. Give them anything they need on the science front, and keep track of progress on the second project."

"Fine," said Camila. "That's what we were going to do anyway."

"Before you go," said Lemieux. "And you too, Armen, please stay." He glanced over at Driver.

"We have something to tell you."

Camila clapped her hand over a giggle.

The two men looked so serious and embarrassed, I could for a moment almost believe they were about to declare their long-standing love for each other.

"We've been listening to you," Driver said. "Sorry about that."

"How?"

"Camila," Lemieux said, "I know you are not a spy, because if you were, you would know that your anti-surveillance device works very well against E.U. wet-tech bugs, but not, unfortunately, against the latest U.S. microbots."

"The Federal Security Bureau," said Driver, "never uses anything else."

"Well, I hope you had fun," I said.

They exchanged another embarrassed glance.

"We are sorry to have violated your privacy," said Lemieux. "But it is the political and not the personal element in your conversations which was of interest to us. We think misconceptions may arise if we don't take you into our confidence, and we can't afford that."

He looked over at Armen. "And you, too, are clever enough to figure things out eventually, and clever enough to get them wrong. We all have to trust each other, because the next few days are going to be very dangerous indeed. Matt, you spoke of a chain of links, and you were right. You said you did not know what is at our end of it. It's time you did."

17

Judgement of Krakens

NIGHT HAD FALLEN, with the suddenness characteristic of that latitude, while they had been in the bar. Lights marked out the long street around the shore. Gregor hurried through the now denser crowd on the esplanade's pavement, and fell in beside Lydia. Elizabeth and Marcus walked quickly ahead of them.

Lydia smiled and caught his hand, swinging it as she strode along.

"It's good to see you again," she said. "Even in such a difficult situation for your friend Salasso."

"How did you come to find out about it?"

She took a small rectangular box from a deep pocket in the side of her skirt, then slid it back.

"Radio. On shore, most of us carry them. I was out shopping this evening when I got a call from Bishlayan, one of our saurs. She knows Salasso, and they were talking when the trouble started. She lent her radio to Salasso, who gave me a list of places where I might find you."

"What kind of trouble is Salasso in?"

"Nothing violent. The saurs are not like us—they do not *brawl*. As to what it is, best you see for yourself. It is very tense. I'm really glad I found you as quickly as I did. It was such a relief to see you and Elizabeth."

Gregor couldn't hear any hint of irony or reproof.

"Uh . . . About Elizabeth, she and I—"

"Yes," said Lydia, "I see that you like each other."

Again the same uncomplicated note. Gregor frowned.

"You're not . . . upset?"

She gripped his hand tighter. "Why should I be? I could see that she liked you back in Kyohvic, that day at the lab. I'm pleased that you have someone to be with."

"I still don't understand."

"It's possible to love more than one person at once," Lydia said earnestly. "My father does."

"Yes, but that's *different*—"

She shot him a look. "Don't be so naive."

Before Gregor could collect his confused thoughts, let alone say anything, Marcus turned sharply left, leading them up a narrow stairway of worn, wet stone. The doorways of small taverns and shops interrupted the mossy walls every ten or so steps. Gregor concentrated on keeping his footing and following Lydia's heels; an upward glance, dangerous but interesting, showed the walls going up like the sides of a canyon, the street- and window-lighting obscuring any strip of sky above.

After about a hundred steps they reached a final flight, broader and less slippery but no less worn, which ended at a street. Halfway up that flight, Marcus stopped. He indicated a door to their left, a few steps farther up.

"This is the place," he said. The door was half-glazed, the windows dim, the sign brightly lit but indecipherable. It might have made sense, to other eyes; Gregor could see only swirls and blocks.

"What kind of place is it?" Elizabeth asked.

Marcus grimaced. "The saur equivalent of a tavern, or a . . . place of assignation. Been in one before?"

Gregor and Elizabeth hadn't.

"It's quite safe to go in, but it is very important to be polite, not to stare, and not to make loud noises or sudden movements. Otherwise we may be thrown out. Clear? Right. Elizabeth, maybe you should stay beside me, and Gregor with Lydia. If there's any trouble, let us do the protecting. Follow me."

Marcus held the door open until they were all crowded behind him, and Gregor let it swing back behind them as they went in. It took a moment for his eyes to adjust to the low lighting. The air was rank with fish and meat; the sweetish whiff of hemp only made it more sickly.

It was the eyes he saw first, slanted obsidian ellipses reflecting the faint glow of the suspended lamps. Then he made out the shadowy shapes of saurs, sitting on chairs at wide circular tables. There was no bar, just a darker opening at the back, a source of clattering noises and strong smells. In front of that opening two saurs in belted robes faced each other, hands raised, in crooked, edgy postures. They were moving very slowly, as though in dance or ritual combat. Dishes and cups lay on the tables. Glowing pipe-bowls moved up and down and about, like mysterious lights in a dark sky. Saur conversations went on quietly, a background hiss rather than a murmur. Above it and behind it, some rhythmic sound he couldn't quite hear worried at the sockets of his teeth.

Lydia clutched his hand. Together they followed Elizabeth and Marcus—also holding hands, he noticed—toward a corner table at the back. From behind the table, five pairs of eyes observed their approach. As he got closer he recognized Salasso, who nodded. He was sitting beside a saur who wore a dark but shiny gown. One of the other saurs stood up and indicated four vacant chairs on the near side of the table. Following Marcus's lead, the humans sat down. The chairs were of the same corky substance as they'd seen in Saur City One. The table, made of a single block of the same stuff, had a sharp inward curve from the top to the base to make room for knees, though not quite enough for human knees.

"Bishlayan," said Marcus. The saur in the black gown ducked her head briefly.

"Salasso," said Gregor. "Are you all right?"

"For now."

Of the other saurs, the two to Salasso's right were in the familiar one-piece coveralls, the one to Bishlayan's left in what looked curiously like one of the bulky leather jackets favored by airplane pilots; almost comical on his—or her—slender frame. A fur collar added to the impression, and the incongruity.

"Let us introduce ourselves," said the saur at the opposite end of the group. "Gregor, Lydia, Elizabeth, Marcus, your names and sexes and occupations are known to us. Salasso and Bishlayan you know. The one beside them is Delavar; he is, as you may surmise, a local skiff pilot. My name is Tharanack, and I am of the male sex. My female comrade is called Mavikson. We are citizens of New Lisbon and are employed as what the humans call 'peacekeepers,' and what we call 'fighters.' "

He spread his hands, splaying the four digits on each. "You may ask for our documents, or you may call for peacekeepers of another species if you wish. No? Very well. I cannot ask Marcus and Lydia, but I must ask you, Gregor and Elizabeth—are you armed?"

Gregor turned to Elizabeth and felt heartened by her wry smile.

"No," she said. "Apart from our knives, of course."

"You are well-armed," said Tharanack. "That is good. We would not want you to feel intimidated."

Gregor didn't believe for a second that the sturdy, sharp lock-knife in his pocket would make much difference in a fight with saurs, but he reckoned the whole significance of the question was symbolic anyway. This preliminary palaver probably wasn't even saur custom, just police procedure in the multispecies municipality of New Lisbon. He realized that his companions were looking at him, waiting for him to speak.

He laid his hands on the table and rolled them, palms up. As a gesture of peace and open-mindedness it probably came across as theatrical to the saurs, but he was acutely conscious of the need to err on the side of caution. If that meant doing the equivalent of throwing himself on his knees and baring his chest, so be it.

"What seems to be the problem?" he asked. Out of the corner of his eye he noticed Marcus's slight nod of approval. The pilot Delavar leaned forward sharply, hissing some epithet; Mavikson silenced him with a glance.

"The problem is this," the female peacekeeper said. "Delavar, Salasso, and Bishlayan have a relationship of long standing. Salasso and Bishlayan, of course, have most recently met in Kyohvic. A certain tension arose when Salasso turned up here, while Bishlayan was with Delavar. In order to reassure Delavar that he was not here in competition for Bishlayan's attention, or some other ulterior motive, Salasso explained his real purpose. Delavar, and others here who, ah, quickly became aware of the conversation, were even more disturbed by this than by his initial jealous suspicion. Assistance was called for. So here we are."

The irritating background rhythm stopped. Behind him, Gregor heard four bare saur feet slap into a different position. A different, but still subtly annoying rhythmic sound began. Off to the side, he could see a lot of black eyes watching him, and a few, apparently, on the dancers. The sight brought him out of his astonishment at the idea of a relationship, or a rivalry, that had spanned centuries.

"Ah," he said, fixing his gaze on Mavikson. "And what would you say was Salasso's true purpose?"

"You know that as well as I do, Cosmonaut Gregor Cairns."

Gregor bowed slightly, acknowledging his error. The saurs weren't given to verbal games.

"Very well," he said. "But what I truly am not certain of, and what I ask your indulgence to explain, is what the objection is to this purpose."

Delavar's right hand shot forward and down, clawing into the table. The two peacekeepers hissed sharply. Bishlayan laid a hand on his forearm, and stroked it, and said something in his ear. Slowly, and with a body-language of bad grace that easily jumped the species barrier, the pilot sat back.

"He understands your language," said Bishlayan, still stroking his arm. "But he is too angry to speak it. I will speak for him, though I do not have an opinion on the matter, myself."

Her other hand was plucking and stroking her chest, claws now and then snagging the gown's fabric. Gregor had a strong impression that for a saur this indicated almost unbearable distraction and distress. He raised his hands, palms open and bent back, as though offering her his wrists to slit.

"Please," he said.

She seemed to recover some composure.

"My lover Salasso has angered my lover Delavar, and others here, with his idea of helping you, the . . ." She said something he couldn't catch.

"Hominidae," said Salasso.

" 'Monkey-fuckers,' " translated Mavikson, in a tone of weary honesty.

". . . to become navigators," Bishlayan continued. "He believes that this will anger the gods. Salasso was surprised at his opinion, which he referred to as . . ."

Another saur phrase.

" 'Perhaps irrationally conservative.' "

" 'A steaming pile of stinking dinosaur shit.' "

". . . because they have long been friends, and he had thought they were of similar views. The argument became extremely heated. They were both doing *this*."

She drummed her fingers on the table, then made quick flopping gestures with her hands to emphasize that she hadn't really meant it.

"When that happened I asked the keeper of the house to call the keepers of the peace, and called up my shipmate Lydia, and let Salasso speak to her on the radio to fetch you."

She sat back, sliding her hands into her wide sleeves, Gregor could see under the cloth each hand's fierce grip on the opposite elbow.

Salasso leaned forward and turned to Mavikson.

"I do wish," he said, "that you would not translate our idioms so literally. And I urge our human friends not to take offense."

"None taken," said Lydia, speaking up for the first time. "Apart from that, would you both say that Bishlayan has given a true account of your quarrel?"

Salasso and Delavar glanced at each other, turned sharply away, and nodded.

"Good," said Lydia. "Gregor, Elizabeth, I have a suggestion to make. May I?"

Elizabeth shrugged; Gregor, who had no idea what do next in any case, nodded. Lydia smiled at them both and turned back to the saurs. She turned her head farther, turning her shoulders with it, then put her hand under her ponytail and lifted it to display to the saurs the back of her neck. Gregor stared, fascinated by the fine wispy curls on her nape. The saurs all inhaled at the same moment.

"As you see," she said, facing them again, "I am very young. I have little experience and no wisdom. How could I know what may or may not anger or please the gods? And I see that you yourselves, who are so much older and wiser than I, cannot agree. So I ask you to consider for a moment taking your disagreement to someone who was old and wise when everyone here was less than an egg. One who has talked to gods. Would you accept such a judgement, and remain friends whichever way that judgement fell?"

As though unconsciously, artlessly, her hand had crept again to the back of her neck, lifting the tuft of the ponytail to the top of her head. She held the pose for a moment.

"I only ask," she said.

Her hair fell back.

Gregor realized that his fingernails were digging into the table. He relaxed them hurriedly and rolled his hands over again, but no one had noticed. They were all staring at Lydia.

Delavar reached across in front of Bishlayan and took Salasso's hand, tentatively at first, then in a firm mutual grasp.

"We would," he said.

"Good," said Lydia briskly. "Let us go to the ship, and consult the navigator."

For a giddy moment Gregor misunderstood her, then realized she was referring to the kraken.

•   •   •

Delavar was willing to accept one of the peacekeepers as a fair witness, and was in any case anxious to resume his interrupted tryst with Bishlayan, so it was only Salasso and Tharanack who left with the four humans. Salasso, very conscientiously, stayed close to the peacekeeper and said nothing. Lydia and Marcus led the way. Rather than go back down the steps, they turned into the street at the top, which, like most streets in the city, sloped down to the shore and ended at a convenient quay. Gregor and Elizabeth brought up the rear.

Gregor drew a deep breath, trying to drive the smell of the saur dive from his nostrils. People streamed up and down the street, free of any traffic but the overhead cable cars.

"It's good to be out of there," he said.

"What the hell's going on?" said Elizabeth.

"I still have no idea why Marcus was after—"

"That's not what I'm talking about. What's going on between you and Lydia?"

"I don't know."

"I saw her walking along, holding your hand and chatting blithely as if she'd never seen us back in the bar. I didn't like that—it was as if I didn't exist."

"She saw us, all right. She didn't mind; in fact she seemed quite pleased about it."

"Did she indeed? How very enlightened of her. How philosophical. I'm sure she's very happy that you have someone to ease the pain of love with until you and your family have got your bloody ship up there ready to go haring off after her."

She stared straight ahead as she said this. Gregor felt himself actually trembling as he walked beside her. Their kiss in the bar had made what Elizabeth felt for him real in a way that Salasso's report of it had not. It had shaken him, and Lydia's arrival before they'd had time to talk had left his own feelings in upheaval. His conversation with Lydia had only made it worse. The tense minutes in the saur hostelry had come as a relief and distraction.

There, he'd admired Lydia with a curious detachment, unclouded by adoration; her tactical, tactful skill in talking to the saurs was, perhaps, what he should have expected of a space-merchant's daughter but it had astonished him nonetheless. It recalled the unexpected understanding she'd shown of the deep questions about the kraken, when she had visited the lab, although then he'd suspected she was showing off. This time she'd shown herself capable of thinking on her feet.

"Elizabeth . . ."

"What?"

Still looking straight ahead and walking fast.

"Can we stop for a moment?"

She stopped and faced him. He had a second of sharp and clear perception of her, a sudden sum of his knowledge of her. She was taller and stronger and older than Lydia, and not as pretty, but at that moment she looked far more vulnerable and far more beautiful. It stung him and stunned him that he had not seen her like this from the beginning.

He held her shoulders, as before.

"I love you," he said. And as he said it, it became true, all his tension and confusion resolved, became sharp and straight and singing, a bowstring that still twanged from sending an arrow on its flight.

"I've always loved you," she said.

When they unlocked from the embrace he was still shaking, and they had to run.

The reflection of the starship's lights smeared across the water like spilt petrol on a puddle. Up close, it was too vast to be strange. It could have been one of the factory ships or the bulk carriers in the harbor, apart from its size, which dwarfed all of them. Water lapped its sides, but it definitely was not floating; if it had been, Gregor vaguely thought, it would have had to be lower down, with a greater displacement. The fields smoothed the sea around it, replacing the waves and swell with complex racing ripples, and made hair prickle and ears hum.

Above the hull's overhang, the occasional skiff flitted in or out of long, narrow rectangular openings, their lens-shapes flashing reflections of the lights within. At one end—whether fore or aft Gregor could not guess—a slanted, rounded opening on the lower side gaped like a mouth, partly in the sea and partly just above it. The water around it and below it was brightly lit, greenish, swirling with kraken whose full-spectrum chromatophore communications sent flickering rainbow flashes through the upper levels of the water.

Their own point of entry was more modest: a wide doorway in the lower curve of the hull, with a pontoon of wood and old rubber tires and tubes moored to its sill. The boatman throttled back the petrol engine, hove to and made fast, and the two saurs and four humans climbed off the boat.

"You'll wait for us?" said Marcus, as he paid for the outward journey.

231

"I'm not going anywhere," the boatman assured them, settling back in the stern and firing up a smoke.

They walked along the swaying planks, Elizabeth and Gregor more confidently than the rest, and stepped over the high threshold into the ship.

Elizabeth glanced downward as they entered, nudged Gregor. "Barnacles," she said. He grinned back at her.

A young crewman sitting on the mooring, reading a book, glanced up and nodded as they arrived. Behind him, a large receiving-bay, planked with wood and slopping with seawater, was almost filled with crates. Marcus led them past the crewman and turned right, into a corridor along the side of the ship, in the direction of the circular opening they'd passed in the boat.

"We're all related here," he explained, over his shoulder. "Don't stand much on ceremony. This way."

There was no other way. The corridor went on and on, for hundreds of meters, or so it felt. White-painted metal plates with big rivets, caged electric lights overhead, the occasional hatch on their left, and bulkheads every ten meters or so. They might have been in the bowels of any large ship. Or an airship built of steel, Gregor thought, this corridor passing along the space between the outer and inner skins.

After about five minutes they reached the end of the corridor, and stepped out onto a wide, wet metal shelf that rang under their feet. Three saurs stood at a railing about ten meters in front of them. Beyond it, the opening to the sea lay like a small lake, about a hundred meters across, lit from below and from the sides as though for some extravagant festivity. Two krakens floated there, their twenty-meter tentacles extended. From that lake, on their left, a channel fifteen meters wide ran back into the interior of the ship. The sides of the vessel curved up around the pool, to meet a convex floor of glass high above it. Above the glass other lights shone, and two other krakens swam, among darting shoals of fish and drifting weeds. From the far side of that gigantic aquarium, a glass column extended down to beneath the far edge of the pool. Inside the column, a lift—or the piston of a pump—was gliding slowly upward, carrying a kraken holding a vertical position, its tentacles curled to its head, its mantle rippling in powerful pulses.

"That," said Marcus, pointing upward, "is the navigator's cabin and bridge, and this is his private mess-hall, where he meets and entertains his guests. Channels and sluices of seawater connect it to other parts of the ship."

He indicated the channel beside them, and then led the way to the railing. Leaning over it, Gregor found himself looking into the largest pair of eyes he'd ever seen. Even thirty-odd meters away, they still seemed uncomfortably close. The thought of the size and complexity of the brain that must lie behind them was even more disturbing to contemplate; apart from the gods, *Architeuthys extraterrestris sapiens* was the largest intelligent species, and almost certainly the largest intelligence, that humanity had ever encountered.

It was also, considered merely as an animal, frighteningly large. The thought that it was a mollusc was not especially comforting.

"Let us consult our navigator," said Lydia.

"How do you know which one it is?" Gregor asked.

"We have to ask," said Lydia. She spoke to one of the ship's saurs, who led them over to the corner between the main pool and the channel where a sloping display-screen and control-panel was mounted on the railing. His long fingers danced across the panel, and complex patterns of light flowed on the screen.

While the saur was doing this, Marcus leaned over the railing and pointed downward. When Gregor and Elizabeth leaned over, too, they could see a much-larger version of the screen, about four meters by seven, shimmering directly below them in the water and obviously repeating the patterns displayed on the screen above. One of the krakens had sunk beneath the surface, and after a minute or two resurfaced, facing in the opposite direction, its tentacles away from them and its broad back toward them. The eyes regarded them as before.

Patterns of light played briefly across its back.

The saur at the screen turned to them.

"That is our navigator."

"Well, that's lucky," said Lydia. She gestured to Salasso. "Please ask your question, as you wish, in your own language. Tharanack will translate it—and any answers—into ours, and Voronar here will translate to and from the language of light."

Salasso stepped up and asked his question. Voronar recoiled slightly, glancing over at Lydia and Marcus as though appealing for support. They both nodded firmly. The saur bowed again over the panel, his fingers unsteady at their task.

"Salasso has asked," said Tharanack, "whether the navigators appointed by the gods know if the gods would be angered, and if they themselves would feel at all offended if some of the, ah, hominidae were to take it upon themselves to guide ships between the stars."

The effect of the question, once Varonar had transcribed it into the colorful ideoglyphs and displayed it on the underwater screen, was like lighting a fuse to start a fireworks display. The krakens in the pool, and others now visible in the sea beneath, and those in the overhead aquarium, burst almost simultaneously into rapid-fire exchanges of racing, flashing colored light.

Gregor felt Elizabeth's arm clasp his waist, and clasped hers in response, but more firmly. He felt that they needed to cling to each other to remain on their feet. Lydia and Marcus and the saurs were gazing at the display with almost as much amazement.

"It's rare to see anything like this," said Lydia. "So long, and so intense. The volume of information being exchanged must be enormous."

Eventually, after about five minutes, the lights died down and the navigator's body darkened. Then, quite slowly, a much simpler series of patterns scrolled across his back. Varonar began to speak, and Tharanack translated into English.

" 'The gods are all around us, and care little of such things. It is their felicity to contemplate the universe as it is. Nothing can anger the gods which does not threaten the variety and beauty which they see in it. Others, not the gods, lifted our ancestors from the seas of Earth long ago. These others incurred the anger of the gods, and we lifted the ancestors and relatives of the saurs from the lands of Earth, to escape that anger which destroyed the others. The saurs have lifted the hominidae and other species. Recently some of the hominidae have lifted themselves, and traveled here without us and without the saurs. We must assume that the gods approved of their coming, and will approve of their further traveling.

` " 'As to ourselves, we are happy to be navigators, but would be as happy to be passengers. Our home is the great ocean that spans the worlds. If we lost one specialization, we would find others. Species change, the niche remains. If the hominidae can fill our niche at a lower price, we will only gain from it, as will all the other intelligent species. Peace and trade to you.' "

Salasso spun around and embraced his two friends.

"I knew it!" he said. "I knew it!"

"It's not as simple as that," said Varonar, the translator. "The navigator just told you that he and his kind will not fight you, and neither will the gods. But they will compete. And so will we."

Gregor smiled at him over Salasso's head.

"Peace and trade," he said.

He gently disengaged himself from the saur and from Elizabeth, and stepped back and looked at Marcus and Lydia and their crewmates. "We have a navigator to find," he said.

Marcus said good-bye with a swift handshake and a thin smile, Lydia with a sudden kiss. Then they walked with Tharanack back along the long corridor to the floating pier and the waiting boat.

Tharanack parted from them at the end of the quay.

"I will take the navigator's judgement to Delavar," he said. "By morning it will be all over town. By noon, all over the world. Nothing will change. The humans still have to work things out for themselves."

"Of course," said Salasso. "But at least they will not face ignorant opposition."

"We may hope so," said Tharanack, and left.

Salasso waited until the peacekeeper had disappeared in the crowd, then struck a pose like one of those assumed by the saur dancers. After a moment he stood straight again, and looked away as though embarrassed.

"That was undignified," he said. "But still, it is good news. Better news than Tharanack imagines, but he will soon find out. He'll repeat the judgement word for word, and others of us who are not so concerned about the question of humans will hear a different message in the answer, a message about our past."

"What message?" asked Gregor.

Salasso's nictitating membranes flickered.

"That the gods were not angry with us in the deep past. They never were angry with us, but with others. This is very good news. I feel like climbing onto a roof and shouting it. I will tell it to everyone I meet."

"Don't," said Elizabeth. "Unless you want to end up nailed to a cross."

"Your pardon?"

"Thrown from a cliff," said Gregor, making a guess at the likely mode of saur martyrdom.

"Such a thing has not happened in many thousands of years."

Aha.

"But I'll consider what you say." Salasso dismissed the matter. "Meanwhile we have to decide what to do next. Have you found any of the old crew?"

They told him about Volkov.

The saur's eyes narrowed.

"So Marcus, and possibly others from the ship, are searching for them too. That is alarming."

"It is indeed," said Gregor. "How come the merchants know about the First Crew at all?"

"I told Bishlayan, back at Kyohvic, that some of them were alive. She knew that Athranal, our old teacher, would know where they were. So she took a skiff to Saur City One en route, and asked her."

"Did Athranal tell you this?"

"No," said Salasso. "Bishlayan told me tonight."

Gregor stared at the saur, then shrugged.

"They're probably just hoping to cut them some kind of deal. After all, the original crew must know how to navigate."

"Cut them a deal and cut us out?" said Elizabeth.

"Quite possibly," said Salasso. "I think they may also want them for something much more valuable—the knowledge of the long life."

"They may not have it," said Gregor. "They have the long life, all right, but that doesn't mean they know how to give it to anyone else."

"They don't need to know," said Salasso. "They carry the information in their bodies. And if there is one place in the human societies that could extract that information, it is in the academies of Nova Babylonia."

Gregor was getting impatient hanging around.

"I doubt it," he said. "Remember what Esias de Tenebre said? That our lab was more advanced than the academies of Nova Babylonia? Let's just go back to the Hot Squid and find Volkov."

"Yes," said Salasso, "and as quickly as possible. You said Volkov arranged to meet Marcus at nine tomorrow. We have to meet him first, or we'll be left out in the cold."

"Marcus could offer an inducement to the old crew that would be enough to make them cut us out?"

"Oh yes," said Salasso. "He could indeed."

But back at the Hot Squid, Volkov and his companions were nowhere to be found. By the time they'd checked all the other likely places along the front, it was well after midnight.

"Let us try to intercept him in the morning," said Salasso. "In the meantime, let us return to our lodging and go to bed."

Elizabeth and Gregor looked at him and at each other.

"What a good idea," said Gregor.

"Yes," said Salasso. "We all need some sleep."

"Yes," murmured Elizabeth, as they followed him out, "but not all of us will get any."

18

Social Engineering

I FLOATED ALONG a dim-lit corridor, propelling myself with occasional touches of my hands or feet against the sides. The green fronds of plants now and then brushed against me. In the spex I kept the view constantly shifting back and forth between the reality in front of me and a three-dimensional diagram of the layout lifted from the station library. The only sounds I could hear were the constant sigh of the air supply, and my own breathing.

Over the past two days I'd explored the station like a scuba diver sounding out an undersea cave system. I didn't make it obvious—whenever anyone met me, I was plausibly on my way somewhere, or plausibly lost. I was on call all the time, and often had to visit the fabs, in real or virtual space, to help sort out some discrepancy between the plan and the practicalities of construction. The rest of the time my work consisted of rehashing the procedure we'd gone through for the craft, this time for the second project: the engine.

In a way, the second project was easier. I'd already met most of the bugs in the project plan while working through the details for the craft; and the engine itself was a simpler construction, more straightforward and robust, less finicky, than even the stripped-down version of the craft currently taking shape in the fabs. It would require more actual material, including such exotica as black-hole atoms, but it might take less time to actually build. Consulting the interface had become easy and habitual, and that, too, clarified matters and speeded things up.

At the end of the corridor I heard voices. I caught a stanchion and let my bending arms take the strain of my sudden halt. Listening more closely, I could make out two voices speaking in Russian, too low to quite make out and too fast for me to follow. One of them sounded male, the other female. A tab to the station map showed a big storage depot off to the right; although pressurized, most of the handling required in it was robotic, and it didn't seem a likely place for people to be. Especially as one of the depot's features was that it was a big metal box—a Faraday cage, impervious to electromagnetic radiation, and hence to our spex' comms.

I kicked off again, aiming for the doorway. The door was, for good safety reasons, unlockable. I swung the lever to open it and gave what I thought was a convincing impression of blundering in, arms windmilling as I drifted across several cubic meters of empty air before snagging the upper edge of a lashed-down plastic crate with my foot.

Snugly braced by their feet and backs between rows of crates, side by side and face-to-face, were Aleksandra Chumakova and Grigory Volkov. They looked up at me guiltily, as if I'd caught them in some clandestine assignation, then instantly recovered their composure, covering their confusion with indulgent smiles as I covered my own with more newbie flailing-about.

Aleksandra I'd seen before, leading the opposition at the mass meeting and later speaking for her team at Driver's debriefings. I'd never seen Volkov, but I recognized him at once. His Slavic cheekbones and crew-cut fair hair had made him the most photogenic cosmonaut since Gagarin. The first—and last—man on Venus, who'd risked his life for the glory of a landing that was about nothing but glory; and, of course, a CPEU member, one of the Russian hard core, a CP loyalist and E.U. patriot.

"Hi there, Matt," he said, in English with a perfect Voice of America accent. "Are you lost, or have you come here for some peace and quiet?"

Chumakova was fanning a hand by her ear and shaking her head. "I know how it is; sometimes you can't hear yourself think back there."

I grabbed an edge and maneuvered myself into a better position, out of reach and a bit above them.

"Yeah, that's it," I said. "But as it happens I'm very glad I found you."

"Problem in the fab?" said Volkov, shading his spex, then clearing them. "Ah, I see your difficulty. We've been working offline."

My spex had gone offline as soon as I'd entered the room. The only way you *could* work inside this metal sheathing was offline.

"Ah, it's not that kind of problem," I said, making myself more comfortable. "I've been thinking about what you said at the meeting, Aleksandra. You remember, the Baku one?"

"*That* circus? I remember it very well."

"Well," I sighed, "you seem to have been right about some things. This so-called information campaign is costing scores of lives back home every day."

Chumakova nodded. "*Of course* people riot when every rumor comes across as a just-cracked state secret!"

"Yes," said Volkov gravely. "Even where the stories are true, they're very misleading when they're taken out of their proper context."

"Provocations," I said. "I've seen what they've done to my own city, Edinburgh. But apart from any, you know, personal concerns, what worries me is that the unrest will actually strengthen the militarists on our side, and the extremists on the American side."

Volkov was nodding and smiling. "Of course, of course," he said. "It's only to be expected that the excesses of the so-called 'left' play into the hands of the right, both in our Party and in the capitalist world. Don't get me wrong, Matt, I totally agreed with exposing the militarist plotters, but this anarchistic campaign is just the kind of excuse the real hard-liners need for a crackdown, and perhaps a foreign adventure . . . some confrontation that might be symbolic at first—the Siberian concessions, perhaps—but such things can get out of hand, and turn real, and ugly, real fast."

Chumakova gave me a sort of friendly frown. "But Matt," she said, "this is something of a sudden conversion for you, is it not? As I understand it, you are a member of an anarcho-syndicalist union yourself."

"Oh, I haven't changed my views," I said. "I know they're not the same as the Party's. You know how it is—in my line of work you get your nose rubbed constantly in the few areas where U.S. tech is still ahead of our own. It's impossible not to be a bit critical of official policy."

"That's very understandable," said Volkov. He took his spex off and smiled wryly. "We know how you must feel. A good worker appreciates good tools."

"Exactly," I said. "But, well, it's good to talk over a few worries with people who, you know . . ."

They both nodded and smiled at that. Like many Russians, they were unshakeably convinced that most sound, ordinary working people were basically loyal to the socialist brotherlands, even if some of them did vote for parties other than the Party or go to church or dye their eyes in funny colors.

But Chumakova persisted in her caution, still sounding me out. "You seem to have plenty to talk about with your Yank pilot," she said. "Of course, that is your affair, so to speak. And according to the newsfeeds, you had some kind of relationship with the American spy."

"Yes," I said, squirming a bit, "I feel very guilty about Jadey. Not because of Camila, she's . . . a friend, and you needn't worry about her, she doesn't have a political bone in her body."

"As I'm sure you would know," said Volkov.

We laughed.

"So why do you feel guilty," Volkov went on, "if you are not being moralistic about it?"

"It's . . . Well, I suppose it *is* moral, or maybe political. Jadey Ericson is in jail because of me. Not just because she was arrested while I got away—and you must remember, we had good reason to be afraid at that time—but because she's being held on trumped-up charges. There's already a warrant out for me—contempt of court because I didn't come in as a witness—and I can't help wondering if she isn't going to be used at some point to put pressure on me."

"To do what?"

I shrugged. "I don't know; that's what worries me. Anyway, I've been assured the Reform faction is doing what it can to get her out, so for the moment I can't afford to antagonize Paul."

"Lemieux is in the Reform faction?" Volkov asked.

"Oh, sure," I said. "I didn't know he kept that a secret. Shit. Don't let him know I told you!"

"No, no, of course not," said Volkov.

"Aha!" said Chumakova. "So *that's* why Driver's made such a big deal about that bastard Weber."

"Who?" I asked.

"The Trotskyite MEP, the one who was arrested—"

"Oh, yeah, right. I remember, but—I'm sorry, I don't see the connection."

"The Reform faction are a bunch of Trotskyites, basically—rights posing as lefts," said Volkov, with the confidence of a man confirming a long-held prejudice. "Look at how they renamed the station: *The Darker the Night the Brighter the Star*. After a book about Trotsky! Ridiculous."

"It does seem to have annoyed a lot of people," I said. "After all, Marshall Titov was a real Soviet space hero."

"First space-walk, yes," said Chumakova, with a sidelong glance at Volkov. "They can't take that away from us."

"No," I said. "They can't. And we can still do some great things here."

"We already are," said Chumakova. "First Contact, my God! And building an anti-gravity vehicle! What the Yanks would have given for that."

I pushed up and rolled over.

"Ah well, screw the politics, the project's still worth doing. I better be getting back to it before Driver gives me an earful. Catch you later."

"Yeah, see you soon," said Volkov, as I sailed to the door. Urgent messages blinked up as soon as my head passed the jamb.

"Where the fuck have you been?"

I clipped my belt to the webbing and resettled my spex.

"Ah, I just needed to get away for a while," I told Avakian. "Sometimes it just feels a bit crowded in the living-quarters."

"Yeah, I guess some people find that," he said, in a tolerant but uncomprehending tone. "You gotta watch it, man, maybe get some meds."

"No, I'll be fine now," I said. "Now I know there's places on the station where you can't be reached."

"Well, don't go to them without letting someone know," he said.

"Okay, okay, it was a bit irresponsible; I'll let you know in future. Now, where were we?"

"Have a look at this," said Avakian.

We patched in to a shared space.

"Oh wow," I said.

" 'Wow,' fuck indeed," said Avakian. "I've done it. Well, to be honest, we've done it, but I just realized that what I've just done had actually finished it, and I wanted you to be the first to see it."

It was the engine. Only in VR, of course, but it meant that the entire production process had been run through successfully in simulation. It gleamed on its smoothly integrated pedestal like an anvil from another dimension, or a mounted rocket-motor from some museum of the far future. I'd seen the sketches, the 3-D diagrams in the plan, but this was different: a hyperreal rendering of how it would look when built. It was about four meters long, less than a meter across at its widest diameter, and its maximum height was about two meters. I could reach out and touch it, and I did.

"Thanks, Armen," I said. "What a sight."

"Yeah," he said. "Fundamentally it's a weirder sight than the craft. See the four small holes in the corners of the base? I reckon what you're supposed to do with it is fucking *bolt it to the floor*. Just one little problem though."

"Control system?" I hazarded, thinking: *Not again!*

"As in, there ain't one."

"Wait a minute," I said. "There is on the plan."

I rummaged the pages up. "There, that plate—it's obviously a control system, it's covered with switches, even if we can't use it without—"

"Yeah, take a look at how that turned out."

He rotated the view and zoomed on a completely featureless blank rectangle on the pediment.

"Shit."

"For all we know," he went on, "that could be a goddamn name-plate, and what looked like switches in the plan could be just the equivalent of a company name engraved in brass."

"Okay," I said, "there's no reason the aliens would have given it to us like this. Maybe if we take the question to the interface, they'll come up with something we can use."

It took us the rest of that day to formulate the query. What it came up with was not an answer, but a picture and a set of coordinates on three axes, which pinpointed to the nearest centimeter a place within the interior of the asteroid.

"I reckon they're telling us to go and get the answer there," I said.

"You first," said Avakian.

"Oh hell," I said generously. "There must be somebody here who'd be a lot better than me at getting around in the big picture."

"I wasn't talking about that," said Avakian. "I meant you can be the first to tell Driver."

Driver was too tired to explode. He didn't even seem particularly annoyed.

"We never expected to actually test the big engine straightaway," he said. "It's the craft that's something we can hope to actually use. Even an unusable but unarguably real version of the engine would be enough to get people excited. I mean, don't get me wrong, it's great you've got this far, and you can see if you can sort out this control-system problem if you like, but don't let it delay the other stuff."

"Okay," I said, relieved and a bit disappointed.

"Tomorrow's the big day," he said. "We shift the little engine from the fabs to the receiving-bay, and then maneuver it into the *Blasphemous*. That'll require some EVA. Mikhail, how are your boys and girls?"

Telesnikov, physically present, gave him a thumbs-up.

"We're ready to go," he said. "In fact, we're quite keen on doing the whole shift as an EVA—take it out of the fab's door and lug it around to the *Blasphemous* directly, instead of maneuvering through the corridors. It'd be more straightforward, for one thing, and for another, we know the engine can handle vacuum—it's in vacuum already in the fab—but we don't know how it'll cope with exposure to biologicals."

"That's not a bad idea," said Driver.

Telesnikov grinned. "Yeah, it's so obvious I wish I'd thought of it myself."

"Who did think of it?" I asked.

"Grigory Volkov."

I swallowed hard.

"Uh, can we just discuss this further for a minute?"

Driver raised his eyebrows. "A minute."

"Okay," I said, "I know I'm not an expert on space-working, but I do know that machine we've built as well as anyone can without understanding it, and I'd swear it's totally robust against biological contamination. I mean, come on, every moving part is sealed. The control systems are our own kit, and we know how tough that is. Whereas, uh, no offense to your team, Mikhail, but the longer something's being handled in EVA the bigger the chance of an accident. One slip and we could send the thing spinning off into space and lose it for good."

Telesnikov waved a hand.

"It'll be in a mesh, tethered all the way," he said. "There's no question of its being unsafe."

"Ropes can break," I said.

"Not these ropes," said Telesnikov. He gave me a reassuring grin. "NASA spec. And we have the most experienced EVA operator in the Solar System—as far as we know!"

"Who?"

"Grigory, of course." His eyes widened suddenly. "Oh, I see! You may have heard that ESA just assigned him here for reasons of prestige, but that's the kind of envious rumors that spread around in the bureaucracy. No cosmonaut believes them. Grigory is far from just a pretty face."

"But—"

Driver raised his hand. "You've had your minute, Matt. We do it as EVA all the way. Next business."

Camila was shaking my shoulders.

"Matt! Wake up!"

"Wha'?"

"Your *bleep*'s going off. Can't you hear it? Everybody else bloody can!"

I woke and fumbled for my reader and spex. When I thumbed off the *bleep* it became obvious it wasn't the only one sounding in the vicinity. They fell silent one by one as I slid the spex on over eyes grainy with tear-salt.

"Patch me in?" said Camila.

"Yeah, sure." I opened a channel to her spex as the report floated up in front of me.

PERSONAL PRIORITY NEWS:

Opening shot of someone being bundled up the stairs of a United Airlines 777. Zoom and track: Two Scottish WPCs holding Jadey. She seemed to be struggling, but in a theatrical, pro forma way. At the top of the steps they let go of her and just pushed. She stumbled, caught the doorframe, and turned.

She raised an outstretched arm and extended index and middle fingers and a thumb, the current version of a defiant salute.

"Death to Communism!" she yelled, and backed into the aircraft.

SURFACE:

The American spy Jadey Ericson was released at midnight tonight and is now on a plane to the United States. The murder charge against her has been dropped in the light of new evidence, and she leaves a full confession exposing the anti-European, anti-socialist conspiracy in which she was a pawn.

DEPTH:

The subversive Human Rights Federation, financed in part by the military-industrial company Nevada Orbital Dynamics, which recently sent aid to the mutineer-held space station *Marshall Titov,* is linked to the fascist and nihilist gangs behind the violence of the past few days, and with the CIA agent and space mutineer Colin Driver. Driver's partner in the cabal that has temporarily seized the station, to the dismay of its honest scientists and cosmonauts, is Paul Lemieux, long identified with the so-called "Reform" grouping in the CPEU, who was a member of the Trotskyite LPR in his student days at Lausanne. Further CIA influence on factionalist elements in the CPEU and on the Trotskyite LPR have been clearly established by the investigations into the connections of the former MEP Henri Weber. The motivation of the current campaign of disinformation and claims of access to "alien spacecraft technology" appears to be to strengthen the self-styled "Reform" faction in the CPEU, which parades itself in the E.U. as a popular, democratic current and internationally as the only Communists ready and able to "do business with" the United States. The demagogic and contradictory nature of this "platform" should be obvious.

ANALYSIS:

At that point I switched off. Camila's arm was around my shoulders. "That's great news, Matt! Jadey's free! Wow!"

"Aye, thanks," I said. "It's brilliant, it's a big relief. But, shit, they're saying she confessed all that stuff. . . ."

"Ah, crap," said Camila. "Nobody'll believe that! Especially when they said she was a pawn. How could she possibly have known all that?"

"She couldn't," I said. "And as far as I know, she didn't."
"It's all commie paranoid gibberish anyway."

I took off my spex and rubbed my eyes and stared at her in the dim light of our alcove.

"It isn't," I said. "Modulo the comical prose of the Party press release, it's exactly what Driver and Lemieux told us the other night."

"It *is*?"

"We get used to doing translations."

I grabbed her and hugged her, for no other reason than comfort.

"You don't seem very happy."

"I'm happy," I said. "God, I'm so relieved I could cry. But we're still in a very dangerous game."

"Yeah, you said it." She stroked my back. "Go back to sleep. Jadey should be home by morning. I'll wake you up when the news comes in."

I slid the spex back on and flexed my fingers in their infrared feedback.

"No need," I said. "This thing will."

Before I could take them off and go back to sleep, an incoming message flashed. I accepted it and Grigory Volkov's handsome features filled my view, like a poster on a teenager's bedroom wall.

"I think congratulations are in order, Matt," he said, smiling. It was a canny sentence; nobody listening in could have guessed that he was asking, rather than offering.

"Yes," I said. "Congratulations all around. Thanks, Grigory."

By the time the reader woke me with news of Jadey's debarkation—at McCarran Airport, Las Vegas, much to my relief—Camila had gone. She was due in the receiving-bay under the *Blasphemous* from the beginning of the day shift. Slightly miffed that she hadn't even said goodbye, let alone roused me with her usual morning cuddle, I washed and dressed and made for the refectory. Over breakfast (salted rabbit meat and fried-egg sandwich—not recommended) I scanned the news with the thought at the back of my mind that I'd got very used to Camila's morning cuddle. But it was Jadey who was at the front of my mind. As soon as she'd got out of E.U. airspace she'd put out a statement repudiating the confession, denying she'd made it, and ridiculing its contents as summarized.

Most comments I tracked seemed to agree with her there, but disagreed over whether it was a complete fabrication or whether it was based on some encrypted information the FSB (or some random hacker) had managed to crack, and were releasing in this way so as not to compromise their real sources. To add to the tortuous confusion of the whole labyrinthine affair, the smartest analysts—whether on *Europa Pravda* or the *Daily Web*—were pointing out that the FSB itself undoubtedly favored the Reform grouping, and that the CIA usually kept well clear of backing violent opposition in the Socialist Democracies, being far more likely to try to exert its influence on the FSB . . . which, of course, itself . . .

I switched off. The world has become one big grassy knoll, crawling with lone gunmen who think they're the Warren Commission. My own take on the matter was that my heavy hint to Grigory the previous day had led him to believe that Jadey was being held as a bargaining-chip by the Reform faction, and that releasing her would help his cause— that of the straight-down-the-middle centrist faction, conservative but not outright reactionary like the militarist hard-liners. We would see.

I routed a phone message for Jadey through the station's mailbox. She wasn't online, but it went through to Nevada all right. After a good jolt of coffee, and with my breakfast settling in for a protracted stay in my stomach, I headed for the fabs.

The fabrication units occupied a separate wing of the station. This was my first visit to them outside of VR; for which, after slogging through a dozen airlocks and blast doors and decontamination bays, I was quite grateful.

The control room was crowded with at least twenty people, apart from the five operators, who were mercifully able to ignore it all in their spex and full-body rigs. Most of the people here were familiar to me only as names that had popped up in my workspace, or called me into theirs, with a construction problem. Driver and Lemieux were at the front, Chumakova beside them. Avakian hovered at the back. I jostled in and managed to find a position with a clear view ahead.

The fabrication unit itself lay beyond a thick partition of diamond-laminated glass. The multiple, multiply-subdivided robotic arms of the fabricators—the closest anyone had got to a Moravec bush robot—bristled and sparkled. In the tips of their toughest fingers they held the engine and control system of the craft.

Despite all my familiarity with it in VR, there was something of a thrill in seeing it in reality, with actual photons that had just reflected off it entering my own eyes. I greedily absorbed the sight, which in truth was nothing more than a smooth metal bulge with a flat base, attached by three meters of electric cabling to a block of polystyrene cladding which I knew contained an instrument panel and a racked array of levers.

The outer door of the fab was already sliding up, to reveal a ten-by five-meter rectangle of black. This frame was quickly filled by two cosmonauts in EVA suits, deploying a barely visible net around the doorway. Cables trailed behind them. The movements of ropes and net in vacuum and microgravity were different enough from the familiar to give me a sense of unease.

Or to provide a focus for the unease which I already felt. I tuned my spex to the comms channel and listened in to the cosmonauts and the control-room crew. They were speaking Russian and neither my own language skills nor those of the spex were able to make much of it.

The mechanical fingers flicked, and the thing sailed out to be caught in the net. The net was closed at the mouth with a simple drawstring, and was hauled off to the right, out of view.

I patched to an outside camera, and watched the mesh bag and its contents being lashed to a basic sled, the free-fall equivalent of a forklift truck. It consisted of several cubic meters of crate with a fuel tank underneath. At each end, fore and aft, were mounted four jets, a set of controls, and a step for the pilot to stand on, with the jet nozzles safely behind. The bag was now free, except from the sled. The sled, with the kind of belt-and-braces caution alluded to by Telesnikov, was itself teth-ered. A long, loose cable with one end fixed at the fab and the other just beneath the half-kilometer-distant *Blasphemous Geometries* passed through two sturdy metal half-rings projecting from the sled's side. Five cosmonauts, the tubes of personal rocket-packs curving from their shoul-ders like the outlines of cherubic wings, were spaced out along the sled's path.

The sled's pilot fired up the jets briefly and the tug moved forward in a straight line at a low speed. It had passed two of the cosmonauts and was halfway to its destination when something went wrong.

The rope snagged and stopped playing through the loops. The abruptly-halted sled swung around and at the same moment its forward jets began to flare, far more intensely than the rear jets had done. It shot backward and away from the asteroid's surface, stretching the rope in-stantly to a flattened V. As I racked the view into close-up it became evident that the rope had stuck not just along the side but around the front of the crate. As suddenly as it had stuck, the rope broke at both sides of the sled, which soared away at an angle, jets firing for a few more seconds. By the time they stopped, the sled was beyond even the swiftly tracking camera's zoom.

Everybody in the room was either yelling or shocked into silence. The cosmonauts' comms channel remained calm. Discipline was holding. I heard the tug-pilot's voice in crackly, halting Russian:

"The sled's fuel is exhausted and the sled is tumbling."

Volkov said, "We have you on the radar. Jump clear, stabilize with your own rockets, kill as much outward velocity as you can, and we'll pick you up."

"*Nyet.*"

"For the love of God, Andrea! Abandon it now!"

The reply came through, still crackly, in English.

"This isn't Andrea, this is Camila, and I'm not going to abandon it."

I yelled out at that, a completely futile howl because I was unable to transmit to the comms channel. Even its discipline seemed to be breaking up, in a sudden babble. Through the camera I could see cosmonauts jetting about, toward or away from each other.

Camila's voice broke through again, fainter.

"Stand by," she said. "I'm bringing it in."

I tabbed frantically between camera viewpoints until I found one directed outward. In the starfield a point glowed like a blue nova, slowly brightening and becoming fuzzy. Within seconds it was in full view, hurtling straight toward us. The camera back-zoomed and stabilized and I could see the sled and its pilot within the blue nimbus.

She brought it right up to the door and then to a dead halt. In her hands was the engine's control panel. Chunks of shattered polystyrene swirled around her as though in atmosphere, a sight as flagrantly impossible as her spectacularly non-Newtonian arrival. She waved, and skittered the sled off to the side, to bring it to another abrupt stop beside her own ship.

"EVA transfer complete," she said. "Unscheduled flight-test complete. Engine and controls nominal."

By this time the arrests, too, were complete.

Lemieux squatted in his habitual upper corner, practicing a new and irritating and dangerous stunt: He'd place his Aerospatiale 9-millimeter in the air, and then tap the end of the barrel sharply down, making the weapon spin in front of him, and letting it drift away a little. Then he'd grab it from orbit. Over and over again. He seemed to pay attention to nothing else. Short of trimming his fingernails with a combat knife and whistling through his teeth, he couldn't have come up with a less subtle display of instability and menace.

Driver, meanwhile, was hamming the soft-cop role, complete with occasional worried glances at Lemieux. He reclined behind his desk, in front of which Chumakova and Volkov looked as though they were standing to attention, their arms looped through the webbing. They weren't tied; it was all very civilized, apart from Lemieux's routine.

I hung off to one side of them, jammed against some shelving; Camila floated by the door. Almost everybody else on the station, including the forty-seven in detention at various improvised places, was watching the show on their spex.

"Come on, comrades," Driver said. "If this was a goddamn NASA accident inquiry, I could maybe believe that what happened was an overdesigned safety system going wrong. Some chemical deterioration in the cable that made it sticky and easily broken, an unpredictable sloshing of fuel in the tug's engine, a burnout. These things happen, right?"

Volkov shrugged. "So we are told. Sometimes it's a mistake to rely on U.S. tech and NASA procedures instead of our own skill."

"Yes," said Driver. "But it was your idea, wasn't it?"

"There was nothing wrong with the idea," said Volkov. "If you are suggesting sabotage, it is ridiculous. I thought it was Andrea Barsova on that sled. I wouldn't risk a cosmonaut's life. You know that, Colin."

"But you weren't risking anyone's life," said Driver. "Barsova is an experienced sled operator, and you would have expected her to jet clear at the first sign of trouble."

"This is all speculation," said Chumakova.

"It isn't," said Driver. "We know you're in touch with elements in the Party and government. After Matt spoke to you, you relayed the conversation to a contact in Brussels. Someone quite high up in the administration. Within hours, Jadey Ericson was released and a fake confession was in circulation, calling me a CIA agent and so forth. I don't think that was a coincidence, and I don't think the people you immediately contacted within the station just happened to be colleagues."

"How do you know—?" Volkov stopped, and glared at me.

"All right," he said. "So Matt told you, and then you followed every contact we made afterward. What of it? It's not a crime."

"Some of your people have talked, and they admit it was more than talk," said Driver.

Volkov laughed. "You won't catch me with that one."

"Maybe not," Driver allowed. "But we'll catch you with the recordings."

Chumakova made a convulsive movement. Lemieux stopped spinning his pistol, and cocked it. Driver gave him an anxious look.

"Easy, easy, Paul," he said. "Aleksandra, you were saying?"

"Nothing that we did was a crime! We value our work, and we will not let you hand it over to the Americans! You're a spy and a filthy traitor, Colin Driver, and when order is restored you'll be shot."

"I'll take my chances on that," Driver said. "Now, I'll ask you to step outside and accompany the detail to the brig."

Volkov shot me another look of disgust, then shrugged and nodded.

"Very well," he said. "It's an honor. We won't have much time to enjoy it."

"What do you mean by that?" said Lemieux.

"Look at the news, everyone," said Chumakova, over her shoulder. "Order is being restored."

19

The First Navigator

ELIZABETH, STRADDLED ACROSS his hips, leaned forward, hair swinging, cheek catching the dim light, and teased his nipples with her fingertips. "What are you laughing at?"

He reached up, returning the favor. The breasts so soft and smooth, the nipples so hard and rough, and so much bigger than his two tiny tips. He wondered, in a kind of detached way, whether her pleasure at this manipulation was greater in a similar multiple. If it was, he envied her.

"I'm laughing at me," he said. "I've been a fool."

Her hair made a broad brush-stroke down his chest.

"That you have, Cairns, but not as big a fool as me."

His hand was in her hair, another marvel. He wished his response could be as inexhaustible as the stimuli, so many of them, so much jungle and ocean, mountain and hillock, the long white beach of her back, the whole unending planet of her body, the blazing dark sky of her mind. A world that he had explored for hours, and which had explored him right back.

"I don't know if that's going to work, this time," he said.

Her tongue did something shockingly clever with his foreskin, by way of reply; an experiment that refuted his null hypothesis. She was a biologist, and she knew her subject well.

Third block, Quay 4, Ferman and Sons. At eight in the morning the quay was a vile place, the wind off the sea carrying the stench from the killing-cliffs and the closer, chemical reeks from worn refrigeration and harsh disinfectants on the factory ships. Bone-chips underfoot and a slippery mixture of mineral and animal oils. Haulage vehicles creaked and rumbled on the cobbles. Among the dockers and sailors the saur and the two humans were inconspicuous. They found a waterfront cafe opposite the office building's entrance, and lurked around a table by the steamy window. Elizabeth and Gregor munched their way through smoked-fish sandwiches; Salasso picked at strips of brackie beef. Gregor kept lookout, wiping the window every so often with his sleeve.

"Lipids colloidally suspended in water droplets formed around smoke particles," he said. "You could write a whole thesis on this place without even starting on the biology."

"Have another coffee," said Salasso. "Your brain is undergoing early consequences of sleep deprivation."

Gregor yawned and nodded, smiling at Elizabeth as Salasso raised three fingers to the waitress. The cafe was full of manual workers having a late breakfast and office workers or business owners having an early one. Most of them were human, apart from a gigant docker and a couple of saurs.

"This man Volkov," said Salasso after the waitress had brought the refills. "You got the impression he knew Matt Cairns?"

"Oh, definitely. He was with a man who mistook me for Matt, from the back, anyway."

"So we know your ancestor has hair similar to yours, and perhaps a similar stance and build," said Salasso. "That may be helpful, but I wish you had spoken more to that man."

"To tell you the truth," said Gregor, "I was so shaken by meeting Volkov that the other man seemed less important. And I was being cautious, because we know *they* are cautious. Didn't want to ply him with questions."

"Even so—"

"Look," said Elizabeth, grinning across the table at them both, "the fact is I distracted Gregor from his research. Don't be too hard on him."

"I'm pleased for you both," said Salasso, "but this liaison has happened at an awkward time. And now you are both suffering from sleep deprivation."

Gregor didn't take his attention away from the blurred view through the window. The memory of his night with Elizabeth seemed imprinted on every part of his skin, and all her curves and angles remembered in his hands.

"I wouldn't call it 'suffering,'" he said. "And while we're on the subject of awkward times, you yourself were . . ."

"There is that," said Salasso. "But the consequences of my personal entanglement were *fortunate*."

To Gregor this sounded uncharacteristically defensive. Whatever emotions were involved in Salasso's evidently centuries-long affair could only be intense. He decided not to press the matter.

"Anyway, about Volkov," he said. "He wasn't at all eager to let Marcus know who he was, so I don't think he'll be selling any secrets to the merchants."

"Then why's he coming here?" said Elizabeth.

"Assuming he is. . . . He didn't say right out that he would. Maybe he does just want to set up some deal involving marine-engine lubricants."

"There is more going on than that," said Salasso. "I am irrationally certain of it."

Gregor laid his cheek against the damp glass, not sensually—the greasy feel was quite unwelcome—but to see farther up toward the street end of the quay. The clock on the cafe wall showed half past eight.

"That's one of the things I like about your people," he said idly. "Humans don't call their certainties 'irrational,' especially when they are."

"Rationality is a worthy aspiration," said Salasso. "For your species."

Gregor was still chuckling when he recognized a man walking slowly along, a bit farther up on the other side of the quay, pausing occasionally to peer at doorways and signs.

"Don't all jump," he said, "but I've just spotted Matt Cairns. Wait here."

He stood up and was out the door before anyone could object, and barely remembered to look both ways before crossing the road.

The man stood on the pavement by the third block's doorway, looking at the names of businesses listed beside their bell-switches. He was just raising a tentative finger toward them when he noticed Gregor's approach, and turned.

Gregor stared at him, transfixed. The only thing about him that looked old was his jacket, its dinosaur hide worn so soft it hung like cloth. Despite what he knew, he'd subconsciously expected his ancestor to look ancient, the image of the young man in the castle portrait gravitating toward the lined features of James. Even seeing Volkov hadn't dislodged the assumption. This man's face looked younger than the one Gregor had blearily seen in the shaving-mirror a couple of hours earlier. It betrayed no recognition or surprise.

"Can I help you?" the man said.

Gregor blurted the first question on his mind. "Did Volkov send you here?"

"Volkov? Shit!"

The man immediately turned away and walked off, up the quay toward the street. Gregor hurried to catch him up.

"Excuse me," he said. "My name's Gregor Cairns—"

"I know your name," said the man. "And I'll thank you not to say mine."

Gregor almost missed his stride. "What?"

"Shut up and keep walking and we might just get out of this trap."

They'd reached the junction of the quay and the street before the man relaxed a little. He stood with his back to the corner of Block 1, where he could watch all three of the possible approaches.

"Okay," he said. "What's this about?"

"I was going to ask you—"

"All right. Last night I heard about your inquiries, and the merchant's." His gaze kept shifting as he spoke, with unsettling effect. "And I heard the merchants would have someone at Ferman's about nine. I didn't know Volkov was behind me hearing it. Somebody's going to get a good kicking for that little omission."

"Volkov—"

"Fucking hates my guts. Not like he'd stick a knife in them, but anything he sets me up for is unlikely to be much fun." He met Gregor's gaze full-on for the first time. "What are you after?"

"We were hoping you had some old tech from the ship."

"What for?"

"Navigation."

The response was a rude laugh.

"What's so funny?" Gregor was finding the man's manner as annoying as his shifting gaze, and was beginning to glance around uneasily himself. The street was unfamiliar in the daylight, the traffic light, the pavements cluttered with the flapping canopies and bare tables and detritus of the market winding down. The quay was loud with the squeal of metal and the hiss of rubber on cobbles.

"I'll do the watching," the man said. "You look at me, and tell me what you see."

"I see Matt C—"

"Like I said. Shut the fuck *up* with that name. The second one. Yes, I'm Matt. Matt Spencer. Side branch of the family. Interesting resemblance, isn't it?"

"You mean you're *not*—"

"Yes, of course I'm the goddamn navigator. That's worth far more to the merchants than anything to so with navigation. They have navigation. They don't have this."

"Ah," said Gregor. "That's what Salasso said."

"Your saur pal figured it out, did he. Good for him. If I know Volkov, he thought the same, and made fucking sure that if anyone turned up for the meeting with the merchant, it wouldn't be him."

"Would meeting the merchants be all that dangerous?"

Matt's gaze fixed on him again.

"Would you like to find out?"

Gregor walked back down the quay in a dino-hide jacket from whose pockets an interesting collection of weapons had been removed. Imagining that extra kilogram's weight on his shoulders helped him get Matt's walk and stance more or less right. He resisted the temptation to glance across at the cafe.

The sheet-metal door of the block stood open, to a concrete passageway ending in a spiral stair. Beyond the stairwell another door stood open to a narrow lip of quay. He checked the faded labels pasted beside the doorbell buttons:

Ferman & Sons, 3rd Flr. Marine Engnrs.

He bounded up the three flights of stairs and arrived a little dizzy. A big door with the firm's name on a brass plate stood slightly ajar. It swung back on a gentle push. Across a couple of meters of stained carpet was a heavy wooden desk. The female pithkie behind it looked up and smiled.

"Good morning," she said. She glanced down at an open diary. "Are you expected?"

Gregor's head lowered and his shoulders hunched involuntarily as he stepped into the office, a warehouse conversion, open-plan, partioned at head height. Keyboards clattered and conversations hummed. Narrow floor-to-ceiling windows overlooked the harbor. Nobody waited at either side of the door.

257

Still looking around, he stopped in front of the desk.

"Good morning," he said. "I'm not expected, but I'm here to meet Grigory, uh, *Antonov*."

"Engineer Antonov should be along in a moment," the receptionist said. She picked up a pen. "And your name?"

"Cairns."

She noted the name, then rippled her long-fingered, long-nailed hand to indicate a leather sofa to his left.

"Please, take a seat."

"Thank you."

He sat on the edge, fists in empty pockets, and then willed himself to sprawl, if not relax. After a minute Volkov strolled in. He was walking past when he must have noticed Gregor out of the corner of his eye, and turned around sharply. The edges of his hands came up like knives in front of him; his knees crooked. Then he straightened and backed off. Gregor had jumped up to meet the expected attack, for all the good that would have done.

Volkov laughed and stepped forward, hand extended. Gregor shook it gingerly.

"Good morning," said Volkov. "My apologies—for a moment I mistook you for our friend Matt." He looked pointedly at the jacket. "I see you've met him."

"Yes," said Gregor. "And if you hadn't been mistaken?"

Volkov shrugged and smiled. "He might have tried to attack me. He's a bit paranoid, as you'll have noticed."

"Uh-huh," said Gregor, in as neutral a tone as he could manage.

"I suppose he expected the people from the ship to shanghai him or something, and that I'd somehow set him up for it." Volkov shook his head. "And why did you come here in the first place, before you ran into Matt?"

Gregor looked around.

"Uh, can we talk privately?"

"Of course," said Volkov. "This way."

Behind the maze of partitions was a corner office on a raised concrete dais with two glass walls. From its convenient supervisory vantage Gregor could see about a dozen people within the partitioned spaces, working at drawing-boards or keyboards or calculating-machines. Volkov spun a well-worn castor chair over to Gregor and sat behind the desk.

"When are you expecting the merchants?" Gregor asked.

"Any minute now, so make it quick."

"I'm here because we're after the old computing-tech for navigation, as I mentioned, and quite frankly we think the merchants are after the same thing. We're also concerned that the merchants just might find it very tempting to take one of you with them and, uh, extract the life-extension tech from you one way or another. For that they might make you an offer you couldn't refuse."

"And Matt thought I'd set him up for that? Well, well." Volkov shook his head again. "As for your other concern, I doubt if anyone has any functioning tech from the ship. I certainly don't."

He stood up and stepped to the glass wall. "If I had it, I would use it—secretly, of course—to get an edge on my competitors, instead of paying people to crank out calculations on the clunking monsters down there."

"This firm is yours?"

"No, no. I have this office, various contracts with the staff—I do most of my work at sea. I'm genuinely interested in what the de Tenebres have to offer. Speak of the devil, here they are."

He left, to return a minute later with Marcus de Tenebre and one of his crewmen. Marcus gave Gregor a raised eyebrow, and Gregor moved to leave.

Volkov raised his hand. "Gregor, I'd like you to stay. This is not confidential. I want you to report on this meeting to Matt, and to your colleagues, and to the Families." He shrugged. "And the news-sheets and the radio if you like."

Marcus took the chair Gregor had vacated, Volkov sat back down at the desk, and Gregor followed the crewman's lead and slouched against the wall.

"Gentlemen," said Volkov, "am I right in thinking that you aren't here to sell fine-grade lubricants?"

Marcus nodded.

"Good. So let's not waste time. I gather you intend to leave shortly. I would like to leave with you. In return for my passage, and obviously for some hospitality and initial assistance in Nova Babylonia, I offer you my full cooperation in rediscovering the medical procedures which have enabled me to live as long as I have."

Marcus's face remained impassive. The crewman simply gaped.

"That's a generous offer," said Marcus. "It seems almost too generous. You offer us the long life, in exchange for your passage? a house? some help in finding a *job*?"

"I ask more than that," said Volkov. "I ask for a guarantee of my freedom." He waved a hand. "I'm not afraid of being of being cut up in a laboratory—I've met enough Nova Terrans and emigrants over the years to know that I have nothing like that to fear. But I don't wish to be tied to your family, or to your ship, though of course you will get the first benefits of any success we may have. And I offer less, by the way—I have no guarantee that the research will be successful."

"That's reasonable," Marcus said. "How do you expect to hold us to this?"

Volkov slid a piece of paper across the desk. "I have a contract. Naturally, it's not explicit as to the nature of the knowledge, but it's watertight enough. I know it's in your interests to honor contracts, because for you repeat business depends on a *very* long-term good reputation. Copies have been lodged with my solicitors, and young Gregor here can witness it and take one too."

Marcus scanned the document and nodded.

"I'll sign," he said.

Volkov signed, Gregor witnessed. Then they all signed the copies.

"You have no one you wish to take with you?" the crewman asked.

Volkov's lips compressed. "No," he said. "The long life can be a lonely business."

"And your practice here?" Marcus glanced around the busy office, evidently impressed.

"I'm happy to leave it." Volkov stood up. "Are we ready, gentlemen?"

"In a moment," said Marcus. He rose, propped himself on the edge of the desk, and turned to Gregor. "You are skilled in the life sciences, perhaps more than our philosophers. You could help us in the research. In Nova Babylonia, you could become a great scientist, a man of renown. I know of your conversation with my uncle. I can assure you that he would regard this both as a proper use of your gifts, and a gift worthy of his daughter."

Gregor didn't doubt a word of it. He could imagine it all, clear and vivid, glowing and glorious. He shook his head.

"What I want is here."

Marcus extended an open hand.

"Your friend Elizabeth can come too, if she wishes. Or if you prefer to depart without good-byes—our skiff is on the quay out the back."

"No," said Gregor. He felt slightly dizzy. "No, thank you."

He picked up the document, and paused a moment until his mouth was no longer dry.

"Perhaps it would be best if I leave before you, gentlemen. Give Lydia my love, all the same. If I see her again, it'll be in one of our own ships."

Marcus nodded, Volkov smiled skeptically, the crewman stood aside.

It seemed a long walk through the office. As he came around the partition into the reception area, he saw Elizabeth and Salasso sitting on the sofa. Elizabeth jumped up.

"Everything all right?"

"Everything's fine," he said.

"We were keeping an eye on you," said Salasso. "Matt told us it was a bad idea, but we disagreed."

Gregor clapped them both on the shoulders. "Thanks. It wasn't necessary, but thanks. Where's Matt?"

"Still in the cafe, I hope."

"Good," said Gregor. "I have some questions for him."

"Well, that's it," said Matt. "Nothing to be done about it now."

They had left the cafe and walked to the end of the quay, and had conducted most of their conversation sitting around on bollards, out of earshot of anyone. The ship was about to lift. Their hair prickled. Odd currents of wind whirled scraps of news-sheet and fishwrap into small vortices.

"Nothing to be done about what?" Elizabeth sounded edgy.

Matt gestured at the ship, rising above a bulge of water. The last of its skiffs scooted to the long slits in its side.

"Volkov," he said. "You've done Nova Terra no favors, letting him go. Nor your friends the merchants, for that matter. Nor us, in the long run."

"He seemed a reasonable-enough man to me," said Gregor.

"Of course he fucking did! When you've lived as long as I have, you'll know that anyone can seem reasonable if they want to."

Yes, but why would anyone want to seem like a paranoid git? Gregor felt like asking.

"You," said Salasso, "do not seem very reasonable. Is that because you don't want to?"

"Maybe I will when I've lived as long as you," said Matt. "Or maybe not. Us monkeys don't get any better from living longer. We learn nothing and forget nothing. We get worse. My way of getting worse is a lot better than Grigory Volkov's, believe you me."

The ship floated upward, like the airship it so blatantly wasn't. High in the sky it began to move forward, on a horizontal line that would soon take it out of the atmosphere, and which much sooner took it out of sight.

"Gone to Croatan," said Salasso. "I know the course."

"What do you mean, you're better than Volkov?" said Gregor, in a sudden gale of disappointment and rage at his ancestor. "Volkov's a successful businessman. You're a bum."

"Volkov's been a bum in his time," said Matt. "And I've been rich. *C'est la* fucking *vie.*"

He stood up, still staring after the ship. "The point is, Volkov could be a successful politician. What a man who doesn't age could do to the politics of Nova Babylonia is a bit worrying. Still. What's done is done."

He turned around. "Now, what can I do for you?"

"For a start," said Elizabeth, "you can tell us whether you do in fact have any of the old tech."

"Yeah," said Matt. He dug into a deep pocket and pulled out an aluminum case that Gregor had seen already among the knives, pistols, and key-rings. "Come and have a look."

They gathered around the bollard he was sitting on.

He opened the case and passed a pair of wraparound sunglasses to Gregor.

"Go on, try them."

Gregor's hand shook a little as he opened them. The earpieces had tiny speaker-grilles at their curved ends, and still-bright copper and optical connections at their hinges. He slid the glasses on. When he looked at the sea it sparkled with tiny, perfect reflections of the sun.

"Wow," he said. "They really cut down the glare."

"Exactly," said Matt. He held out his hand for them. "That's all they do. Anyone else want a go?"

"What happened to them?"

Matt shrugged as he folded them away.

"Accumulated errors, radiation damage, general fouling-up of the directories . . . in short, everything that didn't happen to me."

He stood up. "Look, we didn't know," he said, sounding defensive. "We didn't know how well the fucking treatments worked. They hadn't been running long enough, I mean, sure, the biotech companies made big boasts, but they always do. The telomere tabs were one-shot things, right, most people got them in their early twenties. Fix and forget. We didn't have them on the ship, and we didn't have the spec for them. It's not like we kept something back from you."

His face was bleak.

"It's all right," said Elizabeth. "We'll get there ourselves."

Matt grinned at her. "That's the spirit. Speaking of getting there ourselves, when can I see this navigation solution of yours?"

They walked up the quay, back to the city.

It was a small window, and the light came through it in a narrow beam. They followed its hot yellow pool around the floor, shifting position unconsciously as Gregor talked Matt through the calculations that summarized the Great Work. Elizabeth and Salasso filled in details of the model of the squid nervous system.

A last sheet of paper lay on the floor: the bottom of the stack. Gregor slashed a pencil line below the last line of figures, and rocked back on his heels.

"That's it," he said.

He stood up. His knees hurt a little. Matt rose more quickly, and walked to the window. The sun, low and orange, threw his dark shadow back.

"Well," said Elizabeth, "what do you think? Have we cracked it?"

"I don't know."

"What?" Gregor heard his voice crack. Salasso silently handed him a chill bottle of beer—the local stuff; tasted of chemicals. He gulped gratefully.

"You must know," Gregor said. "You're the first navigator. You navigated the ship across ten thousand fucking light-years. You set the problem. You must know if we've solved it."

Matt stepped away from the window and sat down on the bed. It was still rumpled, as Gregor and Elizabeth had left it. The One Star Hotel, aptly named, didn't do room service. He reached for his jacket and fished out a pouch and some papers.

"Thank the gods you people had this," he said. "I never could have stood it otherwise. I'd have gone bugfuck crazy."

His hands shook a little as he wrapped the leaves.

"Knowing that the baby in your arms will get old and die before you. Knowing that your grandchildren will die before you. We made a choice, see. We were scientists, on the whole we were civilized people.

We didn't want to become gods, or kings. So we had to disappear, and keep on disappearing, generation after generation, decade after decade. Some of us took ship to other suns. The rest of us . . . well. Enough self-pity. Let's just say, it's been tough, and the dope and the drink help, and they don't even kill us, like they should."

He inhaled deeply. Gregor resisted the impulse to clout him, and accepted the joint. The soothing smoke dissolved his rage.

"All right," he said, after Elizabeth and Salasso had partaken. "You've got all of us mellow, Matt Cairns. Now tell us why you don't know."

"I'm an artist, not a technician," said Matt. "I'm a mathematician, a systems manager, a programmer. I've followed every step of your reasoning, and I have to say it strikes me as sound. I set up the problem for my descendants to solve, yes. I'm good at that. I think you've solved it, but I don't know for sure, because . . ."

He looked down, then up. "I'm not the first navigator."

"So who *was* the first navigator?"

"There was no first navigator," said Matt. "But there is now. You are the first navigator."

20

Blasphemous Geometries

CHUMAKOVA WAS RIGHT. Order was indeed being restored back in the European Union. While we were dealing with Volkov's abortive conspiracy, a rather better-planned coup was being launched in Brussels and the regional capitals. Oskar Jilek, a Major-General in the European Peoples' Army, popped up on screens, goggles, and desktops to announce the formation of an Emergency Committee and the honorable resignation of General Secretary Gennady Yefrimovich. Firm action would be taken against rioters, provocateurs, military-adventurist elements, revisionism, dogmatism, and corruption within the Party and state apparatus, and agents of imperialism within the state security organs. Urgent negotiations would be opened with the United States over *genuinely* collaborative access to recent advances in space exploration.

Rather cleverly, the Emergency Committee rescinded all "administrative measures" against members of elected bodies. Weber and other MEPs and councillors who'd been arrested were immediately released. This eliminated one democratic grievance and instantly clogged up the elected bodies with Party-initiated procedures to get rid of them through proper channels. It also distracted attention from a swift roundup of less well connected citizens, mostly for offenses that had long been winked at. Import controls and safety regulations shut down hardware and software bazaars like Waverley Market within hours. Corrupt officials who'd lined their pockets by allowing black-market racketeers to endanger the livelihoods and lives of E.U. citizens were exposed and arrested with a great show of shock and indignation.

"They'll be overthrown in a few days," said Camila. "It's 1991 all over again, you'll see."

"Not this August," I said.

One more news item was given a lot of play: a ship was being readied at Baikonur to rescue the scientists and cosmonauts of the *Marshall Titov* from the small rebel cabal currently holding them hostage.

Shots of boosters lifting heavy equipment and a large number of personnel to orbital rendezvous with a large craft. It had to be large because it held a complement of about a hundred.

Two were ESA cosmonauts. The rest were EPAF Special Forces: space marines.

I looked up from my plate to see Driver moving crabwise behind the long table. He squeezed in opposite us with a plate of tonight's sticky rice-and-meat concoction and a liter plastic bottle of red. It was the first time I'd seen him in the refectory; now that I came to think of it, the first time I'd seen him outside his office.

He pressed the plate to the table and passed the wine across.

"Help yourselves," he said.

We ate for a while, pausing occasionally for a squirt of wine. Driver drank rather more than we did.

"You're looking very relaxed," said Camila.

"Oh, I am," said Driver. "The anti-gravity actually works! Weight off my mind, know what I mean?"

We laughed politely.

"Nah, it's actually getting Volkov's little conspiracy lanced that did the trick," he said. "Christ, it does get tedious knowing people are plotting against you, and not knowing when they're going to make their move. Tomorrow I'm going to shove all the responsibility for running this station onto whatever committee the scientists see fit to elect. Let somebody else take the strain for a while."

"You'll still be managing the projects?" I said.

He shrugged. "If they still want me to."

"I hope so," I said.

Camila was looking from one to the other of us.

"I don't *believe* you guys," she said. "There's just been a goddamn *military coup* in your own country, and you're carrying on like something good has happened."

Driver crushed his plate and glowed up a smokeless.

"It's not good," he said. "But it's not as bad as it looks. It's still the Party that's in power, not the Army, and not the FSB, thank God. And it's the Party centrists, not some ideological dingbats."

"Huh!" she said. "That commie gibberish that Jilek came out with sounded ideological enough to me."

Driver and I both laughed.

"That ain't ideology," said Driver.

"Well, what is?"

"Do you believe," he said, "that human beings are endowed by their Creator, or by their nature, with certain inalienable rights?"

"Sure I do!"

"Why?"

"It's, well, like the man said, it's self-evident. You get it, or you just don't get it."

"Fine," said Driver. "Now, *that's* ideology. What the Major-General appealed to in his serious little talk is *vocabulary*. It's just a structure of ideas and symbols and organizations that helped the Russkis get their act together a generation ago, and helped the Europeans to unite shortly after. What our people really believe in isn't microwaved Brezhnevism but the Party's *real* ideology, which is something a good deal more insidious."

"And what's that?"

He shrugged. "Protectionism, I reckon. Anyway, fuck it. The coup's a bit of a relief. It's like we're not waiting for the other shoe to drop anymore."

"It's you that's gonna drop," said Camila, "when they come out here."

Driver shook his head, narrowing his eyes as though against imaginary smoke.

"Nah," he said. "We don't do hanging. Nor shooting, not even for spies and traitors, despite what Aleksandra said. Nor your horrible Yank electric frying." He made a chopping motion. "Guillotine. Quick and humane—at least, nobody's ever complained afterward."

I folded my plate over the remains of my dinner and took a quick squirt of wine. Asteroid 2048. Rough, definitely not a good vintage.

"Do you really think—"

"Let's not kid ourselves," Driver said. "You guys should be all right. Camila, you're an American just doing your job, they can't touch you. Matt, well, maybe if they throw the book at you, but I don't think so. Emigration isn't a crime, even if you did it illegally. As for the rest of the crew—"

He sat back, and at that moment I realized that everyone else in the refectory had stopped talking and started listening. No doubt this was all going out on more than one set of spex. Driver pretended not to notice.

"Most of the scientists should be all right, they can claim they didn't have much choice. At worst they'll be taken off the station and given other work. Even my good mate Paul—well, hey, they don't want to hand a martyr to the Reform faction. Five years, tops, in a temperate climate." He grinned and winked at me. "I hear the Highland lumber camps aren't too bad, apart from the midges. I've seen guys who'd sweated out a tenner up there, no bother. Paul has the connections. I don't."

"Is that because you're English?" Camila asked.

"Yeah. My parents were English lefties. We were on holiday in the south of France that summer the Russians rolled over the Yanks in the Urals and just kept on coming. Didn't see any reason to go back to London. I got a good education and I've done all right in the FSB, but, you know how it goes. If there was ever anybody who'd make a perfect candidate for the chop, it's me."

He stood up and stretched. "Still, it's been a good run. No complaints. See you tomorrow—we'll skip the debriefing tonight and have a general meeting in the morning. Make sure the teams know, okay?"

He was off before either of us could say a word.

Not much work got done that evening. People hung in the station's intranet, talking or watching the news. The Emergency Committee was making frantic efforts to mend bridges: with its own populations, with China and India, and with the United States. They made hostile gestures at Japan. As Avakian pointed out, it was safe enough to annoy a country about which nobody gave a shit.

I was following the arguments in a fairly desultory way when a call from Nevada blinked up.

"Well, hi there, Matt," said Jadey. She smiled, bright across the light-seconds. I felt a surge of joy; and a pang of guilt, which I had not expected.

I propped my reader where its camera could see me and replied.

"Hi," I said. "It's great to see you! Are you all right? You're looking well."

After forty-odd seconds' delay her answer came back.

"Yeah, I'm fine. It's great to see you too, Matt! They treated me all right, apart from that pack of lies they put in my mouth—I'm still

mad about that. Thanks for your messages, though, they did get through
and they were a big help. You know, this is more like instant messages
than phoning? Like, it's *not* instant? So I'll just keep talking and then
let you come back, otherwise we'll be talking across each other all the
time. You're not looking too hot yourself, Matt."

"Ah, I'm all right, just knackered. We've been busy. You heard we
got the flying saucer to fly?"

I watched her waiting.

"Uh-huh. Camila Hernandez has been in touch with Alan. But look,
Matt, you're not getting this, you have to talk for longer than that,
otherwise we spend half the time waiting. So give me your news, and
what you make of this commie coup and so on. And while you're thinking about that, I can tell you things are getting a bit hot over here too—
all kinds of legal hassles. The Feds are accusing us of stealing the alien
tech from the commies without authorization, *and* of giving it to the
commies. It's like they got us coming and going."

When she stopped I was still thinking over the implications of Camila's having been in touch with her home base. Not that there was anything wrong with it, but she hadn't told me about it; not that she had
to, but . . .

"I've been missing you," I said. "I think it might have been me
who got you out."

I recounted my social engineering with Volkov, and what he had
been up to.

"And," I continued, "your so-called confession was a fake, sure, but
basically I think it was more or less true. Your Feds—the CIA or whatever—and some factions in the E.U. have been using us, and they must
have some plan to wrap it all up."

"Yeah, yeah." She nodded impatiently. "They all dream the same
dream—a stable society with themselves on top. Statist shits! Full marks
to you guys for splashing the code-cracking math all over the Net, but
they're already talking about ways around that: keep secrets on paper
or in people's heads, use trusted messengers instead of electronics. I
can tell you, the nukes are now invulnerable to cracking, they moved
real fast on that one, which is a good thing, I guess. But they're gonna
try to keep the alien tech in safe hands—theirs! Think about that, Matt.
Uh, I've gotta go, this is one of the few secure channels we've got left,
and there's a queue. But keep sending the voicemail, and I'll reply when
I can. And thanks for getting me out. Try and get yourself back in one
piece, okay? Just for me?"

"I'll do that," I promised. "And you look after yourself. Watch out for the black helicopters."

"You're tense," said Camila. She was massaging my shoulders, her thighs gripping my hips.

"Yeah." I laughed. "I've been talking to Jadey."

"Jeez, is *that* what it's about? Hey, come on. This isn't hurting her, and it's helping you. And me, I have to say, nothing's changed. So give the conscience a rest, okay?"

"It's not just that," I said. We rolled around and I began returning the favor. "It's all the stuff that's coming up. Not that I ever expected the information campaign to change the world, but I expected it to do something better than make the governments even more paranoid than before. And—God, this sounds so childish—I didn't ever expect us to get in trouble for what we've been doing."

"Ah," she said. "Don't let that bother you. This is endgame, sure, but we ain't beaten yet, not by a long way. And come on, Matt, today I near enough flew a goddamn flying saucer! *Nothing's* gonna make me feel down after that!" She shifted her shoulders under my hands and sighed. "Just you keep doing that for a while longer, and see if I can't make you feel a lot better real soon."

The amphitheater at Ephesus—not a bad place for a meeting. This time Avakian had resisted the urge to fiddle with the dials. The scan was recent: ruins, scrub, litter, and lizards. Everyone appeared in their own avatars, a small crowd in a space built for a large one. Aside from that, and the site's subliminal implications of elite democracy, the virtual venue seemed neutral enough.

"It's like a football game," Camila said, sitting down beside me and gesturing at the people taking their places on the worn tiers.

"No, that would be in a *stadium*."

She punched me, her avatar's fist swiping through my avatar's chest. "I won't do that again," she said. "Makes me queasy."

"Me too," I said. I shut my eyes. It was something like travel-sickness.

When I looked up again I focused on the stage down at the front, where Driver had taken his position. When he looked up, he held out one hand, palm uplifted like a classical orator. I couldn't guess whether the imitation was deliberate.

"Okay, comrades," he said. "We all know why we're here." He

looked around. "Okay, some of us aren't here. I've given the, uh, comrades in detention the opportunity of taking part. None of them have.

"Right—we can assume the marines are on their way. Those shots yesterday of the ships being prepped wouldn't have been released before launch. Trouble is, we don't know when they actually were launched, but we have a minimum of eight days, a maximum of thirteen. We have to decide now what we're going to do, because we have quite a wide range of options, starting with unconditional surrender and working up from there.

"Up until now, you've all had the option of claiming that you did what I told you, and you obeyed me for whatever reason—coercion, or the belief that I had some constitutional authority, or for want of any alternative. That option ends here. As of now, I'm stepping down from provisional command of this station. What you decide to do about the, ah, rescue mission, and what to do about me, is entirely up to you."

He then literally stepped down, to take a seat a few rows up from the stage. For a moment everyone looked at each other, uncertain what to do next. I glanced over at Avakian, hunched over his virtual keyboard. He shrugged and shook his head. It wasn't like Driver to leave something like this to chance; I was certain he'd have sounded out someone else to step in at this point. Lemieux, also sitting near the front, stood up without taking the stage.

"For different reasons, I take the same position as Colin."

Out of the uneasy silence that followed, the scientist Louis Sembat jumped up and bounded to the speaker's dais.

"For the moment, unless there is any objection, I will chair this meeting."

No objection.

"Very well." He pointed. "Angel, you wish to speak?"

Pestaña stood up, turning around as he addressed the crowd rather than the chair, though he maintained the formalities.

"Colin must know," he said, "that his comments last night were widely discussed. Nobody, other than some of those in detention, is going to let him take all the responsibility. We are certainly not going to see him executed, or Paul imprisoned. Above all—let us be quite frank about this—we are not going to have our work taken away from us."

"You might be given the choice," said Driver, from his seat. "Let them have me and anyone else tagged as a ringleader, and keep your work."

Pestaña shook his head. "It wouldn't be politically possible to condemn you for inciting us to do something that we would still be permitted to do. Also, you have done nothing that we have not done. Replacing us would be difficult. I say there is room for serious negotiation."

The mathematician Ramona Gracia spoke next.

"I would not be too sure of that," she said. "They could retain our colleagues who are not present, and these could train a new influx of scientists. Some work would be lost, but it might be considered worth it for a reliable crew."

Jon Letonmyaki, a Finnish cosmonaut: "Perhaps I could ask what it is we—or indeed Colin or Paul—have done that is illegal? We are acknowledged to have prevented a very dangerous move by the militarists. We have released some information to the public domain, but the General Secretary—the former General Secretary—had already called for international collaboration. Colin resigned from the FSB and, I presume, from the Party in a rather demonstrative manner, but that is not a crime! So what have we done?"

Driver raised his hand. "May I?"

Sembat nodded.

"Okay," said Driver, clambering to his feet. "Let me tell you what I've done, and what you've done. I deliberately transmitted the news about the alien contact and the crypto-war plans to the Americans. That was conscious and deliberate treason, which I took care to conceal from my friend Paul Lemieux. He's only up for trying to exploit it politically. As for the rest of you, you've all collaborated in releasing mathematical tools that have made most existing forms of encryption useless, and destabilized most of the governments of the world. That may not get you jailed, but you can bet it'll get you off this kind of work—or any potentially security-sensitive work—for the rest of your goddamn lives. If the E.U. authorities regain control of this station, your careers are over."

There was no rush to speak next. Most people here, I guessed, had figured this out already, but at some level they'd still clung to the kind of hopes so naively expressed by Letonmyaki—and, less naively, by Angel Pestaña. A lot of them seemed to acquire a sudden interest in the realistic rendering of crushed Coke cans and hardened chewing-gum on the steps, or the haze and cypresses in the middle distance.

Telesnikov, whose card I'd long since marked as Driver's man within the cosmonaut cadre, stood up and strode to the front.

"Enough of this!" he said. "We are not helpless, we do not have to sit and wait for the marines. We can elect a committee to represent us in negotiation with ESA and if possible this new EC. We can appeal to the world public, preferably along the lines that Jon Letonmyaki suggested: do our best to sound innocent and reasonable. And while we are doing that, we can prepare for the worst.

"We have the most advanced aerospace vehicle in the world, just awaiting completion. We know that it works, and we have only the beginnings of an idea of its capabilities. Avakian has told me he believes it can reach Earth in a matter of hours. There is much we can do with a machine like that!

"We also have the space-drive, which we can construct in perhaps ten days. It is just possible that we can complete it before the marines arrive. And if we do . . ."

He paused, and looked around, daring us.

". . . we can use it, and when they arrive we will be somewhere else!"

This time, so many people wanted to speak that Avakian could barely fend the rush.

The Bengali astrophysicist Roxanne Khan had the strongest objection, after most of the obvious what-ifs had been argued into the ground. If the thing didn't work, we were no worse off. It was unlikely to blow up, or otherwise destroy us, unless the alien intelligences had some very warped motives indeed; and if they did, we were safer dead than at the mercy of murderous or suicidal gods.

"The problem, as I see it, is one of navigation," Khan said. "Mikhail speaks of making a small, controlled, jump of a few light-minutes—a proof of concept which would indeed be quite sufficient to give us the whip hand in negotiation. But we already know that the information we are given is sometimes ambiguous, difficult to interpret. What if we make a mistake? Let us leave to one side morbid thoughts of ending our jump inside a sun. What if we find ourselves halfway across the galaxy? Or halfway across the universe?"

Telesnikov had an answer for that. I suspected he'd been thinking about this for some time.

"There are about three hundred of us, about equally divided between the sexes. That is not a bad number to begin a colony."

"Using what?" somebody shouted, through a clamor of more ribald comments. "Cometary resources?"

273

"Mine the gods," said Avakian, as though under his breath, but so that everyone heard, and most laughed.

"Not all the small bodies in the Solar System are . . . inhabited," Telesnikov went on, unperturbed. "We have no reason to think this is exceptional. So in principle, yes. We could."

That didn't exactly end the discussion, but somehow it took the edge off it. From what I picked up afterward, most of us were glad to have something to do other than wait to be arrested, and the knowledge that if negotiations failed we had an outside chance of escape.

There was also the strangely comforting consideration that at worst we might die, but we would not *die out*.

"I'm ready," I said.

My breath was loud in the helmet. Ten meters away from the face-plate, in a direction I refused to think of as "down," was the surface of the asteroid—the nightside, at the moment, its clinkery detail faintly visible in the dim light from my suit. In every other direction were the stars, sharper than frost. I couldn't think of them as a destination. The Copernican hypothesis seemed absurd. These scattered points of light could not be suns.

"Turn the light off," Armen said.

In front of me now, nothing but black.

"Pull very gently on the ropes, and stop when you see it."

The paired ropes, one for each hand, were stretched between two tall masts a hundred meters apart. I'd moved along them about forty-five meters, sliding the clip of my tether under one hand. I tugged myself farther, peering into the black. Beneath me—in front of me—I saw the alien apparatus. It glowed just enough to be visible. It looked like a bush, or a bush robot, just big enough to fall into.

"Now," said Armen, "just pull the ropes toward you and let go, and let yourself drift into it. Don't worry about missing it, you won't, and remember you're still attached to the ropes. Turn the radio off."

I did, then tugged as gently as possible, and let go, and sank forward between the ropes. In the seconds it took to traverse those few meters, the apparatus looked ever more crystalline and fragile, as though I were about to crash very slowly into a snowflake chandelier.

When Avakian had shown us what he called "the big picture" of the asteroid's interior, I'd assumed we were seeing a direct view of it, of something that was relayed to us in a vastly diminished, user-friendly form through the interface. Actually, what we'd seen was recordings from previous encounters such as the one I was about to have. The interface aside, there was no ongoing direct view of the interior. The interface was fed by a fiber-optic cable as thick as my arm extending from the bush down the side of the asteroid to the station, but for the real live action we had to use this other interface, constructed—or grown—by the aliens themselves. For what reasons, the gods only knew; and for once that flip phrase was a literal truth.

The apparatus didn't shatter as I collided with it. Some of its branches moved and parted, others gathered, to mesh at their tips into shapes like huge petals. It absorbed my momentum and held me. One of the flat shapes covered my faceplate. For a second of complete darkness I felt, quite irrationally, as though that covering would suffocate me. Then I found I could still see the coordinate readouts on the faceplate, printed on the upper left corner in faint red digits. That display, and an input jack on the helmet, and the orientation controls under my splayed fingers, were the only interactions with the apparatus which the aliens had deigned to allow.

There was a small increase of light, or perhaps my eyes adapted. I saw obsidian walls passing on either side, then faster and faster the viewpoint rushed me down endless branching corridors, each one slightly wider than the last. The red numbers on the readout flickered. It occurred to me that I might be seeing the branches of the crystal bush, from inside. The sensation of movement was inescapable. I closed my eyes, and found that I still saw the black corridors down which I helplessly hurtled. By means I could only guess at, this scene was being played directly on my retinae. Only the readout vanished from my sight. When I opened my eyes I saw it again, the numbers a red blur.

Down one final straight, smooth shaft I went, and was sent flying out of it into the asteroid's interior space. Beauty flooded my brain. If closing my eyes could have stopped me seeing it, I would have grudged a blink.

This time I didn't have the chill splash of Avakian's laughter to save me. It took all my mental strength to turn my attention to the three long numbers of the coordinate display, and to press my fingers against the apparatus to take control of my virtual flight. And once I had, the temptation to use it to play, to swoop and soar, was almost irresistible, but not quite. I moved until the numbers matched the coordinates we'd been given, and found my viewpoint hovering inches above an intricate, floral, fractal pattern like a bank of moss.

My viewpoint was being provided by an icy chip wafted by molecular gusts, transmitting information back to the apparatus and thence to the input jack. So it was supposed. My face plunged into that minute and perfect garden, and some plant in front of me was ripped out by the roots. The sense of damage done filled my eyes with tears as fast as the structure repaired itself. I blinked, and the view vanished. The apparatus pushed me away with as much force as my arrival had delivered to it. As I drifted backward, it was all I could to grab the ropes.

"That's it," said Avakian. "Do you want to have a look?"

I shook my head. "Just tell me."

"I'll show you," he said, waving from his spex to a screen stuck to the wall, and tapping his thumb.

In the hours since returning from my encounter I'd been unwilling, and possibly unable, to go into VR. Even the interface, on recollection, struck me as unbearably clunky. Avakian had assured me the effect would wear off: "It's like a drug—burns up your endorphins, or something. You'll bounce back."

With a dull pretense of interest I watched as a diagram and sheets of data appeared on the flat screen. High-res, but to my jaded eyes it was crude, as if I could see the pixels. The engine was displayed, subtly changed. I couldn't see the difference at first. Avakian threw a laser bead on the screen.

"There," he said. "A control system, and it looks like a human-oriented interface. The data columns underneath are *settings*. We're in business, man. All we have to do now is build it."

All I could think of was the tedium of churning through the project plan yet again, tweaking it bit by bit to bring this changed result.

"Good," I said. "I'll get on with it."

"You will not," said Avakian. "We may be going to the stars, but *you* are going to sleep."

"Will that help?" The notion sounded vaguely intriguing, but irrelevant.

"Trust me," he said. "I'm a doctor."

"Did I wake you?"

Camila had climbed out of her overall.

"Yeah," I said, "you must have bumped into me. What's the time?"

"Midnight," she said.

"So I missed the meeting."

She hooked a foot through webbing and pulled me to her, wrapping her arms around me.

"You didn't miss much," she said. "The new committee's still getting the cold shoulder from ESA, not to mention the junta. The good news is, we've got the *Blasphemous* fitted out. I take it for the first proper test flight tomorrow."

"Hey, wow! That's great!"

She caught my shoulders; her own shook with restrained laughter.

"Matt, wake up properly! That was routine, we knew we were going to make it. Everybody was talking about what you did."

"What I did . . . Oh!"

The memory of what I'd done came back, but it was like the memory of a dream remembered not on waking, but later in the morning, already breaking up into elusive, colorful fragments. At the same time I felt a surge of well-being. My endorphins, or whatever, were onstream again.

"The data you got back, what Armen calls the settings, Roxanne and Mikhail have checked them over and they definitely are for a short jump, just like you asked for. And you went right in among the aliens to get it!"

"Yes, I did that. I can hardly believe it now. And, oh hell—"

I laid my forehead on her shoulder for a moment.

"What is it?"

I swallowed. "I can see why they were so keen to volunteer me to do it. If you've done it once . . . you'd never want to do it again."

A shiver shook her warm body. She pushed back and looked into my eyes.

"Is it *that* horrible?"

"No! No, it's beautiful. It's the most beautiful thing I've ever seen."

"More beautiful than me?"

"Yes," I said, without hesitation. "It just ravishes the mind, like a packet storm overloading a buffer."

"My, what an evocative vocabulary you've got."

I had to laugh.

"But I'm forgetting it," I said. "And I want to forget it. The beauty I'm seeing now is a lot more real."

"Now you're talking," she said.

Some synergy of Camila's excitement at flying the *Blasphemous Geometries* with its new engine at last, and my endorphin overshoot, and perhaps my last shreds of memory of that garden of intelligent machines, filled us with energy and invention and affection, and kept us awake most of the night.

I didn't feel at all sleepy in the morning; indeed I felt immensely refreshed. I followed Camila to the receiving-bay where we'd first arrived, so few days and such a long time ago.

A small crew of cosmonaut techs was waiting for her. Roxanne Khan was nominally in charge as chair of the recently elected committee. Colin Driver hung about in a purely advisory capacity.

Camila dragged her g-suit from a mesh crate.

"Is that necessary?" Driver asked.

"Maybe not," said Camila, sliding into it with a neat somersault. "But just in case."

Helmet under her arm like an astronaut posing for a pre-launch photograph, she drifted toward me and parked the glass bubble in midair before giving me an unexpectedly firm hug.

"Wish me luck," she whispered.

"You'll be fine," I told her. "You're the best. Good luck."

"You too," she said, and turned away like a fish. She vanished through the hatch. Her routine checks and messages began to come through on the comm, until they were complete.

"All systems nominal."

Driver glanced over at a tech by the wall. "Shut the airlock," he advised. "Okay, everybody out of the bay."

"Why?" asked Kahn. "It's safe enough."

"We don't know that." He scratched his throat, making noises in the mike. "There might be some, uh, electromagnetic phenomena."

"What makes you think that?" I asked.

If he hadn't been standing in the air at an angle to me I could've sworn he shuffled and looked down.

"If, well, what one hears about close encounters with these kind of machines is anything to go by."

Oh.

We all went out of the bay and patched to the surface cameras. The ship was outwardly unchanged, its aspect as improbable as ever. The sounds of disengagement clicked and banged through the walls and floor.

"Ship is clear to go."

"Firing secondary jets," said Camila.

A two-second burn took the ship clear, another stabilized its position a kilometer out from the asteroid.

"Engaging AG."

No blue nimbus was visible this time, nor any change in the ship.

"Okay," came Camila's cheerful voice. "That's it powered up in neutral. I'm going to ease it forward."

The ship moved. One moment it was there, the next it had stopped dead a kilometer away. Even those of us who'd seen the performance of the sled could hardly believe it. Roxanne Khan, who hadn't seen it, actually covered her eyes for a second. She saw me looking, and her briefly paler cheeks reddened.

"Rest in peace, Sir Isaac," she said under her breath. Then, in a clear voice:

"Cosmonaut Hernandez, take it away."

"Thank you, ma'am," said Camila. "Engaging forward motion."

The *Blasphemous Geometries* went away.

An instant replay of the view in the cameras, then of that on the radar, showed only the briefest dwindling glimpses before it vanished from both.

Driver let out a long breath.

"Like a bat out of hell," he said.

He turned to the technicians.

"Can we raise her?"

"Sure."

He nodded at Kahn.

Very formally, she said: "Space station *The Darker the Night the Brighter the Star* calling *Blasphemous Geometries*. Report, please."

No reply. Kahn repeated the call.

After another second, Camila's voice came back.

"*Blasphemous Geometries* to *Bright Star*. Craft operation is nominal, systems are nominal."

"Very good," said Roxanne. "Disengage forward motion, reverse direction, and return to station."

"*Blasphemous* to *Bright Star*, uh, that's a negative."

"Is there a problem?" Roxanne asked.

This time the delay was about two seconds. It suddenly dawned on me that the craft was already a light-second away: three hundred thousand kilometers.

"No problem," said Camila. "I'm returning to base—Groom Lake, Area 51."

. . .

Sometimes it's only when an assumption is destroyed that we realize what it was, or that we'd made it all. I had assumed that if Camila were to go home she'd take me with her. I'd also assumed that because I was in love with Jadey, I couldn't be in love with Camila.

I alternated between rage at Camila and hope that she would come back. That was a dream. Camila and Jadey were both—very definitely and for the foreseeable future—in the real Dreamland. A voicemail message from Jadey came in a few minutes after Camila landed there.

"Uh, Matt, there's something I've got to tell you. The disk I gave you wasn't the one I got from Josif. *That* disk had the information Driver leaked to one of our agents in the ESA apparat, about the alien contact and the alien math and what it meant for crypto. I zapped it across to Nevada from my office at work that morning. I didn't know what was on it, natch, but I doubt it was even encrypted. No point, right? And the FSB must've read it, which started the whole ball rolling, bounced the E.U. into making the announcement. The data on the disk I gave you is on sites all over the Net, and has been for over a year. I downloaded it from one of them.

"We think the aliens spammed the space-drive info to widely dispersed sites without the knowledge of anyone on the station. It was in the form that the ESA systems on the station defaulted to for production specs. Nevada Orbital Dynamics has people who do web searches for flying-saucer stuff. This is because the company has turned up a few, uh, anomalies in the records. You know what I mean. Enough to make this sort of thing worth at least keeping half an eye on. Most of it's total crap, of course. They found the data in all that clutter and checked it out and it looked interesting, but they didn't have the necessary skills to deal with the ESA conventions and to actually run the systems analysis and production-planning because, as you know, these actually require hairy, kludged combinations of U.S. and E.U. tech.

"However, they knew a man who did—you, via me. And we always knew you could be counted on, politically. They hung back, though, until the thing could be authenticated. I'd already taken a download, lightly encrypted—I didn't know what it was. When I sent them Driver's message confirming the alien contact, they replied with a prearranged phrase which meant I should take the flying-saucer datadisk to you, and once you were convinced, to get you to America. The data wasn't important—*you* were important. If it hadn't been for Josif getting killed, which was sheer bad luck, and the crackdown, I'd have gone with you. As it was, my arrest at least served as a distraction.

"Because it was you we needed, and it was you the cops should have gone after. The data was out there all along."

I hung in the webbing for a while, on the side of a busy corridor, watching people pass like fish, their mouths working almost silently as they talked in the other, invisible web. I took out my hand reader, pulled down the completed production plans, and routed them through the station's transmitter to as many nodes as possible.

It wasn't really necessary, but it gave me some small satisfaction.

I wasn't the only one who'd made false assumptions. The entire ship watched agog as recriminations flew around the science committee.

"None of us imagined that Hernandez would take the craft to Earth," said Roxanne. "Because we *assumed* that our security expert had good reason to trust Hernandez, or he'd never have allowed her to make the test!"

"Oh, I trusted Camila, all right," Driver said. "I absolutely took it for granted that she'd be off at the first opportunity. Like a bat out of hell."

"So why did you allow it?"

"Because that's what I wanted."

After the noise had died down, Lemieux said:

"Colin, my friend, please tell us, now there is nothing more to lose or gain—are you, after all, an American agent?"

"No," said Driver. "Hand on heart, mate, I'm not. I'm not now, nor have I ever been."

"So what *are* you?"

"I'm an Englishman," said Driver.

The CNN bulletins showing shaky amateur video from Groom Lake had barely faded when Major-General Oskar Jilek appeared on an E.U.-wide broadcast.

"A grave situation has arisen with regard to the rebel-held space station *Marshall Titov*. The scientific knowledge obtained by its historic achievements, which by rights should have been used for the benefit of all humanity, have been usurped by foreign agents and unilaterally applied to endanger the peace. The Emergency Committee of the European Union regrets to announce that its patience with the rebels is exhausted.

Their escalating provocations and insolent demands have crossed a threshold. From this moment, the European Union is in a state of war with them. Their actions equally endanger the United States, and we urge upon that nation's government a course of action appropriate to the gravity of the situation.

"We have nothing to negotiate with the rebels. Any further communications to ESA, by anybody on the station other than Major Sukhanov, will be regarded as another hostile act. Major Sukhanov and his fellow hostages must be unconditionally released, and full authority over the station returned to Major Sukhanov within one hour. Otherwise, the Special Forces of the European Peoples' Aerospace Force will respond with all necessary force and without further warning."

Driver, too, didn't waste time. He ignored the scientists' committee. His face and voice filled the ship.

"Jilek is bluffing," he said. "We now know when the expedition left Earth orbit. An astronomer in Kazakhstan caught the picture, and some hacker in Sydney has just zapped it through to us. The burn was seven days ago. We have five days to build the engine and disengage the station from the asteroid. And then, people, *let's jump.*"

21

The Darker the Night the Brighter the Star

S HE NEVER CAME back?"
Elizabeth's voice sounds sad.

The hour is late, even for New Lisbon. The pithkie and the gigant at the bar are almost asleep, but they pride themselves on outlasting their customers. The pub is empty except for them, us, and few saurs, and who gives a fuck what they overhear?

I've told them my story, in a long wander that has taken us from the One Star Hotel through a succession of bars. We've eaten, at some point. I've kept the parts of the story I don't want humans to hear for our swift staggers through the streets, or the dives of the sister species.

"Of course she fucking never came back," I say. She flinches slightly, and I soften it. "She contacted me. We talked. She loved me, I think, but there was no way she could fly off in the gods-damned hell-spawned *Blasphemous Geometries*. The U.S. Air Force was all over it like flies on a shit."

"You still haven't told us," says Gregor, "what went wrong with the navigation. Did you miscalculate, or what?"

I stare at him. Sometimes I wonder, I really do. The myth of our navigation has served us well, but it must have served the locals too. It must fulfill some deeply-felt needs, to survive so long in the face of its brazen unlikelihood, to say nothing of its falsehood.

"We didn't navigate anywhere," I tell them. "The data I recovered might have been authentic, for all I know, but maybe only a kraken— or your artificial squid—could have made sense of it. Or it might have been complete garbage, intentionally or not. Whatever. I suspect the engine had a preset instruction to go here. All I know is that we set up what we thought was a jump across the Solar System, and we found

THE ENGINES OF LIGHT

ourselves in polar orbit around Mingulay. We'd just figured out that it was definitely not Earth and definitely not the Solar System, when Tharovar's skiff turned up. A skiff—that wasn't the scary bit, we kind of expected that. The scary bit was when he dropped out of the airlock."

I fix on Salasso what I hope is a hard stare, but which is probably just a bleary look.

"You people have a lot of explaining to do."

The saur spreads his long hands. "I can't help you there. None of us knows anything of what any saurs in the Solar System may have done in historical times."

I wonder how much you would know if I stuck a probe up your arse.

I hope I didn't say that.

"I wonder," says Elizabeth, "if the computers on the ship still work."

"They probably do," I say. "Radiation-shielded, you know? All the equipment to reboot them. Hell, I could do it now. Except that Tharovar and his mates took us off the ship in a great hurry, and made a big fuss of us, and never, never let us back."

"That should not be a problem," says Salasso, "now that we know you can navigate. We never believed you had found Mingulay on your own, though we never contradicted you. We believed the gods had sent you here, and wanted you to stay here. Perhaps they did. They have some purpose in setting up this Second Sphere, but neither we nor the krakens know what it is. However, now that the krakens have given their judgement, there is no reason to stop you."

Gregor grabs the saur's arm.

"You mean we could try out the navigation on the *Bright Star*?"

"Yes."

He grins at Elizabeth, and even in my drunk and stoned state I can see that she, perhaps, does not entirely share his delight.

He turns to me.

"What's it like?"

"Come on out," I say.

We haul ourselves up and, arms around each other's shoulders, sway into the street. I lead them away from the streetlights, into a square where no lights burn. We look up at the Foamy Wake, at the blazing god, and we wait awhile, until we see the shuttling spark cross the sky from north to south, the *Bright Star*.

"You go there," I say.

• • •

You make your way through the ship's long corridors, with nothing in your hands but numbers. Your shipmates, your colleagues, your comrades clap your back and congratulate and encourage you, with an anxiety in their eyes that you hope you are not showing, yourself.

You approach the engine, diving down to its base, and you hope that what you are doing is entering the numbers in its alien mind. You confirm that everyone is ready.

You press what you hope is the right switch, and you—

jump, becoming light.

dark light

To Andrew and Lesley

ACKNOWLEDGMENTS

Thanks to Carol, Sharon, and Michael, for more than usual.

Thanks to Farah Mendlesohn for reading and commenting on the draft and for historical information about Rawliston (any mistakes are mine); to Catherine Crockett for details about the sky people; to Rachael Lininger for help with the folk song; and to Mic Cheetham and Tim Holman for holding out for an ending.

Don't fear that philosophy's an impious way
—superstition's more likely to lead folk astray.

—Lucretius, *De rerum natura*, Book One
   paraphrased by Joanna Taine

Contents

I

Urbi et Orbi

R AWLISTON SPRAWLS; from space it's a grubby smudge, staining the
glassy clarity of the atmosphere along fifty kilometers of coastline.
Biggest city on the planet, home to a million or so human and other
beings. Seven centuries old and ever renewed; two centuries on from
the biggest jolt it ever got; hours away from another. It's coming like
an earthquake, coming like a runaway train, coming like a lightspeed
ship.

Stone froze in a cold sky. Around him, the glider's struts creaked and
its cables sang. Hundreds of meters below his feet, the valley crawled.
The Great Vale stretched fifty or so kilometers before him and the same
distance behind him, its fields and towns, rivers and screes filling his
sight. Through the imperfect glass disks of his goggles he couldn't quite
see the mighty rockfalls at either end that had, thousands of years ago,
isolated the valley, but he could just make out the distant gleam of the
lake formed by Big River against the natural dam at the eastern end.
The midmorning sun glimmered on a series of meanders in the river's
fat, lazy length along the valley's broad floor. *The word for world is
"valley,"* he thought, *and the word we use for ourselves is the "flying
people," and the word the savages use for themselves is "people." Oh,
but aren't we a sophisticated and self-conscious Stone Age civilization!*
He hung in a leather harness; the handles he gripped were made
from the paired humeri of an eagle; the fabric of the wing above him
was of hand-woven silk doped with alcohol-thinned pine resin; the
craft's singing structural members were tensed bamboo, its cables vine
and its stitching gut. Flint blades and bone needles and wooden shuttles
had been worn smooth in its manufacture; no metal tool had touched it.

No man, either; the whole process, from harvesting the raw materials through building it to this, its test flight, was women's work. It would be bad luck for a man to touch it until it had been brought safely back from its maiden flight and formally turned over. Stone wryly reflected on the canny custom that assigned the rougher and riskier parts of glider production—finding the eagle's carcass, tapping the resin, testing the craft—to women like him. He enjoyed the excitement and the solitude of these tasks, though they would not have been so welcome without the background of days he spent in the secure and companionable society of other women, working in long, airy sheds with the needle or the loom, the glass saw or the stone knife.

He banked into an updraught and followed its upward spiral, almost to a level with the mountain range on the western side of the valley. Below him, a pair of wing-lizards skimmed the corries. Two black flecks, their wingspans almost a third that of the glider. He kept a cautious eye on the upper slopes as he drifted past them; sneaking across the skyline was the preferred approach route for savage scouts and even raiding parties, and firearms were one product of the metalworking peoples whose use none of the stoneworking peoples—including his own—dared to disdain.

From his high vantage he could see the other aerial traffic of the valley: a few hot-air balloon-trains lofting to cross the eastern barrier on the way to Rawliston, dozens of other gliders patrolling the slopes or carrying urgent messages and light freight from one town to another. A quick upward turn of his head caught him a glimpse of a high, fast glint as one of the snake people's gravity skiffs, on some incomprehensibly urgent mission of its own, flashed across the sky like a shooting star. The skiffs were a common sight, starships rarer. Every few weeks a ship would follow the line of the Great Vale in a slow, sloping descent to Rawliston; it'd be at an altitude of two kilometers when it passed above the western end of the valley, down to a thousand meters by the time it reached the other.

Swinging out of the updraught, he set the machine on the long descending westward glide that would take him back to the launching-and-landing slope of the airfield above his native town, Long Bridge. He was following the course of Big River at a few hundred meters—an altitude quite low enough for him to smell the smoke from the kilns and see and hear children pointing and yelling at him from each village he passed over—when he heard a screaming from the sky to the north and west. Stone looked up.

DARK LIGHT

Something huge and black hurtled in a second from the zenith to behind the hills, just ahead of him and to the left. Reflexively he closed his eyes, flinching in expectation of a crash and an explosion.

None came.

He sent a quick and self-consciously futile prayer of thanks to the indifferent gods and opened his eyes. What he saw made him almost shut them again. Behind the brow of the mountain range a vast, ramshackle contraption was rising like a malignant moon. Evidently the object seen falling, it moved forward, almost scraping the summit. Lurching and yawing, it careened to above the middle of the valley. Then it stopped, hanging in the air half a kilometer away, right in front of him. It turned around.

The air crackled; Stone could feel every hair on his body prickle. He was still rushing forward, on a collision course that in seconds would splatter him and the glider across the front of the thing like a fly on goggles. He swung his upper body forward and his legs up, and tipped the the bone levers to tilt the glider into a dive. Down and down, he aimed for Big River, in the slim hope that if he couldn't pull out in time he might just survive a crash into water.

The shadow of the unidentified flying object passed over him. Something, not the air and not his own efforts, slowed his descent, at the same time buffetting him as though with invisible fists. He felt, incredulously, that he was actually being lifted. Then the shadow and the strange lightness passed, and he began to plummet again, but now he was able to pull back. At fifty meters above the river he was in level flight, at a speed that a small and cautious upward flex on the controls turned into a shallow climb.

The long bridge that had given the town its name whipped beneath his feet like—so it seemed—a just-missed trip wire. He banked leftward above the rooftops of tile and thatch, slowing and spilling air as the field came into view, closer and closer, he could see the blades of grass, and then he was down with a thump that jarred every cartilage from his ankle joints to the top of his spine and running, running faster than he'd ever run before, sprinting up the slope as fast as a man running full pelt down it to take off, the glider still flying at shoulder height and no weight at all, and then he could slow and finally stop.

He stood for a moment, unbuckling the harness and lifting the wing, then stepped out from under it and let it sag to the grass behind him. His breath came in deep sighing gusts; he could not control it. His legs shook; he could control them, and he walked stiffly away from the glider

299

toward the sheds at the top of the field. Later he would ache. For now, he just felt an immense surge of exhilaration carrying him along.

Slow Leg, the pilot for whom Stone had been testing the new craft, waited for him under the eaves of the glider shed. In his twenties, a few years older than Stone, lounging elaborately against a log pillar, Slow Leg was clad in nothing but a short pleated skirt and a pose that showed off his chest, arm, and leg muscles to advantage.

His calm cracked to a wide grin as Stone approached.

"That was magnificent," he said. "That's a well-tested wing."

Stone grinned back, in unabashed gratitude for the laconic praise.

"It is yours," he said, controlling his breath as best he could. He took off his goggles and wiped sweat from his forehead, then removed the feather helmet.

Slow Leg nodded and walked past him and picked up the glider and carried it reverently to the shed, where he lifted it into an overhead rack and returned to the post and the pose.

"Thank you."

Stone dipped his head, then, formalities over, looked up and asked the question at the forefront of his mind: "What *was* that thing?"

"A ship."

Stone laughed. "That was never a ship. Unless the sea people have taken to crossing space in *rafts*."

"It did look like something lashed together from a bedstead and barrels," Slow Leg admitted, "but I don't think the sea people made it."

He had the look of someone waiting to tell a joke.

"The sea people don't *make* their ships," Stone said, teasing him with precision.

"All right," Slow Leg said. "It was not made by the snake people for the sea people, like every other ship we have seen."

Stone stepped behind the straw-mat screen where he'd left his clothes and began unpicking the fastenings of his down-quilted jacket and trousers. Most pilots flew in nothing but a breechclout, but modesty and frailty were allowed for in test flying. Only men had to be tough enough to bare their skin to the high-altitude winds.

"So how do you know that, Slow Leg? Did the gods make it, and tell you in a dream?"

"I saw it with . . . my own vision!"

Slow Leg guffawed at his own joke; Stone laughed politely. He untied his long fair hair and shook it out, ducked into his knee-length blue silk tunic and stepped into the matching trousers, strapped on the sloping compressed-bark wedges of his sandals, and emerged from behind the screen. When he met Slow Leg's eyes again he noticed, as he had so often in the past, the subtle, swift shuttering—something as quick and involuntary as the nictitating membrane flicking across the eyes of one of the snake people—that signaled the sudden shift in the basis of their conversation. Slow Leg's literal stance shifted: He stopped leaning against the log and took a step back, and hooked his thumbs in his belt.

"Vision," he said, tapping beside his eye. "There was a name written on the side of the ship, and I read it."

Phenomenal visual acuity was normal among pilots; literacy was not. Slow Leg had some justification for the lazy self-satisfaction in his tone.

Stone let his eyes widen. "What was it?" His voice had taken, quite without artifice, a slightly higher pitch and lighter note.

Slow Leg sucked in his lips and gave a small shrug. "There were several words, or names," he said, "some of which had been painted over, but there were two words that were quite clear, in the Christian language and lettering . . ."

He paused again, playing a smile.

Stone spread his hands. "Please."

"Bright Star."

Stone mentally translated from the Christian.

"Bright Star?" He felt the pitch of his voice rise out of control, to an undignified squeak.

"That was what it said." Slow Leg shrugged. "Whether it was indeed that ship, I don't know."

He turned and gazed down the valley, as if he could still see it. "But it looked as one would expect that ship to look, and as for its piloting . . ." He chuckled.

"If that was flown by one of the sea people, they are in a bad way indeed. No, I think that was flown by a—you know the Christian word, a *human*."

"Or by one of the snake people?" Stone suggested. "A very experienced skiff pilot?"

Slow Leg passed a hand over his eyes. "Or a very inexperienced one!"

Stone smiled slyly. "It takes a very experienced pilot to dive down to ground level and then pull out. . . ."

Slow Leg shook his head in self-reproof, slapped Stone's shoulder, then let his arm drop awkwardly.

"Of course, of course," he said. "I forget myself. I must pour you a drink, Stone."

They walked along the front of the glider shed, mostly empty at this time of day, Slow Leg padding barefoot on the grass, with the almost imperceptible drag on the left foot that had inflicted his name, Stone stepping carefully in the short-paced gait imposed by the built-up heels of his sandals. Against the far end of the shed was an unattended table with a skin flask of beer propped in a wicker frame and a few pottery cups. Slow Leg ignored the beer, ducked under the table, and fished out a glass bottle of corn-mash spirit.

"Ah," said Stone. A smuggler.

Slow Leg smiled and winked as he filled two cups with the rough liquor, then hid the bottle again. He leaned an elbow on the table and raised his cup, then noticed Stone wasn't leaning on the grubby, sticky table.

He waved for a pause and hurried to drag up a stool.

"Thank you," said Stone, taking the seat.

Slow Leg resumed the toast. "High flights!"

"Safe landings," Stone said, heartfelt. The reaction was already getting to him, his body belatedly assimilating the reality of his narrow escape and beginning to tremble. He gulped, steadying himself, blinked as his eyes stung.

"Wooh!"

"Good stuff," said Slow Leg. He licked it off his lips, looked away, took another sip. He seemed to remember something.

"If that ship really was the *Bright Star,*" he said slowly, "then many things will change. Others will have recognized it too. It will be the talk of the valley within hours."

"You're right there," Stone said. His mind was still racing through the implications. They unfolded as though before his eyes, with the slow-motion inevitability of a glider crash. The *Bright Star*'s arrival, over two centuries ago at a world that he vaguely thought of as five years' journey away, was so fundamental to the sky people's whole existence that it was part of their religion. A late part, of course, but already seamlessly incorporated in legends that went back through countless generations to the Cold Lands, to what the Christians called Earth. The gods had brought that ship to the New Worlds, with its message of deliverance. Without it, the sky people's religion would in all likelihood no longer exist, and the sky people themselves would be miserable wretches.

If it had now arrived at Croatan, it could only be a portent.

"You realize," Stone went on, "that what happened today will be remembered in the stories of our people?"

"Of course," said Slow Leg. "It will be called something like, let me see, 'The Story of How Stone Fell from the Sky.' "

Stone laughed. "That sounds about right. Or 'How Slow Leg Almost Lost His Wing.' "

"That's how the women will tell it, yes," Slow Leg said wryly. "Oh, well, I suppose we will know the truth about the ship soon enough, and the consequences will be what they will be."

Stone nodded agreement with this profound but entirely uninformative remark. Slow Leg made a small chopping motion with his hand, to indicate that as far as he was concerned they'd said all there was to say on the subject. Stone waited politely for the man to introduce the next.

But Slow Leg hesitated, drank a little more, stared moodily into the distance for a minute before turning and saying abruptly: "You really are a very good pilot. That was truly amazing."

Stone looked down, as though modestly, thinking *here we go again*. He raised a hand and let it flap down from the wrist.

"I was lucky," he said. "The ship's spirit, its *field*"—he used the Christian word—"pulled me out of the dive."

"Even so. It took great skill and presence of mind. You are as good as a man."

There it was, the usual clumsy, well-meant but unwanted compliment. At least it was done. He smiled and, again as usual, fluttered his eyelashes. Slow Leg put down his cup and gave Stone a hard, steady look.

"I would be happy to have you flying with me."

"What is this?" Stone said. "A marriage proposal?"

That would have flustered him less than the kind of partnership that Slow Leg was, ever so deniably, suggesting: to join him in his smuggling.

Slow Leg laughed and threw a pulled punch in the direction of Stone's shoulder.

"One wife is enough! More than enough, to tell you the truth. No, seriously, Stone. Let me ask you, then: Would you be interested in flying with me?"

"That is not possible."

"Yes, it is. If we are careful."

Stone sipped the liquor and held up the cup. "I take it you already do some very careful flying."

Slow Leg nodded. "There are things we have that the councils of the Christians disapprove of, and they have things—such as this—that our elders frown upon. There is profit in the trade, if you are careful. But not enough profit—almost all our traders will stuff a few such items into each trip. I have been thinking. There must be some Christian things that the women want and that the elders and the councils forbid. Simple and light things, easily carried." He shrugged. "I would not know what they are. But you might."

"I can think of plenty," Stone said. "Steel needles, small sharp blades, scissors, eyeglasses . . ."

There were already a few such treasures in some of the women's hands, discreetly used and jealously hoarded; he knew of them only from glimpses and grumbles. The thought of joining in Slow Leg's scheme expanded as warmly in his mind as the drink did in his belly. To fly regularly, and to see the city, and to be the prestigious source of such valuable tools . . .

"Yes," he said. "I would like to do that."

"Very good," said Slow Leg. As though emboldened by this agreement, he leaned forward and continued, intently: "You're a natural flyer. With practice, you could be a great one. Instead you let your ability run to waste as a woman and fritter your days in weaving and stitching and gossip. Why don't you turn your back on all that petty stuff and become a man while you still can?"

Stone was unsure as to what would be an appropriate response. He compressed his lips, took a deep breath, smoothed the lap of his tunic. Reactions to his status ranged from good-natured joshing to fascinated admiration, with most of that range occupied by a matter-of-fact acceptance. An active attempt to persuade him out of it was unheard of: Neither tradition nor what he could recall of the books of anthropology afforded a precedent.

But he had just seen one event without precedent; he wondered if Slow Leg's boldness was somehow incited by the feeling that had gripped them both of great changes to come. So instead of taking offense, or laughing it away, he took it seriously and calmly.

"There is some truth in what you say, Slow Leg," he replied. "I love flying, and I wish I could do more. But I also love the women's work and the women's company, which is not as petty as you imagine. But besides all that, the fact remains that I chose it for a reason, which you well know. I may be good at flying, but I couldn't be good at fighting."

He spread his hands.

Slow Leg had listened with an expression of growing frustration and now burst into eager, urgent speech.

"I could train you!" he said. "Fighting is just a skill. To tell you the truth, a woman could do it, if she practiced enough and didn't mind the pain—and I've seen birth, pain I couldn't imagine. Women have their own pain, so don't tell me they couldn't endure some blows and cuts. Don't tell me *you* couldn't. We could practice, somewhere quiet, until you were ready for the challenge."

Stone winced inwardly at the mention of the challenge but kept his expression carefully bright.

"Ah, that's just the trouble, you see," he said. "Nature, the spirits, the gods—call the power what you will—has given mothers the strength to give birth, and fighters the strength to fight, and to me and my like neither. I accept that, and I'm happy to be as I am."

Slow Leg still fixed him with a stern gaze.

"I knew you when you ran and fought and hunted with the other boys," he said. "You had the makings of a man, and you still do. You're no coward." He frowned for a moment. "If it's that you"—he made a quick vulgar gesture with his fingers—"to tell you the truth, some of the men, the hunters and warriors, they too . . . with each other, and nobody thinks any the less of them."

"I know that," Stone said with a sigh of exasperation. "That's not the difficulty."

"So what is?"

"It's as I said."

Stone wished he could have said more, but what he felt was so chaotic, and threatened so much to make him weep, and so difficult to put in words either in Speech or in Christian, that he left it at that.

"All right," said Slow Leg. "I am sorry I raised the matter."

"It is forgotten," said Stone. "But I will fly with you, as we agreed."

They finished their drinks. As Stone left, Slow Leg called after him, "See you soon!"

Stone glanced back over his shoulder and gave him a sly smile and a friendly wave. The path from the glider shed to the road was paved with flat, irregular stones, leavings from the paving of the road, and therefore equally ancient. He walked down its left-hand side, on the outside of the pair of ruts left by centuries of identically spaced cartwheels. The roofs of Long Bridge's streets of stone houses and long wooden industrial sheds looked like broad steps in a jumbled collection of giant stairways descending the hillside to the river.

That was itself a detail of the pattern of much larger steps, the terracing of the fields, which earthworking in turn was laid over the succession of the raised beaches that appeared at various points along the sides of the valley. The airfield had been formed in the slope between two of them; after the next downward slope, the field was on a level with the roofs of the uppermost street, and on that field's trampled grass the town's boys and young men practiced their sports and the arts of war. As he walked past he was recognized by some of his former companions, one of whom shouted a suggestion after him. Stone waggled his hips defiantly.

"I wouldn't have you fuck me," he shouted, looking back, "if you were the last man in the world!"

Matt Cairns peers at the city through a window frosted with micrometeoroid impacts, troubled by the sense of height induced by looking at it from space but not from orbit, and by the feeling that *none of this has happened yet.* Some clock or calendar at the back of his mind is still tidal locked to Earth's distant turning; for him *the present* will always be 2049 plus however many years he lives, and most of that time up until now has been lived in *the future,* piled on top of an already dizzying stack of light-years.

So here he is, uncounted thousands of years and light-years away from *now* and *home,* standing in the drive's local gravity on a ship built for free fall and looking at a city that hangs improbably in front of his face and grows larger by the second. He turns away.

The ship's control room, the subject of several iterations of retrofitting and hacking, is about two meters high by three deep and ten across. At the other end of its long, low window stand a young man and a young woman, as intent as Matt had been on the planet's looming surface. Gregor Cairns resembles Matt in his swept-back black hair, narrow nose, and thin mouth—and the set of his shoulders, which is that of a man ready for trouble. Elizabeth Harkness, her left hand straying like a persistent-minded small animal on Gregor's back, stands a little taller and noticeably bigger in build; her black hair tumbles thick to a sharp, impatient-looking cutoff at the level of her chin. The ship's pilot, perched on a high stool between Matt and the couple, is himself intent on the surface of what looks like a tilted lab bench, to which various pieces of apparatus are strapped, lashed, or wired. His arms are elbow-deep in the cluttered array.

Matt gets the uneasy impression that the pilot is deliberately ignoring the proximity of the globe filling the window.

"Is this the right way to come in?" he asks. He can hear faint overspill of the planet's radio traffic from a speaker, vaguely wonders why such transmissions had never shown up on the Solar System's most sensitive radio telescopes in their most meticulous SETI sweeps, and remembers, again, that *this hasn't happened yet . . .* quite possibly in 2049 the lightspeed ships carrying the very first human specimens from Earth's deepest antiquity had still not reached their destination.

"No," the pilot replies, not looking up from the jury-rigged controls. "It decidedly is not. We must swing around and approach by the normal flight path. Please, everyone, hold on to something while I adjust—"

The direction of the field sways sickeningly for a moment, then stabilizes. The apparent size of the planet stops increasing.

"Okay," says the pilot, standing up and turning around and dusting his palms. "We are now in a stable position. It may take some time to plot the approach."

"You mean you don't know?"

Matt stares at the pilot, caught by another mental glitch: Just as the present sometimes seems to be the future, so he can't help seeing the pilot as an alien. Salasso isn't an alien—saurs and humans have a common terrestrial ancestor, an undistinguished vertebrate somewhere back of the Triassic—but he has an eerie, almost comical resemblance to the image of the alien that was iconic in Matt's ancient youth. Long familiarity with the saurs hasn't entirely erased that early imprinting. It can still make the hairs on his nape and forearms prickle. Not even the image of the truly alien, the garden of the gods that still glows in his mind after two centuries, can displace the sinister semblance: the hairless head with huge eyes and tiny mouth above a scrawny body, the long arms and long four-digited hands are species markers of the classic mythical alien, the Gray.

Matt has long harbored a dour suspicion that this is far from a coincidence. The saurs' disk-shaped gravity skiffs lend some weight to the notion.

And the fear and anger, still there like trace elements of a poisonous heavy metal, or an isotope with a long half-life, not yet nearly spent . . . he's ashamed of it, he fights it and tries to hide it, from others if not from himself.

"We know in principle," Salasso says stiffly. "From here on in it's partly skill, which . . . I am learning, and partly calculation—ah, Gregor?"

The young man moves away from the window and the woman, and joins Salasso in a huddle over a monitor and keyboard on the table. After a minute of watching them scribble, mutter cryptically, check readings, and punch data, Matt reckons this was not going to be quick. He walks past them and stands by Elizabeth. She doesn't look away from the view.

"It's wonderful," she says. "I can hardly believe I'm seeing this. Croatan, wow!"

Her finger traces in the air the outline of the eastern coast of Croatan's western continent, New Virginia, on which Rawliston stands out like a blemish on a cheek. West and north and south of its smoke haze spreads a patchwork—from this height, more a stitchery—of green and gold and black; beyond that, a deeper green of forests and then the gray slopes and white tops of a mountain range that roughly parallel the coastline at a distance of between one and two hundred kilometers. Clouds are piled up along the range, like surf. East of the town, the ocean shines blue.

"It is beautiful," Matt agrees.

She turns, her black hair swinging, her black brows lifting.

"Did you ever see Earth—like this?"

Matt sighs. "Yeah, for a few seconds, just as I was leaving it. In real life, that is. Lots of times on screen, of course. Live pictures, VR, wallpaper . . ."

She wouldn't have known quite what he meant, but she looks at him sympathetically.

"You miss it."

He scratches his chin with a thumbnail. As usual after spending time in space, he feels he needs a shave. He doesn't: This journey has been that short. "Yeah, I miss it. I've had some time to get over it."

As though reminded that she herself has more pressing reasons for homesickness, Elizabeth looks quickly down, then back at the new world below. After some minutes the view begins to slide to the right, as the ship moves west. In a moment they're looking straight down at the mountains.

"Please take your seats," says Salasso. "We're about to attempt a controlled vertical descent."

"I bloody *wish*," says Matt, heading for the seats, "that we'd brought that skiff. I'd rather risk a Roswell crash than a fucking *Tunguska Event.*"

The others know better than to ask him what he means by that. They don't have a skiff. They'd hired one, back on Mingulay, to use as a shuttle while they renovated the *Bright Star,* but it had been too expensive to take with them and anyway would have been missing the point, which is to set up a human-controlled spacefaring capability. They've left most of the fabs and labs behind, in the same old orbit, along with most of the ship. What they have now are modules of the life support and living quarters, some modules with carefully selected scientific equipment from the labs, a vast corpus of knowledge downloaded to an assortment of still-functioning computers, a cargo hold stuffed with Mingulayan manufactures, and the lightspeed drive.

A drive that, throttled back to some infinitesimal fraction of its capacity, can be used for gravity work—in-system space and air travel. Your standard strange light in the sky.

Matt straps in alongside the others, in cannibalized, bolted-down seats that were originally designed for minor jolts and unscheduled burns in free-fall maneuvering. The belt looks as though some small animal has taken bites out of it, leaving crescents of acidic spittle to fringe the bites with interesting burn marks—just a couple hundred years of slow-motion, vaccuum-resistant bacterial rot, but leaving the belt something he wouldn't have wanted to rely on in a car.

Salasso eases what looks worryingly like a rheostat a millimeter or two forward, and the zoom effect begins again. A brightening glow and rising screech indicate that they've hit stratosphere. There is no shudder; the field surrounds the ship like an elongated bubble, which is just as well because otherwise they'd be shaken apart like an oil drum raft in rapids. The mountain range expands rapidly from a rendered contour map to a papier-mâché model to the real thing, a planetary surface about to come through the window. Matt glances sideways at Elizabeth and Gregor. They stare straight ahead, rapt but untroubled. Their only experience of air travel is in airships and gravity skiffs. Matt's is a little wider, and his grip on the armrests is hurting his hands.

He opens his eyes as the howl of the air stops. The view ahead is filled with tough tussocky grass and boulders gray and yellow with lichen. The ship's gravity and that of the ground a few meters below are perfectly perpendicular to each other. He looks away queasily. Salasso rotates his big black eyes and eases back the control. The ground pulls away again—Matt can see rabbits scattering—and sky suddenly swings down and fills the screen. Most of the screen. The lower quarter shows a rugged ridge. They lurch upward then forward—Matt's toes curl, waiting for the scrape—and then they're hovering above a big, wide valley between that ridge and the next. Salasso pokes a long finger into something, and the ship swivels, looking straight down the valley. Matt glimpses a great river meandering along its floor, green and black fields in a landscape dotted with white towns.

And straight ahead, coming at them like a fly at a windshield, a black shape like a gigantic bird or medium-sized pterosaur. Salasso takes the ship a few tens of meters up as the object plunges into a dive. As it flashes past below, Matt can see it's a wing, without a tail and with some kind of struts and lots of colorful decoration.

"What the fuck was that?" he yells.

"Hang glider," says Salasso imperturbably. "No doubt its pilot is asking the same question."

Through the angled inward slope of the lower part of the window Matt can now make out more of what they're passing over. The valley stretches for at least fifty fast-diminishing kilometers before them. Its breadth varies from two to five kilometers, densely inhabited; fields and cultivated woodlands extend from the fertile floor to the terraced lower slopes, with contours that he guesses are raised beaches; watermills where the current flows fast in the loop of meanders; a circuit board tracery of irrigation and drainage ditches, with the white blocks of low buildings its capicitors and switches. Thin, wavering columns of rising smoke. Beasts in the fields that flock like cattle but seem far too big. Boats and barges and—

"Watch out!" Matt yells. Salasso shoots him a pained look and lifts the ship yet farther, above the path of a drifting . . . blimp, Matt thinks at first, then realizes it's half a dozen linked balloons from which a single long gondola hangs swaying.

"Shit," says Gregor, jumping from his seat and peering forward through the glass. "There're dozens of them, balloons and gliders. We're in somebody's *airspace*."

"I'm more concerned about being hit from behind," says Salasso. "If we stray into the regular starship approach path."

"Not very likely," says Elizabeth.

At the eastern end of the valley, the river broadens into a lake behind a natural-looking rockfall dam, over whose rim it cascades. After that the valley floor drops sharply, and far on the horizon they see the blue gleam of the sea and the yellow-gray haze of Rawliston. They cross above rough country which, as the mountains dribble to densely forested foothills, opens out to a wide floodplain, farmed and fertile, across which the river fattens and snakes. Swift as a descending airliner, silent as a balloon, they drift forward until the city fills their sight.

"Like L.A." Matt says.

"What?"

"City on Earth, ages ago." He waves a hand. "Forget it."

He's too busy staring at Rawliston to talk about it. Elizabeth too falls silent; like Gregor, she's never seen a city of this size—a human city, anyway—from above. The primate brain is hardwired to respond to complexity with fascination, as Matt knows too well. The asteroid habitat of the aliens still haunts dreams from which he wakes bereft. A city from the air is but a crude outline of that and still the most complex object of human devising you can grasp in a single gaze.

First the suburbs: shanties with allotments, on the outermost fringe where they merge with the poorer farmland close to the city; then the shacks are replaced by more substantial dwellings, and all the roads, not just the main throughfares, are visibly paved, gleaming black rather than dusty brown. Water tanks on stilts like marching Martians, instead of rain butts and culverts; decorative floral gardens and lawns, instead of tiny, frantic fields. The traffic too has changed—out on the fringe it was human or animal, interspersed with great laboring machines farting smoke, and small overladen contraptions buzzing among them, and lots of bicycles; closer in, the vehicles shine, the large trucks and haulage vehicles gleaming with vivid colors and polished metal piping, the small ones carapaced in enamel, their shapes like oval, painted fingernails. Bridges, large and small, unite the two sides of the broadening river that divides the city.

The average height of buildings rises, as does their mass. Built of stone rather than concrete, brick or wood or corrugated iron, just before the seafront they rise like a stone wave, this crest breaking to a lower, less salubrious splash of industrial and commercial buildings, docks and quays on either side of the river mouth and around the curve of the bay.

Beyond that the harbor, crowded with ships; and beyond these ships, out in the roads, two kilometers out to sea, the starship berth is flagged by buoys. Three starships lie there, floating more in air than in water.

"The de Tenebre ship," Salasso remarks, bringing them in alongside one of them. Matt has always felt that identifying a starship by the merchant family who travel in it makes about as much sense as naming

THE ENGINES OF LIGHT

an oceangoing vessel after some lineage among its complement of rats. The starships—or motherships, as he sometimes can't help calling them, in another mental glitch—are, well, as he thinks now, *big* mothers: hundreds of meters long, bigger than any other machine he's seen apart from oil tankers and heavy-lift boosters. Close up, the de Tenebre starship looks even bigger, reducing their own fifty-meter-long lash-up of modules and walk tubes to a raft bobbing alongside.

As the drive powers down to the minimum required to keep them afloat, or aloft—they can see the waves break against the invisible screen of the field—a babble of radio voices breaks through, along with a lot of hissing and howling as Salasso, slightly rattled, twiddles the dial. He finds the channel he seeks.

". . . yourselves please," says a voice with a twangy accent. "Ship in the roads, identify yourselves please."

Matt leans forward as Salasso hesitates.

"Tell him," he says, "that the *Cairns* ship has come in."

2

There Dwelt a Lass in Rawley's Toun

GAIL FRETHORNE'S GRIP on the spanner slipped as Joshua's yell startled her, and her hand grazed a raw flange. She saw the red blood on the black oil for a moment as her hand went to her mouth. Sucking her barked knuckles, she slid the low-wheeled platform she was lying on smoothly out from under the car and wound back a load of curses to hurl at Joshua.

He stood in the garage workshop yard a couple of meters away, gazing up openmouthed. From her low vantage, the apprentice looked like an allegorical statue of Astonishment. On her back, conveniently placed to look at the sky, she tracked the direction of his gaze.

"Holy fucking shit," she said, her ready-primed profanities sliding into reverence. The thing that floated by a hundred meters overhead was too big for an airship, too small for a starship, and surely the wrong shape for either. Christ, there were *holes* in it! You could see the sky through them.

She scrambled to her feet, not looking away from the thing. It was coming down, sinking in the sky as it headed east across the city. Joshua shot her a reluctant glance.

"Some kinda new airplane?"

She could tell from his tone that he grudged consulting her on the question.

"No," she said, trying not to sound scornful. "Not the right shape for a lifting body, too fast to be an airship. If it had jets or rockets we could see them and hear them. I think."

"You don't reckon," said Joshua, watching it out of sight, "it could be something new the heathens have lashed up, out of, I dunno, gliders and balloons or something?"

"The heathens don't go much for *new,*" Gail said. "No more nor the saurs or the krakens. Nah, that's a fucking ship or maybe skiff all right, man, and it's a kind we've never seen before. Nor heard of, neither."

"Hey!" Josh put his knuckles to his brow and waggled his forefingers. "Aliens!"

Gail laughed. Joshua's sole evidence of literacy was his painfully slow but persistent reading of sensational pulp comics.

"There ain't no aliens, 'cept the Powers Above."

"We don't *know* that," Joshua said stubbornly.

"Yes we do," Gail said absently, still gazing at the sky. Then she turned sharply to him, a big grin stretching her face. "And you know what that leaves?"

God, he was slow.

"People!" she said, clasping her hands above her head. "Our people! It's the ship from home! They've come here!"

Joshua frowned. He looked over at the big blaring radio, balanced precariously amid engine parts, jars of hazardous liquids, and tins of nuts and bolts on the shelf by the garage doorway.

"No need to *speculate* about it," he said, surprising her. "If it's anything special it'll be on the news, right?"

"Oh, yeah." Gail reached for the tuning knob and twiddled it through howls to the news band. After a minute of the usual midday prattle about crimes and traffic, the announcer's voice changed. You could hear the rustle of paper and the clunk of telephone switches.

"News just in," she said. "A starship has a few moments ago berthed off Rawliston and has identified itself as the *Bright Star.* We're sending out an urgent message to Chris, our eye in the sky, to give them a buzz, and meanwhile we'll keep you informed."

Some crackly exchanges followed with the man in the light aircraft whose job it was to keep an updating eye on the city's endlessly snarling traffic flow, and some old geezer from the university was roused from a siesta by the sound of it to talk incoherently about how marvelous and historic all this was, and with a defiant look Joshua wrenched the dial back to music.

"That's it, then," he said. "You were right. It's the cosmonauts."

He sounded disappointed. Gail gazed at his sullen face, pondering what depths of stupidity and disproportionality might lie beneath that expression. What daft dreams of aliens had been dashed by the discovery that the pilots of this unprecedented craft were merely, gloriously, human? To her it seemed the best and biggest news of her life.

"It's a big deal," she said. "You'll see."

Joshua shrugged and wandered back to disappear under the raised hood of the car on which he'd been working, halfway across the yard. The other two mechanics were in the dim interior of the machine shop, still welding—she blinked away the floating afterimages of her quick glance—and seemed not to have seen the ship or heard the news on their radio. The boss, scowling over dockets behind the window of the office that jutted from the yard's other corner, was equally oblivious.

She turned away quickly, before he could look up and catch her idle, and licked the still-welling blood from her knuckles. With one part of her mind she considered how to shift that recalcitrant nut. To play a flame on it was tempting but far too dangerous. Several sprays of penetrating oil seemed not to have penetrated at all. She ambled over to the cupboard where they kept the tea break stuff and nipped a twenty-centimeter strip from the coil of plastic heating element, about the amount they usually took from it to boil a liter can of water.

Back under the car, she wrapped the purloined strip around the nut and flicked it hard with her thumbnail. After a few seconds it glowed yellow, then orange. After it had burnt itself out she blew away the crumbling ash and applied the spanner again, and managed to loosen the nut just before the heat crept up the spanner and made it too hot to hold.

She abandoned the task until everything had cooled down a bit and hauled herself out again just as David yelled from the machine shop, "Abigail! I thought I saw you making some tea. Where is it?"

"Coming *right* up," she shouted back. "Davy!" she added, a variant of his name he detested as much as she did the one he'd used of hers. Making the tea was part of Joshua's job, but Gail felt obscurely obligated to the apprentice for her uncharitable thought that had marked him down as dimmer than he actually was.

She wiped her oily hands on her oily overall, hurried to the cupboard and the tap, and repeated the trick with a length of the disposable heating element. The boss had once wasted an hour or two laboriously proving to his own satisfaction that this saur product was cheaper than electricity. As she waited for the tin kettle to boil, Gail wondered idly why it wasn't more widely used and turned over vague notions about economies of scale and so forth, but eventually (as she threw a handful of tea leaves into a blackened earthenware pot, poured on the boiling water, and let it stand) concluded that it was just another example of the odd criteria the saurs had about what they would and wouldn't trade. They'd sell their leaf-thin solar panels and plastic tubing from the genetically engineered jungles that they aptly called the manufacturing plant, and they were downright helpful about petroleum extraction. But they left most human industry to muddle through on its own. They wouldn't sell skiffs and grudged even to rent them out. They were considerate and conscientious in selling restorative surgery, and swift to limit the spread of diseases introduced by interstellar trade, but they certainly weren't about to share the secret of their own long lives.

She poured the tea, and David, Mike, Joshua, and the boss gathered around for their half-past-ten break. The garage yard's usual din was replaced by the tinny tone of the radio, the creak of metal and glass and wood differentially expanding in the rising heat, and the low murmur of conversation and laughter. The three older guys were a lot less sanguine than Joshua about the arrival of the ship. As they talked, one aircraft after another buzzed over, heading from the airfields on the edge of town toward the sea. Eventually, Gail could stand it no longer.

"Uh, Mr. Reece," she said to the boss, "do you mind if I knock off for the day? The engine mount job is coming along fine, and, well, I'd like to get out to the runway."

She could almost see the calculations clicking away behind Reece's narrow eyes. It was a rare request on her part, she normally worked longer than necessary anyway, the job was ahead of schedule and the car's owner couldn't pick it up earlier than arranged . . .

"Yeah, okay," he said. "Just so long as you're in early tomorrow."

She grinned at him and at the lads, put down her mug unfinished, and set off for the washroom at a run.

An hour or so later, just before noon, she racked her bicycle in the club shed and walked out on to the grass, feeling that she needed another wash, this time to remove not oil but sweat and dust. The garage was on the fracture zone between the suburbs and the shanties, and most of the westward roads beyond it were rutted and rough. The green open space of the airfield was like cold water after all that.

Its perimeter was about five hundred meters by two hundred, its fences marking off an area of rough grass on relict riverbank soil too pebbly and gravelly to farm. Hangers, huts, a wind sock, a token mooring mast—most airships docked much farther in toward the center of town, or down at the quays—the circular concrete blockhouse containing the kerosene tanks, and a row of fabric-and-bamboo monoplanes and biplanes. The club had a dozen aircraft, all but three of which were at present in the air, no doubt buzzing the newly arrived starship.

Away off in one corner was a wide patch of grass—trampled by landings, blackened by liftoffs—where the heathens arrived and departed in their hot-air balloon trains. Around it was a wider area, torn and tire-rutted, where the much rarer gliders landed and from where they were relaunched by towing them—the pilot standing on a slatted wooden platform with six bicycle wheels until he'd built up enough speed to take off, and for a minute or so afterward was towed through the air as he soared, until he let go of the handle and the rope snaked back down to earth behind the club's car.

It was that car, at this moment parked neatly behind the clubhouse, that had given Gail her way in a couple of years earlier, when she was sixteen and just hanging around on the edges, unregarded, watching the aircraft take off and land, or herself circling the perimeter of conversations among the pilots and mechanics, catching snatches of information and jargon, assumed to somebody's kid sister.

She'd seen, a hundred meters away, the tall half-naked heathen heft his curious contraption, step lightly on the undercarriage, and shout and wave. The car had coughed into life, revved up, roared forward. The heathen stood braced between the wing above him and the wood at his heels, bouncing across the grass. And then the car had stalled, and the line slackened, and he'd tumbled forward, caught himself, and run for a little before going all of a heap, the glider tipped and sticking up above him at an angle.

She'd run up. The heathen was on the ground, clutching his knee, whey-faced but tight-lipped. The glider appeared undamaged. People were ignoring him, standing around the raised hood of the car and shaking their heads. As she'd elbowed her way in she'd realized that none of them had a clue: Their expertise with aeroengines didn't extend to those of cars.

Hers, as she rapidly demonstrated, did, and that was it. She'd fixed the distributor cap that was the source of the problem, and an hour later the heathen—who'd done something nasty to his left knee but was studiously, stoically ignoring it—was up and away. From then on Gail was in with the lads, just like at the garage; she had credibility, she had a regular role here, maintaining the old car. She'd done more than maintain it; she'd tuned and tweaked the engine until it ran reliably and smoothly every time.

The heathen pilot had not forgotten her. Two weeks after his accident, he had returned, startling her with a silent approach as she worked on the car. The proposition he put to her had startled her even more, but in the time since then, it had resulted in a welcome addition to her income, albeit one that occasionally nagged at either her conscience or her fear of being found out.

She strolled past the clubhouse and spotted Paul Loudon flight checking the Kondrakov-LeBrun 3B, a two-seater high-winged monoplane. Paul owned the small engineering company that had built it, under license from its Mingulayan designers. In his midtwenties he was already independently wealthier than most of his landowning family, and looked it: tall, with sharp dark eyes, fine cheekbones, a proud nose. He never gave the slightest indication that he noticed her sex, or her class, for that matter; Gail wasn't sure whether the reasons for this were good or bad, but she counted the result entirely to his credit.

"Oh, hi, Frethorne." He slid shut a tiny hatch above a fuel valve in the side of the fuselage and wiped his fingers on a white handkerchief, then raked them absently through his swept-back brown hair. "Just caught the fuss by chance on a radio at work. Probably missed most of the fun. Bloody nuisance."

"What sort of fun? You can still go up and have a look."

"Oh, to be sure, that's just what I'm about to do. But all the other chaps have no doubt got reporters and photographers along for the ride and are raking in fees by the fistful."

She knew it wasn't the money that mattered to him; it was missing the cachet of having been among the first to witness and record a little bit of history that was pinching his brow and mouth.

"Well," she said, "that means none of them are taking pictures for the club. . . ."

"Aha!" He slapped his thigh. "Good point!" He looked somewhere above her, then below. "Ah, I don't suppose, you wouldn't mind awfully much coming along and shooting a spool or two?"

"No," she said, keeping her face straight. "I wouldn't mind that at all."

She'd been hoping he'd let her spin the propeller.

•   •   •

Lydia de Tenebre knew exactly what the black rectangular structure was, even before its dangerously low passage, skimming the rooftops of Rawliston, had brought it close enough for her to glimpse through the haze its crudely painted name. She had hoped to see it someday but had never quite believed that she would, and certainly not so soon, after a mere three months of her life.

Trying not to run, she hurried down the crowded waterfront street. The low-slung, carbon-coughing vehicles lurched and paused, lurched and paused, in a typical downtown morning traffic jam. People mostly made way for her: The extremes of beauty, like those of ugliness, could part crowds, and Lydia used her beauty like a scythe. Only the occasional gigant or pithkie grudged her passage and stepped aside with a grunt or a flash of bright, sharp teeth.

The walls of the warehouses and offices cut off any view of the starship's landing. When she arrived at the street that opened to the quays, the coppice of masts in the harbor blocked any sight of the sea. She paused in a convenient shopfront doorway and pulled her radio from the hip pocket of her dress. She flicked it on, wincing at the babble and howl—the frequencies were more crowded in Rawliston than anywhere else in the Second Sphere, more even than in Nova Babylonia itself, where strict regulation kept the numerous channels well distinct. Here, it needed all the fine discrimination built into the set to find the correct wavelength.

"Lydia on shore to the ship," she said.

"Come in." The operator sounded distracted.

"Has the other ship landed safely?"

"If you can call it a ship," replied the operator. "Yes."

"Praise the gods," said Lydia. "Signing off."

She looked up and down the long shorefront street. A recent rainfall had left it gleaming and puddled; cars and buses and trucks threw curls of water from their wheels as they passed, splashing the sidewalks. The traffic flowed faster than on the side streets; along here the street was a continuation of the broad boulevard that bordered the more residential and commercial, less industrial and mercantile segment of the seafront and retained its sweep though not its trees, umbrellas, and cafés.

She waited for one of the inexplicable halts in traffic that happened at random every few minutes and dodged across the road. A quick jump over a low chain fence took her onto the tarry timbers of the pier, from which long quays fingered out. She dodged among bollards and barrels, carts and trucks, dockers and hauliers, the crowd less dense but its components faster and heavier. She stayed nimble and alert until she'd crossed the swing-down customs barrier that restricted entrance and exit to the landing stage that had been set aside for boats to and from the starship berth. Then she relaxed with a long, shuddering exhalation and strolled its hundred-meter length to the end. She was in her own territory now.

An inflatable dinghy rocked on the water at the bottom of one of the stairs. She called down to the crewman, a distant cousin, snoozing in the stern. "Hi, Johannes! Can you take me out?"

Johannes started awake and waved up at her. "Yes, come on in."

She descended and sat down facing Johannes on a seat made, like most of the rest of the boat, from thin plastic that had once been transparent and had by now been scratched and stained to a watery translucence. Johannes cast off, shoved clear of the barnacled stanchion, and fired up the outboard motor.

As the dinghy puttered out through narrow gulfs between the hulls of wood and steel, Johannes grinned at her and said, "What's the rush? Didn't expect you back before evening."

"You didn't see it?"

"See what?"

"The Mingulayan ship coming in? You know, the cosmonauts' ship?"

Johannes scratched the back of his head. "Hells, no, I missed that. Good gods, they actually did it?"

"Yes," said Lydia. "They navigated here themselves." She shook her head. "I never expected Gregor to crack it . . . so soon. I'm impressed."

Her cousin was looking at her with sly amusement. "I bet your father will be even more impressed. Changes things a bit for you, eh?"

"That's for me to decide."

She smiled, just to show that the firmness of her tone didn't indicate a reproof, and turned away to look forward, beyond the dinghy's rounded prow. As they emerged into clear water they could see both starships far ahead. The Mingulayan ship was a dark, flat shape, barely discernible beside the circular aspect of the de Tenebre starship's cylindrical length seen end-on. As the dinghy bounded across the waves, Lydia began to make out a line of light between the small ship and the sea; it wasn't even big enough to make a significant depression in the water. She found herself wondering idly what exchanges might be going on, between the *Bright Star* and her family's ship, and between either of them and the Port Authority, and then realized that her speculation need not be idle.

She pulled out the radio again and thumbed the switch and turned the tuning knob very slowly through a small part of the dial.

"... in your ship," a voice was saying. "I repeat, remain in your ship. A Port Authority vessel is on its way."

"Acknowledged," returned another voice, which she didn't recognize. She looked astern and saw another, much larger inflatable boat powering out from the harbor, far behind in their wake.

"Can you make this go faster?"

Johannes nodded. "Sure. We'll get a bit wet. . . ."

"Do it, please."

The crewman leaned on the tiller, and the engine's note deepened. The boat surged forward; salt spray began splashing in. Lydia raised the radio again.

"Calling the *Bright Star*, come in, please."

After a few crackling noises the reply came back: *"Lydia?"*

Her heart jumped like the boat; her eyes filled with water like the spray.

"Yes, it's me! Gregor?"

"Hi, Lydia. Good to hear you." His voice sounded more level this time. "Where are you?"

She told him.

"That's great," he said. "But let's keep off air for the moment, we don't want a swarm of—"

The hum of an aircraft engine drowned out his words; a seaplane flashed by about fifty meters above her head. She stared after the rickety craft and saw it slice the sea with its floats and rock to a stop beside the ships. Within moments a converging flock of small airplanes was circling the starship berth. From somewhere behind the harbor mole a blimp wallowed in the same direction. She rolled the dial to the data-transfer channel: It was buzzing; fuzzy photographic reproductions were obviously being transmitted to Rawliston's newspaper offices. The radio news channels, too, were busy, with no news she didn't already know.

"Damn!" she shouted above the sound of the outboard and the growing racket overhead.

"What did you expect?" Her cousin's amused look had returned. "That ship is legendary! This is historic!"

"I know," Lydia said. Her notion of a quick, quiet reunion with

Gregor now seemed naive. "I just didn't expect the locals to catch on so *fast*."

But that too was naive, she realized as soon as the words were out of her mouth. She grimaced and turned again to face forward.

It had been less than a quarter of a year ago, in her own life, that she'd heard of the *Bright Star*'s first arrival—not at Croatan but in polar orbit around its daughter colony, Mingulay, five light-years distant. In that time Croatan had made about two hundred circuits of its sun, two hundred years that had been radically affected by the event. The buzzing aircraft themselves were one of its consequences, as was much of the surrounding industrial landscape. Not that Croatan hadn't been industrializing quite effectively on its own, but interstellar trade with the rest of the Second Sphere and even the limited technology trade with the vastly more ancient and advanced saurs just couldn't hold a carbon-arc lightbulb to the effect of a shipload of downloads from the Earth and Solar System of 2049, which had begun to arrive in the seasonally adjusted Year of Our Lord 2057. The current approximate anno Domini was 2270-something, according to Croatan's calendar, which quite sensibly discounted the countless millennia lost in lightspeed transit. Elsewhere in the Second Sphere, Nova Terra's year was standard, and its zero date was the founding of the city now called Nova Babylonia, which had recently celebrated its tenth millennium. Lydia felt some patriotic pride in that, though she well knew that to the older hominid species, let alone to the saurs or the krakens, this was all very novel, and to the gods it was as yesterday in their sight. She herself was, like everyone on the merchant ships, a one-way time traveler, skipping into the future with every subjectively instantaneous lightspeed jump; in her two score years she'd left her date of birth centuries in the past, and in that sense she was older than Rawliston. The town had changed faster than anything else she'd seen in her travels: *My, how she's grown!*

The dinghy dodges around the seaplane's floats and into the gap between it and the *Bright Star*. Matt and Elizabeth crowd behind Gregor, who stands in the opened hatch of what was once an internal doorway. Their own dinghy, deflated and folded around its gas cylinder, is stashed alongside that hatch in another piece of botchy retrofitting. The whole ship is scarily unsuitable for space flight: only one airlock, in a very awkward corner; ESA-issue EVA suits that haven't been tested or used for centuries; life-support hydroponics incorporating decades of unedited mutation, which occasionally give off rank swampy whiffs. The humid air from the outside feels fresh by comparison. The saurs have kept the *Bright Star* maintained and ticking over, mothballed in Mingulayan orbit, but they've done the work by the numbers, painstakingly following instructions they've recovered from files: Whatever life-support engineering skills they ever possessed has atrophied over the millions of years in which they've never had to spend more than a few hours at a time in actual hard vacuum. The digit they're missing is the human's green thumb.

Over Gregor's shoulder Matt sees the woman crouched in the dinghy's prow, straining forward. Through the side of his arm he feels Elizabeth, peering over Gregor's other shoulder, tense. Wavy black hair blown in the wind, light brown skin, a really quite beautiful face; Matt understands some of the reasons for Elizabeth's tension at the sight of Lydia and on an impulse gives her shoulders a brief, fortifying squeeze.

She glances sideways at him for a moment and blinks.

The dinghy heaves to. Gregor catches a flung rope and steps back into the control room, scattering his companions behind him. After a moment of puzzlement he lashes the rope to the fixed stanchion of one of the seats. By the time he's turned back Lydia has climbed in, followed by the lad who has steered the boat. Lydia's dark blue dress is cut in pleats and concertina folds; its skirt flares, and when she shakes the salt spray from her hair the drops slide off the fabric leaving no track.

Lydia embraces Gregor for a long moment, then steps back, her hands on his.

"You did it!" she says. "You made it! Oh, I'm so proud of you! I'm amazed."

Gregor shrugs modestly. "It wasn't all my own work. . . ." Then he grins broadly. "But mostly it was! Thank you."

Lydia spins away and grabs Elizabeth, who gives her a very uncertain hug in return, then shakes hands with Salasso and introduces her cousin and crewmate, Johannes.

"And this is Matt Cairns," Gregor says, "my ancestor."

Her awestruck look as she grasps his hand is strangely gratifying, after a protracted lifetime of secrecy on that very point.

"Hello, Lydia," he says. "Very pleased to meet you. I've heard a lot about you."

"Likewise," she replies, smiling.

"Oh?"

"Your friend Grigory Volkov speaks well of you."

"I'm sure he does," Matt says, as smoothly as he can manage. "I look forward to meeting him."

"Of course," says Lydia, dropping his hand with a final flare-up of her smile and turning to Gregor.

"We don't have much time," she says. "The news people and the Port Authority will be all over you in minutes. I just want to say that you're all welcome on our ship and that my father is eager to meet you and has much to discuss."

"As do we," Elizabeth says pointedly.

The two women look at each other, and Gregor looks, rather helplessly Matt thinks, from the one to the other.

"Excuse me," says Salasso. "However personally fraught this situation may be, the matter of the Port Authority is considerably more urgent. What can we expect from them?"

Lydia frowns. "Shouldn't be a problem."

Gail had cadged a few flights before, but only as a passenger. There had always been the feeling of being indulged. This was different. In the borrowed leather helmet and the navigator's goggles, with the strap of the heavy camera tugging at the back of her neck, she was part of the crew of the KL-3B. She had a job to do. She'd written her name in the club's logbook in block capitals and signed it, just below Paul's, and beside it he'd scrawled, *photographer.*

She had to crouch a little to keep her face behind the plastic windshield and out of the slipstream. Paul, though as tall as she, didn't have to. She guessed he had a lower seat. Her fingers, cold in far-from-windproof gloves of silk with rubber fingertips, fumbled a little as she adjusted the few knobs and levers of the camera that hadn't been previously set up for her by Paul.

"Just slot it on the bracket," he'd said. "Point and shoot."

Easy for him to say. The bracket was clamped to the lip of the rear cockpit. You couldn't mount the camera on it before takeoff—too much risk of its being sheared off by the bumping. She heaved it up from her quivering knees and levered it out on her elbow-propped forearms, twisting around awkwardly to do so. By the time she'd got it slotted into place, Rawliston had passed beneath them in a jerky series of glimpses like blurred snapshots, and they were banking into a long swing around the starship berth.

Paul waved and yelled something over his shoulder to her, his words whipped away by the wind. She guessed he meant it was time to get busy and folded out the periscopic apparatus of the viewfinder so that she could look through it right in front of her, then with her other hand found the shutter button. Looking through the tiny viewfinder with goggles on was just about impossible; she slipped them up to her forehead, shielded her eyes with one hand, closed one eye, and screwed up the other.

The view juddered constantly. The larger starship made a complete diagonal: *click*. Another aircraft skimmed dangerously close; sky and wheels filled the view for a moment: *click*. Down now, so that only the *Bright Star* and a seaplane and some little dinghy were in the scope: *click*. Curving around it, back for a low pass. A much larger boat cut a white V toward the berth. Gail recognized the stylized turret-on-shield of the Port Authority ensign, snapping sharply in the boat's own slipstream. By the time Paul had pulled back and returned, that boat had hove to, and three or four dark figures were moving up its deck toward some opening in the *Bright Star*'s side: *click*.

Down again, so low that the highest, lightest droplets of spray from the wave tops salted the breath, and the seaplane rocked as they roared past it. Gail pulled on a lever that angled the camera upward, for a straight sideways shot of two men entering the starship: *click*.

Their rifles showed clear and sharp.

Gail almost yelled. An armed boarding of a ship was rare—of a starship, unprecedented. She could hardly believe it.

The two remaining on the deck had rifles too, and they brandished them at the KL-3B and the other buzzing aircraft: *click*. When Paul ignored, or failed to notice this and made another low run over, the two dark-uniformed men dropped to one knee and brought their rifles to their shoulders, the muzzles swinging around as they followed the airplane's swift, low flight.

At that point Paul got the message and veered off and headed for home—but not before Gail had got the picture: *click*.

3

Customs

M ATT HOLDS HIS hands well clear of his dinosaur-hide jacket's weapons-laden side pockets and glares at the boarders. Each has a rifle slung on one shoulder, and he has no idea how fast their reflexes might be, or how twitchy their mood. More reassuringly, they are both middle-aged men, with weathered, outdoor complexions, their build burly rather than tough. One of them is tall and clean-shaven, the other short and bristly. Their uniforms look more suitable for pirates than for customs officers: cravats and loose shirts with broadcloth jackets and lots of braid and frogging and general macaroni, worn with blue jeans under open orange waterproofs blazoned with the Port Authority name and flash.

"Who's in charge of this ship?" the taller of the men demands.

Gregor twitches.

Matt steps forward. "Who wants to know?" he asks.

With an air of practiced weariness, the big guy fingers a folded sheet of printed paper from a vest pocket. " 'Rawliston Port Authority, Customs Division, under International Commerce Regulation 453C of the local common year 2234, requests and requires in the name of the sovereign people, et cetera et cetera, full access to all information respecting but not limited to cargo crew master owner provenance origin destination of all ships entering the harbor."

"That doesn't apply to starships," says Lydia, "as well you know."

The officer gives her a grudgingly respectful glance, looks back at his paper, and runs a fingernail along a footnote, apparently in small print to judge by his labored delivery: " 'For the purposes of this regulation 'ship' shall be construed as any vessel whether surface or otherwise on or above the surface of the harbor waters as defined above subparagraph 86E and owned or operated by members of the Adamic races.' "

He looks at Matt, then flicks his gaze over Gregor and Elizabeth. "That means you, you, and you." A smile at Lydia, a nod at Johannes, a carefully blank blink at Salasso. "Not you, you, or you."

Matt reckons he's sussed that Lydia is from the de Tenebre ship— probably by her dress—and her companion by his crew fatigues, and that he has assumed the same of Salasso, or has wisely decided that his authority doesn't extend to saurs, no matter what ship they rode in on. The thought of claiming that the undoubtedly non-Adamic Salasso is the *Bright Star*'s owner tempts Matt for only a moment. He nods at Gregor, who takes the cue.

"I'm in charge here," Gregor tells the customs man. "On behalf of the Cosmonaut Families of Mingulay. Now, what do you wish to know?"

"Uh, that's still to be decided. We have to ask you to accompany us to the Authority office on shore, where you'll no doubt have to fill in a manifest and provide a bill of lading and other documentation, which we'll check when you unload, or before that by inspecting the ship in your presence."

"Couldn't we just get that over right now?"

The officer shakes his head. "No, because what comes after the check is a tariff, and that has to be determined on shore, not by us out here. To prevent corrupt arrangements, you understand."

Or to reserve them for a higher level of officialdom.

"All right," says Gregor. "We'll come along. But I want you to note that we do so under protest, and that we don't accept that human-crewed starships are covered by your regulation—"

"When it was written," the other officer breaks in, sounding apologetic, "there weren't any human-crewed starships."

"That's as may be," says the first officer. "But right now it does cover them, and if the assemblies meant anything different, it's them who're going to have to change it."

Gregor reiterates his objection, and with that point made they rummage up the ship's scant documentation and follow the officers onto the big inflatable boat. Salasso, Lydia, and Johannes remain on the ship.

Dark Water was sawing through a bundle of bamboo with a gut rope on which ground glass had been glued. The rope was wound around an arrangement of wheels and pulleys, powered by a foot pedal. She looked up, keeping the saw humming, as Stone walked carefully past her.

"Ha!" she said. "You've been drinking spirits. If Slow Leg comes home with that stuff on his breath I'll beat the shit out of him."

Stone steadied himself with a surreptitious hand on the bench behind him and faced her glare with a grin.

"Come on," he said. "It was only a mug to celebrate my successful flight."

"A mug of beer's one thing," Dark Water said, bending again to her task. "Whiskey is something else."

Inwardly Stone had to acknowledge the truth of this. His senses of sight and balance seemed affected—things went out of focus very easily and swayed a little all the time. But he couldn't help defending his friend.

"Slow Leg will be all right," he said. "He'll be busy with the wing all afternoon, anyway. The wing, remember?"

But nobody was talking about the wing. All along the the shed the talk was only of the ship. Women's voices floated up and down, swooping around the hum of pulleys and rasp of saws, the clatter of shuttles and the hiss of spinning wheels, the slap of wet clay and the roar of kilns. The scent of their sweat mingled with that of fresh sawdust and wood shavings, of burning logs, of vegetable and animal oils and hot glue, and of the fragrant breeze off the hillside fields and meadows that kept the air in the long shed breathable.

Ignoring the giggles and barbed comments that his carefully steady progress provoked, Stone made his way to the area where he usually worked. Children scooted and scampered and screamed around and between the benches and looms.

He looked down at the scored surface of his workbench, at the small stack of seasoned wood and the rack of flint tools with which he had to turn the wood into the complex, interlocking shapes of a glider harness attachment. The thought of getting hold of good steel blades was a lot more attractive than the task before him.

Outside, the sound of drumming began. Stone looked up and saw in the glaring sunlight a shaman's apprentice bashing the taut skin circle with evil-spirit-scaring enthusiasm, as the shaman himself ducked into a smoke-filled tent to consult the spirits of the ancestors, which were contained in the sacred book whose title Stone had once heard whispered: Christopher Dawson's *Autochthonous Hill Tribes of New Virgina: A Preliminary Anthropological Survey.*

• • •

The small boats that approached the starship berth have by now turned tail; the small aircraft have either departed or are circling at a much safer distance. Wet from spray and splash, sweating in the muggy heat, Matt huddles morosely between Gregor and Elizabeth on one of the boat's seats and tries to look as interested and surprised as they are by the endemic features of Croatan's native life.

This isn't his first visit to the planet, but he isn't about to tell his companions that, not just yet. He had, one long evening, given them a long and rambling account of the vicissitudes that had brought him and others with the *Bright Star* to Mingulay: his early life on Earth in the mid-twenty-first century, his journey to the asteroid research station, and his initiation into its real discoveries: the alien life within the asteroid, and the gods' revelation and specification—Greek gift or Trojan Horse—of the lightspeed drive and antigravity craft. He has told them little of his long, clandestine life on Mingulay, and nothing of his life off it.

So he stares and points and looks wide-eyed with the rest of them. Here, small pterosaurs fill the niche occupied by seabats back home on Mingulay; their narrow, angled wings, harsh cries, and vertical dives sending up high fountaining plumes remind Matt poignantly of gannets. The boat passes close by a swift-leaping group of sea animals, known locally as "seals" and homologous to porpoises or ichthyosaurs; Elizabeth excitedly points out the long, yellow serrated beaks and the tail-equivalent fused webbed feet that mark them out as birds, though with aquatic adaptations far more extensive than those of the penguins from which they're descended.

Another difference between Croatan and Mingulay becomes apparent as they get closer to the shore. The haze that hangs over Rawliston isn't fog—as, Matt guesses, his companions have assumed—but smog. Coal smoke and petrol-engine exhaust; the smell brings on some nostalgia, as well as a roughness in the back of the throat.

Elizabeth wrinkles her nose and looks at the bearded customs officer sitting across from her. "How do you *breathe* this stuff?"

"What stuff?"

Then he cracks a smile, relenting. "Yeah, I know. But it's part of the terraforming—greenhouse effect, yeah? The saurs say it's helping to hold off an ice age."

"Didn't think this planet *needed* terraforming," Gregor says.

"Call it fine tuning," says the officer.

"What's intriguing me," says Elizabeth, "is where the fossil fuels came from in the first place. When were the coal measures laid down? How long has this planet had Earth life on it?"

The Authority man shrugs, turning away to look over the prow. "You'd have to ask the saurs, and they don't know or ain't telling."

Well, you could do more than ask the saurs, Matt doesn't say. *You could ask the gods.*

He's still brooding on that thought when they've hove to, climbed up the quayside ladder, and walked into the Port Authority offices by the back entrance, avoiding the baying crowd of reporters and photographers around at the front.

The office has a row of orange plastic chairs along one wall, by the door, and a heavy hardwood desk opposite them across a couple of meters of frayed gray-green carpet. A wide window overlooks the harbor sound, but the minuscule crack by which it's opened does little to refresh the air of the room. A case of thick leather-bound books stands against the rear wall. The big comfortable-looking swivel chair behind the desk is, for the present, unoccupied, and on top of the desk lies nothing but an ornamental inkwell and long dip pen, a leather-bordered blotter, a telephone, a broken-handled old mug containing a clutch of dip pens and a single ballpoint, and a globe of Croatan.

"Looks like we've been left to our own devices," Matt says, after they've sat waiting for no more than a minute. The damp patches on his clothes are beginning to dry out, as well as to chafe. He stands up and strolls over to half sit on the desk and idly spin the globe, ignoring the disapproving looks from Gregor and Elizabeth. In their short and relatively privileged lives they've never encountered any authority that wasn't light-handed and legitimate, and Matt's pretty sure they don't know how to behave when they encounter the other kind. For himself, he'll try disrespect first, and if that doesn't work, and resistance isn't an option, he'll grovel. The important thing is not to pretend that voluntary consent is involved, either way. Matt studies the globe and waits for the door to open.

New Virginia, the continent they're on, is in roughly the position of North America and roughly the size of Australia. Croatan has seven other island continents, none of them particularly close to each other. Only the indentations of their coastlines indicate that they'd ever been joined; local scientists have wryly dubbed that past supercontinent New

Gondwana. Nobody's yet measured continental drift, instrumentation—
and funding—not having yet caught up with the theories that the *Bright
Star*'s files downloaded long ago. But the indications are that the continents are still dispersing across the globe; tens of millions of years in
the future, some of them may collide, throwing up, perhaps, New Alps
and New Himalayas, but for now they inch apart, hurrying away from
each other like the galaxies after the big bang: Nova Europa, Elizabetha,
New Hindostan, Arctica (joined to New Virginia by the polar ice), St
Paul's Land, Discovery, Havenbless.

The coast, and much of the interior, of New Virginia has been well
mapped; the outlines of the other continents look more artistic than
scientific, and large areas of their interiors are, on close inspection,
essentially blank. All of them, however, have human inhabitants, descendants of at least two episodes of involuntary human arrival: the
more recent one that founded Rawliston in historical times, the other,
or others, prehistoric, and the origin of the various pockets of heathen
savages, as they're called here. In a time before even prehistory, in some
epoch reachable only by palaeontology, the other hominidae and the
large mammals were brought; and still earlier, drilling down into geo-
logical time now, the saurs and the kraken and the megatheria and marine birds, the pterosaurs that rule the skies, the insects and insectivores
and all the rest of the ecosystem made their varied ways to this world.

Whatever the origin of the planetary body itself—and Matt has his
suspicions about that, given the paucity of Earth-like worlds and orbits
in the Solar System's vicinity, and their abundance in the Second
Sphere—it's long ago been established that its whole biota bespoke a
created world, on which the transplanted products of an original evolution have themselves evolved further: distant descendants of Earth's
stolen and unknown children. Matt tends to think of this pattern, prevalent throughout the habitable planets of the suns of the Second Sphere,
as a *backup file*. What catastrophic losses of data this backup was intended to forestall, the gods only know, but Matt has every intention of
finding out.

The door opens, and a man comes in, with a file.

Lydia turned away from watching the customs boat's disappearing wake
through the open hatchway and found herself looking at Salasso, who
returned her gaze with an expression unreadable even by saur standards.
She tugged her radio from her pocket and raised her eyebrows.

"Please," said Salasso.

She tuned the dial to her ship's channel, switched on the scrambler, and raised the Traders' House.

"Lydia on the *Bright Star,* to the house."

"Hi there, Lydia," Esias de Tenebre said, in the accented English he staunchly stuck to when on Croatan. "Good positioning, my number-seven daughter! Consider your back clapped. Any idea what the hell's going on?"

She recounted the Port Authority's arrival and departure.

"That sounds heavy-handed," her father remarked. His sigh was a white noise in her ear. "It seems not long ago when such travelers would have been welcomed royally, not bureaucratically!"

"I remember," Lydia said soothingly. "I miss the dear old king, myself."

She was anxious to deflect Esias's standard canned rant against democracy, a political system that Rawliston had recently and violently adopted. As a member of the Electorate of the Republic of Nova Babylonia, the senior de Tenebre took a dim view of universal franchise.

"However," she went on, "I think this is more than just a case of local officialdom overstepping its mark. The news channels and the populace seem pretty excited and enthusiastic about it, and I can't imagine what the Port Authority thinks it's trying to accomplish by delaying our friends' making contact with them."

"You've put your finger on it," her father said. "Delay is exactly what they're accomplishing. And if some jumped-up winner of the administrative lottery decides to embargo the ship while his minions crawl around it . . ."

Again the white noise, from spluttering this time. Lydia held the earpiece away until her father's voice resumed, in a calmer tone: "Could be some onshore agents of our competitors behind all this—some loose-lipped third cousin or lazy servant has no doubt been bragging in a bar about how we've been expecting the cosmonauts' ship to turn up any day now."

"I certainly wasn't expecting it," Lydia said.

"But you were hoping," her father said wryly. "Weren't you?"

"Yes," she said. She paused for a moment, to indicate that she wanted to change the subject. "What would you like me to do now?"

"Oh, stay on the ship," Esias said hastily. "If they'll allow you."

Lydia raised her eyebrows at Salasso, who would have overheard every nuance of both sides of the conversation, inaudible though the faint sound from the earpiece would have been to Johannes, only a meter or two away. The saur nodded firmly.

"Salasso's happy with that."

"Salasso, by the gods! He's there too? Well, let him know we'll send someone out to see him."

"I will," Lydia promised unnecessarily—Salasso's usually impassive face was indicating bright delight already. "Signing off for now."

"Signing off," Esias said. "Take care."

Salasso looked at her. "Thank you," he said. "I shall look forward to that meeting."

"Well," said Lydia, with an awkward, light laugh, "I don't suppose you could show us around your ship, while we're waiting?"

"Certainly," said Salasso. "Except for the cargo itself, which is commercially confidential."

"Of course." Lydia wondered if Salasso could read her small smirk at the presumption of thinking that competition from the *Bright Star*'s cargo was likely to worry the de Tenebre family business; probably he could. His nostrils widened fractionally, the corners of his lips extended sideways a little: a smile.

He glanced at Johannes, who still stood, almost at attention, by the exit hatch.

"Both of you?" he asked.

"Uh, no," Lydia said. "Johannes, would you mind just . . . keeping an eye on the door?"

"Not at all," said her cousin, in a tone that indicated he minded a bit, but not enough to make a big deal of it. She'd have to make it up to him, afterward with a detailed description over drinks.

"Let us begin where we are," said Salasso. "This is the control room. The controls themselves are mounted on this table, and are undeniably crude. However, as we have demonstrated, they work."

Lydia had not expected that the clutter of data-input devices, tangles of cable, and cannibalized electrical apparatus on the tilted table could be the controls. She'd assumed it was some bits of legacy junk and had vaguely imagined a shining console with wraparound screens in the bowels of the ship. But then, she had never actually seen the controls of a starship—for all she knew, the kraken might play their tentacles over something equally uneasy on the eye. Though not, she guessed, with such shoddy insulation.

She ducked after Salasso through an oval hatch that led to a strip-lit tubular corridor with free-fall handgrips along the sides and retrofitted planking along the bottom. After a few paces the saur pointed sideways at a doorway.

"Fabrication unit," he said as he passed it. Hurrying to keep up, Lydia caught a glimpse of a module dominated by a floor-mounted cluster of glittery, spidery machinery that looked sinister and alien and that she suspected—but it could have been a trick of the light—was in tremulous motion.

"What do you plan to do with it?"

Salasso glanced back, pausing at another doorway. "It may have industrial applications," he said. "But that is for the long future. We took it in case we needed to make repairs."

He led her quickly on, pointing out habitation units, cargo bays, labs, and finally, as they turned a corner at an intersection and stopped before something huge and bolted to the corridor floor, the drive.

She stood looking over the saur's shoulder, struck silent by the sight. Smooth, as though cast in one impenetrable piece, its flowing curves and fluted flanges and flared, funnelled ends were those of a jet engine designed by gods. It stood on a pedestal, and by moving about she could take in its approximate dimensions: two meters high, one across, and four long. From any angle, it looked as though streamlined to move in that direction. The beauty of its form was fused with its fitness for some incomprehensible function, making it irresistible and at the same time uncomfortable to look at.

"It plays tricks with the eye," said Salasso. "It makes the head hurt."

"Yours too?" she asked.

"No," said Salasso, turning away. "You have never seen one before?"

Lydia closed her eyes and put her fingers to her temples and turned her back on the drive. She could still see it, in her mind.

"No," she said. "The krakens don't give us tours." She laughed weakly. "Just as well."

"I have not seen one on a ship," said Salasso. "Only newly built ones, in the manufacturing plant."

Lydia gazed, unseeing, at the far end of the corridor. "I still can't believe Gregor actually figured out how to control that thing." She gave the saur a shrewd sidelong glance. "It wasn't you, was it?"

"No indeed!" Salasso sounded slightly indignant. "I could not, even if I would. No, Gregor's work was the culmination of generations of hand calculation by members of the Cosmonaut Families. It was implemented on this ship's remaining functional computers after Gregor had independently achieved the key insight."

"Oh," she said. "And what was that?"

The saur's large black eyes regarded her, his expression verging on something like humor.

"Octopodia."

There was a feeling in her back as though she were being watched. "Take me somewhere else," she said.

"I think you have seen all you need to see," said Salasso. She followed him as he headed back to the control room by a different route. On the way she glanced into a lab module through a glass pane in its doorway.

She stopped. "What's that?"

Again, it was something she couldn't look away from, more alien by far than the complex fabrication tool kit or even the drive itself. Like an enormous model of a snowflake rendered in fine sheet metal, partly folded and partly crumpled, it almost filled the room.

Salasso turned and looked back at her, impassively.

"That is the device that the crew of the original ship—when it was a research station on the surface of a god—used to communicate with that god."

"Oh," said Lydia. She shivered, as though the snowflake sculpture were making her cold. "It seems a strange item to bring with you."

"It might have been necessary," Salasso said, "in an emergency, if Gregor's navigation calculations had been mistaken."

"I see," said Lydia. "Like you brought the fabrication unit."

"Yes," said Sallaso. "Like that."

Lydia followed him to the control room without further interruption and stepped through its hatchway with a sense of relief. She had found the tour fascinating but disturbing; all her life she had traveled in a ship piloted by giant squids; a ship built, crewed and serviced by saurs, and whose original design, she knew, had come from the gods themselves. That remote and limited interaction with those distant and indifferent divinities had been mediated by the two known species of greater intelligence and antiquity than the human. Now she was standing in a ship built by human beings that had touched the very face of a god, and she now knew that at least two men of her acquaintance, Matt and Volkov, might have had even closer communion with it than that.

No wonder, then, that these two old cosmonauts seemed ageless.

Perhaps it wasn't, as Volkov had claimed, some advanced medical treatment received long ago in the Solar System that had bestowed this gift, unexpected as it had been. Perhaps some cold fire from the icy mind of the god had entered their nerves. As always when she thought of Volkov, a hot fire entered her own.

As soon as she'd cleared the hatchway she saw that Johannes was no longer alone in the control room. A saur stood in the external doorway, behind which an extending ladder sloped back and up to the just-visible underside of a hovering gravity skiff.

"Bishlayan!" Salasso said. The two saurs met in the middle of the floor and held each other by the shoulders for a moment. Keeping his hand on her shoulder, Salasso escorted her to one of the battered seats and almost lifted her into it, then swung back and up into another.

"It is good to see you," Bishlayan said.

"Likewise," said Salasso. The two saurs, politeness satisfied, dropped out of Trade Latin and into their own language, of which, like most humans—even her father—Lydia knew little more than a few everyday phrases and the odd technical word. Their body language of mutual affection, subtle but intense, she found almost embarrassingly understandable.

It suddenly ocurred to Lydia that the de Tenebre ship's last-but-one visit to Mingulay had been less than a year ago in Bishlayan's life, and in Lydia's, but more than four hundred years in Salasso's if he'd spent all that time on the same planet. A long time for lovers to be parted, even though the saurs saw love from the different perspective provided by their millennia-long lives.

The thought of parted lovers, and of long lives, brought a pang. Gregor Cairns and Grigory Volkov, the one young and bright, the other old and sly, might between them provide the solution to both problems . . . though the two of them presented her with a different problem and the prospect of a difficult choice. Lydia looked away from the saurs' sibilant, sinuous conversation and ambled idly about the control room, looking out of the forward window—and it was a window, not a viewscreen—at the shipping, looking over the shoulder of Johannes, who'd slumped in one of the chairs behind Salasso's back and was carefully inspecting, and carefully not touching, the control system.

Like black rocks perturbing a smooth current, the names "Volkov" and "Cairns" suddenly cropped up in Salasso's speech. Johannes, not as attuned as Lydia to the language or to the names, and still tracing wires with his gaze, didn't seem to have noticed. Lydia moved around to get an inconspicuous sidelong view of the saurs. They were both leaning forward. Salasso's long fingers were gripping his knees. Bishlayan's hands were held in front of her, quivering. Both spoke more quietly than before, and sometimes—almost unthinkably for their kind— at the same time, interrupting each other. The cosmonauts' names came up again and again, each time more harshly dissonant than before.

Then Bishlayan leaned back slightly—in a human, it would have been a violent recoil. Her hands—open, palms down in front of her— moved sharply apart: *cut.* She grasped the arms of the seat and slid out of it, stalked across the floor to the exit, and ascended the ladder. In a moment the steps slid back into the craft, and its shadow passed across the forward window as it flitted away.

Salasso sat bowed over, with his elbows on his knees and his head in his hands.

Matt takes his time about shifting his buttock from the desk, as the official strides over, nods with a passing frown, and arranges himself in the chair. His sallow-skinned face projects above the high collar of a uniform too big for his short and skinny frame: knee breeches to mid-calf, epaulettes that almost reach his ears, the blue, brass-buttoned coat's sleeves turned back at the wrists to reveal a square foot or two of greasy silk lining. He shuffles the papers he carried in and adjusts the blotter, looking sternly downward as Matt eases himself back to an orange seat.

Then his sharp, dark eyes look up.

"Good afternoon," he says. "Citizen Obadiah Randolph, secretary of customs, at your service."

They return greetings in an awkward chorus.

Randolph smiles. "Well," he says, "I suppose I had better welcome you to the city, and the planet, and I do, but I shall spare you any disquisitions on the historic significance of your arrival. The chatterboxes will no doubt stuff your ears with plenty of that before the day is out. It's their job. Mine is to ensure that you are not carrying any prohibited products, to apply any applicable tariffs, and to make arrangements for currency conversion. May I see your bill of lading, please?"

Matt fiddles with the flimsy sheets for a moment.

"What we would like to query," he says, "is whether this whole procedure is applicable to arrivals by starship, given that the established interstellar merchants don't have to go through any such clearance. In short, and with all due respect, we question whether your authority extends to our ship."

"Ah!" Randolph leans forward, steepling his long fingers. "I'm afraid it does. The great merchant families"—he waves a hand vaguely at the window—"such as the de Tenebres are, as you say, established. Tariffs, by immemorial custom, are not applied. As for quarantine regulations—well! The ships in which the established merchants travel are owned and crewed by beings whose experience in this regard can, I think, be safely reckoned to be vastly greater than ours." He smiles again, not so warmly. "And in *my* experience, the krakens and the saurs are our mental and moral superiors, and the difference in both knowledge of consequence and sense of responsibility is . . . noticeable."

"I'll give you that," Matt says dryly. "It just seems odd that you'd be ready for something that's never happened before. I mean, come on. An independent starship arrives—and not just any starship, at that— and the first thing you think of is to drag it through *customs*?"

Obadiah Randolph's lips narrow. He spreads his hands. "It's true, we've only recently realized that such an event might be possible, and made . . . contingency plans. A thousand apologies if it seems burdensome, but if it does, would it not be better to get it over with?"

Contingency plans, huh? Matt has a good idea how the Port Authority just happened to have them worked out recently.

"Fine," he says, rising and passing the papers across the desk. "Let's get it over with."

Randolph shows no signs of hurry to get it over with, as for the next hour or so he queries every line in the manifest, hauling book after book down from the shelf and looking up obscure precedents and arcane definitions, all for tediously innocuous items of Mingulayan manufacture— high-value stuff, jewelery and precision intruments and so forth, as the economics of the trade dictate, but nothing of obvious malign use or biological origin. Matt kicks his heels, stares out of the window, wishes for a drink or smoke; Gregor and Elizabeth talk quietly and, in the end, desultorily.

The telephone buzzes once. Matt notes that the apparatus isn't cabled; still using radio, then. Citizen Randolph listens intently, murmurs briefly, returns the handset to its cradle and his attention to a musty volume. About ten minutes later he replaces it on the shelf, brushes its dust from his fingertips, and slumps back in his chair. Then he reaches into a desk drawer, produces a tinned inkpad and a large rubber stamp, and thumps an imprint onto each sheet of the cargo manifest with an air of a job well done.

He slides the papers back across the desk.

"That's it," he says. "All in order, as far as I can see. No embargoed products, and nothing in your cargo appears on the schedule of imports on which tariff is liable. A small fee of five hundred talers is due for my services, of course, but as long as it's paid at my office downstairs before your departure—"

Gregor raises a hand. "Excuse me." He pulls a bundle of Croatan currency from his pocket, peers at it, peels off five, and slaps them on the desk with ill grace. "There."

"Thank you," says Randolph, vanishing the cash.

Matt picks up the documents, smiling for a moment at the blurry curlicues of red ink.

"Thank *you*," he says. Out of the corner of his eye he sees that Gregor shares his looming, forward-leaning stance and seizes the moment of psychological advantage. "Now, citizen, could you please enlighten us on what the point of this whole rigmarole has been?"

Randolph leans back and blinks. "I beg your pardon?"

Matt gestures out of the window. "I've watched a dozen surface ships come in this past hour, all heavy-laden merchantmen, and by their rig and flags I guess they must have have come from at least four different distant shores, and you have the time to personally inspect our documents in the most pernickety detail?"

"I doubt that any of their cargoes are as significant as yours. If human starship traffic is possible—and you have shown it is—it will be repeated and extended. The cargoes of our surface shipping will change and multiply. We'll have both the need and the ability to map and explore our own planet much more intensively then before." He waves a hand at the globe on his desk. "No more of that 'here be dragons' nonsense. Besides"—he leans farther back—"the cargo is the least important part of what you have on your ship. The past hour has given us time to initiate an independent inspection of the rest, for ecological, biological, chemical, or other hazards. I have just heard that the boarding has been successful."

Matt has a strong impulse to tip the chair right back and send the man sprawling, and an equally strong conviction that this won't do them any long-term good.

•   •   •

The loud-hailed warning from outside jolted Salasso out of his hitherto unshakeable gloomy trance. He walked slowly to the exit hatch and leaned out, then stepped back.

"It's an inspection," he said.

The man who came through the hatchway was younger and slimmer than his predecessors and more elaborately dressed, with tall boots and a plumed hat, which he doffed with a bow to Lydia.

"Citizen Charles Cargill," he said. "Your servant. Customs, excise, and public safety."

They introduced themselves. Cargill turned to Salasso. His black hair hung in a pigtail down the back of his green coat.

"You are in charge here?"

"For the present," said Salasso.

The inspector pulled a radio from his pocket and spoke into briefly, too quickly and quietly for Lydia to catch. He clicked it shut and put it away.

"You'll be glad to know," he said, "that your documentation is in order. Your declared cargo is cleared for landing, pending inspection."

"You are welcome to inspect it," said Salasso.

"Thank you," said Cargill. "But that is not my purpose. You are free to leave the cargo sealed for the moment. It will of course be checked on landing. My duty is to inspect the ship for possible public hazards."

Lydia had a brief surge of the feeling she associated with the gravity's being switched off.

Cargill looked about, frowning, and pointed at the table in the center of the deck. "Perhaps you would care to start by explaining *that*?"

"Certainly," said Salasso. "This is the control panel."

Cargill studied the apparatus warily, noting the dodgy insulation with pursed lips and a shake of the head.

Salasso stood by the door to the ship's interior. "I will now show you around the ship," he said.

Lydia thought she could detect a strained note in his voice. He stepped over the bulkhead, beckoning Cargill after him.

They reappeared some twenty minutes later.

Cargill made his way to the nearest chair and sat down in it, visibly mustering his composure. His clamped hands stopped the quivering of his knees, but one of his heels, apparently without his awareness, kept tapping on the floor.

"This ship . . ." he said. His tongue flicked along his lips. "This ship is impounded."

4

The First Man on Venus

THE STEPS INSIDE the Port Authority building are of worn concrete; those outside, spilling down to the street from the double swinging doors, are of chipped but clean marble. The sunlight is harsh against the white stone as Matt emerges blinking, Gregor and Elizabeth at his heels. At the bottom of the ten or so wide, shallow steps are a couple of dozen people, holding up heavy cameras or holding out thick black microphones. Many of them are clutching radios to one ear and talking, and scribbling on pads of paper. Behind them in the broad street huge trucks and small cars are alike trundling by in low gear. Drivers and pedestrians loiter and stare. The din of voices and vehicles is distracting. A few brown-uniformed men sweating under polished steel helmets and clutching two-meter staves are urging people to move on, but beyond preventing a complete standstill they're not accomplishing much.

There's no surge up the steps, though, so Matt ambles down to face the thicket of microphones. A woman holding one of them shoves a big flapping sheet of paper into his hands. The paper is warm, and the black lettering smudges under his thumbs. A bold masthead in antique font announces it's **The Hourly Electrostat** over a blocky headline screaming **STARSHIP SEIZED**. The rest of the top half of the page is a grainy but perfectly distinct photograph, obviously taken from a low-flying aircraft, of the two customs men boarding the *Bright Star* and two others pointing rifles at the camera. Matt is impressed: The event happened less than two hours ago. Maybe the masthead's boast is justified.

Matt has no time to read any more of it. A microphone is thrust in front of him.

"Mr. Cairns, do you have anything to say about what the Port Authority's doing?"

Other reporters crowd around, shouting questions about why and how the *Bright Star* has made the lightspeed jump. Matt turns to Gregor, who is after all in charge of the ship. Gregor shrugs and mouths silently. Elizabeth shakes her head. Matt realizes with some irritation that the other two have decided that he has to speak for them.

He smiles at the woman who gave him the paper and says, "No, I have no comment at all on what the Port Authority has done."

"Don't you think it's—?"

But he's already turned to answer someone else.

"We're here on a trading mission," he says. "And to test the ship. That's all. Navigator Gregor Cairns here has solved the problem of navigating the jump between Mingulay and Croatan. We're of course relieved that it works"—he pauses, smiling for a camera until someone smiles back—"and we're delighted to be here."

The woman from the *Electrostat* fixes on him again and swings her microphone dangerously.

"Why have you come? You personally, all of you?"

He nudges Gregor to take this one. The younger man shrugs and scratches his head as though this is some deep question. Typical scientist. The dead air stretches for twenty seconds.

"I'm here," Gregor says, "because I did the navigation, and I would not ask anyone else to bet his or her life on my calculations and stay behind myself. My, uh, relative Matt is here because he had some expertise on the working of the ship itself. He has, ah, made a special study of it. And Elizabeth, uh . . ."

"I'm here," Elizabeth says firmly, "because I'm a scientist. A marine biologist. I'm here representing the university, not the Cosmonaut Families."

"Isn't there anyone back home you'll be missing?" the reporter asks her, with a sly smile.

"Of all the people I know, Gregor is the only one I could not bear to be away from for ten years." That raises a laugh and some whoops.

Another microphone pushes in front of Matt's face. "Is it true that the saurs are helping you?"

"A few are," Matt says.

He turns away sharply from that mike and answers some more questions fulsomely but evasively and makes sure to clasp his arms around the shoulders of his companions, partly for the cameras and partly because he can see both of them beginning to look a little dissociated. He knows the feeling: It's culture shock, combined with the even bigger shock to the human animal brain of finding itself on a different planet, with the gravity ever so slightly off so that your heels come down a bit wrong and you thump things and the air carries unfamiliar smells in a slightly different mix of gases that your brain can't quite make sense of but that you notice in every cell.

And all the while he is wondering how they are going to get away from all this and where they can go when they do, when suddenly he sees a delightfully familiar and welcome sight, a real taste of home: A flying saucer slides above the rooftops of the high buildings opposite and begins to descend, reflecting the entire scene in a wondrously distorted image in its perfect-mirrored lenticular surface as it settles slowly on the street. Vehicles and people shift out of its way, in a cacophony of squealing brakes, crunching fenders, tinkling glass, engines revving and people shouting. Its three legs telescope out and its entrance hatch opens like a liquid eye, and a dull-gray stairladder extends to the foot of the Port Authority steps.

The de Tenebre girl, Lydia, takes a few steps down the ladder and glares around at the crowd, then grins down.

"Come on in," she says. "We can take you to the Star Traders' House."

Matt sways on the spot as first Gregor, then Elizabeth ascend. It's as if his leg muscles have locked. Then, with a shake of his head and an effort of will, he follows them up into the skiff. The hatch seals soundlessly behind him. Inside, it's exactly like every other flying saucer he's ever been in, with a wraparound screen showing the outside clearer than a window, and a sort of angled soft shelf all the way around the bottom of that, with a small arc of it recessed to the control panel before which the saur pilot sits. Another touch of home.

Salasso is already on board. Matt smiles at him and sits down beside Lydia on the circular bench whose comfortably padded back wraps around the central faring over the craft's engine. The floor is cluttered with suitcases, among which he recognizes his own.

The pilot looks back over his shoulder. "Everybody ready?"

"Yes," says Lydia. "Take us away, Voronar, if you please."

There's no sense of motion, but the view in the screen tips and slides down. For a moment Matt looks down at the crowd of reporters, some of them still holding their microphones skyward, or more rationally their cameras, and then the view swings up again and there's nothing but hazy sky ahead.

"So what happened out there?" Matt asks.

Salasso exhales a long, hissing sigh and gestures at Lydia as though he is beyond speech, which he may be.

Lydia is herself furious. "That *fop,* that *bureaucrat* Cargill marched all over the ship and impounded it as a hazard! We just managed to get your stuff off. None of you are allowed back on except Salasso, and that's just because he persuaded Cargill that the drive needs regular attention or it'll be a *bigger* hazard. They have two armed patrol boats moored alongside now. You can unload your cargo, but that's all."

Gregor frowns and leans forward awkwardly around the curve of the bench. "Do you think Cargill really was genuinely frightened by the sight of the drive and the other bits of advanced kit?"

Lydia laughs, and when she speaks the spitting rage has gone out of her voice. "I know it scared him—and it scared me! But that's not a rational reason to embargo the ship. No, it's a pretext."

"So what's the real reason?"

"We'll discuss that at the house," Lydia says. "My father knows something of the matter."

She stands up and looks out of the viewscreen. The air is clear outside, the sky bright blue. The skiff has sped beyond the city's edge to fly low along a coast road. Between the road and the long white beaches, large villas and mansions are set in broad gardens. Toward one of the largest of them, it dips, then yaws and sideslips like a falling leaf into a paved, palm-lined courtyard where fountains play with rainbows. Its legs and ladder, extending, neatly straddle the central bathing pool.

"Here we are," she says. "Welcome to the Star Traders' House."

Lydia led them to a table under the courtyard's interior colonnade. A couple of distant cousins had run up for the baggage, and the skiff lifted off over the roof to immediately descend again, this time on the long lawn of long grass between the house and the beach.

Her father, Esias, and his third wife, Phoebe, rose to greet the new arrivals. Esias, evidently relaxed, wore an informal loose toga, Phoebe a similarly Nova Babylonian light robe of green cloth flecked with silver threads. Much handshaking and backslapping ensued; Matt was the only one who needed an introduction. Phoebe started filling glasses from a large, ice-clinking jug and signaling to some cousins across the courtyard for more drinks at about the same time as Voronar strolled in through the open passageway from the front and joined Salasso as they all sat down.

Lydia found herself on Gregor's right; his left arm was around Elizabeth, who had no attention for anything but the tall glass that had just appeared in front of her.

"You once asked me where we lived, between journeys," Lydia murmured. "This is where we live when we're here."

"It's wonderful," Gregor said, craning his neck and gazing around. "How do you keep it, between visits?"

"We don't," Lydia said. "It's rented to any merchant family that happens along, and betweentimes, I imagine, to local rich folk who want some time out of the city." She leaned back and looked around, noticing as if for the first time the weathering of the slates and the flagstones, the lichen and the creeper on the walls. "It's changed a lot, in the last few months, I mean centuries . . ."

Gregor looked at her wryly. "Yeah, I'll bet. Are there any other families staying here?"

"No, no, just us. Four wings, three stories—it's just about big enough for all of us. Sixty-odd humans, thirty or so saurs—that's a fairly typical trader clan and crew, and the others in at the moment have other villas up and down the coast."

"Better than the Keep, do you think?"

Lydia smiled, recalling the vast prehuman castle that the Cosmonaut Families maintained outside Kyohvic, Gregor's native town on Mingulay.

"More comfortable, perhaps, but not as interesting, with no one staying here to give us hospitality. No dinosaur heads on the walls, and no clifftop walks, either."

Gregor smiled momentarily over the shared memory, then reached for his drink. Matt Cairns and Esias were already talking quietly and intently; the two saurs were passing a pipe of hemp back and forth between them, puffing fragrant smoke rings from their narrow mouths, and Phoebe was drawing out Elizabeth with some sympathetic small talk across the table, a conversation to which Gregor turned his attention.

Lydia didn't need to ask whether Gregor and Elizabeth were still in love with each other—Elizabeth's presence here was earnest enough of that—but she had no idea whether this passion excluded her. She suspected it did. Mingulayan custom was sexually tolerant but emotionally constrained, holding up mutual physical attraction combined with friendship as the only worthy basis of marriage, and disdaining romantic love as a dangerous but transitory disorder of the mind, a flimsy foundation for any protracted partnership. The predictable result was that infatuation flourished in a furtive manner, its stems not tall and flowering but creeping along the ground, pallid and twisted and entangling. She couldn't help but regard her own culture as much healthier and more natural, giving fleeting romantic attachment an honorable but ornamental place alongside the more businesslike affair of marriage.

At that moment, her father's second wife, Lydia's mother Faustina, walked in from the passageway accompanied by Grigory Volkov, both of them naked and dripping from the beach, chatting and toweling and teasing each other, and Lydia almost cried out with the hot fury of her jealousy. There was nothing to it, nothing; of course there was not; Volkov could swim with anyone he liked, and he did. Right now he was grinning straight at her, his white teeth gleaming against his new tan, his blond hair palmed casually back in inch-long damp spikes. He knotted the towel around his waist as he noticed the new guests, and his smile subtly changed as he greeted them and swung around the table to drag up a chair at the corner beside Lydia, while Faustina snuggled damply up to Esias opposite.

"So you made it," Volkov said, to Matt rather than Gregor. His soft baritone and the indefinably cultured accent of his English gave Lydia, as always, a sensation like that of stroking a cat's back. Or, she fancied, of being a cat and having its back stroked.

"We made it," Matt said firmly. A cousin had wheeled up a rattling trolley of bottles and was slowly orbitting the table. Matt glanced away from Volkov long enough to make a selection, then fixed him again with his gaze as he absently tipped several fingers of clear vodka into his fruit juice.

"Good to see you all," Volkov said, flashing his smile around. "I could hardly believe it when I heard it on the radio." He chuckled. "So I went swimming. Ah, large vodka. Thanks, Arianne." He smiled up at the cousin serving and raised quick eyebrows to Esias. "Have you got to business yet?"

Esias shook his head, frowning a little. "I thought that could wait until after dinner. Our guests need to relax."

"Naturally," said Volkov. He fingered water from his ear and looked around again, head tilted, as though shyly. "I'll be going in the pool and the fountains to wash the salt off, and I'm sure Faustina will do the same. Would any of you like to join us?"

"What an excellent idea," said Esias. He shed his toga and, wearing nothing but his immense dignity, picked up his second wife and walked to the pool, threw her in, and jumped after her.

Volkov looked sidelong at the startled expressions of Gregor and Elizabeth.

"But we have nothing to—" Elizabeth began.

" 'When in Rome . . .' " said Volkov, and after a little more persuasion, they did as the Nova Babylonians had done.

Esias is a broad-beamed, sturdy man in his midforties, with springy, gingery hair and a spray of freckles across his flat nose. From the head of the table, flanked by his first and second wives, he chairs the after-dinner conversation with nothing more obtrusive than a narrowed eye or a cocked ear. With intent that might be mischievous or tactful, he has seated Volkov between Faustina and Lydia—his seventh but, for this occasion, most-favored daughter—and Matt directly opposite Volkov, between Claudia and Phoebe. Gregor, then Elizabeth, are to Lydia's left; Salasso, Bishlayan, and Voronar to Phoebe's right. Farther on down the long table are other senior clan and crew members, saur or human; as seems customary, various junior relatives have done the serving, and the rest of the shop's complement are scattered among other tables, on this outer verandah or on the tussocky seaside grass in the house's long shadow that, with the sea breeze, makes this a cool and pleasant location for an early evening meal. Harp music from nearby merges with the tinkling of the fountains from down the passageway in the courtyard behind them, to provide a similarly soothing and cooling effect on the mind.

Matt has found conversation with the two ladies on either side of him interesting but something of a strain. Like the rest of the de Tenebres they know of his—and Volkov's—untoward longevity and are intrigued by his recollections of Earth. Matt has had little experience of recounting them to people who hadn't been there themselves, and there's a fine line between mystifying them with too little explanation and making their eyes glaze over with too much. Volkov, he notices, has no such difficulty, chatting easily to both Lydia and her mother, calling across to other people whose acquaintance he's obviously cultivated during the past quarter, and always making a point of thanking the younger folk on waiting duty rather than taking their attentions for granted like their relatives do.

Matt dourly reflects that Volkov was always good at winning people over. It's entirely possible that his genuine competence as a cosmonaut, and the authentic if scientifically worthless heroism that took him to and from the hellish surface of Venus, were themselves effects as well as causes of his political ascent through the bureaucracies of the European Space Agency and the Communist Party of the European Union. In the past couple of centuries these achievements have been entirely moot, but he's had several business careers since then under different identities, and each one has usually left a nice little nest egg for its successor to hatch for the benefit of the reappearing Volkov, billed as a long-lost son or other legitimate inheritor. Unlike Matt, whose typical transition from one incarnation to the next has involved arson, major insurance fraud, and faking his own death to escape angry creditors. Avoiding any reference to these serial suicides, self-embezzlements, and so forth has been not the least exacting part of his small talk with Claudia and Phoebe.

Gregor, too, is having an awkward time, talking mostly to Elizabeth and almost cold-shouldering Lydia, though she's hanging so much on Volkov's conversation that she may not have noticed. At least Gregor and Elizabeth look like they've got over their planet shock, though Matt expects them—and himself—to crash down to an early night. The three saurs at Matt's right are silent, torpid from their hearty eating—each has a plate in front of him or her piled with the bones of the main dish, small pterosaurs that taste like chicken—and whacked out of their heads by a recently shared pipe of hemp. Matt absently accepts a joint from Claudia and finds his gaze drawn away from the table to where the harpist is sitting, her back half turned, leaving her cheekbone, jawline, and pensive mouth as visible and as fascinating as the straight blond hair that hangs to the waistline of her leather trousers.

Matt is shaken out of the resulting erotic reverie by the sound of Esias elbowing the table and clearing his throat, so he leans past the vacant black eyes of the nodding saurs to pass the joint to starboard and settles back and looks to the head of the table.

Esias makes a big deal of lighting up a fat cigar with a fancy new device he's just imported from Mingulay, which Matt does not doubt he is inordinately pleased with and has high hopes of franchising elsewhere. The lid of the knockoff Zippo clicks shut and Esias puffs smoke to clear the petroleum whiff.

He coughs again, just to make sure. It's discreet but as emphatic a signal as the rap of a gavel to the few who hear it. The only person other than those around the head of the table who responds is the harpist, who stops playing and turns around (another moment of distraction, as Matt catches sight of her lean, pale features). Esias plays air harp for a moment, urging her to resume playing. She does. Salasso, Bishlayan, and Voronar jolt out of their trance. Esias leans forward on his elbows and speaks quietly.

"Before we've all had too much to drink—which, I expect, we will—we have some business to attend to. Everybody here is guest or family, so we needn't worry about being overheard, and doubtless everything I say will get around, but we have a moment of not-too-obvious semiprivacy, so let's use it by getting the, ah, more delicate matters out of the way first. . . ."

He closes his eyes momentarily, and sighs, and combs greasy fingers through his shock of hair. Lydia suddenly blushes and looks, desperately, as though she doesn't know where to look and settles on staring fixedly across at Matt. Baffled, he returns her what he hopes is a friendly and reassuring smile.

"As some of you know," Esias goes on, "I promised Lydia's hand to Gregor here, a few months ago back on Mingulay, if he could meet us in his own ship. He has done that. I also repeated that promise, on different terms, at another time. Lydia's consent was"—he smiles at her, briefly—"evident at both times. We consider ourselves bound to it. Gregor, the decision is in your hands. You need not make it now, but it would be . . . convenient if you did."

Matt is shaken. He knows there's some tension between Gregor and Elizabeth over Lydia but has assumed it no more than the normal jealousy over an ex not over an outstanding arrangement. Are the interstellar master traders really as primitive and patriarchal as *that*? Bride-price? Christ, by 2049 we'd stamped that out in fucking *Afghanistan*. . . . He realizes that this is the first time in years that he's thought *we* and meant the European Union.

Gregor and Elizabeth have clasped hands firmly above the table. Esias takes this in but speaks to Gregor only. "Your relationship with Elizabeth is not an obstacle to your accepting the offer, as far as we are concerned."

Gregor, floundering until now, seizes on this like a thrown line. "It is, as far as I am concerned," he says. "I appreciate what you're saying, and I thank you for it, but we—on Mingulay we have a different way of looking at these things."

"Indeed you do," says Esais wryly. "But I must ask you formally: Do you release Lydia from my promise?"

"I release her," says Gregor, then surprises Matt by turning to Lydia with a big grin and adding, "but, you know, no offense . . ."

Even Elizabeth joins in the laughter at that; even Lydia, though she's blinking a little rapidly and at the same time looking released and relieved.

"Thank you," Lydia says. "I'm sure I'll live down this rejection."

"It's not a—" Gregor begins hotly, rather blowing the wit and tact he'd a shown a moment ago.

Lydia puts a hand over his mouth. "I'm such a tease," she says.

Too much of a one, Elizabeth's dark glance agrees, but the whole strain of the situation has been collapsed by Gregor's apparently artless compliment. Matt is sure that no one else but Elizabeth has noticed that beneath his light tone was a note of regret.

"Very good," says Esias. He looks around his wives, who all seem as cheered as he is by the settlement of that particular item on the agenda. "Let's, um, move on. About the ship and its impounding. Since our last visit here this city has adopted a new political system: legislation by assemblies of the entire populace, with almost all public offices filled by citizens chosen by lot. Out-and-out democracy, if you ask me." He shakes his head sadly. "Well, they'll learn. That kind of straightforward tyranny of the majority has many disadvantages, one of which is that it makes officeholders difficult to bribe, beyond the most routine grease and graft, and makes it even more difficult to place sympathetic people in useful positions."

Matt laughs, then realizes from the surrounding silence that the merchant is being quite serious.

"Nevertheless," Esias continues, "it does seem to me that more is involved here than some petty bureaucratic enforcement of a regulation in an area to which it was never intended to be applied. Not that they *have* a bureaucracy, as such. Just those gods-damned jumped-up lottery-picked citizens. The only exceptions are the Port Authority itself— which, as it happens, *is* a bureaucracy, albeit a notionally private corporation—and posts requiring specialized knowledge: the military cadre, and public health and safety officers such as our friend Citizen Cargill. He might have provided the entering wedge."

"I got the impression from Citizen Randolph that the regulation has recently been taken down from the shelf and dusted off," says Matt. "He mentioned that they'd made contingency plans for the arrival of a human-crewed ship."

"Did he indeed? It would seem that I was right about someone's blabbing in a bar. Oh, well. Nothing to be done about it now. The puzzle is that the local populace would undoubtedly benefit from an increase in trade, and the local compradores—the import-export representatives of the great shipping families—would not, but the former have a much more direct lever on the authorities than the latter. Possibly one of our competitors—the Rodriguezes, the de Montforts, the Vari, any of that lot—has managed to get some leverage over elements in the Port Authority. Perhaps via Cargill. Hmm. I shall have my local agents look , into it."

The de Tenebre clan is itself one of the shipping families Esias has mentioned, with a considerable starship fleet to its name, and no doubt has a great onshore encrustation of compradores and agents of its own to match. Unlike the others, however, it has cut a deal with the Cosmonaut Families of Mingulay to get in on the ground floor of any new trading patterns that their independent navigation may establish. Its rivals, Matt guesses, must be fuming.

"What about getting the decision reversed?" Gregor asks.

Esias waves his cigar. "Within weeks the matter will have been raised at most of the neighborhood assemblies, by which time we'll have used our contacts to make sure people realize, if they don't already, that putting inconveniences in your way is not a good way to encourage future trade."

Weeks? Matt doesn't have weeks. He keeps his spontaneous remark to this effect firmly behind compressed lips.

So he asks instead, "How long are you staying here?"

Esias draws breath through his teeth. "Naturally, we're impatient to get back to Nova Babylonia, but we're going to be here on Croatan for another three months—our ship's schedule and route are all determined by the kraken, not by us. Which is one reason why we're so keen on human-controlled ships. Our ship is due to move to ports on the other continents in, ah, seventeen days from now and return here about six weeks later to eventually leave on St. Teilhard's Day."

"One of the cults of the local Anglican church," Volkov explains, grinning. "Three months from now they have a big carnival in celebration of St. Teilhard of Piltdown, the patron saint of evolution. The procession is quite spectaular, I'm told. Drums, costumes, dancers filling the streets, the lot, all headed up by the bishop, bearing a reliquary."

"Now wait a minute," says Gregor, frowning. "They can't possibly have relics of Teilhard de Chardin."

"Avowedly faked bones," says Volkov smugly.

"The Christians never cease to astonish me," says Esias. "We have them in Nova Babylonia, too, of course. Descended from Christian Roman soldiers, caught up to heaven with some lost legion long ago. May their God help them when they find out what their Croatan brethren have made of their gospel, let alone what was made of it on Earth." He sighs, then looks up with a determined smile. "On a more cheerful note, you at least have your cargo, if not access to your ship, and I think you'll find that our onshore agents can offer you some mutually profitable arrangements in disposing of it. . . ."

Esias slips into a detailed discussion with Gregor and Elizabeth, and the others around the table begin to rise and drift off. Matt looks hopefully at the harpist, but she's still busy, lost in that absorbing absorption with her work. Maybe later. Matt looks across the table at Volkov, who's becoming thoroughly restive now that Lydia and her mother have joined Esias in shop talk.

"Grigory Andreievich," he says, "would you care for a stroll on the beach?"

Volkov nods, eyes narrowed. "Walk off some of this? Good idea."

As he makes his way around the table, Matt taps Salasso, now fully alert again, on the shoulder.

"Let's walk," he says.

The saur scrambles up and follows him.

Croatan's sun is just above the low hills and long buildings along the shore, and the sky is blue at the zenith and yellow at the horizon, the colors between shading imperceptibly through evanescent limes and greens. The sea looks dark and choppy and colder than the breeze coming off the mountains. The two tall men and the short saur cast long shadows across the white sand, their terminations indistinguishable in the surf.

Volkov has taken a course to the left, and they're walking slowly northward. Eyeing him sidelong across Salasso's bobbing pate, Matt realizes that there's still a trace of envy in his mind that Volkov's apparent age is at least ten years greater than his own. Back in the twenty-first century, all kinds of antiaging nostrums had been peddled, in the socialist bloc even more than in the capitalist. Matt, like everybody he knew, swallowed them by the handful. The Russian must have been in his thirties when whichever one of them—or whichever synergic and serendipitous cocktail of several—had kicked in to give even more longevity than had ever been promised, with the aging process not just delayed but—so far—abolished. It's an odd thing to envy, but the impression of maturity has certain advantages over Matt's stubbornly youthful appearance.

"Well," says Matt, "you've been here three months. What have you been doing?"

Volkov shrugs, kicks to send a pebble skipping across the sand as he walks. "I had to abandon my business on Mingulay," he says, "when the traders offered me a place on their ship at very short notice. But I still have contacts here, in marine engineering and so forth, and I've been cultivating them. Arranging some forward shipping of devices and techniques that Esias assures me are novelties in Nova Babylonia. It'll give me something to trade on in case the deal with researching our common, ah, condition doesn't pan out as profitably as Esias hopes."

"Very wise," says Salasso. "If they wish to find the secret of your longevity in Nova Babylonian laboratories, then your longevity will itself be of considerable advantage."

The two men laugh. "We'll see if the experimental method doesn't shake their scholars up a bit," says Matt. "I'll make sure the works of Francis Bacon are among the de Tenebres' cargo."

"Take the *Novum Organum* to Nova Babylonia," says Salasso. "Yes!"

"Presumably," says Volkov, "the two of you have not come out here to tell me which epistemological tips to slip to the alchemists."

"Ah, no," admits Matt. "Salasso and I have a plan, which we have, to be frank, not shared with the nice young couple back there. We believe you might be interested."

Volkov turns, eyebrows raised. "Something commercial?"

"No," says Salasso. "Something scientific."

"Go on."

"You remember Armen Avakian," says Matt.

Volkov chuckles. "The scientist? How could I forget him?"

"He made it his business to be forgotten," says Matt. "But I know that he took ship to Croatan some years ago, and I suspect that you know where to find him."

"Ah," says Volkov. "And what if I do?"

"We brought the alien interface device with us on the ship," says Matt. "Do you know how to operate it?"

"No," says Volkov.

"But Avakian does," says Matt. "And you know how to fix the old EVA suits, or to make new ones if needs must."

"Uh-huh," grunts Volkov. They are laboring through tough, tangled grass that has caught the sand and consolidated it into a dune. "I'm interested. So what's the plan?"

The three walkers pause at the top of the low rise. Matt points upward. The sun has set about fifteen minutes ago, and in that time the dark has dropped enough for the first stars to be visible. Croatan's moon, even more cratered and pitted than Luna, is rising full above the sea.

"You set us up for EVA, Armen sets us up for communication. We take the ship out to this system's equivalent of the Kuiper belt, and we talk to a god."

Through the passageway, in the courtyard, the lights are bright and people are drifting around, some of them dancing informally. Somebody's drumming quietly, someone is playing a fiddle. Out here, the tables are emptying. Background music for conversation is no longer needed. The harpist's hands drop from the strings to her knees, and she straightens her back and tilts her head up; her fine hair almost brushes the small seat. Matt pauses, waves Salasso and Volkov on toward the courtyard, and walks past her and stops in front of her.

"That was beautiful," he says.

"Thank you." She flexes her long fingers, rubs her thumbs over their tips. "The trouble with playing an instrument is that nobody talks to you."

Her face is narrowed by her long jaw and sharp chin; her eyes and lips look too big and soft for it. A faint tracery of lace is visible where her small breasts push out the thin silk of her white shirt. Her feet are bare and gritted with sand.

"Let's talk now," Matt says.

She busies herself with lifting the large, awkward instrument.

"Allow me," says Matt. He hefts it lithely, with a well-learned precision of movement—a score of score of years has made him mindful of his lower back—and grins at her through the strings. "You are—?"

"My name is Daphne de Charonea," she says. "Of a minor sept of the de Tenebres, from Nova Babylonia."

"Pleased to meet you, Daphne," he says. "I'm Matt Cairns. From Earth."

She probably knows this already; word has got around. But hearing it from his own mouth has the expected effect, and as he follows her to the brighter light inside she's already plying him with questions, and he's already sending a small prayer of thanks to the appropriate goddess, Venus.

5

The Apothecary's Traffic

W HEN HE WENT to his work shed the morning after his test flight, Stone's head was still a battleground of violent and malevolent beings. His previous afternoon's woodwork had been subtly damaged overnight, or so he suspected: Nothing at all had seemed the matter with it when he had left it, and now it was almost all unusable. The flint blades of several of his planes and chisels had been blunted and chipped. No wonder that the drink was said to contain spirits.

"I told you so," Dark Water said, as he stood staring glumly at the task before him.

He gave her a sour smile. "Did you give Slow Leg a thumping?"

She shook her head. "He did not come to the house drunk. Perhaps he is more familiar with the spirits than you are. Which is not a good thing, but as long as he is careful not to bring them home in his body, I will tolerate it."

Stone tried to ignore the pain in his head and concentrate on the possibilities of the situation. Dark Water had never alluded to any of Slow Leg's illicit activities, and Stone had not known about them until yesterday.

He looked around. The place was filling up, but none of the other women were within earshot. Nevertheless, he spoke in a low voice.

"Do you tolerate his smuggling?"

She looked at him sidelong. "I say nothing about that."

"And I know nothing. But I am wondering, what would you think if some things more useful than the drinks with spirits were to be smuggled?" He picked up a chipped blade, turning it over and over in his fingers, and with a sigh dropped it in the basket of shavings and broken stone under his bench.

"They do say," replied Dark Water, in the same tone of idle speculation, "that 'a clumsy woman blames his tools.' You are in danger of being such a clumsy woman, my friend. Try to be a clever and crafty woman."

With that she winked and sashayed off to sit at her treadle saw. Stone's gaze followed her, then turned sharply back to his bench. The cloth garment that constrained his loins, so that he always presented a flat groin and smooth lap, felt painfully tight. Women such as himself were not supposed to feel, and certainly not expected to show, desire for other women. But he did feel it. He put that troubling thought out of his mind and set to work replacing the broken blades and starting over with fresh wood.

Over the rest of that morning, he took Dark Water's advice to heart and used his occasions of wandering around and gossipping to drop less heavy-handed hints.

The sun was high in the sky when he heard outside the low twittering whistle of a mountain pterosaur. Some of the other women looked up idly; it was a sound seldom heard at that altitude. But only Stone recognized it not as the call of a winged lizard but as a hunter's signal. He took his time to clear up his bench, then saun- tered out.

The call was repeated. Stone followed it to the edge of the practice field, now mercifully deserted except for the great slow-moving bulks of a couple of grazing megatheres. Slow Leg was lying on his back behind some bushes, chewing a stalk of sweet grass and gazing at high cumulus clouds. Stone squatted politely beside his feet and waited to hear what he had to say.

"Don't try to squat like a man," said Slow Leg, still studying the sky. "You look like a woman pissing. Sit properly."

"My trousers will get damp."

" 'My trousers will get damp,' " Slow Leg mimicked. He reached behind his head and threw a rolled small reed mat at Stone. "Here."

Stone spread the mat and knelt on it, sitting back on his heels. Slow Leg rolled over and leaned on one elbow.

"There," he said. "Now we look as though we are flirting, not planning a raid. Or a flight. And even if everybody knows we are—and after your blundering around the workshops this morning, the dogs in the street will know it—they cannot swear that they saw us doing so."

Stone blushed and suppressed a giggle. From where he sat he could see right up Slow Leg's skirt.

"Perhaps we are flirting," he said.

Slow Leg snorted. "Dark Water would kick me in the bollocks if she thought we were really flirting. You're a pretty enough woman, but not that pretty."

"Hah," said Stone, averting his eyes from the growing evidence that Slow Leg might be finding him more than pretty enough. "So let us plan a flight."

Breakfast in the Star Traders' House is a comfortably communal affair. Tables along one side of the courtyard are laid with platters of melon, bread, olives, cheese . . . Matt hopes and expects to find hot food in town. At least there's coffee. He hasn't had much sleep. Matt sits opposite Daphne and takes more pleasure in watching her eat than in the bread and black olives. They keep looking at each other and grinning and discovering again they can barely tolerate their separation across that meter of pale, old wood. Her fingertips are rough, her toes smooth.

"You're both being insufferable," Volkov announces, clapping Matt on the shoulder and sitting down beside him with a laden plate and a steaming mug. "Some people are here to eat, you know."

Daphne flushes slightly, her glance darting away. Matt reassuringly strokes her calf with the sole of his foot: never mind him.

But then she looks back at Volkov and says tartly, "You can talk, when everybody knows with whom you have spent the night."

"What everybody knows is one thing," says Volkov, unperturbed. "What everybody sees is something else. My lady and I don't paw each other in public."

He chomps silently for a while and then leans forward on his elbows, observing Daphne across the rim of the mug from which he slowly sips.

"Matt and I," he says, "and the saur from his ship, Salasso, are going into town today. We'll be visiting machine shops and talking to engineers and accountants. Lots of figures, lots of detail about machinery and money—millimeters and millilivres, so to speak. Would you like to come along?"

Matt is surprised by the clumsiness of this attempt to put the girl off. "You'd be welcome to come with us," he says, as though he means it. Daphne, to his mingled satisfaction and concern, looks actually interested.

"Music is mathematics," she says. "I know a lot about figures. What are you planning to have manufactured?"

"Space suits," says Volkov.

Daphne repeats the word, then says, "Vacuum . . . garments?" She's mentally translated the concept into and out of Trade Latin, Matt realizes. "What for?"

"Extravehicular activity," says Matt.

She understands that, it's barely out of the Latin already, and she rocks back, eyes widening.

"You want to go outside a ship? In space? Why?"

"When you've seen our ship," says Matt dryly, "you might get one answer: emergency repairs. But mainly we want to make it possible for us to land on and explore other celestial bodies, such as planets."

He gestures at the setting moon, pale and huge above the roof. "There, for instance. Or"—he searches his memory for the planets of Croatan's sun—"on Adonis or Cybele or Chronos."

"What a strange thing to wish to do." Daphne giggles suddenly. "You know, until we called at Croatan on our last round-trip, before your ship came to Mingulay, I did not know it was possible to land on these planets. I did not know that the worlds we live on were themselves planets, or that their suns were among the fixed stars."

Both men start speaking simultaneously.

"But—"

"Surely you—"

Volkov waves Matt to proceed.

"Were you not taught any astronomy?" He grins, suspecting he's discovered some sex distinction in education. "Just told to concentrate on your music, or something?"

Daphne shakes her head. "Of course I knew astronomy! It is part of harmony, like music. Every child knows that."

"And what," asks Volkov, "is every child taught?"

"The polycentric Ptolemaic system of astronomy," says Daphne. "It is rather complicated."

"I'll bet," says Volkov. "Could you explain it to us, a little?"

"Um. I'll try."

Daphne dips her finger in slopped coffee and starts doodling on the table, describing circles.

"Each world is surrounded by concentric spheres, upon which the suns and moons and planets revolve, for days, and times, and seasons, and years. There are holes in the spheres, through which the great ships pass. While traveling between the spheres, the ships and their occupants are in eternity and outside time, although time continues to pass within the celestial machinery of the spheres, which manufactures time as a clock does but of course on an inconceivably greater scale. That's why our journeys seem instantaneous to us, though upon returning we find that time has passed."

She looks up. "What is *your* explanation?"

It occurs to Matt that the anomalous experience of travel by light-speed ship, before the travelers had had any grasp of the notion that light had a speed at all, was probably responsible for the persistence of this entire ludicrously complicated cosmology.

"Ah, that would take . . . some time," Matt says. "But surely it's obvious that the appearance of the fixed stars from Croatan is very similar to that from Mingulay, and so on all the way to Nova Terra." He pauses, frowning. "Do they look much different even from there?"

Daphne shakes her head. "Some of the major constellations are different—the Archer, the Hand, the Hind. But many of the stars are in very similar positions, yes. That's because the spheres of each world have small differences, which vary in proportion to the years spent in eternity between them."

"And it has never occurred to anyone that it might be simpler to suppose that the stars are suns, seen from very far away, and from a different viewpoint on each world?"

"Oh, yes, it has, naturally. But only a minority of astronomers hold to that hypothesis, which has difficulties of its own." She laughs. "But it seems to be true. I like the idea of landing on planets. I cannot help imagining them as small bright objects that one could walk around, not as worlds."

"What about the comets?" Matt asks.

Daphne shivers slightly in the early morning sunlight.

"Whatever the planets may be, we know that the comets are the gods, coming in from the intramundane spaces to look more closely at the works of men and saurs and navigators. They are harbingers of misfortune."

"Our friend Salasso," Matt says idly, "has been making some other saurs angry, by telling them that the gods are not."

Daphne compresses her lips and stands up.

"I have work to do," she says. She smiles at Matt. "I will see you tonight."

"Yes, see you."

He watches her out of sight.

"Looks like it's not just the saurs who think Salasso's a bit of a heretic," Volkov says.

"I don't know if it was such a good idea, talking about what we're going to do today."

Volkov rips a piece of bread and smudges up an olive with it.

"Ah, fuck it," he says. "It'll come out eventually that we're trying to knock off some space suits. Trying to be secretive would only arouse suspicion. Your harpist has very sensitive hearing and gets to overhear a lot of conversations while she sits there strumming away. She's one of old Esias's sources of information about what goes on among his crew and family, not to mention *other* crews, when they have their rather fraught social get-togethers. Same-same for them, of course."

Matt wonders if this isn't some subtle ploy by Volkov to make him wary of Daphne, but he lets it pass. He has no intention of letting Daphne in on the secret of their bolder aims anyway.

"You're a bit paranoid about me, aren't you?" says Volkov.

Matt tries to keep his hands busy with rolling a New Virginia cigarette. Volkov politely disdains the offer to share.

"Yes," says Matt, past his lighter flare. "I don't like the thought of what you could do in Nova Babylonia, given time. And time, you have."

"We all have." Volkov turns toward Matt on the bench and leans back, arms spread, theatrically defenseless though not, Matt well knows, in reality. "Would you kill me?"

Matt feels the chill of an inhibition so ingrained it has become superstition, and shivers at the thought of killing a fellow immortal, just as Daphne did at the thought of the gods above. The mutual nonaggression pact between the surviving members of the original crew has never been explicit; it has grown, over their unexpectedly extended life spans. The very length of their disputes and vendettas, pursued down decades of scheming, bonds them like brothers.

"You know I wouldn't," he says. "But short of that . . . What *are* you planning, by the way? Becoming the dictator of Nova Babylonia?"

Volkov laughs. "Of course not. What a bore that would be." He leans on his elbow and cups his chin, suddenly serious. "But think. We've all kept our little secret, and for its sake lost lives' worth of work, abandoned families, lost love over and over. Now some of the saurs have seen fit to share it with the merchants, or at least with this clan, who I'm sure are clannish enough to keep it to themselves. But when I get to Nova Babylonia, it won't be a secret, not if they want their scientists to reverse-engineer the process. If they succeed, it'll change everything and thoroughly disrupt their famous mighty and ancient republic and eventually the whole of the Second Sphere. I want to use whatever influence I can get along the way to make sure that the treatment is available to everyone rather than just to the ruling class and that the outcome is progress rather than collapse."

"I can see it now," says Matt. "A progressive, dynamic, socialistic republic, like the European Union, in which you are once again somebody close to the top of the heap."

Volkov spreads his hands, grinning. "And what's wrong with that? A young man should have ambition!"

Matt smiles back, his suspicion not at all disarmed. But he is fairly confident that by involving Volkov—as he must—in the project, he has found a good way of keeping tabs on him, and that if necessary he can find some nonfatal method of screwing up Volkov's plans.

And if it's longevity that is going to be the cosmonaut's apple of discord, it's entirely possible that Matt can play the same game on Mingulay or Croatan, with faster results. . . . He's lost in a moment of calculation of light-years and centuries and rates of growth, when a long oval shadow falls across the table, and he turns with a start to see Salasso.

The automobile that Volkov has selected from the house's motor pool has a noisy and exhaust-rich petrol engine and a heavy steel chassis. Its bodywork and most of its fittings are of shabby polymer; the lilac shell and bubble canopy give the whole thing a teardrop shape when the rear half of the canopy isn't retracted around the vehicle's stern, as it is now. Matt sits in the front passenger seat, Volkov drives. Salasso has taken a skiff into town, on some errand of his own; the declining of the offer of lifts has been mutual.

"Used this since we came here," Volkov yells above the engine noise and grating gear changes as they lurch out of the front gate and into a gap in the traffic. It's a dangerous combination of a sparse but speedy succession of commuter vehicles and a slow but steady flow of long, lumbering trucks carrying produce and livestock from the coastal farms. "It's great. It's like the cars they had in America!"

"Not very," Matt replies. The impression of speed is terrifying: The wind is roaring past his ears and whipping through his hair; buildings, street fixtures, and slower vehicles blur past. The speedometer reads only 50 km/h; he doesn't believe this for a second. Within minutes the growing heat of the sun and the heat of the engine itself warming up the vehicle fill Matt's nostrils with a nostalgia-inducing fragrance that he recognizes from his childhood as that of polystyrene cement: model-kit glue. He tries not to think about what this may imply about the car's structural integrity and gazes outward at the rapidly passing landscape.

Out on the shimmering sun-hammered sea the glare is broken by long low smoke-trailing ships, by sails, and at the horizon by tall derricks that he takes to be oil wells. The beaches become less and less white and uncluttered as they approach the edge of the town. Then the road and the shoreline diverge, and the mansions along the other side are replaced by close-packed villas, and within minutes they're between tenements and warehouses and offices, and the traffic has slowed to a rush-hour crawl.

"Fuck," says Matt, as exhaust fumes from the huge idling truck they're stuck behind roll over them, "*this* is more like America."

"You were there once?"

"Yeah, briefly. Yourself?"

Volkov laughs. "Just Washington, D.C., to shake hands with the vice president, all that, then a motorcade in New York. Strange place."

Matt's looking around. "But not as strange as this, huh?"

Close up, it's not very like twenty-first-century America, or even Rawliston as Matt remembers it from decades ago. The streets are tarred, but potholed and filthy; the sidewalks are broad and crowded and crumbling. The current fashions strike Matt as an odd jumble of several different period styles, into which the jeans and loose shirjacks that he and Volkov are wearing will fit as workingmen's clothes, but in the less utilitarian outfits on display he can see an evolution toward showiness and elaboration since he was last here: Trousers and skirts are narrower, jackets shorter, shirts and blouses frillier, hats and heels taller; it reminds him of the early nineteenth century. There's a similarly intense density of detail on the street, with posters and placards and banners everywhere, shop windows small and crammed, hawkers jostling and calling in cries as recurring and as incomprehensible as those of the wheeling and swooping small pterodactyls whose bright red, blue, yellow, or particolored leathery wings flash past faster than those of the pigeons, sparrows, and seagulls whose urban niches they occupy here.

Even the other hominidae seem to have been infected by the decorative urge, as they've found new slots in Rawliston's booming economy. Gigants, their fur dyed in garish hues and coiffed all over, loll in large open vehicles, talking on radiophones. Pithkies, lithe and tough but much slenderer than their rural, mine-working cousins and ancestors, dart about on urgent errands, the females in fluttery shifts, the males in gaudy shirts and shorts. Matt has long concluded that despite appearances, the pithkies are not the sharpest blades in the hominid tool kit, and the gigants are. But in Rawliston they're both officially Adamic races, fully human, citizens with savable souls, so any speculation or skull measuring along these lines is (laudably, in his opinion) considered impolitic and impolite.

The only obvious underclass here are the converted and civilized descendants of the heathen, blond and light-skinned, whose few representatives in this part of town are either doing heavy manual work—digging holes in the road, to yells of annoyance from everyone else—or lurching about drunk.

Volkov follows the traffic slowly forward for about half a kilometer, then turns right into a narrower street with higher buildings and more human and animal-powered traffic. The draught animals are giant tapirs, three meters high at the shoulder, looking down long noses, arrogant as camels. Small, ragged children dash between wheels and hooves, scooping dung into reeking sacks. The pavements have no fewer prosperous-looking pedestrians, however; the ladies occasionally cough and *faugh* through evidently scented lace handkerchiefs, the gentlemen flourish pipes and cigars. Matt's just beginning to appreciate the difference the frequent whiffs of marijuana and tobacco smoke make to the ambient odors when Volkov hauls on a lever and the canopy comes rattling up from behind, closing with a rubbery clash and automatically starting up a racketing air conditioner that fights inadequately against the immediate greenhouse effect of the canopy but at least keeps out the worst of the stinks.

A couple of hundred meters up the street the buildings on both sides have been recently levelled, and the cleared site has been chained off for a car park. Volkov finds a vacant place, makes a payment or bribe to the attendant, and leads off at a brisk pace into a maze of alleys.

"Ah, here we are," he says, stopping under a sign suspended from above a frowsty shopfront. Matt looks up at a painting of a mortar and pestle and a bramble of barbed serifs, which he eventually makes out as *Armen Avakian, Physician and Apothecary*.

"Good gods," he says. "He's using his own name?"

Volkov shrugs. "Hide in plain sight. It's worked for me, sometimes."

Matt can't imagine Avakian hiding in anything but obscurity.

The shop is a lot cleaner inside than outside. Clumps of dried or drying herbs hang from the ceiling. A quarter circle of counter in the corner guards shelves of racked potions and unguents, and a doorway to a dark inner sanctum. The other sections of wall have fold-down, polished wooden benches, every foot of them occupied by people in various states of discomfort or distress. Sawdust on the floor absorbs most of the spittle, phlegm, and blood. The walls above the patients', customers', or supplicants' heads are plastered with urgent advice and improbable testimonials.

A sallow-skinned young man, slim and crop-haired and clean-shaven in a neat white coat, stands behind the counter writing on the label of a small bottle.

"Excuse me," says Matt. "Could we speak to Dr. Avakian?"

The man barely glances at him. "You're speaking to him."

A son, or a more distant descendant? Matt detects a similarity in the dark eyes, sharp nose, full lips.

"Could we speak to, ah, the *senior* Dr. Avakian?"

This time the doctor stops scribbling and stares at them. "Matt!" he shouts. "Grigory! Holy fucking shit!"

He ignores the tittering and tutting this outburst provokes in the queue, he can't shake their hands fast enough.

"You guys, you haven't changed a bit!"

"You have," says Volkov.

Avakian glances downward, then up. "Losing the beer gut took a while," he admits. "The hair and beard, well, that was easy."

His raucous belly laugh hasn't changed and confirms the update in Matt's mental image of the man.

"Didn't you see the photos of me in the newsprints?"

"Crummy dot-matrix," says Avakian. "Didn't recognize you at all." He remembers something. "Just a minute."

He finishes the labeling with a signature flourish and hands the bottle to a young woman with a feverish ten-year-old in tow.

"No more than twice a day," he says firmly. "And keep giving them twice a day until the bottle's empty, even after it's all cleared up. That's very important."

"Yes, Doctor. Thanks." She departs and the queue shuffles up. Avakian pokes his head around the backroom door and yells, "Hey, Collis! Take over out here, please."

He sheds his white coat, revealing a pea jacket, a pin-tucked shirt-front, and a pair of denim trousers that look like jeans but that come up to above his waist. He lifts a section of counter and steps out and gestures to the door.

"Gentlemen," he says, "after you."

． ． ．

The coffee shop is quiet at this time of the morning, after the breakfast rush and before elevenses. Avakian orders a liter cafetiere and leads them to a dark corner niche table. He declines Matt's offer of his tobacco pouch with a regretful shake of the head.

"I have to set the locals a good example," he says. "Don't worry, I don't try for miracle cures. I'm just another quack, but one who gets results. And I'm getting a lot of good stuff from the heathen pharmacopoeia and off the merchant ships. Laying a bit of cash aside from the two-way trade, there, for when I have to—you know. Train up young Collis, turn the shop over to her, then move on before people start wondering if I have the elixir of youth stashed at the back."

"Why not work up at the university?" Matt asks.

Avakian grins. "I don't think they'd recognize a degree from Yerevan University."

Matt's eyebrows twitch.

"Look," says Avakian, somewhat defensively, "it would be completely maddening to help them reinvent the wheel. All that twenty-first-century state-of-the-art information that got downloaded from the ship and printed off and shipped from Mingulay two hundred–odd years ago—it's *still* being reprinted, in big leather-bound volumes. Most of it is still incomprehensible, and what they do understand they dogmatise. It's not just medicine, it's everything. The different encyclopedias have become the basis of fucking *schools of thought*. Grolierists and Britannicists at each other's throats in the faculties, with a strong faction of Encartists among the students and junior staff."

Avakian depresses the plunger of the cafetiere and pours. They inhale and sip for a minute of grateful silence.

"I doubt if anything that came on the *Bright Star,*" says Avakian, putting his cup down, "has brought as much innocent, unalloyed pleasure as coffee. Just as well we had the beans in our hydroponics. And speaking of the ship, guys, I'm impressed." He narrows his eyes at Matt, lowers his voice: "Your descendants completed their Great Work?"

"Yup," says Matt. "And once they had done that, the saurs, for a wonder, agreed to take us back up to the ship. So here we are. My descendants' navigation worked, unlike"—he drops his voice further—"mine."

He still feels his ears burn, at the thought of that little fuckup, when the navigational programming he'd been certain was for a short-lightspeed hop across the Solar System had turned out to be for—or had been overridden to produce—a lightspeed leap of unknown but vast length.

"Do the Families know about . . . us?" Avakian asks, just as quietly. Volkov and Matt trade uncomfortable glances.

"Well, uh," Matt begins, with a conscious effort to stop his feet from audibly shuffling, "some of them do. One of the saurs on their ship told the de Tenebres, when they turned up at Mingulay. They then started hunting for us, and another saur, Salasso, helped them find us. The de Tenebres are taking Grigory here back to Nova Babylonia to, ah, see if they can crack the fix, whatever it was. My two companions know about me, of course, and so do the heads of the Families back on Mingulay. That's the state of play yesterday, or five years ago."

"Hmm," says Avakian. "Well, let's hope they haven't blown our cover. It's a fucking miracle we've kept it quiet this long, even with the, ah, *help* of our little gray friends."

The three apparently young men share a moment of grim silence. Avakian ends it by exhaling noisily, as though he's been holding his breath.

"So, gentlemen, to what do I owe the pleasure, as they say here?"

Matt decides to dispense with preliminaries. "We've brought the interface," he says. "We want to talk to the gods again—and this time get some *answers*."

Avakian takes this in with almost saurian calm. "I understand you have a problem with access to the ship."

"All in good time," says Matt. He pats his shirjack pocket. "I have some specs here. Right now, we're going to visit an engineering company and talk about pressure seals, and faceplates, and air supply."

"Oh, right," says Avakian. "Suits. Good luck finding someone who can build that around here."

Volkov grins. "We don't need luck. I'm a marine engineer, remember? In the past three months I've checked out every reliable engineering company in this town, and I'm going to start with the best. Paul Loudon."

"I thought he was aviation," says Avakian.

"Exactly," says Volkov. "Precision milling. Pressure differentials. Air hoses. Critical tolerances. I'll go to a diving-equipment manufacturer if I have to, but the aviation industry is where astronautics began, and that's where it's going to begin here, if I have anything to do with it."

Avakian smiles wolfishly. "Quite right," he says. "Pilots cost more to replace than divers, and if I'm going to be manhandling that fucking interface in a vacuum I want to do it in a suit designed by someone who thinks I'm very expensive indeed."

"You'll come?" says Matt, hardly daring to believe it.

"Of course," says Avakian. He glances about with an expression that Matt has seen on Volkov's face and, he suspects, sometimes shown on his own. "What else is there to do around here?"

Loudon's Engineering Works is in the light-industrial semicircle around the city's commercial area, which is crowded around the harbor. There's no zoning; dwellings of varying quality and size, from middle-class villas narrow and shiny as top hats to teetering high-rise workers' flats to a sort of scurf of squatters' shanties around the feet of both, are squeezed between the workshops and distilleries and breweries, all loomed over by the flaring high vents of an oil refinery and the high smokestacks of power stations and the bigger factories in the heavy-industrial zone.

"*Serious* fucking terraforming going on around here," Matt remarks.

Volkov parks the automobile, half on the sidewalk like everybody else here has done, and leads the way to Loudon's factory. It's in an aggressively modern building of glass and steel and concrete with its owner's name in bevelled aluminium sans serifs above the revolving door at the front. Inside it smells of plastics and polish. Workers and technicians in neat blue overalls are conferring around a circular table behind the first of many glass partitions beyond the reception area. The receptionist, fashionably and expensively a female pithkie, is sitting tapping at a manual keyboard behind a curved desk of chrome and inlaid Bakelite. She looks up and flashes bright teeth from a foxy face fringed in golden fur.

"Good morning, Mr. Antonov," she says, momentarily confusing Matt until he remembers it's the pseudonym under which Volkov has been trading for the past twenty years or so.

"Good morning, K!kh!thashth!kh."

Matt can't even mentally transliterate the mashed syllables of the name Volkov pronounces, evidently well enough to charm its bearer. She registers Matt's bafflement.

"Just call me Cath," she tells him and looks again at Volkov. "You have an appointment?"

"Yes," says Volkov, rather to Matt's surprise. "I radiophoned Citizen Loudon early this morning. He's expecting me around eleven-thirty."

She peers at an open desk diary, shaking her head a little, then turns the book around and looks closer.

"Ah, so he is." Another flash of teeth. "He must have jotted it down himself on his way in. His writing's terrible."

She presses a switch and speaks into a clunky telephone, then nods and waves them through.

"Third on the left, then up the stairs."

Loudon's office is spare, its only decoration posters advertising the company's products and a few framed photographs of Paul Loudon posing beside biplanes and monoplanes. Volkov introduces Matt and, after exchanging pleasantries about the significance of the *Bright Star*'s arrival, they sit down and explain their requirements.

Loudon almost pounces on the space suit specs. His finger races down each page, the fingers of his other hand drumming on the desk. When he's scanned them all, he pushes the papers away and leans back and scratches his nose.

"Hmm," he says. "Interesting. Very interesting."

He jumps to his feet and stalks around the desk to the window overlooking the street and the city and stares out for a minute or so. He turns back to face Matt and Volkov, hands clasped behind his back.

"We have the skills and machinery required to make your suits," he says. "Even the fabric components—used in aircraft, you know. I employ outworkers for that, of course. However, the problem is, gentlemen, that while normally I'd be delighted to take your order, at the moment and for the foreseeable future we're working flat out on other projects. There's a bit of a boom on, as you may have noticed. Overheated, to tell you the truth. Skill shortages and bottlenecks all over the place. Between ourselves, the popular assemblies are running the printing presses a little too hard."

"Printing presses?"

"Inflation," Loudon explains. He nibbles his lower lip. "I really would like to help you. I can see all kinds of applications for this type of suit, even a simpler version, for high-altitude aviation. But . . . now wait a moment, gentlemen."

He sits back at his desk and swivels a big apparatus that looks to Matt like an antique computer monitor. The screen lights up, and Loudon starts sliding sheets of transparent plastic across a sort of hopper underneath it and cranking a brace of knurled knobs at the sides. The images on the screen—lines of text, diagrams, pictures—change with dizzying speed.

"Microfiche," Loudon murmurs. "Latest thing. Very useful. Could replace paper entirely, they say. Now, let's see . . . ah, yes."

He looks up, smiling. "I see I have one rather elderly technician who doesn't seem to be fully occupied at the moment. He can take charge of this, but he'll need someone to help him, and I can't spare even an apprentice—aha! Got it! I know just whom I can poach."

He jumps up, rubbing his hands, and keys his desk phone.

"Cath?" he says, "can you fax a message through to the flying club, with all my numbers and a request to contact me *immediately*? For the attention of Gail Frethorne."

He listens for a moment, then very patiently spells the name.

The two-man glider was heavy, but not too heavy for one man and one woman to carry. Slow Leg and Stone took it from the hangar shed in the time in the hot early afternoon when most people were sensibly asleep and carried it up the long slope of the hill. Slow Leg was weighed down with bulging leather bags hung from his shoulders, but he walked as though they—and the machine he and Stone bore above their heads—weren't there. Stone tried to emulate him. With his clothes and sandals packed away in a pouch and with his quilted flying suit knotted bulkily around his waist, his gender wasn't obvious at a distance, and he tried to keep its traces from his walk.

They stopped at the top of the ridge and looked along the valley. Slow Leg's sense of the weather had been sharp: A strong breeze cooled their faces, and a series of cumulus clouds hung above the whole length of the Vale, marking thermal stepping-stones all the way to the city and the sea.

Stone climbed into his flying gear, while Slow Leg attached himself to the forward harness. Stone ducked behind him under the wing and got into the rear harness. He clutched a bar in front of him—it was part of the glider's rigid frame and had no connection whatever with the control surfaces.

"Have you ever flown *with* anyone before?" asked Slow Leg over his shoulder.

"No," said Stone.

"It's easy. All you have to do is run behind me when we're taking off and again when landing. The rest of the time, stay like you're lying on your belly and do nothing unless I tell you to. Don't even swing your legs."

"All right," said Stone. It didn't sound easy at all. It sounded terrifying.

"Ready?"

"Yes."

They ran down the slope for a dozen or so meters, and then the air spirits caught the wings and bore the glider aloft. Stone swung his body back to a prone position and fought the spirits in his arms and hands that urged him to fly the machine. His knuckles whitened on the bar. He and his friend had both been right. Taking off as a passenger was easy, and flying as a passenger was terrifying.

6

Dawson's Night

G AIL FRETHORNE FOUND the fax with her name scrawled on it folded behind the slats of the notice board lattice just after she'd ridden her bicyle up to the club after work. As she read it her hands shook and sweat dripped on the paper, smudging the sooty print. She had to read it again very carefully to make sure it said what she thought it said.

She folded it carefully and slipped it inside her shirjack pocket, went to the washroom to freshen up, then walked thoughtfully to the club bar. It was an open verandah with bamboo furnishings and a big four-bladed propeller turning slowly, powered by an electric motor mounted on the ceiling. She seldom used the bar, preferring to save her money for more congenial venues. Today, however, she had spare money in her pocket. Paul Loudon had faxed the photographs she'd taken straight to an hourly paper within minutes of landing, and they'd wired twenty talers to his account at the club. He'd split the money with her, over her not very sincere protests, and bought her a drink as well. So now the old guy at the bar, a booze-sodden heathen capable of little else in the way of work, recognized her and even smiled.

She smiled back with stiff politeness (the sight of his teeth made her throat spasm) and took her blueberry-flavored long vodka to a seat by the railing overlooking the airfield. After a few relaxing sips she spread the now almost illegible paper in front of her and read it again, just to make sure. There was no doubt about it. He was offering her a job, starting immediately. Day after tomorrow, if possible. He would even pay her boss a week's wages in lieu of notice.

Her feelings, she realized, were mixed. She was excited and delighted with the new prospect, but she liked her job at the garage. David and Mike had taught her most of what she knew, and Joshua was all right in his gormless way, and Mr. Reece was a fair enough employer. She had no idea what working for Loudon would be like, or of his qualities as a boss or of conditions in his works. If they were anything like the factories she'd worked in when she was younger . . .

But that was the wrong attitude, she was sure. It was to quail at change. The pay he was offering was half as much again as she could earn at the garage even in a good week. And the job title rang like good metal: *machinist.*

She folded the fax away, her mind made up. She would take it. As soon as she'd decided, and imagined herself going in to Loudon's works two mornings hence, she realized that she'd done so without one consideration so much as crossing her mind: that Loudon might be making this unexpected and unexplained offer because he fancied her. Strange. It was such an obvious thought, such a romantic cliché—Gail had, in her early teens, and even then rather guiltily, read some of her mother's stash of romantic novellettes—that perhaps that in itself explained why she hadn't thought it could happen to her. She still didn't think it had. He'd been favorably impressed with her competence, and her sharpness in snapping the photos had merely brought it home to him, that was all.

She drained her glass and ambled to the club office, fired off a fax with her acceptance and the details of Reece's garage, and returned to the verandah for another long vodka—well deserved, she thought as she settled down with it, and would keep her occupied while she waited for her drug smuggler. It was the usual day for Slow Leg's fortnightly flight, and the weather had been perfect. She turned a little in her rattan chair and gazed at the city. The view was less hazy than usual, these updrafts were lifting the smog a bit, and the red flare above the refinery blazed like a false sunset among the columns of sharply rising smoke. Rain on the way, maybe late tonight or early tomorrow.

More smoke than usual, and not just from factories. It was as though here and there in the suburbs and shantytowns there were a lot of small fires, a lot of—

"Bonfires! Oh, *shit!*"

Stone forgot his fear when he saw the city. He had known about it, of course, but no description or even photograph could prepare his mind for the sight itself. How many people there must be, with all those houses. How rich they all must be, with all that smoke.

Slow Leg banked the craft slightly—by now, Stone's urge to throw his own weight into the maneuver had calmed to a mere twitch—and corrected again to bring them about a hundred meters above a black road. The heat liked to hide in black roads during the day and then escape to the sky as the sun's gaze slanted. The rising thermal spirits lifted the craft a few tens of meters. Down below on the road, vehicles bigger than megatheres trundled along, and smaller vehicles faster than horses overtook them, their paths moving in and out of the gaps like a needle through cloth.

After following the road for a few minutes, Slow Leg brought the craft around and began to descend toward a green field among the buildings at the edge of the city.

"Swing down now and get ready to land!" he yelled.

On the field were aircraft, bigger than any Stone had seen but whose wings looked oddly stubby. The glide in seemed frighteningly faster than it did when he was doing the piloting himself, and by the time his feet were skimming centimeters above grass, the fighting energies from his chest were firing his legs to run. The landing was gentler than he'd expected, Slow Leg having skillfully slowed the craft to a near stall before touching down, but they still had to pelt along for a dozen meters before they came to a complete stop.

They undid their harnesses one-handed, holding the craft up, then stepped carefully out from beneath it and let it collapse behind them. Stone felt like collapsing on the grass himself. Slow Leg turned and grinned. He looked fine, standing very straight under the weight of the heavy bags, his skin pouring sweat and his muscles quivering beneath the skin. If the change from the cold of the slipstream to the heat of running hard and then the heat of the city had been painful, he was not showing it.

A very strange-looking woman came running up, carrying a bundle in one hand. She was tall, with big breasts that jounced under her shirt, and short hair whose small curls glowed like copper in the low sun. But she ran like a man and clapped Slow Leg on the shoulder and laughed in his face.

"Hey, ya big heathen, good to see you! Even if you did pick the worst day to come here!"

She turned around, still with one hand on Slow Leg's shoulder, and added, "Even if you've brought your girlfriend!"

"This is . . . Stone," said Slow Leg, accurately translating his name into Christian. "He is not my girlfriend. Just a woman who is a friend."

"Yeah, that's what they all say. Pleased to meet you. My name's Gail."

She shook Stone's hand, smiling but staring at him with unabashed curiosity. Her face was regular, not bad-looking but not pretty either, with a rather heavy jaw and big mouth. Her eyes were a sort of greenish gray, bright and curious; her skin, clean under a recent sheen of sweat and dust, was very fair. She wore a cotton shirt with some kind of crisscross pattern, and long blue trousers.

"Look, guys, we have to move fast." She tossed her bundle to Slow Leg. "Get these on right now, you'll look less conspicuous. Then let's get this wing under a roof and make tracks."

Stone couldn't quite follow the Christian colloquialisms, but she was acting out her words as she spoke, grabbing one wingtip of the glider and unceremoniously motioning Stone to grab the other. They lugged it toward a low, open-sided hut, in which some big objects made of bright primary-colored fabrics and metal rods stood racked. As he got closer Stone figured out that they were dismantled gliders, their spars separated and their fabric folded up. A good trick; he found himself considering ways it could be copied.

When Slow Leg joined them to help lift the glider and attach it to one of the roof's crossbeams, Stone had to smother a giggle. The man had put on shoes and blue trousers and a white shirt that looked just like women's clothes except that they were made of a coarser material. He wore them as if he'd worn them before. A swift glare forbade comment.

While Slow Leg trotted off to retrieve his bags, Stone removed his feather helmet and shook out his hair. Gail looked at him critically.

"Uh, Stone, you don't happen to have any sort of girl's clothes you could change into? You look like a goddamn mollyboy."

"I have my own clothes with me."

"Well, get changed as fast as you can. Stash your flying gear here."

Politely, again like a man, she turned her back on him as he began to unfasten his suit. He didn't bother to tell her that this respect for his modesty was unnecessary.

"Hmm," she said when he'd finished and stepped out in front of her, "not bad. You still look like a heathen, but at least you look like a heathen *woman*." She grinned, making an obvious glance at his chest. "A skinny one, mind you."

Stone rejoined them, and Gail casually took one of the bags from him and slung it over her shoulder.

"Right," she said. "I think we want to leave this place by the back."

She led them down a rough, stony path worn in the grass to the airfield's perimeter fence, which was made of three-meter-high wooden posts between which were strung lines of what seemed like, but surely could not be, metal stretched into strands.

"Why are we going this way?" asked Slow Leg.

Gail pushed through a creaking wooden gate, held it open for them, and carefully closed it behind her.

"It's a bad night to be a heathen in some parts of town," she said as they continued on down the dusty and now widening path. "I passed kids stacking up wood and rubbish on my way out here, but I never made the connection until about half an hour before you arrived. It's Dawson's Night."

"*Dawson?*" Stone asked. "The anthropologist?"

"That's the one," Gail said over her shoulder. "Here they call him a heretic."

Stone had no idea what that last word meant, but something in her intonation suggested *sorcerer*.

"People remember him here too? And this is his night? Why is that bad?"

"Because tonight they fucking burn him in effigy, just like they once burned him in real life, that's why."

Stone felt such a cold shock, like a splash of water across his neck and shoulders, that he almost stopped walking. Instead he increased his pace, difficult though it was in his sandals and on the uneven track, to walk right beside Gail.

"You are saying that people hate his memory so much that they burn *images* of him?"

"Yes. Don't look so worried; it's only some people, not all, and not many around here. Hell, most of the burnings are just for fun, lots of people have more or less forgotten what it was all about."

Stone did not feel reassured. The dusty path had sloped down, like a rivulet into a gully, into a little street of buildings of two or three stories, built of stone or brick, washed or plastered in white or in other colors. Projecting eaves and awnings provided shade. He found himself eyeing the people they were passing on the road and was relieved to find that their glances were curious rather than hostile.

Three young men, talking and laughing loudly; an old woman trudging up the street, lugging a net bag of vegetables; an old man sitting against a wall, smoking a pipe; a young mother with four small children running around her feet and one baby on her hip; a girl pushing a barrow load of scrap metal, its handles almost as high as her shoulders . . . More and more people. The street had more people in it than an entire village.

They did not seem as rich as he had imagined. The younger ones were thinner, the older heavier, than seemed healthy. He quickly ceased to be surprised by the sight of men wearing trousers and women wearing garments that looked like elaborately decorated or cunningly shaped versions of the short skirts of warriors or the long robes of elders. That was mere custom, and he was well aware that custom varied. It was the bodies the clothes covered that disturbed him. Too many of them seemed worn or tired. But this physical deterioration didn't seem to have affected their spirits. For the most part they seemed lively and, if not always cheerful, at least not ground down.

The vehicles in the street were fortunately traveling slowly in comparison to the ones he'd seen from the air, but they still moved fast enough to startle him, and without beasts to haul them they looked strangely incomplete. He was very conscious of the need not to appear perturbed by them and carried his deliberate insouciance too far when Gail led them across the road.

A noise like a mammoth trumpetting, a bright green blur, a violent yank on his arm that almost dislocated his shoulder—

"Jesus! That was close!"

Gail stood looking at him, shaking her head. Then she smacked the side of her head. "Sorry," she said. "I was forgetting. You guys must be shattered. Let's sit down for a bit."

A small walled yard with trellises of climbing plants between the top of the wall and a straw-mat awning was a few steps away. Gail led them in, and they sat down at one of the round wooden tables. A boy appeared at her elbow.

"Would you like some beer?" Gail asked.

"Yes," they both said.

The beer was pale and so lively that the bubbles tickled Stone's tongue. The cups were large and made of fine glass. He revised his opinion of the wealth of this people sharply upward.

"You look puzzled," Gail said.

Stone had many questions but decided to ask one that would not show how many questions he had. He leaned forward, flicked back the fall of his hair, and spoke quietly. "What is a *heretic*?"

"Oh!" Gail frowned, and Stone worried that he had asked an ignorant or impolite question.

"That's a good question," she said. "It's kind of difficult. You people—your people, you have . . . priests?"

"No!" Stone said. "We do not sacrifice animals. That is what the savages do."

"Sorry, I mean . . . people who consult the spirits."

"Shamans, yes, they speak to the gods and the spirits."

"All right. Suppose a shaman was to say that the spirits didn't agree with what the elders say, or with what other shamans have said that the spirits say? That would be a heretic."

Stone and Slow Leg looked at each other and laughed.

"Then our shamans are all heretics," Slow Leg said. "Perhaps I may explain it, Gail?"

She waved. "Please do."

"Very well." Slow Leg glanced around. The people at other tables, mainly ancient men playing a game with small pale rectangles of wood or bone that clacked on the tabletops, were paying them no attention. But still he slid his chair closer to the table and leaned in, hunching his shoulders and circling his arms as though guarding his beer from being snatched away.

"This is one of the secrets men are given in their initiation, after the challenge," he began. "I should not really be telling you this, but we are not in the Great Vale now, so the spirits are not listening." He lowered his voice. "There is one god, the father almighty, who made the sky and all the worlds. The other gods and spirits are lower to him than the ants beneath our feet are to us. All men and women are his children."

He looked so shamefaced that Stone had to look away. Gail was evidently deeply shaken by this secret; she had her hand over her mouth.

"Obviously," Slow Leg went on, "we cannot tell that to women and children."

"Obviously," Gail agreed solemnly, from behind her hand.

"But that is what the Christians believe!" Stone said.

"Yes," said Slow Leg, sounding exasperated. He glanced around again. "There is no need to shout it out. When the Christians first came here, they took great pains to teach our forefathers their religion, because they believed that theirs was the only way to reach the sky father. They won over many of the sky people, but those they won over became lost and sad and did not thrive, because they had lost all the teachings of their forefathers, and they knew not where to put their feet. Then the

Bright Star came to the world nearest ours, and the knowledge it carried included the teaching and the disputing of many of the Christian wise men, who had studied and spoken many years after the Christians of our world had been taken from the Cold Lands. Christopher Dawson was a young man who was preparing to be sent to preach to the sky people, and he studied these new doctrines, and he was inspired to go among the sky people to learn their ways, not to try to make them change them. He took the challenge and was initiated as a man of the sky people, and he wrote his book, and he said that the sky people did not need to become Christians to reach the sky father.

"The elders of the Christians called him back to Rawliston and accused him of bending the words of the sky father. That is what is meant by *heretic*. Dawson replied that the Christians' own book says that the man they say was the son of the sky father once said: 'There are many rooms in my father's house.' They quoted other words from that book, and he said these words had been put in the mouth of the sky father's son and his followers by later scribes, and they had a little more disputation, and then they burned him."

Any note of pathos in Slow Leg's voice was seared away when he added, "So our forefathers rose up and killed or drove out all the Christians in the Great Vale, and defeated the warriors sent from Rawliston to avenge them, and those of them who had forgotten the teachings of their forefathers learned them again from Dawson's book."

Slow Leg sat back and took a long swallow of his drink. "That is the story of Dawson."

"Yeah," Gail said. "That's the story. The way it's taught here, Dawson was a preacher who taught the heathens they could keep right on being heathens, and who mocked the bishops of the church to their faces, and whose followers tortured and massacred every convert they could find up in the big valley. There're lots more churches now, of course, and some of them regard Dawson as a saint and martyr, and some of them burn him again every year. Lucky for us, in this area most of the churches are of the former opinion. The other ones call them Dawsonites, when they're having a proper Christian spat, as they do."

Once again Stone felt he was not quite understanding her, but she drew the conversation to a close by draining her glass and saying it was time to catch a bus. Stone didn't know what that meant, but he soon found out.

．　　．　　．

Gail sat on one of the hard, horsehair-padded seats in the minibus. Crammed on the seat beside her was a stout grandmother clutching a basket containing a chicken whose occasional startling sounds could almost have made her suspect that the bird anticipated its likely imminent fate. Stone and Slow Leg sat in the seat opposite, Stone facing her directly, pushed up against the window like herself. Every seat and every available space in which to stand was taken. Only the open side doors prevented the noisy little vehicle from becoming intolerably hot.

The two men looked like a man and a girl, though their fair hair— absolutely goddamn *golden,* she couldn't help thinking—Stone's loose with its curls and waves around his shoulders, Slow Leg's braided and beaded close to his scalp and knotted at the nape—made it obvious enough that they were heathens, as did Stone's blue silk tunic and trousers. But it wasn't as obvious that they were tribals—some of the younger folk among the Christian heathen affected traditional costumes and hairstyles.

This wasn't her usual route to the Back-o'-the-Docks. She'd chosen it, starting with the back path from the airfield, to avoid areas associated with the more conservative churches, the bigotry of whose nominal adherents often seemed in inverse proportion to their grasp of the doctrines of their own sects, let alone of Christianity.

As the bus finally emerged from the backstreets and turned onto the wide street to the docks, running parallel to the left bank of the Big River, Gail realized that her plan for avoiding trouble might not work. The evening was shaping up to be the liveliest Dawson's Night she could remember. In the gathering dusk there seemed to be bonfires everywhere, their flare and the glare of fireworks reflected on the river's dark water. Most of the commercial properties along the left side of the street were boarded up or shuttered; on the right, the embankment and esplanade were thick with people drinking, throwing ripped railings and broken benches onto illegal fires on the pavement and down by the river, or wandering in fast-moving, shoulder-barging groups from one focus of firelight and noise to another.

Most of the earlier passengers had already completed their journey from work to home, and the bus was filling up with people partying. Mostly kids, she saw with relief, boys and girls with a few beers in them, out for a good time and more interested in each other and in their own raucous conversation than in anybody else on the bus.

The bus was just pulling away from a stop when it rocked and the driver yelled as four, five young men ran up and leaped on the running board and then pushed in, grabbing the overhead bar with whatever hands they could spare from holding bottles. They passed money forward to the driver with loud laughter and bad grace, and swayed and sang and swigged for a bit as the minibus picked up speed. They were all dressed in a similar style, short black jackets and narrow trews and shirts frilled at the front and cuffs, their hair piled high and combed back. The quieter kids and the remaining two or three older passengers ignored them, one or two of the kids—admiring or intimidated and sucking up—joined in their singing and shouting.

The seat beside Gail was vacant, and one of the new arrivals, after breathing sour vapors in her direction for some minutes, occasionally leaning down and peering at her directly and pulling faces and passing remarks that she supposed were intended to make her laugh, finally swung down and sat beside her.

He waved a half-empty bottle of corn-mash whiskey in front of her.

"Want a drink, gorgeous?"

"No, thank you."

He stuck out his right hand above the bag on her lap. "Pleased to meet you anyway. My name's Phil."

She decided to humor him, to placate. Stone and Slow Leg were staring straight ahead, as if they couldn't see anything. She shook his hand awkwardly.

"I'm Gail. Hi."

She let go of his hand, but he held onto hers.

"Let go, please."

He dropped her hand and leaned forward, twisting to stare at her.

"What's the matter with you, ginger? You upset about something?"

"No," she said, staring straight ahead again.

"That's a very hard hand you've got," he said. "For such a soft face."

He fingered her cheek.

She jerked away, then whipped her head around so fast that his finger almost went in her mouth—if it had, she'd have bitten it to the bone.

"Don't you fucking *touch* me!"

He recoiled as though she really had bitten him.

"Okay, okay," he said. "Ease off."

He looked up at his friends, who were laughing at his rebuff. For a few moments he seemed to accept it. Gail looked out of the window,

THE ENGINES OF LIGHT

checking her location. The next stop was just five minutes away and a short walk from Back-o'-the-Docks. Stone gave her what she guessed was meant to be an encouraging smile, but it betrayed just how nervous he felt.

"You two together?" Phil said, as though trying a different tack. He turned his attention to Stone. "Hey blondie, what's your friend got against a bit of fun?"

Stone responded with another scared smile, this time trying to look compliant and interested. Gail watched sidelong as, with the unexpected perceptiveness of someone just drunk enough to be uninhibited, the youth's face took on a look of pleased enlightenment as he turned to his mates.

"Hey," he said, "that isn't a girl, it's a goddamn mollyboy!"

"Yeah, and *you* fancied her for a minute!" jeered one of the others, whooping and jerking his bottle in front of his crotch.

Slow Leg seemed to snap into awareness. His eyes were suddenly focused on the man opposite him.

"You will be quiet," he said. His voice was like an announcement coming out of an iron grille at a great distance. "You will not say another word to these women."

Phil leaned back, taking a relaxed pose. He glanced up at his mates, who were hanging forward, intent. Gail tensed her legs and moved a little farther into the corner, watching them and ignoring Phil.

"What women?" he said. "I don't see any women here." He looked at Gail, then at Stone. "Nah. Just a fucked-up dyke and a cock-sucking mollyboy. And what's it to you, anyway, you heathen sodomite?"

Slow Leg's fist came out of nowhere and smashed Phil's nose.

In the moment that followed, Gail saw a bottle flash down toward Slow Leg's head. Her hand shot forward, the rest of her body following like a striking snake, and clamped onto the descending wrist. The deflected blow broke the bottle across the back of the seat. Gail hauled the wrist down farther and head-butted the guy in the face, then punched him in the stomach. She let go as the driver stamped on the brakes. Everyone standing, herself included, was thrown toward the front of the bus. The four guys who'd been standing in the aisle went all of a heap, sliding forward along the floor. Phil, his hands over his face, slammed into her hip as she made a simultaneous impact on Slow Leg. Stone had ducked into the space where Gail had been sitting a moment earlier; the rapid deceleration rocked him back, then he sprang up as the bus stopped.

Slow Leg caught Gail with one arm and straightened her up, at the same time reaching past her and pushing Phil's head down and pulling and pushing him to the side, sending him sprawling onto the floor.

Gail found herself looking straight into Slow Leg's eyes. He was smiling.

"We leave now," he said.

His voice sounded quiet, but that might only have been because it was hard to hear above all the yelling and screaming. The violent braking had cleared the space between them and the open side door. Phil's mates were just sorting themselves out and off the floor. Gail jumped off the bus, followed by Stone and then Slow Leg.

They were on a fairly empty stretch of esplanade pavement; the nearest groups of people were around fires tens of meters away in either direction. The traffic had been thin enough not to pile into the back of the minibus and was now flowing past it.

"Across the road," Gail said.

Stone kicked off and picked up his stack-heeled sandals, and looked up at her with a complicit, apologetic grin. Slow Leg grunted something. Together they sprinted and dodged speeding cars across the broad boulevard without incident to the shoreward pavement, darker and almost deserted. A side street leading eventually to Back-o'-the-Docks opened at the next corner ten meters away. Gail glanced back across the road. The minibus had moved on, leaving all five of the gang on the pavement, scanning the street. They caught sight of her at the same time and launched into a rush across the road. Brakes squealed and horns blared.

"Run!" Gail said.

"No," said Slow Leg, with a light touch on her arm.

She turned to see him and Stone stand stock-still a couple of meters apart, facing the spread-out oncoming gang. At the last moment the heathens leapt farther apart and lashed out with feet and fists, taking down the two of the attackers who'd gone straight for them. One of the others ran at Gail, a broken bottle held high. She bent her knees, ducked forward and to the side, caught his arm, pivoted, and let his momentum send him over her shoulder, his head hitting the pavement with a satisfying crack. The next one loomed above her as she rose. To her utter surprise she saw Stone spring into the air beside him and floor him with a perfect floating kick between the ribs and the hip, then land on all fours like a cat. The fifth was on his back already, Slow Leg looking down at him.

"Now we can walk," Slow Leg said.

"Make it fast," said Gail. The melee had stirred a commotion on the esplanade, drawing attention and people from both of the nearest groups around fires. It looked entirely possible that some of the separate crowds would join and surge across.

Stone slipped his sandals back on and picked his way past the sprawled bodies. They were all writhing and moaning—nobody killed or crippled, by the look of it. Stone joined hands with Slow Leg and ran. They were around the corner in seconds; Gail, bringing up the rear, kept glancing back, but after a minute without sight or sound of pursuit she relaxed a fraction and caught up with the heathens. The narrow street was empty and ill-lit. She put an arm around Slow Leg's waist, and they walked together, commanding the pavement like a swaggering gang.

"Wow," she said. "You guys." Her voice felt shaken and giggly. "I thought the deal with you lot was that women *didn't* fight?"

"That was without weapons," they said together, then laughed.

"That doesn't count, then?"

"Fighting with weapons," said Slow Leg in a tone of patient explanation, "is what men do. Anybody can fight without weapons, but it is mostly boys who learn to do it."

"I was a boy," Stone said. "I have not forgotten what I learned. *You* fought well." He leaned forward and grinned at her through a tumble of blond curls. "Were you a boy too?"

"Ya know," she said, grinning right back, "if I was to do like Slow Leg I'd punch your face for that." She felt his muscles tense in the crook of her arm and added hastily, "But not to worry, I'm not that touchy."

"Nor are we," said Slow Leg lightly. "But please, do not make threats again, even in a joke."

"All right."

She felt she had some air to clear between them.

"Since you ask, Stone, no, I wasn't a boy. I was a girl, and I am a woman. I do work that some people think is men's work, that's all. And I can fight, with weapons and without. I own a pistol and a big nasty knife, though I don't have either of them on me tonight, worse luck or maybe good luck. And my neighborhood militia has a very old and very long rifle with my name on it, and the law makes me practice with it twice a year, for all the good that might do."

"Women here fight with weapons?" Stone asked.

"Oh, yes. In theory. There hasn't *been* any fighting here since the last civil war, apart from against pirates, but we're supposed to be ready."

"I see," said Stone. "Then there is no difference between men and women here."

"None at all," said Gail. "Glad you've got that cleared up."

The sarcasm went over their heads.

"In our society," Stone said, "You would count as a man."

"I suppose I'll take that as a compliment."

This time Stone caught her dry tone and laughed.

"I know just what you mean," he said.

In all the months of her connection with Slow Leg, Gail had never arranged any dealing at the airfield. It was not exactly illegal, though with the assemblies making law by tumult and show of hands you never knew when it might become so. Evading the various taxes and tariffs that had been slapped on at various times to discourage the trade was certainly illegal, though it was hardly considered immoral or unusual and was widely winked at. But it would have been discourteous and would certainly have got her thrown out of the club.

Hence their trips, hitherto by a more direct route, from the airfield to Back-o'-the-Docks, Rawliston's traditional unrespectable district. Even in ancient times, when the Anglican church had dominated the early colony, it had been simultaneously reprobated as a sink of sin and tolerated as a safe containment thereof. Nowadays its hundred or so blocks were the bright and lively haunt of alcoholics, agnostics, artists, atheists, beggars, cutthroats, deserters, drug dealers, evangelists, footpads, gentry, heathens, informers, jays, knife grinders, lesbians, libertines, mollyboys, musicians, navvies, ostlers, physicians, queers, recruiters, reformers, sailors, socialists, trulls, users, vagabonds, watchmakers, xenophiles, and yuppies.

Gail had compiled the list once in her head, and ever since had kept an idle lookout for a Zoroastrian.

The pub was called the King's Head. The sign above the door was a bloody axe. Gail led the heathens in, sat them down, planted beers in front of them, and prowled the room for her regular dealer. She spotted Zachariah Tompkinson soon enough: In this crowd, the cultivated shabby gentility of his suit and haircut and general air of being a thirty-year-old clerk with no prospects stood out like a drag queen at a funeral. Apart from Paul Loudon, he was the richest man she knew.

"Hi, Zack. Got a minute?"

"For you, two."

She indicated the table with her eyes and sat down. In a few minutes Zack joined them and began his usual dickering over the contents of Slow Leg's satchels. Nothing addictive, that was where she drew the line. She was high already herself, or coming down from a high, jittery with reaction from the fight, her head spinning alphabetical lists. Aphrodisiacs, euphorics, hallucinogens, herbs, spices, and stimulants . . .

She turned to Stone, who was observing the pub's customers and was well out of the business dealing beside him, and was about to say something to him when she caught in the corner of her eye a penetrating look from a man a couple of tables away. She faced him and found herself locked in mutually embarrassed recognition with Paul Loudon, who was sitting with his arm around a mollyboy.

7

Ancient Astronauts

MATT COUNTS NINE separate silvery lines of bubbles rising to the surface of the tank. This is not good, this is not good at all. He takes the grease pencil from behind his ear, plunges his arms into the water, and draws a circle around each fizzing source. Most of them are at the seams and joints. The water comes past his elbow and seeps up his rolled-up sleeves. He straightens up and shakes off drips.

"Okay, you can turn it off now."

The din of the air compressor stops, leaving the small annex—it was originally some kind of washroom—echoingly quiet. He reaches in again and releases the straps holding the suit to lead weights at the bottom of the tank. Sagging already, it bobs to the surface. Plasticized canvas in a bloated human shape without head, hands, or feet, like the trawled-up victim of a particularly gruesome murder, the half dozen red patches on the torso its stab wounds. He disconnects the tube plumbed to the plastic collar where the helmet will go and hauls the clammy carcass out.

"Shit," says Gail. "It'll take hours to dry enough to put more sealant on."

"I don't think more sealant's the answer," Matt says. "Or more patches."

"Do these tiny holes really matter?" Gail asks.

"For diving, they wouldn't," Matt says. "In a vacuum, they most certainly would. Any of them could start a total blowout."

"Even after we've got the tension layers wrapped around it?"

"Hmm," says Matt. "I'm not sure. I'm seriously beginning to wonder if adapting a diving suit is any kind of shortcut. Maybe it would be quicker in the long run if we were to scrap this approach and pitch in with Volkov's start-from-scratch scheme."

Volkov has been running himself ragged between the university library, which contains in its vaults encyclopedic accounts of EVA suit construction, and various plastics companies and Loudon's factory, trying to simplify the spec down to the local tech level. Matt has, by agreement, followed the superficially simpler path of seeing whether something can be cobbled together from aviation and diving gear. So far, it's been the worst of both worlds: crash and leak.

Gail looks glum. "You mean we've wasted a whole week?"

Matt grins. "Finding that something doesn't work is never a waste of time. How's the helmet coming along?"

She shrugs. "Frank Kemble's a great believer in off-the-shelf. He just mutters every time I ask just *when* I get to learn to use the milling machine, then sends me off trotting around the workshops and stores for odd components and bits of scrap. Or tells me to go and help you. Like now. But we have made a good start with adapting an aviator's oxygen supply apparatus, and Frank seems finally to have made a neck seal that you can open and close without actually having to screw your head on and off."

Gail has in fact turned out to be very good at rounding up bits and pieces and wangling some work on the side from other projects all over the factory and in knowing exactly what might be needed to improvise solutions to problems as they come up, and is thus contributing far more to the work on the helmet than she would if she were turned loose on a lathe. Matt carefully doesn't say this and instead says brightly, "Well, that's progress. I guess old Kemble will give you the right training in his own time, but meanwhile just badger him occasionally, okay?"

"Okay," says Gail. She pokes at the deflating suit's tied-off ankle cuff. "What about this?"

"Ah, leave it. Let's mosey over and see if we can be of any use to Grigory."

They bang out through the swinging doors into the factory yard and cut across to an equally neglected room where Salasso and Volkov have set up their drawing office and test lab.

Volkov looks up from a workbench as they come in and keeps on working as Matt recounts the latest dismal results. He himself has set up a sort of railing at the end of the workbench, upon which a roll of aircraft fabric, a roll of sheet plastic, and a roll of metal mesh are mounted. He's feeding them across the bench and trying out various techniques for laminating them, which judging by the discarded scraps stacking up at the other end of the bench have so far involved rivet guns, brute-force stitching, various glues, heat treatment, and several combinations thereof.

Salasso has perched himself on a high stool by the bench at the wall, which is loaded down with volumes borrowed from the university library: massive, musty volumes of reverently reprinted twentieth- and twenty-first-century American and Russian astronautics texts, which he can scan and assimilate a lot faster than Matt or Volkov can. Volkov has a lot of practical knowledge of EVA in his head, but it's more from the end-user than the production angle. Since starting work on this project, Salasso has taken to wearing an open-necked check shirt and black trousers—boys' sizes, and even then fitting very badly—in a rather vain (in both senses) attempt to make his presence less likely to freak out old Kemble, not to mention any members of Loudon's workforce who may encounter him unexpectedly. At the moment he has his feet up on the bench and his head down over a garish paperback, one of a big tottering stack beside the leather-bound tomes.

"I don't know if I'm making any better progress myself," Volkov says. "If we could get at the original suits, it might be a boost."

"How are things going with that?"

"It's out of my hands," Volkov says, turning up his palms as though to confirm it. "Esias and Lydia are working their political contacts. Loudon's been putting a word in for us at the big capitalists' watering holes. He claims to have got at least one of the local scandal sheets agitating the proletariat on the issue. Not much use when most of the rest are running scare stories about dangerous machines and space-mutated Earthborn plague viruses."

"It's something," says Matt. He's been rather hoping that Volkov might be using his own local contacts to put pressure on the still-stonewalling Port Authority but guesses that the project hasn't left him much time for that, just as he himself hasn't seen much of Esias and Lydia.

"There's a meeting in my neighborhood this afternoon," says Gail. "I'll be going along. Why don't you come, Grigory Andreievich?"

Volkov's got them all used to calling him that; the patronymic helps to avoid any slipups with his surnames.

Volkov makes a face. "I don't think I can spare the time. I have spoken to a few people I know in that area, Gail, so maybe you could hook up with them?"

Gail nods. "Yeah, give me their names and I'll track them down, no problem."

"Good idea," says Matt, pleased that Volkov has been working his contacts after all.

"Meanwhile," he adds, "it might speed things up if I just throw in my lot with you."

"Maybe," says Volkov skeptically. "It strikes me that boots and gloves would be worth having ready for when we get a functioning suit, and you could concentrate on that instead of getting underfoot here. Thanks for the offer, but you know how it is. Too many cooks and all that."

The mention of boots and gloves sets Matt off thinking vaguely about leather and wondering if a skin-tight leather suit is just the kind of radical low-tech departure that they need, and that brings up thoughts of Daphne and her leather trousers. He follows this line of speculation for a moment, sighs, and distracts himself from the distraction as Salasso chucks aside the book he's just finished and picks up the next and Matt notices the cover picture, which is of a Gray alien.

Matt registers for a moment the weirdness of the sight—it's like Salasso is reading a book with his own portrait on the cover—and peers closer at the spines of the rest of the stack: ancient astronauts and flying saucers and alien abductions and Roswell and Area 51 and conspiratorial cover-ups, locally produced editions of books that, gods know how, were included in the *Bright Star*'s library files but that, thankfully, were never reprinted by the university press. Evidently Rawliston's entrepreneurial publishers have taken up the slack.

Oh, well. Matt doesn't feel it's his place to question the saur's reading priorities, and he doesn't want to start a conversation that might stray into awkward territory for himself and Volkov.

Gail has no such inhibitions. "What the *fuck* are you reading that stuff for, Salasso?"

The saur looks up, the nictitating membrane flickering across his huge, black, almond-shaped eyes.

"I'm searching," he says, "for evidence that my species has given your species some technological assistance in the past, back in the Solar System. If there is any, it might help me to rebut the claim that what I have been doing is unprecedented."

Matt stares at him, torn between the impulse to guffaw and a sudden surge of sympathy, and over and above both feelings is a momentary shiver of the uncanny. The saurs in the Second Sphere have always said that they have no idea what their putative counterparts in the Solar System have been up to, and there's something almost touching in the sight of Salasso hacking his way through the same jungle of disinformation as any human interested in the question would have to. It's also rather worrying. The saurs understand fiction and imagination perfectly well, but sustained, deliberate downright lying, not to mention delusion and hallucination and insanity, is more or less beyond their ken.

"I don't think you'll find much there that might count as evidence," Gail says scornfully.

"Oh?" says Salasso, peering over the cover in another trompe l'oeil moment. "You've studied it, have you?"

"Yes," says Gail. "There was a lad at Reece's Garage, where I used to work, who read that kind of rubbish all the time, as well as *science fiction*. Aliens, starships going faster than light, crap like that."

Volkov looks across sharply. "There's no doubt there's *some* truth buried in that rubbish, somewhere," he says. "Your own people and all the peoples who came here before you have traditions of their ancestors having been taken from Earth by beings who can only have been saurs."

"Yeah," says Gail. "But Salasso, can you seriously imagine saurs kidnapping people and sticking probes up their asses?"

"No," says Salasso rather coldly. "But the question of whether they made any other interventions remains open."

"Besides," adds Volkov, "there were well-attested records of sightings of what seem very like gravity skiffs. Even in the socialist countries, not to mention the United States."

Matt laughs harshly. "It's said that Camilla Hernandez once dropped a hint that there were some traces in her employers' records, but she flew only from Area 51 to the *Bright Star,* and then flew a flying saucer back, so what did she know?"

One of the few disadvantages of not aging is that losses stay sharp. Matt looks out the long window at the cluttered yard for a moment, then tells Salasso to keep searching and joins Volkov at the bench. Gail, momentarily at a loss for something useful to do, starts idly flicking through the books herself.

Gail was refreshing her acquaintance with the archaeological discoveries of Erich von Däniken when she heard a commotion in the yard. A sharp knock sounded on the lab door, and two brown-uniformed militiamen, one militia woman, and three saurs came in without waiting for a reply. Gail stood up and stared for a moment.

"What's all this?" Grigory Andreievich demanded, in the truculent tone of a man with a lot on his mind and nothing on his conscience. Gail shut her mouth and determined to keep it shut as long as possible. For the entire week she'd been working here she had been worrying about her actions catching up with her. Damage and casualties from the Dawson's Night celebrations had been unprecedented, and the gang she and the heathens had tangled with had given their side of the story to the militia—two of them from hospital beds, where they were being treated for broken bones and internal injuries. And then there was the matter of her unauthorized drug trading, which Paul Loudon had made perfectly clear could not continue if she was working for him. She had told the heathens just before she'd launched them in their glider, laden with small metal goods, from the car-and-chariot arrangement the following afternoon, that drug trading was right out. They had just looked at her impassively and said they would see her in a week.

"We're shutting this project down," the militia woman said. "We expect your full cooperation."

Gail tried to hide her relief, as she had hidden her guilt. The others seemed to be looking to her for a lead, presumably because she was a citizen and they weren't.

"Why?" she asked, with as much indignation and surprise as she could rally. "We aren't breaking any laws."

One of the saurs stepped forward. "You are not breaking any human laws," he or she said. The tone was almost sympathetic. "However, what you are doing is causing dissension among our people, and under our agreement with your city, we have a right to ask your peacekeepers to make you desist."

"I protest," said Salasso.

"Your protest is recognized," said the other saur. "But the agreement is clear."

"First I've heard of such an agreement," said Gail.

The saur's thin lips twitched. "It was made shortly after the founding of your settlement. The original of it is in a glass case at the city hall."

Gail remembered, as a child, standing on tiptoes for a brief glance at this vellum relic, written with a feather in crabbed italics where every *s* looked like an *f*. She decided to appeal to a more immediate authority.

"What does Citizen Loudon have to say about this?"

The militia woman smirked and made a ball-tossing gesture toward the phone.

DARK LIGHT

"Ask him."

Gail picked up the phone and dialed the number for Kemble's workshop.

"Hello, is that Paul Loudon's office? We've got some militia and saurs down here telling us the project is shut down."

"Oh, Powers Above," said Kemble. "They're not here yet. Want me to get the gear out of the way?"

"Yes, yes. Sorry, wrong number."

She knocked on her forehead and dialed the right number.

"Loudon speaking," said Paul.

"Paul, uh, Citizen Loudon, it's Gail Frethorne, we have some—"

"—militia and saurs in the lab. I know. Their officers have just had the courtesy to call on me, to tell me that they are already, ah, deployed. No choice but to comply, I'm afraid, but do make sure anything they take is documented and signed for."

But they weren't interested in taking anything. They merely politely escorted them all from the room and taped up and sealed the door and slapped a notice with an official stamp on it. Gail looked disbelievingly at the stamp.

"*Port Authority?* What's this got to do with them?"

The militia people laughed.

The saur who had spoken previously was more polite. "It does not have much to do with the Port Authority," he or she explained. "But among all of your institutions that signed the original agreement, it is the only one that remains."

"Then it's *about fucking time,*" Gail said over the saur's head to the militia people, "that the assemblies did something about that! The Port Authority's getting too big for its boots! I'll raise this at my neighborhood meeting this afternoon."

"You do that," said one of the militiamen. "And now, you do this." He jerked his thumb over his shoulder. "Off."

Off they went, straight to Loudon's office. Paul waved them in and they all sat, except Salasso.

"Well," said Loudon. "Kemble managed to stash the breathing apparatus before they got round to his lab. Sharp thinking on his part, and on yours, Frethorne. At least that's one thing saved from this sorry mess. Militia tramping around *my* factory! As if we were some kind of criminal enterprise! I think you owe me an explanation, friends."

"This is my fault," said Salasso.

The rest of them stared at him.

"What?"

He looked at Matt and Grigory.

"Shortly after the ship landed," he said, his voice as heavy as his big head suddenly seemed, "I discussed our plans with my lover, Bishlayan. She very much did not approve. She must have mentioned it to others."

Paul Loudon glanced around with an expression more reptilian than the saur's.

"You're telling us," he said, "that the other saurs disapprove of your helping us to build *space suits*? Or do your plans involve something else, which I have not been told?"

"It's possible," said Grigory, "that they object to a . . . notion we had of landing the ship on other celestial bodies, to explore."

Loudon seemed to find this notion plausibly outlandish, but Salasso shook his head sadly. "You know that is not the whole truth, Grigory Andreievich."

Loudon rested his chin on steepled fingers.

"Well, chaps, I'm waiting for somebody to do the decent thing and bloody well tell me the whole truth." He flopped a hand. "Unless it's commercially confidential, of course."

Gail felt relieved that he was keeping his sense of humor. The three star travelers looked as uncomfortable as guilty schoolboys. Matt broke the awkward silence.

"We'll be happy to tell you," he said. He glanced uneasily at Gail. "It might not be fair to include your employees."

Loudon raised his eyebrows. "I've already assigned Frank Kemble to another project and told him to keep well out of this. Chap's got a grown family and a retirement to think about. Frethorne"—he grinned at her—"any risks you wish to take with the law are up to you."

"Thank you," said Gail. "I'll stay."

She wouldn't miss this for anything.

There are times when the world changes, Gail thought, half an hour later. Not just the world, *your* world. When something you were sure was solid melts into air.

The world, Croatan, had changed the day the *Bright Star* arrived, but *her* world had not changed until today. She felt some small measure of the shock her ancestors must have felt, when the strange silvery shapes had first been glimpsed through the trees, and their small gray pilots had walked inexorably forward, invulnerable alike to musket fire and exorcism.

She'd known since childhood that the original crew of the *Bright Star* had talked to the Powers Above and learned from them how to build a lightspeed drive. Now Matt and Grigory wanted to talk to the Powers Above again and find out if they could explain the reasons why the Second Sphere existed at all and what the gods wanted of the intelligent beings within it, the humans and hominids, the saurs and the krakens. That was why she felt as if everything were dropping away from beneath her feet: the thought that all these worlds and the very ground beneath her might exist for a purpose, and that they might (therefore) never have existed, and that the immense intent of their existence could be divined.

"What I want to know," Loudon asked, "is why you want to do this now, and not at some other time?"

"I would like to try to find the answers before I leave for Nova Babylonia," said Grigory Andreievich.

"And I need him to do it before he leaves," added Matt. "I don't have anyone else who has his knowledge of the original ship and of the space suits."

"And your expertise is just as irreplaceable, is that it?"

Matt nodded. "Yeah," he said bleakly, "that's about the size of it. So let's talk about space suits. It looks like we're shit-creeked as far as building them here is concerned. If we tried it at another company, we'd just get shut down again. If we defy it on your property, Paul, rip that tape off the door, we'll get you into worse trouble, no matter how unpopular we manage to make the actual shutdown. So I'm in favor of throwing all our efforts into getting the embargo on the ship lifted and then work on repairing and renovating the old EVA suits."

Grigory Andreievich shook his head. "The more I think about trusting my life to one of these, the less I like it. They're very complex, very software-dependent, and they've had a long time to degrade in ways we might not even recognize. I'd feel a lot safer in a new one, even if it was a crude one. Precisely because it would be more basic, there'd be less to go wrong."

"Good old Soviet design philosophy," said Gail. They looked at her.

"I've read about it in books," she protested.

"Well, your books got that right," said Grigory. For a moment, as he looked sharply at her and said that, she felt—not for the first time—a niggling recollection of having seen him somewhere before they'd met. Something in what had just been said had almost brought it back, but now it was gone. Grigory turned to Loudon. "What, if anything, can we save from the project as it stands?"

Loudon spread his hands. "Breathing apparatus, air tanks. I'll see to that. All that leaves is—everything else! Damn."

"Suppose you did somehow get other suits built," said Gail, "and the embargo isn't lifted, at least not before you leave. You'd still have the problem of getting the ship back."

"Remember that I have access to the ship," said Salasso. "Even though there are guards on board, this should make it not too difficult to get them off. If I were to 'check' the engine and tell them it was about to malfunction, I imagine they would leave the ship very quickly."

Laughter greeted this optimistic scenario. Gail had little doubt that it would be more difficult than that. But the notion of deception was a good one.

"How about," she said, "simply announcing that you intend to return to Mingulay? They'd let you back on the ship then, and you could go off and do what you want."

Matt shook his head. "I've thought of that, and it wouldn't work unless our two scientists from Mingulay went along with it. And they won't—they're very serious about setting up good trading relations, and they're unlikely to do anything that might alienate the Port Authority, or risk the ship in any adventures out in the cometary cloud."

"What gives you the right to take these risks?" asked Loudon sharply.

"Hmm," said Matt. He stood up and walked to the window, then turned around and looked straight back at them.

"Legally and morally," he said, "that's a matter internal to the Cosmonaut Families. Gregor Cairns and Elizabeth Harkness have different priorities from me and Antonov here, but their judgment doesn't necessarily override ours. We feel we have a right to take this chance, maybe the only one we'll ever get, to find out why the ship and its crew were taken here in the first place."

"Well," said Loudon, "I'm not entirely happy about that. But this is all moot, it's so much hot air unless you have space suits. The Authority could let you back on the ship tomorrow, your friends could tell you to go right ahead, and it wouldn't do you any good if you couldn't get out of the ship to set up your device."

"And we've agreed to build them," said Gail. "And we made the agreement with these guys, not with the others."

"Good point," said Loudon, with a slight lift of the eyebrows at her boldness. He looked down and started doodling what Gail recognized as a critical path analysis on a scrap of paper.

"Let's focus on that, shall we? What are people's plans for the day?"

A movement in the sky caught Gail's eye. It was a heathen balloon train. She remembered, with something of a shock at having forgotten, that her heathen friends were due to return to the airfield tonight. She stared at the glowing object drifting down to the rooftops, like the ship had done just the other week. Niggled by a thought just beneath the surface of her mind, she looked down and noticed that she was still clutching one of Salasso's crazy old books, the kind that Joshua had devoured so eagerly, about ancient astronauts meeting Stone Age civilizations. The cover picture showed a line drawing of some heathen witch doctor in an outfit and headgear that looked vaguely like a space suit—

"Yes!" she yelled. "Yes! That's it!"

She jumped up and everybody turned and stared at her. She waved a hand at the window.

"*Look* out there! What do you see?"

The rest of them spared it no more than a glance.

"Heathen hot-air balloon train," said Loudon. "Ingenious contraption. What about it?"

"Space suits," she said.

"Yes," said Paul Loudon, with heavy irony. "We *were* talking about space suits, before—"

"You know what I see?"

They looked again at the craft, then back at Gail's excited gaze as though they were missing something, or she was.

"Ceramic braziers," she said. "Airtight fabrics. Glassware."

"Uh—" began Matt, her point clearly dawning on him. But she wasn't about to let him get ahead of her.

"What I see," she said, "is a technology that can build your space suits. No sweat."

If anyone had asked Lydia who she was, she'd have told the truth. To that extent, she wasn't in disguise. She was, however, hoping that her locally fashionable outfit would let her blend in as a middle-class young lady on the fringe of this lower-class assembly crowd. She hoped so:

Squeezing into the ugliest outfit she'd ever worn—watery blue silk dress with a tight buttoned bodice and a narrow skirt with rows of frills from the knees to the ankles, underpinned by some very uncomfortable underwear and matched by a hat, gloves, purse, fan, and parasol in the same fabric and style—would have been pointless otherwise. It made her sweat so much she suspected she already *smelled* like a local, though she rather hoped not.

Fanning herself and sniffing a pomander, she pushed her way through the lines of reporters, children, beggars, hawkers, and idlers to the row of trestles that marked off the assembly itself. A couple thousand people from the neighborhood packed out a games pitch adjacent to a local school. Some of them were sitting on folding chairs, others were standing up and milling around. They hadn't been called to order yet, and the din of conversation bouncing around the high wooden walls—the pitch was for a ball-and-racquet game, something like a team version of squash—was almost deafening. The crowd had come straight from work at midday, some of them via a grogshop. If democracy, as Esias was fond of saying, was mob rule, here was the mob.

Somewhere in this mob—ah, there he was, up near the front—was Andrew Burnaby, the de Tenebres' agent for this neighborhood. She'd spent half the morning briefing him in a coffeehouse. It had been something of a strain. Burnaby was more skilled in putting forward sly arguments for a tariff here or a tax concession there, or rebutting similarly self-interested proposals from rival agents, than in making a populist case for free trade and against Port Authority meddling and bungling. She'd had to present it in the most venal possible light for him to grasp it at all, and even so she suspected he'd be out of his depth.

This working-class suburban neighborhood, optimistically named Verdant Heights when it had been jerry-built a hundred years earlier on an inadequately drained malarial swamp, was of no great importance in itself. It just happened to be the first to hold an assembly since the *Bright Star*'s impounding, and steering a protest through this meeting might be crucial in starting the ball rolling. So Esias had explained when he'd briefed Lydia over breakfast. She felt herself on trial, and on her mettle.

A low wooden stage had been dragged into the playing court for the afternoon and placed at the front, with two chairs and a table upon it. Up the three steps at its side climbed a fat, middle-aged woman swathed in black skirts. She puffed her way across the creaking planks and sat down heavily. A thin and nervous-looking young man followed her, clutching a briefcase. When he'd sat down and laid out a pad of yellow notepaper and arranged two ballpoint pens and a sheaf of printed papers to his satisfaction, the woman thumped her fist on the table.

A hush fell at once. The woman opened the meeting, the man read out minutes and matters arising, people spoke to the points from the floor. The young man took notes and recorded votes. When Lydia had got over her surprise at how orderly it all was she found it tedious. An hour of people popping up and down and spouting off crawled by. Lydia bought herself a very small cup of fruit juice and sipped it very slowly. Somebody was talking about drains. Her attention wandered. She began to hope that the heat and discomfort of the venue—the sun on the field was *fierce*—would help speed up movement through the agenda. Burnaby wouldn't get much chance to intervene until Any Other Business.

Her idle gaze reached the rear of the enclosure and lit upon a small huddle near the gate, in which she recognized Volkov talking earnestly to a tall red-haired woman. Lydia was jolted by a sudden surge of jealousy. Two or three other people were listening just as intently. As she watched, the woman turned away and plunged into the crowd, assiduously elbowing her way to the front; the others headed for the middle and the sides.

Volkov, his gaze following them, spotted her. He smiled and made a sort of drowning wave above the heads of the throng. Intrigued, Lydia began the slow process of joining him, meeting every grumble with a fixed smile of apology. By the time she reached him ten minutes later, her cheek muscles were as sore as her toes. He had moved to the very edge of the crowd, and he turned his head to glance at her for only a moment, then faced forward again.

"Hello," he said. "You look rather glamorous."

"I don't feel it," she said. "I just feel tied up and *hot*."

The corner of his mouth twitched; she wondered if she'd said something unintentionally amusing. She was quivering inside a little.

"What brings you here?" Volkov asked.

"Oh, politics. You?"

"The same. The tall redhead is working with us on the project. She happens to live around here. The others are a couple of local workers I've met on business. They're all going to try and get a word in about what the Port Authority has been up to."

"I'm expecting someone here to raise the matter too."

Volkov glanced sideways again, approvingly. "Good. That gives us quite a spread of speakers."

"Depends on whether the chair recognizes them," Lydia said.

Volkov looked right around at her with a broad smile, as though she had said something quite charming.

"Yes," he said. "Not the sort of thing one would want to leave to chance, eh?"

With a chuckle, he turned away.

After a few more minutes of discussion of drainage and subsidence had drawn to a close and several amendments and a motion carried, the woman in the chair rapped her knuckles on the table and said, "Any other business?"

She said it as though hoping there wouldn't be any but knowing all too well that there would. Hands shot up all over the place; the half dozen or so gigants in the crowd had an advantage there, and Lydia noticed one pithkie perched on another's shoulders, arm up and waving. Some people present took the arrival at this point in the agenda as the occasion to take their leave; others took it as the end of the so-far two-hour-long smoking ban and lit up; others pushed forward, or started rapid and noisy conversations. It all seemed much more the sort of chaos Lydia had expected democracy to be like than the main part of the meeting had been.

"This is where it gets interesting," said Volkov out of the side of his mouth.

The young man on the platform was glancing around the crowd and scribbling notes on his pad without looking down at it. He leaned sideways and conferred rapidly with the chairwoman, then pointed discreetly with his pen. She nodded, raised her arm, and pointed very clearly at someone.

"You, second row, tall, red hair—"

"Thank you, Madam Chair," said the woman who'd been speaking with Volkov. She pushed forward and jumped on to the corner of the platform, where she could face most of the crowd while keeping up the polite fiction that she was addressing the chair.

"Citizen Gail Frethorne," she said. "With your permission, Madam Chair, I'd like to bring to the attention of this assembly a quite unprecedented action by the Port Authority. Just this morning, they ordered the militia into Loudon's Engineering Works to shut down a project—"

She paused. "Interest," she said. "I work there, on the project they shut down."

"Noted," said the young man, scribbling.

"The project was to build some survival equipment for the space travelers who have recently arrived and whose ship has been so rudely embargoed by the Port Authority."

"Treaty! Treaty!" someone shouted. There was a moment of commotion, during which Lydia nudged Volkov.

"Is this your *space suit* project that's been shut down?"

"Yes," said Volkov. "I'll tell you about it later."

"The chair recognizes the interruption," said the big woman on the platform. "You on the right, halfway along—yes, man in the hat."

A high-crowned, long-plumed hat waved above the left flank of the crowd.

"Madam Chair, citizens, this project has been cancelled at the request of the speakers for the local saur community, which the Port Authority is bound to—"

"Interest! Interest!"

The man stretched up and glowered toward his interruptors. "Port Authority clerk," he said. Laughter followed.

He plowed on: "They have appealed to the treaty, so this is a matter for the Port Authority and is out of order and ultra vires of a neighborhood assembly—"

Uproar. Lydia made out some of the indignant shouts:

"The assemblies are *all* sovereign!"

"Nothing's out of order except you!"

"Recall! Recall! Recall 'em all!"

"What country d'you think *you're* living in? Fuck off back to it!"

Madam Chair almost broke the table.

"Order!" she shouted, just once. The shouting stopped. "The matter raised by Citizen Frethorne," she went on, "is indeed out of order, but not because it's a matter for the Port Authority. It's out of order because anything involving the treaties is a matter for the courts. Citizen Frethorne will please stand down."

Gail Frethorne hopped off the platform and returned to where she had been standing. Lydia felt disappointed.

"Damn, that's a bit of a—"

Volkov was shaking his head. "Wait."

"You at the side, red shirt, hand up—yes, you!"

"Whatever they did this morning," a man said loudly and confidently from the floor, "I reckon the Port Authority wants a good looking at. What do they think they're doing interfering with the Mingulay starship, anyway? They never lay a finger on the big merchants' ships, which carry only capital goods and luxuries. Not that I've anything against that, but there's *loads* more stuff we could trade if there was a regular run between here and Mingulay—"

"What's the difference who flies the ships?" somebody else shouted. "It wouldn't change the ten-year turnaround time!"

"Order!"

"That it wouldn't," the man in the red shirt went on. "But having *lots* of ships, shuttling back and forth so there's a continuous stream going each way, and a simple system of export-import advance orders like the big merchants have—that would make a difference. It would make the imports we already have cheaper and make bulk imports and exports profitable."

The concept of ship streaming was familiar enough to the crowd for this to go over all right, but the objector shouted out again.

"And where are these *lots of ships* going to come from?"

"Well—"

But he'd lost the initiative. Volkov clicked his tongue, irritated.

"He should have come back on that right away," he said. "Oh, well."

A very tall old man with a long white beard and a long black coat spoke next.

"I don't think there should be even *one* more ship," he said. "We should send the *Bright Star* back where it came from, to the goddamned pagan heresiarchs of Mingulay, and tell them to stick right there where they belong. If the Powers Above had meant human beings to navigate ships, they'd have given us, they'd have given us—"

"Tentacles?" somebody called out.

"They'd have given us some better evidence of it than a story told by these there godless cosmonauts, whose ship has brought this world nothing but heresy and sedition these past two hundred years. I remember when I were a lad—"

"And the ship arrived the first time?" the same wag hollered.

"The folks who were as old then as I am now, and as you will be one day *if* the Lord spares you, used to say that the Powers Above taught the krakens the way through the passages the Lord has provided in the crystal spheres of the firmaments, and that it was only of the Lord's mercy that the *Bright Star* had not broken the spheres when it came from Earth and released upon us the waters above the firmament, as in the days of Noah."

He paused for a moment to draw breath and then continued, louder, shouting down a further outburst of heckling: "Assuming it came from

Earth in the first place, of course, and not from the father of lies. Because the books they brought with them and that these there professors up at the university treat like Scripture itself are full of nothing but lies, and there's only one place *they* could have come from—"

He continued in this vein for five minutes, then sat down abruptly to catcalls, amens, and scattered applause.

"With all due respect to the previous speaker," said the woman who spoke next, "I'd like to point out some other objections to the proposal of extending human-controlled trade that may be more, ah, widely shared. The Port Authority has warned us that the ship is full of health hazards, of viruses and bacteria from the Solar System that have had centuries to mutate in the radiation of space. Starship engines are—as we all know—designed to be controlled by the krakens, the great navigators. We are told that the one on this ship is in fact controlled by a calculating machine, programmed by a student! And that the inexperienced pilot on board is a saur whose actions are strongly disapproved of by many of his fellows. *My* only complaint about the actions of the Port Authority is that they've let this plague carrier and potential nuclear bomb sit in our harbor, instead of sending it straight back to Mingulay, or—as the citizen here has just suggested—to hell!"

A significant minority cheered that one.

"Goddamn gutter press," muttered Volkov. "It's worse than a whole regiment of priests."

"It's all right," said Lydia. "Our agent's got the floor."

Andrew Burnaby had just jumped on to the platform.

"We all know your interest," said Madam Chair wearily, "but tell us anyway."

Burnaby started off well enough, but the increasingly skeptical and scoffing interjections—especially the growing cry of "What ships?"—almost drove him from the platform. Competent enough at raising minor details of taxes and regulations, at demagogy he was hopeless. Lydia would have jumped up and down with fury and impatience if her dress had allowed her to. She turned to speak to Volkov and found that he wasn't there. He had somehow insinuated himself to the front, and a note had been handed up to the platform, literally bypassing Burnaby while he was still floundering.

Madam Chair and Mister Secretary had their heads together, and suddenly the woman nodded and beckoned. Volkov bounded onto the platform almost before Burnaby had time to get off. Cameras were popping and microphones extending all over the place.

"Thank you, Madam Chair," he said, his voice already easily commanding the room. "Thank you all. My name is Grigory Antonov, from one of the Cosmonaut Families of Mingulay, and I'm working very closely with the crew of the *Bright Star*. Let me assure you that it doesn't contain any plague germs, its engine is not about to blow up, and it didn't make any holes in the sky.

"Some citizens here have spoken of the benefits that will come from having human-owned ships trading between the worlds. Others have asked, 'Where will all these new ships come from?' We're unlikely to be able to buy them from the saurs, after all! Even if they were willing to sell, we couldn't afford to buy them. Where will we find other ships?"

He paused and looked around. Lydia felt, for a moment, that his eyes had met hers and realized that everybody else here had—even if only for a fraction of a second—felt the same.

"I can tell you," he said quietly. "The *Bright Star* was built by human beings like ourselves! Ordinary men and women in the European Union, a great democracy like your own, built the *Bright Star* long ago. The technology they used was not much more advanced than ours. The lightspeed engine of the *Bright Star* was built by human beings not long after. They were given the design directly by the Powers Above, and the tools they used to build it are still on the ship. Someday, you may want to learn to use these tools yourselves.

"So that's my answer to the very good question, 'Where will the other ships come from?' They will come from Rawliston, from Mingulay, from other human worlds. We can *build* them for ourselves! The *Bright Star* is only one ship, yes. But with your skills, your hopes, your strength, you can know for sure—*there will be other ships.*"

He looked around again and smiled. "Thank you," he said and stepped down. The cheers and jeers stopped and hands went up.

"It's all very well him talking about us building the ships, but *where*," the next speaker wanted to know, "is the *money* going to come from?"

After another half hour or so, a cry went up to close the matter. This was carried by acclamation. Then a vote was taken on a motion to challenge the action of the Port Authority. It passed by a narrow majority, just big enough to register on a show of hands.

After that it was all anticlimax, or so it seemed to Lydia. Ten slips of paper were pulled at random out of a big bucket holding the names of all citizens present. The ten would go on to represent Verdant Heights at the next municipal assembly, in a couple of weeks, where the votes taken here and at other neighborhood assemblies would be discussed.

Lydia watched the crowd stream out. Small groups hung around, still talking. Volkov was at the center of one of them, walking toward her and talking and gesticulating. He stopped in front of her, and the others stopped too. He introduced her to the man in the red shirt and the other man he'd conferred with earlier, and to the woman, Gail Frethorne.

Gail had a broad smile and a firm handshake, and she didn't seem to have any special relationship with Volkov. Lydia hoped her insanely intense suspicion didn't show in her face.

"Pleased to meet you, Trader Lydia de Tenebre," Gail said.

"Likewise, Citizen Frethorne . . . Gail."

Gail suddenly smiled in a different, more relaxed way. "I wouldn't have taken you for a trader; you have the accent just right, and the look is so stylish . . . that's such a lovely dress.'

"Thank you," said Lydia. Gail, in trousers and shirjack, rough-handed, didn't seem like she would care about such things, but her eyes shone with genuine admiration.

The thin young man who'd been on the platform had joined them. His name was William Endecott. Pinched features, bright sharp eyes, thin pale red hair combed back, plain suit. He transferred the briefcase clutched under his elbow to his hand for the handshake, then put it quickly back. Well, she'd had as much trouble with her various fashionable encumbrances.

Lydia noticed Volkov's unobtrusive nod at Endecott, a look that said, "Well done!" and understood what he'd meant about not leaving the recognition of speakers from the floor to chance. A thought struck her.

"Citizen Endecott," she said, "isn't it just a matter of chance that the delegates you send to the municipal assembly will reflect the feeling of this meeting? Ten out of—what, two thousand? It's well within probability that they could all take the minority view."

"You're quite right," said Endecott. "It's a problem, but there are more than a hundred neighborhood assemblies, and—"

"It all comes out in the wash," said Gail. "And it's the way we've always done things."

"Nevertheless," said Endecott. He glanced at Volkov, as though checking something. Volkov's nod was, again, barely perceptible. "We've been discussing, just throwing ideas around you understand, just

405

considering the notion that it might be a good idea some time in the future to change the constitution so that neighborhood meetings *elect* the delegates, to ensure that the majority view prevailed beyond cavil."

The two workingmen nodded firmly.

Gail looked shocked. "What about the minority views? Who would represent them?"

Endecott made an impatient chopping gesture. "Oh, the minority would be bound to get some delegates, and anyway they'd be quite free to try to become the majority themselves. I don't see how it could be a problem. Like you said about drawing lots, it all comes out in the wash."

"That's *ridiculous,* that's completely different," said Gail. "Drawing lots is *fair,* even if it sometimes throws up a freak result. With elections you're actually building the minority problem right in at every level, and lots more with it—parties, money, fame, graft, just for starters. What chance would that leave ordinary people, what chance would we have of being heard or of making a difference? Elections are completely undemocratic, they're downright *anti*democratic. Everybody knows *that!*"

Volkov's expression was entirely neutral, but the three men looked at him and waited for him to say something. He shrugged.

"I understand," he said thoughtfully, "that in the socialist democracies, the representation of minority views was never a problem."

He slapped one hand with the other. "But come on. Enough of politics. Let's go to the coffee shop."

The shop was crowded, the coffee was good, the conversation was lively. By the sound of it, there was quite a lot of dissent and discontent in Rawliston, more than she'd thought. The compradore magnates, and their influence over the Port Authority, didn't seem popular at all. While this sentiment was useful to the de Tenebres in the present circumstance, it might not bode well for the future—after all, they had their own compradores. Lydia said nothing about this. After an hour the two workers and Endecott took their leave—another meeting, they said—and sometime after that, Matt and Salasso strolled in. Volkov waved and slid along the bench to make room. Salasso edged in and Matt swung in after him, shouting an order for coffee and hemp.

"Ah," said Matt as he settled, "so we found the place at last. Here we all are." He rubbed his face—hot, sweaty, and tired. "Oh, hi, Lydia. Wow, you look amazing." He blinked and glanced across at the overflow of skirt at the side of the table. "That's a beautiful dress."

"So everybody keeps telling me!" She tried to keep the irritation out of her voice.

Matt chuckled and turned to Volkov. "So how did the meeting go?"

"Very well," said Volkov. He lidded his eyes over his steaming mug. "Lydia, now, she got an agent to make quite an effective intervention—"

Flatterer! thought Lydia, but she couldn't help feeling pleased.

"—and Gail probably turned the whole meeting around."

"Flatterer," said Gail mildly. "You know it was your speech that did it."

Matt looked up from his rather shaky rolling of a joint. "It's in the hourlies already, Grigory Andreievich. You were always a good politician."

Gail looked across sharply. "What do you mean?"

Matt scratched his head. "Ah, there's a lot of politics in business," he said. "A persuasive guy like Grigory here can get a lot more engineering done than somebody who knows more about slide rules and steel than the insides of people's heads."

"You could say that," agreed Volkov, looking almost sleepy. He glanced more alertly at Matt, Salasso, and Gail, then at Lydia. "When we've, ah, finished our coffee, we have an appointment with Paul Loudon. . . ."

That sounded like a hint. Lydia drained her cup and busied herself with her gloves and bag, angry with herself that she felt so disappointed and shut out.

"Why shouldn't Lydia come with us?" said Gail.

Another unspoken consultation flashed between the two cosmonauts. Matt lit up his joint and gazed at Lydia as if he had never seen her before.

"Yes," he said. "Yes, why not."

"What are you seeing Loudon about?" asked Lydia. She was glad she'd pulled her gloves on; her knuckles would be white.

"Oh, the space suit project," said Gail. "You might find this very interesting."

"I have a lot to do," Lydia demurred, trying not to appear too eager and curious. "My father has given me a lot of responsibility for the politics of lifting the embargo on your ship. Like today."

"Yes." Volkov nodded and leaned forward, gazing into her eyes as if he and she were completely alone. "Now, doesn't that seem like a good reason for you to come with us this evening and find out more?"

That would do, that was a good reason to be persuaded, along with all of her bad reasons.

"Yes," she said. "Thank you."

Gail was becoming increasingly worried as she scanned the early evening sky and saw yet again that it remained empty of heathens in hang gliders. She wondered if her friends had been offended by her breaking off the drug traffic, or if they had found nothing else worth trading. Or, for that matter, if they'd run up against a more concerted opposition to their technological innovations than they'd led her to believe they expected.

She'd left her colleagues and her rich new friend Lydia at the coffee shop, nipped home for a wash and a quick change and a routine warning rant from her long-suffering mother (who'd been startled to see Gail's face under screaming headlines on the newsprints), and rejoined the group at the coffeehouse and guided them through the complicated chain of bus routes out to the flying club. Lydia had admired the green silk heathenwoman suit Gail had changed into, an early gift (or payment, she wasn't sure) from Slow Leg, and they'd all chatted inconsequentially along the way.

Loudon had booked a private table with a shade and an overhead electric light, out in the open a hundred meters from the clubhouse, and laid on cold beers and cold snacks. It was a much better way of ensuring privacy than hiring one of the small rooms off the bar, with their thin walls. He'd accepted Lydia's unexpected presence with polite curiosity and good grace.

Lydia had grasped the point about how the heathens might be able to help, and now they were all discussing the matter, heads down over sketches and calculations. Every so often Gail would find that she'd lost track of time and that another half hour had passed, without any sign of the heathens' arrival.

She looked up again, saw that the sky was almost dark. Oh, shit. It didn't look likely that they'd be coming now. She sighed and turned back to the discussion, hoping that it wasn't now academic.

"Now," Loudon was saying, "we need to look at ways of fitting a threaded metal sleeve to a ceramic helmet. How about, um, a rubber seal—is that vacuum-resistant enough?"

"No," said Matt, with a vaguely distracted air. "Uh, excuse me for asking, but can someone tell me what I'm seeing up there?" He pointed. "That, uh, strange light in the sky?"

Stone cautiously, at arm's length, poked a short stick at the sliding door of the brazier, knocking it open, pumped the handle of the fire-spirit container, and simultaneously squeezed on the bellows. Flames shot up with a searing whoosh into the balloon above him. With a lurch that almost threw him on his back in the long basket-work gondola, the balloon train's forward pitch was corrected, nearly overcorrected. With another hasty swipe, he closed the brazier's door, and the flame moderated.

"Easy back there," Slow Leg called from his perch at the bow. "Now damp back the others. Quick, quick!"

Clutching the sides of the basket with each hand as he clambered over bales, Stone worked his way along its thirty-meter length and slid the other two brazier doors shut. After closing the sternward one he looked down. The ground seemed to be coming up very fast in the dim light. Then a cloud of dust and dirt drifted by beneath him; Slow Leg had released some ballast, and the descent slowed.

"Hold tight and bend your knees," Slow Leg advised. Stone needed no second urging. He half crouched, knees on a bale of soft stuff, and waited tensely. The balloon train yawed a little to the right as one of the side sails flapped out like a fin. The thump of landing still took him by surprise, but it wasn't as violent as he'd feared. As he'd been drilled to do, he vaulted out as soon as he'd recovered his balance and ran to grab the nearest coil of rope attached to the side. Beside it, inside the basket, a mallet was conveniently stowed. On the end of the rope was an anchor. He paid out the rope and hammered the sharp stake into the hard earth, then ran forward to repeat the process. Slow Leg was meanwhile doing the same on the other side, and they finished off at the bow and stern. At each end was a bottle of water, with which they hastily dowsed the braziers. The three huge hot-air bags were already sagging; by turning the craft Slow Leg had ensured that the breeze would carry them to fall at an angle rather than directly on top of the basket, but the risk of fire was always present. After they'd dowsed the central brazier they stood looking at each other, laughing. Slow Leg clapped Stone's shoulder.

"We made it," he said. "Thank the gods."

"Thanks to you," said Stone.

"That too."

THE ENGINES OF LIGHT

They laughed at this outrageous immodesty. Slow Leg peered around. In the middle distance shone the lights of the airfield's low buildings, against which a dozen curious watchers were silhouetted. Closer by, three dimly visible figures were hurrying across the grass.

"Gail and two men," said Slow Leg. "Let us go and meet them."

There's a minute of confused and confusing introductions—Slow Leg is the tall tough one in the short kilt, Stone is the small pretty one in the quilted suit—then Matt finds himself lugging a big felt bag bound with leather straps across the field to the table where they've been sitting. Then he's running back and doing the same again. Eventually they have the balloon train's cargo laid out on the grass in the puddle of yellow light from the lamp, and the heathens are proudly unwrapping them to display their contents.

"Ho-ly fucking shit," Gail says reverently.

It's treasure, even Matt can see that. He knows that his aesthetic sense may not have been much to write home about to begin with, but it's had a couple of centuries to wise up, and what he sees makes the hairs on his neck prickle. Carvings of mammoth ivory, intricate woodwork, ephemeral-looking but oddly substantial confections of feathers and dried flowers, ceramic wares and glasses that would not look out of place on the classiest tables he's ever dined at. Images of gods and demons that make his materialist soul shiver.

"What's this *for*?" Gail asks.

"These," says one of the heathens, Slow Leg, "are the goods the women traded for the goods we brought."

"That's, that's—" Gail is lost for words but sounds indignant.

"Profitable, yes," says Slow Leg. He slaps his bare thigh and laughs.

"What goods did you bring?" Lydia asks.

Stone, the other heathen, speaks up. "Blades, mostly. Scissors and knives, razors. Needles and thimbles. Eyeglasses."

"This," says Loudon, "is a ripoff."

"Unequal exchange," says Volkov.

The two heathens nod eagerly.

"Let us make the most of it while it lasts," says Slow Leg.

"Um," says Paul. He turns away from them and glances covertly around his guests, raising his eyebrows and rolling his eyes a little, then looks directly at the two new arrivals.

"I expect you are hungry?"

"Possibly a little," says Slow Leg, sitting down.

Stone climbs out of the quilted suit, revealing a very pretty blue silk sort of salwar kameez underneath, and sits down too.

"These are interesting pictures," says Stone after a while, looking down at the scribbles and sketches.

It's been agreed that Gail will put the proposal to them. She leans forward eagerly.

"There is something we would like to ask you to make for us," she says. "Something we wish to trade with you for. Not medicine, not beautiful things. We could pay you very well for it."

"Let us see what you want us to make," says Slow Leg.

"Well," says Gail, turning one of the sketches the right way round for them. "We would like something like the suit and helmet Stone wears for flying, but made with different materials. This here, for example, would have to be of strong fired-clay ware, and this would be glass, and this would be perhaps of the fabric you use for the balloons and the wings. It is very important that it could all be made in such a way that no air could pass in or out, except through this hole here. If you were to pump—to blow it full of air, and stop up this hole, and place it under still water, not even the tiniest bubble could rise from it. Do you think you could make two such suits in the Great Vale?"

"Ah," says Slow Leg. "This is very like the kind of suits the women of the Great Vale used to make for the forest people, the gigants, long ago." He waves a hand behind his head. "Before the *Bright Star,* before the Christians, before . . . well, a long time, spans of hands of mans of years ago—"

He glances at Salasso.

"—before even your time, or your mother's time, the snake people built a city on the moon. But they needed strong workers to build it, so they asked the forest people to help them. And the forest people asked our ancestors to make the garments they would need to live on the moon, because there is no air there. So the women made them. They were called—"

He frowns at Stone for a moment. "What would they be called, in the Christian?"

"Space suits," says Stone.

"Yes!" says Slow Leg. "Would that be close enough to what you want?"

It's settled. Matt, Gail, and Salasso will take their specifications and designs and—more importantly—the breathing apparatus to the Great

Vale, and women there will build the suits. Lydia will show the heathens' trade goods to her family's marketing department. She and Volkov will work together on regaining access to the ship and will maintain radio contact with the others while they're up in the Vale. They've exhausted the subject, and themselves. Now they're winding down, talking about anything else.

Slow Leg is talking to Volkov and Gail and Loudon about ballooning and gliding. Stone is explaining to Matt and Lydia and Salasso the complex traditions and customs governing and limiting the trade relationships the Great Vale clans have with Rawliston, with the savages in the hinterland, with the nonhuman species, and Matt is increasingly puzzled by what for him is an entirely new kind of embarrassment in social intercourse. He doesn't know what sex Stone is, and he can't figure out a way of asking without risking offense. The heathen's smooth face, slight but wiry build, and light voice give no definitive cues either way, and the style of hair and clothing are obviously feminine, as are the gestures, but at some moments something in the light, or a movement or a turn of speech makes Stone suddenly seem to be a long-haired blond man in blue pajamas, and then Stone does something like twine a lock of that hair and Matt mentally kicks himself and decides that Stone is obviously a woman, and then . . . It's like superposed quantum states, or one of those visual illusions that can be seen in two completely different ways.

"When we returned, the shamans had gathered for a council in one of the larger villages," Stone says. "They are still arguing. Rumors are spreading of big disagreements. The arrival of your ship is a mighty portent."

"Why?" Matt asks.

"Our society is in many ways an artifice, maintained by conscious holding on to old ways and conscious holding back in adopting new ones. Of course there are exceptions—the strong drinks, the steel tools—but until now they do not change things because they are not . . . recognized?"

"That's the word," says Lydia.

"Now, the whole reason for this is that we very deeply believe that different societies should walk in different paths, and that only unhappiness comes from confusing the paths. You see—and we see—what happens to those of us who live in this city. We remember how that began, when the Christians tried to lead us onto their path. And we see

DARK LIGHT

in the sky and all around us how the different . . . peoples? like yours,
Salasso, and the sea people and the forest and mountain people, the
saurs and krakens and gigants and pithkies as the Christians call them,
do not share their tools and machines, or do so only in a very small
way. Every people has a place in the great order of the universe. Or so
we thought, until you brought the *Bright Star* here."

"So you're saying that because we're walking on the paths of the
saurs and the kraken, your people have started wondering if they
shouldn't walk some different paths of their own?"

"You have followed me," says Stone.

"It's quite a jump," says Lydia.

Stone laughs. "It is, but you must remember, the *Bright Star* has
always been a totem for all the sky people, the tribes of the Great Vale."

Oh, yes. From a morning last week quizzing Gail about the messy
aftermath of Dawson's Night, Matt has learned something of the sky
people's version of liberation theology and of the local objections to it.

"It must have been quite a shock actually to see it."

"Oh, yes!" says Stone. "Especially when it almost collided with
me."

"That was *you*? In the glider?"

"Yes."

"Amazing!" Matt ponders this apparent coincidence and realizes it
isn't one, that it makes sense in the autochthonous worldview that the
person who first encountered the ship should be the first to act on the
implications of its arrival.

"I thought you said that flying was men's work," says Lydia.

"It is," says Stone. "But building and testing the gliders is women's
work."

Matt, relieved to have his quandary resolved, smiles at the heathen
woman. "And building space suits!"

"Yes."

"I can't imagine what we can give you in exchange for that," Matt
says.

"Oh, more of what we have already taken will be very welcome,"
says Stone.

"Still," says Matt, "there must be something more than needles and
knives that would be even more welcome."

"There is something I have thought of." Stone looks at Matt and
Lydia shyly, through eyelashes. "Your robe, Lydia, I . . . begin to see

how it can be suitable for a woman to wear such a garment, and I think it is possible that other women might see it in the same way. I wonder if, perhaps, tomorrow I could borrow it, or one like it, to show them?"

Lydia splutters with laughter. "I'll offer you better than that," she says. "You can *have* this dress, right now, if I can have your suit."

It's an instantly done deal. They disappear together and return about ten minutes later. Stone sashays around showing off the dress for Slow Leg's benefit, but it's Gail and Loudon who seem most taken with the display. Lydia sits down again, beside Matt.

"You look stunning," Matt says. He looks over at Stone. "So does she."

"Oh, boy," says Lydia, grinning at him mischievously. "Have I got news for you."

8

A Man You Don't Meet Every Day

L YDIA BLEW SEAWATER and snot from her nose and mouth, laughing at how unladylike she was, and turned her back to the next incoming swell. This time she got it right, jumping up as the wave came in and swimming smoothly up its retreating slope, letting it buoy her with an exhilarating sensation of being borne aloft, then reaching the crest and riding it forward, swimming steadily, flying along above the sand in that ridge of water with a meter-deep dip of air in front of her face until the wave curled over and at the same time her knees hit the soft sand and she was kneeling in foam and spitting and laughing again. She flicked her hair back and stood up, calf-deep in the surf, and was about to wade out again when she saw her father about thirty meters away, striding out from the beach.

She yelled hello and waved. He splashed up, shading his eyes and peering at her in the low sun. .

"You're up early," she said.

"Same reason as you," he growled, walking on past her. "Sleeping alone. Faustina's with her immortal hero, and Claudia and Phoebe spent the night with each other. Pah!"

He looked back at her. "Don't just stand there."

She followed him out to a depth where the waves' troughs reached their waists, the peaks their chests. He stood and ducked his head in and emerged gasping and shaking off drops, then turned around, leaning back against the incoming swells, letting his arms bob beside him.

"Woo-hoo-hoo!" he said. "Chilly at first!"

"I'll be chilly again if we don't go deeper."

"Can't talk and swim," Esias said. "At least, not in the sea. Never quite got the hang of that."

He backed out a little way farther.

"That was well done yesterday," he said. "At the meeting and out at the airfield. Making contact with the heathens and setting up the beginnings of a deal was certainly worthwhile—that kind of craftwork sells very well back home. But keeping on our friend Volkov's tail was even more important."

"Oh! Why?"

"He's up to something," Esais said. "I don't know just what, but my sources tell me he's been talking to a lot of people that he doesn't seem to have any kind of business relationship with. People such as those workers at the meeting, and that busy clerk, Endecott. There was some kind of political organization among the cosmonauts, back in the Solar System—"

"The one he calls the Party?"

"Yes. It had some very strange and unsound ideas, by all accounts. Communism, indeed!"

"What's that?"

Esias waved a hand. "Look it up sometime, I think you'll find it in Plato. Volkov seems to have some odd hankering after it, heaven knows why. I rather suspect some of the old cosmonauts may share his views, and I'd appreciate it very much if you could keep an ear out for any of that sort of talk."

"I'll be happy to do that."

"I'm sure you would," Esias said dryly. He looked at her sideways. "I hear you've been flirting with him."

"That's not true!" she said hotly. "Who told you that?"

Esias tapped the side of his nose. "Like I said—sources. Walls have ears. Which is why we're talking out here. Anyway, I've seen how you look at him."

"Well, what—"

—*business is it of yours?* she didn't finish, realizing that it was indeed his business.

"—have I got against that?" Esias finished for her. "None at all, number-seven daughter. Except . . ."

He frowned at the distant house, as though trying to see through its ancient walls, to pry through the low sun's dazzling reflections on its windows, to listen in on pillow talk in its rooms. Then he turned on her a softer gaze.

"I'll be frank with you, Lydia, because you've shown maturity. Just as I tolerate his discreet dalliance with Faustina, so I will smile through my teeth upon any affair you and he may have—a decent interval after Faustina, of course; I won't have the air of my house poisoned by mother-daughter jealousies. But I would worry about his intentions toward you. He's a man of guile and charm. I'm sure he seems very excitingly . . . wise and experienced to you. Zeus above, he's almost old enough to be your father, eh?"

"I'm listening," said Lydia, devoutly wishing she wasn't.

Esias scooped up water and splashed his face, rubbing his cheeks.

"What's easy to forget," he said, and at this point she realized that he too was blushing, "is that he is much, much older than that. He is a man with a long past and a long future, and he has long plans for it. He has ambition."

"How do you know?"

"Credit me with *that* much experience," Esias chuckled. He waved his right hand vaguely at Rawliston, northward along the curve of the coast. "What was it their actor fellow said? 'Let me have men about me that are fat . . .' " He looked down, laughed, and looked up. "I'm fat and contented. He is lean and has a hundred years of hunger in his eyes. He moves among us as we move among the people of the shore, knowing they'll be dust when we return."

"Well, he wants us to share in that."

"No doubt he does," said Esias. "Though whether our science can get that secret out of his . . . secretions is another question. Still, what does it matter to us, eh? We drop him off at Nova Babylonia, set him up with a sound investment fund to sustain him and the research, and after a few months of raking in the money from this trip, leave him in the scientists' capable hands. Two hundred years later, a year or so in our lives, we pop in again to see how they're getting on. If he's outlived six generations of savants, none of them any closer to extracting his elixir, what's that to us?"

"I don't quite see your point," said Lydia, paddling. The tide was coming in. By now they both had to tread water with each wave.

"My point," said Esias, spluttering a little, "is that a man like him will not have spent those two centuries sitting on his hands. We might come back to find him an emperor, or a god."

By unspoken accord they kicked off and began swimming shoreward. Mindful of what Esias had said about talking while swimming, Lydia said nothing until they were both wading ankle-deep through the shallows.

"What does that have to do with his intentions toward me?"

"I'm afraid," said Esias dourly, "that he might get a notion to ask you to *marry* him."

Lydia looked down, too embarrassed and startled to respond. A broken wave hissed up the beach, spreading white froth like a trailing train of lace.

Matt tries not to look down at the rocks as the last of the early-morning sea wind and the first of the midmorning thermals loft the balloon train over the natural dam, to drift not very far above the Great Lake of the Great Vale. A brazier roars up at the bow, and another answers behind him, and a minute or two later he is comforted to observe that while he can still see the spreading circular ripples and the bright flashes of leaping fish he can no longer see the patterns of the scales on their backs.

He grins in relief at Gail, who sits facing him. They've been warned not to talk, because clear communication between Slow Leg and Stone, yelling at each other from either end of the craft, might be crucial at any moment. She smiles back, then her gaze flits past him again, at Stone. Then she sees that Matt has noticed and she looks away. Salasso is huddled on the floor between Matt and Gail, his head lolling against Matt's knees. He resists the urge to stroke it, feeling that this comfort would offend the saur's dignity. Rendered completely insensible, if not unconscious, by a full pipe of hemp urgently smoked before takeoff, Salasso needs all the dignity he can preserve. Matt himself would have much preferred to travel to the Vale by gravity skiff, but—security considerations apart—the fraught divisions among the saurs has put that out of the question.

The mountain ranges on either side widen out as the lake narrows to the river mouth, and the valley's plain opens before them. It seems much more extensive than it did from the ship, and not quite so densely populated—it's easy, from this height, to see the spaces between the villages. The bits that aren't simply wild are meadows and gardens rather than fields, indicating an economy that is pastoral and horticultural rather than agricultural. The sky is startlingly busy with slow balloons and balloon trains and swift gliders; among them, and sometimes not much smaller than the gliders, the pterosaurs soar and swoop.

Even from this height—just within earshot of children's yells—it's clear that the people tending the garden plots or herding the great and various megatheria are all almost naked and therefore probably men. The women, in their brightly colored trouser suits, are the much rarer tiny figures he glimpses hurrying along the village streets. Matt guesses that they work indoors and realizes that this is the basis of the hitherto baffling division of labor between the sexes: women work indoors, men work outdoors. So gardening and herding, digging up and chipping flint, and building houses and chopping down trees and so forth—and yes, fighting; he can see a skirmish line of a dozen spear chuckers in enthusiastic practice—are all men's work. And women's work is everything else: woodcarving and weaving and pottery and glassblowing and gods know what.

Building gliders, too, but not flying them, except for test flights. He wonders how common people like Stone are here, and how many other dangerous bits of supposed women's work they tend to specialize in. Pretty expendable, he thinks with a wry grin, glancing over his shoulder at Stone, who is moving back and forth between the mid and the aft braziers, tweaking the hot-air supply. It's only the practicalities of this task that have got him into his flying suit this morning, and out of his new frock, which is neatly folded in a bundle.

After about an hour the two heathens start tamping the braziers and hauling on the ropes that spill hot air from the balloons and on the tougher cables that tug the steering fins. The balloon train sinks toward a cluster of several hundred buildings on either bank of the Big River, joined by a long stone bridge. The whiff of megathere manure wafts up from the kitchen gardens and middens, and the more fragrant smell of peat smoke drifts from chimneys. The craft passes low above the rooftops and just reaches the lower end of a long sloping field above the town, at the top end of which are low wattle sheds and parked gliders.

The grass comes up fast, then slows at the last second as the braziers give a final coordinated *whoomph* and the basket hits the ground, not too hard but not too gently to wake Salasso. He starts up and vaults over the side as readily as the two heathens, who're running to make fast the guy ropes and dowse the braziers. Matt and Gail follow, teetering on unsteady legs like newborn lambs for a few moments. Some heathen men come running up to help catch and stow the deflating balloons, and the three visitors stand aside. To Matt's surprise, they aren't stared at. Rather the reverse: He feels that they are being deliberately ignored. Beyond the landing field, their arrival seems not to have made any stir.

Maybe it's rude to stare. Matt turns away from watching the unlading of the cargo and the swift dismantling of the craft and instead gazes over the village below. His first impression is that the place is old: The stone-paved path alongside the landing field is rutted, the house roofs are furred with broad patches of orange and gray lichen. Walls are covered with creepers, and culverts are fringed with thick green moss. The streets are, from what he can see, fairly clean. The sky people don't seem to take horses or the larger mammals into their villages. There are plenty of dogs, cats, and turkeys on the streets, and in most backyards small dinosaurs about the size of geese strut and peck.

Gail joins him in his survey and breathes in and out noisily and appreciatively.

"The air up here's a lot fresher than in Rawliston," she remarks. "And it's cooler. And it's quiet."

"Yeah," says Matt. "You know, it kind of worries me that we seem to be setting this place up for increased trade. One generation from now, I can see it becoming a holiday resort for your compradore magnates. In two generations, for anyone—for car mechanics!"

Gail snorts. "Nah, there's too much bad blood between Christians and heathens for that. The only way Rawliston could swamp this place is by outright invasion, and there's no way our little gray friends will let that happen."

Salasso has unobtrusively stepped between them and is impassively regarding the village and the Vale.

"I would not be too sure of that," he says.

Behind them, Slow Leg whistles. They turn to see the other heathens trotting off up the slope, six of them bearing the balloons' long basket on their shoulders, other groups lugging the folded silk. Stone and Slow Leg are left standing with their bales and with the more elaborate packages containing the breathing apparatus.

"That's a strange lack of curiosity," Gail says.

"It is politeness," says Slow Leg. "There will be a lot of questions for you later."

He stoops and hefts a bale. "Come."

Volkov joined Lydia at the breakfast table in the courtyard about an hour after her swim. She was on her third coffee and second sheet of paper, as she made plans for the next few days. Number-one item on her agenda—meeting Volkov—wasn't written down. She looked up and smiled as he sat down opposite her, wrapped in a big white toweling robe.

"Good morning," he said almost warily. "If I recall last night's discussions correctly, you and I are supposed to be coordinating our efforts."

"That's right," said Lydia. She fingered her scribbled notes. "I've been going through a list of the family's contacts, upcoming assemblies, and so on, for the same kind of thing as we did yesterday. I can't help thinking it's not enough."

"Oh, it won't be," he agreed cheerfully. "What we need to do is combine legal and illegal work."

"Illegal work?" That sounded alarming.

He waved a melon rind. "Figure of speech. What I mean is, we need to try and get the embargo lifted, yes, but we also need to prepare for direct action if it isn't lifted, or isn't lifted in time."

"In time for what?"

Volkov gave her a very direct look. "Well, we need to get the ship out and the suits tested and Matt trained in EVA before I leave. Maybe do a little exploring."

"All right," Lydia said. "So what would the direct action involve?"

"Get Salasso back on board, legitimately. He then panics the guards with some plausible-sounding nonsense about the drive becoming unstable. Matt and I and maybe another old cosmonaut—there are a few in this town, and I've been trying to track them down—nip on to the unguarded ship, and off we go."

Lydia just stared at him.

"I am not *stupid,*" she said.

"What?"

"I can think of a dozen ways that plan could go wrong. People getting hurt, even killed. Don't tell me you'd take that risk for a bit of field testing and safety training. So what are you planning to do—steal the ship?"

"Hmm," said Volkov. He rocked back a little and sipped his coffee. "Sorry, Lydia. We should have told you the whole truth in the first place." He leaned forward again and spoke more confidentially. "Matt and Salasso and I want to take the ship out and talk to a god."

That sounded like a reasonable explanation.

"Do Gregor and Elizabeth know about this?"

He shook his head.

"What about my father?"

"Likewise, no."

"And you don't want them to know?"

"Indeed not."

Lydia shut her eyes for a moment. She had a mental picture of wheels spinning in some moral calculating engine. When they stopped, the numbers came up black. She was going to feel guilty about this though. Rather to her surprise, it was the thought of Salasso's involvement that tipped the balance. A saur would not do something insanely dangerous or wrong.

"All right," she said. "Presumably you are not doing this out of idle curiosity."

Volkov shrugged and smiled disarmingly. "I knew I could trust you," he said. "As to idle curiosity, that's what took me to Venus once, and it's had a long time to grow. The intellectual passions are the strongest in the long run."

She didn't know what to say to that; she could think a lot of passions right now that were a lot stronger than curiosity.

"You mentioned looking for other cosmonauts," she said carefully. "Don't you . . . keep track of each other?" She laughed. "I'd have thought the advantages of being a conspiracy of immortals would be considerable."

"Oh, they are," said Volkov lightly. "Fortunately or otherwise, it hasn't worked out like that. We made a conscious decision to live unknown, as the philosopher says, for, well, obvious reasons." He waved a hand, taking in everything around them. "Can you *imagine* the mess places like this and Mingulay would be in by now if we hadn't? We'd either be hunted down like, I don't know, vampires or witches or something, or be venerated like gods walking the earth. I'm not sure which would be worse. So we chose not to, and by now we're dispersed across the Second Sphere, and only small groups of us know each other, personal friends and, ah, acquaintances."

"Which of these is Matt?"

"A friend," said Volkov. He stood up. "Would you like to meet some of my acquaintances?"

The heathens had led them down a paved pathway, and then turned right along the village's upper street. The noonday heat lay on it like a hush. Flowers and hanging plants poured over every eave and windowsill. By the time they'd walked fifty meters, almost a hundred people had appeared in the street, emerging not from the two-story stone houses—which were deserted, apart from old folk dozing in front of them—but from alleyways and adjoining streets or, it seemed, from thin air. Children raced around and chattered, women nudged each other and giggled, men stalked up and stared in silence, then backed away to pace alongside or behind. Gail followed their guides' example and walked as if the street was empty. The weight of her personal pack on her back and an air tank over one shoulder was beginning to tell.

The growing procession was stopped in its tracks by the frightful apparition of a heathen sorcerer who leapt sideways into the middle of the road in front of them. His feather-crowned mask looked like an elongated skull, or possibly a contorted saur face. His flapping cape was fringed with rattling seashells and pinned at the shoulders with saber-tooth canines. A hollow gourd on a long stick made a noise like pouring rain as he swung it from side to side. His feet, bare and dusty under the cape, slapped the paving as he capered in a surprisingly brisk jig.

The crowd spread out and flattened themselves against the walls of buildings, facing outward and staring straight ahead. Children without an adult to huddle against covered their eyes. Stone and Slow Leg stood stock-still. Matt, Salasso, and Gail moved closer together, a couple of meters behind them. Gail lowered her burdens, and after a sidelong dubious glance, Matt did the same. Salasso had nothing to carry anyway, but stood in a willfully relaxed pose.

A long sentence in the heathen tongue rolled booming from the mask's mouth. Slow Leg answered at similar length. Gail didn't know what he was saying, but his voice sounded calm and patient, as if he was explaining something, without defiance or apology.

The sorcerer leapt back as if stung, then skipped so high in the air he seemed to levitate for a moment before descending. Gail could see his feet still flicking up and down, and the cloak spread like black wings. When he hit the ground he jigged more violently than before. He waved his stick and the gourd made a noise like a struck hive. Then he held it still, and in the sudden silence spoke again, at greater length.

This time it was Stone who replied. He too spoke firmly, but Gail could hear the strain in his voice, the self-control that was stopping it from shaking. She felt a surge of protective feeling toward him, as strong and unexpected an urge as the lust and affection that had over-whelmed her the previous night, when she'd seen him in Lydia's pretty dress, which had disturbed her ever since.

The sorcerer didn't take Stone's reply anymore kindly than Slow Leg's. He didn't jump, but he made a keening noise that lifted the hairs on the back of Gail's neck and made small children scream.

Salasso stepped forward and walked deliberately up between the two heathens and then past them toward the sorcerer. The saur walked as though he wasn't about to stop. The sorcerer fell silent and at the last moment jumped back, then turned to one side and darted into the alleyway whence he'd come. Salasso kept walking and didn't look back.

After a moment's pause, Stone and Slow Leg followed, then caught up with him, and Matt and Gail walked forward too. For some reason, it seemed very important not to look back. Gail heard the noise of bare or sandalled feet behind her, and mutters and murmurs, and then another sound from the crowd. They were laughing and talking loudly. Within a few moments they again surrounded her and Matt. This time, there was a lot of light touching and poking. Three men and two women were asking questions in English, and translating others' questions, and as quickly translating the answers back.

"Who are you?"

"Are you a man?"

"What about her, is she a man too?"

"Why have you come here?"

"Why can you not make them yourselves?"

"What can you give us for them?"

"Will the Christians come after you?"

"What about the snake people?"

Powers above! It was like being surrounded by five-year olds! Gail was immensely relieved when they reached the end of the street and turned up a steep road that led up the bank behind it, and the curious crowd fell back.

Stone walked in front this time, to the front of a long low building with short stilts, a wooden roof, and no walls, though it had rolled-up straw screens between the tops of its carved wooden pillars. Standing in front of it or sitting on its raised floor were a few score women. Within seconds they had crowded around, and the touching, the jostling, and the questioning had started again.

Gail sat on the air-tank cylinder, elbows on her knees, and sipped from an earthenware cup a black drink that tasted bitter and slightly alcoholic. Stone had called it beer, but Gail suspected that this was a social rather than a literal translation. She tried not to let her imagination dwell on what she'd heard about heathen methods of preparing alcoholic drinks, which tended to involve stripped bark, steeped leaves, protracted communal chewing and spitting to remove poisons from essential ingredients, and weeks of fermentation in deep straw-lined pits.

Most of the women had returned to their work. The long industrial shed was humming and buzzing and clattering with the sound of tools and machinery. Voices filled the spaces between these notes and discords. A dozen or so women sat outside, legs curled under them, on scattered mats. One of them was talking earnestly to Slow Leg, squatting on his heels at the edge of her mat. The others were engaged in apparently idle chat with each other and with Stone, who was sitting among them in exactly the same pose as they had. Matt sat next to Salasso on the other air tank, sipping his drink and smoking a joint. The gear they'd brought from Rawliston—their equipment and the heathens' Christian trade goods—was all still bundled up.

"Evidently," said Matt, leaning sideways and passing her the joint, "this is not going to be a matter of looking over the space suit specs and cutting a deal."

"Oh, it will be eventually," said Gail, putting down her cup and puffing. "They just need to circle around the subject for a few hours first."

"Yeah. Like pterosaurs waiting to make sure something is dead before they come down."

"No!" she said, more sharply than she'd intended. "This is very important to them, and to us. They have to make sure everything is"— she waved her hands—"all of a piece. It's more like a spider joining its web back together again after it's caught a big fly."

Matt laughed, taking the joint back and handing it on to Salasso. "All right, I'm willing to be patient."

Gail didn't feel impatient at all. She was content for the moment to sit and watch Stone and to catch his voice when he spoke. So as not to make this obvious, every so often she'd pointedly turn her gaze somewhere else, but she found herself always coming back. It was all incomprehensible and embarrassing. She wasn't particularly attracted to women, though she got on all right with women who were. Unlike some of her friends, women she knew down at Back-o'-the-Docks, she wasn't even fascinated by mollyboys. But there was something about the polarity she'd suddenly seen between Stone's sex and his behavior and appearance that was like—well, like the two poles of a battery, which made her jump every time she touched them in her mind.

She turned her face away to the sky and the hills, and her mind away from the thought of a wet finger.

The next time she looked back, Stone and Slow Leg had opened some bundles. The glittering blades, and the dress, were passed being around. After very little inspection they were handed indifferently back, to lie unregarded on the spread cloth of the bales.

"What I'd like to know," Matt was saying, "is what our friends said to that witch doctor."

"Slow Leg told him," said Salasso, making Gail look around sharply, "exactly what we had agreed, about making the space suits, and that this was a traditional industry of the Vale. The sorcerer replied—to summarize a rather long discourse—that he would be the judge of what was traditional. Stone then pointed out that other shamans disagreed with him, and that in any case the snake people were older than he was, or, ah, something to that effect. This did not ease the situation. At that point I decided to intervene."

Gail joined Matt in staring at the saur openmouthed.

"Uh," she croaked, "you've understood what they've been saying all along?"

"Of course," said Salasso. "I understand most of the languages of the Second Sphere." He made the dry throaty sound that passed, among his kind, for a laugh. "The various saur languages are much more different, and difficult, than the human."

"Oh, duh," said Matt, knocking his forehead. "For all my life I've thought you all spoke the same language."

"There are those," said Salasso, "who think we all look the same too."

Matt cleared his throat. "Anyway," he said, covering his embarrassment, "what *are* this lot powwowing about?"

"They are coming to an agreement on prices, and on protocol. The course of the former discussion has conformed quite intriguingly to the standard model of a market under conditions of monopoly and monopsony."

He leaned forward and with the claw of one long finger scratched two complicated lines that crossed each other in the dust, then straightened back and looked at Matt and Gail as if he'd just delivered some enlightenment.

"It's called haggling," said Matt. "And your point is?"

Salasso pointed. "That they are about . . . there, and there, on the curves. I anticipate agreement within the hour."

"Thank the Powers Above for that," said Gail, shifting on her awkward seat.

"What about protocol?" asked Matt.

426

"One of you is going to have to work with the women, in this shed," Salasso said. "Whoever it is has to be a woman."

"Well, yeah, obviously, they seem to have a pretty strict division of labor—"

"Yes," said Salasso. "And they have already decided that Gail is a man."

After the lunchtime spit-and-sawdust bars around the port, and the smoky afternoon coffee shops hot with argument, the university's grubby, dim-lit refectory was almost a relief. Almost: Lydia could see, at the far end, some student musicians setting up sound-amplifying equipment on an improvised stage and hear them tuning up their guitars and pipes. She didn't know if she could bear to stay in the room if they actually started singing. Hadn't she already suffered enough?

It had been an exhausting and somewhat depressing day. She felt that she'd been dragged around, largely because she'd had very little to say, and had had to disagree silently with most of what was said, especially by Volkov. He'd been introducing her as a student—her disguise for this role had been to wear her brother's locally bought denim jacket over her muslin empire-line dress, also local, and a lot more comfortable than yesterday's dreadful confection—and introduced himself, to anyone who didn't know him already, as an engineer. He seemed to have plugged into a whole network of contacts among discontented workers and eccentric autodidact study circles, and they'd listened with respectful attention to class-war doctrine and cynical tactical advice that were making her blood boil. What made it all the more infuriating was that she could see all the ways in which he was right, and that he had—surprisingly, she thought, for an engineer—a considerable fluency in political economy—not only the kind she had been taught, about how supply and demand usually balanced, but also some deeper theory that showed beneath all of that the interchange of human activity. Now he was putting on the same performance for some students who, in her opinion, had too much time on their hands.

All the same, Lydia had to admit to herself that her eyes had been opened a bit to the seamy and squalid underside of a town whose thriving businesses she'd hitherto seen only from the viewpoint of their owners' offices. And she had met one or two people who had struck her as more significant and influential in these circles than they tried to appear, and who—Volkov had privately explained, on the run between meetings—were old cosmonauts.

"The important point," Volkov was saying to a circle of philosophy students around the table, "is for students to play to their strengths, so to speak. They have a very specific contribution to make to the movement. In the first instance, of course, students can be moved into action by almost anything—from great questions of intellectual liberty to the most mundane grievances over conditions." He picked up a gristly remnant from his plate, let it drop. "For example, food."

They all laughed.

"Yeah, the food's atrocious," said one young man. "But, come on, there are people in this town living on worse."

Class-guilty, earnest nods all around.

"Of course," said Volkov. "You're right, and it's a disgrace. But you're not going to help them by living on pig swill. And you're not, heaven knows, going to help them by quitting your studies and getting a job in a factory. There's enough competition for unskilled jobs as it is without the sons and daughters of the better-off adding to it. You have opportunities that are denied to many—perhaps most—workers. You're privileged, that's true. But your greatest privilege is your opportunity to learn, to aquire knowledge, to discuss ideas. And that's exactly what the most intelligent, the most politically conscious workers need and want. Look at the trade unionists, the political societies, the study circles! They need people who can write leaflets, who can edit newspapers, who have access to books. They need people who can see the big picture—that it's not just this stinking factory or that lousy slum or the other stupid law that's the problem, but the whole oppressive system."

"Now wait a minute," a girl said. "If people feel they're oppressed, and we agree that they are, right, we have democracy here."

"Exactly!" said Volkov, smiling at her as though she'd just grasped an abstruse point. "We *have* democracy—all we have to do is *use* it. And what's keeping people—working-class people, that is—from using it in their own interests and against those of the magnates and compradores?"

"Well, what?" asked another, sounding thoroughly skeptical.

Volkov looked around the circle. "Lack of knowledge," he said, counting off one finger. "Lack of alternative sources of information." Two. "Above all, lack of organization." Three. "There's an old motto that explains how to end these lacks: Educate, agitate, organize." His extended fingers wrapped back to a fist. "And the first task, the central one, is to break the unconstitutional power of the Port Authority and get some much more effective democratic control over it, because it's what the magnates use as their private state . . ."

After some more discussion, the students departed to a meeting, an invitation to which Lydia politely declined. She went up to the bar and bought a couple of beers and sat down again. Volkov put away a notebook.

"Thanks," he said, taking a bottle. "That's us finished for the day."

"Good," said Lydia, exasperated beyond tact. "I don't know if I could bite my tongue and sit through much more of your demagogy."

Volkov smiled. "You should find tomorrow a breeze, then. Very respectable businesspeople in polite salons, eager to hear of the advantages of free trade and the prospects for opening spaceship yards. There's already a whole speculative bubble building up on the local stock exchange, I gather. I'd certainly like you to contribute to that."

"Better make sure there's nobody there who knows what you've been saying at today's meetings," said Lydia. "Otherwise their boom and your schemes will go bust pretty fast."

"Don't worry about that," Volkov said with a shrug. "They're not likely to take socialistic notions among the lower classes anymore seriously than you do."

"Oh, I take it seriously," Lydia said. She hesitated, then plunged on. She could only be honest.

"I think it's utterly pernicious and dangerous drivel, and I'm ashamed of myself for even seeming to give it any countenance."

Volkov's cynical expression vanished.

"Look, Lydia, I understand your concern. In fact, I share it. Everything I've said has been to urge some moderation and rationality on people who are already fired up by injustice and inequality. Much wilder talk than anything you've heard today—let alone anything I've said— is rife in the poorer quarters. You should hear some of their street preachers, or read some of the scandal sheets."

He drew a finger across his throat.

"Oh," she said, feigning disappointment, "I thought we'd at least get the choice of the wall or the lamppost!"

He chuckled. "Believe me, Lydia, free trade and some kind of basic social responsibility for keeping people out of destitution is the safest bet in the long run for the local capitalist class. Capitalism has a long way to go here, and lots more to do, if it isn't aborted by a bloody, chaotic, and desperate uprising. Or even by demagogic but counterproductive measures voted through by the assemblies—debt repudiation, protectionism, hyperinflation, that sort of thing."

"But you—"

The sound of a finger tapping a microphone with its speaker's volume control set too high interrupted her. Like everyone else she turned to the stage, on which a group of rather sheepish-looking students, some holding instruments, was dimly discernible. A young man with a beard of patriarchal length stood wringing the microphone like the neck of an unexpectedly resilient chicken.

"Sorry about that. Well, at least I've got everyone's attention. Without, um, any further ado I'd like to introduce the university Traditional Song Group, who'll kick off this evening's entertainment with the ever-popular 'A Lass in Rawley's Toun.' "

"Gods above," said Lydia, rising. "Let's get out now."

Volkov touched her sleeve. "Wait."

She resettled herself reluctantly in her seat. Somebody struck up a guitar, a girl played opening notes on a flute, and a woman with long red hair and a long russet suede waistcoat and skirt took the microphone and sang:

> *There dwelt a lass in Rawley's Toun*
> *I thocht that she was mine*
> *But I must go to Mingulay*
> *and she go up the line*
>
> *I must away, and she to stay*
> *her business for to mind*
> *We swore we'd meet another day*
> *and she went up the line*
>
> *She said for sure she'd follow me*
> *in two score weeks and nine*
> *I waited two long year for her*
> *but she'd gone up the line*
>
> *She need not bide another day*
> *and oh! the ship was fine*
> *She took that ship to Mingulay*
> *An' it took her up the line*

A cunning work the sea beasts are
the gray folk they are kind
and man and woman travel far
but all go up the line

And aye we're told o' powers above
this world o' yours and mine
We're told they hold us in their love
but they send us up the line

Now many a year my lass I've sought
in th' streets o' Rawliston
but gods have battles to be fought
and she is light-years gone

Aye many a year in Rawliston
I've sought my lass to find
Bit I am here and she is gone
Light-years up the line

Lydia blinked hard before looking again at Volkov.

"How did she *do* that?" she whispered. "I never heard anything like—"

The singer waited out the applause and then, just as clearly and confidently, launched into another song:

My name is Jock Stewart, I'm a canny gun man
and a roving young fellow I've been
so be easy and free when you're drinkin' with me
I'm a man you don't meet every day

She finished that song, and then the bearded man took the microphone. His voice sounded quite different when singing than when speaking: Instead of being diffident and hesitant, it was clear and confident and resonant. After he'd sung a couple more songs the band took a break. Lydia jumped up and clapped hard.

"Looks like folk music has won another convert," Volkov said dryly, as she sat down.

Lydia shook her head. "It was mainly that woman. She made my spine tingle. That first song, it might have sounded sentimental, self-pitying, if it had been sung by a man like I suppose it usually is, but the way she sang it was . . . electrifying. All that loss and betrayal! What was it about? What does 'up the line' mean?"

Volkov's gaze was more troubled than it had been when they'd argued about politics. He hesitated before replying.

"It's a . . . a belief you'll find among people who work in starship ports. A rumor, if you like." He sucked his lips for a moment. "You know how starships are sometimes lost? Like, they go to lightspeed and never arrive?"

Lydia shivered. "So I've heard. Well, okay, I know it's true. Accidents will happen. But it's very, very rare."

"No doubt," said Volkov. "Perhaps not as rare as you might think. Anyway, the rumor is that these are not accidents. That the gods know that some great battle, or war, or emergency is going to come to a head, far away and far in the future. A million years, a million light-years, two million, who knows? And they know they'll be hard-pressed. They need to conscript reinforcements, so sometimes they send ships . . . up the line."

"I've never heard of such a thing," Lydia said. "It's crazy!"

The truth was, it was too horrible to contemplate—the thought of being thrown into some incomprehensible battle, far away in time and space, with no prospect of coming home.

"Is it?" Volkov said quietly. "It's what happened to the *Bright Star*."

"But—oh! I see what you mean. That *you* were thrown into the future, yes! But there's no battle going on around here."

"Not yet."

"That's even crazier. The whole Second Sphere couldn't possibly be just a—what, a *forward base*—"

"We don't know," said Volkov. "But it's something we intend to find out."

Lydia stared at him, struck silent for a moment. So it wasn't idle curiosity that was driving him. It was for no trivial end that he was manipulating Rawliston's politics and people. Beneath his political, even moral, differences with her there was a deeper agreement.

"That's worth finding out," she said.

Whatever it costs I will pay.

There had to be a feast that evening, to welcome the guests. Nobody had made any obvious effort to organize one, but as the sun sank and the flint diggers and flint knappers trekked in from the quarries, and the gardeners from the fields, and the hunters came over the mountain carrying the huge joints of huge beasts, and children swarmed in from the scrubby woodland bowed under bundles of brushwood, it had become evident that a consensus on this point had somehow been reached.

Now meat was roasting over fires inside circular stone walls along the paved bank of Big River, down by the bridge, and ancient stone tables and benches that, if isolated examples of them had been dug up by archaeologists, would probably have been identified as altars, were piled with food and drink. The noise and smoke and light and general drunkenness reminded Gail curiously of Dawson's Night back home. Some of the men were surreptitiously passing bottles of spirits, and Gail had taken more than one swig herself.

Salasso, religiously avoided while unconscious by the heathens, was sitting propped up against the river wall, his hemp pipe slipping from his fingers. Stone had disappeared off somewhere. Matt was sitting on a bench among dozens of young and presumably unmarried women. He was chatting to the few who spoke English and patiently listening and politely replying while they translated for those who did not and altogether seemed to be enjoying himself—and his newly redefined gender—hugely.

Gail was not. If she got one more friendly slap on the back or poke in the ribs or punch on the biceps she was going to fucking flatten someone, she was not going to be fucking responsible for her actions. Now she sulked at a table of men and married women, between Slow Leg and his wife, trying awkwardly to converse with both of them. Dark Water didn't speak much English, and Slow Leg's grasp of the language was rapidly converging to meet hers. Not that that was preventing him talking.

"Pterosaur," he said. "The big goddamn wing lizards. Came right at me—"

He leaned forward and peered past Gail at Dark Water and said something.

"I see it too," she said. She spread her hands wide apart and raised her eyebrows and rolled her eyes. "Up there, I think he die—"

Slow Leg continued with another burst of heathen gibberish, then swayed majestically forward and closed his eyes, his nose inches above the table, moving up and down as though repelled from the stone surface by an invisible force field like a ship in the bay. Powers Above, why could these guys not hold their drink?

"I wait and take him home," said Dark Water, getting up and moving around behind Slow Leg. "In the morning I kick him."

"He'll be sore enough without that," said Gail abstractedly. She had just noticed that Stone had returned, replacing Matt as the center of attention at the girls' table. He'd changed into his new dress, and the other young women were reaching out to touch it. Their discussion was getting very loud and giggly. Matt was laughing and shaking his head.

Gail said good night to Dark Water and waved vaguely at the others around the table, picked up her cup of the heathen beer, and walked over to the girls' table. She realized at the last moment that it would be impolite of her to sit down there and just smiled at Stone as she passed.

She walked to the river wall and leaned her elbows on it, letting the sound of the rushing water clear her head. After a while Stone came up and leaned likewise beside her. He said nothing. She noticed the smell of his body, underneath the lingering traces of Lydia's perfume.

They turned their heads to each other at the same moment, both about to speak.

"You first," said Stone.

"I was just going to say, Matt seems to be having a good time."

Stone laughed. "He is, yes. He seems to find the situation very funny."

"I was just wondering," Gail said, "what would happen to him, if he, ah, forgot he's supposed to be a woman while he's here and, you know, found one of the young women here attractive, and perhaps, she did too, and they, ah, went together?"

"Oh! You mean if they fucked?"

"Yes. Not that it's likely," she hastened to add. "I mean, he has a lover back in the city, and I think he means to go back and see her sometimes while we're working here."

"But it is possible," Stone said. "He'll be sleeping in the young women's lodge and working with women all the days, and we can be very immodest among ourselves."

"So what would happen to him, if he and a woman fucked?"

Stone shrugged. "He would have shown he wanted to be a man and couldn't be trusted to stay a woman, so he couldn't be a woman anymore. So he would have to take the challenge and be initiated as a man and of course marry the woman if she would have him—or leave and never come back."

"What's the challenge?"

Stone turned away and stared into the river.

"You go out over the hills with your—brothers? Not sons of the same mother, but boys who have grown up together?"

Gail nodded. "Right."

"Not more than"—he held up one hand, fingers spread—"in a party, or it would not be . . . fair. And you go to the savages' lands and seek out one of their warriors, and you kill him and bring back his head."

Gail felt slightly faint. She swore as blasphemously as she knew how.

"No," said Stone, "it is a *head* 'on a stick.' On a spear."

"Oh, Christ," she said, more mildly, "I can't *believe* every man here has done that. I mean, Jesus." She turned to him. Behind him, the noise and the feasting and drinking were going on. It seemed unreal. "That's—that's *murder.*"

Stone's eyes widened. "You mean it is the same as killing a man of the sky people who has not attacked you?"

Gail thought rather guiltily and desperately about the state of war, and about pirates and outlaws—but no, no, that was different from this bloody *ritual,* and she had to give them the chance to justify it.

"Well," she said, "if the savages are actually raiding you at the time, or on their way to a raid, killing one of their warriors would be all right. But is that how it happens?"

Stone shook his head. "Raids are fought off by men, by our fighters. Boys—and some girls—who are ready to be men go out and kill when there is no war." His smile twisted. "In a war, it would be too dangerous."

"Then, yes," Gail said, "it is murder. It is the same as if it was one of your own people who was not attacking you."

She was feeling terrible about this; she hadn't been here a day and she was already attacking her hosts' culture, already kicking them right in the balls, already thinking maybe the goddamn Christians who'd burned Dawson had a *point*—Christ, she suddenly thought, Dawson must have killed a savage himself! Some bloody enlightened reformer he had been!

But Stone, to her surprise and relief, was smiling.

"That is what I have always thought," he said. "That is why I would not take the challenge, and that's why I am not a man."

Gail's eyes stung. She blinked and looked down at him standing there in his curls and frills, and she wanted to grab his shoulders and say, *Oh, but you are!*

"Oh," she said, "I thought it was because you were, like, uh—you

435

remember the man Paul Loudon was with, in the bar at Back-o'-the-Docks? Like that."

Stone looked away again at the river.

"No," he said. "Some women are like what you call mollyboys, but I am not, though I am happy being a woman. Some men are like, like Paul, but I am not that either. Being a man has nothing to do with whether you want to fuck men or women. It has only to do with whether you are willing to help kill another man, and— and—"

He was choking on his words. She could not bear it. She put her arms around him and held him. He hugged her firmly right back and after a minute looked up at her.

"Perhaps," she said, as his hand went up to the back of her head and exerted a gentle pressure to draw it down, "we had better not be seen like this."

He sniffed, blinked, and smiled. "Nobody would mind," he said. "I'm a woman, and you're a man, so it is all right."

She kissed him. Time passed.

"Can we go somewhere alone?" she asked.

"Yes," he said.

"Good," she said. "And I'll show you who's a woman, and who's a man."

There was a long, low wooden building at the edge of the village, and it had a lot of small rooms with doors and a bed inside. It was very busy that evening.

"Very civilized," Gail said.

There was a stone plate on the floor, and set upon it was a small bowl of oil with a wick. Stone lit it and stood looking at her, suddenly nonplussed. He looked down and began fumbling with the tiny buttons.

"I can do that," Gail said. "You can open mine."

Her breasts were contained in a strange garment of thin cloth with ridged patterns of flowers. It felt pleasant to touch her through it, for her too, and they did that for a while. But he wanted to touch her skin.

"It opens at the back—it's all right, I'll—"

The unfastened dress slithered off his hips at the same time. He stepped out of it. She caught his hands as he reached for the shoulders of the other dress that Lydia had given him, to wear under the first.

"Oh, wait," Gail said. She had all her own clothes off now. "You are so, so beautiful in that petticoat."

She held him at arm's length for a moment, then pushed him back on the bed and fell on him. It was a long while before she let him take the underdress off, but he didn't mind at all.

In the morning he woke up naked beside her, and she had all the quilt around her, so he put the cotton garment back on because he was cold and didn't want to wake her with his cold skin when he went back under the quilt. She woke anyway and immediately began to nuzzle his nipples and stroke his hips through its thin cloth, and to spread its wide skirt across her own bare legs and look at him and laugh and then suddenly sit up and dive in under it, and so it went, and that was the morning gone.

The salon was a different affair, in a different class entirely from the previous day's dockside discussions. Carpets and cocktails and canapés, chairs with gilded frames and padded seats. Lydia knew several of those present already, including Paul Loudon—who arrived late, dressed smartly but still smelling faintly of oil from the factory. Some of them knew her, and they all knew who she was. She was here as herself, as the star merchant's daughter, in a simple and elegant Nova Babylonian gown and her hair up on jeweled skewers. She sat beside Volkov, facing the small, select crowd, and waited for the shuffling and rustling to stop.

"Good afternoon," she said, standing. "I thank you all for coming, and I thank our gracious hostess, Mistress Spangenburg. I'd like to introduce a man who, I am sure, to many of you needs no introduction, the engineer and political economist, Grigory Andreievich Antonov—"

She paused, half turned to him, and they waited, hands poised to clap politely, and for a moment she saw them as Volkov did, as bearers of certain historically determined relations of production, who could be neither blamed nor praised but who had their part to play as necessary, temporary, disposable stages of ascent, and she smiled as she waved him to his feet.

"He's a man you don't meet every day."

9

Vaster than Intellects and More Cool

D RY RUN.
Dry mouth. Lydia stood between Volkov and the apothecary Avakian on the star merchants' quay. The view through her binoculars shook a little as she watched the power dinghy steered by her cousin Johannes carry Salasso toward the *Bright Star*. The Port Authority motor boat, moored to a buoy alongside, loomed large beside the tiny yellow speck. A man stood up on deck and hailed it, waving.

The dinghy pulled in. Salasso waved his arms above his head for a minute. The man on deck was joined by two others. They conferred, then one of them gave a casual salute. Salasso bobbed back down, and the dinghy disappeared behind the Authority boat. Lydia lowered the binoculars.

Volkov's radio crackled. He turned to Lydia and raised his thumb. "He's inside."

"Great!" said Lydia. "How many guards?"

They'd agreed a word-order code with Salasso beforehand.

"Just two," said Volkov.

Endecott, sitting on a bollard beside them, his thin face more pinched than ever in the brisk morning sea breeze, his briefcase across his knees and a radio pressed to his ear, also turned and gave a thumbs-up.

"The boys are ready to go," he said.

Lydia spared him a smile before lifting the binoculars again. A longshoremens' dory was pulling away from the quay, heading out toward the starship berth. Two ships stood there, but the de Tenebre ship, with most of the saurs and a few of the family on board, had moved off to visit other ports. Hardly ever more than a few kilometers from the ship in her life, Lydia felt this as an additional cause of insecurity.

The previous evening Loudon had called in from the flying-club airfield, having taken delivery of a perfectly legitimate balloon train cargo of heathen ceramics. Along with it had come Salasso, with the news that the space suits were complete. One of Loudon's company's trucks had taken Salasso to the Traders' House, and the cargo to the quay, where two long, straw-packed crates of fragile ware had been nodded through by the Authority men at the gate. The crates were now outward bound—again quite authentically—to the Rodriquezes' ship, with whose fleet's traders Avakian had a longstanding relationship, exchanging rare but legal heathen materia medica for Nova Terran exported remedies.

Meanwhile—ah, there they were—a couple of boatloads of harbor maintenance workers were heading out from a different pier, on a route that would take them past the starship berth to do some routine work on its riding lights. On the docks, a small, tightly knit group of politically motivated men was standing by.

Lydia's tracking view of the harbor workers' boat was interrupted by another boat cutting across, slightly out of focus, then another and another.

"God damn!" said Volkov.

Lydia lowered the binoculars and saw that a dozen Port Authority boats, including a heavily armed cutter, had suddenly and unmistakably converged in a flotilla, their arrowing wakes heading out to the starship berth and cutting off the two boats with the men and the cargo. Volkov's and Endecott's radios were squawking, and Avakian was looking distractedly up the quay, to where a clot of brown uniforms and yellow oilskins had gathered at the gate.

"What's going on?" Lydia demanded. She already knew.

"Loudon's just called in to say he's heard that the yellow jackets are all over the airfield, searching for contraband and commandeering planes," said Volkov.

"Hold on," said Endecott, lowering his radio and clicking off the transmitter switch. "They've started pulling in the comrades on the docks. Militia, Port Authority—claim it's a crackdown on smuggling." He scratched his neck. "The lads are ready to go, one shout and they'll mix it up with these goons—"

Volkov nodded. "Are enough comrades still free to get some more boats out there?"

Endecott nodded. "Sure, no problem—"

"Tell them to go ahead, but not to call out the men or tangle with the cops just yet. Dodge arrest as long as they can, but go quietly if caught."

Endecott started rapping out clipped commands.

Lydia stared at Volkov, appalled.

"What are you *doing*?" she said. "No amount of boats can beat that lot out there—it'll be a massacre. On both sides!"

"This isn't a dry run anymore," said Volkov calmly. "This is the live action. We could not get through a reinforced guard around the ship—unless our men get there first."

He scanned the harbor and pointed to the far end of a distant dock, from which three boats were racing out to overtake the Port Authority fleet.

"Good work, Endecott."

"Three?" yelled Lydia. "They'll be slaughtered! Call this off now!"

Volkov pointed silently to similar departures from other quays. At the same moment, some of the Port Authority boats peeled off from the rest and doubled back to confront them.

"Militia are through the gate," observed Avakian, still gazing up the quay.

Lydia whirled, outraged afresh by this new complication. A knot of militia with two Port Authority men at their head was jogging down the quay toward them, staves glinting in the sun.

"Total fucking territorial violation," she said. She balled her fists by her sides and was about to stalk forward when she remembered that this was not the most urgent matter and turned again to Volkov.

"Call it off, it's hopeless, we'll have to try something else—"

Volkov was listening to his radio, not to her. He smiled, eyes narrowing.

"Okay, Salasso," he said. "Lift!"

Then he turned to Endecott. "Call them back," he said urgently. "And tell the comrades to stand down."

"What?" Endecott said. "That's—" He shook his head. "We're committed now, we have to go through with it, this is our only chance—we can do it now!"

"Perhaps," said Volkov dryly. "But you don't have to."

He jerked his head. "Look out there."

The *Bright Star* was already ten meters above the water. Two yellow-clad figures emerged from the exit hatch, teetered for a moment on a ledge, then leapt into the sea. The boat that had stood by the ship cast off and moved to pick them up. By the time they were out of the water, the *Bright Star* was a dwindling dot at the zenith, and in another second it was gone.

Endecott had got his mouth closed enough to speak and was relaying Volkov's stand-down call as the militia clustered around them all.

"Ah, good morning, officers," said Volkov smoothly. "What can we do for you?"

"You have some questions to answer," the leading officer fumed. "And as for that goddamn agitator—"

"Excuse me," Volkov interrupted. "Citizen Endecott is an elected trade union official and has just called off a potentially unpleasant industrial dispute, if I correctly interpret what I've overheard."

"And we don't have to answer any questions!" said Lydia. "The question I have for you is, who the hell gave you the authority to barge in on an extraterritorial facility?"

"Sorry, ma'am, but this is an emergency—we're here to stop an attempt to violate the embargo on the Mingulayan starship."

Lydia raised her eyebrows. "What attempt?" she said. "The saur crew member had Port Authority permission to board, as he has had all along. He reported that he'd found an irregularity in the drive and bravely volunteered to move the ship away from where it can present any danger to the city."

"That's as may be, but what are all these boats up to out there?"

"You tell me," Lydia said. "I've no idea what the Port Authority is doing with all of them."

"The *other* boats!"

They were all heading back to shore, as far as Lydia could see. Johannes and his dinghy were being towed behind the Port Authority boat.

She shrugged. "I think you'll find they all have legitimate business to attend to, at least they had before the Authority started cutting them up. That, or they're involved in this labor dispute you seem to have on your hands."

"Speaking of which," said Endecott, still looking baffled but taking his cue, "I have to go and see some of my union brothers, who have been accused of smuggling and pilfering. These are serious offenses, you know."

With that he hurried off, carrying his briefcase and talking into his radio, head cocked.

The Port Authority officer shook his head and breathed in through his teeth.

"Sir, ma'am, I've been instructed to order you confined to the Star Traders' House while this matter is fully investigated."

"What—" Lydia began, enraged anew.

"We quite understand," said Volkov. "We're just on our way there in any case." He glanced at Avakian. "Our personal physician will accompany us. I'm sure you'll be reassured to know that he can witness that there has been no rough handling."

"Maybe not rough handling," Lydia muttered as they walked together back to the gate, "but I sure have been under a lot of *undue stress.*"

Avakian glanced at her and patted his big black bag.

"Cannabis," he said. "I'll make you a small infusion when we arrive."

They piled into the lilac plastic car in which Volkov had delivered her and Salasso to the quay only half an hour earlier. Volkov gunned the engine and was into the traffic before Lydia had got over the reflex to grab for a nonexistent seat belt. Avakian, leaning in from the rear seat, directed Volkov off the main drag and through backstreets and perilously narrow rat runs until they unexpectedly reemerged on the coast road out of town.

Lydia relaxed slightly.

"Well, that was quick thinking," she said. "Getting Salasso to take off."

Volkov snorted. "It was not quick thinking, it was plan A. It was *always* the plan."

He coughed and looked over at her, a little apologetically. "That is to say, mine and Salasso's."

If he hadn't been driving she'd have throttled him.

"Oh, great," she said. "So why did you put us all through all that?"

"I knew the plan would leak—stool pigeons, if nothing else—and also that an attempt to board the ship was just what the PA was expecting, so I played along with it. Even if the Port Authority hadn't shown up in force, Salasso would have taken off today. All that mattered was getting Salasso on the ship, and they couldn't legally stop him from doing that."

"But they might have anyway!"

"Indeed, but it would have been hard to sell to the guards—they're all genuinely scared of that drive. Especially those who've been on board, jumping at every weird noise the ship makes. I'd bet they've sneaked a look at the drive, too, and got that funny feeling that it's looking *back*. Besides, when did you last see someone facing down a saur?"

"Well, fine," said Lydia. "That's Salasso on the ship. I suppose you also have a great plan for getting you guys and the space suits out to the ship. What is it—Salasso waits offshore and you fly out by hang glider? Hot-air balloon? More boats stashed somewhere?"

"No," said Volkov. "But I'm pleased to hear you're thinking that way, because I'm sure the Port Authority is thinking in exactly the same box."

She frowned. "What box—?"

Then she thumped her hand on the dashboard, in lieu of banging her head on it. Behind her, Avakian was laughing like a slightly manic donkey. It was not a pleasant sound, but he seemed to enjoy it.

Volkov looked in the rearview mirror.

"Nice," he said. "Port Authority van. Following along just to make sure we keep to our house arrest."

Volkov drove even faster, giving the van a hard time keeping up. He pulled the car off the road at the house and jumped out, Lydia and Avakian following. The Authority van screeched up, and as she glanced back from the driveway, Lydia saw two yellow jackets taking post on either side of the gate.

Volkov hurried in to the house, pausing only to pick up a small backpack and—with a smile of thanks at one of Lydia's junior relatives—a sack of provisions. He padded across the courtyard, past the pool with a cheery wave at Lydia's mother, and proceeded down to the beach.

Lydia and Avakian caught up with him as he stood on the sand, squinting into the sun, speaking into his radio.

"Why the rush?" Avakian asked.

"Speed," said Volkov slowly, "is of the absolute fucking essence."

He looked around at Lydia, dropped his bags and—to her surprise—opened his arms. She stepped straight into his sudden embrace. He didn't kiss her, just lightly brushed the top of her head with his lips and drew in a long breath through his nose, as though inhaling the smell of her hair. A shadow fell over them and something screamed in the sky.

"Ah, Lydia," he said. "Good-bye for now."

"Good-bye, Grigory Andreievich," she said, through the rush of air and sand as the *Bright Star* settled on the beach. He ran, clutching his luggage. Lydia shouted after him: "And good luck! Go with the gods!"

He paused, looking over his shoulder as Avakian preceded him inside.

"That's *exactly* where we're going!" he shouted.

He couldn't, she thought as he ducked inside, resist the jest; nor she him.

The ship lifted, making grains of sand hang in peculiar moiré patterns for a moment, then rose at an ever-increasing speed straight up.

This time, it didn't vanish in the blue. Its ascent stopped, and then it shot forward, inland, to the west.

Matt and his colleague Falling Leaf carefully lower the second space suit onto the thick layer of straw in the bottom of the crate and stand looking at it for a moment. It's a curiously beautiful thing, and the feeling that they're putting it in a coffin is momentarily solemn. It's all white ceramic, except for the bulbous and imperfect glass faceplate, and the joints, the section connecting the front and back of the chest pieces, the waist, and the gloves, which are of tough laminated fabrics. Matt vaguely recalls having seen such a suit of white armor in some movie he saw as a kid. If armor it is. He has been assured that the ceramic is not fragile, toughened as it is with handfuls of minute fibers of some mineral that he hopes is not asbestos. He has been shown other pieces banged with flints and bounced on rocks. But it still *looks* fragile. It's definitely waterproof, though, and capable of containing air under pressure.

He and the other woman pack on more straw around it and on top of it, wrap the hoses and connections of the breathing apparatus around the feet, then pile on more straw. Matt drags the lid into place. Falling Leaf covers her ears and shuts her eyes as he nails it down. Then she smiles at him and he lifts first one, then the other end of the big box as she twines vine rope around it. Using some deft finger judo that he can't follow, let alone imitate, she ties it all off in a knot that leaves all taut.

She stands back and gives him a high-five, to which he responds enthusiastically, amused that this gesture at least has passed from him to them. Her blond hair, blue eyes, perfect teeth, and general prettiness, set off by the blue suit that shows off her big breasts and hips, give him as always a lifting of the spirit. Living and working constantly among so many women, and so many of them of all ages so beautiful in their

444

different ways, and all of them completely off limits sexually, has not been as frustrating as he'd at first expected. It's partly because he's been happy and satisfied by his weekly trysts with Daphne, who like all the trader women has a refreshingly recreational and impressively knowledgeable approach to sex. But that has certainly not exhausted his sexual capacity, and what remains seems to have been sublimated into a continuous glow of affection toward all the women he sees.

He looks around the busy workshop and realizes he's going to miss this place, and miss the women. He's going to miss them *badly*. He feels quite quivery inside at the thought of saying good-bye to them all before departing on the evening balloon train flight. Perhaps he won't— the sky people are reserved about good-byes. They regard anything too emotional in partings as bad luck.

"We move it," says Falling Leaf, in her own language. It's one of the phrases he's had ample occasion to pick up. Together they lug the box outside and lay it down beside the first one, then wait beside it looking conspicuous until a couple of men working in the nearest kitchen garden happen to notice them and saunter up and in passing offer to carry the crates to the airfield.

Matt gives Falling Leaf a chaste hug as though she were his sister, grabs his dinosaur-hide jacket off one of the wooden hooks that grow like branches out of the intricately carved pillars, and follows the two men and their burdens down to and through the street, like some pathetically ill-attended procession at a double funeral.

It's been a long, hard month since they first walked up this street and confronted the medicine man. Gail has been on a work team that has foraged out many kilometers most days for increasingly remote deposits of the rare clay, and the rarer fibrous mineral, replenishing the rapidly diminishing stocks lavished both on the space suit parts and the increased production of trade goods. Infuriatingly often, the carefully hand-moulded or wheel-thrown components of the suit have cracked with a loud *ping* as soon as the kiln was opened, or have turned out to be the wrong shape or size once baked and fired and cooled. Getting the helmets right has been a particular bastard of a job. The joints and gloves and lining have all had their failures and frustrations, too, and have required further searching or trading for essential ingredients.

The sense of satisfaction that it's finished is enhanced, for Matt, by the reflection that they've made space suits, all except the breathing apparatus, by entirely Stone Age and traditional techniques. No doubt trade with other societies and other species is what ultimately makes

445

this, along with much else in the lives of the sky people, possible. But still.

Gail and Stone are already at the airfield, working on the balloon train. Putting the thing together is a much longer job than taking it apart, because there's so much that has to be checked and rechecked before a flight. Stone is crawling about on the spread fabric of one balloon, minutely examining its seams for rips; Gail is cleaning out braziers. She exchanges some banter with the men as they put the cases carefully down. Matt spreads out his jacket, sits on it, and waits for her to speak.

"It feels strange," she says to Matt as the men stroll off without looking back. "We've finished the job, and it's great, but I feel kind of . . . flat."

"Yeah, I know. These folk seem to go for celebrating when something starts, not when it ends. Well, maybe tonight I'll take the team out for dinner."

She smiles. "A restaurant dinner in Rawliston—ah yes, that's something I can really look forward to."

"Oooh, arr, a bit of Christian food, lad, I haven't had that for . . ."

Matt is in the middle of an extended riff on this Ben Gunn impression—cracking up Gail, for whom the antiquated English and the accent have quite different associations—when the scream starts in the sky. It's echoed below as people all over the place look up and see the black shape hurtling down upon them. It's slowing rather than accelerating—however reassuring, this is slightly disturbing to the eye, and to the brain's hardwired physics circuit—but the backwash of air as it comes to a complete and impossible-looking stop a meter above the ground and twenty meters downslope almost bowls Matt and Gail over. Stone is flat on his face, hands over his head. He slowly gets up.

Matt stares at the *Bright Star*'s clunky, unignorable, enormous presence and realizes just what a neat job someone—Volkov?—has pulled. Because the great merchant starships are piloted and navigated by krakens, they have always landed on the sea. Everybody has been completely locked in to the unconscious assumption that the way to get people and stuff onto the *Bright Star* is by boat, or—at a stretch—by gravity skiff, just like every other starship from time immemorial.

"Oh, ya beauty!" he yells.

The airlock exit hatch swings open and Volkov peers out, does a slight double take, and beckons urgently.

"Matt! Got the suits?" he shouts.

"Yes!"

"Get them on board now!"

Gail shakes herself out of a daze and effortlessly shoulders one of the crates. Matt grabs up his jacket, and he and Stone shift the other crate crabwise to the side of the ship. The force field is like a sticky bog around their feet as they near it. Volkov manhandles the crates back to someone inside and then reaches out a hand for Matt.

"Get in now," he says.

Matt looks around at Gail and Stone, who still look a bit stunned. There's a faint but fast-increasing sound in the sky, which Matt recognizes. He suddenly shares Volkov's sense of urgency.

"Make your own way back, Gail!" Volkov calls above Matt's head. "And thanks, Stone, tell them all!"

He cocks his ear to the growing noise in the sky.

"Oh, and take cover! Now!"

With that he grabs Matt's outstretched hand and hauls him in bodily, Matt still clinging to his heavy jacket, walking his feet up the side through the diminishing resistance of the field. It releases him and they both tumble inside. Matt turns around to see Stone's head appear in the portal.

"Get back!" Volkov shouts.

Stone comes in almost head over heels, and a second or two later Gail scrambles through after him. Volkov lurches at them, then stands still.

"Ah, fuck it," he says. "On your own heads be it."

He steps past them and dogs the outer and the inner doors.

"One thousand meters," he says calmly. Salasso is at the controls, and Avakian is leaning on the table as if it's a bar counter. He gives Matt a quick, amused glance and then returns his attention to the window.

The ship lifts.

Matt shoves Gail and Stone into seats as the forward view swings around giddily. They cling to armrests or the table surface, even after they've realized that they aren't being thrown about. The ship is flying slowly down the valley, above or past the usual balloons and gliders. Right ahead, just coming over the dam, are a couple of fast-enlarging black specks.

Airplanes. Feeble cedar-and-canvas, petrol-engined kites that can chew up anything the heathens can put in the air. Unheard of for them to overfly the Vale.

Salasso drives the ship slowly but implacably toward them. The distance has closed to half a kilometer, whites-of-the-eyes stuff, when the two planes bank sharply away from each other, turning tail and heading back toward Rawliston. Salasso keeps the ship just behind and above them for the next few minutes, until they've reached what Matt recognizes as the flying-club airfield and they begin their descent.

The ship hangs above them until they've landed.

Then Salasso slides back the control mechanism, and in seconds the sky is black and the planet below is blue. Stone and Gail gaze out with rapt amazement. The others are more blasé.

"Well, Matt," says Avakian, as everybody relaxes a little, "I must say you do look pretty."

Matt looks down at his tunic and trousers, of which he's been quite unselfconscious until this moment. He steps out of his sandals and shrugs on his jacket. The weight of the weaponry in its pockets is comforting. He glowers at Avakian.

"Shut. The fuck. Up."

They go a bit wild after that. They go around the back of the moon and land beside the ruins of the city the saurs and gigants built millennia ago. The sight is somehow sobering. Matt and—at his own insistence— Stone test the suits with immense caution, first in the airlock and then on the ground. On their return the suits are grubby with black dust.

"So what's the plan?" Avakian asks, when Matt, Stone, and Volkov have stowed the suits again. He looks around. "I don't see a radio telescope."

Matt laughs. It took ESA's most sensitive radio telescopes and most sophisticated signal-detection software to detect the gods, and that was only because they knew what to look for and where. Avakian, of course, is well aware of this.

"Or are we going to apply the well-known needle-haystack search algorithm?"

"No," says Salasso. "Volkov and I have been searching the university library. They may be backward in some ways, and overly dependent on the *Bright Star*'s knowledge base in others, but they have a long and quite respectable tradition of optical astronomy. They have detected almost a hundred of this system's larger asteroids, one of which is distinctly anomalous, its albedo and apparent size being too large for its mass as calculated from its orbital dynamics. Its name in their catalogues is Tola, or the Contested Judgment, or the Enigma. Its orbit is highly eccentric, passing from the asteroid belt between Adonis and Cybele to the Kuiper-equivalent region beyond Chronos."

"Sounds like a good candidate."

Salasso nods. "The Croatan astronomers themselves have of course speculated that it is one of the Powers Above."

"Don't the saurs know?" Matt asks.

Salasso regards him coldly. "The saurs do not investigate such matters, or trespass on the gods' domain."

Matt jerks his head toward the window, indicating the shattered towers and crumbled blockhouses on the near horizon, and the beaten tracks between.

"Looks like they trampled over this bit of it once upon a time."

"A long time ago," says Salasso. "And you will note that these ruins are not the result of natural processes. There are random heaps of dust and improbable stacks of rock on this moon that have been stable for longer."

Matt's curiosity is fired. "What happened to it?"

"I do not know," Salasso says. "The story of the city on Croatan's moon is not one that I was told."

Matt has a sudden thought. "What about the sky people, Stone? Do you have any legends?"

"The elders have no stories about that," says Stone. "We know only that we have never since then been asked to make space suits, until now."

There's one of those silences where the temperature seems to drop.

"All right," says Avakian, with a graveyard laugh. "Do you know how to get to to, uh, Tola?"

"Yes."

"Well, let's see the calculations, if you don't mind. I'd like to check them."

"There are no calculations," says Salasso. "I have closely studied many volumes of the book they call the ephemeris, which gives the orbital data and current position of the known celestial bodies in this system, including Tola."

"That's a lot of use," says Avakian.

The sarcasm whizzes past Salasso's head.

"Yes," he says, "it is a lot of use. From it I know how to get to Tola."

"Without calculation?" Matt asks.

Salasso shrugs. "Do you need to calculate to catch a thrown object?"

"He does now," Avakian cackles.

"Fuck you," says Matt absently. "How long will it take us to get there?"

"Depends on our speed," says Salasso, with that target-homing instinct for the bleeding obvious that he occasionally displays. "An attempt at a lightspeed jump might be ill-advised."

The idea of doing that hasn't even occurred to Matt, and he decides to let it lie.

"We estimate," says Volkov, "that we can do it in about two days at one-tenth lightspeed. We could go slower, but we have at most a fortnight's supplies." He glares momentarily at Gail and Stone. "Probably less, now. We could go faster, but we need the time to set up the communications device. Armen, maybe you want to concentrate on rebooting the interface? Matt and I can do the outside work."

Avakian is looking straight at Matt but not seeing him. He's focused on something far away and long ago.

"The interface," he says. He licks his lips with a dry tongue. "Yes."

Matt walks through the corridor with an obscure feeling that he should be floating down it, the tug of memory being more insistent than that of gravity. Even in this lopped offspring of the ESA station, he can recognize places from its original impressive extent, catch a play of shadows and faint odors that reconstruct a moment of the past.

Volkov follows him. Matt stops and opens the air-sealed door of the lab module containing the communications device. They step inside, taking care not to step on any part of its folded, fractal, metallic structures. It's the most alien object Matt has ever encountered in physical space, having been manufactured by one of the asteroid research station's fabrication units under the direct, real-time control of the asteroid's alien intelligences. These minds had used this device, cabled to the ship's computers, to set up the hypnotic, encyclopedic virtual reality environment that everyone had called "the interface."

That interface had been seductive enough. At the hub of the device itself was a more direct interface, which had projected on the user's faceplate and retinas a physically accurate view of the asteroid's interior and of the aliens themselves. These crystalline low-temperature, quasinatural, and endlessly self-transformed entities had appeared as an infinitely intricate jeweled garden or huge congeries of minute machinery, a masterpiece of the blind watchmaker operating with nothing more than a faint wash of solar and stellar energy differentials and the self-organizing properties of extremophile nanobacteria. On some intermediate scale these interactions produced minds, countless trillions of distinct but collaborating individuals; on the scale of the asteroid itself, the collaboration of these minds produced—so the cosmonaut scientists had concluded—something greater: a god.

From the asteroid belt, the Kuiper and the Oort, the ESA astronomers had detected the electromagnetic whispers of pantheon upon pantheon, in conversations that extended—according to the aliens themselves, and to reasonable hypothesis—to the cometary shells of star upon star, perhaps galaxy upon galaxy.

"Wonder if this bugger's multiplatform compatible," he says, with the deliberate irreverence that's the only defense of the human mind against such thoughts. "What a laugh if after all this we slap it up against Tola and find that it's about as much use as sticking a dick in a datadisk."

"Or that it has no answers to our questions, or is simply unwilling to communicate."

"Huh," Matt grunts. "I'm not too worried about that. There's been communication between the gods of the Solar System and of the Second Sphere, surely. I think we'll get talking to Tola, unless Tola turns out to be some fucking freak object whose shape has nothing to do with its being a god at all." He waves his hands. "Something diffuse, a cloud of cometary snowflakes or something."

"Your physics is rusty," says Volkov. "Things don't *stay* diffuse like that. If it is something unknown to science, we ask Salasso if his intuitive orbital mechanics extends to the position of other asteroids, odd or not." He scratches his head. "Our one whatever it was, Lora, looked like any other dull carbonaceous chondrite from the outside, after all."

He looks down, kicks at a coil of cable. "This stuff, is it still connected and plugged in?"

"Sure," says Matt. "We checked before we left Mingulay. It's sound." He gestures past the device to the window wall of the lab. "Seal the door, open the window, the whole lot sails gracefully out."

Volkov raises an eyebrow. "You've tested that too?"

"In one of the old suits? Do I look like a fool?"

"No," says Volkov. "But that would be a useful job with which to occupy ourselves en route: blow it out and haul it in again. I want to be sure we can deploy it with some despatch when the time comes.

Good EVA training for you and practice for me too." He stretches, turns around. "Let's go and see how Armen's getting on."

Armen is on his back under a console in another of the old lab modules, this one stuffed to the gunwales with computer kit. He has an antique multitool splayed in one hand and a chunky battery-powered torch in the other—Maglite it ain't, Matt's thinking—and something else between his teeth. It's a reel of insulation tape, long past its sell-by date, which he's somehow manipulating with his teeth, opening and shutting his mouth to pay it out in little jerks. The other end of the tape is attached to a cable somewhere in the dark clutter.

He completes whatever he's doing and heels himself out and stands up. His shirt and high-waisted trousers are stained and crumpled, but he puts the pea jacket back on as though about to meet a client and dusts off his hands.

"Are you *sure*," he asks Matt, "that there really aren't mice on board this thing?"

Matt actually has to think about this. It's not entirely impossible that there were lab animals on the space station, or even pets, and some kind of closed ecosystem has been maintained here all this time, and—nah.

"It's all bacteria and mold," he says.

"Well, what's down there looks like fucking teeth marks to me. Want a look?"

He holds out the torch. Matt shakes his head.

"That's wise," says Avakian. He settles into a chair and puts his feet up, unconsciously adopting the pose he usually took, unsupported, in microgravity. "Well, I've found one, count 'em, one set of spex that haven't degraded like the rest"—he holds up the precious object—"and a fair old stack of still-functioning screens and boards and so forth, so in among all this junk there is the potential for something that can sustain the interface programs without blowing every fuse in the ship."

He gazes balefully at the mess, waving his hands in vague curves like a sculptor seeing a shape in a rough block of marble. "It's there already," he says. "Virtually."

They leave him to it.

Gail found it annoying that she and Stone were assigned the task of making coffee and cooking, but all she had to do was show Stone how to handle the electrical heating elements. Once he'd grasped that he took over the galley. Gail left him to it and wandered about, looking for things to fix, puzzling over mechanical and electronic contrivances, leafing through manuals.

The first evening—or so her body regarded it, though the light was quite unchanged—they all sat around in the control room and ate boiled vegetables and bread that had been fresh in the morning, and drank coffee.

"You two are taking this very calmly," Avakian said.

"I didn't feel very calm when Stone took a running jump at the side of the ship," Gail said. "But it was that or wait for the airplanes. I recognized the sound, you can't mistake the Kondrakov-LeBrun 3B. Two-seater, and they can mount a rifle as easily as a camera. Port Authority sometimes use them against pirates."

Matt looked troubled. "I hadn't thought of that. I was expecting them to land and try to stop us. Do you think we've left Long Bridge and the Vale open to air raids?"

"Nah," said Gail, more firmly and dismissively than she felt. "Trying to stop us is one thing, but there'd be an uproar if they did anything more."

"I agree," said Stone. "And our men have rifles, too, though they do not use them except in war."

"Not even to hunt mammoths?" Avakian asked.

"If we did that there would soon be no mammoths," said Stone. "The snake people taught our ancestors much about that when they came from the Cold Lands."

Matt laughed. "I must tell you sometime how the saurs hunt dinosaurs on Mingulay. They panic entire herds of them over cliffs."

Stone looked a bit shocked and disappointed.

"It is a sustainable yield," said Salasso. "The principle is the same, Stone. We do not say one thing to your people and do another ourselves."

"What's all this about the Cold Lands, anyway?" Avakian persisted. Gail guessed that he'd had little to do with heathen, or he'd have known not to be quite so direct.

Stone tore some bread and mopped up the remains of his meal.

"Our ancestors dwelt in valleys that were cut off by the great ice. Their numbers were dwindling, and the hunting was bad. The snake people came in their gravity skiffs and said they could take us to warm lands where the hunting was good. The elders and shamans went first in the skiffs and came back to say that the skiffs took them to a big boat in the sky and that there was room in it for all of us. They said we would not have to stay in it long, but to take all that we could carry to the skiffs. So we went and found that they spoke the truth. The sky was black and the world was blue and white. The big boat closed its doors and then opened them again. The sky was still black, the world was still blue and white. Other snake people met us and took us to the warmer country."

He looked up and laughed. "We did not know it was another world. For many years our name for the place where we lived was 'the South.'"

"I guess that's not much different from calling it 'Croatan,'" said Gail. "We never knew why we were taken here either." She looked around at the cosmonauts. "And now we're going to find out! Jeez!"

She hugged herself. No, she was not taking this calmly at all.

"I have a question," said Stone. He looked at Avakian, at Grigory and Matt, as though awaiting their permission. It was a habit that Gail had tried to talk him out of, but it kept coming back. She'd been quietly entertained over the past month by observing Matt beginning to pick it up.

"Yeah, go ahead," said Matt.

"I have seen you all today working in this ship," Stone said. "I have not seen you make mistakes, or take the wrong turnings in the corridors. I have seen you reach for things without looking and find them to hand. This is not the way Gail and I have been working today."

"Uh-huh," said Grigory. "So?"

"I know that Matt has been on this ship, but not you and Armen, yet you move about on it as if you know it well."

Grigory glanced at the others and shrugged.

"We've studied this ship. I myself have read everything there is to read about it—plans, details. I could find my way around the original ship, not just this one."

"That may be true," said Stone. "And you, Armen? You are— what?—a shaman of the Christians? Do they study the plans and workings of the *Bright Star*?"

"I don't know about that," said Avakian. "But I certainly have."

"I do not say you have not," said Stone diffidently. "But I know the difference between seeing a place in a picture and knowing it well. You are like men who have been on this ship a long time."

Gail felt her knees trembling. The three men had the strangest expressions of unease and embarrassment she'd seen since—since that time in Loudon's office, when Matt and Grigory had been challenged about what their real plans were. She remembered from the same occasion one of the moments when Grigory had looked familiar, when they'd been talking about books, about Soviet—

"*Cosmonaut Heroes!*" she said.

They all stared at her.

"What?" asked Grigory.

"It's a book," she said. "I read it I was a little girl. It's a child's history of space exploration by the Soviet Union and European Union. There was a picture in that book of a man who looked just like you, Grigory. His name was—" It was on the tip of her tongue.

"Grigory Andreievich Volkov," said Grigory Andreievich.

"Yes! The first man on Venus!"

"Yes," said Avakian dryly. "The resemblance is uncanny."

"Was he your ancestor?" asked Stone. He sounded as if he felt this might be an adequate explanation for what had puzzled him.

Grigory hesitated. He looked at Matt and Armen and at Salasso.

"You might as well tell them the truth," said the saur. "We have to trust each other."

Grigory swallowed. "No, he was not my ancestor," he said. "He was me."

"We were all on the original *Bright Star,* in the Solar System," said Matt almost apologetically.

Gail frowned, trying to puzzle this out. "Have you been traveling, ever since? To Nova Babylonia and back?"

That would do it, that would explain it—no.

They were all shaking their heads, and then Stone said, "Oh, I see. The snake people live a long time, and so do you." He didn't sound at all surprised.

"Yes," said Matt. "We don't know for sure why, and we can't give the treatment to anyone else. Perhaps in the future we can."

By the time Gail had wormed the rest of the story out of them she felt dizzy just thinking about its implications, though not for any possible application of it to herself. She knew intellectually that she was too young to take that aspect of it seriously. It was a solution looking for a problem as far as she was concerned. She was giddy at the thought that the three men here were ancient, that they had lived so long, that they had lived on *Earth!*

She could understand why Lydia was (so obviously and so unselfconsciously) fascinated with Volkov. Gail had been deeply suspicious of his politics, but she could now understand that his favorable references to socialism and to republics could be explained as a sort of patriotism and loyalty to his original country rather than some subtle subversion of hers, and thus in themselves were commendable. He wasn't just a handsome and to all appearances young man, he was a hero stepped out of an old book. She could remember the smell of its pages, of something heady in the ink.

"There it is," says Salasso, passing a long brass Mingulayan telescope sideways.

His voice carries an odd vibration in its tone. Matt hasn't known the saur for long, but he knows that if Salasso sometimes seems even more restrained than most of his kind, it's because he has a lot to restrain. No other saur would contemplate what Salasso is doing now.

They've stopped the ship dead in space, relative to the fuzzy dot that is the most prominent object in the starfield ahead. The controloom lights are dimmed. Matt takes the telescope and aims it at the dot. The brass cylinders slide the lenses smoothly into focus for his eye.

It's like another eye is looking back.

The pupil is the dark spot at the center, maybe ten kilometers across, which he guesses is the cometary nucleus. The rest of it is the iris, its veins and tendrils branching out in a circle maybe two hundred kilometers in diameter, and within that structure millions of tiny flecks of every color in the visible spectrum. A fractal stained-glass circular window, a butterfly wing, a dish aerial made of flowers . . .

With some reluctance, Matt passes the telescope on.

Avakian and Volkov each in turn say something blasphemous or prayerful in Russian. Stone and Gail just gasp.

"This is a new thing," says Salasso.

10

The Gods Ourselves

THE BREATHING MASK is clammy over Matt's nose and mouth, the straps are tugging hairs on the back of his head, and the faceplate is flawed and fogged. His thick-gloved hands fiddle the crude knurled knobs that control the flow and the pressure, and the plate clears enough to see.

The *Bright Star*'s underside is a meter away from the surface of Tola's black nucleus. Matt's face is closer to it. He and Volkov, attached to the main airlock by ropes, are deploying the communications device. It has unfolded itself, and Matt is pushing that giant snowflake ahead of him with one hand and propelling himself along above the surface with the other, while Volkov pays out the communications cable.

The arm of the device that his hand is holding suddenly evades his grasp. The whole thing flexes like a grasping hand. The tips of its extended arms touch the sooty surface and dig in. Matt feels an uncanny vibration in his fingers. He pushes off a little and sees that the hub of the device has also lowered itself to the rock. It's hunkered down like a foil origami spider. He knows there's some kind of incredibly fine probe, or needle, that goes in like a sting from that hub and suspects that was the vibration he felt. He has no idea where the energy for these movements is coming from.

He raises a hand with an upturned thumb—no radios in the suits, natch—and Volkov lets go of the cable. Matt grabs his rope, and he and Volkov, one by one, hand over hand, return to the airlock.

Avakian has the spex on and isn't likely to pass them around, but he's set up a wall-to-wall bank of screens in the computer lab module so that the rest of them can share most of what he sees. Text-input devices are strategically positioned. At the moment, the screens are a uniform white. Stone and Gail are, for the first time, looking scared and out of their depth. Volkov is grasping the back of Avakian's chair, leaning over. Matt stands behind Salasso and in a forgetful moment puts his hand on the saur's shoulder. It's trembling, so he keeps his hand there. After a moment, Salasso's hand comes up and his chill, rough fingers wrap across the back of Matt's hand.

"Taking its time," says Volkov.

"You know what I think it's doing?" says Avakian. "I think it's *downloading* the stuff we got from 10049 Lora."

The screens light up with moving pictures and scrolling text and control surfaces—the whole wall in front of them is showing at any one moment far too much information to take in. At the same time it looks familiar: It's a stripped-down version of the same intense, feature-rich virtual environment that he remembers from the long encounter back in the Solar System.

Avakian makes a groping motion. Matt guesses he's interacting with the virtual reality in his spex, then sees Volkov lean over and silently place a water bottle in Avakian's hand. Avakian sips and swallows. He puts the bottle down, and his hands start scuttling on keyboards.

The text and pictures change in response. Avakian must be seeing and assimilating more, but he narrows the view, selecting a pictorial story line that plays across the bank of screens.

Earth, unfamiliar at first, until Pangaea splits into Laurasia and Gondwanaland, then these into smaller plates, some of them recognizably rough outlines of the modern continents. Matt mutters a commentary to Gail and Stone. Salasso is silent and intent as the Cretaceous world of the dinosaurs is evoked.

The view cuts to the oceans, diving deep. Giant squids swim by, moving in complex, stellate dances, hundreds of individuals at a time sharing information in the data-dense flickering of their chromatophores. The view shifts back and forth between these aquatic displays and the interiors of asteroids. Somehow, perhaps by a slow drift of molecules into and out of the atmosphere, or more likely by the subtle electromagnetic whispers to which the gods are so exquisitely attuned, communication is taking place.

Into this serene scene, an alien presence irrupts. Cylindrical lightspeed ships appear in the Solar System, then in Earth's atmosphere; discoid gravity skiffs spin to the ground and to the sea. From them emerge extraterrestrials. Radially and bilaterally symmetrical, with eight long limbs, each with eight digits; eight eyes clustered on the central thorax or head; fuzzy fur in various colors. Their behavior matches their appearance: They're spider-busy, monkey-clever. Unclad, they scamper and swing in the forests, cling to tree trunks and the necks of brontosaurs. In protective suits, they swim beneath the oceans, swarm across the surfaces of asteroids. They talk to the gods and to the krakens. At the isthmus of two continents, they establish a base. Other than that, they build nothing of their own on Earth. In cycad glades they find small, flitting tribes of stone-wielding, small-brained, bipedal, tailless dinosaurs.

They steal their eggs.

(Salasso makes a sound like tearing metal.)

Some time later, saurs troop down the ramps of skiffs. Their big heads and spindly limbs look grotesque and feeble against the stocky proportions of their wild ancestors, but their metal tools give them the edge. They flourish, spread around the world, work with the monkey-spider folk.

They build ships and skiffs. Great craft settle and sink into the ocean; krakens swim inside. The ships rise, seawater pouring off their sides, and accelerate into space. Some blink away, lightspeeding; others cruise the Solar System, talking to the gods. Krakens, saurs, and monkey-spiders work together. Some of the indwelt asteroids sprout strange growths—tendrils of cable, flowers of aerials.

None of them notice, until too late, the faint outgassings from some of the Kuiper-belt bodies, the gavotte of orbital nudges that, out of nowhere, send an uninhabited metallic asteroid on collision course with Earth, targetted—there is no room for doubt on that score—at the monkey-spider base.

The Cretaceous world ends.

All the surviving monkey-spiders flee, along with some of the krakens and saurs. The krakens and saurs who remain work with the gods, rescuing what organisms they can from the mass extinctions, finding them new homes on a multiplicity of Earth-like worlds. The time scale speeds up, as the traffic continues through the Tertiary and the Quaternary; it ends with saurs lifting human beings. Any further development—the whole history of the civilizations of the Second Sphere—passes in less than a blink.

Then there's a simple diagram to show the distance between the

Solar System and these new worlds. A light beam flashes across the screen, Earth's blue dot makes one circuit of the sun. A black square is blocked out. This happens ten times, and there's a pause.

"Okay, okay, we get it, ten light-years," Avakian mutters.

The bar of black dots doubles in length, then triples, then by similar increments extends to ten times its original size: one hundred blocks, one hundred light-years. The scale shifts, and the new line is itself extended ten times.

A thousand light-years, my god, Matt thinks. He's not too surprised when this line, too, is multiplied by ten—for whatever reason, the phrase "ten thousand light-years from home" has been kicked around long enough among the cosmonauts.

Beneath it, nine more lines of the same length rattle into place like the bars of a gate. At this point the display stops. Matt is shaking. In part it is shock at having his irrevocable exile confirmed. In part it's a kind of grudging relief. For a horrible moment, he'd expected the ten-thousand-light-year line to form one side of a square. . . .

"One hundred thousand light-years," says Avakian. "We're on the other side of the galaxy."

As though on cue, a picture of the galaxy swirls up. Quick zoom in to scenes of conflict—lightspeed ships exchanging laser fire, a gutted asteroid habitat swarming with monkey-spiders, a ruined monkey-spider city, a saur manufacturing plant forest in flames. There are humans and saurs on both sides, monkey-spiders on only one. The view pulls out, until the war they've just been shown is represented by a red dot. In the picture of the galaxy, red dots spread like a rash.

The view on the screen fades out. Avakian takes his spex off and looks around. For a minute it seems that he can't see anyone. Nobody speaks.

Avakian finds his voice. He waves a hand at the banked screens. "You can read the commentary for yourselves. It's—it's not a war, and that is not war propaganda. The fuzzy spider things were just explorers. They weren't conquering, they weren't doing any harm. The gods—the majority of the gods, that is—are into contemplating the universe. This lot came along like a crowd of kids with loud music and lots of energy, running about all over their peaceful ashram. The gods just stamped on them to *keep the fucking noise down.* And the krakens and the saurs who stayed on the gods' side are their hired muscle, putting the boot into intelligent life wherever it gets too obstreperous. And that's what they want us to do too. Tread on the fingers of the spidery people, or any race that climbs too high up the tree. That's why we were given the lightspeed drive, that's why they moved us here. It wasn't just some kind of backup against a catastrophic loss of data back in the Solar System. They were *conscripting* us and kick starting a mobilization among their reserves."

"I don't see any mobilization," says Gail.

Avakian laughs. "On the time scale they're working on, everything that's happened in the two centuries since this ship arrived has been a scramble to arms. Shit, even if we did nothing now, nothing at all, all this capitalist development we've triggered off would have the place swarming with starships—human crewed or not, it doesn't matter— within another century or two."

"Wait a minute," says Matt. "I got the distinct impression that run-away development was precisely what the gods wanted to prevent." He forces a smile at Avakian. "Remember—what you a long time ago called 'spamming'?"

"Oh, it won't be allowed to *run away*." Avakian glares, for a moment, at Salasso. "Our little friends are around to put a damper on that, just as we're among them to stir a bit of primitive primate energy into the mix. 'Damper' is the fucking word, actually—the whole Second Sphere is like a well-designed fission reactor, where they're the absorbers, we're the emitters, and between us we'll provide a very smoothly controlled chain reaction. And if it does get out of control anywhere, well—there are a lot of mass-extinction-level asteroids out there."

Salasso shrugs Matt's hand off his shoulder and stalks forward and turns to face them all.

"That is not how I see the relationship between your people and mine," he says. "I am disturbed that—"

Everybody is staring straight past him. Salasso looks back at them, then turns around.

Spelled out on the screens behind him are the words:

I AM THE SUM

Salasso steps away from in front of the screen and stands again in front of Matt. The words disappear and more words scroll up, in cool italics. Gail whispers them to Stone, who can read, but not that fast. This quiet accompaniment makes them seem all the stranger.

I speak for the sum of the minds of this world, though I am not that sum. I have shown you the story of your worlds, as it would have been shown to you by the other minds around this star, and those around your star. You may visit other minds and confirm this. I have recently entered this system. I am not one of those minds. I am one of their enemies.

Avakian lunges for his keyboard and rattles out a query that seems to take a long time. The answer is shorter.

You do not have to destroy others or be destroyed. There is a way out. Here it is.

What comes up next is a three-dimensional map. Matt peers at it, recognizing the numbers along its pathways as instruction sets for light-speed jumps. If the sketchy star map among which the paths are entwined is on the scale he thinks, the routes shown can take them into regions in the immediate neighborhood of the Second Sphere—and for kiloparsecs beyond it. He even recognizes the pattern of the map—it's something like the old Landis percolation model of galactic colonization, whereby species could expand without ever actually running into each other. There's enough unused real estate around to amount to a fractal fraction of infinity. Tola's map is showing them how humans can expand through it, without necessarily even impinging on resources already claimed by the higher intelligences or by other expanding species.

Avakian is staring at the screen. He looks over his shoulder.
"What—"
Volkov glances at Matt, catches his emphatic nod.
"Tell it," he says to Avakian, "that we understand."
Avakian blinks, shrugs, returns to the keyboard.

Good

There is a long pause. Then the letters start scrolling past, almost too fast to read.

The information from the mind at your star that you brought with you on this ship contained other information that you did not know about. It is destructive to minds such as mine. I have been fighting it, but my resistance is at an end.

I die now.

Gail felt the breath stop in her throat. The screens went blank. Stone looked at her as though afraid that by saying those words she might die herself. Matt and Volkov were looking from the screen to each other. Salasso was standing stock-still, nothing moving except the nictitating membranes flicking across his eyes. Avakian had crammed the spex back down over his eyes. He hammered his fingers across the keyboards, paused, and started again.

"It's gone," he said. "There's nothing there."

"What happened?" Gail asked. "Did we—did we just destroy a—a Power Above?"

Avakian threw his spex at the empty screens.

"We did more than that," he said. He banged the sides of his head with his fists and stalked up to Gail and Stone. "You don't understand what we've done. Imagine all the stars in the sky had worlds around them, and that all these worlds were crowded with people. Imagine them all killed. That would be the tiniest *fraction* of what we've just done."

Volkov seemed to come out of a trance. "*We* didn't do it," he said. "It was the other powers—or one other power—that did it. We were innocent carriers of an infection. But if the infection was deliberate— Christ, talk about murder."

Matt stirred himself too. "Are we—can we be sure?"

Avakian turned to him with a snarl. "I don't think it was kidding."

Matt silently walked out of the room. They followed him down the corridor to the control deck. From the forward viewing screen they gazed beyond the horizon of the cometary nucleus to the vast upward curve of Tola's dish aerial. It curled inward, darkening by the second, like the petals of a dead flower.

Closer to the ship, just a few tens of meters away, the alien communications device had disengaged itself from the surface. Salasso pushed past the others and took the controls of the ship. The surface of Tola dwindled as the *Bright Star* backed away, the long and now disconnected communications cable trailing out straight in its path.

Gas, glowing in the solar radiation, gouted from a suddenly opened rift in the side of the ruined body. Almost imperceptibly at first, Tola began to move, sideways relative to the ship.

Salasso did not look away from it.

"Gregor Cairns," he said, "once told me he wondered why the gods should ever leave their long orbits and burn off their substance close to our suns and become visible comets in our skies."

He turned away and looked at the humans, his nictitating membranes flickering again.

"I will tell him the answer."

They're all a bit numb as they sit down around the table in the control deck. For a while, nobody has much to say. Matt gets up and makes coffee. He doesn't trust either Gail or Stone at the moment. Their faces are wan, they aren't taking this at all well. They're like kids who've just learned for the first time that their parents fight, and what all the cracks and chips and dents and crashes and broken crockery that they've always taken as part of the order of nature in the background of their lives have been *about*. The cause of the scars on the moon's face wasn't an accident in a meteor shower, it was a fucking *battering* . . .

Matt himself . . . as the hot water drips through the filter he gives himself a ruthless introspection and realizes that while he is appalled at the enormity of what's happened, he is at the same time rather guiltily feeling a surprising thrill of optimism and hope.

He stares at the saved screen shot of Tola from their initial approach that somebody—probably Avakian—has thumbtacked to the wall of the galley. It's like a computer-generated math poster from his geeky teenage years. The feeling that's making his blood surge is almost as old. It's the one he got centuries ago when he left socialist Europe and found himself on American soil. Well, okay, on an American *ship,* but the principle was the same. It's that sense of suddenly enlarged possibility, of a low ceiling that he'd always taken for the sky being rolled away like a scroll to reveal above it a topless depth of blue.

The world of the Second Sphere has always struck Matt as entirely congruent with the ideology of the Party, for all the continuing conservatism and capitalism of the elder species. It's a steady state of population and production, a sustainable society, one in which a broad scope for talent and ambition is ultimately constrained by limits defined as physical. There's a great chain of being, almost, from the gods down through the krakens and the saurs to the humans and the affined fellow Adamic hominidae. There's a division of labor, a turnover of resources, all within a hundred-light-year radius of Nova Terra.

It's a fucking big box, but it's a box.

What Tola has told them—at such unthinkable and, surely, unexpected and uncounted cost—is that they can go outside the box, that the gods can be defied, that the universe is open. There are cracks in the box.

By the time each of them has drunk about half of his or her first mug, they're beginning to recover, to assimilate, to argue.

"Let's take a paranoid possibility," Avakian's saying. "Suppose that sending that . . . virus, or whatever it was, was the whole purpose of our being sent here in the first place? Suppose the *Bright Star* has all along been a Trojan Horse?"

"A way of fooling an enemy into letting your soldiers into his city," Matt interjects, for the benefit of Gail and Stone.

"I know the story," says Stone. "What does 'paranoid' mean?"

"It means to assume that events are part of a hidden plan against you," says Volkov.

Stone nods. "Ah, sorcery," he says. "Go on."

Volkov puts down his coffee and puts his elbows on the table, gesticulating as he speaks in a way that suggests confidentiality and passion.

"Armen, I don't think your first suggestion is valid. There was no way for the mind in 10049 Lora to know of the existence of Tola, or that it would be the first 'god' that we reached. It's possible that whatever destroyed Tola was engineered to attack a—an enemy god, yes. But it's also possible that it was simply the equivalent of a disease to which Tola had no immunity. We might have had the same effect on a god who was on the same side as the one who sent us here. Who knows?"

He bares his teeth suddenly. "On the other hand, perhaps you are not being paranoid enough. What is the net effect of our encounter with Tola? We have some new information that may or may not be reliable and that casts doubt on anything we may learn from other gods. We have no way of knowing that Tola was itself a site of consciousness, as it claimed, and not simply a mechanism created for no other purpose than to act as a honey trap, with its conspicuous location and unusual form its attractive features."

Matt shakes his head. He doesn't want to let go of the genuineness of the grief and shock he's felt.

"I can't believe that," he says. "It's too neat and too crude. Armen, did you"—he doesn't know quite how to put it—"feel anything a bit *off* in the communications?"

Armen stares out of the window at Tola's increasingly distant wreck.

"It was very responsive, very Turing test passing, if that's what you're asking. It was like the interface I remember." He shrugs. "Not that that's necessarily relevant. Once you start questioning at that level, where does it end? We could raise the same questions about any other gods we may encounter. Or the ones back in the Solar System, come to that." He grins at Matt. "There never was a general solution to the trusting trust problem."

Stone leans forward, visibly fighting off diffidence. Matt nods encouragement.

"The truth is," says Stone, "We cannot trust the gods at all, and we never could. What is good or right for us to do may not be the same as what the gods—any of them—may want us to do." He looks down for a moment, then back up, challenging. "I have thought for a long time about this matter."

"I'll bet you have," says Gail, giving Stone a smile and squeezing his hand.

Matt doesn't quite get what's behind that, but his sense of freedom takes another upward spiral turn.

"Moral autonomy," he says. "Of course, of course. We have to decide for ourselves."

Volkov cuts in impatiently. "Yes, yes," he says. "That's all very well and good, but we have to understand the actual situation we're in, the actual balance of forces, before we decide what to do."

Then he looks at Matt and Stone and, disarmingly, his eyes widen and he smiles.

"Aha!" he says. "Yes, I see now what you mean. That in terms of decisions, we are on our own *is* the analysis. Very clever."

Stone just looks puzzled, if slightly flattered.

Avakian's lips twist a little, something between a wry smile and a sneer.

Gail frowns. "Huh." she says, "All that sounds like is that we haven't learned anything, we might as well not have come." She glances out of the window. "In fact it would have been better if we hadn't."

"No, no!" Volkov insists. "We have learned something that we could not have learned any other way. We've always had at the back of our minds the thought that there was an explanation that would justify what has happened to us and that would give us a guideline, a map, a line of march into the future. Now we have an explanation—which may not be true, and if it is true, it shows only that our whole existence, the whole purpose of our being here is as absurd, as arbitrary as the most nihilistic philosopher has ever proclaimed it to be!

"And you know, I think that this would be true of any explanation that the gods could give us. Their purposes—whatever they are—are not ours. Whether we adopt them, adapt to them, or rebel against them is a matter for us to decide in terms of our purposes and ours alone."

He turns to Salasso. "Of all of us here, I think it's you who might find this most difficult."

Salsso gives him a black, unblinking stare.

"I have tried to tell my people that the gods are not angry with them," he says, "that the great disaster in our past was not a punishment. Now I have to tell them a harder thing: that it is we who should be angry. We should be angry at the gods."

Matt finds the solemnity of all this a bit much but decides to keep his own counsel. He knows too well that Volkov—as he's just virtually admitted—will let nothing divert him from whatever large ambitions he has. Matt has no intention of repaying him in any less genuine coin.

"We still have to check," he says. "We have to find one of the gods that Tola was opposed to, and ask."

Salasso spreads his long fingers. "The ephemeris data indicates another candidate site, at twenty-two hours' journey time away."

As Salasso sets the new course, Matt looks out at Tola, now a distant, shining sphere with the beginning of a nimbus, and any regret he feels at its destruction is outweighed by the liberating thought of the map it has shown them, which genuine or not opens a very different future from anything Volkov may have in mind.

O my America, my newfound land!

The gray object visible through the window of the ship looked like a piece of clinker from the grate of a brazier. Stone did not know whether to be relieved or disappointed that it did not resemble the beautiful and enigmatic Tola. Its name in the Christian language was Othniel.

Closer they crept, until it filled the view, and then Salasso rotated the ship, and they were no longer approaching an object in front of them; they were above the surface of a small world. The cosmonauts and Salasso jabbered numbers. Again the spidery device was deployed;

again it attached itself to the surface. Volkov and Matt returned to the ship, and they all crowded once more into Avakian's room of windows. Avakian tapped his spells onto his instruments.

"Downloading the Lora and Tola information," he said. "Looks like."

Stone pressed his side against Gail's as they waited. The screens remained white for a hand of breaths. Then they filled up with black numbers.

"Well, that's a response," said Avakian. He took the goggles off his eyes and looked at Matt and Volkov, who were peering at it and reading along and up and down. You could follow the movements of their heads and see where they had reached.

"What do you make of it?" Avakian asked, when they'd finished.

"It's a set of coordinates," said Matt. "It maps a position in the interior of the asteroid. Maybe physical, maybe an address space. It's telling us to go out to the device and use the direct interaction."

"Why can't it just put stuff up on the screens?" asked Gail.

"Good question," said Avakian. "But when you think through what's happened here—there's been data collected in the Solar System, organized and translated and retranslated by the minds within 10049 Lora. Then that's been downloaded to Tola, and Tola's response integrated. Now this lot has all been assimilated and processed by Othniel, maybe for the first time it's ever encountered data like this. In human terms what it's accomplished in the past few minutes is something like the entire scientific and cultural effort of the whole of human history. The amazing thing is that it can communicate with us at all, not that some of the final fine grain of the interface mechanism has a glitch."

"So one of us has to go out and use its own interface?" Gail said.

"Yes," said Avakian. He grinned at Matt and Volkov. "So which of you is it to be?"

"I take it that means you're not volunteering," said Volkov.

Avakian shook his head firmly.

"Me neither," said Volkov. "I've done it before, and I don't think I could do it again. Matt?"

Matt wet his lips. "It's tempting," he said. He looked at the floor, grasped his chin, and rasped his fingers on stubble. He looked up, shamefaced.

"No," he said. "No way am I going through that again. Sorry."

"What's the problem?" Gail asked indignantly. "Is it a horrific experience or something?"

468

Matt and Volkov both laughed bitterly.

"No," said Matt. "That's not the problem. It's not horrific. It's so beautiful it's—"

He closed his eyes. "I can still see it," he said. "Even now. It's afterward, after you've been there, you've seen so much beauty that for hours and hours nothing else seems . . . any good. Everything that isn't dull *hurts,* and for weeks after you get flashbacks, it's like coming off a drug."

"Oh," said Volkov. "You too? You never said. I thought it was a—a personal weakness."

As they stood looking helplessly at each other, Stone suddenly realized that he knew what they were talking about. He felt his knees become rubbery.

"I know this," he said. "The men of the sky people also speak of it."

Everybody stared at him.

"In their initiation," he said, "they take herbs, and smoke, and paste, and mushrooms, and they see visions of the gods and they feel pain for a day or a night afterward. They say it is the most wonderful thing they have ever done, and they say they would never do it again." He shrugged. "I would like to do that. I will go out and see what the god Othniel has to show."

Matt gave him a very worried look. "You do understand," he said, "that this is not the same thing? What your people do, with drugs and so on, is not really speaking to the gods. It's all—" He tapped his head.

"That may be," said Stone, "but they talk about it the same way."

"You have a point there," said Avakian. He turned to Matt and Volkov. "Yeah, it's subjective for the heathens, but subjectively it might be a very similar experience to what you had. The sensory and endorphin overload, that kind of one-shot addictive quality—"

He scowled thoughtfully at Stone.

"So long as you can come back with something that makes sense. . . ."

"I can tell you everything I see," said Stone.

Gail faced him, caught his shoulders. "You'd be taking a big risk," she said.

He shrugged under her hands. "So are we all," he said.

"All right," said Matt, after a moment. He pointed at the screens. "These numbers, how long do you think it would take you to learn them and remember them?"

Stone looked at the screens and closed his eyes, opened them again, checked.

"I see them," he said.

The ship's field had a sucking pull like quicksand. Clear of it, Stone found that moving felt like falling. Holding still felt like falling. He followed the cable, not hauling himself along it but gripping the clinkery rock with his fingers and moving as though climbing without effort. A rope was attached to the back of his suit, so he couldn't fall off, upward into space. It was something like flying, something like a dream. It was all new. His breathing was loud in his ears.

When he raised his head and looked forward he saw the device, like a squatting spider up ahead of him, and above its angled knees the black sky and bright stars. Even through the glass of the faceplate they were hard and sharp, and so many. He turned his head and looked cautiously from side to side and saw that the stars came right down to the surface. It was like crawling on a flat mountaintop on a very clear night, except that there was not the slightest diminution in the brightness of the stars as they came closer to the horizon. He could fix his sight on the lowest of the stars and make them blink on and off just by rolling his head a little.

But there was no time for that. He moved forward again. The tip of one leg of the device glided in front of his face. He raised himself and with the tips of his own fingers maneuvered up its angled length until he was hanging above the curious machine. Bafflingly complex and diverse, it called to mind a tangled thicket sprouting with flowers and jagged leaves. At its heart was a dark space about big enough for a human face to cover, and on either side of that a couple of queer contraptions against which fingers could be pressed.

He placed his hands on them and pulled himself down so that the faceplate kissed the dark surface. It reacted instantly, unfolding and wrapping around the convex glass. Stone fought down the feeling of panic, breathing slowly to convince his body that he was not being smothered.

Like afterimages in front of his eyes, rows and columns of numbers floated. He rippled his fingers experimentally, and the numbers raced sideways and upward, then stopped. After doing this a few more times he could see how the numbers changed, and without thinking too much about it he began pressing with different fingers until the numbers before him matched the numbers in his head.

At that moment the view before him changed. It seemed that surfaces streamed past him as if he was swimming down a narrow passage. Then everything opened out around him, and he was flying—it was as though the passage had opened out into a truly enormous cave, as big as the Great Vale and the sky above it, walled and roofed and floored with faceted surfaces in more colors than he had ever seen. Like banks of flowers and the lively scales of fish and the glitter of mica.

His headlong movement came to a halt, as it seemed, a few meters away from a place on the floor. Lights moved and flowed and then came together quite suddenly, to form a picture in blue and white, green and brown. Stone recognized it at once as the picture of the ancient Earth with which Tola had begun its exposition.

Far more quickly than at first, the story pictures flashed past his eyes. The images, however, were exactly the same as before. Once more the tale ended with saurs walking beside humans clad in animal skins, into skiffs. They might have been his own ancestors, Stone thought, with some pride.

Then a new tale began.

Lydia drifted, thankful that she was in a big house that she didn't know and in which she could get plausibly lost. The house arrest had been lifted after a day of baffled interrogations, exhausting radio interviews, and urgent representations, and this long-planned social occasion hosted by one of her family's commercial rivals provided a welcome respite from the still somewhat fraught atmosphere of the Traders' House. The Rodriguez clan's favored onshore rented dwelling was, like the de Tenebres', between the coast road and the beach, but it was much larger and less open. It had fountains and an expensively maintained lawn rather than a swimming pool in its courtyard, the opening to the beach was narrower, and the general style had been developed by several generations of Croatan architects fascinated by the rococo and the baroque.

Lydia leaned a bare elbow against a bulbous pillar of stacked plaster pineapples, sipped a tall cocktail, observed a mirror-walled ballroom around the corner, and reflected that the different historical times and pseudohistorical styles experienced by the different clans on their variant journeys probably accounted for their differences in taste. It was a kinder thought than to write off the Rodriguezes as incurably vulgar and philistine, as she had done before encountering Volkov's characteristic habit, which he obscurely called "materialism," of explaining such things by social experience rather than innate traits.

The view of the room in the mirrors indicated that the coast was clear. About twenty couples in a variety of overelaborate finery were twirling elegantly; others stood around the edge of the floor, eyeing each other up or talking. Her own currently best dress, an iridescent blue shift, looked severely understated in this company. She walked confidently around the pillar, scanning the wallflowers for some conveniently disposable partner among the Rodriguez lads and almost collided with Gregor Cairns.

The one man she wanted most to avoid, and whom she'd spent the past couple of days avoiding, stood awkwardly in front of her, clutching a tall glass of beer and frowning, first at her and then down at it. Gregor was wearing a flouncy local shirt and high-waisted trousers; everything about his stance indicated that he felt both uncomfortable and ridiculous. Lydia glanced around, checking the room again. Elizabeth, at least, was nowhere in sight. Small mercies.

Gregor looked up, lips compressed. His eyes were bright and his expression stiff. In the past few seconds his face had grown visibly paler under its weatherbeaten, ruddy tan.

"Well, hello, Lydia," he said flatly. "Hot in here, isn't it."

"Would you like to go somewhere cooler?"

He nodded. She turned and led him around the dance floor to an open doorway leading to a balcony overlooking the beach. Black water stretched to the horizon. Lydia leaned on the ivy-covered stone balustrade.

"Um." Gregor took a gulp of beer. "Lydia, I don't know what to say, but the least, ah, offensive thing that comes to mind is that you owe us an explanation."

"Us?"

"Us," confirmed Elizabeth, materializing out of a shadow and standing behind Gregor. She looked, if anything, angrier than Gregor. She wore a formal dress of russet silk and organza as though it was an old T-shirt she'd pulled on. Her face was flushed and her black hair mussed; Lydia smiled politely at her as she raked her fingers through it again, apparently unconsciously.

"*You've stolen our ship,*" she said. "What the hell did you think you were doing?"

"I didn't think I was stealing your ship," Lydia said. "It wasn't just Volkov and Avakian who took it, it was Salasso and Matt too, and they—"

"Have no goddamn right to it!" said Elizabeth. "Jesus, leave aside

472

the morality of it, it's fucking *illegal*. It's *mutiny*. Matt and Salasso—
Matt, anyway—could literally *swing* for this, back on Mingulay."

"By the neck until dead," said Gregor, filling in. "And maybe here,
too, if the Port Authority's efforts to extend maritime law to starships
prevail in the assemblies."

"Oh, yes," said Lydia, thinking on her feet. "And speaking of the
Port Authority, we did at least get your ship out of their hands."

"So you did," said Elizabeth. "Hell, I almost forgot. And now it's
safely out in the fucking *asteroid belt,* and the whole city's in an uproar
and the Port Authority's breathing fire down our necks. Good move,
that."

Gregor glanced sideways at Elizabeth in a desperately placatory way
and then gave Lydia a disloyally apologetic smile that Elizabeth, still
standing slightly behind him, fortunately didn't catch.

"What we'd really like to hear from you," he said, "is, like I said,
an explanation."

Lydia sipped her cocktail and gestured toward a small round table.
"Could we, ah, sit down?" she said.

They did, Gregor with alacrity, Elizabeth with some ill grace and a
noisy rustle of skirts. Lydia seized her chance to take an embroidered
pouch from her blue leather purse and, with elaborate casualness, began
building a joint. She wasn't entirely comfortable with the drug herself,
but she didn't discount the efficacy of the ritual in putting the Mingulayans at something like ease.

"All right," she said, "I do accept that I owe you an explanation,
and an apology. My only excuse, if that's what it is, is that I found
myself caught in a conflict of loyalties, and—"

"And we came second," said Elizabeth. "You surprise me, you
don't."

"What was your first loyalty?" asked Gregor, still working hard on
the personal diplomacy. "Was it to your family?"

Lydia licked papers, laid them out, and spread some grass along
them.

"Not exactly," she said, looking up. "Well, maybe indirectly. In the
first instance—"

She cupped her hands to her nose, inhaling the fragrance of the
unburned weed from her fingers. Then she sighed and opened her hands
to her friends.

(And yes, they were her friends.)

"It was to Grigory Volkov," she said.

That got through to them, particularly to Elizabeth, who smiled for the first time, albeit without warmth.

"You're a fast mover," she said, with a sort of withering admiration. "Gods above, all this time I've been worrying that you wanted to pull *Gregor* into your . . . arrangements, and meanwhile you've been getting your cl—" She stopped herself. "Setting your sights on Volkov."

Lydia rolled up the joint and sealed it, meeting Elizabeth's gaze— still hostile, but in a less personal way—head-on.

"There's more to it than that," she said, wishing she didn't sound quite so defensive. "Our family has a contract with him that well, obliges us to give him a certain latitude."

That argument had cut a lot of ice with her father, once he'd calmed down a little, but she could see it wasn't doing much for Elizabeth. Lydia sighed and lit up, and after a quick puff passed the joint to Elizabeth, who accepted it with an ironic quirk of her brows.

"I also thought," Lydia added, as Elizabeth inhaled deeply, "that anything Salasso was involved in wouldn't be, well, fundamentally wrong or crazily dangerous."

Elizabeth coughed a cloud of smoke and spluttered, passing the joint hastily to Gregor, who for a moment couldn't use it for laughing. Then he took a long hit and breathed out slowly, sharing a smile with Elizabeth that they both, in some mutual relenting, turned on Lydia.

"Salasso," said Elizabeth, "is the most reckless, amoral, and crazy saur you're ever likely to meet!"

Lydia had to agree, and had to laugh.

"All the same," she said, passing the joint quickly again, "I can understand their reasons for wanting to go out there, for wanting to get *answers*."

"You know what really pisses me off?" said Elizabeth. "It's that they didn't *ask* us. They just assumed we'd be against it."

"You'd have been for it?"

"Of course we would," said Gregor.

"We're scientists," said Elizabeth. "We take risks for knowledge all the time."

"Yes, but now you're—"

"Traders," said Gregor heavily. "Yeah, and therefore we're cautious and conservative and watching the bottom line. Hell, we risked everything just coming here. If we're traders, we're not traders like, well—"

"Our hosts?" said Lydia.

"Well, yeah." Gregor glanced sideways at Elizabeth. "Uh, what's the state of play at the moment, politically?"

Lydia looked at the recirculated joint and stubbed it out on the balustrade.

"I don't know," she said cautiously. "But it's something I mean to find out. And this function might not be a bad place to pick up something." She raised her eyebrows. "Would you both be interested in, maybe, joining forces with me on this?"

"Now that you're not busy avoiding us?" asked Elizabeth.

"Exactly," admitted Lydia.

Elizabeth shrugged one shoulder. "Why not? All right, say we meet back here in an hour."

"Unless we're in the middle of a really interesting conversation," said Gregor. "In which case, check again in another hour."

"And so on."

Elizabeth's giggle as she said that made Lydia wonder just how reliable, not to mention discreet, the two of them were going to be, but she wasn't particularly bothered. The point was that she'd patched things up with them. Any new information they managed to sniff out tonight would be a bonus.

"Okay," she said. "You go now, and I'll wait a minute, then go inside too."

They departed laughing, and Lydia, after staring out to sea for a while, followed. The lights around the house were too bright for her to see the stars.

"Citizen Cargill?"

The Port Authority safety inspector who'd originally impounded the ship looked up at Lydia, startled. He was sitting at a small table in a room with a bar. The room's only other occupants, in a corner at the back, were a couple who were otherwise engaged. Chamber music from the ballroom floated through the doorway on a more turbulent current of talk and laughter.

"I'm surprised to find you on your own," Lydia said.

Cargill shifted his plumed hat—his uniform evidently did service as a formal outfit of green coat, white shirt, black knee breeches and tall boots—moved a bottle to the center of the table, and reached over to the unattended free bar for a clean glass.

"Please join me," he said.

Lydia sat. Cargill tapped the bottle. "Whiskey? Or something else?"

"Thanks, I'll have the whiskey, Citizen Cargill."

She wanted to encourage him to drink; sharing the bottle might help the process along.

He poured.

" 'Charles,' please, Mademoiselle de Tenebre."

"Oh, and likewise, do call me 'Lydia,' " she said, raising her glass. "You were going to tell me why you're alone."

"I was? Oh, well, if you say so." He sighed. "I'm usually in great demand at these functions, though I haven't, ah, received any invitations from your house recently."

She smiled. "Well—"

"I'm sure it's nothing personal on your family's side anymore than it was on mine, though I quite see—" He waved a languid hand. "But where was I? Oh, yes. It seems I'm in some bad odor with this family too. I will have to be more careful. At this rate I shall acquire a reputation for incorruptibility, and my wife and mistress and their poor children, some of whom I am reliably informed are also mine, will suffer the pangs of want."

His tongue, Lydia thought, was well-loosened already. Or perhaps not. She glanced at the half-empty bottle. Her first cautious sip had confirmed that it was fierce stuff, at least a hundred proof.

"Should you be telling me this?"

Cargill took a far from cautious sip and laughed.

"It's common knowledge, Mamz—Lydia. I keep a record of all bribes, of course, and hand in the entire proceeds less fifteen percent to my superiors, along with a chit. It's called an expense account."

"You aren't tempted to leave some off the record and keep the whole bribe for yourself?"

Cargill mimed shock. "Of course not. Why should I? I value my reputation for honesty. Besides, the clients receive a copy of the receipt and would query any discrepancies."

Was he drunk, or was it her own head that was spinning?

"Are you telling me that corruption is *institutionalized* here, that you just blatantly sell favors?"

"Are you telling me that you didn't know this?"

Lydia nodded.

Cargill closed his eyes for a moment, then reached in a vest pocket for a small, ornate box the lid of which he flipped open with a lazy, affected wave of the hand. He took a pinch of dark powder from it, placed it at the base of the thumb of the other hand, and snorted it up.

He closed his eyes again, inhaling deeply, tears welling, then blew his nose on an elegant handkerchief.

"Care for some?" He held out the box.

She peered into it. The dark dust within smelled minty and peppery. "What is it?"

"Snuff—powdered tobacco."

"No, thank you."

"Clears the head remarkably," said Cargill. He gave his head a quick shake, as though to settle it back. "Now—ah yes, checks and balances. As you may have noticed, dear lady, there's a certain amount of suspicion in this city about officialdom and bureaucracy and so forth. At the same time, there is a need for a competent, permanent civil service, whose responsibilities seem to become more onerous the more the city prospers. Tax collection, other than tariffs at the harbor, is a joke. Consequently, the Port Authority has made a virtue of necessity, and—as you say—raises revenue for its services by blatantly selling them for whatever the market will bear. Thus neatly confirming the prejudice of the populace, that all permanent officials are necessarily corrupt, and the whole thing muddles merrily along."

Lydia didn't know quite what to make of this; she still had a small suspicion that he was pulling her leg.

"So does this mean," she asked, "that we could have got the ship out of hock just by paying you enough?"

Cargill scratched the back of his neck, somewhere near the root of his pigtail.

"You did, dear lady. Or rather, your persuasive passenger the engineer Antonov did so on your family's behalf." He frowned. "On somebody's behalf, anyway. In the name of the—what was it?" He snapped his fingers, staring away into space. "The Liberation Front, that was it. A rather obvious name for a dummy company, don't you think?"

"Hmm," said Lydia, treading water. "So why did we, uh, he have to physically seize the ship back?"

"My dear, one has to observe the formalities. These things require a certain . . . finesse, if they're not to become public before the publication of the end-of-year accounts."

"And, if I may ask, how much did, ah, Antonov pay you?"

"Ten million talers."

She accidentally drank a mouthful of the whiskey. It was like being scalded.

"What?"

477

"On account," said Cargill soothingly. "To be paid in installments."

"All the same," said Lydia, "it does seem rather a lot, just to get the ship back."

Was Volkov expecting to find a fortune out there in space? To sell information from the gods?

"Oh, it wasn't just to get the ship back," said Cargill. "It was to change the entire policy of the Port Authority. To shift its support from the compradores and shipping families to the new human-owned trading fleets that Antonov has convinced us are the coming thing."

"That's a very long-term prospect," said Lydia. "Surely you can't have accepted a promise of payment out of—what?—some garnish on top of tariffs decades or centuries hence?"

"Indeed not," said Cargill. "But futures in such payments are already doing a brisk business. In the nearer term, a big expansion in sea and indeed air traffic can be expected. Our friend will have had no difficulty raising the amount on speculation alone."

"Ah," said Lydia. Even to herself she sounded strangled. "I see." She found she could take a larger sip of the spirits; possibly her mouth was becoming numb.

Cargill smiled. "And you also see, I'm sure, why I've become persona non grata at this event. The Rodriguezes are deeply offended at having been outbid by upstarts. The de Tenebres—well!" He spread his hands and smiled. "They continue to treat me as though I was not on their side."

Lydia flashed her eyebrows. "Perhaps they are being careful not to show their hand, so to speak."

Cargill chuckled. "That would be wise. It won't be necessary for long, in any case. Soon everyone in the city will know about the Port Authority's new stand."

"How soon is 'soon'?"

"Tomorrow morning," said Cargill. He fingered a gold watch from a fob pocket, fingernailed its lid open. Its two hands lay almost side by side. "That is to say, today."

11

Catastrophic Loss of Data

THE BLADE IS a sliver from the shell of a large freshwater mussel; it gleams with mother-of-pearl and keeps a better edge than steel. Matt dips it in the bowl of hot water and begins to shave Stone's soaped face. He's never gotten the hang of shaving face to face, as the sky people—suspicious of mirrors—always do, so he's kneeling behind Stone, making essentially the same movements as he'd make when shaving himself.

When Matt has finished he steps into the galley, pours out the scummy, hair-flecked water from the bowl, and refills it from the coffee machine's hot-water jug. He then refills the jug and sets the coffee machine on its proper task. He walks around Stone and sits cross-legged in front of him, setting the bowl between them, and soaps his face. Stone leans forward and applies the shell razor to Matt's upper lip. He works with frightening swiftness. Matt has learned to hold still.

"I see you are wearing your old clothes," says Stone.

"Uh-huh," grunts Matt. They're not really his; they're fatigues and socks and shorts from the ship's original and still vacuum-sealed supplies, not too degraded but definitely a bit scratchy.

"This is because you are going back to the Christians?"

"Mm-hmm."

Stone leans back, looks at him critically, and passes him the soggy towel. Matt wipes off the remaining suds and strokes his face. It's very smooth. He dips his finger in a small jar of red paste and applies it to Stone's lips, and then—with another finger—some blue-black paste around Stone's eyelids.

"You could stay with the sky people," says Stone. "The other women spoke well of you. They said you could be a good woman."

"I'm honored," Matt says, "but, well, I'm . . ."

"There are other men like Gail," says Stone hastily.

Matt laughs. "You know, the thought of shacking up with one of your Stone Age amazons and doing what you call women's work is kind of tempting. But—"

It's only at the moment he actually says it that he realizes just how tempting it is, not only in a slightly perverse erotic way but in the sense of settling down, of being able to stop running, stop fighting, stop having to look after himself and look out for the main chance all the time. His month at Long Bridge has left him with a tantalizing taste of what that different life could be like, and a taste for it too, which he'd never have suspected in himself.

"I have other work to do," he finishes, rather lamely.

Stone nods. "There is other work to be done," he says, "but perhaps you are not the one who has to do it?"

This thought is something of a jolt for Matt, but Stone just throws it off, sounding rather offhand and preoccupied. His expression becomes troubled. Matt waits for him to speak, worried that another flashback from his encounter with Othniel is about to hit. Their frequency has diminished over the past couple of days, though not their intensity.

"Matt," says Stone, "I have something to ask you, and I would like you to answer it without being afraid of offending me, but also not to tell anybody else I asked you."

While saying this he's looking around and cocking an ear for sounds, but the rest of the crew are still asleep, and the corridor outside the galley—the ship's only reliable source of hot water—is empty and quiet. Still, Stone leans forward and speaks in a low voice.

"Do you think I am becoming a man?"

Matt rocks back. "Ah, why should I think that?"

"I have done what a man has to do," says Stone quietly. "I have been on a killing party, and I have talked to a god."

Well, yes, that picture of Tola after the virus had finished with it might count as an enemy's head on a stick. . . . Competing with that morbid thought is the amused and irritated reflection that Matt's been repeatedly wakened throughout the past night by the uninhibited sounds of Gail and Stone fucking each other senseless. Not that that's relevant to Stone's question, but . . . Matt has to make a bit of a conscious effort to take it as seriously as it's meant. He sighs.

"Look, Stone, do you *want* to be a man?"

He has to bite his tongue not to include a qualifying phrase like "thought of as," or to launch into some patient explanation of how equating gender with sex is a mistake no matter which direction the ascription points.

"No!" says Stone. Then, less emphatically, "There are some things that men do that I want to do, or do more often, but that doesn't make me a man."

Yeah, no more than it makes Gail a man, Matt thinks but doesn't say, knowing too well that it would only make confusion worse confounded. Instead, he uncrosses his legs and rocks forward onto his knees and takes Stone in his arms.

"Then don't worry about it," he says into a mess of unkempt curls. "You're a woman if you want to be, no matter what you want to do."

He disengages and stands up, and as Stone gets up too he gives him a light, comradely punch on the shoulder. The smell of coffee is filling the air.

"Come on," he says. "Let's tell the lads to wake up and make their own fucking breakfast."

Croatan looms blue and white and green and brown, vulnerable and small, heartbreakingly reminiscent of Earth. So many more worlds to protect, so much to save. Matt has to will his jaw to unclench and discovers as he does so that a long-loosening molar has finally let go. He reaches into the back of his mouth, tugging and twisting, and wrenches it out. His head fills briefly with pain, his mouth with an iron taste. He swallows blood and tongues the empty socket. He can't quite feel the replacement tooth pushing out, but he knows it's there. This particular tooth has regrown two or three times already. Dental replacement isn't even part of his inadvertent immortality; it was one of the earliest genetic hacks he ever bought, and it hasn't let him down yet. He should offer a testimonial.

"Two hours until landing," says Salasso from the control table. Gail is watching over the saur's shoulder. Avakian sits in a spex-masked trance, still trying to integrate the flood of data from Tola with the much less tractable and user-friendly uploads from Othniel. Volkov and Stone are head-to-head over another table, talking in low voices. Of all of them, including Matt and even Gail, Volkov has had the easiest time adjusting to Stone's paradoxical gender conundrums. Perhaps because he has no personal stake in the matter, or because he retains some of his Party training in a sort of tongue-biting tolerance on "the sexuality question," for him it simply isn't an issue. From what Matt can overhear of their conversation, it's all politics.

"Where will we land?" asks Salasso, in the tone of someone about to start drumming his fingers.

"How about Long Bridge?" Matt suggests. "Keep us from falling straight back into the hands of the Port Authority."

Volkov looks up sharply. "No," he says. "We land at Rawliston harbor. That is very important."

Matt shrugs. "So what do we do about the Port Authority?"

Volkov smiles wolfishly. "That will not be a problem."

For one petrifying moment, as she sits bolt upright in bed, her mouth open for a scream, Lydia thinks that Faustina has come to kill her. (The notion of insane jealousy over Volkov flashes across her mind.) It's the sound of a tremendous bang outside that has awakened her, but her mother has flown into the bedroom before Lydia has had time to begin to react. She has never seen her mother so distraught. Hair in disarray, nightgown flapping open, she's shaking Lydia's shoulders and yelling, "Get up! Now! Down to the shelter!"

The words produce their conditioned adrenaline jolt. Lydia has known shelter drills since childhood. She bounds out of bed and hits the floor running, her mother close behind her. Slap of feet on cold marble. A brief thunderous din overhead tells her that this is not a drill.

Arrows, discreetly incorporated in the artwork of the corridor's mosaics, point the direction of the nearest brass sliding post. She halts her headlong run by catching the pole. The impact is enough to confirm that it's still sound. She steps over the low safety rail around the hole, catches it in hands and knees and crossed ankles, and slides down. The nightgown protects most of her from the friction, but her palms burn. She hardly notices as she makes a smoothly decelerated impact on the cellar floor and steps smartly away. Faustina arrives seconds later, others pouring down after her, almost but not quite on each other's heads. Poles at other locations in the house are also fully occupied.

An enormous *whumff* shakes the air, and a cloud of plaster and dust drops down through the pole hole and expands as it reaches the floor. There's a thud and scream. Two cousins stagger out of the dust cloud carrying Angela, a small cousin who has one shin at a bad angle and a shocked face pale even under the dust. Lydia sees all this more or less over her shoulder as she runs, tugging Faustina, for the halfway-open blast doors.

Inside the shelter at the center of the cellar it's all huddle and babble, emergency-generator-powered lights throwing weird shadows as they swing back and forth overhead. Esias is organizing counting and first aid. After a few minutes it becomes clear that—apart from twisted ankles and Angela's broken leg and lots of flying-glass cuts—casualties are low and everyone seems to have made it. Esias bolts the blast doors.

Lydia shoulders her way to where her cousin Marcus is manning the periscope.

"What's happening?"

He doesn't look away from the eyepieces.

"Port Authority cutter shelling the house," he reports calmly. "Sounds like we've been lucky so far. The first thing they hit was our spare skiff—waste of a shell—and it woke us up. Couple of boat loads of PA marines heading for shore," he adds in a louder voice.

Esias takes note of this with a nod. He's already in radio communication with the family's ship, by the sound of it.

"They must be crazy," Lydia says. "We can get skiffs from the ship here in—what?—an hour?"

She can't wait to see the attackers, whoever they are, frazzled in the skiffs' plasma blasts.

"Yes," says Esias, signing off. "The enemy expects this operation to be complete in less. Hence the bombardment."

"Who the hell is the enemy?" Lydia is more confused than shocked. Yesterday, when the Port Authority's change of policy had been announced, the town had been tense, buzzing with discussion, but peaceful.

"Recalcitrant elements in the Port Authority," says Marcus, still not turning around. "The marines are on the beach."

No time for politics. Esias has already unlocked the armory safes—like the shelters, they've been standard facilities in traders' houses since the last civil war to rip through Nova Babylonia, centuries ago in historical time, a frightening childhood memory for Lydia. Fully automatic rifles and pistols, better than the local ordnance. No high-energy weapons, unfortunately—these are jealously monopolized by the saurs and stashed in the skiffs or on ships. Right now, that means they're thousands of kilometers away.

Lydia, like Faustina and the other women and the saurs, take their pistols and herd the children to behind the shelter's interior blast partitions. Esias hands out the rifles to some of the men and leads them off into the maze of tunnels around the shelter. There are concealed exits by the road and on the beach, and pop-up points throughout the grounds, hidden in bushes and garden features. It's not much of a defense against professional military assault, but it makes the house a hard target for pirates, criminals, and factions in local political disputes. Lydia hopes the last is all they have to contend with now.

With Marcus gone, the nearest periscope is unattended. Lydia breaks from behind the barrier and darts over to it, ignoring yells of protective protest from Phoebe and Faustina. The eyepieces are still warm from Marcus's cheeks. It takes her a moment to adjust the focus—this instrument isn't as simple as binoculars—and by the time she has steadied it the view is almost filled by a pair of boots. She guesses that the objective lenses are concealed in a flower bed in front of the house, over which this attacker has just trampled.

Knowing that any movement might betray its location, she holds the periscope steady until the boots clump away, then studies the now-clear view ahead. A few hundred meters out to sea, the cutter stands, its light guns silent for now, their smoke long since drifted away. The landing boats lie empty on the beach. Closer to, the one skiff left by the house for casual transport is on its side, its extended legs sticking out over the lip of a five-meter crater in the grass, its underside scorched but otherwise apparently undamaged. The only visible attacker is a brown-uniformed, steel-helmeted man writhing on the grass about ten meters away, his arms around his entrails. No sound is audible, but in the clear focus of the periscope Lydia can see his screams. One of Volkov's throw away phrases—"There is nothing sacred in the life of an invader"—comes unbidden to her mind. She shuts her eyes for a moment as she swivels the periscope, tracking to the left. Beyond the side of the house she has a clear view of the sweep of the coast road around toward Rawliston.

Above the distant city, columns of smoke are rising; whatever heat is driving them is evidently enough to punch them straight up through the smog-haze and the temperature-inversion lid that keeps it in place. The road seems at first empty, but after a few seconds Lydia makes out the rows of vehicles pulled in at the sides and the few small, dark dots of those vehicles that are moving. They're moving fast, some going into town, others out. Over the sea an airship is trailing smoke and losing height. Another blimp floats, so far undamaged, in the farther distance.

Elsewhere in the sky small airplanes are flitting about. No skiffs are airborne that she can see—the two starships in harbor, barely visible at this distance, are after all owned by families who are likely to be on the side of whatever the recalcitrant elements behind this coup may be and are, probably, wisely keeping well out of it.

Whether they—or their saur crews—will continue to keep their heads down when the de Tenebres' skiffs come on the scene is an open question. Lydia just hopes she stays alive for the next fifty minutes or so to see the answer.

Salasso doesn't bother with the glide-path-like approach of their first arrival. Instead he takes the ship vertically down through the atmosphere like a dropping elevator to come to a visually shocking halt one meter above the sea at the starship berth. He slowly rotates the ship, bringing into view the great bulks of the two other starships and the seven Port Authority vessels that are circling them all. There are a lot of aircraft in the sky, but they're not buzzing the berth this time. Matt's the first to grab for the telescope. The boats are crowded, overloaded even, and their flag is different: Around the Port Authority turret-on-shield logo has been stencilled the outline of a clenched fist.

Without a word, Matt passes the telescope to Volkov, who snatches it and stares for a few seconds.

"Somebody's trying to hail us," he says. "It's Endecott."

"Who?"

"One of the local radicals."

Salasso stops the movement of the ship. Volkov opens the airlock exit hatch and leans out. Matt peers over his shoulder. The PA launch has swung in almost alongside, and from its deck a thin young man with a briefcase under his elbow is grinning and waving up at them.

"Welcome back, Comrade Volkov!" he shouts. "To the People's Republic of Rawliston!"

"Oh, bloody hell," Volkov says, just loud enough for Matt to catch. "This was not supposed to happen."

Matt steps back and stares at Volkov's back. His hand clenches around the nastiest of the knives in his jacket pocket. For a moment he savors the image of taking it out, opening it, and slamming its half-serrated blade between Volkov's shoulders.

Instead he just says, "You stupid, stupid Stalinist son of a bitch."

Volkov looks back at him, with the grin of a rider on a roller coaster. "You're too kind," he says.

Salasso, Gail, Avakian, and Stone stand around the radio, thumbing the dial and listening to a bumpy succession of fragments of disturbing news. Gail is monotonously saying, "Shit shit shit shit . . ."

Volkov has given Endecott a hand up. The radical stumbles on board, clutching a briefcase and a bullhorn, a radio slung on a strap around his neck bouncing on his chest. He straightens and glances about. He takes in the control deck in about a second, nods an "Oh, hi!" of recognition to Gail, smiles at the others, and finally fixes on Matt.

"You're the other cosmonaut?"

"Yup," says Matt. If he doesn't know Avakian, that's none of Matt's business.

Endecott shakes his hand. "Good, good," he says. His quick glance takes in Volkov. "Any arms on board?"

"Maybe a couple of pistols," says Matt.

"Are any of you good shots?"

Volkov gives a downturned smile. "Me, him, and Gail."

"Okay," says Endecott. He darts to the exit hatch, leans out, and starts shouting, and within half a minute has passed back four rifles and, with more difficulty, an ammunition box. Then he turns to Salasso and looks at him with his first hint of not knowing quite what to say next.

"My name is Salasso," says the saur, "and you want me to take this ship somewhere else."

"Yes," says Endecott, with relief. His shoulders sag briefly, then he pulls himself straight. "There are a lot of other places where you could help, but I have to tell you: The Traders' House is under attack."

"Go there," says Volkov. He grabs Endecott's shoulder. "Do you have to come?"

Endecott dithers for a fraction of a second. "Yes," he says. "You might need me to negotiate."

By this time it's pretty much moot. Salasso is already taking the ship up. The hatch is still open, but the field keeps the slipstream at arm's length. Gail has about a minute to familiarize Matt and Volkov in the workings of the rifle, which she calls the Chapman. Matt imagines leaning out of the hatch and firing it, reloading after every five rounds. Along with the hope that their opposition is easily terrified, he has a thought.

"Will this thing punch through the field?"

Salasso's concentration on the fiddly, crude controls doesn't waver. "Yes," he says, "but the velocity of the projectile will be reduced." The ship halts again. The view in front is tilted upward. They're a couple of hundred meters up and about the same distance out to sea from the Traders' House. Its roof has three huge holes in it and the walls are pockmarked. Men in ones and twos are skirmishing through the garden. A few bodies sprawl on the ground.

Gail gets on one knee behind the exit hatch and pokes her rifle out, waves behind her back at Salasso.

"Take us around," she says.

For a petrifying few seconds the contradiction between the wildly moving view and the rock-steady one-gravity local field makes Matt almost sick. The bangs of the rifle are shocking. Gail rolls aside and sits and reloads; Matt takes his cue and takes her place as Salasso brings the ship around for another low pass. Matt sees a flashing blur of wrecked greenery, scurrying dark figures, a wall. As the ship soars and then swings around again, Matt is shouldered roughly aside by Volkov. He crawls sideways, rolls to a seated position, and notices that the rifle is hot and its magazine is empty and he can't hear a thing. Gail mouths words at him around a fixed grin as she finishes reloading just before Endecott takes the firing position.

Next time around, Matt is back on the door and Salasso brings the ship to another intuitively impossible halt. A few meters away Matt sees a man with his arms above his head and a rifle at his feet. Other men are running past, fleeing. Matt takes aim at one, fires. He falls, thrashing and screaming. The others stop; some throw themselves on the ground, then join the others in standing with their hands up. Matt vaults out, Endecott just behind him, and covers that scattered half dozen defeated men. It's over.

Not quite. With a vast rush of air the ship lifts and skims out to sea at about ten meters altitude, straight for a low, armed craft a way offshore. Matt watches in fascinated horror as the ship stops directly above it. With preternatural clarity he can see a long gun barrel moving above the deck.

Then the *Bright Star* descends implacably on the craft, pushing it down into the water. When the starship lifts again there's nothing below it but a roiling froth of bubbles and a few small, bobbing objects. It stays above them. Matt has a busy few minutes rounding up men and weapons while Endecott runs through impromptu interrogations, and then the ship's shadow falls over them again. It descends onto the remains of the house's back garden, and a handful of soaked militiamen drop from its side and join the other prisoners.

Meanwhile a lot of to-and-fro yelling has been going on, and men from the de Tenebre clan have started popping out of the shrubbery. One or two of them are checking the casualties, distinguishing the dead from the wounded and giving the latter what help they can. The smell of blood and shit mingles horribly with the garden's scents. Matt is in no compassionate or regretful mood. His blood is still up; he feels nothing but outrage that the house has been attacked and anxiety for those inside it.

Volkov jumps down from the ship and sprints to Endecott. Matt, seeing that the prisoners are now adequately guarded and in any case have the fight knocked out of them, steps over to the two men, who're already exchanging information and speaking rapid-fire into radios. He waits for the first slight pause, then grabs both of them.

"*What* the fuck is going on?"

"A good chunk of the PA didn't stay bought," says Endecott. "Their attempted coup has been met by an uprising of the people. Barricades are up all over town."

"Who's *supporting* this coup?"

Endecott waves a hand. "Oh, some of the magnates and compradores. And their hangers-on. Usual riffraff, some of the Back-o'-the-Docks elements—"

Volkov holds up a hand. "Face it," he says, "the city's pretty much split on this, yes?"

"You could say that," Endecott acknowledges, "but the core industrial workers are out on strike—"

"And how many are out for the 'People's Republic'?"

Endecott shrugs. "To be honest, that's a slogan that has been raised spontaneously by the loyal sections of the militia. We've picked it up and we're running with it, but—"

"Excellent!" says Volkov. "However, right now the key issue is to isolate and defeat the conspirators, so I strongly suggest you ask your comrades to stop defacing the flags, and so on, and get the maximum unity possible among the forces opposed to the coup. You know all this, Endecott. Don't get carried away."

He turns to Matt. "Can we ask Salasso to take Endecott back to the harbor and possibly do a little more intimidation along the way?"

"You can ask," says Matt. "It's up to him. See if the others want to get off first."

"Go to it," Volkov tells Endecott. He claps the radical's shoulder. "Don't worry, man, you're doing a good job."

Endecott runs to the ship. A moment later, Stone, Gail, and Avakian scramble out. The ship lifts again, climbs, and heads for Rawliston.

"If this is a good job," says Matt, "I'd hate to see a bad one."

Volkov gives a wry grin. "It's their revolution," he says "and their people. Now let's go and see to our own."

Lydia climbed up one of the exit shafts and stood on damp grass and looked around. This shaft emerged at the front of the house, on the side where the road passed it. A white vehicle with a red Maltese cross painted on the side was parked in the driveway, and the Hospitallers were stretchering people out or dragging long heavy sacks. All of the deaths and serious casualties were among the attackers, but now the relief of that thought was clouded with a kind of nausea and guilt. Not that it had been wrong to defend themselves, but that she had, without much knowledge or care, contributed her might to bringing these things to pass. *Whatever it costs I will pay,* she had thought. But it was not she who was paying.

Warned off from entering the house, where masonry still unpredictably crashed every minute or so, she wandered around to the back and found most of the clan there, milling about, half dressed or naked or in nightwear, all of the adults carrying some weapon or other, like armed sleepwalkers. The family's own cuts and bruises and broken bones were being dealt with by the medically trained among the cousins, by Avakian, and by the saurs. Esias was in a huddle with the people who had come off the *Bright Star,* interrupting his conversation now and then to speak to relatives or speak on his radio. Lydia pushed her way through.

Volkov smiled and took her hand, very formally and properly. "It's good to see you," he said.

"Likewise," she said, equally formally. "Thank you for—"

At that moment Matt's lady friend, Daphne, hurtled out of the crowd and threw herself on Matt, almost knocking him over, wrapping her arms around him and twining one leg behind his knees. Lydia smiled to herself. That was what she wanted to do with Volkov, but not in public. Not in front of her father. At that moment Faustina arrived and gave Volkov a barely decent embrace. Esias and Lydia noticed each other pretending not to notice and almost laughed.

"It's Endecott you have to thank," said Volkov, when Faustina had stepped back. "He made stopping this raid a priority. Maybe he had some political reason for doing that, or knew he would have me to reckon with if he hadn't, but I'm still grateful."

"I'm just glad you're back." She looked around. "All of you," she added. "Did you do what—you set out to do?"

"Yes," Volkov said. Gail nodded. Matt's face, and Stone's, took on a strange, withdrawn expression for a moment. Then Stone looked down, and Matt turned back to Daphne's hair. He closed his eyes and breathed deeply, as Volkov had done in Lydia's hair just before he'd left.

"Talk about all that later," he mumbled. Then he stretched and looked around over the crowd.

"Are Elizabeth and Gregor here?"

Lydia shook her head.

"They're holed up at the university," Esias said.

"There's some fighting, not very serious—different gangs of students laying into each other with fists. The main fight seems to be over the university radio station, which has fallen into the hands of some of the extreme democrats." He smiles. "It's under seige by the less extreme ones."

"This is all so chaotic," Lydia said.

"It isn't," Matt said, with a glare at Volkov. "It's all bloody predictable. You got most of the personnel of the Port Authority to change sides, all right, but those who benefitted from its previous policy have struck back with those who didn't. And that's roused the workers and the city poor, or at least sections of them, and I bet they aren't going to settle for a few trade policy changes that won't show any benefit to them for decades. Especially after you've been cynically stirring them up."

Volkov returned him a thin-lipped smile.

"It's not my responsibility that a long-overdue reform is being brutally opposed." He shrugged. "And if some on the people's side are in the grip of illusions, at least it inspires them to fight, in a way they might not for the small improvements that are all that is possible at the moment."

Esias, to Lydia's surprise, agreed.

"We can make a difference here," he said. "Judging by the attack on us, and from what my contacts have been saying on the radio, we have a certain symbolic importance for both sides. So does the *Bright Star,* and so does Grigory Volkov. We have to get him into the town, into the thick of it, and onto the airwaves."

Lydia had a moment of inspiration.

"The university," she said. "It's in a commanding position, and the radio station—"

Esias looked around and beckoned urgently to one of the saurs. "Let's get that skiff upright and check that it can fly. We don't have time to wait for the rest to arrive."

He organized Volkov and the saur pilot and a few extra hands, and they hurried away.

"I'm going too," Lydia said.

"No, you are not," said Esias.

He looked into the hot rage of her eyes for a second, then covered his retreat by adding, "Not like that. There are clothes down in the shelter."

She surprised him with a hug, and ran.

"Don't you want to go too?"

Matt, sitting on rubble and gratefully sipping coffee, looks up at Stone and Gail.

"No," he says. He motions them to sit down.

"Why not?" Gail asks.

"Look," says Matt, "I'm not a very political animal, and all the political instincts I do have would only make things worse. I would be inclined to urge people to, you know, take their affairs into their own hands, not to trust anybody in authority. Which would be fine if I was going to stick around for the consequences, but I'm not. And I'm a stranger here, so why should anyone listen to me?"

"Volkov is a stranger," says Stone, "but people listen to him. And he is going away, too, but he is not afraid to urge people to do things now."

"Yeah, well, there is that," says Matt. "Volkov's a political animal, all right. And he expects to be living with the consequences."

"Ninety-odd light-years away?" Gail scoffs. "Sounds like he'll be well out it."

"What happens here in the next few months or years," says Matt, "will start feeding through to Nova Babylonia in the next few months or years of our friend's life. And of our other friends' lives, the de Tenebres', come to that." He laughs. "You know, when I met him here after we arrived, he said he was arranging forward shipping of devices and techniques new to Nova Babylonia, to give himself something to trade on if the research into his longevity didn't pan out."

"What's so funny about that?" asks Gail.

"That's exactly what he's doing now, with all his political tinkering."

Gail snorts. "He wants Croatan to export revolution to Nova Babylonia? That'll take some doing!"

"Yeah," says Matt. "It will, and he's just the man to do it. The mighty and ancient republic has some creaking timbers of its own, and he knows just where to apply the levers."

"Nah," says Gail. "Nova Babylonia is rich. Nova Terra's like a huge park. Life is easy for everybody. Not like here."

"Hmm," says Matt. "Yet it had a civil war, maybe worse than any you've had here, just a few centuries ago. And unless they've made some huge jump in their machinery and technology since the de Tenebres left, *and* had a social revolution into the bargain—all of which I wouldn't rule out but I wouldn't bet on—they still have many people working for a few. And that's all it takes."

"You are more of a revolutionary than Volkov is," says Stone. "He has said nothing like this."

Matt grins, drains his coffee, and stands up. "See what I mean?" he says. "Anything I can say here would only make things worse."

"I don't see why," says Gail.

"People can be free and equal only when they're all rich, or all poor. Anything in between, they can't. And Rawliston's in between and will be for a long time to come. The Great Vale, though—"

"We are not all poor!" says Stone.

"No," says Matt. "You're all rich."

And what's going to happen here will make you all poor.

He gazes down at Stone, transfixed by the guilt of this thought. The development triggered by the *Bright Star*'s arrival, and that of its almost inevitable successors, will be enough to destroy Stone's society in decades. The likely outcome of the revolution here will only speed that up. An expanding, industrializing capitalist society with a state that will, for the first time, be well adapted to that kind of society—the outcome that Volkov undoubtedly wants—will absorb the Great Vale into its hinterland. Matt can see it all now; the trinkets turned out for money in airless workshops, the young people drifting to the city factories, the drunks and drug addicts, the deserted villages become bijou holiday homes, the servants and gardeners and prostitutes. He can see it now because he's seen it all before.

And the devil of it is, he can see how Volkov can think it's all justified, in the light not only of his own ideology but also in the light of what they've learned from the gods about what is really going on in the universe.

Well, it may be inevitable, but he's damned if he's going to justify it to himself. He's damned if he's just going to let it happen. And damned, he realizes, is exactly what he will be, his whole life might as well not have been lived, if he doesn't do something about it.

Now.

Gail and Stone are watching his silent seconds of troubled thought with puzzled concern. He forces a reassuring smile.

"You know," he says, "I've thought of a way I can get involved here, a way that won't make things worse."

Gail gives him an encouraging grin. "Better than doing nothing," she says.

"Stone," says Matt, "what exactly was Volkov saying to you, in the ship?"

"He was talking about how more trade will come here, with the new ships," says Stone. "And he said that the Port Authority will still tax it, but that the new ships can land anywhere, not just on the sea. So perhaps, he said, a place like the Great Vale could become a port, too, one that did not tax the trade, and could compete with Rawliston. It could declare itself a free port. I said I would raise the matter with the elders."

Matt blinks. *Gods above, the man's clever.*

"Stone," he says earnestly, "I entirely agree with that. You should raise the matter with the elders and tell them that this is one thing they absolutely must *not* do."

"Why not?"

"How long do you think Rawliston would let you take trade away from them?"

"How could they stop us? The treaty forbids them to interfere with us."

"I'm just guessing here," says Matt, "but I think you'll find that the treaty forbids your two societies, Christians and heathens, from *interfering with each other*—and it wouldn't take much to convince people that stealing trade, as they'd call it, was interfering, and anything Rawliston did to stop it was self-defense."

"I understand that," says Stone. "But the treaty is with the saurs, too, and they will stop Rawliston from making war on us."

"Think about what we've learned from the gods," Matt says. "Now think about what the saurs will do, when they learn it too. And the humans, for that matter."

Stone's face is stricken. "Then we must not tell them!"

Gail jumps up. "Yes!" she says. "That's it! We have to keep it secret."

Matt stares them both down.

"Not a fucking chance," he says. "If Volkov and Salasso—or you, or Avakian—don't spread the word, I will. We can win only with the truth." He grins at them. "Well, maybe the truth and a bit more. But we *can* win."

People are already busy clearing rubble; Esias has taken to supervising this task. Matt looks around until he spots the nearest unattended radio, lying on one of the small picnic tables among cups and litter. He goes over and picks it up and raises the ship's hailing channel.

"Salasso? Matt here."

"Ye-es," says Salasso, a strained note in his voice.

"When you've finished scaring the shit out of pikemen," says Matt, "could you come back to the house and pick us up?"

"Give me a few minutes," says Salasso. After a pause, during which the channel fills with chaotic noise, he adds, "Bring Bishlayan, if she will come."

From the skiff, the most obvious difference from a normal morning rush hour was the relative absence of vehicle and animal traffic. Entire streets were packed with pedestrians, who were not on their way to work. Even in the thin spread of the suburbs, the shift in the proportions held. The reduction in exhaust fumes and factory smoke made the haze thinner than usual, and the columns of smoke from burning barricades and looted shops more prominent than they might have otherwise been. All of the main bridges seemed to be closed to other than foot traffic, and that itself was being filtered by squads strung out across the approaches.

Lydia spotted the *Bright Star* performing frightening maneuvers above one of the industrial districts, diving and not so much pulling out as reversing. Volkov was flipping between radio channels, speaking to Salasso in the ship and to Endecott, now back at the dockside. He signed off and grinned at her.

"Salasso seems to be doing all right," said Volkov. "So are the popular forces, as far as I can see. Somebody down there knows how to organize an insurrection."

She looked at him sidelong. "Nothing to do with you?"

He chuckled darkly. "That was not among the tips I passed on," he said. "In small city-states such knowledge becomes traditional."

The saur pilot swung the skiff in the direction of the university, a great multilayered pile of a place near the center of the town.

"No," said Volkov. "Landing at the university would be a mistake."

"Why?" asked Lydia, as the pilot brought the craft to a midair dead halt.

Volkov shrugged. "Instinct. I have a feeling it would give the wrong impression. Let's land at the docks, instead."

"You have some friends there," Lydia acknowledged.

"It's no accident," said Volkov, "that Endecott's 'People's Republic' at the moment consists mainly of the docks, some boats, and a stretch of harbor water." He laughed. "Yes, put us down there."

They landed on the shore street, at the entrance to the star merchants' quay. A hundred or so dock and harbor workers were gathered outside it, along with some arguing truck drivers and a huddle of radio reporters. The skiff soared away, and Volkov and Lydia walked toward the crowd, which quickly surrounded them, the reporters stretching microphones over shoulders from behind.

Lydia recognized one of the workers who'd been with Volkov at the neighborhood assembly and one or two other faces familiar from his swift succession of meetings. But everyone here seemed to recognize Volkov, who was shaking hands and slapping shoulders and (when asked) introducing her as "a progressive trader—the de Tenebres are all right, they're on our side."

He left her to field questions from the reporters—mainly about the attack—while he went off into another conspirative huddle, involving much radio communication and scribbling on bits of already printed paper. Then he strolled back and waved over the reporters' heads.

"Looks like we may have a deal," he said.

Then he stretched, almost on tiptoe. "Anyone want to come up to the university?" he called out. "The progressive students need a bit of reinforcement."

"Huh," said someone, "haven't seen any of that lot down here."

"We'll send some down to the picket line, don't you worry," said Volkov. "And it'll take only a handful of us to make a difference up there."

Within minutes a dozen or so dock workers and one hurrying reporter were walking alongside as Volkov and Lydia walked through the waterfront office area, then Back-o'-the-Docks, and up a slope to the university. Lydia found the presence of their companions reassuring. Some of the people hanging around the streets were friendly, others hostile, but none wanted to tangle with the dockers. A lot of windows had been broken overnight. Most of the people they passed were too busy talking among themselves or clearing up damage to pay much attention. A fair number were either drunk or sleeping it off.

"This is a bit of a bohemian area," said Lydia. "I'd have expected more, well, revolutionary enthusiasm."

"In Back-o'-the-Docks?" Volkov shook his head. "This is about what I would expect—very divided and not very reliable either way. You'll see more enthusiasm in the respectable districts."

He talked, all the same, to anyone who wanted to walk alongside and argue or enthuse and to the dockers: The latter conversations were in a clipped argot and accent that Lydia found hard to follow.

The university entrance, a big opening in a small version of a city wall, stood open, its wrought-iron gates dragged wide. Inside was a broad quadrangle of gravelled paths and trampled grass, upon which about a thousand people were sitting or standing about in large groups, or sleeping in small clumps. The air smelled of coffee and sausages and smoke. A lot of those present looked too unrespectable even to be students. Perhaps this was where whatever revolutionary enthusiasts Back-o'-the-Docks could throw up had congregated. Sheets scrawled with slogans hung from every window: Free trade and socialism got about equal billing. The quantity of handbills, newspapers, and general litter was astounding; it was like walking on a carpet of discarded paper.

They'd walked only about ten meters in from the gate before they were surrounded, the dockers getting almost as much attention and conversation as Volkov as they walked along. The party around them grew by the minute. Lydia recognized some of the students Volkov had talked to on his tour of agitation.

By the time they'd gone through the other end of the quadrangle and across a paved plaza to a more modern building with a radio mast topping its five-story height, they had hundreds behind them. It was almost frightening. It was certainly enough to frighten off about fifty students outside the building chanting, "Democracy yes! Socialism no!" who took one look and vanished in a flurry of dropped placards.

Lydia and Volkov, the dockers, and a similar number of students all ascended the stairs inside to the radio room. It was already packed and their new crowd seemed as if it couldn't possibly go in, but it did.

A bearded student who looked as if he hadn't slept took off earphones and glared, while with one hand he played over a bank of switches. Music leaked from the headphones. Smoke filled the room like a stiff jelly.

"What's—oh, it's you, Engineer Antonov! Come on and sit down. My name's Chris Hewett."

Lydia grabbed a coffee while students fussed over everyone. One young woman began eagerly taping interviews with the dockers for later transmission. Another, apparently transmitting live to judge by the bulk of equipment she carried, asked Lydia for the de Tenebres' view of the situation.

"Well, naturally," Lydia said, "we're entirely in favor of the legitimate majority of the Port Authority and entirely opposed to those who're trying to thwart the will of the people. The rebels attacked our house this morning! I'm happy to tell you that this cowardly attack was defeated, with heavy losses to the attackers. Quite frankly, I hope that's the kind of reception they get everywhere."

"What about the proposed changes to the constitution?"

"It would be improper for us to take a position on any kind of detailed proposals," Lydia temporised. "I understand that our friend the engineer Antonov has been asked by some of the democratic forces to publicize their positions, and I'm as eager to hear them as you are."

Volkov patiently listened to explanations of electronics and electrics that, Lydia guessed, he could have operated blindfold. Finally, after a rambling and embarrassing introduction from Hewett, he was given the microphone. The reporter who'd accompanied them poked his microphone over, too, presumably for another channel.

"Good morning," Volkov said. "Thank you for this opportunity to speak to you. As you all know, I'm a traveler here, but not, I hope, a stranger. I've been asked to put before you a proposal that may settle your constitutional conflict.

"I've also been asked to pass on an appeal to those of the militia who are fighting on the side of the rebels. You have been lied to. Your officers may not have lied to you, but others have lied to them. The people of Rawliston are not on some rampage against private property, law and order, and public decency. They are for peace, freedom, and prosperity, just as you are. They want you to think, think hard, before you go out to die for men you have never met, men who work in the shadows, men who are loyal to nothing but their own money. Come over to the side of the people, the side of your neighbors, the side of your friends. You'll be welcomed.

"Now, the proposal, which I've heard discussed all over this city—from trade unionists, from businesspeople, from students. Leaflets outlining it are already being circulated, and details will be in the electrostats within hours. It's very simple. Your Port Authority has become a state within the state and a law unto itself. It regulates the traffic in the streets, the public health, the public works, the terms of trade. Tomorrow it will regulate more, and it'll still be accountable only to the merchants who set it up long ago—to dredge the harbor and maintain the lighthouse!

"Parliamentary democracy is the standard solution to this sort of problem. The people of Rawliston can elect a council of their own chosen representatives to control the Port Authority. The representatives could stand for whatever policies they wanted the Port Authority to follow. Everything would be out in the open, everybody would know where they stood.

"Just as you know where I stand.

"Thank you."

Volkov handed the microphone back and pushed back his chair, then closed his eyes and let out a long breath. Lydia almost laughed. All this subversion, and all the time he was trying to sell them a republic! Nothing could have been more beneficial to the de Tenebres, or to the local businesses that would benefit from free trade. But would they buy it? Suddenly she saw the point of Volkov's well-cultivated contacts with the local radical organizers: If he could sell this to them, even if only as a necessary stage in the revolution, they could probably sell it to the people.

"Uh, thank you for that contribution, Engineer Antonov," said Hewett. He looked around the room, silently jabbing a finger at the microphone. Someone shoved through and grabbed it. Lydia recognized the red-haired woman folk singer.

"Yes, that was very interesting," she said. "Pauline Tydway here again, you heard me singing earlier. I have a few questions for Engineer Antonov. First, where do the people's assemblies fit into this scheme?"

"The people's assemblies must remain sovereign," Volkov said. "But most people don't have the resources or the time to oversee the day-to-day decisions of the Port Authority. An elected Port Authority Council could do that, and more."

"It's the 'more' I'm worried about," Tydway said. "What's to stop this *parliament* handing the Port Authority more and more power?"

"Only the vigilance of the people," Volkov said mildly. "In my view, there *is* more that needs to be done by the public authorities, to deal with destitution and oppression. But that's for you to decide. And remember, if it doesn't work, the assemblies can simply abolish it."

"If it hasn't abolished the assemblies first!"

Volkov smiled. "No parliament could do that, if the people didn't want it."

She scowled at him dubiously. "Well, no doubt this will all be thrashed out . . . meanwhile, there's a question many people have been asking: Where have you, and the *Bright Star,* been for the past few days?"

"If I'd known you were going to have a revolution the minute my back was turned . . ." Volkov said, raising a reluctant smile from Tydway and a laugh from the packed room. "But seriously. We took the ship on a mission of exploration. All the data we recovered will in due course be made available to the scientists here and to the public. That's all I can say at the—"

He stared past Tydway, past Lydia, at something outside the window. Lydia looked over her shoulder and saw through the big plate-glass panel the *Bright Star* descending. By the time the surge to the window was complete, the ship had set down in the campus plaza. Hewett grabbed the microphone and began a breathless running commentary. Salasso emerged, looked up, waved, and trotted to the building's entrance. A moment later, Matt followed.

When Salasso walked into the room, everybody stared and pulled back slightly, so those closest to the room's walls were pressed against them. Matt, his overalls and jacket whitened and his eyes reddened by dust, was hardly less intimidating.

"There is nothing to be afraid of," said Salasso. Matt's evil grin around the room was perhaps intended to convey the same message, but it didn't. Hewett wound up his commentary and gestured them toward the microphone.

Matt leaned into it and said, "Thank you, good morning, everyone. I'm not too happy with what my colleague, uh, Antonov has just said. I mean, screw this parliamentary democracy swindle. You'd do better to scrap the Port Authority and have the assemblies and any other democratic bodies run the whole show. You can't control bureaucrats by electing politicians, that's not what democracy is about. But you know that already, and you don't need me to tell you."

Volkov looked about to throttle him, or at least grab the mike. Matt fended him off with one hand and with the other beckoned behind his back.

"However," he went on, "that's not what we've come here to talk about. My crewmate Salasso has more urgent news."

Salasso stepped forward and glanced at Hewett, who nodded. Hewett and Tydway, Lydia was interested to see, made way for him with alacrity. Volkov backed off more reluctantly, and Matt placed himself between the other cosmonaut and the saur. Lydia glowered at him; he smiled back. Whatever annoyance Volkov might be feeling, Lydia suspected she could double it. The idea of scrapping the Port Authority entirely was not one that her family would profit from and—even given Matt's lack of local connections—was an incendiary one to throw into such a volatile situation.

Salasso sat by the table and pulled the microphone closer.

"I have two items of information. The first is that the coup's fighters on the ground appear to be in disarray. Surrenders and desertions are spreading and could well be encouraged further by appropriate measures."

His thin lips quirked. "As my colleagues here have been saying, all of you listening know what to do. What I wish to tell you, however, is something that you could not hear from anyone but me.

"The *Bright Star* indeed went on a mission of exploration. The second item of information I wish to give you is to tell you what we sought and what we found. We wanted to know why the worlds of the Second Sphere were populated by the species that live on and among them, and why the *Bright Star* was made to come to Mingulay two hundred years ago. Contrary to the impression that its crew sought to give, its arrival here was not by their intention. The only possible conclusion is that it was sent here by the powers in the Solar System with which they were in contact. At the same time, these powers gave the instructions for building the engines of the lightspeed ships and the gravity skiffs to the human beings who then lived on Earth.

"The first power we approached, the large cometary nucleus known as Tola, gave us the answer to the first question. The Second Sphere was established to provide a haven for the first two intelligent species to evolve on Earth: the great squids and my own species, the saurs. It was necessary to do this because the powers were warring with another intelligent species, and among themselves, and they visited great destruction upon Earth. The power, Tola, that gave us this information was itself destroyed shortly after it did so."

Lydia heard a collective gasp and uneasy movements in the room. Hewett, she noticed, was staring at Salasso with a kind of fascinated horror; Pauline Tydway, the folk singer, with something like admiration. Salasso glanced sideways and continued.

"We then approached another power, which resides in the asteroid known as Othniel. From Tola, we knew how far from Earth we are— one hundred thousand light-years away, clear across the other side of the Foamy Wake. And from Othniel we learned that there may be no going back to Earth, even if we could.

"The powers gave the secret of the lightspeed drive and the gravity skiff to the people of the Solar System to equip the human race for another conflict with a race of extraterrestrial intelligent beings. Since then, no information from the Solar System has reached the powers in the Second Sphere. No lightspeed ships, no radio whispers have brought any news. It is entirely possible that there was a war in space, which humanity lost."

He paused and closed his eyes for a moment. Tydway leaned forward, biting her knuckles, eyes watering. Hewett stared intently at the dials of the radio apparatus and reached to make some fine adjustment. Nobody else moved.

"It is also possible that the human race itself became a threat to the powers. They do not take sides between the few intelligent species that have evolved independently in various parts of the galaxy. Instead, they use each species to suppress any of the others that disturb their peace. There is a fine line between being strong enough to suppress another species and becoming too strong for the powers' liking. We do not know on which side of this line we are, but we do know that most of the powers in the Second Sphere are happy that the humans intend to build starships of their own. Most, not all.

"The powers argue among themselves, but they agree on this: The Adamic races, the saurs, the kraken, and any other intelligent species out there, are all lower forms of life. The powers do not know which side they will take when the ships of another intelligent species arrive here, as they soon will, or which side will win.

"In the meantime, they continue to take occasional ships from our traffic and hurl them into battle far away. They do this by hacking into and altering the settings of the ships' engines. Your old song is true— we all go up the line."

He glanced at Pauline Tydway, his lips stretching. She nodded with a wry smile.

"At any moment ships of another species may be sent up a line that ends here, to war with us. There is no right or wrong in these wars. The powers care no more for us than we do for the germs that infect us, the cells that die to fight them, and the pus that we wipe away.

"I think we can do better for ourselves than that, but whatever we do, we must do quickly. The aliens are on their way, and we have to be ready. We must—"

He was interrupted by shouting from the stairwell, then a commotion at the door. Somebody posted outside the door jumped aside, and ten saurs marched in.

They stood in the middle of the floor, a compact group, shoulder to shoulder. Lydia had never seen a saur angry, and now she saw ten. Their rage might have been taken as mild irritation by anyone less familiar with the species. The students whose passage wasn't physically blocked by the saurs streamed out of the door nonetheless, leaving Hewett and Tydway, Volkov and Matt and Lydia to face them. Salasso was not facing them. After one quick look to take in the situation he had turned back to the microphone and continued to talk.

"We must all work together, hominids and saurs and krakens. We must be ready not to fight the aliens but to avoid fighting them, and if possible to win them over to our side. Together we must be ready to fight the Powers Above."

He handed the microphone to Hewett and spun around in his seat and stood up.

The saurs said something that to Lydia sounded like a collective hiss. Salasso shrugged and spread his hands. Perhaps it was this human gesture that provoked the next escalation of fury against him. The entire group of saurs strode forward together, their arms reaching forward, hands clawed.

Matt was suddenly standing between Salasso and the other saurs. He reached into a side pocket and an inside pocket simultaneously. A quick shake of the wrist, and an ugly serrated blade jutted from one fist.

The leading saur's hand struck too fast to see. The knife fell, and Matt staggered. In a moment the saurs were past him and had grabbed Salasso. They made a concerted rush, bearing him to the window. Lydia sprang up and threw herself past them. They stopped. Volkov and Matt were beside her in seconds.

The saurs held Salasso above their heads. He had his eyes closed and was not struggling. Lydia stared at the front rank of the saurs, half a meter in front of her, fighting down every mammalian instinct to flee or capitulate. Matt vaulted onto the windowsill and stood there against the glass. He was shouting.

"Gail, lift the ship! To the window! Now!"

The saurs stared up at him, nonplussed. Then a couple of them let go of Salasso and leapt forward to tug at Matt's legs.

Even Lydia was shocked when he kicked at their heads—they dodged his boot easily—and tried again. The others were heaving Salasso back, about to throw him forward.

"No!" Lydia yelled.

"Dodge *this*," Matt grunted. Out of the corner of her eye Lydia saw a pistol waving. The saurs hesitated for a second or two, backed off, then ran forward again. Matt fired, left-handed, wide. Somebody screamed.

The saurs pitched Salasso into the air and straight at the window. Matt made a sideways lurch like a goalkeeper and fell to the floor. The window shattered.

Lydia saw the glass falling in front of her and felt bits of it crash on top of her head and shoulders, for what seemed like forever until she realized what it and the room's sudden darkness meant.

She turned in time to see that Salasso had landed on his feet in the airlock hatch of the *Bright Star,* whose side filled the space where the window had been. Matt hopped on the sill and hurtled after him. The ship vanished upward.

The saurs stared at Lydia and Volkov, and at the gaping space behind them, then turned about and marched out. Lydia felt something warm running down her face and was almost relieved to find that it wasn't tears.

12

Lights in the Sky

THE SHIP HUNG at a steep angle, the forward view showing the
university's ancient and modern buildings, its paved squares and
green patches like a camera obscura scene. People were fleeing from
under the ship. Even with the rock-steady artificial gravity, Gail still
had the impulse to grab on to something.

She also, despite the seriousness of the situation, had the impulse
to say, "Whee!" She slid the control widget along, and a slight tremor
in her hand set the ship yawing wildly as it retreated skyward.

"I will take over now," Salasso said. His scalp was bleeding and
his limbs trembled.

"You will not," said Bishlayan, guiding him to a seat and pushing
him down in it. "And you, Cairns, you will sit down too."

Matt sat by the window. He looked in a worse way than Salasso,
though this was partly because his clothes and hair had already been
covered with dust. He had several cuts on his head and face, and he
clutched his right wrist with his left.

"That was nothing wrong with that knife," he said regretfully. He
closed his eyes and manipulated his forearm and winced. "Nothing broken."

Stone walked over and stood beside him. "You need to get these
cuts seen to." Bishlayan was already dealing with Salasso's injuries,
applying sticky-looking liquid oozing from a tiny tube, one of several
in a flat box she'd pulled from inside her suit. Glue, probably, Gail
thought uncharitably, though Salasso's blood was as red as Matt's.

"Not just yet," said Matt. He looked over at Salasso. "Do we have
time to pick up the others?"

"I hope so," said Salasso, eyes closed as Bishlayan's fingers probed

504

around his orbits. He reached inside his torn shirt for a radio, which he powered up and tuned in one-handed.

"Salasso here," he said. "Where are you?"

He listened.

"Go up on the roof," he said, "and wave something conspicuous. Do it now."

Salasso said something saurian to Bishlayan, who nodded. Gail stepped back from the controls as Salasso rose and came forward and stood behind them, gazing intently forward. The entire university area, about a square kilometer, filled the view.

"There they are," said Salasso.

He fingered the controls, and the view zoomed to the flat roof of a building on which two people stood looking up, both waving some white cloth. After another fine adjustment the ship was horizontal again, feathering in to stand beside them. Stone opened the airlock's outer door, and a young man and a young woman clambered through, clutching lab coats.

They smiled at Salasso and Matt and Bishlayan, stared at Gail and Stone. The man looked very like Matt.

"Close the door," said Salasso. Stone jumped to it, and as soon as the last bolt was shot Salasso took the ship up so far the sky turned black, and so fast it was like a blink.

"Stone, Gail," said Matt as the unfelt motion stopped, "meet Gregor and Elizabeth, the owners of this ship."

"Who have not had much say in its disposition," said Elizabeth. "And now—" She sighed. "Salasso, what have you done?"

"You heard me speak?"

"We sure did," said Gregor. "And we heard what happened afterward—live commentary. Gods above, Salasso, we told you before where that sort of preaching can get you!"

"I was not preaching," said Salasso. "I was conveying the results of a scientific investigation."

"Whatever," said Matt. "No time to argue. There's only one safe place for Salasso, and that's Mingulay. You must leave now." He waved a hand. "Well, after you've put us down, I hope."

Salasso took the ship into a descent as Gregor and Elizabeth exchanged dismayed looks.

"Leave everything?" asked Elizabeth.

"What's to leave?" Matt asked. "Science work at the university? You've both given that place a good kick up the ass already. Any work

505

you started, others can finish. The money from the trade—I'll make sure that's banked. The de Tenebres will handle it, and it'll be ready for the next Cairns ship to come here."

"We've made friends—" Elizabeth stopped. "You mean you're not coming?"

"Maybe on the next ship to Mingulay. Right now I have work to do here."

"You're in almost as deep shit as Salasso," said Gregor.

Matt laughed. "I can handle that. Speaking of work, there's stacks of new stuff in the ship's computers. Dig it out. And if you two want to do some more biology, see if you can hack the longevity fix." He passed Gregor a sheet of paper. "Here's how to contact some of the other old cosmonauts. Try to lure them out. See if you can get any of Salasso's fellow heretics to help you study them. Getting a century's start on Nova Babylonia would be worth doing, apart from the obvious, uh, personal benefits."

"We have arrived," said Stone. He was already opening the door.

Startled, Gail looked out of the window and saw the green landing field of Long Bridge.

"Safest place," Matt grinned, "for us. For now."

"Oh, hell, take care," said Elizabeth.

"Say good-bye to Lydia for me," said Gregor.

He and Elizabeth shook hands with Matt, who then, to Gail's astonishment, put an arm around Salasso's narrow shoulders.

"Look after yourself," he said.

Salasso's nictitating membranes flickered.

"You also," he said.

He looked at Bishlayan. "You have not changed your mind?"

"No," she said.

"Good," said Salasso.

Gail and Stone said their good-byes. Gail felt an unexpected pang that she might never see the saur again.

"Thank you for saving me," said Salasso. He was looking at the sky. "Go now."

One by one, Gail, Stone, and Matt leapt down to the grass. Gail caught a glimpse of Gregor closing the outer door, as the ship rose. At a thousand meters it began to move forward, and then its path became a red streak to the horizon.

In the sky high above, as Gail blinked at the afterimage and her ears rang with the sonic boom, she saw two silver specks flying in the same direction, then stop and turn back, cheated of their prey.

The flying club airfield is quiet in the dusk, and the heathen trader who's brought Matt to Rawliston has nothing to say to him and therefore says nothing. Thank the gods for heathendom, where people ignore you just to be polite. Matt shoulders his pack and pauses for a moment as the heathen lugs a couple of heavy bales up to the clubhouse and considers following him. The lights are inviting, and Loudon might be up there. He wants to meet Loudon again, sooner rather than later.

No, later. He turns and takes the path out of the lower end of the airfield, down toward the streets. The path is rough, dusty, and stony. Christ, but it's good to have his boots back, and his own clothes, both retrieved from Long Bridge. It's been a long and involved afternoon up in the Vale. Radios have been among the recent imports, and accounts of the *Bright Star*'s journey are already becoming folklore. Good though it was to see Falling Leaf, Dark Water, Bright Shell, and the other women again, Matt has found that the sketchiest hearsay of what he's done has meant that everybody treats him as a man. Wham, just like that, as sudden as a slap on the back. He hopes Stone doesn't have this same jarring experience. They have had a long discussion about what Stone should and shouldn't say about what he's done. A lot depends on how Stone manages to put across his visionary encounter with a god.

The streets around here are wide, their edges indefinite. The density is somewhere between village street and suburban sprawl. The wooden houses go up to two or three stories. Some have front yards with flower beds and vegetable plots, trickle-irrigated with perforated pipes, amid patches of trampled grass. Nobody bothers with, or can afford, lawns. Cement mixers and old cars and odd agricultural implements are sometimes hauled up there, rusting or under running repair. Shops and cafés and stalls squeeze in between or in front of the houses, lit and advertised by strings of lightbulbs and bended strips of saur-manufactured plastic neon tubing.

People of all ages are on the streets, sitting at stalls or café tables or on their front steps, talking and drinking and smoking. Couples stroll and old men clack dominoes and suck their teeth. Children race everywhere. The younger ones act out barricade battles; the older ones and the teenagers strut in small patrols or make believe their street-corner hangout is a turnout of revolutionary guards. Matt is used to this sort of milieu, he knows just how to slouch and where to look so as not to attract more than a passing glance.

He savors the feeling, which he hasn't had since arriving on Croatan, of being anonymous and alone—a free agent, his own man. He'll miss his Mingulayan friends, little though he's seen of them recently, and he'll miss Salasso a lot. But there's a weight off his shoulders in knowing that they're off his hands.

What he doesn't expect is the acute pang of nostalgia that the smallest hints of a revolutionary situation bring. The raised fingers and raised voices of argument over a crumpled newspaper in a pool of light at a table, the flag on a shop's pole with the Port Authority logo cut out of the middle, the girl on the intersection self-consciously fiddling with her rifle's shoulder strap,—they all sting his eyes and stop his thoughts like a familar but forgotten scent. It triggers memories that go back to his childhood. Despite or perhaps because that revolution had come in the aftermath of military defeat, it had been a relaxed affair, almost lackadaisical. The Russians had done all the hard work, and their version of socialism—a significant upgrade on the one that had crashed in 1991— had turned out to be mutiplatform-compatible and easily enough installed.

Not so easily uninstalled, Matt reflects, though he wasn't around for that.

The streets become narrower, the buildings taller. Matt drops into a bar, a low, wide room hung with bad pottery and wire vines and paper leaves. A score or so of locals are sitting at its tables, and the counter is lined with people on tall stools. Matt buys a liter of beer and a hot smoked sausage with mustard, slings his bag at his feet, and stands at the counter, listening with half an ear to the talk. It's a working-class place, and most of the men and women here are well-dressed for this time of the evening; normally they'd be coming off work about now, still in their sweaty work clothes, but not many have worked today. The revolution is still in a holiday mood. It still smells of soap and cheap perfume and cologne.

The electrostat in the corner chatters, on the hour, and folded sheets of paper fall into the hopper and are passed around—free, if you don't count the advertising. The defeat of the rebel faction of the Port Authority earlier today is no longer news, though above the masthead a line of print still proclaims it's the "Victory Edition!!!"

Almost all the news and comment spins around panicky speculation about ALIENS and POWERS. It's like an invasion is imminent. It's all feeding in to the politics, heating up discussion about the urgency of industrializing, uniting, arming to meet this new threat. The various religious factions have been shaken up as well. The conservative sects, ever ready to see demons in the sky, are crowing. The official church—hitherto confident that the Powers Above are benign—is on the defensive.

Way down on the inside pages, Matt learns that a coalition called the Liberation Front has popped up to plug the program that Volkov relayed earlier today. Parliament and free trade are its bullet points. It's all very moderate. Even parliament won't be an innovation—there's a half-forgotten Council of Notables, elected on the nod, which can be pressed into service simply by reelecting its delegates. Meanwhile they'll serve in consultation with the popular assemblies, the reformed Port Authority, and the Liberation Front. . . .

"Shit!" yelps Matt.

A young couple sitting to his left, who've given the paper the most cursory glance before returning to more interesting matters, give him curious looks.

Matt smiles and shakes his head.

"I beg your pardon," he says.

"What was that about?" the woman asks, amused.

Matt hesitates for a moment. If he starts a political conversation now, he'll be anonymous no longer, even if still alone. Somebody's sure to ask who he is, and he has no intention of lying about it.

"Something in the paper," he says.

"Oh, yeah," says the man. "It's all looking pretty good, isn't it."

"A lot of it is," says Matt cautiously. "It's just that I've realized this city has suddenly got itself a provisional government."

"What?" says the man. "Nah, there's nothing about that."

"Come on," says the woman, "we haven't exactly *read* it yet."

"Yeah, but—"

Together they frown over their own copy. Then they're stabbing their fingers at the exact same inside paragraph that stung Matt.

"You're right," says the man reluctantly. He looks at Matt, shaking his head, then sticks out his hand.

"George Wotton," he says. "And this is my wife, Beth."

"Pleased to meet you. Matt Cairns."

"Oh!" says Beth. "You're the—"

It goes on from there.

Hours later, Matt has wandered all the way down to Back-o'-the-

Docks, repeating and refining the procedure. On the way he runs across several members of the Liberation Front, one or two of whom are, he suspects—though they're cagey about it—also members of the Rawliston branch of the CPEU. (That's what it is, he reckons, that's the clandestine network Volkov has so readily plugged into, and he marvels at the persistence of their unlikely vision.) These know exactly who he is, without any introduction, and eye him warily. But he also meets a rather larger number of radicals who have no connection with Party or Front and who have networks of their own. Their clubs and societies go back at least as far as Rawliston's last revolution, the one some fifty years ago that cost the king his head.

By taking very great care not to have more than one beer in every bar he steps into, and to intersperse bars and beers with cafés and black coffee, he is no more than red-eyed and loquacious by dawn in the King's Head and is able to find on the esplanade an unoccupied bench on which to sleep it off. He wakes at noon with a hangover and a sunburn and a sense of a job well begun, and hitches out the coast road to the Traders' House and pitches in with the repairs, talks to Lydia, has a swim in the sea, and falls asleep, most uncharacteristically, the moment his head hits the pillow of Daphne de Charonea's bed.

Stone woke to such a sense of dread that he wished he could go back to sleep. The small upper room that he and Gail shared was flooded with early sunlight and the crowing, hooting, and honking of the various species of small dinosaur in the village street's yards and pens, and the quarrelsome chirruping of leatherwings roosting under the eaves.

He rolled, under the blanket, and put an arm and a leg around Gail. She stirred, and gradually her lips and eyelids stickily opened. She drew him closer, and they lay silently in the warmth of their mutual nakedness.

"God," she mumbled, "what time is it?"

He glanced at the slope of the sunlight on the stone wall opposite the window. "An hour after dawn."

"God," she said again. She disentangled herself and sat up, gulped water from a mug by the bedstead, splashed some on her fingers, and wiped her face.

"Why are we awake so early?" She blinked wet eyelashes. "Oh. Yes. Big day." She yawned. "I suppose we'd better get up."

"There is no need to get up at once," said Stone.

She slid back down under the blanket and ran her hands over him.

"Are you always like this in the mornings?"

"Yes," said Stone, affecting a complacent gaze at the ceiling.

"This really is something that's different for girls," she said, as he rolled under her touch. "I'm not at my best, you know. And your chin is scratchy. And your . . . mmm . . . ah . . . well . . . waste not, want not, I suppose . . ."

She was quick to slide under him; there were times, as now, when she liked to take his slighter weight on top of her, and it was at those times when he felt most that she was in control, her whole body holding him in its grasp: her heels pressing down on the backs of his legs, her thighs gripping his hips and pacing their rocking rhythm, the swift spasming clutch of her vagina around his penis, her elbows jagged at his shoulders, and her hands full with his hair.

She hauled his head down, held it still against her shoulder, while everything else moved. As she released him he released himself, shuddered, spent, wasted, and wanted.

"Don't stop."

He slid out and moved off and let his fingers take over, marveling anew at the sheer capacity of the woman, at the way she could throw herself at her pleasure again and again.

They flopped together after a while.

"And don't go to sleep again," she said.

"Mmm."

"And don't . . . oh, fuck . . ."

Still sleepy, soon again, but he felt a lot more ready to face the day.

The field above Long Bridge, not the airfield but the meadow that the boys practiced in, was the site chosen for the council. Children carefully gathered dried dung for the fires, but the megatheres, pushed off to rougher pasture, had left fresh steaming pats behind, which not a few of the congregating shamans put a heel down in, or trailed a tattered hem through. The sachems, less fuddled, took better care of their dignity. By foot or boat or glider, they arrived from up and down the Vale. Tents for the shamans and canopies for the sachems formed a vast circle in the field, in the center of which the fires burned. Dried, entire plants of hemp burned along with the dung and brushwood. The mingled sacred and profane smoke lofted a succession of small paper balloons, bearing tiny animal sacrifices or scribbled prayers, to the midday sky and to the gods. The shamans' apprentices capered about, banging drumskins to drive off malign or mischievous spirits. The population of Long

Bridge and its neighboring villages wandered in and out of the circle, or sat on the grass and awaited developments.

Stone waited too, on the paved path. He could feel his knees quivering. The drumming stopped and shamans emerged from their tents, smoke gusting behind them, and converged on the central fire. Sachems ducked out from beneath their canopies and strolled behind or among the shamans. Apprentices hurried to spread straw mats for them all to sit on.

"It's time," said Stone. Gail squeezed his hand and grinned. Together they walked to the middle of the field, the center of the circle, a long hundred meters. The fire heated his face, the smoke made his head swim. Odd details sprang into focus and significance: a crushed flower, a smoke-stunned bee fumbling the air with slowmoving legs as though trapped in honey, a toy glider on the grass.

A space in the circle around the fire had been left for them, and a mat. Stone sat down on it, legs curled. Gail squatted beside him, her forearms resting on her thighs, her hands open and loose between her knees.

Cups of beer and pipes of herb were passed around, along with the most idle comments about the weather, the fishing, the hunting. Gossip about couplings and births, feuds and deaths, more appropriate for old women than for men with deep-lined faces or frightful masks, mingled with jests more apt for boys. In this way an hour passed. To Gail, not understanding most of what was said, it must have dragged even longer than it did for Stone.

Then a sachem away to his left remarked, "They say that Stone from Long Bridge has a message for us from the gods."

It was spoken like gossip, laughed at like a joke, passed on with nudges. Stone joined in the derision himself, and Gail, after a startled glance, did so too. And then everybody looked at her. Silence waited.

"Woman talk to a god," she said. "Sky not fall. Not happen."

Stone winced, but her bad grammar set them all shaking back and forth with indulgent laughter. One shaman fell backward and had to lift his mask a little to recover his breath.

"Perhaps Stone is here," someone said. "It could be that he has something to say."

"We might even have time to listen."

"There is not much to do today."

"It might be a good time to leave, now."

With that they all stood and picked up their mats. Gail looked around and almost rose too. Stone caught her arm in the nick of time.

The shamans and sachems shuffled themselves into two semicircular rows, facing Stone and Gail. As they settled down again Stone turned about, his back to the fire, and urgently gestured to Gail to do likewise. When she had done so he stood up.

"I am Stone from Long Bridge," he said, "and I have come back from a journey on the *Bright Star* into the sky above the sky, where I met a god and was shown visions. I was shown the snake people and the sea people take the sky people from the Cold Lands, as our ancestors have told us. After that, the god showed me many new things." He paused. "We know that the gods do not always agree."

A chuckle came from behind some of the shamans' masks and smiles from the sachems.

"We did not know that the gods at times fight among themselves, as men do, or that they use the different peoples in the worlds of the sky to fight for them. The gods look upon the peoples as we look upon the beasts. We do not hunt the wolf and the great knife-toothed cat, though they hunt the same beasts as we do. The snake people have taught us that if we do that, the grazing beasts will multiply and eat too much grass, so that they all perish together, hunter and hunted alike.

"So it is with the gods and the peoples of the worlds. The god showed me wars in the sky between peoples we know of and peoples we know not, and whichever side wins, the outcome is the same to the gods. They say, it is well.

"It is well for them, but it is not well for the peoples who perish like beasts. I have seen cities greater than the Rawliston of the Christians burn like an oven. I have seen domes on cold moons, filled with hands of hands of crowds of the snake people, crack like a bad pot in a kiln. I have seen forests of people from other worlds, busy and bright and strange, swept away like a fallen branch in a flood. All the different peoples do this to others of themselves, or to other peoples, and always it is the same to the gods. The peoples of the worlds are at war, so that the gods remain at peace, and they say it is well.

"War is coming to our worlds. The god that showed me these things did not know when, but it is coming. We must be ready for it."

What he was saying frightened even him. He fell silent and watched the council rock back and forth on their heels and whisper together. Outside the circle, the crowd of women and warriors and children pressed forward until the bolder children were sent scurrying back by fierce masks glancing over shoulders.

"He is telling us that the gods are evil," said a shaman, the words booming from the mouth trumpet of his mask.

"It is said that the snake man Salasso has been telling the same to the Christians," said a sachem.

Other comments, inaudible to Stone, bounced back and forth among the council members. Their heads swayed from side to side in a ripple that traveled like a gust over grass. Stone waited for it to die down before he spoke up.

"Salasso," he said firmly, "traveled on the *Bright Star* with me. He and I are not saying that the gods are evil. I am saying that what is good or evil in their sight has nothing to do with what is right or wrong in ours."

"It may be," said a Long Bridge sachem, "that the god who spoke with Stone has told him what would be right for us to do."

They all laughed at this.

"No," said Stone. "But Matt Cairns from the *Bright Star,* whom many here have met, has told me some things that we might consider."

The council, and the crowd behind it, stirred again.

"Now *there*'re two names to conjure with," Gail muttered.

"We might consider these things," said a sachem.

"The Christians in Rawliston will soon have a new council," said Stone. "They will make ready for the wars to come, and one of the ways they will do it is by trying to make the Great Vale a part of Rawliston."

He waited for the uproar to subside enough for him to make out the loudest question: "Why would they do that?"

"We have seen," Stone said, "and the Christians have seen, how the *Bright Star* can land wherever its crew pleases, and not only on the sea like the ships of the sea people. They have seen how we are trading for the first time with the star merchants. They know there will be more ships like the *Bright Star,* in the next few hands of years. They expect more traffic on land and sea also. The councils of Rawliston live by taking a small part of the goods that are traded, and they know that our fliers can take our trade high over their heads and out of their hands. They will fight to keep it."

"And what," asked the sachem from Long Bridge, "could we do, if this is to come?"

"What we must do is this," said Stone. "We must trade for rifles, and train all men and women in their use. We must build spears of fire that can destroy the flying machines of the Christians."

The enthusiastic uproar went beyond the council and into the crowd: whoops, yells, brandishing of weapons, drumming of spears on shields. So far, so good. Stone took a deep breath. The last part of Matt's program was the most dangerous and contentious, but it had to be said.

"And at the same time, we must make friends in Rawliston, and not enemies. We must make peace with those of the sky people who have become Christians, and with any Christians in Rawliston willing to take our side. There will be more than we now think. In years to come, if the Christians make war on us, they will arm and lead the savages against us. To prevent that we must make peace with the savages."

He faced a hostile silence. A sachem stood up and walked toward him and peered into his face.

"You are finished?" said the sachem.

"Yes," said Stone.

"You may go."

Stone nodded at Gail to rise, and they walked past the sachem and through the half circle of his fellows. Stone noticed the women from the workshop talking among themselves, grinning, aiming imaginary rifles.

A word of Matt's came to his mind, and he said it.

"This is progress."

"Son of a bitch," said Volkov.

Lydia watched Matt ambling along piling his plate at the breakfast tables and felt like saying the same. His explanation of the *Bright Star*'s sudden departure and his relaying of Gregor's good-bye had been more perfunctory than she felt she deserved. And she had still not forgiven him for his troublemaking intervention on the radio; nor had Volkov.

Matt walked around the drained swimming pool and past neatly stacked rubble, toward their table. Apparently oblivious to their hostility, he sat down opposite them.

He grinned and raised his mug of coffee. "Here's to Rawliston's revolution," he said.

Volkov glowered. "Which you're doing your best to wreck!"

Matt sipped, unperturbed. "Why do you say that?" he asked.

Volkov rubbed his face with his hands, and sighed.

"Very well," he said. "The whole future of this city was being put at risk by an unstable combination of direct democracy and that relic of mercantilism, the Port Authority. By establishing a representative democracy, the people will gain an efficient administration and a social safety valve, both of which are necessary if the next ship from Mingulay isn't to find this place a ghost town or a heap of ruins."

"How dialectical," Matt said. "I suppose the idea of using the direct democracy to reform the relic hasn't crossed your mind."

Volkov sighed his exasperation. "Matt, you really should have lived down your anarchist illusions by now. Free trade and parliamentary democracy are the boringly obvious solutions to this city's problems, and any idea of going beyond that in the next century or so is as futile as it's ultimately reactionary."

Matt nibbled around the stone of an olive while listening to this, then put the remains on the side of his plate as if for later and turned to Lydia.

"This," he said histrionically, "from a member of the party that forced *socialism* on half a continent!"

Volkov looked wearily unimpressed. "Europe was ready for it. Rawliston is not. Get that clear in your head, Matt, and stop trying to muddle the heads of others."

"The night before last," Matt said, "I found a lot of heads that were very clear indeed about what the Council of Notables adds up to. And they didn't like it one bit."

Volkov slammed his fist on the table's bare planks.

"You're playing into the hands of the enemy," he said. "You're playing with fire. You're playing with people's *lives*."

"At least I'm playing through to the endgame," said Matt. "You're leaving in—what, five weeks?"

Volkov shrugged. "That's time enough for the situation to settle down, as long as reckless provocateurs don't blow it all up."

"Speaking of reckless provocations," said Matt, "what do you call urging the heathens to declare the Great Vale a free port?"

Lydia felt a chill in the belly. "Who has done *that*?" she asked.

Matt inclined his head at Volkov. Lydia turned to him, the movement so swift she slipped away a little from him on the bench.

"Tell me you didn't!"

Volkov gave her a baffled look. "I suggested it to Stone, yes."

Lydia felt the gravity fail, felt that endless drop begin. "You must be—" She stopped and shook her head. "No, you're not crazy, or stupid. You must have known what that would do. I've seen scores of cities like this—trade is their life. They'll fight for it. People always do. And if their trade rival is a rabble of hunters and gardeners—gods above, they'll walk over them!"

Volkov smiled and nodded. "Exactly!" he said. "That is the whole point!"

"What do you mean?"

"Look," said Volkov, leaning toward her, spreading his hands, "the idea is bound to come up anyway. The heathens are sharp enough to think of it themselves, if some city entrepreneur doesn't put it to them first. Or the Port Authority will anticipate the possibility. However it plays out, it ends with Rawliston integrating the Great Vale. Potential trade rivalry aside, they can't indefinitely tolerate an enclave of barbarism athwart a strategic position a few tens of kilometers away."

"Yes," said Lydia. "And so?"

"So why not get it over with, while it's still an easy conquest and the cost to both sides is low?" He shrugged. "I don't know if the heathen will fall for it just yet, but it's worth trying. And a short, sharp war with the heathen would consolidate the new regime here. All in all, it would save a lot of lives in the—well, not even the long run, actually. More like over the next decade."

He said this with such expectation of her agreement that she did not doubt he believed every word of it.

She heard Matt's voice as if from a great distance. "You're wrong, Lydia," he said. "He *is* stupid."

Her flaring anger suddenly turned on Matt. "You're no better!" she said. "If you're trying to stir up the people, you're encouraging *civil* war, and that's the worst kind there is!"

"I'm not trying to stir up the people," he said, "and civil war is exactly what I'd like this place to avoid. And they can avoid it, if they dislodge this new government before it's had a chance to consolidate. I don't expect them to launch any wild social experiments, either—just keep open all the possibilities of their existing and quite admirable democracy. Peace with the heathens—inside the city as well as outside—is essential for that. Just as war with them is essential for Volkov's stupid little scheme for an ever-expanding capitalist republic."

"Progress and industrialization," said Volkov. "That's what we need here and on every world. Stagnant little backwaters won't stand a chance when the aliens arrive, or if the gods decide we're getting too big for our boots. Like Salasso said, we have to be ready, we have to work together. Within the next century every human-settled planet will need a space defense capability—one that can handle not just aliens but also asteroid bombardments from the gods. That means heavy industry and nukes, like it or not. And they'll need to actually understand the light-speed drive, make it invulnerable to hacking from the gods any time they want to flick us away like flies."

"You told me about a map," Lydia said. "The one that Tola showed you, a way out of these confrontations, by spreading out through the galaxy. Wouldn't that be an alternative to your"—she screwed up her eyes and shook her head, restraining her words—"*vision* of war with the gods?"

Volkov shot her an impatient glance.

"We have no basis for trusting that map, or that idea, because it itself was a move in whatever game the gods are playing."

Matt looked about to say something, but Lydia got in first.

"That doesn't *matter*," she said. She put her fists to her forehead, as if to stop her head from exploding.

"The point—the point—the point is, if we're being manipulated from above, it's no answer for us to manipulate those below us, because that could just be . . . an extension of the same strings, farther downward."

Matt nodded enthusiastically. "Yes!" he said. "But—what do you mean, exactly, by 'those below us'?"

"Oh, *you* know," Lydia said, waving her hand. "The people of the shore."

Matt placed rinds and crusts on his plate and stood up. "That was what I thought you meant," he said.

As he walked away through the passageway to the beach, Lydia was surprised to feel within her as much regret and reproof as she had heard in his voice.

"What was that about?" she asked Volkov.

He waved a hand. "Matt likes to pretend he is an ordinary worker, a man of the people. It's as decadent an affectation as any I've come across in the great houses." He smiled. "Not in yours, I hasten to add."

"I thought you believed in equality."

"Yes, I do treat people as equals, whenever possible. Life is more pleasant that way, believe you me. But I am not going to pretend there is real equality between people who live and die in one small span of space and time, and people like us who stride across centuries. You are right—the people of the shore are below us, and cannot *but* be below us. We have responsibilities to them, but they are measured on a different scale from our responsibilities to each other."

"Oh?" she said. "So the people you've been working with, your comrade Endecott and so on, they're just tools to be used?"

He shook his head. "By no means. No more than your family's shore agents are to you. But, in all honesty, look around you." His wave took in the growing breakfast crowd of the clan. "You'll all be back here in another couple of centuries—a year in your life. These walls will be more worn, that ivy will be thicker, the glass in the windows will be less transparent, and you will be more beautiful than you are now. And the people of Rawliston will be the descendants of the people you have met on this visit. The events of the present will be history, perhaps proud history. The name of Endecott may be one that children read about in school. This is real to you, yes?"

"Yes," she said. "I've been here before, and—yes."

"All right," he said. "These people you'll meet a year from now are real to you, as real as the people in the cars buzzing by outside. How do you do the right thing by them?"

Lydia thought about it. It was like a logic puzzle, something that you could work out, but it was one for which she knew the answer already. She had been taught the answer, back when she was almost too young to understand it. Esias had stood over her while she frowned at the black numbers in the big books.

"Well, you, you—for a start you trade honestly with the people here now, you make sure the finances and the funds and the contracts are all in order, so that, you know, you aren't leaving some terrible speculative bubble behind that'll wreck their economy or anything, because then there'll be nothing here for you to come back to. You make sure the shore agents' businesses are sound. You make sure the crew doesn't spread diseases or leave any uncared for pregnancies, and so on."

Volkov looked at her with evident disbelief.

"In other words," he said, "you behave no differently from how you would if you were meeting the same people again a year from now? Treating people ethically in the present is exactly the same as doing the right thing by their descendants?"

"Yes!" She smiled at him, delighted that he had got the point. Then she recalled their preceding argument, and frowned. "So how can you justify trying to start a war now, in the hope that it'll make things better for people in ten or a hundred years?"

"I am *not*," he said, "trying to start a war. You know as well as I do that a clash between the people of the Great Vale and Rawliston will take place, regardless of anything we may do. The question is, will that war be soon and swift, or late and long?"

"You've said that before," she said. "And that is not the question. It is not the question *for you*. Or for me, either. It's a question for the political leaders of the two societies—kings, councillors, elders, bureaucrats, whatever. They can make that decision, for good or ill. It's *their* responsibility. And who's to say that something you haven't anticipated at all won't make the whole issue redundant?"

Volkov smiled. "That's just leaving it to chance," he said, "and that, too, is a choice."

"I see what you mean," she admitted. "All right. You tell me how you see our—or your—responsibilities to those people I'll meet in a year."

"Very well," said Volkov. "It's worthwhile, it's in our interests and in theirs, that they should have as good a life as possible. Anything we can do now to promote the progress of industry and society means more, richer, and very likely happier people up the line."

Up the line, indeed! You are not a god, she thought, and said, "Even if it means sacrificing people in the present?"

" 'Sacrifice' is not a word I would use," said Volkov. "But some additional suffering now for the sake of less suffering and more happiness later—yes, that is acceptable."

"It's for those who'll bear the suffering to decide whether it's acceptable!"

"They rarely can," said Volkov. "Every militia officer here may have to order people to certain death, in an attack on a pirate stronghold, let's say, for the sake of, oh, some greater good like a reliable margin of profit on shipping."

"That's war itself, that's different—"

"It's no different in civil life. When this benighted hole finally introduces adequate sewerage in the poorer quarters, the number of laborers who'll die in the diggings can be predicted—in round figures, to the nearest ten—by any experienced actuary or civil engineer. But the number of lives saved by that sewerage system can also be calculated, in the hundreds of thousands."

Lydia shook her head. "All the people involved in that are reckoning their own risks, whereas you are reckoning people as costs. I don't deny that people in a position of responsibility have to make hard choices, but that responsibility is itself a cost. You're making that calculation without any cost to yourself. If your friend Endecott were to urge war sooner rather than later, fine, I could respect that, because he'd be taking the risks—political defeat, assasination, or even the thought that two hundred years from now children will know his name only because their mothers use it to frighten them."

Volkov rubbed his temples. "I take a risk, too, but I still say that the future well-being of the people—"

"You mean, the well-being of future people!"

"Yes. It's something we can legitimately take into account because we will live to see it, and the people of the present, here, won't."

"We take it into account in the present," she said, "by honest accounting." She smiled as she said it, hoping somehow to stop this difference becoming a dispute.

Then Volkov said, "You may see it differently when you've lived long enough."

And that got to her; she was furious. She stood up, scraped her thighs as she stepped sideways between the table and the bench, and stalked around in front of him and leaned forward, fists on the table.

"Listen," she said, "I may be younger than you, but I've lived through history hundreds of years longer than you have. I've seen dozens of worlds, I've seen cities rise and fall, and my family have seen more and longer and they have taught me what is right, and I *know* that it works, I know that doing right by people who may live *now* is the same as doing right by people who may live *then,* and I know that what you've tried to do is wrong."

"Lydia, wait—"

She turned on her heel and walked away, down to the beach. The early sun boomed on the water. An onshore breeze made the sand hiss at her feet. After a few minutes her lips tasted salty. She found Matt sitting on a tussock a few hundred meters to the north of the house, morosely chucking stones seaward and doodling on the dune's slope with a bit of driftwood. Any patterns he made were being obliterated by the sand dislodged by their making.

"Hi."

"Hello." She sat beside him. They both stared out to see for a while, then Lydia exploded again.

"Bastard! I—like him a lot, but he can be a patronizing, arrogant, strutting, stupid bastard sometimes."

Matt turned a twisted smile on her. "Now you know what it's like," he said, "to be one of the people of the shore."

"But *we* don't treat them like that! That's what I've just been arguing with him about!"

"Oh, Lydia de Tenebre," he said, "if you just knew. You traders, you don't see what you do to people, to societies. You fuck them up! You kick them forward, or off their tracks, you change them forever with the new ideas and new goods you bring, and you come back in two hundred years when the dust has settled, and you do it all again."

"But we do it *honestly*."

"You do it blindly. It isn't your fault. But Grigory Andreievich and I have lived through in slow motion what you see in time lapse, and it . . . gets wearing, after a while."

"Maybe when everybody lives as long as you do," she said, "it'll be different."

"Yeah, it'll be different all right. Very different indeed, for Nova Babylonia." He laughed. "Especially if Grigory gets to work there like he's doing here."

"We have to take him to Nova Babylonia," she said. "We agreed, we made a contract. But—I'm afraid, my father is afraid, of what he'll do when he gets there."

"Join the club," said Matt.

"You're the only person who can stop him, or act as a balance, or something," she said.

"Yeah," said Matt, with some bitterness. "And I've a lot still to do, right here. I've been intending to stay until it's done."

"There's more to do on Nova Terra," she said. "Truly, and so much more at stake! And—and—"

She stopped. He smiled at her, a warm and open smile this time.

"You'd take me there?"

"Yes."

He stared out to sea, then after a minute turned sharply. "All right," he said. "St. Teilhard's Day. It's a date."

She looked at him, puzzled. "I know it's a *date*."

He laughed and explained, and they walked together back to the house.

Later that day, Matt moves out of the Traders' House and into a single room with a single bulb at the back of Back-o'-the-Docks. He has a small stash of money from the ship's trading profits, more than enough to live on. But he takes a job all the same, casual labor at the docks. He's desperate to find out what's really going on and what people are really thinking, and he can't do that from the Traders' House, or (regretfully) from talking to people in bars.

Over the next week some events move faster than Matt expects, others slower. The anxiety about the news brought by the *Bright Star* doesn't so much subside as seep into the groundwater of people's awareness, becoming a background radiation in every serious discussion. It fuels the street scuffles between gangs of youths from Dawsonite and anti-Dawsonite neighborhoods, and between heathens and Christians, that are a regular part of the annual buildup to St. Teilhard's Day. A few unions, emboldened by the response to the political strike, press claims on their employers. Most of them are settled quickly, all of them without serious trouble.

The neighborhood and municipal assemblies are in more or less continuous uproar about the new and still fluid arrangements but are just as continually one step behind events as the Port Authority is reformed, its militia purged and reorganized, and the Council of Notables hurries to forestall objections, to meet disagreement halfway, to draw dissenters into labyrinthine committees, and to rush through a few social reforms: Primary education is to become compulsory, street cleaning is to be municipalized, the poor are to get scrip to pay for medical attention. Elections are duly scheduled for just after the festival, and the Liberation Front fields a slate on which Endecott is the candidate for Verdant Heights. Volkov vanishes from the public prints and the radio channels.

Matt isn't bothered. Daphne keeps track of Volkov's activities and passes on the information by radio or in person. He himself keeps track of Volkov's influence and ideas, which keep cropping up: The "Great Vale problem" is mooted in every forum, from the serious radio panels to the hourly sensation sheets. The drug traffic, sectarian and racial tensions, possible military dangers are all attributed to its anomalous autonomy.

It's a radio message from Loudon that Matt most eagerly awaits. Near the end of the week, he receives it. Gail, Stone, and Slow Leg have arrived at the airfield.

The three of them meet him in a shebeen in the heathen area bordering Back-o'-the-Docks and pass on their news very quietly.

The council of the sky people have decided to attack Rawliston.

"They decided *what?*"

Gail looks about anxiously. "Keep your voice down," she says.

The whole dive is full of scores of heathens busy getting drunk or preparing for the one big colorful event in their year, the St. Teilhard's Day parade.

"All right," Matt says, leaning in and speaking more quietly. "So what the fuck *happened*?"

He's doing it again, his voice rising in indignant incredulity.

"I said just what you asked me to say," Stone tells him, looking apologetic. "Something may have got lost in the translation."

"You're not fucking kidding," says Matt. "I mean, didn't the women object?"

"They're all for it," says Gail, with infuriating enthusiasm. "The sachems—these elders and wise men and brave warriors and so on who make up the councils—they're elected by the women. The council went on for three days and nights, and I think most of the real decisions were made in the nights."

Stone nods. "Yes. The women talk among themselves, and the sachems talk things over with their women in the evenings, and they go to the council the following day and puff out their chests and talk big and say what their women tell them to say. More or less."

"I know how your system works," says Matt. "I just don't understand what's in it for them."

"War industry," says Gail. "More prestige. Less alcohol and more useful tools getting in. Stuff like that."

Stone and Slow Leg nod soberly and sip their beers.

"I can see some problems with the logistics," Matt says dryly.

"Ah, but you gave us the answer to that," says Slow Leg. "We make friends with the sky people in Rawliston, and they will help us. They will be what Gail calls a 'fifth column.' "

Matt makes a show of looking over the people around them. Men in grubby work clothes or luridly natty suits drink cheap beer and bad whiskey and talk raucously among themselves above the maddening sound of the fiddlers at the back. Overweight mothers tipple gin while stitching sequins on festival costumes for their skinny daughters, some of whom are looking after their younger siblings by plying them with dilute drinks. Others look far too young to be talking to the men they're talking to.

"This lot?" says Matt. "They're hopeless. Every year they get dressed up for the carnival, and every year the young men get tanked up for it and start a riot afterward—payback for Dawson's Night, I guess—and every year they get hammered."

"We can give them hope," says Slow Leg. "We can bring them back to the ways of the sky people."

"Something did get lost in translation," says Matt. "I wanted you to be ready for an attack *from* Rawliston, not to . . . Have you any idea what that could provoke?"

Slow Leg bristles. "It is we who are provoked," he says. "We are provoked by the way our people are treated in this city. We are provoked by what we hear spoken about us on the radios, which is as you said— some people in the new councils of the Christians are preparing to attack us. We have to stand up for ourselves, because we know now that the gods do not care about us. The gods are happy if the peoples fight each other. Very well, we will make them happy."

Matt feels cold with dismay. "Is that how you understand the news from the gods?"

"Yes," says Slow Leg.

"I too," says Stone.

Matt turns to Gail for help. "We have to stop this."

Gail looks back, poker-faced. "As well try to stop an avalanche," she says. "You know what the sky people are like, once they make up their minds."

Matt sighs. "All right," he says. "And when do they intend to . . . make their move?"

Stone looks away from a process of fairy-wing construction that has held his gaze for the past five minutes.

"St. Teilhard's Day," he says.

13

St. Teilhard's Day

A DINOSAUR HEAD grins in through the window, and when Matt wakes up the sight makes him jump. He takes in the green and red and white painted colors just as the papier-mâché shape sways away. He hears again the sounds that woke him: the rattling whack of sticks, rhythmic shouts. It's intimidating enough to be reassuring.

He rolls out of the bed and moves sidelong to the window at its foot and slides it up and leans out, into the air of a fine morning, the blue of the sky still pale above the roofs, sea smell faint on the breeze. In the street below, the front half of the dinosaur is waltzing around independently of the rear, and along fifty meters of sidewalk a hundred or so half-naked young men are facing off each other and practicing attack and defense moves with staves.

"Hey!" *Thwack!* "Hey!" *Thwack!* and the thump of feet wearing good industrial boots that kick up dust as the men leap from one stance to another.

Farther down the street the festival's floats—or very large costumes—are marshalling, the nearest being a brightly colored representation of a balloon train complete with red silk streamers sent fluttering up by a gust from a bellows arrangement. Lithe heathen girls prance or pose in gorgeously embroidered tunics and trousers or in gaudy silk costumes of insects and fairies and leatherwings. Their big mamas sail out of the doorways in Sunday best dresses and wide-brimmed flower-laden hats; their fathers strut in dandy suits, twirling canes, while their brothers, bare-chested in Christian casuals, toyi-toyi and flourish spears and staves.

Time to get moving. He wraps a towel around himself, hurries down the greasy-carpeted corridor to the washroom, splashes water on his face and on the back of his neck, returns to the room, and climbs into clean clothes and hauls on his jacket and checks the contents of the pockets. The knife he lost has been replaced by one heavier and nastier. Pistol and ammo, check. Radio and earpiece, check. Something else. Look around. Plastic half-liter water bottle, he'll need that too. Fills it at the washroom. Remembers to piss.

Clatters down the wooden stairs, careful not to snag the cleats of his boots on the frayed death-trap carpet, and out into the street. Glances up at the heathen lads, sees Slow Leg, who doesn't see him. Good. No complications. Matt ducks away down a side alley. A few more turns and he's in Back-o'-the-Docks.

The streets are already filling up with people and floats taking their places—it's a big, big day here, as big as it is for the heathen. Stilt walkers and jugglers, acrobats and dancers, gigants and pithkies, costumes and floats—some of which even celebrate the revolution: hardboard mock-ups of armored cars with broom handles poking out the windows and people in real or fake militia uniforms trotting alongside. Or they will, when they've got moving and stopped milling around. Every mollyboy in the place is out, in tarty gear or posh frocks or outrageous drag or costumes with long nodding feathered headdresses and hoop skirts up to three meters across.

He jogs and dodges through the streets, out of the district and into the warehouse zone, long wasteland streets with no windows and then out to the front and the shore road beyond that spread the docks and the quays. Traffic is diverted and in any case slack for the holiday. The cranes, and some ships in the harbor, are decked with bunting and banners. Two starships out in the roads—the Rodriguezes', due to leave for Mingulay tomorrow, and the de Tenebres', which will leave later today for its next stopover on the way to Nova Terra. Skiffs are already flitting back and forth.

Lydia will pick him up on one of them, at nine this evening. If he lives that long.

Had a good run anyway. Like a Galápagos tortoise. Memory of looking on television at eyes that had looked at Darwin . . .

Slows to a juddery walk, breath heaving, sweat springing. Slings the weapon-weighted jacket over one shoulder and saunters in to the first rendezvous, a dockside greasy spoon. Long counter, a few tables, smell of coffee and onions. Not busy today, ten of the dozen customers parked along the counter are his lads. All of them work at the docks but only two of them are dockers, guys who actually load and unload cargo, that being a tightly closed shop and one that Volkov's local Party branch has been well dug into for generations. The men who aren't dockers are casual or low-grade, rough and unrespectable and young. He's worked a few days with them, off and on, in the past weeks. They know he's off the *Bright Star* and they think he's a Mingulayan. He has found them already more hostile than he is to the new government, and they're ready for action today.

He greets them and slides on to a tall rickety chair by the counter and orders a big fry-up and coffee, skins up a quick cigarette while he's sipping the first cup and waiting for the food. The nicotine and caffeine deliver quite a hit in oxygenated blood.

Smudged electrostat paper passes along to him.

"What d'you reckon to that, Matt?"

The sensation of the hour is an announcement that the Great Vale is about to proclaim itself a free port. It's made all the more urgent by some unsourced speculation that the Mingulayan Cosmonaut Families have built lots more ships already, they aren't going to wait for the *Bright Star* to come back before sending them out, packed to the airlocks with goods and adventurers. This part of the story has a lot of plausible detail about how the drive's more exotic components could have been bought from saurs influenced by Salasso, who has plugged just that sort of cooperation.

The waitress places the plate in front of him. He smiles thanks and takes a bite or two, thinking. Mustn't show himself bothered at all about this. The lads are joking with the waitress or calling new orders; the cook, short and fraught under a cap, is yelling obscure personal insults back.

Matt puts down his fork, swallows, hands the paper back to Dave Borden.

"Load of bull," he says, loud enough for everyone to hear. "No way did they have more ships on the go when we left, and no way at all could any have been built in three months."

"You sure about that?" one of the dockers asks, leaning in and looking along. "Once you've got the drive, all you need is a fucking *airtight box*."

"Not if you don't know for sure where you're going," Matt says. "We didn't, not definitely. Anybody who leaves before the *Bright Star* gets back won't know either. Leap in the fucking dark, man."

"What about the heathens?" Borden asks. "Looks like they're trying to shaft us after all."

Matt grins at him. "I told you, didn't I? Told you somebody would set up a provocation. This is it."

"Thought you meant the heathen buggers making trouble, or some of the anti-Dawson crowd mixing it with the parade. You didn't say nothing about this."

"No, I didn't," Matt admits. "Wouldn't make any difference if I had. Both these stories are lies."

He finishes his breakfast. Rolls another cigarette and says, "Okay, anyone got the map?"

Somebody has the parade committee's flyer, showing the routes. Matt slides it into the electrostat's copy facility, marks a few points on the copy, then copies that nine times, hands them out.

"O-*kay*. The actual church contingent assembles on Piltdown Rise, in front of the cathedral. The rest arrive by feeder routes from Back-o'-the-Docks, the heathen district, the university, and the three parks uptown. All of them fall in behind the bishop's lot, by the numbers, as it moves off. Down the hill, along the riverside, wheel around over the bridge, onto the shore road, along past here, then the religious procession itself goes on to the quays to watch the bishop splash holy water in the harbor while everyone else swings around into Back-o'-the-Docks by midafternoon, the militias peel off, and . . . then it's up to them. All we have to do is stop trouble breaking out along the parade route. Everyone clear?"

Everyone was.

"Right, these X's on the map are good points for an attack—awkward corners, open stretches, narrow streets with alleys, that sort of thing. We'll have at least a dozen good lads and lasses at each of them, tooled up."

Matt flashes a grin along the long counter.

"And down here," he adds, "we have us."

Gets a laugh. Small pang of conscience.

"Lucky for us the other groups peel off one by one if the parade goes past without trouble, and by the time it reaches here—flashpoint central, thanks to the docks, the PA goons and that crap in the paper—they'll all be ready to back us up."

"Show them," Borden says. "Fucking PA scabs."

Bit of back-and-forth follows, but by the time he leaves they're all on line about what to do. His breakfast is too heavy for him to jog so he walks fast and consults the bus timetable on the side of the map. The heat of the day is beginning to build up. Bored militia people in crisp new uniforms stand at the junctions of a shore road still almost empty of traffic. The reformed and expanded Port Authority militia, not the neighborhood militias controlled by the assemblies.

That story, now, about the heathens, and the ships coming soon, that's a good one. He wonders who's behind it; it strikes him as too reckless a provocation even for Volkov. The folk most likely to be agitated by it are the dockers, and behind them the people who rallied to the rebel elements in the Port Authority: the compradores and their employees. They're like retainers of some great family that has lasted for centuries and whose empty castle they tend for generations. Every century or so the castle floods with light and dancing and wealth, then the lights go out again, the party's over. . . . There's something feudal about the relationship. Dependence. The people of the shore.

Thinking about Lydia again, and about Daphne. Stop now or accept another two-hundred-year obsession. That is not funny. If you outlive everyone you love, what you accumulate is losses. It's too frightening.

So run around that corner, swing onto a bus, grinding up the long, gradual incline to Piltdown Rise. Strap-hang amid chattering people. Think. If some of the dockers are swayed by the story, a big part of the plan, one of its thrashed-out selling points, is in big trouble. His side absolutely has to command the docks by evening. It's been a promise and one he dare not break.

He looks at the baffling, tiny-printed instructions on the back plate of his radiophone, works through the fine-tuned wavelengths for the other groups in his bootstrapped organization. Everybody's in place and on the ball. No trouble so far. He calls Gail and passes on the warning.

Gail let the hood of the club's old car fall shut. It made a tinny clunk rather than a satisfying slam, but she was happy with the work she'd done under it. The engine note was as clean as it would ever be, even if it could never be described as a purr.

"Okay, you can turn it off!" she shouted. Stone leaned in through the open door and groped under the dashboard. The engine stopped, without so much as a cough. Stone grinned out at her and stuck a thumb up. She smiled back at his small triumph. Together they walked across to the shed where the heathens stashed their gliders. Normally there would be only two or three at a time in it. Today, there were dozens.

Gail and Stone spread them out on the grass to let the dew, still present on the wings, dry off. A heady scent rose from the doped silk as it warmed up. When they had finished, a great expanse of the field looked as though a flock of giant butterflies had landed on it. Then they had to gather them up again, beginning with the first ones they'd laid out, now dry but in danger of warping if they were left too long in the sun.

"Oh, Christ," she said as they slumped, shoulders aching, in the shed's shade. "I hope this works."

As if in answer, she glimpsed a party of warriors from the Vale, trotting through the long grass at the edge of the field. They reached the dusty path to the streets and disappeared down it at a run.

"It'll work," said Stone. "Matt is cunning."

"Cunning isn't enough," Gail said.

Matt's warning about trouble down at the docks was preying on her mind; it could throw the plan off course. Those weeks of agitating and organizing, of calling in favors, of words in the right places, could all come to nothing.

"Timing is everything," she said. "And keeping the plan secret, from both of our sides, both columns"—she moved her hands together—"and from the other side."

She turned and looked into Stone's eyes. "And hitting the right targets."

"That's a lot of everything," he said.

The bus climbs slowly through the industrial zone, turns on to a broad avenue, and stops a few hundred meters from the assembly point. Everybody piles out, and Matt accompanies them to the big tree-lined public square in front of the cathedral. A crowd has already gathered there, a thousand or more. It's more respectable looking than the one Matt woke up to, but its folk art is no less colorful. The bishop, clergy, and choir are gathered around a crucifix and a large gilt omega symbol. Silk banners with portrayals of the saint's mild, studious features flap from long poles. In among the suits and Sunday best, kids cavort in costumes of dinosaurs, megatheres, ape-men, saurs, and krakens. Scores of the congregated parishioners are gigants and pithkies themselves, and their encounters with hairy-costumed, prognathous-masked *H. sap.* children are droll and, as far as Matt can make out, good-humored.

He makes his way to the ornate black notice board that projects above the churchyard wall and scans its gilt lettering while waiting for the procession to move off. The Anglican Church of Rawliston. A branch of the Extraterrestrial Episcopal church. Matins, choir practices, communions. Christenings first Sunday of the month. Visitors welcome.

It's no more absurd than any of the other institutional continuities with Earth that abound in the Second Sphere, but it strikes Matt as simultaneously ridiculous and magnificent. There's a dauntless defiance in its stubborn mundanity, its refusal to let mere distance make a difference to the spirit.

A murmur and a hush ripple concentrically across the crowd, and Matt turns to see the bishop hold aloft, in succession, a cranium, a mandible, and a femur, while intoning in a resonant, nasal voice into a silence broken only by the inevitable shuffles and coughs. Matt catches the occasional sonorous phrase: "... teach us to see in these fraudulent relics the many levels of Your truth . . . in the stumblings of our science the mystery of Your ways . . . Your wisdom in our foolishness . . . unity in multiplicity . . . all Your children, whatever our outward form . . ."

This is enough to kick Matt's atheist reflexes back into action, and he irreverently rolls and lights a cigarette. Drumbeats and flutes and jangles announce the imminent arrival of other contingents. Through the trees, Matt can see banners waving and drumsticks spinning up in the air on two of the square's four approach roads. The bishop replaces the fake bones in the reliquary and, bearing it on one shoulder and carrying his crozier in the other, leads off. Matt lets the crowd move out of the square before stubbing out the cigarette and falling in at the rear, behind a tinfoil imitation of a gravity skiff in which children with big saur heads on their small shoulders bob and wave.

The first of the feeder marches closes the gap behind him, and before long he's walking immediately in front of the marching band of a merrier and noisier but still relatively restrained contingent from the nearest middle-class neighborhood. Their particular kick is historical military reenactment, and they're in the helmets and cuirasses of the colony's early militia; the companies of men behind the band shoulder obsolete but real rifles. Matt moves sideways onto the sidewalk for a bit, checking it out. The women stride along in russet skirts and checkered shawls and kerchiefs, and their rifles or maybe muskets look even older and longer, but no less real, than those carried by the men. Matt suspects that this whole theatrical display has the unspoken function of protecting the congregation up ahead as well as the other denominational contingents immediately behind.

One lot less to worry about, then. Let the faithful look after their own. He lets the church groups go by and falls in behind the first of the Christian heathen sections of the march, which forms a long and flexible shock absorber between the religious groups and the overtly secular revellers from the working-class districts, the university, and Back-o'-the-Docks. For the first time the smell of marijuana smoke is heavier in the air than that of incense.

Ten of the heathen infiltrators have taken the lead in stewarding this section and have got the rest of the young men running and toyi-toying up and down the sides, handling their fake spears as real staves. They're enforcing a strict alcohol discipline as well, forcibly swapping beer bottles for spirit bottles with anyone caught swigging out of the latter.

Matt slow-walks back into a factory section. He feels out of place among all the matching logo-flash overalls and the floats of sheet-plastic replicas of steam-driven machinery, and drifts back again, bypassing the company's sponsored neighborhood militia unit, until he's in a union section. An oompah band and banners and another tight militia platoon bringing up the rear. He sticks with them until they reach the first potential flashpoint, a corner with a small park opposite and an anti-Dawsonite district just across the grass.

He ducks out and joins up with the squad there, local kids whose slightly unconventional appearance and attitudes have got them roughed up a few times by local toughs. They're sitting on a couple of dilapidated benches and watching the procession and sipping beer. One or two of them are lolling on the other side of the benches, keeping a lookout across the park at the row of rundown shops and houses opposite. A few furled banners are stacked alongside, with strong, thick poles sticking out and easily removed.

"All quiet so far?" he asks, sitting down on an iron curlicue of armrest and gratefully accepting a beer.

"Yeah, fine," says Annie Gibbs, who seems to be the unopposed leader of this particular cell of anarchists. She's light-skinned enough to be a heathen and has her fair hair done in braids, heathen man style, and wears a formal shirjack over scuffed leather trousers. She has read a lot about anarchism.

"Time to move on?"

"Don't think so," says Matt. "Let's stick around, run on to the next unit after a few of the obvious easy targets go past. So far it's all been well defended."

"Noticed."

"This usual?"

She gives him a *where-you-been?* look.

"Nah," she says. "See the factory militia groups? None of that last year. Bosses didn't like them, then, see." Grins ironically. "It's the revolution, wow!"

"Could be," says Matt, carefully noncommittal. "Or maybe just that there's a bit more tension about anyway."

"Same thing, kind of. See that report about the heathens up the Vale?"

"Yeah," says Matt. "What do you make of it?"

"Somebody's fucking winding us up," she replies without hesitation. "War is the health of the state and all that, and somebody wants the state a bit healthier."

Sharp. Matt nods eagerly, keeping one eye on the procession.

The kid sitting on the back of the bench taps Annie's shoulder. "Trouble," he says quietly. "Don't all jump up."

Matt doesn't even turn around. He keeps looking at the section of the passing parade that's coming around the corner. It's not Back-o'-the-Docks yet, but it's definitely more colorful now, lots of mollyboys, lots of girls and women, hoopskirts and headdresses, glitter and glitz; the heathens in this lot are just strolling along or dancing behind the band, and there's no defense group in sight, and the next group up the hill is from the university, not much help there unless—ah, yes, somewhere way up there he can see the banners of the cadets.

This all takes a second or two. The back of his neck prickles. He turns around slowly. It takes him a moment to spot what the potential trouble is, and he almost laughs: Outside a grogshop a hundred meters away on the far side of the patchy, littered park, a group of about twenty men has gathered, and they're waving bottles and jeering and gesturing.

"Fucking chimps," he says.

Annie moves slowly to the stacked banners. "That pub can hold a hundred, and believe me it can empty fast."

Shit, it's serious. It'll be hand-to-hand in seconds: bottles, knives, staves, and fists. And his two pistols, if need be. He can't let it come to that.

"Pick up the poles," Annie's saying, "one by one, and just kind of saunter over to the side of the march and spread out in line, holding them horizontal. Face out."

They do that. More crawling feelings arise on the back of his neck until he turns around. The knot at the grogshop has grown but hasn't moved forward. Matt leans back, looking to his right; every time he sees a heathen man capering by he nods and glances at the hostiles.

Some of the lads just laugh, or are too drunk or stoned to comprehend or care. One or two respond by taking a place in the thin line. Annie starts calling out something in the heathen speech, and after a couple of minutes their group of ten has been joined by at least as many again, forming a solid human barrier at the outer side of the corner.

The grogshop's customers go back inside, just as the student cadets' first drum majorettes swing around the corner. The heathens jog off to catch up with their own section.

Matt checks his memories of the order of the rest of the procession and looks back up the street as far as he can see, to check, and decides that it's safe to move on to the next danger point. He passes this on, and he and Annie's group set off at a fast pace, cutting through some backstreets to where a dozen heathen road workers are awaiting them, resting casually on their picks and shovels at a junction, and just as casually eyeing up a small but militant fundamentalist congregation massed in a side street with placards denouncing heathens, sodomites, and Dawsonites.

That too passes peacefully, and the road menders join the squad as it moves briskly on. The weight of their shouldered tools doesn't slow them down. They have the hunter-gardener physique. Matt doesn't, and he welcomes the cooler air down by the Big River, after two more such standoffs and subsequent reinforcements to the flying defense squad. He accepts every friendly offer of water or beer that comes his way.

By the time Matt reaches the bridge he has almost forty people with him. They split up, a score on either side of the bridge's debouchment, not really noticeable among all the other bystanders crowding the pavement and the way, and once again watch the parade pass and keep watch. Let it all get past this chokepoint, follow it over the bridge, then overtake the more vulnerable sections and join up with the dockworkers for the final potential flashpoint. That's without a doubt the most dangerous of all, what with angry dockers, heathen lads with a bit too much alcohol and cannabis and adrenaline in their blood, and the nervy new PA militia in the mix.

Annie's standing beside him, grinning, barely out of breath. Matt shares his beer with her, and as he watches the now-familiar forward half of the march go by—there go the science students again, and their giant cardboard microscope with a white-coated student, a giant foil pin projecting from his midriff, wriggling on its slide and waving cheerfully—his brain catches up with what its subroutines have been mulling over all the while.

It's the sight of a truck bed with two-meter-high imitation test tubes racked on it, with plastic extensions to the exhaust pipe ingeniously funnelled through to make fumes come out of the tubes, that suddenly crystalizes a suspicion from his inchoate thoughts: Avakian!

All the connections click into place. The apothecary has a commercial relationship with the Rodriguezes, heathen contacts who trade in legitimate (and possibly other) medicinals, and knows enough about the fabrication units and the drive's construction to supply convincing details.

Matt turns around, leans over the stone parapet, and drops his empty bottle on the low-tide boulders below. It shatters with a satisfying crash.

"Bit antisocial of you," Annie reproves.

"You're right. Damn." Matt turns back, slightly contrite. "I just figured out who's behind today's big provocation, and it's a guy I thought was a friend."

"Just because you're paranoid doesn't mean they aren't out to get you," says Annie.

Matt marvels momentarily at the staying power of old anarchist saws. She probably thinks that if voting changed anything they'd make it illegal, and . . . but this is being patronizing, she's the most solid and reliable and political person he's met all day. A big boxy float negotiates the corner on to the bridge, then one stacked with multicolored bales, and the next is a four-meter-long model of a starship, very light because it's being carried on poles on the shoulders of just four men, and behind them another big cardboard imitation crate, planking sketched on it in splashy lines of black paint . . . Matt suddenly realizes that he's watching the dockers' union contingent.

And strolling along with them, chatting amiably, is a skinny young man with a briefcase under his arm. Endecott sees Matt at the same moment and makes a gesture of apology to the docker he's speaking with and nips smartly out of the parade and over.

"Hi, Matt," he says, with a quick polite nod to Annie and a wary glance over her comrades. "Christ, I've been looking for you everywhere."

"I could say the same," says Matt, though in truth he has almost forgotten in the heat and rush. "I'm afraid there'll be trouble down at the docks."

"Yeah, tell me about it. Since that story broke I've been . . ." He jerks a thumb over his shoulder. "Half the goddamn union branch didn't even come on the march. They're probably sitting in pubs working themselves up to bash some heathen heads."

"Bad news. What about the Party branch?"

Endecott's sandy eyebrows twitch, very slightly.

"They're solid. Most of them."

"What party?" Annie asks suspiciously.

"Uh, later," says Matt. He has an absurd flash-forward of her taking Endecott to task over Kronstadt, Makhno, the Barcelona Telephone Exchange . . . "Think your backsliding dockers are likely to throw rocks at the parade?"

Endecott winces. "Worse. Lading tackle. Big lumps of metal."

"Christ! Got any plans to deal with it?"

"Damn right I have." He glances again at the squad, and its counterpart across the road, and at the heathens just now war-dancing their way toward them at the front of the Back-o'-the-Docks contingent. "Looks like somebody else has plans too."

"Everybody's stepped up their security a bit," Matt says truthfully but economically. "That's why it's been peaceful so far."

"Well, I better get going, catch you later."

And he's gone, sprinting after the departing dockers' floats, now cresting the middle of the bridge.

"You know," Annie says, "these floats are very *dull*, except for that starship thing. Look like last-minute jobs, if you see what I mean."

Matt nods, winks, and gives a thumbs-up.

"Oh, look at the boys," she says.

The vanguard of the heathen lads are going by, dusty but with energy undimmed, still keeping up their high-stepping dance, still giving the spirits of the air a bruising with their staves and spears. Several of them shout what sound like admiring or jeering comments at Annie, in the heathen speech, and she yells back in the same language.

"Meant to ask," says Matt. "You a heathen yourself?"

"Grandparents were," she says. "So yes, I'm a heathen. Had to learn the language myself, mind. My parents are kind of touchy about it."

The Back-o'-the-Docks and heathen contingent, the last of the parade, the least respectable and the most influential and imitated and talked about, now fills the riverside road and turns on to the bridge, rank after rank, and between the ranks open spaces to make room for a particularly energetic dancer or extravagant costume or gigantic stilt walker or dangerous juggler making swords spin in the sun. The bands, discordant at a distance, become harmonious as they pass, the sound of each temporarily drowning out the rest. Mollyboys pout and pose and blow kisses at bystanders, or navigate ships of skirt with entranced panache. The heathen girls skip and pirouette, energetic as the boys who toyi-toyi along the sides of the parade. And at regular intervals among them, rifles at port arms, marching to a different drum, are the members of two militias: the one from Gail's neighborhood, and the one from Loudon's factory.

He calls up Gail on the radio.

"Time to go," he says.

"Acknowledged," she says.

It doesn't seem long before the whole of the rest of the parade's gone by, and the two halves of the squad nip in behind it before the bystanders who want to join in can get in front of them. So with that growing crowd behind them, they make their way across the bridge and out on to the shore road, toward the docks.

Eleven gliders were already in the air, circling up on the thin thermal above the nearest buildings. Gail brought the car around and drove back to the starting point, the launch trailer bumping across the grass, and saw that Stone was the next in line. She turned the car and trailer around, braked, idled the engine, and stepped out. Stone stood with one hand holding the frame of the wing, the other arm coming around in an awkward hug.

"Oh, Stone, take care," she said.

They only had a moment. Timing was everything.

"I will," he said.

He lifted the glider over his head and his shoulders, settled the harness around him and buckled up, and carried the glider over to the trailer and stepped on. For a sentimental moment Gail saw the glider as his carnival costume. Then she swung back into the seat, checked that the launch path was clear and that Stone was properly braced on the trailer, and gunned the car forward, faster and faster, and after a hunder meters his shadow passed over her, and the glider soared to join the bottom of the circling stack.

The glider at the top of the stack broke away and swooped toward the far side of the town, toward the shore.

Annie and Matt chivvy the squads into a run, and they overtake most of the parade. Just before they reach the long front of the quays, about twenty dockworkers detach themselves from the side of a building and fall in beside them. They all slow to a walk.

"Shit, this all we've got?" Dave Borden says.

"Never said there'd be more," says Matt. "But it's not all."

"The militias, and some heathens hopping about? Don't make me laugh."

"We'll soon see who's laughing," says Matt. "What's it like up ahead?"

"I've had a look," says Borden. "There're hundreds of 'em, not just dockers, on the quay just past that warehouse. See that line of PA cops? The crowd's about twenty meters to the right of that. They're just yelling for now, but you wait, soon as they see the heathens and the Back-o'-the-Docks lot, they'll start chucking stuff. And then they'll walk over the cops—it's a token line, a dozen or so—and steam right into us."

Matt can imagine all that, and for a moment it's not the political consequences of such a riot that fill his mind but an image of all the fragile beauty of the girls and the mollyboys getting stamped on like butterflies. He wishes that Rawliston's version of queer masculinity had run to tough gays, all muscle and leather and chains, instead of trans-genderal effeminacy. But history hasn't given them that, and—

"You fight with what you have," he concludes aloud, and Borden, surprisingly, gives him a thumbs-up and dodges away to liaise with Annie and the other squad leaders.

In a minute or two they've arrived. There's an open space of a couple of hundred meters in front of a wide quay whose edge is about a hundred meters back of the shore road, and the now twenty-odd PA militia members are spread out just in from the sidewalk, with huge gaps between them, backs to the parade, facing a crowd of, oh fuck, something near a thousand and something like a stone's throw away. The section of the dockers angered by the story have built a popular front in reverse, pulling in a coalition of the discontented and bigoted and scared. The dockers form a disciplined front rank, and behind them is a disorderly and noisy crowd, like the one that had gathered outside the grogshop but more determined. It bristles with staves, and a scatter of anti-Dawsonite and other placards, and here and there helmets glint beside rifle barrels—some of the PA militia who fought on the wrong side, discharged but evidently not disarmed, must be in the mob. It's still growing—there's a steady stream of people arriving along the quay from the same direction as the parade's moving, and Matt speculates sickly that some of the people deterred at other flashpoints have had the same idea as he has and concentrated their forces on this.

There's no point in trying not to provoke them. They're already provoked. So the squads form up on the sidewalk between and behind the cops, in five groups, with their staves up and the picks and shovels clearly visible. This is exactly the kind of situation they're good for. Matt can hear nothing but the booming of drums and the booing of the enemy. Which section's going by? He glances over his shoulder. The students. Their militia officer cadet group has already gone past. Damn. Shouldn't have expected anything else, unless they came under attack themselves.

But the first heathen boys are running up and gathering together in the gaps between the squads. There are a lot of gaps to fill in that two-hundred-meter line, and the spaces still gape, but Matt hopes that the main heathen group doesn't run ahead of the contingent it's supposed to be guarding.

A clattering din behind him and a rush of booted feet. Matt turns to see Endecott's dockers' floats slowing, men swarming over them, and the cardboard crates collapsing outward and the brightly colored covers of the bales flapping away. The clatter and the rush are the sounds of dockers throwing down pallets hacked and adapted as wooden shields and picking them up and running forward. They're also grabbing and carrying short thick sticks and, terrifyingly, long steel hooks.

Scores of them run through the gaps and form a line a few meters in front of the cops. Others form a similar line behind where Matt's standing. They have far more shields than they need themselves and are urging passing heathens and militia members to grab them and raise a shield wall along the line of the parade.

Matt is jostled again and sees more and more heathen lads filling in the line and hears the distinctive beat of the heathen drums, and he glances over his shoulder and sees the pretty people passing, hurrying, and he glimpses behind the still-forming shield wall Slow Leg directing another line of heathen boys with their spears horizontal, holding back any of their fellows who want to plunge in from the crowd.

There's just enough space for the squad members to move. Matt props his stave against his shoulder just as the first black shapes come hurtling down. The first volley falls mostly on the line of union dockers up front, thudding on the shields, or just behind them, and then the second shower of scrap arrives, this time striking home—screams, bleeding heads, somebody nearby falls thrashing. The enemy crowd surges forward, stops, the dockers fling again. This time Matt sees the objects hurtle overhead, hears the freak hailstorm rattle of them on the wooden shields behind, and more screams.

He's pushed forward, out in front of the cops, just behind the union dockers' line, and they're glancing back and everyone on either side of him is looking at him, and he sees Annie's full-beam grin ten meters to his left, and they nod to each other and turn away and Matt says quietly, above the uproar, "In your own time, comrades, please."

And runs forward.

Rawliston crawled beneath his face. The air was warmer than he was used to flying in, the thermals stronger. Heat haze and sweat distorted his view. Once or twice he riskily removed the goggles to spit in them and wipe smearily with a thumb and to blot his eyebrows with his wrist. Ahead of him and to his left, those who'd taken off before him were spread out in a straggly V formation like migrating wing-lizards.

The pistol was heavy at his waist, the two bombs a drag on either wing. Stone, like the others, had practiced flying with weights beforehand, but something—perhaps the knowledge of the danger these earthenware pots contained—made the real thing more awkward.

The leading flyer banked away from the road they were following, and they all wheeled after him, flying along and down, toward the docks.

Matt clears the union dockers' shield line, and his racing feet are off the cobbles of the street and on to the thundering timbers of the quay. The distance closes fast because the other side is running forward too. The last thing Matt sees before they close is the now useless wooden shields flying over his head and into the enemy's faces. He's unaware of how he's carrying his stave until he sees the man whose chest it cannons into stagger and fall, under feet that take him down like a quicksand.

Matt brings the stave up just in time to deflect the slashing downward swing of a stave wielded by the man behind the man he hit. And then the end of his stave is under his opponent's chin, and they're both pressed forward by those behind them, and that's it. Blood sprays Matt's face, slicks the stave. He sees the man die by inches, inches away.

Then it's too close even for that; it's the crushing furious intimacy of fist and face, forehead and nose, fingers and eyes, elbows and kidneys, knee and groin. Matt feels, or rather hears, his own lips mash and teeth crack. He spits blood and a tooth in a face, head-butts, then he's sliding down and unable to move.

A whirring and whizzing noise overhead. A snatched upward glimpse of a whole flight of staves hurled as spears falling into the crush in front. Then another, and another. The locked crowds sway backward and forward, but neither yields.

Then a different sound comes from above, and at the same time a shadow passes overhead, swift as a blink.

How hard it was, at this speed, at this altitude, to tell the crowds apart. The two struggling masses were one, and the fault line between them all but invisible. All that Stone could do—following the example of the first flyer—was to aim for the half of the crowd nearest to the quayside. He swooped low, just above the level of the tall four-story buildings on either side of the crowd, and tugged the toggles as he passed over the roadway and the long colorful line of the parade.

The glider jolted upward as the bombs were released. Stone fought to control it and couldn't follow the forward arc of the fall. He zoomed into a climb that carried him above choppy gray water and masts that seemed to reach up for his feet, and banked around. A quick glance down and to his left, to see the bright flames blossom, and then he had to concentrate on flying.

Bangs and flames and screams. The chest that Matt's face is shoved up against suddenly eases its pressure, and Matt gets enough clearance to drive a fist into its solar plexus. Then he's stumbling forward, shoving the man back, then gaps open out in front of him and then it's running fights all over the quay. The firebombs have splashed blazing petrol in dozens of places. Some people are rolling about, clothes and hair burning, others are trying to beat out their flames, and a few are running frantically to jump into the sea. Those who haven't been hit are scattering. Matt picks up a stick and joins in the fury of the pursuit, lashing at fleeing backs. He sees out of the corner of his eye a heathen mollyboy, with nothing but blue tatters around his bare legs, deliver a perfect floating drop-kick at a face full of surprise. He sees Annie cracking a renegade militiaman's rifle with her stave. He sees more burns than he ever wants to remember. And then it's a rout, and then it's over.

•   •   •

Matt leaves Borden to organize some of the union dockers for their next big task and then he and Annie run back to the main street and jog up past the procession, much of which is oblivious to what's just happened, though rumors are spreading fast.

Up ahead, the religious part of the procession has passed on down the street and is turning a corner to the main harbor entrance. The colorful, carnival part of it is turning in the opposite direction, into Back-o'-the-Docks. Some of the heathen lads—from Rawliston and the Vale—are forming small groups and sprinting off down alleyways and streets.

A growing number—hundreds, now—of other heathen warriors are forming up in ranks, right here where the factory and neighborhood militia platoons are falling out, leaving the main sections they accompany to move on, to the ceremony or the big street party according to taste. Heathen and Christian unit commanders are liaising and negotiating, sometimes quite loudly.

"That's it," says Matt. "We're done."

He stops running and leans against the wall of an office building. His back slides down it until he's sitting on the ground, hands on his crooked knees, looking up at Annie.

"What's going on?" she asks.

"Just another coup," he says. "The neighborhood and factory militias are about to march off and unseat the Council of Notables, seize a few public buildings, and so forth. Together with the heathens, who think they're invading and conquering Rawliston with some help from local allies, poor chaps. Between them they should walk over the PA militia."

She glares down at him. "You set this up?"

He shrugs. "More or less."

"Aren't you going to take part in your coup?"

"No," says Matt. "They can look after themselves, and anyway there's a bigger fight brewing. All these people we chased off are going to regroup, spread the news, and sometime in the next few hours they and the anti-Dawsonites and all the other rabble are going on the biggest rampage through Back-o'-the-Docks and the heathen district this town has ever seen."

"Shit," she says. "Yeah, I can see that, all right. We'll have to be ready."

He struggles to his feet. Annie is scanning the street, spotting and beckoning her comrades. He looks at her with a sort of hopeless admiration. She really is a heathen amazon. There's nothing he wants to do more, between now and the pickup, than to join the street parties at Back-o'-the-Docks until the fighting starts, and then slip away.

She's rounded up the posse.

She cocks him an eyebrow.

"Oh, all right," he says.

Stone brought the glider down in the middle of a street in Back-o'-the-Docks, just in front of the first flood of people into the beginning of the street party. He ran on hard cobbles, slowed to a stop, ducked out from under the wing, and found himself looking at hundreds of people, all of whom were cheering. It took him a few seconds to realize that they were cheering for him.

He walked forward, carrying the glider, and waited at the edge of the crowd—most people were already turning their attention to drinking and dancing—for one of the sky people's captains to find him. A man from Long Bridge strode out of the crowd and held up a spear and a rifle, and shook them.

"Well done, woman," he said to Stone. "Now let us put away the glider and join the people who have gone to build barricades."

"I have a radio message to send first," said Stone.

He borrowed the captain's walkie-talkie and let Gail know he was all right. They stashed the glider in an alleyway, agreed that there wasn't much chance of their ever recovering it, and gathered up some more sky people and some of the locals and walked away from the music and noise and smoke, down empty streets to the edge of the quarter.

"Here," said the captain, whose name was Hard Fist.

They stopped. The street was narrow and opened on to a square from which other, wider streets radiated into a hostile neighborhood. Every shop in this street had its windows boarded up—it was a traditional route for the traditional back-and-forth running fights that annually broke out as the festival came to an end.

A couple of hours of hard work followed. Vehicles, doors, and furniture—some of the material volunteered by its owners, most of it not—were dragged into position across the street. Bottles were filled with petrol, bricks were stockpiled, and stashes of both carried up to rooftops and upstairs rooms with windows overlooking the square. The team that Stone had joined coordinated with other teams by radio, and more and more people drifted out of the street parties and pitched in. Militias of any color were nowhere to be seen—they were all fully occupied with either overthrowing the provisional government or defending it. Occasionally a distant rattle of gunfire echoed, or a piece of news became amplified into rumor.

Stone heaved and dragged, sucked splinters out of his hands, pushed and hauled. The sun was lowering but the air was still hot. He was filthy and sweaty, but he didn't care. There were about sixty people in the street now, heathens and mollyboys and sky people and local residents, and the whole process had become a small carnival in itself, despite or because of the seriousness of its purpose.

The barricade was barely completed when the first attack came. A group of about forty young men suddenly charged out from one of the side streets of the square, gathered behind the defunct fountain in the middle, and started throwing stones. Then, when everyone behind the barricade had ducked down, a petrol bomb crashed in front of it and set it alight.

Hard Fist stuck his rifle through a gap and fired off a couple of shots. The attackers scattered, giving the defenders just enough time to dowse the fire.

"No more shooting," said Hard Fist. "We save that for if they break through."

The next attack came within half an hour. This time, the crowd filled the square. Stones, bricks and bottles, and petrol bombs hurtled in both directions. Skirmish parties from both sides forayed and clashed. For Stone, events became disjointed; at one moment he was reaching for the last brick in a pile, the next he was behind broken glass, looking down at the square and seeing a petrol bomb burst and knowing he had just thrown it but not knowing how.

An old heathen woman, gap-toothed, was yelling in his ear, "Why don't you *use* your bloody *gun*?"

He turned to her, as she rummaged in the wreckage of her bedroom for something else to throw.

"Just hold on," he said, "hold on," and ran down the stairs. Outside, he could feel the evening breeze, the wind from the mountains and the west, and he looked up and saw the first lights from the braziers of the hot-air balloon train fleet drifting toward them across the sky.

Then, above all the shouting and the crashing and the occasional shot, he heard the drone of aircraft.

．　　　．　　　．

Gail took the radio message and leaned past the windshield and tapped Loudon's shoulder. He looked back. She pointed down. He gave a thumbs-up and took the plane into a dive. Away below them, at about a thousand feet, the primitive airship fleet they'd circled above for the past twenty minutes wallowed across the town, painfully slowly. Columns of smoke rose from the streets around the docks; here and there across the town, Gail could see flames. Ahead, from somewhere up the coast, came two Port Authority seaplanes, frighteningly fast.

Matt's plan had allowed for the possibility that not all the Port Authority's aircraft would be in the hands of the assembly-loyal militias by the time the second wave of the Great Vale's air force—bomber command, as he'd wryly called it—had arrived over Rawliston.

Gail checked the mounted machine gun's ammunition belt and made sure the sights were adjusted for the probable range. She clutched its double grips, swung it into the firing position, and moved around on the seat until she was uncomfortably crouched behind it.

For a moment the two seaplanes looked like sitting ducks as they headed straight for the balloon trains. The Kondrakov-LeBrun had the advantage of surprise and the low sun behind it. But a burst of machine-gun fire from somebody in a swaying gondola—Gail could imagine it, all too vividly—missed wildly and sent the first seaplane into a steep evasive climb. It flashed past Gail's eyes, a couple of hundred feet away, quicker than she could do anything about. She tracked it as it banked at the top of its ascent and dived toward the KL-3B.

Loudon took the plane into a screaming loop. Gail felt that all the bones in her spine were being compressed. The maneuver worked: The seaplane, slower and heavier and with greater air resistance, couldn't match the turn. The other enemy aircraft had overflown the slow balloon trains and was now turning around. She had it in her sights, steady, for a second or two, and squeezed off a burst. The ammunition belt thrashed across her knees, the spent casings sprayed past her face.

Missed.

The KL-3B dived, banked, and they were in level flight again, and the first seaplane was flying in parallel a hundred meters away. Its pilot made the fatal mistake of banking away. Gail's next burst raked the underside of the craft, and it fell, spinning.

She didn't have time to follow it. The second seaplane was now on their tail. Neither aircraft had a forward-firing gun, and she couldn't swing her own gun around to fire back. The enemy stayed behind them despite Loudon's attempts so shake it off. He swung around again and flew toward the leading balloon train. The seaplane followed, and a burst from the balloon train, better aimed this time, took it down.

Matt crouches at a street corner behind an overturned cart and watches an entire riot scatter as petrol and blast bombs rain from above. He can see, in the darkening sky and through smoke, other lights moving and fires falling. Somebody in the fleeing crowd has the presence of mind to stop and shoot upward at the balloon train overhead.

The hot-air bags are punctured and start sagging instantly, then flames lick up them, blazing faster and faster as the contraption falls. The gondola's ropes burn, too, and it breaks loose and hurtles out of the sky and smashes into the street. Nobody in it has the smallest chance of survival. The burning balloons drift forward and down, onto roofs. More fires spring up.

But the street stays clear, the attack has been beaten off. The sheer shock of being attacked from the air has done more to demoralize the enemy than the physical effect of the bombs has damaged them. Matt and Gail retreat from the front line a few blocks to a secure area. Most of the other balloon-trains, lightened of their lethal loads, are drifting eastward and down, toward the sea.

Matt looks at his watch. It's eight-thirty local time. Annie is grabbing some refreshment. He smiles at her happy, grubby, fierce face as she swigs back the beer and looks at him inquiringly.

"I'm needed down at the docks," he says. He waves skyward and seaward. "Search and rescue—the balloons have to ditch in the sea, and we have to send boats to pull the flyers out."

"Ah," says Annie. "So that's why holding the docks was so important."

"Yeah. Shouldn't take more than an hour." Matt touches her arm. "Catch you later."

She grins widely. "Yeah, I'll be around here. Look after yourself."

He turns away and runs. Maybe she has the heathen superstition about good-byes, maybe she'd have been just as casual if she didn't think she'd be seeing him again in an hour or two. It makes him feel slightly better.

So, just as this morning, he's jogging through Back-o'-the-Docks. Bizarrely, knots of people are partying on, side by side with groups hurrying to or from the fighting. He's running along a dark stretch of road between two pubs when he sees a familiar figure walking briskly along the pavement, alone, carrying a big black bag. Avakian.

Matt doesn't think twice. He comes cannoning out of the middle of the road and has the apothecary bodily displaced two meters sideways and slammed up against a wall in a dark alcove, and a knife at his throat, in about three seconds.

"Matt . . ." Avakian croaks.

"Talk," says Matt. "You blabbed to the Rodriguezes, didn't you? What did they do—threaten you, or just get you drunk?"

"Jesus Christ," Avakian pleads, "what are you talking about?"

He lets his black bag fall. It clinks and rattles as it hits the street.

"I've been doing first aid for hours," he says. "I have no idea what—"

"What sparked most of this mess *off*," says Matt. Letting the blade prick. "That story about the heathens, about the ships, right?"

Avakian blinks. "Oh!" he says. He reflexively makes the smallest possible shake of the head, winces, then holds very still as a bead of blood wells on his neck.

"That wasn't me," he says. "Why the fuck would I do that? The Rodriguezes have been cold-shouldering me ever since we came back. They weren't pleased at how we used them as a cover when we took the ship." He grins desperately. "The party invitations have kind of dried up."

This sounds entirely plausible. The only way Avakian could have been the source of this story would have been unwillingly or unwittingly, and either way he'd be contrite, not denying it.

"Shit." Matt releases Avakian, makes the knife vanish like a magic trick, and takes a step back. "Shit. Sorry, Armen. Shake."

Shaken indeed, Avakian grasps his hand. "I don't blame you," he says. "I knew it wasn't me, so I know who it must have been. Christ, I could kill him myself."

"Yeah." Matt frowns at him for a moment. "Yeah, well maybe I just will. See you again, mate."

He runs on. Strange to be running through the same streets as in the morning. Strange to look up at the passing lights in the sky, to have seen that brief battle in the air, and to reflect that the next battles here could be in space.

He's appalled by the chaos and blood of the past hours but at the same time satisfied with what he's done. Turning the heathens' hopeless assault into an adjunct to the uprising may affect, even determine, what kind of society exists here when the aliens come, whether it's in a year or a century or longer. A society that might just be able to meet them and win them over, as Salasso had urged, instead of a society bristling with suspicion that can only meet fire with fire.

And even if that doesn't work out—and who can say, so far ahead?—he suspects that this will be the last riot on St. Teilhard's Day. The local heathens are no longer without allies, no longer an easy target, and the Great Vale can command respect. For the day, it's enough.

Lydia stood at the foot of the skiff's ladder, on the far end of the traders' quay. Smoke roiled above the nearby streets. Out of it, one by one, drifted the balloon-trains, carried by the wind over the edge of the dock area to sink toward the sea. Some of them had already ditched, far out, floating briefly like ceremonial paper lanterns. Powered boats rushed among them recovering their crews.

Matt was late, and every minute he was late reduced the amount of time she'd have to give him a piece of her mind and increased the time she had for her anger to build. By the time he came panting and thudding up the quay, smoke-blackened and ragged and red-eyed, she had concentrated everything down to one phrase.

"Fuck you, Matt Cairns."

He looked gratifyingly taken aback by that.

"What?" he gasped. He stood with his hands on his knees, his chest heaving, and stared up at her.

"You're not coming with us," she said.

He straightened up. "Why not?" He grinned wryly. "I've shown what I can do to muck up Volkov's schemes."

Lydia felt her fists clench. "Yes, by schemes of your own! You're as dangerous as he is! Either one of you is bad enough! I wouldn't want the two of you on the same *planet!*"

He frowned, then smiled and shrugged. "Shouldn't you be on the ship by now?"

"Yes," she said.

A saur's voice called her, urgently. She ascended the ladder and turned at the top to see Matt looking up.

"There will be other ships," he said.

Engine City

To Carol, with love

ACKNOWLEDGMENTS

Thanks to Carol, Sharon, and Michael, as always; to Andrew Greig for listening about light-years; and to Farah Mendlesohn for reading and commenting on the first draft.

There is no middle path between these two, for a man must either be a free and true commonwealth's man, or a monarchical tyrannical royalist.

Kingly government governs the earth by that cheating art of buying and selling, and thereby becomes a man of contention, his hand is against every man, and every man's hand is against him; and take this government at the best, it is a diseased government, and the very city Babylon, full of confusion.

—Gerard Winstanley, *The Law of Freedom in a Platform* (1651)

Contents

Prologue: States of Mind

T HE GOD WHO later became known as the asteroid 10049 Lora, and shortly afterwards as the ESA mining station *Marshal Titov*, was not unusual of its kind. Around the Sun, as with most stars, gods swarm like flies around a sacrifice. Life arises from states of matter. From some of these states of matter arise states of mind.

In the asteroids and cometary bodies the units of life were extremophile nanobacteria. Regulating their ultra-cold molecular processes, the vanishingly tiny temperature differentials, detecting the quantum signature of usable energy—over millions of years, these and other selective advantages drove the development of delicate networks adapted to processing information. Random variations in the effects of their activities on the asteroid's outgassings and on the glacially slow transport of mass within it were selected for whenever they resulted in more stable orbits and fewer collisions. Increasingly complex networks formed. Subjectivity flickered into being on trillions of separate sites within each life-bearing asteroid or cometary mass.

Those within 10049 Lora found themselves in a society of other such minds, exchanging information across light-hours. They had much to learn, and many to learn from. Billions of years of evolutionary fine-tuning had given the cometary and asteroid minds an exquisite sensitivity to the electromagnetic output of each other's internal chemical and physical processes. Communication, exchange of information and material between cometary clouds, became rumor that ran around the galaxy's outer reaches, which ring like residential suburbs its industrial core where the heavy elements are forged.

Just as minds are built from smaller information exchangers—neurons or bacteria or switches—so from the vast assembly of intercommunicating minds within the asteroid emerged a greater phenomenon, a sum of those minds: a god. It was aware of the smaller minds, of their vast civilizations and long histories. It was also aware of itself and others like itself. Its component minds, in moments of introspection or exaltation, were aware of it. In moments of enlightened contemplation, which could last millennia, the god was aware of a power of which it was a part: the sum of all the gods within the Solar System. That solar god, too, had its peers, but whether they in their turn were part of some greater entity was a subject on which lesser minds could only speculate.

On Earth, evolution worked out differently. On its surface, the multicellular trick took off. Beneath the surface, the extremophile microorganisms that riddled the lithosphere and made up the bulk of the planet's life formed extensive interacting networks which became attuned to the electromagnetic fields of the planet and its atmosphere. Constantly disrupted by processes far more violent than those of the smaller celestial bodies, they attained the level of symbolic thought, but never quite intelligence. Earth's mind—Gaia—was like that of a pre-verbal child or an animal. Its thoughts were dreams, afterimages, abstractions that floated free and illuminated like sheet lightning.

The large squid of the genus *Architeuthys*, which men later called krakens, were the first real intelligences on Earth, and the ones whose outlook on life was closest to that of the gods. They communicated by varying the colored patterns of the chromatophores on their skins. The minute electrical currents thus generated interacted with the electromagnetic flux of the planet and were amplified by it to come to the cometary minds' acutely sensitive attention. Responses tickled back from the sky. As the gods began to make sense of the squids' sensoria—a research project which kept the equivalent of a billion civilizations' worth of scientists happily occupied for several centuries—they modified their own internal models accordingly. The visible spectrum and the visual field burst upon astonished inner eyes. Sight dawned for the gods, and enlightenment for the squid. Megayears of happy and fertile intellectual intercourse followed.

Towards the end of the Cretaceous period, alien ships emerged from nowhere. Their occupants were warm-blooded, eight-limbed, eight-eyed, and furry. Celestial minds were already familiar phenomena to them. They swarmed across the Solar System, cracking memetic and genetic codes as they went. They talked to the gods with their noisy radio systems, gibber, jabber, boasting in technical detail of the lightspeed drive and the antigravity engine. Their discoid skiffs scooted through the skies of all the planets. They flashed banks of lights at the kraken schools. They listened to the collective voice of the Martian biosphere, which in all its long dying never rose above a sad, rusty croak.

They made friends. They found a promising species of small, bipedal, tailless dinosaurs and fiddled with their genes. The new saurs were intelligent and long-lived. The octopods taught the saurs how to fly skiffs. (Gaia took the saurs and skiffs into her dreams, and spun shining images of them in plasma and ball lightning, but nobody noticed back then.) They dangled the prospect of space travel before the kraken. Many of the squids pounced at the chance. The octopods designed ships and skiffs; the saurs built them and flew the skiffs; the krakens embraced the algorithms of interstellar navigation. Long ships, whose pilots swam in huge aquaria, blinked away.

By this time, one thought in the baffled minds of the gods resonated from one side of the Oort cloud to the other: KEEP THE NOISE DOWN! The radiation noise and the endless blether of information were not the worst irritations. Despite all appeals, the octopods persisted in digging on the surfaces of asteroids and comets. They itched like nits. Some saurs and kraken began to see the gods' point of view, but they were unable to convince the octopods. The cometary minds made small, cumulative changes in their orbits, nudging a metallic asteroid onto a trajectory that ended on the octopods' single city and brought the Cretaceous epoch to a cataclysmic close.

The destruction appalled even the gods. The octopods and their allies fled, while the saurs and krakens who remained behind labored to repair the damage done. They still had skiffs and ships. Laden with rescued specimens and genetic material, lightspeed ships traveled to the other side of the galaxy. The saurs selected a volume about two hundred light-years across and seeded scores of terrestrial planets—some hastily and blatantly terraformed—with the makings of new biospheres. Saurs and kraken settled the new planets, originally as ecological engineering teams, later as colonists. Others returned to the Solar System, to bring more species. The traffic was to continue for the next sixty-five million years.

Echoes and rumors of other conflicts circulated around the galaxy. The kraken picked them up from the gods in the newly settled systems and passed them on to the saurs. In those multiple translations, subtleties were lost. Knowledge of the past became tradition, then religion. Gradually, the saurs, in what they came to call the Second Sphere, diverged from those in the Solar System. Meetings between the two branches of the species became mute, and matings sterile.

In the Second Sphere, a quiet and contented civilization was held together by the kraken-navigated starships that plied between its suns. It assimilated new arrivals at intervals of centuries. Some fast, bright mammals increasingly reminded the saurs of the octopods. Lemurs and lorises, apes and monkeys, successive species of hominid; bewildered, furious bands of hunters, tribes of farmers, villages of artisans, caravans of missing merchants, legions of the lost. The saurs' patient answers to their frequently asked questions became the catechism of a rational but zealous creed. Yes, the gods live in the sky. No, they do not listen to prayers. No, they do not tell us what to do. Their first and last commandment is: Do not disturb us.

Slowly, with the help of the saurs and the two other surviving species of hominid, the transplanted humans built a civilization of their own, whose center was a city that never fell.

For the gods in the Solar System, the human civilization of the Second Sphere was a history too recent for them to have heard of. They knew only that the saurs' snatch-squads continued their work with ever-increasing caution as the human population grew. The clutter of images generated by Gaia's excitable response to the saurs' presence provided the perfect cover for their activities. The gods had real aliens to worry about. The starships might bring back news from the Second Sphere a hundred thousand years out of date, but they collected much more recent news in their occasional stops on the way back. From these the gods learned that the octopods were a few tens of light-years away, and heading toward the Solar System.

The god in 10049 Lora had already lived a long life when it and its peers noticed the rising electronic racket from Earth. It volunteered to swing by for a closer look. It absorbed the contents of the Internet in seconds, and then found, microseconds later, that it was already out of date. It was still struggling with the exponential growth when the European Union's cosmonauts arrived. To them, it was a convenient Near-Earth Object, and a possible source of raw materials for further expansion.

The humans had plans for the Solar System, the god discovered—plans that made the past octopod incursion seem like a happy memory.

But the coming octopod incursion might be still worse. If the humans could expand into space without the devastatingly profligate use of resources that their crude rocket technology required, an elegant solution could be expected to the presence of both species of vermin.

Bypassing the local saurs, who were quite incapable of dealing with the problem, the god scattered information about the interstellar drive and the gravity skiff across the Earth's datasphere. Several top-secret military projects were already apparently inspired by glimpses of skiff technology, but their sponsors unaccountably failed to take the hint. (In their mutual mental transparency, the celestial minds found the concepts of lies, fiction, and disinformation difficult to grasp.) The minds within 10049 Lora opened communication with the cosmonauts on its surface, where the ESA mining station *Marshal Titov* was giving the god a severe headache.

Having their computers hacked into by a carbonaceous chondrite came as a surprise to the cosmonauts. In the sudden glut of information, they failed to notice the instructions for a radical new technology of space travel until it was almost too late. Politics dictated first that the contact should be secret, then that it should be public. Political and military conflicts resulted in a mutiny on the station. Before the space marines of the European People's Army could arrive to suppress it, the cosmonauts built a lightspeed drive that took the entire station away. They thought they had understood how to navigate it. They had not. It returned to its default setting, and arrived at the Second Sphere.

Before their departure, one of the cosmonauts made sure that the instructions distributed by the god would not be ignored, and could not be hidden. The gods approved. Soon the noisy humans would be somebody else's problem.

I

The Very City Babylon

I

The Advancement of Learning

T HE JUMP IS instantaneous. To a photon, the whole history of the universe may be like this: over in a flash, before it's had time to blink. To a human, it's disorienting. One moment, you're an hour out from the last planet you visited—then, without transition, you're an hour away from the next.

Volkov spent the first of these hours preparing for his arrival, conscious that he would have no time to do so in the second.

My name is Grigory Andreievich Volkov. I am two hundred and forty years old, I was born about a hundred thousand years ago, and as many light-years away: Kharkov, Russian Federation, Earth, in the year 2018. As a young conscript, I fought in the Ural Caspian Oil War. I was with the first troops to enter Marseilles and to bathe their sore feet in the waters of the Mediterranean. In 2040, I became a cosmonaut of the European Union, and three years later made the first human landing on the surface of Venus. In 2046 I volunteered for work on the space station *Marshal Titov*, which in 2049 was renamed the *Bright Star*. It became the first human-controlled starship. In it I traveled to the Second Sphere. For the past two centuries I have lived on Mingulay and Croatan.

This is my first visit to Nova Terra. I hope to bring you . . .

What? The secret of immortality?
Yes. *The secret of immortality*. That would do.
Strictly speaking, what he hoped to bring was the secret of longevity. But he had formed an impression of the way science was conducted

on Nova Terra: secular priestcraft, enlightened obscurantism; alchemy, philosophy, scholia. A trickle of inquiry after immortality had exhausted hedge-magic, expanded herbalism, lengthened little but grey beards and the index of the Pharmacopia, and remained respectable. Volkov expected to be introduced to the Academy as a prodigy. Before the shaving-mirror, he polished his speech and rehearsed his Trade Latin.

The suds and stubble swirled away. He slapped a stinging cologne on his cheeks, gave himself an encouraging smile, and stepped out of the cramped washroom. The ship's human quarters were sparse and provisional. In an emergency, or at the owners' convenience, they could be flooded. In normal operation, it was usual to travel in one or other of the skiffs, which at this moment were racked on the vast curving sides of the forward chamber like giant silver platters. The air smelled of paint and seawater; open channels and pools divided the floor, and on the walls enormous transparent pipes contained columns of water that rose or fell, functioning as lifts for the ship's crew. Few humans, and fewer saurs, were about in the chamber. Volkov strolled along a walkway. At its end, a low rail enclosed the pool of the navigator. Eyes the size of beach balls reflected racing bands of color from the navigator's chromatophores and the surrounding instrumentation. Wavelets from the rippling mantle perturbed the water. Lashing tentacles broke the surface as they played over the controls.

Volkov was halfway up the ladder to the skiff in which he had spent most, and intended to spend the rest, of the brief journey, when the lightspeed jump took place. The sensation was so swift and subtle that it did not endanger his step or grasp. He was aware that it had happened, that was all. In a moment of idle curiosity—for he'd never been within sight of a ship's controller at such a moment—he glanced sideways and down, to the watery cockpit twenty-odd meters below.

The navigator floated in the middle of the pool. His body had turned an almost translucent white. Volkov was perturbed, but could think of nothing better to do than scramble faster up the ladder to the skiff.

The door opened and he stepped inside, rejoining his hosts. Esias de Tenebre stood staring at the display panel, as though he could read the racing glyphs that to Volkov meant nothing. Feet well apart, hands in his trouser pockets, his stout and muscular frame bulked further by his heavy sweater, his shock of hair spilling from under his seaman's cap. Though in the rough-duty clothes that merchants traditionally wore on board ship, he had all the stocky and cocky dignity of Holbein's Henry—one who did not kill his wives, all three of whom stood beside him. Lydia, the daughter of Esias and Faustina, lounged on the circular seat around the central engine fairing behind her parents, returning Volkov's appeasing look with sullen lack of interest. Black hair you could swim in, brown eyes you could drown in, golden skin you could bask in. Her oversized sweater and baggy canvas trousers only added to her charm. The other occupant of the vehicle was its pilot, Voronar, who sat leaning forward past Esias.

"What's going on?"

The saur's elliptical eyes spared Volkov a glance, then returned to the display.

"Nothing out of the ordinary," said Voronar. His large head, which lent his slender reptilian body an almost infantile proportion, tipped forward, then nodded. "We are an hour away from Nova Terra."

"Could you possibly show us the view?" said Esias.

"Your pardon," said Voronar.

He palmed the controls, and the entire surrounding wall of the skiff became pseudotransparent, patching data from the ship's external sensors and automatically adjusting brightness and contrast: Nova Sol's glare was turned down, the crescent of Nova Terra muted to a cool blue, its night side enhanced. Scattered clusters of crowded lights pricked the dark like pleiads.

"That's a lot of cities," Volkov said.

Compared with anywhere else he'd seen in the Second Sphere, if not with the Earth he remembered, it was.

"There's only one that matters," said Esias. He did not need to point it out.

Nova Babylonia was the jewel of the Second Sphere. Its millennia-old culture, and its younger but still ancient republican institutions, made it peacefully hegemonic on Nova Terra, and beyond. The temperate zones of Nova Terra's continents were placid parks, where even wildernesses were carefully planned landscape features. All classes of its people were content. Academicians and artists assimilated the latest ideas and styles that trickled in over the millennia from Earth; patricians and politicians debated cordially and congratulated themselves on their fortune in knowing, and avoiding, the home world's terrible mistakes. Merchants traded the rare goods of many worlds. Artisans and laborers enjoyed the advantages of a division of labor far wider than any the human species could have sustained on its own. Emigration was free, but the proportion of emigrants insignificant. The hominidae cheerfully tended and harvested the sources of raw materials, and the saurs and krakens exchanged their advanced products and services for those of human industry and craft. As an older and wiser species, the saurs were consulted to settle disputes, and as a more powerful species, they intervened to prevent any from getting out of hand.

The lights of Nova Babylonia shone just short of the terminator, and somewhat to the north of the halfway point between the pole and the equator. Genea, the continent on whose eastern shore the city stood, sprawled diagonally across the present night side of the planet and southward into the day and the southern hemisphere. Its ragged coastline counterpointed that of the other major continent, Sauria, a couple of thousand kilometers west: the two looked as though they had been pulled apart and displaced, one northward, the other south. Much of the southern and western part of Sauria was wrapped out of sight around the other side of the planet, at this moment; in the visible part, even at this distance, the rectangular regularity of some of its green patches distinguished manufacturing plant from jungle and plain.

"Do any humans live in Sauria?" Volkov asked.

Esias shrugged. "A few thousand, maybe, at any one time. Short-term contract employees, traders, people involved in travel infrastructure and big-game hunting. Likewise with saurs in Genea—lots of individuals, no real communities, except around the hospitals and health services."

Hospitals and health services, yes, Volkov thought, that could be a problem.

"What about the other hominidae?"

"Ah, that's a more usual distribution, except that they have entire cities of their own." Esias pointed; it wasn't much help. "Gigants here, pithkies there. Forests and mines, even some farming. More of a surprise than the cities, that; it's only developed in the last few centuries. They've always been herding, of course."

As the ship's approach zoomed the view, the city and its surroundings expanded and sharpened. The immediate vicinity and hinterland of the city was a long, triangular promontory, about a thousand kilometers from northwest to southeast and five hundred across at its widest extent. It looked like a smaller and narrower India: an island that had rammed the continent at an angle. Very likely it was—the ice of a spectacular and recent mountain range glittered white across the join. The west coast of this mini subcontinent was separated from the mainland of Genea by a semicircular sea, three hundred kilometers across at its widest, its shore curving to almost meet the end of the promontory just south of the metropolis. From the mountains sprang a dozen or so rivers whose confluence channeled about halfway down to one major river, which flowed into the sea near the tapered tip. The central, and oldest, part of Nova Babylonia was on an island about ten kilometers long that looked wedged in that river's mouth.

The city drifted off center in the view, then swung out of sight entirely as the ship leveled up for its run into the atmosphere. Why the great starships approached on what resembled a long, shallow glide path was unknown, and certainly unnecessary, but it was what they always did. The air reddened around the ship's field and, following another unnecessary and invariable habit, its human passengers returned to their seats.

Volkov leaned on the rail of the open sea-level deck of the starship and gasped morning-cool fresh air. The starship had, to the best of his knowledge, no air-recycling or air-circulating mechanisms whatsoever, and after a couple of hours even its vast volume of air grew slightly but noticeably stale. Around him, unregarded, the ship's unlading went on, bales into boats and sometimes into skiffs. The machinery that he had imported from Mingulay and Croatan—marine engines and diving equipment, mostly—would be a small fraction of the de Tenebres' cargo, and that itself insignificant beside the wares of the ship's real owners and major traders, the krakens. Beneath him, the ship's field pressed down like an invisible, flexible sheet on the waves, flattening them to a waterbed wobble. Under that rippling glassy surface, the krakens from the ship and from the local sea flashed greetings to each other. Off to Volkov's right, behind the bulk of the ship, the sun was just up, its low full beam picking out the city, about a mile away across the water, in rectangles of white glare and long triangles of black shade. Ten thousand years of heaping one stone upon another had stacked the architectures of antiquity to the heights of modernity. A marble Manhattan, massive yet soaring, it looked like something from the mind of a Speer with humanity, or a Stalin with taste. The avenues that slotted the island metropolis from east to west were so broad that Volkov could see the sky on the far side through the one directly opposite him. Bridges, sturdy as ribs, joined both shores to districts that stood, less grand only by contrast, on either bank.

Starships by the score dotted the broad estuary. Skiffs flitted back and forth between the sound and the city like Frisbees in a park. Long-limbed mammals like flying squirrels—this world's equivalent of

573

birds—skimmed the waves and dived for fish and haunted the wakes of fishing boats in raucous flocks. Above the city, airships and gliders drifted, outpaced and dodged by the flashing skiffs. Between the starships, tall junks and clippers tacked in or out of the harbor and both branches of the river, and among them feluccas darted, their sails like the fins of a shoal of sharks. At this distance, the city's dawn din of millions of wheels and feet rose in a discernible and gradually increasing hum.

For a moment the immensity and solidity of the place made Volkov's heart sink. The stone crescendo that rose before his face was like some gigantic ship against whose bow history itself cleaved and fell back to slip along its flanks and leave a wake of churned millennia. And yet ultimately it was only an idea that kept it afloat and forging forward, a thought in millions of all-too-fragile skulls. Let them lose that thought, and in a year, the place would sink. Volkov had set himself the harder task of raising it, and at that, he felt weak.

He heard and smelt Lydia behind him, and turned as she stepped up to the rail. She gazed hungrily at the city, transfixed.

"Gods above," she said, "it's good to see it again." She smiled at him wryly. "And good to see it hasn't changed much." Another, more considering, look at the city. "Except it's higher."

"It's impressive," Volkov allowed.

"And you want to change it."

Volkov jerked a thumb over his shoulder at the work being done behind them. "You're the revolutionaries," he said. "Bring in enough books and ideas, and the city will change itself. All I want to do is make sure it's still there the next time you come back."

He grinned at her, controlling his features. His heart was making him shake inside. "If I believed in your people's ideas of courtship, I would offer it for your hand. I would tell Esias that I could take this city and lay it at your feet."

Lydia, to his surprise, blushed and blinked. "That's what Esias is afraid of," she said.

She stared away, as though weighing the city, and the suggestion.

"Gregor offered more," she added, "and he delivered it, too, but he didn't want me after all. No, I'm not open to that kind of offer. Not after that."

"I see," said Volkov. "I'll just have to fall back on my fine physique and engaging personality."

Lydia laughed. "I can never tell if you're joking or not."

574

"Neither can I," said Volkov in a gloomy tone. She punched him lightly. "There you go again."

He turned to her, with a smile to cover his confusion, and even more to cover his calculation. He did not know how he felt, or what if anything his feelings meant. A few weeks earlier, his affair with Lydia's mother, Faustina, had come to a mutually agreeable end. He got on best with women of his own apparent age, or older; preferably married, or otherwise unlikely to form a permanent—and from his point of view, all too temporary—attachment. He wasn't in love with Lydia, or even infatuated with her. He didn't think about her all the time. But whenever he saw her, he felt an electric jolt inside him, and he found it difficult to look away from her. It was embarrassing to find himself stealing glances like some besotted youth, but there it was.

At the other end of the scale, almost balancing that, there was the knowledge that in terms of Nova Babylonian—and Trader—custom, they were potentially good partners. Marriage was a business, affairs an avowed diversion; issue, inheritance, and fortune the only serious matters, over which geneticists and astrologers and matchmakers kept themselves profitably occupied.

In between, at the balance point, he and Lydia had developed a sort of tempestuous friendship, which every so often blew up in clashes in which his values and ideas appeared to her as a jaded cynicism, and her passionately held ethics to him seemed ancient prejudices, immaturely held. At the moment, their relationship was going through one of its calmer patches. He didn't know whether a squall would have been better. More bracing, certainly; but there was no need to bring it on. It would come of itself soon enough.

"Can we at least be friendly, for the moment?"

She smiled back. "You may be sly, Grigory Andreievich, but I do like you. Sometimes."

The first skiff slid out of its slot in the rack and skimmed across the navigation pool and out of one of the ship's side openings. It soared to an altitude of a couple of hundred meters and flew into the city, the other skiffs carrying the rest of the clan and the crew following one by one at intervals of about half a minute. Voronar took his time, evidently enjoying showing off to Volkov the city's towers and his own skill in flying between them. From above, the city looked astonishingly green. Trees lined the streets, and stories rose in steps like terraces, many of which supported grass and gardens: the hanging gardens of Nova Babylonia, a wonder greater than their ancient original. Monkeys scrambled and swung on long vines and branches; goats grazed the lofty lawns and capered up or down external stairways; flying squirrels, their fur bright and various as the feathers of parakeets, flashed across the artificial canyons.

The skiff dipped, making the view tilt alarmingly while the internal gravity remained rock solid. Volkov glimpsed a buttress on which was carved an eagle, wings outspread to ten meters, and beneath it the inscriptions "IX" and "SPQR"; and then, before he could quite grasp the allusive stir of memory, they were past it and sidling in to a tower, down whose fifty-meter lower tier a column of neon spelled out DE TENEBRE. The skiff landed on one of the building's terraces and everyone except the pilot descended the ladder onto soft turf, and the skiff flitted away to make room for the rest of the skein.

"Sliding glass doors," Volkov murmured to Lydia, as they walked toward the entrance. "It's been a long time."

"Oh, so they had them on Earth?"

From the sliding doors emerged a crowd of the clan's retainers and office workers, and—as Volkov learned in the swirl of fast introductions as the new arrivals were ushered inside—members of the home-staying branch, the oldest of whom might remember from childhood someone old enough to have been alive when the ship had departed. Also in the crowd were saurs, for whom the past two centuries were an episode in their lives, and who swiftly renewed old acquaintances among their counterparts in the traveling crew. For all of them, human and saur alike, the return of the ship was a major event and a huge celebration. This floor of the building was evidently the function suite, a vast deck whose open space was only interrupted by support pillars, and on it a thousand or so people were partying. Most of them wore some kind of pleated kimonos, with variations in cloth, cut, texture, and pattern that differentiated the sexes in predictable ways. Others wore loose jackets and trousers, likewise varied.

Volkov circulated, nibbled and sipped, chatted discreetly. Esias's family and the few crew members who knew who Volkov really was had agreed to keep it to themselves and to the saurs, at least until the Academy, the Electorate, the Senate, and the Assembly of Notables had had a chance to consider the situation. He introduced himself as an immigrant marine engineer importing some new technology, which was true as far as it went. A slow circumnavigation of the room took him back to Lydia's orbit.

He gestured at his clothes and hers, then at those of the other revelers. "Doesn't this make you feel a little . . . underdressed for the occasion?"

Lydia brushed her hands on her hips, leaving crumbs on canvas. "Not at all," she said. "Traveling gear is the most prestigious garb at this party, I'll tell you that. If we were to come here in what were our best clothes when we left, we'd look as though we were in some kind of antique costume." She looked around critically. "Mind you, I can see where this sort of silk origami style came from, and I'm quite looking forward to trying it, but there's no way I'd change into it straight off the ship. I'd look as ridiculous as I'd feel."

"I doubt that."

Lydia acknowledged the compliment with a shake of the head. "And how do you feel?"

"Somewhat overwhelmed by all this, to tell you the truth. Not just the occasion, but the city."

"Aha," said Esias, looming into view behind a brandy balloon. "I detect a bad case of cultural cringe. I can see it in your eyes, Volkov. Relax, my friend. We're the hosts here, remember. And from our point of view, we attend such occasions every few months."

"Perhaps at the next one," Volkov murmured, "all the people here will be there."

Esias raised a finger, then winked. "But yes," he said, "an interesting thought . . . I've set some wheels in motion about a hearing from the Academy, by the way. It'll take a day or two, of course. In the meantime, I'll deal with the usual turnaround business, and you . . ."

"I'll sell machines," said Volkov.

Volkov spent the next few days wandering around the city, sometimes in Lydia's company, sometimes on his own. From street level, the terracing gave an illusion of its being built on a human scale. From the pavement, the nearby towers would seem only a few storeys high, those farther away like cliffs striated with verdant ledges. Awnings and cloisters, courtyards and porticoes, plazas and fountains, and the long shadows of the buildings themselves, made the air on the streets bearable, almost cool. Higher up, breezes did the same work. Access to the upper levels was by lifts, or interior stairs, or by perilous stairways that zigzagged up their outer walls. The whole city ran on a like combination of muscle power and electricity. Less dense than it had looked from the sea, it contained endless pocket parks and gardens, fertilized by draft-animal dung, whose collection and distribution was a business in itself. Hardly a splash of shit ever reached the streets. Processing human waste was another specialization, conducted with such skill and speed that Volkov for a long while did not catch more than a passing whiff of it.

The gardens in the business district were decorative, but elsewhere, their floral fringes enclosed vegetable patches, small rice paddies, beds of herbs, tiny meadows for the goats, guinea pigs, and other minor livestock; the trees of the avenues and parks were harvested for fruit, and even timber. It was not something Lydia or anyone else explained to him, it was something he worked out with pencil and paper: The city was a permaculture, self-sufficient in at least its basic necessities. The cash-crop latifundia of its hinterland brought in money, not food, or at most brought variety to the diet.

Its biggest external source of food was the sea, or rather two seas: the Half Moon Sea and the Eastern Ocean. The feluccas fished the former, and the big oceanworthy junks trawled the latter. Even the harbor was clean enough to sustain a fishery of its own, conducted by hordes of boys and girls who sat along the piers from morning to evening with long bamboo rods. In the dusk they sold basketloads of small fry to the felucca skippers for bait, and sizzled the remainder on roadside griddles long into the night.

Volkov, too, hawked wares around the docks, every day lugging samples of the smaller devices, models, and plans of the larger, around shipping and fishing companies. He knew from decades of experience where to go, usually not to the offices but the sheds, not to the owners or administrators but the engineers, who, once they were sold on a new idea, did his selling for him. He picked up the local vernacular as he went; gradually, his Trade Latin approximated to a sort of Trade Italian, and he made enough deals to reassure him that even if nothing came of his larger plans, he could make a living here. There was a kind of contentment in the work that warred with his ambition.

Guilds, associations, companies, cooperatives, and corporations combined the hustle of private enrichment or survival with the stability of municipal administration and held the city's economic life in what Volkov—used as he was to the less regulated markets of the outer, younger worlds—could only think of as a strangling net. Even the European Union's "feasible and sustainable socialism" had been, to his recollection, much more dynamic. Artels plus electrification, he thought wryly, added up to something that wasn't capitalism and wasn't socialism. Its exact classification puzzled the residually and obdurately Marxist modules of his mind until he arbitarily consigned it to the conceptual catch-all of "pre-capitalist." From this society, capitalism could emerge, and—with more upheaval and less substantial change—socialism too, but Volkov's fingers still smarted from a previous experiment in detonating a bourgeois revolution.

Identifying a ruling class and state posed no such problem. The upper and usually senior ranks of the various corporate bodies, patricians and patriarchs of the merchant houses, administrators of cooperatives, guildmasters and latifundists, heads of religious orders and philosophical schools, retired courtesans, professors emeritus, and so on and so forth, formed what was blatantly called the Electorate, who just as blatantly elected the Senate and staffed its administration, and that was that. Volkov had no scruples about elites—having been part of one—and was surprised to find himself shocked by the sheer effrontery of the Republic's lack of the forms of democracy. All his experience had been with people who insisted on at least the illusion of popular rule, and it was disquieting to encounter a people who seemed satisfied with the substance of self-government in everyday life while letting high politics and statecraft go on over their heads—as it almost always and everywhere did, of course.

As he walked through mazes of markets and malls, past workshops and mills, glimpsed ranks of pale-faced clerks filing and scribbling and ringing up totals on calculating machines, and marveled at the countless threads of communication—the racing messenger boys' bare feet slapping in echoing stairwells, the cyclists yelling and dodging in the streets, the long sigh of pneumatic tubes and the ring of telephony—Volkov realized that this city could become the hub of a militarily and industrially formidable state without changing a single institution. All it needed was information.

They already had some—news of the arrival of the *Bright Star*, and bits and pieces of the recent knowledge it had brought, had trickled in long before the de Tenebres' ship had set out to bring back as much as possible. And they had the means to disseminate and discuss it—the press here was multiple and full of rude vigor, as were the numerous radio channels. The massive addition to knowledge that had just arrived would set the place intellectually alight. Rumors of it were already setting everyone agog.

The banner of his revolution would be: *Knowledge is power.*

• • •

The Academy's interior was cool—its granite blocks retaining, it seemed, a nip of cold from the previous winter—and quiet. Its air carried a tang of wood polish and disinfectant; aeons of application of the former had given the high doors of the Senate Chamber a patina millimeters deep, and ages of the latter had worn centimeters of dip into the sandstone steps.

"Nervous?"

"No," said Volkov, belying it slightly by fingering the knot of his tie. He was wearing a hastily tailored but reasonably accurate copy of his old dress uniform, made after the photograph taken on the day of his investiture as Hero of the European Union (First Class) which he still carried around in his wallet. Esias, in a magnificent fur-trimmed brocade robe at least two centuries out of fashion, looked scarcely less quaint and exotic.

The black iron handle of the double doors was turned from within and the doors swung back, silent on well-oiled hinges. Volkov had assumed they would creak. A lean, elderly servitor in a long black gown bowed through the widening gap, then stepped aside. Volkov hesitated.

"After you," growled Esias. "You're my guest, not a captive specimen."

"I'll try to remember that," Volkov said, and with a nod to the servitor, marched into the Senate Chamber. It was about thirty meters high, illuminated by electric lamps and a roseate skylight. Semicircular tiers of benches rose from the podium to the rear, and on them sat a grave multitude of ancient men, among whom were a modicum of younger but still mature men and a very few women. One long-bearded, long-gowned sage stood by the podium, a hand out in a beckoning gesture. Volkov reminded himself that he was older and probably wiser than anyone else present, and strode over to shake the extended hand, rather to the recipient's surprise.

"My name is Luke Sejanus," the scholar murmured, "president of the Academy of Sciences."

He turned, threw out an arm with a practised flourish, and announced: "My lords, ladies and gentlemen, I present our distinguished visitor, Grigory Andreievich Volkov! Cosmonaut of the European Union, colonel in the European People's Army, Hero of the European Union . . ."

He rolled on through a list Volkov's achievements, including the succession of his business ventures on Mingulay and Croatan, several of which Volkov had thought he had taken to the obscurity of a marked but empty grave in the centuries during which the Cosmonauts had concealed their longevity. He had, however, mentioned them to Esias.

Esias had taken a vacant place at the end of one of the lower rows. Volkov glared at him; Esias smiled back.

Sejanus stepped aside, sat down in the front row, and added his expectant face to a thousand others. Volkov swallowed hard and wished there was a glass of water in front of him. Or vodka.

"Thank you, President Sejanus. My lords, ladies and gentlemen, I am honored to stand before you. What is unusual about my life is not what I have accomplished—though I can look back on it with more satisfaction than regret, thanks be to the gods. What is unusual about my life is . . . its length. I am here to show you how you too can live as long a life, and in health and vigor—even those of you who are already old.

"To show you, not to tell you. I am sorry that I cannot tell you. In the third and fourth decades of my life, I consumed many drugs and medicines that promised to preserve youth. As you can see, one of them, or some combination of them, worked. I do not know which, and because the formulae of these medicines were commercial secrets, I would be unable to reproduce it even if I knew which nostrum was, in fact, the panacea. I and the other Cosmonauts have consulted among ourselves, and we have failed to discover which medicine or medicines we had in common.

"What I can do, however, is this. I can show you the method by which you can independently discover the nostrum—the elixir—for yourselves. This would involve extracting material from my body and analyzing it—finding out what molecules are in my blood, for example, that are not in the blood of others. Possibly one or more of these molecules would provide a clue. Or perhaps you might find something unusual in the structures of my cells—I do not know, but that is what I would expect. At the same time, I can give you a list of the types of molecule which are known to have been used in the various medicines, and the parts of the human cells which these medicines were intended to—and were known to—affect. These could be tested on short-lived animals—rats and mice, let us say—then on monkeys, and finally on human volunteers. Many experiments would be necessary. Their results would have to be scrupulously recorded and carefully examined.

"It might be a long process. It might be costly. But we would have, to encourage us, the priceless knowledge that what we were attempting was possible, that it had been done once, and that it could therefore be done again.

"Thank you."

He bowed, and stood aside as Sejanus returned to the podium. Esias was nodding and smiling; almost everyone else seemed lost in thought.

"I shall now take questions," said Sejanus, looking as though he had some himself.

A middle-aged man near the front stood up. "Theocritus Gionno," he introduced himself, obviously unnecessarily for most of those present. "Chairman of the Department of Medical Sciences." He preened his robe for a moment. "In recent days, the Trader and Elector Esias de Tenebre has provided us with evidence for Colonel Volkov's remarkable, nay, extraordinary, claim. We have all had an opportunity to acquaint ourselves with it, and we must, I think, admit that it is extraordinary evidence. Documents of undisputed provenance, photographs, fingerprints. . . . Likewise, we and our predecessors have had many years indeed to examine such evidence of the level of scientific knowledge prevalent in the Solar System at the time of the, ah, *Bright Star*'s departure as has trickled in over the past two centuries. We have no reason to doubt the possibility of the treatment of which the Colonel has spoken."

He cupped an elbow in one hand, his chin in the other, and gazed around the auditorium.

"However," he went on, "the method that the Colonel proposes by which we could independently, as he puts it, rediscover the nostrum must surely strike all men—and women!—of science as preposterously cumbersome and, above all, uncertain. This is not how science is done at all! The scientific method is based upon logical reasoning from observation, and from logical analysis of available data. An immense wealth of such data is available to us already. An even greater addition to it has been bestowed on us by the successful expedition of the family de Tenebre, which beyond the memory of the oldest man now living, set forth to bring from distant Mingulay the full fountainhead of that knowledge of which we and our predecessors have long lapped up the veriest drops and trickles. I have every confidence that a few years of careful study and exact reasoning will enable us to deduce the composition of the elixir."

A low hum of approbation greeted this. Others stood up, one by one, and held forth on the power of logic to reason from old facts to new.

"Let us take for example the theory of evolution," one man, depressingly young, said. "Could that have been discovered experimentally? No! A thousand years ago, Alexander Philoctetes stood in this very hall and explained to the Academy how in each generation more are born than can survive, how consequently there is a struggle for existence, and how therefore small variations conducive to survival must necessarily be preserved—and so on, in that masterly deduction of the origin of species with which we are all familiar. If Philoctetes had used this vaunted *experimental* method—fossicking about in quarries, no doubt—he would have found the most misleading results in the fossil record, and come up with some theory of successive creations, or spontaneous generation, or such like."

And more in the same vein. Volkov would have sat with his head in his hands if he'd had anywhere to sit. As it was, he just stood there, feeling his jaw muscles first slacken and then, increasingly, clench.

"Your pardon," he said finally to Sejanus, "but I must speak."

Sejanus bowed him to the rostrum. Volkov gripped it and leaned forward.

"I fully understand," he said, "and deeply appreciate what the sciences of this great city have accomplished by examining and comparing information obtained by your own careful observations and from study of the information won on Earth in the past. You have indeed accomplished great things. But not all, not by any means all, of what anyone can see in this wonderful metropolis was built by such methods. No amount of reasoning, from observation or from first principles, could have built the machines I have seen in the shops, the ships I see on the ocean, the vehicles in your streets, and the crops in your fields. They were designed by the method I suggested, the empirical method, the method of trial and error, of hypothesis and induction as well as— indeed, hand in hand with—deduction. Your mechanics and artisans, your pharmacists and farmers, your fishers and flyers may not be able to tell you the method by which they have so successfully worked, but the fact of that method and its success are surely beyond dispute here. Let us reason and compare, to be sure, when we investigate the discoveries of others. But let us experiment and test when we wish to make new discoveries ourselves."

As he spoke, he glanced from face to face, and here and there he saw agreement, even—and it thrilled him to see it—enlightenment dawn, but these occurrences were few. The overwhelming mood of the assembly was bafflement, even affront. Theocritus Gionno was simmering, and jumped to his feet as soon as Volkov stepped back.

"Of course," said Gionno, "many of us here do appreciate the value, and understand the significance, of what the esteemed Colonel rightly calls the empirical or experimental method. Some here have devoted their lives as scholars to such works of the masters Bacon and Popper as have reached us. The commentaries upon *The Advancement of Learning* alone would fill a not insignificant shelf, and those upon *The Logic of Scientific Discovery* a small library. But there are many deep problems with such a method, and until they are resolved, it is best left to guide, consciously or otherwise as it may be, the crude blundering of mechanics, artisans, and herbalists. Such methods are no doubt good enough for them. The requirements of exact science are considerably more rigorous."

Volkov laughed. He had not intended to, and he saw at once that its effect was bad, but he could not help himself.

"Somewhere in one of the works of science in the de Tenebres' cargo," he said into a shocked silence, "you'll find a quote from a great scientist of Earth, one Poincaré, who said: 'Science advances, funeral by funeral.' I see that its truth is universal, and I bid you good day."

"Well," puffed Esias, having caught up with Volkov in the shade of a cloistered quadrangle, "that did not go down well."

Volkov ran his hand over his brush-cut hair. "No, it did not," he said. "My apologies, my friend. I hope I haven't dragged you down with me. But these scholars, my God! They'd sooner die than think. And they will."

Esias chuckled. "Some of them. Perhaps not all. Let us proceed to the refreshment patio and wait there, in as dignified a fashion as we can muster, and see if there are any exceptions to the rule." He clapped Volkov's shoulder. "The scientific method!"

"I don't want to hear those words again for a week," said Volkov. "But you're right. And I'm parched."

They sat at a table under an awning and gulped one glass and sipped a second glass of what Esias insisted was beer. Volkov knew better than to press the point. He relaxed and watched the students, at the other tables or walking in the quadrangle. Apart from the black bat-sleeved short robes they wore like overalls, they looked on the one hand like younger versions of the Academicians, and on the other like students everywhere, alternately earnest and relaxed. The proportion of female students was a good deal higher than it was among the scholars, though nowhere near parity. What a bloody waste, Volkov thought. Changing that alone would speed up development.

"You know," said Esias, "you may be underestimating the Academy. They are not dullards. They have millennia of experience behind them of teasing out unexpected implications. Your journey here will not be wasted. It may take them time, longer than you might wish, but the knowledge we have brought back will be assimilated and extended."

"All right," Volkov said. "Let the Academy rummage through books if it wants. What I'm more concerned about is the other institutions. Are they as hidebound? Because time is what we don't have. If the aliens turn up before this place has a space defense capability, then the question of longevity is, you might say, academic."

"Ah yes," said Esias. "The aliens." He glanced around. "I think any allusion to that matter is best . . . postponed, until we can put it before the Electorate—in the first instance, the Defense Committee of the Senate."

Volkov smiled. "That's how it was done on Earth. The consequences were not good."

"Oh," said Esias, looking over his shoulder again, "you won't find any of that paranoia here. You'll see."

But Volkov was only half listening; he was gazing away to the shade of the quadrangle, from which a dozen or so black-gowned figures had emerged blinking into the sunlight and were making their way over.

2

Hardy Man

L EMURIA BEACH WAS the worst place in the world, and Elizabeth Harkness was happy to be there. She trudged along the shingle shore, her head down and her left shoulder hunched against the knife-edge wind off the sea. Hooded parka, quilted trousers, fur-lined gloves and boots weren't quite enough, especially when she had to push her hood back or take her gloves off. Big smooth pebbles ground against each other, and dried wrack crackled under her soles. Seabats screamed as they wheeled overhead. Behind all the sounds, the white noise of the white water filled her ears. The abandoned whaling station where she and Gregor Cairns had parked the skiff was a couple of kilometers behind her, its rusted boilers tiny at this distance, like some wrecked laboratory apparatus. Gregor had chosen to spend the morning hacking fossils from the foot of the cliffs, the same hundred-meter-high rockface that rose to her right. Elizabeth was intent on finding more recent signs of life. Although the season was what passed for spring in these latitudes, there wasn't much: Seabat roosts whitened the cliffs, and the occasional wind-dried corpse of a failed fledgling would be caught on the windward side of a boulder; on the lee side of boulders, lichens spread out their wrinkled mats of grey and orange; on the lichens, tiny red arthropods scurried like the dots before a bloodshot eye; and here and there a drift of soil sustained a small tough flowering plant, white as the sea's froth.

The sea itself, choppy in the wind off the ice-capped polar ocean a thousand kilometers southward, was a more hospitable abode of life than anything the island could offer. Every seaward glance couldn't but take in, somewhere between the horizon and the shore, the plume of hot breath from a spouting whale. Seabats of several species, from the tiny

watershears skimming the wavetops to the three-meter-spanning alca-
trazi gliding high above, patrolled and plunged to pillage the inexhaustible shoals that thronged the waters below. Every so often, about five
hundred meters out from the shore, the black bullet heads of seals or
sea-lions or some such seagoing mammal would pop up, peer around
in a disconcertingly human manner, then disappear again in a humping
curve of back.

Elizabeth worked her way steadily along, scraping rocks, making
notes, taking samples and placing them in airtight plastic cases or small,
stoppered jars. Even the minute insect or arachnid specimens found their
way there, via an arrangement of L-shaped glass tube and long rubber
suction tube and rubber bung with holes through it for both, which, in
all its centuries of scientific use, had never been given a more scientific
name than "put-er." The biota of Mingulay, like that of all the other
Earthlike planets of the Second Sphere, shared a common terrestrial
ancestry but had, over megayears, diverged in unique and interesting
ways. Not that the ancient arthropod or other invertebrate lineages
showed much sign of it—she could identify most of the ones she picked
up, right down to the species level, from memory of the standard manuals reprinted from originals published millennia ago on Earth. Mingulay's own geology and biology had been left for several centuries in
something of a mess. The planet's earliest human settlers had barely
sorted out a few recognizably successive epochs—Pelagic, Noachic,
Nevisian, Corpachian, Strontian—and one or two bold philosophers had
just begun to postulate a theory of evolution when the last starship from
Earth had arrived with the disheartening news that while the scientists
were in principle right, the planet they were standing on had indeed
undergone a succession of creations and catastrophes and was in all
likelihood the bodged work of gods.

After forgetting time for a while, Elizabeth glanced at her watch
and at the sun, decided it was time to rest and to turn back, and selected
a large boulder to shelter behind. The pebbles were dry this far up the
beach. She swung her pack off and sat down and pulled out a thermos
flask of coffee. Just as she was unscrewing the cup, she noticed some
whitened thing sticking partly out of the ground, a few meters up the
beach where the pebbles ran out into thin sand below the cliffs.

Curiosity got the better of her tiredness. She wedged the flask
among the stones and stood up, a little stiffly—forty years of life, twenty
of them spent in varied gravities, were beginning to tell on her knee
joints—and stalked over, tugging off a glove, fumbling in her jacket

pocket for the sturdy clasp knife she used for her rough fieldwork's probing and digging. She hunkered down on the sand and peered at the half-covered thing: a fossil in formation, sinking into sand that would one day be sandstone. At first she thought it was the washed-up exoskeleton of a brittle-star or a long-legged crab: There was a handsbreadth roundish central bit with jointed appendages coming off it. She could see three evenly spaced cup-shaped depressions, each with a tiny central hole, in the exposed part of the main bit, and below these concavities other holes, and below these holes a triangular articulation of delicate, roughly rectangular plates, and along the inner edge of each plate a row of something whiter than the rest of it.

Teeth. Jaws. Eye sockets. The cascade of successive recognitions sent a shock of adrenaline through her body. She walked back to take a trowel from her pack, returned and began to dig around it, very carefully. When it was all uncovered, she stood up and took a long look at it. It had eight appendages in all, each about forty centimeters long, with ball-and-socket joints proximally, medially, and distally. On the distal joints were what looked like miniature versions of the whole skeleton— buds, or eight-fingered hands. The central part was at the top something like a skull, curving inward beneath the jaws; the lower part, joined to the upper by a stubby central rod, and to which the appendages were attached on each side in rows of four, was something like a pelvis. The three sockets she'd initially seen had five others like them further around the circumference, all evenly spaced, and the triple-jaw arrangement was repeated, sans teeth, on the opposite side.

Already it was so unlike any invertebrate she'd ever seen that it was making her shake. It was making her almost sick, actually: It was much too like the remains of hideously conjoined quadruplet infant monkeys to be easy on the eye. What clinched it for her was the presence of shriveled but recognizable tendons on the outside of the joints, still holding them together, and in the parts which had been covered, the clinging fragments of leathery, fuzzy skin. Unless she was misinterpreting it completely, what she was looking at was an internal skeleton, not the external skeleton of an invertebrate, not even one unknown to science. It looked like a vertebrate—hell, if that fuzz was hair, like a *mammal*—that had evolved from some invertebrate without losing its radial symmetry. Either she'd stumbled upon some bizarre malformation, or a new phylum, or an organism that had no terrestrial ancestors at all. She could imagine its possible ancestors. She did not have to imagine, because she'd already seen pictures of its probable descendants. Or, if this was a juvenile, its adults.

Still staring down at it, Elizabeth reached inside her jacket for her radio to call Gregor. Just as she was about to thumb the dial, she heard behind her the sound of heavy footsteps crunching up the beach. Startled, but not scared—someone might have landed silently from a boat or skiff while she was preoccupied—she turned around, and came face-to-face with her second unknown species of the morning.

At first, as before, Elizabeth's perception tried to make sense of what she saw in terms of what she knew. The figure stood about two and a half meters tall, and about twenty meters away from her. It could have been a fat gigant in a black wetsuit. But the staring eyes and opening mouth and snorting nostrils were set in the same shining hair-covered skin as the rest of it. The rest of him. He had long hands and feet, and his neck sloped smoothly to his shoulders, but otherwise his proportions and features were human. She realized that he could be one of the marine mammals she'd noticed earlier.

He said something, in a deep, barking voice, but evidently speech. He spread his broad hands wide, palms forward, and then walked towards her, staring with apparent curiosity all the while, and repeating his utterances. Elizabeth backed away. He stepped over the boulder she'd thought to shelter behind, and paused to look down at her gear, with a long sniffling snort. Then he strode forward again, to stop before the small excavation she'd made. The cliff face was pressing into her back. She could feel the revolver in her thigh pocket knocking her leg as her knees quivered.

He squatted down and poked a long finger at the strange bones, stirring them gently. Then he stood up and looked straight at her. He pointed at the bones, then pointed to the sky, then looked up and slowly brought his arm around and down until it was pointing at an angle to the ground. He dropped his arm to his side, raised it and pointed at her, waved his arm about, and made a loud grunt.

The only sound she could make in response was what came from her teeth chattering. He cocked his head, turning a small ear to her, then faced her directly. He rocked his head from side to side, shrugged, turned and walked back down the beach and, without breaking step, into the water until he was waist-deep, and stooped forward and was suddenly gone with barely a splash.

Elizabeth's thumb at last engaged the knurl of the dial, her fingers found the switch. Finding the right channel was easy; there was no other traffic here.

"Gregor—"

"Are you all right?"

Deep breath. "Yeah, I'm fine. But I think you'd better come over here quickly. I've . . . found something interesting."

"Okay. Be right over. Signing off."

Hands shaking, Elizabeth opened the flask and poured herself some coffee, as if to return to her interrupted action, and therefore to her previous equilibrium. She kept looking out to sea—where the round black heads bobbed up as before—and over to her left, to the whaling station. She'd taken only a few sips and slurps of coffee when she saw the skiff rise from behind the tumbledown wooden buildings and the ochre boilers to skim along the beach towards her, its course so steady that it seemed to enlarge rather than approach. The lens-shaped, fifteen-meter-wide craft halted a few meters away and hovered. Its three landing legs telescoped out, their bases grinding into the pebbles as the field was powered down and its weight came back. The hatch on the underside opened, the stair ladder extended, and Gregor descended. He ran over to her and caught her in his arms.

"I'm all right," she insisted.

"You look like you've had a shock."

"Um," she said, pushing him away gently. "One at a time." She showed him the thing she'd dug up. Gregor glanced at her, whistled, drew a long breath in through his teeth, and squatted down and poked at the bones with his forefinger, just as the other primate had done. He stayed looking for a minute, then stood up.

"You know," he said, "we're going to have to find a better name for these than 'the monkey-spider things.' "

She laughed, some tension going out of her as her identification was validated.

"I thought it might be a relative," she said. "As close to them as a monkey or maybe a lemur is to us."

"That or a juvenile," Gregor said. "We'll have to look again at the records."

Elizabeth nodded. "And look again at the island."

"Oh, gods, yes." Gregor frowned. "This isn't what shook you up."

"No," agreed Elizabeth. "What shook me up was that I met a—"

She hesitated, knowing that as discoverer she had the privilege of naming, and that the name would matter, the popular name perhaps more than the scientific.

"A selkie," she decided.

"What?"

She pointed seaward. "Those, out there. They're not seals. They're aquatic hominids. Probably closer to us than the gigants or the pithkies. Same genus as us, I'll bet." She found herself giggling. "Just like Alister Hardy speculated long ago—you know, the aquatic ape hypothesis? We could call them *homo hardiensis*: Hardy Man."

She told him about her encounter.

"You know what's weird about that?" she concluded. "It was like he *recognized* it."

"It's not so much weird as inevitable," Gregor said. He looked down at the bones, then out to sea. "Even if that thing wasn't here, we'd still be thinking *aliens* as soon as we saw the selkies. Because they sure as hell haven't been here long. The last whalers were here ten years ago."

"Are you sure they couldn't have been unnoticed earlier? The Southern Ocean's big enough."

"Yeah, but its islands aren't. And if they're any kind of viable population, they must use islands to breed, if nothing else. I suppose it's just possible that sailors and whalers misidentified them all this time, but I doubt it. Nah, they must be recent arrivals. And that raises the question of who brought them here. I seriously doubt it was the saurs."

Elizabeth knocked on the underside of the skiff. "Assuming they didn't come here themselves."

"There is that," Gregor conceded. He was gazing intently out at the bobbing dots. "You know, not to get too excited or anything, I think we may soon be able to ask them."

Elizabeth realized that they were now only about two hundred meters out. She counted twelve of them.

"Should we get into the skiff?" she asked.

"Just keep our pistols easy to reach." Gregor clicked open the flap on his thigh pocket, and Elizabeth did likewise. They waited silently.

After a couple of minutes the selkies were standing waist-deep in the water and wading ashore. They were all adults, seven males and five females. The females had large breasts, and long hair on their heads. As they stepped out of the water, they were wringing out their hair and twisting it to hang forward over one shoulder. The water seemed to slide off their bodies; they didn't look wet for more than a moment. They paused at the strand and spread their empty hands.

Elizabeth, then Gregor, mirrored the gesture.

The selkies advanced up the beach to about ten meters away, then stood in a semicircle and looked at the two intruders. Elizabeth recognized the one she'd seen earlier. Their height was intimidating. On an impulse, Elizabeth sat down on her heels. The selkies did the same, taking care to keep their hands open, palms upward.

"Body language looks reassuring," muttered Gregor.

"Uh-huh. I just wonder if a smile means the same."

"Try it without baring our teeth."

Elizabeth stretched her lips and crinkled her eyes. The selkies responded with broad grins. Their teeth were not much larger than human teeth, in proportion to their body size. They just looked larger, white in their black, hairy faces. So Elizabeth told herself.

"Hallo," said Gregor, raising his right hand slowly. The selkies responded with a brief, barking phrase and raised their hands also, but hesitantly, as though the gesture was unfamiliar. Everyone relaxed a little. Three or four of them had, as though absently, begun grooming each other and themselves, scratching and snatching and popping things caught between thumb and forefinger into their mouths. It was disconcertingly apelike. But their expressions remained intent, curious, patient.

The one she'd already met stood up. He looked at Elizabeth and opened his eyes wider—no, he was raising his eyebrows. Elizabeth nodded. He walked forward and past them and laid his hand on the rim of the skiff. Then he patted it and made a happy-sounding chuckle, a deep, liquid note, bassy and warm. Elizabeth wondered if he recognized, in the rough pitting of its metal, and in its general appearance of being a copy made from too many generations of copies, that it was a skiff built by humans and not by saurs. The selkie strolled around it, ducking under to examine the hatch, then went over and looked again at the bones, and called back to his fellows. After standing there scratching his head, he turned and strolled back to the group. They began a quiet and orderly sounding conversation, pointing now at Gregor and Elizabeth, now at the skiff. When everyone had spoken—Elizabeth was watching and listening carefully, and she noticed—he came forward again and squatted on the shingle a couple of meters in front of them. Elizabeth could smell the fish on his breath. He leaned an elbow on his knee and held his chin in one hand for a moment, then rubbed a finger along his lips, then nodded as though to himself. He looked about among the stones at his feet, selected one, and picked up another at random. He held the first stone in the palm of one hand and brought the other down sharply on it, splitting it. He held out the two pieces. They contained a fossil of a coiled shell, an ammonite. He raised his eyebrows and grunted on a rising note.

"Yes," said Elizabeth, nodding.

The selkie tapped the fossil with a blunt, ridged fingernail. Then he pointed over to the bones; at the skiff; at the sky; then away at an angle as he had done earlier; pointed at himself, and finally waved his finger back over his shoulder at the others. He settled back, buttocks on heels, elbows on knees, waved a hand to include Gregor and Elizabeth, and repeated the interrogative grunt.

"Translation," Elizabeth said, turning to Gregor. " 'The spidery things carried us in skiffs long ago. Where do you come from?' Agreed?"

"Yup," said Gregor. "But maybe there's more to it than that. What's with that pointing at the ground?"

Elizabeth shrugged. "I don't know. Maybe there's more of the things buried over there?"

"Hey, that's a thought. We can check it later. What do we tell him? And how?"

"Same way as he told us."

Elizabeth stood up and walked over to the bones. Gregor watched her with a slightly worried look. She beckoned to the selkie, who came over but stayed a few meters distant. She pointed down at the alien skeleton, then at herself, then moved her head from side to side. The selkie tipped his head back a couple of times. She hoped this was a nod.

Elizabeth reached for the trowel, still lying there undisturbed, and sketched in the sand a spidery shape. Indicating it, and the bones, elicited another backward jerk of the head. She smoothed over the disturbed sand and drew a semicircle joined to a V to make a crude outline of a saur's head. Four curved strokes outlined the almond-shaped eyes, a slash the slit mouth. She pointed to the saur face, then to the skiff.

The selkie stared at her. He made what she'd taken as the interrogative sound, but this time with a sort of strain in his voice—the human equivalent would have been *"Huh*?!" He squatted beside her and held out a hand for the trowel. She gave it to him; he grasped it confidently as though holding a paintbrush and rapidly added a rendering of a saur's spindly body beneath the head. Beside it, he drew with equal speed and economy an ellipse with three legs, then put down the trowel and looked at her.

"Yes," she said firmly, nodding backwards.

The selkie's mouth and eyes widened. He stood slowly, as though weary, and walked back to the others. They conferred in a huddle. Some of them made downward slapping gestures that puzzled Elizabeth for a moment, until she realized that in water it would have been deliberate splashing at the surface, perhaps as a warning. Then they all jumped to their feet and fled into the sea; but the bold one was the last, and he looked back over his shoulder as he ran.

After marking the spot and photographing it they finished the excavation, laid the small skeleton carefully in a plastic tray, and into another tray they shoveled the sand in which it had been buried and which contained myriad tiny rods that might be small bones or internal parts or otherwise related to it; or perhaps just the spines of sea urchins; in any case, part of the puzzle. They lifted the two trays into the skiff, along with clinking racks of tubes containing the other specimens Elizabeth had collected. By comparison with the apparently alien skeleton, these specimens seemed trivial, but in the long run nothing was trivial in science. Not wishing to hang around where the selkies had been, as much to avoid further alarming them as out of uncertainty about how dangerous the alarmed selkies might be, they took the skiff back to the whaling station and parked it well up the beach. Over a hasty midday ration, they discussed what to do next.

"The first thing we have to do," said Gregor, "is take another look inland."

Elizabeth waved a half-chewed chewy bar at the cliffs. "We've already looked. There's nothing but sea-bats and insects."

"We weren't looking for *that*. What we need to know is whether it's just some waif or part of a breeding population."

"Okay," said Elizabeth. "I'll fly. You look."

The skiff was human-adapted, but its control panel still assumed four-fingered hands: that configuration was buried so deep in the manufacturing-control program that it was impossible to change without a radical redesign of the craft. Elizabeth sat on the padded seat in front of a section of the circular shelf under the encircling viewscreen, a section that contained a few dials and gauges and a pair of shallow, hand-shaped but four-fingered depressions. She rested her fingers in the hollows, her thumbs to the sides, and consciously relaxed for a moment. Control was intuitive, something you had to ease yourself into, dependent on chords of varying pressures rather than any one-to-one correspondence. She let her fingers do the flying, and the craft lifted.

The view tilted from side to side as her initial tremors of hesitation transmitted themselves to the drive, then steadied as the machine rose above the top of the cliff. Higher, and the jumbled landscape of Lemuria Beach opened before them. The island was about a hundred kilometers east to west, and fifty north to south. Behind the tilted sedimentary strata of the southern cliffs were ragged strips of rock alternating with long bands of rough grass, which, after a few kilometers, gave way to a more recent mixture of volcanic rock and tuff, basalt flows, sulphurous geysers, and bogs of lime-green algae, interrupted by snow-covered remnant plateaus and outcrops of the sedimentary rock and lumpy intrusions of even older metamorphic and basal layers.

"Let's follow the clifftop grasslands first," said Gregor.

Elizabeth leaned down on her left hand, spinning the skiff to that side. She pressed her fingertips down and the skiff moved forward, rocked back the heels of both hands and it rose. They settled on a cruising altitude of thirty meters. Gregor paced around the circular space between the viewscreen and the central engine fairing, gazing out with binoculars. Every so often he'd spot something and Elizabeth would bring the craft down, tip it on edge or even right over, so that they could look at the ground just inches above their heads. But the bones always turned out to be of sea-bats, and the momentary excitement of finding in a grassy bank a huge warren of burrows was dimmed somewhat by the discovery, which at any other time would have made their day, that they were the work of a peculiar flightless bird which they provisionally dubbed the "mole penguin."

"I'm amazed the whalers didn't hunt them to extinction," said Elizabeth.

"Probably taste disgusting."

She looked at him sidelong. "And your point would be?"

They laughed and took themselves aloft.

The volcanic badlands were, not to their surprise, an even less thriving habitat for land animals. They chipped some interesting mats of yellow, stinking extremophile bacteria and netted a few specimens of a small spider that skittered across the algae-clogged pools, but that was it. They returned to the whaling station as the short day ended. The wind had dropped, and the sea was calm, smooth on the surface of its ceaseless swells. Elizabeth and Gregor stowed their less fragile specimens, marked and tagged for later collection, in the whaling station. In the long twilight they built a fire from the whitened timbers of a ruined boat and cooked over it their first hot meal of the day. They lingered, huddling closer together against the cold, as the embers faded with the light and the stars came down to the horizon. The southern hemisphere constellations were so unfamiliar they didn't have names. Repairing this omission and identifying the two stars, among the many visible that they'd visited themselves, was keeping them idly occupied when they heard heavy footsteps crunching up the beach.

"Behind the fire," Gregor said quietly.

They scrambled to their feet and backed off, one to each side, and peered toward the shoreline. The footsteps became quieter as they moved from the shingle to the sand, then stopped. Elizabeth could dimly make out a selkie silhouetted against the starlit sea. He spread his hands wide and stepped forward into the dim circle of light from the fire. One arm was raised, shielding his eyes from the glow as he peered over his thick forearm at them. It was the bold one they'd met before.

He began to speak, his deep voice loud above the surf but quiet in itself. There was something in it of frustration, perhaps sorrow, but nothing of anger or fear. He spoke for about two minutes, then trailed off and ended with a gurgling laugh. Then he hunkered down, spread his hands, and looked at them across the fire, his eyes having apparently adapted to the light. Elizabeth stepped over beside Gregor, put a hand on his shoulder, and he joined her in squatting down. She faced the selkie, spread her hands, and leaned forward earnestly.

"What you are saying," she said, her voice speaking to the selkie but her words for Gregor's benefit, "is that you are speaking, and therefore you are a rational being, and that you want us to recognize you as such, and that you find our lack of a common language as frustrating as we do. Well, I understand and agree with that. In fact, I think that for all your nakedness and living in the wild, you are not a savage, a hunter-gatherer, although that may be how you live now. I think you're basically as civilized as we are, and as aware of the nature of the universe. You can draw, you've seen a skiff before, you've met aliens. Am I right?"

Gregor nodded. The selkie responded with another minute or so of speech, looking down a little, as though in abstraction. When he'd finished, he looked up, and his teeth flashed in the embers' glow. He reached for a stick from the fire, motioned to them and began to draw in the sand. They joined him and watched as he slashed in the sand the glyphs of skiff and spidery alien—ten lines, little more. He pointed at himself, waved a hand out to sea, and then raised a hand, palm forward: Wait. He rose and tramped into the dark, beckoning them after him.

When they were all out of the circle of light, a few tens of meters along the beach, he held out an arm stiff with a pointing finger. It started at the angle to the ground he'd pointed at before, then swung smoothly up and around, until it was aimed at a bright red star about halfway up the sky to the east. They joined him in sighting along their arms at the star. Just to make sure they were looking at the right one, he poked a finger in the sand and dotted out the pattern of the stars around it, completing the picture with the one he'd pointed at, jabbing his finger in deep, then pointing again. He pointed at his chest again, then at the sea, then at the star again. Elizabeth and Gregor nodded vigorously. The selkie's lips peeled back from his teeth in a grin that would have been frightening had they just encountered him.

He laid a hand first on Gregor's shoulder, then on Elizabeth's—it was like being a child again, looking up at him—and said something, then walked away into the waves.

"You know what I just figured out?" Gregor said, as the selkie's back vanished.

"What?"

"The way he was pointing downward earlier, and at the start just there? He was pointing to where the star was in the morning, when it was below the horizon."

She stared at him. "Could you do that?"

Gregor had been a navigator for twenty years. He had a more direct and practical knowledge of the sky than most astronomers. He thought about it for a moment and shook his head.

"Which means," said Elizabeth, "that I may have been wrong about the selkies. They're not as smart as we are. They're smarter."

A storm blew up later that night. Gregor and Elizabeth had already stowed some of their kit in the whaling station's gloomy rooms, but they decided to spend the night in the skiff. With its field on it was less moveable than a rock. Its encircling viewscreen picked up enough light from outside to give them a clear view, even with the interior lights on. They sat exhausted, gazing outward. It was like watching black-and-white television—white the surf, black the waves—but interesting.

"Wonder how the selkies are doing," Elizabeth said.

"They can ride it out," said Gregor. "Like seals."

"But they're not like seals. They're not that aquatic. I can imagine them huddled on a beach somewhere. Poor things."

"They look tough." He grinned. " 'Hardy Man,' all right."

Elizabeth saw Gregor's gaze drift back to the plastic tray in which they'd placed the anomalous octopod's bones. Of all the specimens they'd collected, this was the one they could least afford to lose. They had not cared to examine it further with the crude instruments—scalpels, tweezers, pliers, hammers—that were on hand. They hardly dared to think about it. Not thinking about it was making them dizzy.

"This is big," he said. "This is evidence, the first solid evidence we've had of the aliens for a start, and it looks like evidence that they've settled the selkies here. Or that they're still doing it."

Elizabeth smiled wryly. "The long-awaited invasion?"

"Something like that." Gregor sighed. "Whatever. We have to report back." He reached sideways and clasped her right hand, intertwining their fingers. "The journey's over."

"Yeah," she said. "It's the next journey I'm worried about."

It had been a good journey, almost a holiday. It could even have been the beginning of a retirement, or the resumption of their true careers after a long interruption. They'd always promised themselves that someday they would pay their home planet, Mingulay, the attention of a *Beagle* voyage. Marine biology had been, for both of them, their first love. When they'd both been twenty years younger, eighty-odd years ago, Gregor had found in the structures of the cephalopod brain the key to his family's generations-long Great Work—to reverse-engineer the control program of the lightspeed drive, hitherto monopolized by the kraken navigators who plied the fixed trading routes of the Second Sphere. Implementing the program on the ancient onboard computers of the *Bright Star*, the ship in which Gregor's ancestors had been hurled across the galaxy to humanity's second home, had taken Gregor and Elizabeth across the four light-years to Croatan and, a month or two later, the four light-years back.

The lightspeed jumps were subjectively instantaneous. While they'd been away, people had grown up or aged or died. That first experience of skipping forward in time had been a jolt. As the Cairns clan's starship fleet had expanded and new planetary systems were laboriously added to the navigation programs, their journeys' reach had extended, and that first jolt had been followed by many more. Already, the oldest members of Elizabeth's family, who'd had decades yet to live when her starfaring had started, were long dead. Her parents were barely recognizable centenarians. Her children—at least they had kept pace, because they'd traveled with her. Elizabeth was already beginning to feel that disconnection with common humanity, and that identification with her traveling-companions, that was so patent in the long-established merchant families who for millennia had traveled in the krakens' ships, slipping through centuries in months.

—And she thought for a moment of Lydia de Tenebre, still young in the momentary eternity of her century-long journey to Nova Terra, and she blinked that thought away—

It had seemed their task was done. It was no longer necessary for Gregor, the First Navigator, to go on each newly charted course; or for Elizabeth, the Senior Science Officer, to accompany him. They had been able to get away, to leave the pioneering to others, and to return to exploring their own underpopulated and diverse world. And even, for once, to leave the children at home. Weeks, then months, of wandering the planet's oceans and islands in the skiff had not tired them, nor ceased to bring them new discoveries each day. This day's discoveries would end all that.

3

RTFM

MATT CAIRNS, OUTWARD bound from Rawliston on Croatan to Kyohvic on Mingulay, mooches about among a few hundred other milling passengers. There's not much to do. The ship is just a more or less airtight box with an interstellar drive, inadequate seating, and a few refreshment stalls. There isn't even a window. After the light-speed jump, Matt has become so bored that he finds himself reading the orientation leaflet for newbie passengers. It's available in various languages and in a variety of formats, including one entirely in pictures. The one he selects has a little boxed note at the foot in tiny print:

> Literate, largely prescientific (suitable for sailors, traders, shamans, etc. Not recommended for clergy of desert monotheisms.)

Long ago, he had written the first draft of it himself. His private title for it was: *GREETINGS, IGNORANT SAVAGES!* Follwed by:

Welcome to the Bright Star Cultures

This may be your first journey in a starship navigated by human beings. Please take a few moments to read this document, which should help you to understand your journey, and your destination. It explains how we on the English-speaking planets of Croatan and Mingulay explain the worlds in which we live. Your own explanation may well differ from the one given here. We respect your opinion as much as you respect ours.
     When you look up at the sky at night, you see a broad, bright band of stars overhead, which is sometimes called the

Milky Way or the Foamy Wake. What you are looking at is the edge of an immense disk of stars—a galaxy. There are many galaxies in the universe, the nearest of which you may know as the Little Cloud or That Fuzzy Dot There.

The Foamy Wake galaxy contains a hundred thousand thousand thousand stars. The stars are suns like the one you know, but very far away. The worlds on which we live travel around these suns. (See "Copernican Hypothesis, Evidence in Favor of.") They are so far away that the distances between them are measured in light-years. This refers to the distance that light travels in one year. Light travels three hundred thousand thousand thousand strides in one heartbeat. We are at present traveling at the speed of light between two stars—when we arrive, very soon, the sun will be different from the one which shone above us when we left. There is no need to be alarmed by this.

We live in a very small region of the galaxy, which we call the Second Sphere. It is a spherical volume of space that contains several hundred stars. Many of them are the suns of worlds like the one on which you were born. The Second Sphere is about two hundred light-years across. We call it the Second Sphere because it is not the place where human beings first came from. Human beings came from a world which we call Earth, a hundred thousand light-years away, on the other side of the Foamy Wake. So do all the other people, animals, and plants that you will find on the worlds of the Second Sphere. (See "Evolution, Theory of.") When you go from one world to another, you may find that the animals and plants are different from those on your own world. There is no need to be alarmed by this. In your pack you will find a separate leaflet that will tell you which animals and plants at your destination are dangerous.

As well as human beings and the kinds of people who resemble human beings—the tall hairy people and the small hairy people—there are two other kinds of people in the Second Sphere. These are the small grey people, whom we call the saurs, and the very large people with tentacles, whom we call the krakens. You may know the saurs mainly as the pilots of the small round aircraft we see in our skies, and the krakens as the navigators of the great starships that you have seen in the sky or on the sea. The trade routes followed by their starships are what define the limits of the Second Sphere, at about one hundred light-years in all directions from Nova Babylonia, its oldest human civilization, though not its oldest settlement. The krakens and the saurs have lived in the Second Sphere for much longer than human beings.

You will have been told that there are much greater minds in the spaces between the worlds—the minds that some people call the gods, and others call the powers above. This is true. The gods live in very small worlds, like the ones which we sometimes see in the sky as comets. There are many, many such gods around all the suns that we know about, including the sun of Earth. The gods are minds whose bodies are made up from many very small animals that can endure severe cold and heat. They are similar in some ways to the many small animals which we cannot see but which exist all around us. There is no need to be alarmed by this. (See "Disease, Germ Theory of" elsewhere in this information pack. If you already understand this, see "Extremophile Nanobacteria" and "Emergent Phenomena.")

There is much we do not understand about the gods. One thing we do know is that for a very long time they have arranged for saurs who live near Earth to transport people, animals, and plants to the worlds of the Second Sphere. These have always arrived in starships with saurs from the Solar System on board, and have been met by saurs from the Second Sphere, who in turn transported them to the nearest world. This is how the worlds of the Second Sphere came to be populated. The saurs, of course, came from Earth a very long time ago.

The planet we call Croatan was settled in this way more than seven hundred years ago, in the Seasonally Adjusted Year of Our Lord (SAYOL) 1600 (see "Calendar, Croatan") by people from North America. Its daughter colony, Mingulay, was established two hundred and fifty years later by the followers of a heretical prophetess (see "Taine, Joanna").

Almost three hundred years ago, in SAYOL 2051, a starship from Earth arrived near Mingulay. It was a starship built by human beings, and it was called the *Bright Star*. It was left to travel in the sky around Mingulay when the several hundred people on board were met by saurs and taken to the main city of Mingulay, Kyohvic, where they settled. They were different in three important ways from other people who had arrived from Earth.

First, they had traveled into the space outside their world by themselves. These Cosmonauts, as they were called, had encountered a god in one of the very small worlds we have mentioned earlier, and it had communicated with them. It gave them copies of instructions on how to build the engines which enable us to travel at the speed of light, and the other engines to fly in the air like the saurs do. Unfortunately, it had not told them how to navigate, and when they used the engine they found themselves in the Second Sphere, with no idea of how they had got there or where it was. Their descendants, over several generations, had to work out how to navigate for themselves, and succeeded about ninety years ago. The Cosmonaut families went on to build ships such as the one you are now traveling in. The *Bright Star* also contained much new knowledge, discovered on Earth, which we are still learning. That is why we call ourselves the Bright Star Cultures.

This brings us to the second important way in which the Cosmonauts differ from most human beings. Many of them had taken medicines that enabled them to live for many hundreds of years, just like the saurs do. Unfortunately, neither they nor the saurs understood how this had happened, and we are still trying to find out. Many of the original Cosmonauts from the *Bright Star* are still alive today, and some of them are trying to help. They would be very happy if everyone could live as long as they do.

Thirdly, the Cosmonauts were the last people to arrive here from Earth. As of this date (SAYOL 2338) we know of no other arrivals from outside the Second Sphere. It is very possible that people on Earth, or the saurs near Earth, have come into conflict with another star-traveling species, which we call the aliens. It is possible that Earth has been destroyed. There is no need to be alarmed by this. If you have, now or in the future, any knowledge of creatures resembling furry spiders and about the size of a large dog, please inform the nearest militia officer or starship crew member as soon as possible.

And now, a word about the militia. We in the Bright Star Cultures believe that, in general, people should be free to do whatever is compatible with the freedom of others. Here and below, "person," "people," and "human" refer to members of all intelligent species. Some religious, sexual, and other practices of which you disapprove may be permitted by law. Some of your own practices, which you believe to be righteous, may be prohibited by law. For your comfort and safety, it is important that you do not make mistakes in this area. Please study the following carefully:

Permitted practices of which you may disapprove:

All forms of sexual relations between people over the age of puberty.
All forms of attire (other than uniforms worn for purposes of deception) or lack of attire in all public places except places of worship or public ceremony.
All modes of address to people of any rank.
All modes of worship not involving prohibited practices.
All forms of artistic expression, including descriptions and depictions (but not commission or incitement) of prohibited practices.
Self-medication, including for ennui.
Suicide.
Reading books in public.
Writing in the margins of books.
Abortion.
Keeping and carrying weapons.

Prohibited practices (with or without consent) of which you may approve:

Human sacrifice.
Entertainments of lethal combat.
Sexual relations with people below the age of puberty.
Sexual relations with beasts.
Slavery.
Inflation.
Infanticide.
Piracy.
Cattle-raiding.

Dueling.

Nonmedical surgery on people below the age of puberty,
including but not limited to: scarification, infibulation,
circumcision.

Animal sacrifice grossly incompatible with the codes of
kosher and halal.

Interference with public or private practices not on the list of
prohibited practices.

Public exhortation of prohibited practices or heinous crimes,
except in the public reading of scriptures revealed before
the date of the passage of this law (SAYOL 2226) or in
the performance of traditional rites.

Unauthorized possession of nuclear-explosive devices.

Theomancy.

Heinous Crimes:

Murder.

Rape.

Kidnapping.

Trafficking in slaves.

Torture.

Poisoning.

Maiming.

Nonmedical vaginal or anal penetration of a person below the
age of puberty.

Prevention by force or fraud of any accepted passenger or
crew member from embarking or disembarking from a
starship.

Causing a nuclear explosion within a habitable atmosphere.

Theicide.

Anyone convicted of a heinous crime may be sentenced to death
by public stoning. There is no need to be alarmed by this. The
maximum sentence is seldom applied, and when it is, it is usually commuted to death by firing squad.

Have a safe journey, and enjoy your stay.

And *whee!* Back in Kyohvic—"Misty Harbor," as the helpful stab-in-
the-dark translation says in squiggly italics on the skyport sign, dittoed

below in the barred neon of chi-chi Ogham—Matt Cairns shoulders his duffel bag and heads through the concourse for the shuttle train to town. Foam earpieces tab his throat. The contract brokers will already be yammering after him, but he's not ready yet to come online. He needs a break and doubts his skills are obsolete, for all that his want of trying is everywhere evident in shimmering monitors and remote eyes and the infrared flicker of robot scuttlebutt. In the sixty rack-renting days of his contract on Croatan, this place has jumped forward eight years, and seen more change than in the previous sixteen: Matt knows the pattern, he can clock the curve, he's lived through this shit before; they're running up the steepening slope to the lip of Singularity like there's no tomorrow, and if the gods have their eye on the ball as usual, there won't be. Cue cannon ball: Somewhere out there in the long orbits, a shot is being lined up in the godgames of Newtonian pool. Or the spidery aliens will irrupt into the system, and Darwinian dice will roll.

Outside the low, flat-roofed concourse, he pauses to inhale the autumn late-afternoon wind off the sea, its salt tang muffled by the faint freshwater scent of the fog in the sound, and the sharper notes of acetone and alcohol derivatives. The skyport's on a plateau above the town, its traffic everything from buzzing microlites and zippy little skiffs through new lifting-body aerodynes to the great clunky contraptions of human-built starships like the one he's just stepped off. The town has spread up the valleys like a lichen, sprouted towers like sporula—tall, thin hundred-meter spikes of gene-hacked cellulose offshoot. The factory fringe is a fast merge of that sort of biotech or wet nano stuff with the rougher, more rugged carapaces of steel and aluminum, concrete and glass. It reminds him of the Edinburgh he left, centuries ago in his life, millennia ago in real time. The harbor's busier than ever, the tall masts bearing computer-optimized wind panels rather than sails, the steamships wispy and clean rather than smoky.

Out beyond the surface vessels, a Nova Babylonian starship—a quarter-mile of iron zeppelin, its hull running with rainbow colors—is poised above the water as though impossibly halted in the last few meters of a long fall. On the headland that shelters one side of the harbor like a shielding arm, the Cosmonauts' keep still stands, its prehuman megalithic proportions as unyielding to the eye as ever.

The crowd of merchants and migrants and refugee sectaries off the starship funnels, thickening, to the station entrance and packs the carriages. Matt straphangs through the electric down-slope glide, his knees' grip holding the big duffel upright. His reflexes haven't quite adjusted to the fractional difference in the gravity, but he's used to this transition; hell, he's done free fall often enough, he's bounded across the rusty desert of Raphael in a clumsy pressure suit, he's earned his honorary title of Cosmonaut. Others, the first-timers, are thin-lipped and whey-faced, lurching with each sway of the train. The cheap housing slides past the windows, then the University's crag-built complex, sprawling and soaring like everything else here, then the older, richer streets of the town center and shorefront.

Matt detrains at the esplanade terminus and hesitates. He has never quite gotten used to being feted by his descendants. The Cairns are now the richest of the Cosmonaut clans, thanks to their monopoly of interstellar navigation that they're exploiting as blatantly as the old merchants ever did their long-cut deal with the krakens. He has nowhere to sleep for the night, nobody apart from the brokers expecting him home, and the merchants off the Nova Babylonian ship will be at the castle, probably being entertained royally. A good party to gatecrash. On the other hand . . .

Nah. He's not up for it. He needs to find his feet first. The terminus is new since eight years ago, a cavernous glass shed full of hurrying people—the three major hominid species, and saurs—and cluttered with concession stands: coffee, flowers, snacks, drugs. Announcements are murmured from cunningly focused speakers, and displayed in midair holograms that don't quite work. The female gigant at the coffee stall has had all her hair dyed blonde and curled. Matt tries not to laugh at the thought of this car-wash-scale coiffure, smiles politely and takes his cup—thin plastic, but insulating—to a round enamel table.

"Mr. Cairns?"

He starts, almost splashing the coffee, and sets it down with both hands around it and glares into the smile of the young woman swinging into the seat opposite, slinging down a bag. She has a camera behind her ear like a pen, and a mike on a parallel spoke against her cheek. Her hair, eyelids, and lips are a sort of frosted gold. Behind all that she actually looks quite good. She's wearing black leather trousers and a black T-shirt with a broad rectangular panel of multicolored abstract tapestry on the front.

"Susan Harkness," she says, sticking out a hand which Matt clasps as briefly as politeness permits.

"I don't do interviews."

"I'm not a journalist," she says, fussing momentarily with the recording gear at the side of her head. "Well, I am, but I'm here on family business."

(He detects the increment of the local accent's change since he's been away: *fah-armlie*.)

"You're family?"

"Daughter of Elizabeth Harkness and Gregor Cairns."

"Ah." Matt relaxes and relents, smiling. "So I'm your ancestor."

"Yes," she says, looking at him with the unabashed curiosity of a human child seeing its first gigant. "It's hard to believe."

"In a good light, you can see the scars," Matt says.

"You've had cosmetic surgery?" She sounds disappointed. (*Suhdge'*ry.)

"Just two-hundred-fifty-odd years of shaving cuts." He shrugs. "And fights, of course."

"Of course." She tips her head sideways a little and smiles. Matt realizes she's putting up a good show; she's intensely nervous about him, or about something.

"So," he says, over the rim of the cup, "what family business? And how did you find me?"

She waves a hand. "Oh, I knew you had to pass through here. Mam—" She winces at herself—"Elizabeth and Gregor sent me."

Matt doesn't have to ask how she recognized him. Hanging in the castle is his ancient portrait in oils. There've been more recent photos, too, since he came out of hiding. Decades old, but not out of date.

"How are they?"

"They're well. They're just recently back from an expedition."

"Space?"

"No, sea. That *Beagle* tour they've been threatening as long as I can remember."

"Longer than that," says Matt. "Well, I'm glad they finally made it."

"They had to cut it short and come home in a hurry."

"Why?"

Her eyes widen. "Haven't you seen the papers?"

He shakes his head, thinking, *Don't tell me they've reinvented war while I've been away . . .*

Susan runs her thumbnail across the top of her bag. It opens in a way he can't quite see and she pulls out a bundle of newsflyers, hours old and already tattered. Matt spreads them out to see that they're all downmarket—their money pages cover the lottery rather than the stock exchange—and their front sides all have articles and headlines and photos of odd phenomena: a flattened whorl in a wheatfield, a waterspout, the face of a worried-looking man in dungarees, and something that might have been a thrown ashtray. There's a sketch of two grim-faced men in the Puritan-style suits affected by scoffers, the clergy of the local irreligion, captioned: "Sinister visitors—Heresiarchy denies knowledge."

"*This* rubbish?" Matt says.

"It's true," says Susan. She leans forward, voice dropping. "That's what Elizabeth and Gregor found out. The aliens are here. We're being invaded."

Matt sighs, clasps his hands at the back of his head and tilts back the flimsy chair. He's been expecting this for decades, ever since the expedition to the gods, but it still pisses him off. Through the glass roof he can see a couple of silvery lens-shaped skiffs scooting overhead. A couple of tables away, two small grey-skinned figures with large bald heads and big black eyes are canoodling over a shared bloodshake. The blonde person who'd served him at the stall has just shuffled through a spilled sticky drink and is leaving forty-centimeter-long footprints. There's a good chance that several of the commuters striding past had an ancestor on the *Mary* fucking *Celeste*. Three hours ago by his body clock, he was four light-years away. And it was early morning. He's a hundred thousand light-years from Earth and he's hundreds of years old and he feels every meter and minute of it.

"Aliens," he says, looking up again. "Unidentified flying objects. Crop circles. Men in black. This is *too* fucking *much*."

He swings forward, his gaze still focused on the middle distance, and he has a sudden hallucination that he can see right through Susan's T-shirt to a glowing green hologram of her naked torso. He blinks as the chair settles, and it's gone, there's just that pattern of colorful stitchery. He looks away and back, covertly, then meets her eyes. She's smiling.

"Stereogram," she says. "Computer-generated. You just let your eyes go—"

"I know," says Matt. "That's the most indecent garment I've ever seen."

"You haven't seen the skirts."

Matt stares at her face as though it too were a stereogram, and something clicks into focus. He knows she's attractive but he isn't attracted to her. To attribute this to the incest taboo would be absurd—intellectually, there's nothing to it, she's generations removed from him, and emotionally there is no way that inhibition would have had a chance to lock on—it depends on childhood imprinting of siblinghood, as far as he knows. It must be something else. He has the body and brain and appearance of a man in his early twenties, but mentally, inside, he is just too old. That must be it: Susan is too young for him. She's sucking a strand of her frosted fair hair, and tiny fragments of her matching lipstick are clogging the tips. As though realizing what she's doing, she flicks it away.

"Anyway," she says, "Elizabeth and Gregor want to see you."

"Up at the castle?"

"No. Too busy up there. For the merchants, this place is becoming a bit of a culture shock. Along the shore, at the marine biology lab." She stands. "We can walk." She sees his duffel, and his look. "Or take a tram."

The laboratories are single-storey blocks with wide windows, and walls whose pebbledash and roughcast have fallen off in great flakes here and there and mostly been patched up, so that over the years they've acquired a mottled texture like a lichen-covered boulder. The place is old and important enough to have its own tram stop, Aquarium. Inside, there's an atmosphere of barely controlled frenzy: knots of people in white coats arguing in low or raised voices, technicians wheeling equipment down corridors with the urgency of hospital porters in Accident and Emergency. Susan leads Matt through it all. Anyone who gives her a puzzled look or starts to ask her business is tugged back at the elbow by someone else.

At the end of a long corridor with shore-facing windows along one side, she marches into a room with rows of wide white-topped lab benches, aquaria and sinks and display cabinets around the sides, charts and diagrams papering the walls and a broad whiteboard at the far end, in front of which a woman is standing tapping a long pointer at multicolored scribbles and talking to the score of people sitting or standing around. It's her voice Matt recognizes first, just before she recognizes him and interrupts herself.

"Matt!" She walks toward him, arms opening.

"Elizabeth, it's good to see you. Salasso, Gregor . . . wow."

Of his old companions, only the saur Salasso is unchanged, his small thin lips stretched in what for a human would have been a wide grin, his long arms poking far beyond the cuffs of his standard and therefore ill-fitting lab coat. Elizabeth and Gregor have aged fifteen years since Matt last saw them, fifty years ago. As usual it's a jolt but he can hardly see it as a deterioration. Elizabeth's broad, angular features have tightened more than they've sagged, and her walk has gained poise. Her hair is better styled than he remembers and still black, though not (Matt bitchily notes, as she air-kisses beside his cheek) at the roots. She's wearing a sharp, elegant grey trouser suit that looks like, and may even be, a uniform. Gregor's handshake is harder, his thin face looks more worn, and his swept-back hair (which, like his face, distantly echoes Matt's own) grows grey-flecked, and from farther back on his head; his clothes are as casual as ever. Salasso's long hands grasp Matt's shoulders, briefly. Matt smiles down into the huge eyes, black as though all pupil, and wonders if the saur can feel the faint reflexive shudder induced, against all reason, by his friendly touch. If he does, he gives no sign, and is probably wise enough to realize it's just a reflex, not a reflection.

Elizabeth turns back to the gaggle of scientists.

"Take five—take ten," she says. "We'll bring Matt up to speed and get back in ten minutes."

They disperse, some into huddles around the room, others outside. As they depart, Matt sees a table previously obscured by their backs. There are bones on a black plastic sheet, tweezers around them like sated steel piranhas. Matt finds himself drawn toward the array like an abductee to a skiff.

"Jeez H," he says, so close that his breath moves dust. It's the Holy Grail, right there before his eyes: physical evidence. He's seen pictures; by the gods, he has seen pictures, but until this moment he has never seen real hard evidence of multicellular life of extraterrestrial origin.

"That's what we've all been thinking," says Gregor dryly as Matt straightens, still fascinated, still tracing out in his mind how the thing hangs together. Gregor and Elizabeth take about one minute to recount their encounter with the selkies and their discoveries at Lemuria Beach.

"You're all sure?" says Matt, suddenly struck with a doubt. "You don't think it could be just a new terrestrial phylum, I dunno, some kind of Burgess Shale survivor—"

He keeps to himself his momentary hallucinogenic vision of a pre-Cambrian civilization, which had gone off into space and returned to

Earth at the end of the Cretaceous, just in time to meet the ancestors of the saurs, tweak their genes and set *them* off on their travels after the gods' wrath hit Chicxulub. . . .

"No, because that's not all we have," says Gregor. "It gets worse."

And he's pointing to an elaborately sealed vivarium on a bench over at the side. Sand and a puddle and a clump of algae. Something moving. This time, Matt has to force himself close enough to look. He finds he has mild arachnophobia, rather to his surprise. Probably picked it up in a dodgy lodging house years ago. Well, the only way to overcome a phobia is to face its stimulus and extinguish the response. . . .

Considered objectively, it's quite beautiful. Like a golden-furred tarantula, with tiny splayed hands at the ends of seven of its eight legs Tiny eight-fingered hands, each a minature of itself, as becomes evident when it skitters up the glass and walks upside down across the underside of the clamped-down glass slab on top. Matt gropes for a hand lens, peers through it as the animal repeats the manoeuvre. The brief flickering glimpse leaves no doubt. At the end of each appendage's eight fingers there are other tinier appendages, eight of them, and these fingers' fingerlets are what open out to grasp the microscopic frictions of the pane.

"Holy shit," says Matt. "A natural bush robot."

"A what?" asks Elizabeth.

"Kind of like the fabricators off the ship," says Matt, "but freemoving. Manipulators on the manipulators, right down to the molecular level. Early idea, never got built because the fine motor controls get hellishly complicated. But with a natural one, the lower levels could run on reflex, like digestion or something. Maybe it doesn't go that far down, but it goes a hell of a long way."

He looks again at the thing in the tank, and notices a much smaller specimen running around. "Please don't tell me the top-level hands are *buds* . . ."

Elizabeth, Salasso, and Gregor look at each other, and at him.

"That's exactly what they are," says Gregor. 'We picked up a few small ones, which we thought were spiders, on Lemuria Beach. It was only after we came back that we noticed they were still alive.'

"What do they eat?"

"Anything organic," says Salasso. "Their initial sustenance was the ether in the killing jar. Then each other. This is the survivor, and its first offspring."

"Did I see it wrong," asks Matt, "or does it have two mouths?"

"It has," says Elizabeth. "One for eating, one on the opposite side of its head for breathing."

People are coming back. This is a discussion that assimilates interruptions and swirls on. Elizabeth returns to the whiteboard. Matt moves in to perch on the edge of a table; Susan Harkness hangs back, it seems shyly until Matt notices that she is discreetly recording. Fair enough: This is history. No, it's worse, it's evolution . . .

Elizabeth wipes the board and begins scrawling anew. A circle, a tangent, a couple of dots.

"We've identified the star that the selkie pointed out," she says "It's on the edge of the known Second Sphere—actually just over a hundred light-years from Nova Sol—but definitely off the trade routes and about four light-years from here. So assuming we interpreted the selkie correctly, it seems a plausible enough place of immediate origin. Gregor, over to you."

Gregor takes her place at the board. "I've done a first-cut analysis," he says, waving a sheaf of papers. "Because it's so close to us, we already have a solid body of knowledge built up from navigating around the neighborhood, which should enable us to plot a jump within weeks. If we want to go there, that is."

"Why should we want to go there?" someone asks.

Gregor shrugs. "Scientific curiosity?"

Polite laughter.

"Okay," Gregor goes on, "but seriously . . . it looks very much as if these octopods, or whatever we want to call them, have been here in the past few years. Which raises the question of how they got in and out undetected—we've had the skies pretty well covered for decades. I was with Matt here just before and after he went off on the expedition seventy-odd years ago to contact the gods near Croatan, from which most of our admittedly scrappy information about the aliens—the octopods—is derived. I've had a long time to think about its implications. One of them is that we are dealing here with the actual inventors of the lightspeed drive and the gravity skiff, and the species that—"

He glances at Salasso, and at the two or three other saurs in the audience, as though he's about to mention something indelicate.

"—genetically uplifted the ancestors of the saurs, and culturally— at least—uplifted the kraken. We are used to thinking of these species as wise and ancient, which indeed they are, but the octopods are *their* 'Elder Race.' I don't think we should underestimate their abilities, which may include making a lightspeed jump to a point arbitrarily close to a planetary surface; various stealth technologies, et cetera." Expansive handwave. "We can only place the limits of their capabilities as within the laws of physics which, come to think of it, we don't know either. So maybe the stuff we're seeing in the more, ah, uninhibited newsflyers is not entirely out of the question."

In the ensuing hubbub Gregor looks at Matt, rather helplessly. Matt jumps to his feet and strides to the front.

"This is all completely bizarre," he says. He waits for the nods, then goes on. "That's what makes it believable. I know what a planet undergoing alien intervention looks like, because I was born on one! And I can tell you, this is all horribly familiar. Most of what you read about it is rubbish, hysteria, hoaxes, but if you dig deeper you'll find a hard core of cases that remain unexplained. Not that I'm recommending you dig deeper."

"Why not?" Gregor asks, looking baffled. "If we could only clear out some of the clutter—"

"Waste of time," says Matt. "You'll get bogged down. The phenomena are elusive, that's part of what they are, it's definitive, it's how I can recognize the situation." A thought strikes him. "Just when did you and Elizabeth come back from Lemuria Beach?"

Gregor hesitates. "Couple of weeks ago," he says.

"Let me guess," says Matt. "You've been back since, right? With lots of skiffs skimming the sea, lots of people scouring the bogs and moors."

"That's right," says Gregor. He shifts uncomfortably. "And, well, the fact is—"

"The selkies and the octopods are nowhere to be found?"

Everybody stares at him.

"How did you know?"

Matt grins evilly at Gregor, then swings his gaze around the room. "Like I said, it's a feature. Believe me, folks, better minds than ours have been destroyed trying to make sense of this sort of thing. We're dealing with the unknown, with something irreducibly strange."

"That's a counsel of despair," says one of the scientists.

"No, it isn't," says Matt. "It's to recognize that we can never make sense of it while part of the picture—perhaps most of it—is inaccessible. So I concur with Gregor's suggestion—if we have the slightest reason to think we know where these things are coming from, let's go there and invade *them*. Make *them* watch the skies for a change."

•　　　•　　　•

"Were you serious about that?" Elizabeth asked. She'd found herself, not entirely to her delight, walking alongside Matt while her husband and Salasso had got into some deep conversation and her daughter walked behind them recording it. They were on their way along the esplanade from the lab to find somewhere to have dinner and catch up.

"About what?"

"Going there. Invading the aliens."

"Oh, yeah, sure. I'd sign up for it tomorrow. Fuck, I'd go on my own." He cast her a conniving glance. "Just lend me a ship?"

"Not a chance," she said cheerfully. "I wouldn't trust you with a ship even if we could spare one. Which we can't. So that would mean going on a proper expedition, armed no doubt, on what might turn out to be an eight-year-long wild-goose chase."

"That's looking on the bright side," said Matt. "We could blunder into something that would start a war with the aliens."

"Or the war—or whatever—might start while we're away."

Matt grunted and shook his head. "I don't think that's how these things work. This *probing*"—he laughed, nervously she thought—"and assorted anomalous phenomena could go on for at least another century. That's about how long I give us, at our current rate of development, before the gods decide we're getting too big for our boots. And if they do something before that, putting a few light-years between us and it, sounds like a good start."

"Not much help in the long run." She shot a bleak look at Matt. "But then again, what is?"

"Oh, it's all unutterably fucking depressing," said Matt, not sounding depressed at all. "It's like biological pest control—the species introduced to keep down the pest becomes a pest itself, and we're it. Or the aliens are. Whether the gods are setting us or them up as the vermin this time around is as irrelevant to us as it is to them. If we make peace with the aliens the gods can line up something else to come out of nowhere and clobber us both."

"It makes me wonder," she said, "if Volkov wasn't right after all."

4

The Modern Prince

THEY LOOKED, VOLKOV thought, like samurai. The seven men and five women of the Senate's Defense Committee all wore identical black-silk kimonos, very plain, without any of the elaborate folds and pleats of the current mode. The men's hair was cropped, the women's coiled and stacked; their ceremonial swords, too, were in the ancient Roman style, stubby *gladii* in scabbards stuck behind broad sashes. None of them seemed over forty which, after the Academy, was a relief. They sat around a long table, the head of which faced a tall window. The room was on the top floor of the building Volkov had noticed close to the de Tenebres', a neo-brutalist tower surmounted by a sculpture of an eagle and chiseled Latin letters. It was the headquarters of the city's lightly armed militia, and of its external defense force—a smaller but more formidable army—which together were known for some reason as "the Ninth." Like most such forces in the Second Sphere, its main enemies were bandits and pirates. It hadn't been in an external war for several centuries, and the total number of losses in that war were memorialized in the entrance lobby on a far from grandiose plinth. The more frequent, but still rare, civil wars in the city's history were not commemorated at all.

Their lesson, however, had not been forgotten: the Ninth's civilian political oversight was close, and literal. The Committee met weekly, here on the top floor.

Volkov and Esias sat side by side at the foot of the table, cast at a disadvantage by the strong light from the window—a position in which, no doubt, many officials and officers had sat. As the Committee members shuffled papers and sipped water and talked amongst themselves as they prepared to begin, Volkov reached inside his dress-uniform jacket and found two old pairs of sunglasses. He passed the Ray-Bans to Esias and slipped on the ESA-issue reflective-lensed Leica Polaroids. Then he settled back and faced the now much more observable Committee in greater comfort to himself and, he hoped, less to them.

Carus Jin-Ming, at the head of the table, unfolded his hands from inside his sleeves, lifted his briefing papers and tapped the edges of the stack into place. He nodded at Volkov.

"Begin," he said.

"Chairman Carus, my lords, ladies and gentlemen," said Volkov, "thank you. In the documents before you, you will have read how the *Bright Star* came to Mingulay, and how two centuries later it traveled to Croatan and back. What you will not have read, because it is too sensitive an item to entrust to paper as yet, is what was done with that ship while it was in Croatan's system of worlds. News of what happened there will no doubt arrive, in secondhand and distorted form, over the next months—the ship of the family Rodriguez is, I understand, due to arrive here in a matter of weeks. From that and other ships the news will spread uncontrollably, like a flash flood through the streets. It is vital that the people's representatives should have a full and accurate account in advance of popular rumor.

"That account I can give you, firsthand. I and some others took the ship to the Croatan system's asteroid belt, and communicated with the gods within two of the asteroids. From them we learned that ships of another intelligent species will soon arrive in the Second Sphere. How soon, we do not know. It could be today, it could be a century or more from now. We do know that the gods expect our species—the children of Man, and the saurs—to come into conflict with those aliens. And, I regret to say, the gods look favorably on such conflicts, because they provide an apt nemesis to any human or other hubris. I have seen evidence of terrible mutual destruction in the deep past, between saurs and the aliens. As you must know, for such a conflict we are all ill-prepared. I have some suggestions as to what preparations we should make. Whether you wish to attend to my suggestions is of course a matter for yourselves."

Carus stilled the ensuing commotion with a sharp glance.

"I must say that this is a surprise, Colonel Volkov," he said. "From the background papers which you and the Trader de Tenebre have provided, I expected a discussion on possible implications for our security, as well as for our prosperity, from the Mingulayans' apparent recent mastery of interstellar navigation. The discussion of an alien invasion is something for which I am as ill-prepared as, you say, we all are for its eventuality. However, let us proceed. The first thought that comes to my mind is that we have no reason to trust the gods, as is well known." He glanced around, smiling frostily. "Within educated circles, that is." A small, nervous titter ran around the table, like an escaped mouse. "The second thought that comes, nay, springs to mind is that if your information is correct, the first people we should lay it before are the saurs. They are our friends, our benefactors, our protectors, and they have space travel. They have communion with the krakens, and the krakens have communion with the gods. Any emergency from the heavens is their province, and any help we can give, I am sure we will be as ready to offer as they to ask."

Volkov refrained from speaking, preferring to let someone else bring up the objection. As he'd expected, someone did.

"My lord Chairman," said one of the women—Julia de Zama, according to the crib of the seating plan that Esias had surreptitiously doodled—"in the background paper it has been pointed out that some, perhaps most, of the saurs on Mingulay and Croatan were less than happy with human-controlled space travel. They believe that it draws unwelcome attention from the gods, and they may be right. We, in any case, do not have space vehicles of our own. Suppose, then, that we hand this problem to the saurs. What can they do? We have seen the saurs project the fields of their skiffs to use as battering rams, and we have seen them fire plasma rifles. And that, my lord Chairman, is the sum total of human knowledge of saur military prowess after ten thousand years."

She looked directly at Volkov. "Perhaps the Colonel has seen evidence of other weapons in this communication from the gods?"

Volkov shook his head. "No, my lady, my lord Chairman, I have not. The space-going species seem capable of inflicting terrible destruction on each other, but that has more to do with the vulnerability of their habitats and the availability of kinetic energy in the form of metallic asteroids and so forth than any advanced weaponry. I've seen visual displays of conflicts which appear to have occurred intermittently over millions of years, and certainly no nuclear or particle-beam weapons were deployed in them. I suspect that the gods disapprove of their use, particularly in space, and take measures to prevent it. Not that they stopped anyone on Earth from developing them. The empire which I once had the honor to serve, the European Union, had much more destructive capacity at its disposal than anything I have seen evidence of since."

Carus drew a breath through his teeth. "Well, Colonel Volkov, while that may give us as children of Man a certain perverse satisfaction, it doesn't really help us, now does it? We are all well aware of the kind of weapons that were developed on Earth in the century and a half before your departure. Thanks to the saurs, we have never needed them, or anything remotely like them. The saurs have no need of such weapons, and given their well-known reluctance to provoke the gods, are unlikely to wish to develop them, or to help us to do so."

"You have grasped the essence of the problem, my Lord Chairman," said Volkov: "If we are to defend ourselves against the aliens, we must do so with the cooperation of the saurs or without it. We must develop space rockets and nuclear weapons of our own."

Then he sat back to wait for the explosion, and the fallout.

"You are a devil," said Esias as, for the second time in three days, he caught up with the departing Volkov, minutes after the Cosmonaut had stormed out. "You are like the Shaitan of the monotheists, a sower of discord."

"Am I, indeed?" Volkov snarled. "Then I am glad of it."

He realized he'd been stalking along, legs and arms stiff, fists clenched. He stopped and willed himself to relax. The midday sun bore down mercilessly on the deep, wide street. The crowd that flowed along the busy sidewalk spared him curious glances, steering clear. Flying squirrels, in all sizes from mouse to monkey, combining the ubiquity of urban pigeons with the arrogance of urban rats, chittered and gnawed wherever he looked. Rickshaws and cycles whirred, electric-tractored vehicles whined, heavily built horses whinnied. The glare—white off statuary, multicolored off mosaic—hurt him through the sunglasses. Esias seemed genuinely disturbed, sweat oozing from his creased brow, his armpits staining his blue pajamas. In the merchant's borrowed glasses Volkov saw his own reflection, his hair gone spiky and his eyes masked and his suit and shirt rumpled.

His hand loomed in the reflection as he reached for Esias's shoulder. "I'm sorry," he said. "I . . . lost command of myself. Let's do what we did before, and take a beer in the shade."

Esias, mollified but still looking worried, followed him through the glass doorway of the nearest beer parlor. Office workers from the commercial quarter filled it with lunchtime clatter and smoke. Some stared at Volkov's curious garb, and flinched from the blank flash of his shades. He bought two beers and escorted Esias to a corner at the back. After he removed the sunglasses, the world seemed brighter; after a few sips of beer, brighter still.

Esias was giving him a look that said *what do you have to say for yourself?* Oddly, for all his longevity, Volkov felt for a moment the younger man; a distant memory of his father's frown at some wastrelly act stirred uncomfortably, deep in his mind.

"When I was a student," Volkov said, winging it, "I had to attend lectures in what was called the philosophy of practice. It was a bore, and a chore, but a requirement. Unlike most of my cohorts, I paid attention, and got top marks. Strange to relate, that may have been crucial to my career. One of the things I recall from that class was the line we were given on the Epicurean and Stoic philosophers: While the Epicurean philosophy was materialist, and therefore in principle progressive, it had no notion of internal conflict or inner dynamism—no dialectic, as the cant went—and was therefore in practice passive. And indeed, politically it did recommend disengagement—"Live unknown," as the man said. It had no answer to the idealist but even more fatalistic philosophy of Stoicism, which duly conquered the best minds of the time. All of this of course was related to the lack of progressive forces in the slave-based ancient economy, or so the story went."

He leaned forward, relishing Esias's puzzled suspicion. "What none of this prepared me for, but which it should have, was to see the effect of the ancient philosophies' having a further two thousand years in which to stew in their own juice. You have no slaves here, but you have the saur manufacturing plant, and the saurs' friendly advice. You have no barbarians, and few Christians, and fewer Jews. Now they had dialectic all right, they had enough contradictions built into their theology to keep them busy forever. And, yes, one of them was Shaitan. You need a Shaitan here. Because without that, you get the kind of crap I heard from the Defense Committee—'If there is nothing we can do, it is as well to do nothing.' Look at how people on Croatan reacted to our warning about the aliens! Not much Stoicism and Epicureanism there! None of this waiting with folded hands!"

"Not all of us are waiting with folded hands," said a cool voice.

Volkov turned and Esias looked up, startled, to see Julia de Zama and another Committee member, Peter Ennius, standing with drinks.

Both of them had taken the minority argument, though very subtly, in the meeting. Esias jumped up and bowed.

"May we join you?" asked de Zama.

"Of course, of course," said Volkov, standing and shifting a chair for her. She swept forward and lowered herself into it with a smile, set down her glass and took a moment to straighten her kimono. She was tall and thin, her features fine and firm, her piled hair fashionably hennaed, her eyebrows fair under token penciled arcs. About mid-thirties, Volkov guessed, though the combination of saur medicine and local cosmetics made it hard to tell. Peter Ennius seemed a bit older—a short, thin man whose erect posture and black kimono made him look heavier and taller until he sat down. The musculature of his shoulders and forearms was real and impressive enough. An old soldier, Volkov guessed.

"How did you know we were here?" asked Volkov.

"We had you followed," said Ennius. "Discreetly."

"This is hardly discreet," said Esias.

Julia de Zama sipped a lemon-colored liquid from a twisted-stemmed glass.

"Oh, we don't want it to be discreet," she said. "Let people nudge and stare, let news of our meeting you get back to dear Jin-Ming, hot-foot." She waved a dismissive hand, wide sleeve flapping, as though sending messengers on their way.

"I take it," said Esias to Volkov, "that you have inadvertently drawn the attention of some ongoing intrigue." He smiled at the Senators. "That should certainly save him some time. Good day, my lady, my lord. You will no doubt have much to discuss, but as for me, I'm a businessman, and business is pressing."

With that he drained his glass and left, in no hurry not to be seen leaving.

"A wise move," said Ennius, gazing after him.

"He is not as conservative as you may think," said Volkov. "But you have Senatorial immunity, do you not?"

"We do," said de Zama in a lazy voice. "But our intrigue, so-called, is no secret. We are members of a most respectable association, with support in the Senate, the Academy, and the Ninth, as well as on the Exchange and in the streets of the city. Its aim is the same as its name: It is called the Modern Society. We are, you might say, an open conspiracy."

She paused, as though the phrase were some kind of password.

Volkov vaguely recognized it, then the allusion clicked into place. A happy thought struck him.

"You are familiar, I take it, with the history of the Roman general, Fabius Cunctator?"

"Of course," said Julia de Zama. Peter Ennius nodded, grinning broadly.

"Very good," said Volkov. "Perhaps, then, you are Fabians?"

"Yes," said Ennius. "Just as Wells was."

Volkov felt relieved that he'd got the connection right. It was about all he knew about Wells—another piece of trivia remembered from his philosophy classes. Other than that, the name of Wells conjured nothing for him but a vague image of heat rays and tentacles. Where did that come from? Ah, yes, *The War of the Worlds*. And there was something else, another title that had been mentioned in the lecture on the history of socialism. . . .

He raised his half-empty glass. "To the war of the worlds," he said. "And the modern utopia!"

Julia de Zama was inspecting him with a sardonic but admiring eye. She clinked her glass on his.

"To the new Machiavelli," she said.

Lydia twirled, sending the pleats from the waist at the back of her chrysanthemum-print kimono-like robe flaring out, then tottered and grabbed the nearest pillar. She pushed away from it, recovering her balance and holding out her arms, the sunray-pleated sleeves opening like fans. She walked as though on a tightrope across the grass of the roof terrace to the table where Esias sat under a fixed umbrella with a jug of iced fruit juice and a stack of newspapers.

"The platform shoes take some getting used to," she admitted, taking a seat.

So that was why she looked so tall.

"But the main thing I like about this," she went on, "is that it's office wear. Isn't it beautiful?"

"Very pretty," said Esias. "Gorgeous, in fact."

Lydia poured herself a drink and pouted around the straw. "You don't sound too enthusiastic."

Esias rocked his seat back and waved a hand. "No, no, nothing to do with you. You're lovely. I'm a bit disgruntled, that's all. Our friend Volkov is up to his old tricks."

Lydia blushed, as well she might. Esias still simmered with disapproval over her involvement with Volkov's intrigues on Croatan, a few jumps and a few months behind them, and he still harbored a deep suspicion that the Cosmonaut's intentions toward his daughter were honorable. If they were having an affair, it was none of his business, any more than it had been when Volkov and Faustina had been going at it like rabbits. But if Volkov were to make a proposal, and Lydia were to accept, then he would find it difficult—in fact, outright embarrassing—to refuse it. And then he would lose his number seven daughter forever, unless—forlorn hope—Volkov's project of remixing the elixir came to fruition in something less than a lifetime.

But Lydia's reply showed she'd kept her composure. "Trying to assemble a coalition of progressive forces, is he?"

Esias groaned. The smatter of ugly jargon Lydia had picked up from the incorrigible ancient Communist was not the least of his bad influences.

"It's worse," he said. "He seems to have found one."

He told her about the morning's meetings. "This Modern Society"—he flicked at the stack of newspapers—"seems to be quite influential. It's all talk, because the guilds and workshops are as conservative here as they are anywhere else—they'll gladly seize on new machines, but not on great disruptions to their methods of work. Grand ideas about giant assembly lines don't really appeal to them. But they have the most confused and exaggerated ideas about Earth, about the great independent achievements of mankind back in the Solar System, all based on the snippets that dribbled in from the ships that came back before we did. Heaven knows what's going to happen when Volkov speaks to the Senate—they've already summoned him, and everyone knows it. There's not a chance of that session's being held *in camera,* and not a chance of his being discreet. The whole place is primed for Volkov to detonate."

Lydia gazed out over the upper tiers of the city shimmering in the heat haze, then back at her father.

"I'm not so sure about that," she said. "It's not like Croatan was, with all that social discontent in Rawliston and their funny religions and unstable political system. This city's pretty good at assimilating new ideas without changing very much. There've been times in the past few days when I've felt we've been away for two weeks, not two hundred years."

"That's just the trouble," said Esias. "Volkov can completely revolutionize Nova Babylonia—Nova Terra, come to that—without a revolution. The Academy and the Defense Committee have been skeptical of his plans. No doubt the Senate will be, too. But in each case, there was a minority whom he managed to fascinate. And that minority can take it to the populace. Once the ideas get out that people can be as long-lived as saurs, and that they can get into space without the saurs, and that there is a threat from space that the saurs can't help us meet, then—well, frankly, I'm glad we'll be out of here in a couple of months."

"So am I," said Lydia. She twiddled ice in the bottom of her glass. "And back in a couple of centuries, by which time the dust should have settled."

Interesting, Esias thought, that she still didn't take the prospect of an alien incursion seriously. Perhaps that instinctive skepticism would prove Volkov's undoing in the long run. On the other hand, there was something else she wasn't taking seriously, and it was a good deal more important and closer to hand.

"Ah," said Esias. "It won't be the usual round trip this time. We could be back in one century, or even less."

Lydia frowned her puzzlement. "What do you mean?"

"Ninety-six years have passed since we left Croatan. Fifty or so more will have passed before we are halfway back. Time enough, I think, for the Cosmonaut clans of Mingulay to build more starships, to extend their operations, to expand their range. Even allowing for a long time to calculate the navigation for each new jump, I should not be at all surprised to find that they have expanded far enough to meet us somewhere *en route*. And if they do"—he rubbed his hands—"here is the beauty of the deal I made with the Cairns family: They will have wares from the outer worlds that we can exchange for our Nova Babylonian commodities right then and there. We can then transfer to another merchant vessel on its return trip—for a suitable consideration, no doubt, but that shouldn't be a problem, we can cut them in on the deal—and return to Nova Terra much sooner than expected, thus stealing a march on our competitors."

"Oh," said Lydia, "very good!" She thought about it for a moment. "And what if they haven't?"

Esias shrugged. "Then we're no worse off. We return in two hundred years as usual and, as you say, the dust should have settled by then." He smiled wryly. "Assuming the aliens haven't invaded, that is."

"What do you think of . . . all that?"

"Consider the probabilities," Esias said. "The Second Sphere has existed for thousands of years, to our certain knowledge. For millions, according to the saurs, and I believe them. Earth has existed on the other side of the Foamy Wake for even longer, according to the books in the *Bright Star*'s libraries, and I believe them, too. In all that time, there has been no evidence of any other space-traveling species than the saurs. In fact, the only scraps of evidence that *Earth* has been visited turn out to have been because of the activities of saurs, and the saurs originated on Earth. The god in the Solar System with which the crew of the *Bright Star* were originally in contact gave them no hint of any other space-going species."

"It didn't tell them about the saurs, either," said Lydia.

"That's a point," Esias conceded, "but it doesn't affect the argument I find most persuasive in my own mind, which is—given how long the situation has remained as I've said, how likely is it that a huge change in it should coincide with our brief lives? The chances are at least thousands to one against, I should say."

Lydia pondered this. "I suspect there's a fallacy in that argument somewhere, but I can't put my finger on it."

"Hah!" said Esias. "It's true, unlikely events happen, and that argument can't rule them out—merely show that unlikely is what they are. But at an intuitive level, some such reasoning must account for my subjective lack of panic about Volkov's, ah, 'monkey-spiders.' And everybody else's, I shouldn't wonder. Including yours, respected Number-seven daughter."

Lydia let her eyes almost close. "You have something in mind for me to do," she said.

"Yes," Esias said, sitting up. "Show lots of enthusiastic interest in what Volkov is up to." He raised his eyebrows. "If, that is, you can still stand his company?"

"Oh, yes," said Lydia. "I can that."

Peter Ennius had left. Julia de Zama tracked his departure with a cynical eye.

"Off to make a report," she said.

"You mean—"

"Of course. There's always somebody, isn't there?"

Volkov agreed that there was always somebody. "A useful man to have on the inside," he said.

"Exactly," said Julia. She waved a hand, and fresh drinks were placed in front of them.

"So," she said, "it's just us."

THE ENGINES OF LIGHT

"Indeed," said Volkov. He chinked his glass against hers. "Long life!"

She repeated the toast. "You know," she said, "that's a much more interesting prospect than alien invasion."

"I know," said Volkov. "I intend to make much of it."

"A good idea, but not exactly what I had in mind. I have a strong personal interest in it myself."

"You're a bit young to concern yourself with that."

She gave him a severe look. "You need not flatter me."

Volkov raised his eyebrows. "No flattery was intended, but"—he smiled—"if you say so, I must take your word against the evidence of my eyes."

She flushed slightly. "The light is kind, if you are not."

He smiled again, over the rim of his glass. "I expect progress in that area within, oh, ten years, even if half the Academy has to die of old age first."

"Progress," said Julia. "If you only knew how hard it is to find someone who understands the meaning of progress."

Mother of God, he thought, if you only knew.

"Tell me about the Modern Society," he said.

Lydia joined them, without pretense that it wasn't deliberate, about half-way through the afternoon.

"I've been looking over some of the Modern Society's ideas in the papers," she explained, after introductions.

"Your father sent you," said Volkov.

Several empty beer glasses had accumulated on the table; Lydia knew him better than to assume this meant he was drunk. Julia de Zama, on the other hand, looked as if her self-control was less secure. She was sitting back in a louche manner, one arm draped along the back of the seat behind Volkov, and she was giving Lydia a fiercely territorial stare.

"Of course he did," Lydia said, primly arranging her skirts. "He's interested in what you're doing. But that doesn't mean I'm not interested in it myself. This is my city you're messing with."

On reflection, she could have put it better than that. But there was something about Volkov that had always impelled her to be blunt. He seemed to like it. Julia de Zama didn't. She leaned, or maybe (Lydia thought uncharitably) swayed forward and aimed a forefinger.

"It's not your city," she said. "The presumption that it is is half our problem. You people—the Traders—bring changes with every ship, and

626

blithely depart before they take effect, yet always expect the city to be much the same when they return."

Lydia could see the justice of this—it was after all what she herself had said earlier, but expressed in a hostile tone.

"That's not a problem," she said. "It's a solution. We give the city stability without stagnation, progress without destruction."

"No you don't," said de Zama. "You give it muddle and waste and cross-purposes, and evade both consequence and responsibility. And I'll tell you something else. We don't need you. We don't need the Traders, and we don't need the saurs. If we were to rely on our own resources, we should astonish ourselves."

"I'm sure you would," said Lydia. "But how would you do it, exactly? How would you cut the city loose from all the attachments of trade with other stars and other species? How would you manage affairs without saur mediation? Tell me. Go ahead, I'm all ears. Astonish *me*."

And recklessly, passionately, eloquently, Julia de Zama did. She seemed even to astonish Volkov, who for once was acting the part of moderation. Lydia listened and watched the Cosmonaut and the Senator, their voices and eyes and hands, and realized something more astonishing than the Modern Society's ambitions: Volkov and de Zama were falling in love.

Lydia felt nothing but relief.

Volkov had never before in all his long life seen a saur shudder. When Voronar, the saur pilot and translator from the ship, had finished talking, Volkov saw seven saurs shudder at once. Deleneth, the apparent speaker for the group, turned her head slowly to Volkov, and the other heads turned in unison, like caged lizards watching a fly on the other side of a glass pane.

"You *talked*," she said, "to the *gods*?"

Evidently Voronar had given an accurate account. The saurs all understood Trade Latin and other human languages—their linguistic facility was something Volkov admired without being impressed with, vaguely relating it to the imitative knack of birds—but for serious matters they preferred the subtler nuances of their own speech. This meeting was the most important of any he'd attended so far; more so even than the Senate hearing tomorrow. Its calling had been on shorter notice and had been more imperative. He could finesse anything that happened with the Senate, there or afterward. This group of representatives of the saurs resident in Nova Babylonia could not be blindsided.

"Yes, we did," said Volkov, trying not to shift in his seat. The tiny room was built for saur comfort, not human. A back room of a saur dive near the harbor, its lighting was dim, its furniture was made of something like cork and was so small his knees were higher than his waist, and it all stank of hemp and fish. He was the only human present, and the only person who might just possibly be on his side in any contretemps was Voronar, assuming that saur's loyalty to his employers overrode his solidarity with his kind, something on which Volkov was not counting and hoped not to find out.

"We know that the gods are angry with the saurs," said one of the seven who sat facing him and Voronar in a long row like a bench of inquisitors. "If the gods you spoke to made you mistrust the saurs, perhaps that is another expression of their anger. Perhaps they wish to turn the hominidae against us, to punish us."

Voronar hissed some acid comment, then turned to Volkov. "You explain."

"I know this is difficult for you to accept," said Volkov. "I tell you honestly, and you can compare what I say with what Voronar has just said without my understanding—the gods are not angry with the saurs. Some of the saurs on the outer worlds have come to agree with that, but—and again you can see I am being frank with you—most have not. The saur Salasso who first told them that, and who went with us to inquire of the gods, was in my own presence almost hurled to his death from a great height."

A susurrus of hissing consultation followed. Volkov was surprised at the reaction until he remembered that the saur method of hunting, megayears established and ingrained, was to stampede herds of herbivorous dinosaurs off cliffs. To be thrown from a height must be the most disgraceful and terrible death that could be inflicted on a saur.

The saurs all looked at him again in silence.

"I do not mistrust the saurs," Volkov said into the silence. "I would like to work together with the saurs of Nova Terra and other worlds to prepare for the arrival of the monkey-spider aliens. If we are to set up defenses in space, it would obviously be preferable to have the use of gravity skiffs. The god in the Solar System who spoke to us long ago gave humans the instructions for building skiffs and lightspeed ships, and the humans, and some saurs, on Mingulay and Croatan are working together to build them. After some years—I do not know how many— these humans will be here, and humans here will have the skiffs and ships in any case. But by then, the monkey-spiders may have arrived, and made war on us all. So why not work together now?"

"I can tell you why not," said Deleneth. "The gods do not mind that we travel between the worlds on which we live. But they do mind, very much, if we venture into the gods' domain. There was a time long ago when the saurs did that, and the gods showed their anger and struck at them."

Volkov knew that this was true. He had seen the ancient ruins on Croatan's moon himself.

"That is so," he said. "But the defenses that I recommend we build in space would also be defenses against the gods' wrath."

The saurs facing him swayed slightly back in their seats. Three of them went so far as to claw at their sleeves. Even Voronar sat rigid and still. At last Deleneth spoke.

"Very few will help you with that," she said. "If you persist, if you persuade the humans to follow this this course, very few saurs will work with humans at all. We cannot fight against you, because that too would anger the gods, but we can withdraw from you. We can leave your cities, and the ships in which you travel. What the kraken will do we do not know, but we can guess."

Volkov sighed and laid his hands on his knees, palms up. "You will do what you must, and so will I, and so will those I persuade."

"There is nothing further to discuss," said Deleneth. She and the other six rose and withdrew, and after waiting a couple of minutes to let them get out of the building, Volkov did the same. Voronar stayed with him and walked out beside him.

The narrow street was dark. Volkov walked down it and across a broad esplanade and leaned on the rail. Voronar solemnly propped his chin on the same railing and they looked out across the harbor, bright with the lights of ships and starships.

"That did not go well," said Voronar.

"I'm getting used to hearing that," said Volkov. "I'm also getting used to having a small minority agreeing with my proposal."

"In this instance it appears that I am that minority," said Voronar. "Though I cannot help you much, for I intend to travel again with the de Tenebres."

"Good for you."

"Yes," said Voronar. "I think Deleneth was mistaken about the saurs who travel on the ships, and the skiff pilots generally. We are more openminded than the saurs who stay on the worlds."

Volkov smiled. The skiff pilots he'd known back on Mingulay were indeed, by saur standards, rakish.

"Do you think," Voronar went on, "that the humans here can get along without the help of saurs?"

Volkov had thought about this. Apart from space travel and the products of the manufacturing plant—all of which could be replaced, or done without at a pinch—the main saur contribution to human well-being was in their unobtrusive medical help. From the first, as far as he knew, the saurs had patiently explained the germ theory of disease and its consequences, and something like the Malthusian principle of population and its consequences. The saurs supplied contraceptives. They supplied some kind of life-extension treatments, so that the normal healthy human lifespan was about a hundred and twenty years. Nothing for the genetic causes of aging, which—he presumed—had been synergistically and serendipitously found on Earth in the treatment, whatever it was, that had worked on him. Surgery they taught, tissue regeneration they applied, though not for trivial cases. They moved fast to contain and cure the epidemics that inevitably got shuttled around the Second Sphere by starships.

"It'll be tough," he said.

The news broke the following day. Lydia was working in one of the offices midway up the building—a quite pleasant office, open-plan and open to a terrace, and, unlike most offices she'd worked in—including this one at the time of her previous landfall—full of workers in comfortable and colorful clothes. It clattered with telegraphy and teleprinters, most of which were connected with the big calculating machines down in the basement. The work itself was laborious, but interesting, as she and her siblings and cousins coordinated what they knew of the cargo with what the locals knew of the markets. At exactly an hour before noon everyone stopped. The machines fell silent, and radio receivers were switched on. Lydia couldn't be sure, but she thought the sounds from outside of traffic and general mechanical background hum diminished at the same time, as all across the city people stopped work to listen to the news.

It was a direct feed from the microphones in the Senate's council chamber, and the channel was always on whenever the Senate was in session. No commentary was permitted. The citizens of the Republic might not all have the right to elect the Senators, but they had the right to the raw data of what was said in their name.

Esias de Tenebre had just been called before the assembly, and began his address with a concise account of his family's commission to go to Mingulay and bring back as much new information as possible. So far, so familiar. He held forth briefly on the wealth of information from the twenty-first-century Solar System and its significance. Then he moved on to the surprises: the Cosmonauts' longevity, and their first steps toward mastery of the lightspeed drive. This was news to most of the people around Lydia, though perhaps not to most of the Senate, who were sure to have heard rumors. The room rustled with whispers and silk, and Lydia thought she heard, through the open windows, the sound of the whole city drawing in its breath.

After a brief word of thanks from the Senate's chair, the floor was given to Volkov.

Lydia could hardly pay attention to what he said. She knew it all already, knew exactly what he would say and how he would say it. Instead she watched the office workers, saw how their mouths opened and their hands crept into their sleeves to clutch their elbows as they listened to his insidious message and insinuating voice. When he had finished, the newsfeed fell silent. After thirty seconds a brief, nervous announcement followed. For only the second time in the past seven hundred years, the Senate had gone into closed session.

Lydia walked out to the terrace, wanting to shut her ears to the angry or fearful voices that filled the room, but found no respite. From the terrace, she could hear a sound she had never heard before, the clamor of a city of millions arguing with itself, like the buzz of an upturned hive.

5

Tidal Race

A NOTHER BEACH, ANOTHER world.
Elizabeth walked along purple-tinged sand, the skiff keeping pace a few meters behind her. The skiff's pilot, Delavar, was an old acquaintance on whose loyalty and reflexes she was more than ready to rely. Somewhere behind the navy sky the Cairns ships hung in gravity-defying non-orbit, in any emergency a screaming red-hot minute away. The air was thick and stank of iodine. A few tens of meters to her left, the last exhausted ripples of breakers whose surf broke hundreds of meters farther away hissed into the sand. The tide was far out and on the turn. Giant oystercatchers the size of moas stalked the shallows, stabbing the sand with beaks like swords. Kilometers to her right, a row of cliffs defined the horizon. This beach was huge, visible from space as a white crescent like a life-size drawing of a small moon. They'd called it Atlantis Flats. The red sun loomed high in the sky, far bigger than any sun she'd ever stood beneath, but utterly dwarfed by the ringed gas giant that, gibbous, filled an eighth of the sky above the sea. It looked as though it were floating on the ocean beyond the horizon, the colors of its bands and the dark of its nightside segment and a long, wavy ink-black line from its razor-thin ring bleeding into the water.

Just half a kilometer ahead of her, the city of the selkies rose from the beach and the sea, straddling the mouth of a broad river. Built on stone pillars and wooden pilings resting on the bedrock beneath the sand and silt, and rising about twenty meters above them, the city extended to about a hundred meters beyond the low-water mark and spread for nearly three kilometers along the shore. Intricate inlays of shell fragments embedded in its wood-and-stone buildings shone in the sunlight and glittered in the reflected light from the sea. A haze of smoke and steam hung over it, constantly replenished by the funnels and flues of an industry which, going by the expedition's earlier discreet aerial surveys, processed wood, fish, algae, and kelp. It resembled thousands of such settlements dotted along the coasts of the planet's continents and islands; it was twice the size of the next largest. Inland from the coastal villages and towns unpaved roads linked quarries and logging sites. Other than that, all traffic and communication seemed to be by sea or river: small sailing vessels, long canoes, signaling by smoke and flag and mother-of-pearl mirror flash. No aerial traffic had been detected, not even skiffs.

Beneath the pillars in front of her, a sail snapped up and began to move swiftly across the sand toward her. She stopped, and the skiff did likewise.

"Wait here?" asked Delavar, through the beads on her ears.

"Yes," she whispered back, through the bead on her throat.

Their communications, like the visual display of the scene, were being relayed to the fleet.

After a couple of minutes the sail-powered vehicle—a three-wheeled, low-slung frame of wood and wicker—tacked and slewed to a halt not far away. Two selkies vaulted out; another remained on board, one hand on the rope connected to the boom of the sail, the other resting casually on three spears.

The two selkies on the sand walked forward, empty hands spread. Elizabeth reflected the gesture with even greater polite hypocrisy. One walked ahead of the other, and stopped a couple of his long steps away. His looming face peered down at her. She tried to smile.

"Welcome," said the selkie, startling her immeasurably. "We have been expecting you."

Elizabeth stepped back, staring. It was the selkie from Lemurai Beach.

"You may remember me, from another shore," continued the selkie. "I think I recognize you."

"How do you speak our language?" Elizabeth asked. "And how did you get here?"

The selkie scratched his midriff absently. "Those of us who were on that shore returned to this one, on a ship of the eight-armed ones. The same taught some of us your speech."

Once again Elizabeth revised upward her opinion of selkie intelligence. "And how did they know it? We have not spoken with them."

"They listen and watch," said the selkie. He scratched again, and put a fingertip between smacking lips. "They listen and watch us now."

Reflexively, Elizabeth looked behind her, then, more rationally, upward. The zenith was empty. The selkie's deep chuckle welled up.

"They are near, but not there. They wish to know if they can come here safely."

"We will not attack them," said Elizabeth.

Delavar made a sort of strangled noise that set up feedback in her earbeads. She silently willed him to shut up.

"Very well," said the selkie. He looked up, as though belying his earlier statement, and said something in another language. Then he turned again to Elizabeth.

"My name is Khaphthash," he said.

"Mine is Elizabeth."

For a moment, its syllables sounded just as strange in her ears.

Khaphthash smiled, tipping his head back, and looked to one side. "They are coming," he said.

Elizabeth looked in the same direction and saw, as it seemed far out to sea, a tiny silver disk rapidly approach. A few meters away, a small elliptical patch of shadow as swiftly enlarged on the sand. She blinked and shook her head, and saw that the disk was not above the sea, but tiny and above the sand in just the right place to cast the shadow, but it was at the same time unquestionably far away and approaching—no, it was really small and becoming bigger and bigger. The sand beneath it began to move, the grains arcing in precise trajectories quite unlike sand being blown about: She could look down and see it flowing around her boots. A wide circle with a complex internal pattern formed as the disk approached, or enlarged. The perspectives kept shifting until it was suddenly there in front of her, its three legs extending and settling on the beach in the exact position of three internal sworls in the sand circle. The mode of arrival was deeply unsettling and uncanny to witness.

"Did you *see* that?" she whispered to Delavar.

"An incident of high strangeness," said Matt's voice in her ear.

"That was an emergence from a lightspeed jump," said Delavar. "I have never before seen it done in a skiff, or so close to a planet."

"Yep," muttered Elizabeth, "three meters is close to a planet all right. . . ."

Still, that explanation made the arrival, if not comprehensible, at least rational. The skiff's hull was perfectly reflective, a huge lens of

what looked like the surface of a liquid in its smoothness, like me
In a moment, a hatch opened and a ladder extended. An octopodal a
skittered down it and across the sand to her. As it approached she hea
Delavar making small, distressed noises.

"Are you all right?" she whispered.

"I will be," said Delavar. "I am experiencing fear that I know to be
irrational. This is new to me."

Elizabeth was experiencing no fear at all, which at some level of
her consciousness she thought disturbing. The alien's golden fur was
astonishingly beautiful—she had to resist an impulse to stroke it—and
it gave off a pleasant, musky fragrance: laced with soothing pheromones, she guessed. The tips of its limbs, as it walked, were compressed
to hard, sharp points that left deep, small indentations in the sand. As
it stepped closer she saw that the fur was irridescent, and was almost
certainly not simply hair but some kind of optical fiber. Every follicle
must be light-sensitive, for that to make any kind of functional sense.
She tried to imagine the sensorium of a mind that could use so much
input, a flow of information orders of magnitude greater than even the
all-around vision provided by the eight eyes, and failed.

Its breathing-mouth—a triangle of overlapping lips, with jaws but
without teeth—was on the side facing her. The alien raised its two front
limbs and waved them. The palm-buds expanded, opening to the tips of
the tips of the tips, like a ring of dandelion clocks, then contracted back
to eight-fingered hands that it moved together, the fingertips touching
and rhythmically tapping each other in a curiously human, almost effete
gesture. It stood about a meter and a half tall, its head-thorax somewhat
larger than a human head, and more domed than that of the specimens
Elizabeth had seen so far.

Thinking to reduce any possible intimidation from her greater
height, Elizabeth moved to squat. Instantly the octopod whirled around,
presenting its eating-mouth, open in a flash of teeth. Startled, Elizabeth
fell back on her butt, hands scrabbling the sand. The selkie, Khaphthash,
reached over a hand and helped her back to her feet as the octopod
returned to its former position.

The breathing-mouth opened and the alien spoke, in a curiously
high-pitched and breathless voice, like a very old person with emphy-
sema.

"My apologies. Please do not do that. The posture triggers a fighting
reflex."

"My apologies," Elizabeth replied, mentally kicking herself. It

~d too banal to be the first words spoken to an extraterrestrial. "We
pleased to meet you at last."

"And we you," said the alien. "As you can deduce from my grasp
of your language, we have been observing your planet for some time."

"We had suspected that," said Elizabeth. "We have come here to
learn of your intentions."

"Very good," said the alien. It swung its head as though looking
around, a surely unnecessary thing for it to do, and therefore likely
meant as a reassuring imitation of the human. "Let us repair to the city,
where we can discuss these matters in more comfortable surroundings."

It scuttled back off to its skiff, which led the way at a slow pace
along the beach. The selkies wheeled their odd contraption along.

"Who is piloting your skiff?" asked Khaphthash.

"A saur named Delavar."

"Your people were taken to your world by saurs?"

"Yes," said Elizabeth. "We have met some of our people at another
beach, and they seemed troubled"

"Our people have old tales of encounters with saurs," said the selkie.
"They are not pleasant."

"Would there be trouble if Delavar came out of the skiff?"

"Trouble?" The seal-man looked sidelong and down at her, his small
chin disappearing into the blubber of his neck. "No, not hostility. There
would be surprise. It might be a good surprise, for our people. And they
have to meet sometime. Why not now?"

"What do you think, Delavar?"

"I am consulting with the fleet," Delavar murmured back.

"Go for it," says Matt, before anyone can object.

Gregor glares at him, Salasso casts him a heavy-lidded look of reproof, Susan Harkness busies herself with the recording apparatus, and
the Cairns' flagship skipper, Zachary Gould, pointedly looks away out
of the viewscreen. Matt doesn't care: He's the First Contact Convener,
and he decides this sort of stuff, even if Elizabeth did pull rank—and,
to be fair, her prior experience with the selkies—to be the one on the
ground. Anyway, he's on a roll, in a mental state that his distant but
still vivid memories associate with amphetamine-fueled all-night coding
sessions, and which he is sensible enough at some level to recognize as
dangerous, but seductively productive.

The ship he's on is, like its four companions, shaped like the fuselage of a rather boxy aircraft, maybe a World War Two bomber or
something like that (Matt is vague about aviation history) made from

thick steel and armor-plated glass and about fifty meters long by four high and ten across, except for the skiff-docking bay, which is at the stern and is eighteen meters across. The ship is called the *Return Visit.* The others are called *Explorer, Investigator, Translator,* and *Experimenter.* Matt's suggested names (*Rectal Probe, Up Yours, Probably Venus, Strange Light, No Defence Significance,* et cetera) were all rejected at the committee stage.

It's taken years to get here. Two years and a few months, which to Matt's edgy impatience felt longer. Partly it's been a whole lot of tedious politicking, within the Cairns clan, with the other Cosmonaut Families, with the Heresiarchy and with the city-state governments, starting with Kyohvic and working down. Negotiating with the heretical minority of saurs who agree with Salasso and are working in space with the humans has been a whole 'nother kettle of fish, and by the gods Matt knows by now what a kettle of fish actually is, having consumed many of them in the negotiations. Running on the rolling logs of a public discussion of a real alien presence and alien invasion threat, a discussion conducted amid the waterspouts, crop circles, cattle mutilations, sea serpents, and general flying crockery of mass hallucination and hysteria— has had Matt for the first time in his life devoutly if guiltily wishing he could engineer a good old-fashioned government cover-up, not that there's a government on Mingulay or Croatan that could cover its own ass if you handed it a Blue Book.

On top of that there's been the hard technical graft, from the sort of thing he's been making a living at for the past few decades—porting applications from ancient wet and dry nanotech salvaged from the old *Bright Star* across to a renascent technology where debugging really does mean cleaning the moths off the valves—to top-level project management of the teams building closed-system life-support from old spec and first principles. Because of the short journey times neither the established space-going species nor the upstart humans have any experience in the field, or even much in the way of theory. Even convincing folk that breathable air and potable water, not to mention an unopposed landing, at the other end is not the way to bet when you're making a four-light-year jump into an unexplored system has been a wearing, because essentially political, struggle.

Anyway, it's done, and they have carbon scrubbers and distillation kits and filter beds and hydroponics and some icky gunk from the saur manufacturing plant that, allegedly, manufactures plants. They even have space suits. The five ships of the fleet, each with a complement of twenty or so variously warm bodies, human and saur, have primitive ship-to-ship and space-to-ground missiles, none of which would have impressed a moderately competent pyrotechnician of the Ming Dynasty, and a piratical arsenal of firearms and plasma rifles, which would. If the explorers have to convince anyone that their intentions are peaceful and their armaments defensive, it shouldn't be hard. Nevertheless, this is the biggest collective effort ever mounted by the Bright Star Cultures. The human two-thirds of the crews are—apart from Gregor, Elizabeth, himself, and a few other old and unaging Cosmonauts—young and adventurous types who can stand the thought of dying and the even more daunting thought of finding everyone they knew a minimum of eight years older when they get back. And if they are daunted, well, pay reckoned by time elapsed rather than time lived is a big inducement, as it has hitherto been in the Cairns commercial fleet.

One of these young adventurers is Susan Harkness, the Cairns' youngest daughter, who has wangled her way as recorder onto this dangerous expedition by threatening to do something more dangerous if she isn't. Over the past couple of years Matt has stopped seeing her as too young, and she has stopped seeing him as too old, and they have had an intermittent and relaxed relationship, to her parents' fury and disgust.

Right now she's seeing things from her mother's point of view; but only, Matt hopes, literally.

Close up, the selkies' city looked more than ever like an enormous pier. Its stone pillars and wooden piles were crusted with barnacles and limpets, tufted with green algae, draped with wrack. All of the buildings that she could see looked, on this closer inspection, more like scaffolding. There was little in the way of walls or roofs, and few structures seemed entirely enclosed. Elizabeth supposed that the selkies did not set much store by shelter. Much of the wood was rotten, or bored by shipworm. The stonework was pitted and slimed; even above the tide-mark it looked thoroughly weathered. Deep in the structure's dim underside great wheels turned, presumably mills driven by the river; when the tide was coming in, they would revolve in the opposite direction, to just as powerful effect. On this Earth-sized moon of a gas giant with a red giant sun, the tides were swift and fierce.

Crowds of selkies sat or stood on the internal planks and platforms of the structure, or waist-deep in the water beneath, gazing at her. Scattered among them, octopods swung or scampered with the liquid grace of gibbons. Here and there in the city the silvery disks of skiffs glinted; there seemed to be no passages wide enough for them to enter or leave by, and Elizabeth puzzled about that for a moment until she suddenly realized that they could have emerged from lightspeed jumps in situ, right there. No wonder there were no skiffs in the sky!

The two skiffs beside her stopped as the selkies hooked their sailing vehicle to the end of a long rope, which began to be winched up. The two pilots emerged at the same moment and walked together to the foot of a winding wooden stair. A clamor boomed through the piers as the watching selkies craned their necks and shouted, hooted, drummed on the timbers or smacked the water. It was like the din of an enormous kennel. After recoiling for a moment, Elizabeth walked forward and ascended the stair. Khaphthash and his companions brought up the rear. Gradually the noise died down. Above the smells of wrack and sea Elizabeth caught whiffs of the octopods' soothing scent, and wondered if it was this that calmed the selkies.

The steps were soggy and slippery, but fortunately wide enough to accommodate the great slapping feet of the selkies. Its handrails were too high for her, but all the more reassuring for that. As she climbed higher Elizabeth noticed the abrupt change at the high-tide mark, where the encrustations of barnacles gave place to the new, artificial encrustation of colorful shell fragments, and the wood was no longer rotten but smoothed, and treated with some tarry or oily substance. But the signs of age and weathering persisted: the wood was often white, almost papery to the touch, and the stonework crusty with lichen, soft with moss; some of the shells were faded or crumbling.

At length the octopod stepped off the stair onto a long platform with a broad, low table in the middle. The place stank of fish—no, of their bones and of shells, which had been tossed in a loose-woven wicker basket in one corner. Large clamshells, evidently dishes or drinking vessels, marked positions around the table. The selkies, so advanced in other simple technologies, seemed not to have invented pottery. The octopod skittered to the far side of the table; Delawar and Elizabeth hesitated for a moment, then joined the selkies in reclining beside it. As she lay on her side, propped on one elbow, Elizabeth could see numerous eyes—octopod and selkie—peering down from the dim vaults above and around. She could feel through the floor a constant vibration, which came to her ears as a hum overlaid by rhythmic thuds, as the tide-powered wheels sped up on the incoming race.

Khaphthash gave a long, loud sigh. "It is good that you are here," he said. "I wish we could offer you hospitality. But our food might not be palatable for you. We do not treat it with fire, as you do."

Delavar's head bobbed as he looked sideways at the selkie. "My species enjoys fish. Perhaps we shall trade for it, in the future."

"The future, yes," said the octopod, its wheezy voice sounding impatient. "That is what we must discuss."

"We have some questions about the past," said Delavar.

Elizabeth had found herself surreally wondering if all that kept the selkies from venturing farther inland was their ignorance of kippering. The reedy tremble in Delavar's voice shocked her out of it. She looked closely at the saur, and saw the small tremor in his hands just before he noticed it himself and locked his fingers together and pressed the edges of his palms against the edge of the table. By saur standards, this all indicated a serious loss of sangfroid. The unease, the prickling of the hairs, that some humans experienced in the presence of the saurs must be vastly multiplied for a saur meeting an octopod. To humans, saurs were an enigmatic, vastly more ancient, and vastly superior species that had haunted the human habitat and imagination, glimpsed in the shadow and in the corner of the eye, since the Ice Ages. The saurs had not even that dubious tradition to buffer their encounter with a species older and wiser still, and more intimately involved in their origin. For them, to meet the octopods was to meet their makers.

The octopod waved a limb. "We know little of the past," it said. "The past is eaten and assimilated. We do not share the interest of all your kinds, in"—it made a poking, stirring motion of its bunched fingertips—"what remains. We prefer to reach for the new fruit, the fresh fish, the bright strange molecules."

"It is possible to learn from the past," said Elizabeth.

The octopod fixed her with its multiple gaze. "It is not. We have observed your kind for some time, and the saur's kind for longer. We see no evidence of this learning of which you speak."

"Very well then," said Elizabeth. "Let us speak of the present and the future."

The octopod's fiber-optic fur moved as though a wind passed over it. Its fingers flowered to thistledown.

"That is good," it said. It placed fingertips together, cat's-cradling a sphere, then expanded the sketched ball like a child's construction toy. "We are part of a wave-front of our kind that is passing through what you call"—the ball shrank, solidified—"your sphere. Some of it is already deep within your sphere, other parts—such as ourselves—are still outside, but we will soon be within."

Elizabeth winced at the cacophony as Gregor, Matt, and others shouted simultaneously. She snapped her fingers by one ear to tune them out for a minute.

"Do you intend to settle on our planets?"

The octopod fanned two of its hands. "Only the unoccupied portions. There is no need for conflict. Your kinds do not make full use of the biospheres."

Elizabeth stared at the alien—for the first time seeing it as alien.

"You must be aware," she said, "that our populations are increasing, and expanding into what you call the unoccupied portions. That could result in conflict in the future."

"Khaphthash's people are of your people," said the octopod. "They too increase, but they do not come into conflict with us. You share your planets with the other hominidae, with the saurs and with the great squid, and you do not fight. What is one species more? By developing the unused parts of your planets we could offer you much to exchange, as do the species which are there already. We are aware that the world-minds may wish us to fight, to diminish our numbers. We wish to avoid this by becoming that of you as we are that of Khaphthash's people."

"I'm sorry," said Elizabeth. "I don't understand that . . . last thing you said."

"We and Khaphthash's people wish to join the Bright Star Cultures."

Elizabeth and Delavar have returned. With them around the table are Gregor, Matt, Salasso. Zachary Gould, the captain, is chairing. Susan sits to one side, running her cameras and scribbling notes. The room is spartan and terrifying. It smells vaguely of food. Along two walls it has windows, but only an occasional rolling glimpse of the planet below, or a longer and less reassuring look at the gas giant above, make them anything but black mirrors.

The discussion has been going on for some time.

"It's very straightforward," Matt says. "They're telling us"—he shifts to the breathy register of the octopods—" 'Resistance is useless. You will assimilate us.' "

The sough of ventilation and the creak of bulkheads are for a moment loud.

"I'll give you the first," says Elizabeth. "I'm not so sure about the second."

"My view is the opposite of Elizabeth's," says Salasso. "The human capacity for both resistance and assimilation is considerable. The choice is genuine."

"It strikes me," says Gregor, "that both alternatives may be pursued. Our friend Volkov set out to persuade Nova Babylonia to prepare for resistance, after he failed to persuade us. We know he is very persuasive, especially when he doesn't have another Cosmonaut running interference."

Matt smiles in acknowledgment.

"Well, that's all right," he says. "Volkov may have the whole Nova Solar System bristling with nukes and death rays and gods know what by the time the Bright Star Cultures—with or without the octopods—spread to it. If in the meantime things have turned out badly between us and the octopods, well, tough shit for us, but we'll get some posthumous revenge. And if not, if we're walking along holding their eight hands, there'll be nothing to fight about. As the one Elizabeth and Delavar spoke to said, they'll be just another species in the Second Sphere."

"There are times," says Elizabeth, ostentatiously making sure Susan is getting this and not just recording it, "when I don't know whether to be more shocked at Matt's cynicism or his naivety. I'm not interested in posthumous revenge, thank you very much! I am interested in the safety and happiness of our own people." She glances at the saurs. "Of all our peoples. So much for the cynicism. What is naive is Matt's remark that if all goes as the octopods say they hope, there'll be nothing to fight about. Suppose Volkov succeeds, and Nova Terra is all geared up to fight an octopod invasion. Two things can happen. One is that some of the octopod travelers who *haven't* been in contact with us—and we know there are other parts of the migration en route right now—emerge from the jump and blunder straight into Volkov's defenses, which they have no reason to expect. The other is that we—the Bright Star Cultures, now including the octopods—spread there, jump by jump, just as our traders are spreading now.

"We make our final jump into the Nova Sol system, evade the defenses because we're expecting them, and tell the Nova Terrans the good news: the long-feared aliens are now a part of our rich tapestry! They don't want to take over the worlds, oh no! They just want to settle the underdeveloped parts of our biospheres! Do you have any *idea* how that will look, to the kind of paranoid militarist culture that Volkov will have built? Of course you do, Matt, you are not a complete fool."

Zachary Gould coughs politely. "The Science Officer will please address her remarks to—"

"Sorry, Zack," says Elizabeth. She stops glaring at Matt and looks around at the others. "They'll have spent decades preparing for an octopod invasion—perhaps already, as they see it, fought one off—and when we turn up, we will look to them like collaborators with the aliens. The octopod invasion will be *us*."

"This is indeed a problem," says the orange-furred emissary of the octopods.

It's here with two others, one black and the other multicolored. Their arrival, though prearranged, has been unnerving. The sight of an alien skiff emerging from a lightspeed jump right inside the *Return Visit*'s temporarily empty docking bay without the airlock's having to be opened has given everyone on board a vivid impression of just how advanced the aliens are.

The three aliens are huddled at one end of the messroom, which has been used as a conference room. They cling to the edge of the table or the backs of chairs with some of their hands, and with others keep touching each other's hands, and with yet others gesticulate. They keep changing position unpredictably and startlingly. Matt has no doubt that it's only their calming pheromones that are keeping most of the people who are in the room, and especially the saurs, from climbing a few chairs or walls themselves.

"Fortunately," says the black one, "we have a possible solution. We do not have the jump coordinates for any of the stars in the Second Sphere, other than the one you have come from and the one at the center." It makes some agitated movements of three limbs. "The former, we have only recently calculated ourselves. The latter, we have as an item of legacy information. It is very common knowledge among us. Consequently we can jump from here to your Mingulay, and also from here to your Nova Terra. We suggest that most of us and you go to Mingulay, and some of us and you go directly to Nova Terra."

"What good would that do?" asks Elizabeth. "Your other travelers will have already arrived by the time the Nova Terra expedition arrives."

"That is true," says the orange-furred one. "They will very probably be dead. That is unfortunate but cannot be helped. However, the expedition we propose would be armed, and cautious."

643

"Ah," says Matt, leaning forward. "You have weapons?"

"No," says the alien. "Some plasma rifles." It sketches a shrug with several of its shoulders. "But you have."

Matt tries not to laugh. He can see the others doing the same.

"I don't know that we'd get many volunteers for going straight to Nova Terra," says Zack, manfully keeping a straight face. "That's a two-hundred-something-year round trip. Most of the crews are expecting to go home and still see their folks, and even the few as don't haven't signed up for jumping forward a couple of lifetimes."

"I'd go," says Matt immediately. He glances at the two saurs. They both nod slowly: The two saurs have a lover in common, Bishlayan, but long partings are something they are used to.

"Maybe some of the other Cosmonauts, as well," he adds.

"Not much of a crew," says Zack, still making as if he takes the proposition seriously.

The aliens' hands are busy with mutual blurry touch. They do that a lot, Matt has noticed, and he has a good idea why; it's direct exchange of molecular-coded information—memories, perhaps even genes. Social intercourse, or sexual—with their mode of reproduction, perhaps there is no difference.

The rainbow-hued octopod flourishes a blossoming fuzzy hand, and inhales. "Please explain to us the problem about the crews going home."

They explain.

"Ah," wheezes the orange octopod. "We have a possible solution to that problem. Any of your people can live as long as the saurs and the Cosmonauts. Would this help?"

Elizabeth sat in the cockpit (or on the bridge—the terminology hadn't quite been settled yet) of the *Return Visit* and scanned the viewscreens, which were much more useful than the windows. They showed three of the other ships, surrounded by a small cloud of the beautiful smooth skiffs of the octopods (or Multipliers, to use their own troubling term for themselves). A hundred kilometers away the *Investigator* hung in a lower orbit, moving slowly ahead of the other group. Around it were five Multiplier skiffs, apparently keeping pace. How the jump coordinates for the Nova Sol system had been transferred from the Multipliers' drive to the *Investigator*'s she didn't know; it had kept Matt, Gregor, and two of the octopods busy for several days.

In a few minutes the *Investigator* and its tiny convoy would be making a lightspeed jump of a hundred and three years, taking them to one year out from Nova Sol. "Defuse the situation, or defang the defenses," Matt had said. "Hell, if Volkov is still alive I might even be able to *persuade* him."

Even with most of the armaments from the other ships transferred to its arsenal, it still seemed pathetically inadequate for the task. On the other hand, it was hard to see how anything would be adequate, short of a massive military mission, which neither the humans nor the Multipliers were willing or yet able to mount. The ship had a crew of eight humans and two saurs, Salasso and Delavar. She did not underestimate the courage of any of them, but she would miss the saurs most.

The radio crackled. *"Investigator* to the fleet. Jumping in two minutes."

"Gods be with you," said Zack.

"Hopefully not." It was Matt's voice. "But thanks, Zack, I know what you mean."

Gregor shifted in his seat, glancing around the screens. "I hope Susan's getting all this—where is she, by the way?"

"Over on the *Explorer,*" said Elizabeth.

At that moment Susan's voice came over the radio. "Uh, Gregor, Elizabeth, I'm sorry, I just couldn't miss this chance, and I knew you wouldn't—"

Elizabeth felt as if she'd fallen through ice. *"Where are you?"* She already knew; the voice had come on the open channel to the *Investigator.*

"Jumping in one minute," said Matt.

"Abort the jump!" Gregor shouted.

"You know I can't do that," said Matt's voice, maddeningly calm.

"This has nothing to do with Matt," said Susan. "I'm sorry, I love you, but I want to go."

Elizabeth unclenched her teeth and grasped Gregor's hand. "We both love you, Susan," she managed to say. "And we'll see you again. You can be sure of that, darling."

She took another deep breath and spoke slowly, weighing and meaning every word: "Matt, we're going to take the Multipliers' offer. We're going to live for a very long time, and we're coming after you, and when we get you, we're going to fucking kill you."

"Good luck," said Matt, as though he hadn't heard.

"Good-bye," said Susan.

"Okay, people," said Matt. "Let's jump."

6

Bright Star Cultures

NOVAKKAD, THE PRINCIPAL city of a planet fifty light-years from Nova Babylonia, had always been a strange place. More than anywhere else Lydia had visited along her family's trade route, it had struck her as not just different but foreign. Its people were either much darker or much paler than the standard Second Sphere swarthy melange. They wore tall hats of fur in winter and shallow wide-brimmed cones of straw on their heads in summer. Their priests investigated the nature of fire with crude spectroscopes; their philosophers worshiped geometry. Their accents were thick and various, and their dialect of Trade Latin had a way of mutating unpredictably. Claiming that their city was older than Nova Babylonia, they implausibly attributed certain gigantic prehuman and prehominid ruins in its vicinity to their ancestors. Their own buildings were peculiar, tall wedges with sharply sloped roofs curving to ornate overhanging scoops of eave, like tents of brick and tile. In other ways too the city had the aspect of an encampment, clustered along the shore of a freshwater lake the size of an inland sea at the edge of an endless plain on whose grass the Novakkadians raised vast herds of horses and cattle. On the far side of the lake the glaciers of a jagged mountain range replenished its deep cold waters, within which fish shoaled by the million, some growing to lengths of ten meters and weights of three tons. Hardwoods from the lower slopes of the far mountains were harvested by the gigants and floated across the lake in such quantities that from the sky they looked like mats.

Strange and foreign, but more so this time.

Lydia walked, in native high boots and quilted clothes, through the chill streets and alleys of the autumn market. The air smelled of horse shit and fish roe, with tangs of woodsmoke and unfamiliar polymers.

Crowds of several species of people and herds of beasts swirled in slow crosscurrents from one end of the market to the other, like a demonstration of the theory of price. Stalls filled the sidewalks, banners hung across them advertising their wares—new sharp stuff, glittery and colorful and strange; machines that talked and sang, clothes whose fabric and work seemed worth ten times the asking price, ceramic knives that sliced through meat like fruit and bone like gristle, calculators with little glass screens and unfeasible capacities, radios small and cheap enough to hang on key rings and that blatted forth songs whose words were hard to make out but whose tinny tunes made your feet tap and fingers snap along. Medicines were offered soberly by respectable-looking stall-holders with huge companies behind them—the same names and seals cropped up again and again—whose small print offered things that only witches dared promise anywhere else. The local fishing trade had been taken over, completely it seemed, by a new kind of gigant—tall heavy people with black sleek hair all over them and big mournful eyes. These were far from the strangest newcomers here.

Saurs for a start, saurs like none she'd ever seen, all the prickly dignity of their species dropped like an old cloak as they hustled and schemed, haggled and yelled, and accompanied by swarms of their offspring, some so young they still had their hatchling yellow feathers, others toddling along, tiny under their big and heavy heads, the older ones scooting about and screaming or whistling signals between and among their gangs.

The human traders were dark-skinned men in pajamas and turbans, or women wrapped around in long, broad single strips of silk. Their ships stood outside of town. She could see dozens of them, beyond where the streets ran out into stalls and pens, parked on long jointed legs that went with their shape, which was something like enormous flies: faceted panes of glass at the double cockpit front, stubby swept-back delta wings along the top of the tubby, segmented fuselage. The huge insectile machines sank a little in the trampled mire, their gravity fields evidently switched off. Large and many though they were, though, they couldn't account for all the goods she'd seen in the market, let alone the stuff in the city's downtown shops. And there were no new factories. Where did the goods come from?

Where did the traders come from?

"Chandrakhar," one of them told her. Gold-canine grin, jerk of thumb over shoulder. "Couple light-years back." Nod down at the stall. "Mingulayan opticals, lady? Best price in town, you see for yourself."

"Thanks, maybe later." She wandered off. Chandrakhar? Never heard of it. It wasn't on the trade route, close though it might be. This was a whole new culture that had been in the Second Sphere for gods knew how long, which the kraken ships from Nova Terra had never visited. And they spoke English with the broad Mingulayan accent.

But that wasn't the strangest thing, no, not at all.

"What are . . . they?" she asked a saur who sat behind a stall covered with shiny disks the size of sequins. You put them in machines. He wore headphones covered with yellow fur, from which the rocking music trickled irritatingly. He read her lips, followed her glance.

"Oh, they're Multis," he said. "Short for Multipliers. It's what they call themselves." He leaned across the stall, disengaged a blaring phone from his ear, and spoke behind his hand in a low voice. "They're *aliens*, you know."

He rocked back, small shoulders shaking, lips stretched, the big ellipses of his eyes narrowed to slits. He found something funny, but Lydia didn't see it. She knew they were aliens, and they certainly did multiply. The strange thing was that nobody here seemed to mind, or notice. The eight-limbed furry folk scampered and swung, overhead and underfoot everywhere, common as monkeys in a ruined jungle temple, and as unregarded. Except when they ran stalls themselves.

She stopped in front of one, and the Multi perched on two hands at the far side of the table made little model spaceships in bottles from wood and chips of stone. It held one model in front of it, like a template, and with its other five hands it made more, like magic: one moment there would be a fistful of wood and gravel, then something at the ends of the arms would blur and hum, and a minute later the hands would open on a beautiful little object, like an insect in its perfection as much as its shape. And on it would go to the next.

The thing was, it was making them *inside* the bottles.

Other miracles went on elsewhere. At the busiest stalls of the Multis, people were being cured—or more precisely, mended. People shuffled up and strode off; were carried up, and walked away. Lydia distinctly saw a man walk up with one healthy eye and leave with two. It was like the miracle stories of the gospels of the Jesus of the Christians, and it was happening in plain sight and without fuss. The patients were delighted and grateful, but not surprised, not wondering and glorifying the gods.

Lydia stepped around a corner and into an open space where cattle awaiting slaughter inside a fenced corral regarded her suspiciously. She powered up her ship-to-shore radio and raised Voronar. The ship was thousands of kilometers away, over the ocean where the kraken refreshed themselves and did their own deals, but the skiffs were parked along the lakeside quays and warehouses with the cargo for hominid and saur customers.

"Where are you?" the saur asked.

"Behind the market," she said. "I'm seeing things you wouldn't believe."

"I do not doubt it," came the dry reply. "The question your father wishes me to ask, however, is—are you safe?"

"Yes, I'm fine. Why doesn't he ask me himself?"

"He is in a meeting and can only communicate by buzz codes," said Voronar. "I shall reassure him. The city Elders are plying him with something he refers to as horse piss, but he retains his sobriety admirably."

"Good," said Lydia. "I'll endeavor to do the same with my sanity." She smiled at an anxious crackle. "That was a joke, Voronar."

She signed off and walked on through the ragged fringe of the market, toward the alien—no, that wasn't what was strange—toward the *human* ships.

"You're not fucking local," the boy told her, after a few minutes of ostensibly idle chat. "You're a goddam Nova Babylonian babe, you are."

His teeth were as perfect as his language was foul: Mingulayan English with Croatan swear words, blasphemous and obscene. He lounged on the lower steps of the ship's ladder, torn between pride in the responsibility of guarding the ship—a revolver that looked too big for his hands was stuck in his belt—and boredom at having to stay there. Blue-black straight hair flopped over his eyes.

" 'A goddam Nova Babylonian babe,' " Lydia repeated, grinning. "You certainly give good lines. You should keep notes of them, to use after your balls drop."

The crudity put him at his ease. He leaned back against the treads in a way that would have been uncomfortable but for his bulky fur jacket.

"What are you snooping around after, anyway?" The question came out curious, not suspicious.

Lydia shrugged. "Just checking things out," she said. "We only came in today, and we're not sure how things are. Bit of a change since two hundred years ago."

The boy laughed. "Changed a fucking hell of a lot in four, I can tell you that."

"Oh?"

"We were one of the first ships in here," he said. "Four years ago." He wiped a hand over his eyes, as though tired. "Fucking last week, it feels like. Nah, maybe a month. Me Da and Ma, they made a real fast turnaround back on Chandrakhar, loading up new gear. And even then, shit . . ."

He paused. "I didn't ought to be telling you this."

"We're not your competition," said Lydia. "But let me guess. By the time you got here, you were just ahead of the game. All the stuff that was new when you loaded it on Chandrakhar was already being made locally here."

He gave her a look of grudging respect. "Damn near right," he said. "We're ahead on a few lines, but some things you can't even give away. The only thing that'll pull this jaunt into the black is passengers." He sounded as though in his eleven or so years he'd learned all the weight of a merchant's risks. "Fucking Multis," he added, with startling venom; then, more reflectively: "Clever little monkeys, though."

"What have the Multis got to do with it?"

He looked at her as if she had asked where babies came from. "They multiply," he said, "*things*. They make stuff. They make. Fucking. Everything."

Esias felt the tickle of the radio's buzz against his ankle and counted. Three dashes. Lydia was safe. That was some reassurance but, as he sat naked on a wooden bench in a hot-room with three men, a woman, and an eight-armed, eight-eyed green ball of fur that persistently felt him up, he could have done with more. The radio was in a puddle of towel at his feet and he suspected the heat or humidity would soon short it out. He took a squig of the glutinous local drink from the vacuum flask his hosts had provided. Its chill and its high alcohol content were all that it had to recommend it. The Novakkadians called it khiss. Their listing of its ingredients had started with fermented mare's milk and stopped, at Esias's urgent request, when it reached dinosaur-egg yolk. You could live on it indefinitely, they'd told him. There were worse things than death, he'd not told them.

The Elders were the biggest local business people, as well as hereditary chiefs of the herding clans. Esias recognized their names from their ancestors, with many generations of whom he had dealt: Viln, Vladimiro, Sargonsson, Elanom. They were all old but in good shape, and had matted hair to their waists. There was something troubling about their hair, but Esias couldn't see what it was. The lights were dim and when the room wasn't full of herb-scented steam his eyes stung with salty sweat.

It was customary for the Elders to meet the Traders here in the Traders' Lodge, the lakeside house set aside for starship merchants and their crews. It was likewise normal for them to do their preliminary deals in the hot-room over a melting ice slab spread with fish roe and other delicacies and accompanied by flasks of khiss. For them to get through the preliminaries so quickly, and to have virtually agreed to his opening price, was not normal at all. Usually the haggling and the drinking continued to the point where the following day's hangover would be compounded by his regret at not having been more sober for the handshake.

The presence of the Multiplier was disturbing, but in an oddly abstract way. It should have bothered him more than it did. This was one of the octopod alien invaders that Volkov had warned about, and it was in here and thousands of its like were out there, and somehow he was not alarmed by it. It skittered about the room, its multiple manipulators touching faces and heads and skin. Esias found its feathery, tickling touch all the more uncomfortable for its being physically pleasant, warming and relaxing the muscles like a brief massage. The Elders ignored it, apart from moving slightly and with visible enjoyment— again as though being massaged—when it touched them. It had said nothing, though it was, he understood, both articulate and intelligent. The Elders had not introduced it, explaining that the aliens did not have names in the form of sounds. Their names were written in molecules, and if he were more familiar with it he would recognize the distinctive odor that spelled out its chemical signature.

The woman, Sargonsson, stood up and stepped over to the ice block. She picked up a sliver of roe on a shell and sat down beside Esias, who moved a little to make room for her. Despite her weathered and lined face, and the slightly bandy legs that a life in the saddle had left her, she was a fine figure of a woman, shapely and lithe, gleaming with steam and sweat. She smiled politely and scooped up roe on the back of a fingernail and licked it with the tip of her tongue.

"We are almost done," she said. "Your cargo will fetch a good price."

"If it is as we agreed," said Esias. The phrase was formal, just short of a handshake.

"We have another deal we can make with you," said Sargonsson, settling back into the corner. "The goods we have exchanged so far are the same as you and our fathers' fathers' fathers have traded. The hardwoods and the fresh roe, the strong herbs and the fine brasswork. Likewise with you."

Sargonsson glanced around, to nods from the others and a small flailing of hands from the alien. As she did so Esias noticed what had troubled him about her hair. The length of it between her ear and her butt was a salt-and-pepper grey; the first few centimeters of more recent growth out from her scalp were a pure glossy brown. Her head was crawling with lice.

Esias scratched his own scalp. Turning back, the woman saw his reflex and smiled. He lowered his hand, embarrassed.

"They don't itch," she said.

She put a finger to her temple and one of the creatures crawled onto her fingernail, which she held out for inspection. Perched there was not a louse but a spider—no, a tiny version of the alien. It scuttled up her arm and disappeared again into her hair.

"Ah," said Esias with false heartiness, "so that's why they're called Multipliers!"

"It is not," said Sargonsson. Again she glanced around; again they nodded. The alien climbed onto the bench opposite and crouched there. The mouth on the side that faced Esias had no teeth. Vladimiro threw another ladle of water over the coals. The alien's breathing was loud.

"They are called Multipliers because they can make copies of things. Of almost anything, given the right materials. They can certainly make copies of your Nova Babylonian manufactures. Your way of trading is obsolete. We in the Bright Star Cultures do not need to have merchant clans who live on the ships. We can make short journeys of a few years, because we set our own courses. That is how the Bright Star Cultures have spread from Mingulay to Novakkad, without anyone's having to travel more than a small part of the distance, or knowing how to navigate the jump."

"Yes, yes," said Esias. "I expected that, and I've made plans for—"

"Because of that," the woman continued relentlessly, "we need the long life, the very long life like the saurs. The Multipliers gave the saurs long life long ago, and they have given the same to us." She smiled. "Or so they say. We have no way of knowing, yet. But I will say I feel better than I did four years ago."

She wiggled her shoulders. Esias stared at her, for the first time shaken out of his detached acceptance.

"This is astounding news!"

Sargonsson turned her shoulder rotations into a shrug. "They offer us more than that," she said. "They have given us immortality."

Esias took a gulp of cold slime that burned in his throat on the way down and glowed in his belly.

"That is impossible," he said. "Not even the gods are immortal."

Sargonsson held out a hand to the alien. "Tell him," she said.

"In your body," it wheezed, "there are patterns of information that have instructed the building and instruct the working of your body. Some of them are older than the gods, older than the light from the visible stars. Some of my memories are older still. I remember seeing with four of my eyes the galaxy you call the Foamy Wake, and with my other four eyes the one that you call Andromeda. Yet never have I traveled between them. I remember scuttling through the grass by the lake outside, also. I am four years old."

It hopped down from the bench. "We can make you live long, by changing the instructions of your body. To do that, we must read them. By reading them we read your memories, and they can be shared among us, and will be among some of us until our line dies, as are those of the Novakkadians. In that sense we can offer you immortality."

Esias jumped as the radio on the floor buzzed against his skin, once, long. It signaled an urgent call back to the skiffs. He could hear a commotion and running feet in the rest of the house. It did not seem to matter.

"How can you read us?" he asked.

"That is simple," sighed the Multiplier. It raised two of its hands. Fuzz formed around the fingertips.

"The smallest of the smallest of us are too small for you to see. They are small enough for you to breathe in like smoke. They can travel through your body and read you."

"Travel—through—my—body?"

"You hardly notice it," said Sargonsson. "It's like a slight fever for a day or two, nothing more. And then any that have grown larger crawl out of your ears and nostrils and . . ."

Esias was shaking as hard as the insistently buzzing radio. The

Multiplier flicked its hands. Esias stared as a cloud of green motes, some like dandelion seeds, some like pollen, wafted through the steamy air toward him.

He jumped up and ran to the door, bashed it open and rushed along the rickety wooden jetty and dived into the lake. The shock cleared his head instantly. What had passed in the hot-room seemed like a dream. He swam down through the clear cold water until it filled his sinuses, his mouth, his ears. He shot to the surface gasping and spitting and swam at a racing crawl, plunging and surfacing again and again, until a skiff appeared above him. The ladder came down, and he snatched it and hauled himself up and inside. The hatch closed behind him. He floundered for a moment, then stood up, dripping. His wife Claudia, two of his daughters, several nephews, and a saur pilot stared at him.

"What happened to you?" Claudia asked.

Esias shook his head. "Later," he said. His gaze swept the wraparound viewscreen. The skiff was rising fast, Novakkad tilted and dwindling below, an echelon of skiffs behind them. He padded across the corky floor and around the engine fairing to stand behind the saur. "What's going on?"

"The ship is leaving," said the saur. "We will rendevous in the atmosphere above the ocean."

"Why?"

For a ship to make an unscheduled departure was unprecedented. The pilot shook his head, not turning from the screen and the incomprehensible display below it. "The kraken decided, minutes ago. There has been no time."

"Have we got everyone?" Esias asked.

"Safely lifted," said Claudia. "Everyone in the lodge has checked in."

"And Lydia?"

"Lydia?"

"She was out in the town on a mission—"

Claudia paled instantly. "What were you thinking—" She shook her head. "We must turn back!"

"Yes, yes, turn back!" urged Esias.

"If we do, we shall not make the rendevous," said the pilot.

Esias clenched his fists at his sides. "We can catch another." He knew the other merchants' schedules to the hour. "The Delibes will be here in seventeen days."

The pilot glanced from the clear sky in front to the crowded display on the control board. He read something in its complex glyphs.

"Ah," he said. He turned to Esias. "Do you *wish* to join the Bright Star Cultures?"

Claudia looked bemused and distraught.

It would not be so bad, Esias thought frantically. People were not subsumed. They had free will. The Multipliers were friendly. Lydia was his number seven daughter. The spiders crawled on the scalp and their tiny offspring swam through the blood and the brain, and crawled out. His shudder was involuntary even as he opened his mouth to speak.

"You may," said the pilot. "I do not."

Esias stood still, shivering and unseeing. The skiff flew on.

Three comets lit the sky. Out here in the fields, the lights from the market and the town made the silhouettes of the parked ships stark and monstrous. It was dark enough to see the jagged outline of the mountains against the stars, and the comets' converging tails, a chevron pointed at the sunken sun. Novakkad had no moon, and only solar tides stirred its ocean. In the Second Sphere, this made it a backwater.

Dim reddish lights moved here and there in the broad meadow, barely raising a whinny from the resting horses. The lights came on only for a moment, illuminating complex wheel-mounted arrangements of brass and wood, with long tubes poking up like antiaircraft guns. Around these astrolabes the ships' navigators fussed and muttered, plotting the positions of nearby stars. Now and again a green glow from the screen of a hand-held calculator would light up an intent face from below.

Lydia wandered quietly among them, unregarded. Once or twice she heard a low cry of "Hey, Multi! Give us a hand!" and saw a Multi scurry over and poke a limb into a piece of machinery. Other than that they took no part in the observations or calculations. They could make and adjust things, but they did not seem to know everything already, the way the saurs and the krakens knew, or gave the impression that they knew.

Lydia had given a lot of thought to the aliens in the hours since she had been stranded. If nothing else it served to distract her from her plight while she wandered around, looking and thinking. She had heard the evacuation call but no response to her frantic queries had cut through the babble on the radio, so she had no idea why the clan had fled. The only message she had picked up was a crackly, apologetic, anguished good-bye from her father, who told her that the krakens were taking the ship back to Nova Terra and could brook no delay. No explanation was given, and she had no time to ask. It must be something urgent and fearful for them to leave her behind, but she could see nothing so fearful in the city. It was amazing how quickly one got used to the aliens. There was something soothing about their scent, and their variously colored fur and constant activity and curiosity had a charm that evaporated any associations with spiders. What humans toiled for in factories and saurs spun in the manufacturing plant, the Multipliers made for fun, if they could be so persuaded. Which, she had gathered, was not always easy. Their jittery attention span made humans seem like saurs.

She made her way back to the market and bought with the last few local coins in her pocket a fast meal of beef in a spicy sauce parceled in some kind of thin bread and munched it as she walked back to the lodge. It was a big stone building with a sharp-pointed wooden roof. She flicked on all the lights she could find and wandered through the rooms, disconsolate. Everywhere were the strewn signs of hasty evacuation. The skiffs' landing-feet had left deep prints in the soggy lawn. The hot-room, its door swinging open, was cold and stank of warm seafood and spilt khiss. Her father's clothes lay folded outside. She did not touch them, and started clearing the decayed repast and sluicing the room with a wall-mounted hose.

Gradually this displacement activity calmed her. She felt let down rather than abandoned. The next ship was due in just over a fortnight. There was always money in the lodge if you knew where to look. She worked her way through the house, tidying things away. The servants would not be in until just before the Delibes arrived, just as they had been in the previous day, before the de Tenebres. Her ramble ended in the room where her own luggage lay on a freshly made-up bed. At the top of the case lay the Nova Babylonian robe she had neatly folded, in her own hopeful yesterday. She would wash, put it on, go downstairs and put out some of the lights, make herself a drink and go to bed. Why not?

She was sitting at an empty table in the big dining hall, sipping a long voka, when she found herself feeling more cheerful than even the bath and the drink could account for. At the same time she had a feeling she was being watched. She turned to the corridor. A green-furred Multiplier came clicking along the flagstones, into the room. It hopped onto the end of the table, hands spread, and padded along the tabletop, then clambered onto the seat opposite her.

"Do not be alarmed," it said.

She wasn't.

●   ●   ●

Lydia stood alone at the end of the long pier at Novakkad docks, the one reserved for the star merchants. Her suitcase rested beside her, she had her traveling clothes on, and she had a watch in one hand and a radio in the other. High nimbus made the sky silvery and hard to look at. When she glanced back at the watch, it was hard to read, but she kept looking, from the watch to the sky, from the sky to the watch. At last, and right on time, she saw the dark speck, high above, far away up the lake.

She stuck the watch in her pocket and picked up the suitcase and walked to the top of the ladder. The man in the dory looked up at her.

"Now," she said, handing the case down.

The passenger was meant to sit facing the steersman, but she crouched the other way. The electric engine whined and the boat pulled out from the pier. The Delibes' starship was now a solid black, now a wavery worm in the heat haze. She waited until she was sure it was within range and switched on the radio, preset to the hailing sequence.

"Lydia de Tenebre to the Delibes ship, come in please."

There was a long pause, filled with static. The ship was low now, about a kilometer away. The place where Lydia expected it to set down was a few hundred meters ahead of her.

"Ship to de Tenebre, receiving you. What do you want?" The voice sounded irritated and puzzled. A radio operator was always on standby on an approach, and almost never had anything to do.

"De Tenebre to ship. I would like to come on board as soon as possible."

"Huh? Sorry, I mean, yes, that's not a problem, but why? Are you in some—"

More static.

"Ship to de Tenebre. Sorry, I've just had a message. There's an emergency, I don't know what it is. The kraken want to *pull out!*" The voice rose in an indignant, alarmed, disbelieving squawk.

Now the ship stood just two hundred meters in front of her, a stationary, impossible object, half a mile of streamlined cylinder glowing with Novakkadian symbols and words, the water bending beneath its shimmering fields.

. "I know that," said Lydia, with a calm she didn't feel. She had half-expected something like this. "You're safe enough though, you can wait a few minutes to take me on board."

"Hold on a minute."

At the same moment as the radio at the other end clicked off, the boat's engine died. Lydia whirled.

"What's the problem?"

The doryman smiled placatingly and waved ahead. "I can't go on—look."

Lydia looked foward again and saw what she had missed in her attention to the ship. Between the boat and the ship the pointed front end of an enormous mat of logs floated on some fast current, filling the space like an entering wedge. The tugboat that had been riding herd on it had evidently cast loose on sight of the incoming starship and was now speeding away on a diagonal course at, as the phrase had it, a rate of knots.

"Can't we get around it?"

It was a stupid question. "No," said the doryman.

The angled leading edge of the mat was coming closer; the doryman was loyally holding their relative position with small bursts of power to the motor. The side of the mat would pass just in front of the bow.

The radio crackled. "Ship to de Tenebre. The saurs say the kraken agree to hold our position for ten minutes or so. Come on board as soon as you can."

"Can you send out a skiff?"

She overheard some background consultation, indistinct but loud.

"No, sorry." The voice sounded genuinely apologetic. "The saurs are . . . well, they're a bit paranoid, between you and me. I've never seen them . . . like this."

"Okay, thanks, I'll do what I can," said Lydia. "Hold the door."

She put the radio away and looked over her shoulder at the doryman. "How long will this thing take to pass?"

He shaded his eyes and looked up the lake. "Half an hour, maybe more."

"Burning hell."

Lydia half-stood, gazing at the logs that drifted by a couple of meters in front of her. The mat was held together by cables around the outermost logs; within that kilometers-long loop the logs were (another phrase literalizing before her eyes) logjammed, wallowing and bumping like a school of whales in a bay. The trunks were huge, up to fifty meters long and two or three meters on the bole. As she stood there, her balance sharpened by her long familiarity with small boats, Lydia suddenly saw the logs as the backs of a galloping herd of wild horses, and an image of leaping from back to back (the neighing, the dust, the roar of a thousand hooves) was real behind her eyes.

She motioned the boat forward and the steersman, perhaps not understanding, complied. The nearest log was a meter and a half away. Lydia picked up her case and put one foot on the prow.

"No!" yelled the doryman.

Lydia jumped—it was hardly more than a step, but the boat moved backward behind her—onto the wet rough bark. Then she sprang to the next, and the next, dancing across the rolling logs (the bucking backs), from one to the next before each had time to roll further (to notice), with her case (her frantically-held pack of food) a burden but at the same time a help in keeping her balance.

Halfway to the ship, she slipped. She crashed forward, the arm with the case thrown over the top of the log. Her side thumped hard against the bark, her legs in very cold water to the knee. There was no pain but the breath was knocked out of her. She saw the crushing logs converge (the pounding hooves trample) and her whole body convulsed in one complex movement she could never have intended, and she was astraddle the log and then standing, running along its back to regain her balance, and then she leaped sideways.

A minute later her last leap took her through the open deck door of the ship, where her heel skidded on slopped water and she fell hard and slid four meters on her arse and banged up against a bulkhead. Everything hurt. She sat and stared at her grazed palms and cried.

The deck door shut behind her like a snapping clam.

Saurs glared at her, then turned away. The human clan members looked at her with compassion and amazement. A kid helped her to her feet.

"How did you *do* that?"

She looked at her hands. The grazes were already fading. Bits of dirt and bark, expelled from under her skin, flaked away. She dusted her palms and smiled.

"Just luck."

The Delibes were kind; they took her to the senior family's skiff and helped her into dry clothing and gave her hot drinks, even though they were themselves in upheaval over their landing's being aborted. The krakens had set a course back to Nova Terra. The Delibes' route only intersected the de Tenebres' at some points, of which Novakkad was one; they had left Nova Terra a few weeks before the de Tenebres had arrived, so they knew nothing of Volkov and his dire warnings and wild projects, and little of the historically recent arrivals on Mingulay. Lydia spent the hour before the lightspeed jump filling them in. But they were more interested in the Multipliers, and the Bright Star Cultures.

"This is bad for us," said Anthony Delibes, the clan patriarch. "It is a new sphere, intersecting the Second Sphere and supplanting all our routes. The saurs and the kraken are terrified. They seem too shocked even to talk. But—"

He hesitated, stroking his beard. "In itself it does not seem bad. It is not the invasion and war that your Volkov feared."

Lydia nodded eagerly. "I feared much worse myself. But what I've seen on Novakkad is very different from what I expected. The species we know already are mingling much more than before, and the two new species are just"—she spread her hands—"accepted."

She did not tell them all she knew. She could remember touching a carbon atom, and how its springy, slippery feel matched the sight of its wavelength in the spectrum of a supernova; the dissolution of death, and the wild joy of jaws closing on a deer's throat; flying with wings, and swimming with fins. These and myriad other fragmentary memories, random thoughts, equations solved and principles understood, floated in her mind as disparate bright shards, which someday and with untold effort she might assemble to a mirror, and see in it a new self.

Until she saw that new self, she could talk about none of this. She felt restless, and excused herself to take a walk around the ship. She was at the navigator's pool at the moment of the lightspeed jump.

The navigator had recoiled to the side of the pool. Gouts of sepia blackened the water. This was not the normal response to a jump. Within a couple of seconds, alarms sounded. The saurs and humans of the ship's complement rushed to evidently prearranged posts. Lydia scrambled to the nearest skiff. Only the pilot was in it.

"What's happening?"

"I do not know," the pilot said. "We are definitely at our destination, but Nova Terra bears . . . an unfamiliar aspect. And we have been hailed, perhaps even challenged. The kraken are disturbed."

"Indeed they are," Lydia said. "Which suggest that we should be terrified."

The saur himself was trembling slightly. "I am awaiting instructions," he said. "I am ready to die."

Lydia regretted her flippant tone. "Shall we look outside?"

The pilot palmed the controls. Lydia scanned the familiar landmasses of Nova Terra.

"Look at Nova Babylonia!" she said. "The air's filthy!"

"Yes," said the saur, as though something more important had been missed.

Lydia felt an odd sensation on the back of her neck. She turned and saw a huge shape glide—as it seemed—above them, then come to a halt in front of them.

"It is we who are moving," explained the saur. "The other craft is in Trojan orbit."

"How far away is it?" Lydia asked.

"About a kilometer."

The scale of the thing snapped into focus. Toroidal, rotating about a stationary hub, bristling with antennae and what Lydia guessed were armaments, and accompanied by a dozen or so small vessels with long jointed legs.

"Gods above," she said. "It's bigger than we are."

"Orbital fort," said the pilot. "Keeping station on the jump destination."

Lydia had not known that jump destinations were at Trojan points.

One of the small craft burned off a brief boost and scooted toward the starship, closing the gap in seconds. Its retro-flare almost overloaded the screen's brightness controls. As Lydia blinked away afterimages she saw its rockets make a few smaller nudges. It vanished below her line of sight, apparently docking. The saur fingered a control and the view cut instantly to the side of the starship, on which the craft resembled a small spider clinging to a large pipe. The docking bays, Lydia noticed with interest, were compatible.

"We have been boarded," said the saur. His tone carried a faint note of melancholy.

"Can you switch to an internal view?"

He shook his head. "I have no access to the ship's internal sensors."

"No," Lydia said patiently. Saurian thought ran more deeply than the human, and therefore in deeper ruts. "But you do have access to the skiff's external—"

"Ah."

In a moment a band of the skiff's hull had become as glass. On the wall across from the skiff, beside the equivalent rack of skiffs, a stairway zigzagged to the interior deck near the navigator's pool. Three space-suited figures trooped down it, heavy-duty plasma rifles at the ready. As they turned on a landing, their open helmets revealed human faces.

The pilot stared at them and turned to Lydia, and she could see by his expression that he had never seen and barely imagined their like. Their clumsy suits were of obvious human manufacture, their rocket maneuvers were perfect; their fort resembled one of the space stations

Volkov had told her about, the kind the Germans had imagined and the Americans never built, perhaps because by the 1950s the Americans already understood that deep space would never be theirs. They'd abandoned it, too hastily, to the Russians, not realizing that it didn't belong to the skiffs' little grey pilots either. Knowing nothing of this, the Russians were the first to meet the galaxy's real masters. The Nova Terrans in the past century had founded a human space presence more formidable than anything even the Russians had attempted, and they had done so in a full knowledge of its possible consequences. Lydia had to admire them for that. She was afraid of them, but she admired them, and she took a certain malicious joy in the saur's discomfiture at this unexpected display of human capability.

"What are they?" the saur asked.

"Cosmonauts," Lydia said.

It turned out they called themselves astronauts.

Lydia returned to the deck and found the senior Delibes had gathered there ahead of her. Anthony, his pugnacious jaw thrust forward, was making an effort to be polite.

"Naturally," Lydia heard him say, "I share your concern for the security of the Republic. I assure you that nothing and nobody on this ship could compromise it. You have my word. I am a Member of the Electorate!"

"So'm I," said the cosmonaut who stood in the apex of the group. He gestured at the other two, a pace behind his shoulders. "So're we all."

"Ah!" The merchant smiled and relaxed. He held out his hand. "Welcome aboard, fellow citizens. Anthony Delibes, at your service, officers."

"Thank you, citizen." The cosmonaut returned the handshake, then jerked a thumb at his chest. "Astronaut Sarn't Claudius Abenke; Astronauts Alexander Obikwe and Titus Adams. Space Defense Force of the Democratic Republic of New Babylon."

"Oh, shit," said Lydia, unable to stop herself.

The astronauts glowered at her; the Delibes turned, startled.

"You have a problem with that, citizen?" said Abenke.

"Volkov," said Lydia.

The astronauts all looked uncomfortable. Abenke composed his features to a steadfast frown.

"Volkov is dead."

662

7

The Modern Regime

E VERY DAY WAS the same. Reveille, canteen breakfast, assignment. For most of the steadily growing number of inmates—a thousand or so, increasing by scores every day as new ships came in—the assignment was to light work, or recreation. For Lydia it was to interrogation. Torture had been abolished.

One interrogator sat on the other side of the table, the second over to her side, just at the edge of sight. Every so often they would change places.

"What do you know of the aliens' plans for invasion?"

"Nothing."

"What happened to you on Novakkad?"

"I've already told you."

"Tell us again."

Sometimes there was a different tack. "What was your assignment from Volkov?"

"There was no assignment."

"What were your relations with Volkov?"

"I've already told you."

"Tell us again."

The detention center was on an island in the Half Moon Sea, within sight of the city. Concrete blockhouses, barbed wire, a jagged shore and hungry currents—nobody tried to leave. Every day a few dozen people were released and loaded on a boat to the city. Grim rumors circulated about what happened to them, but nobody thought in their hearts that they were fed to the whales. Every day a few score more people arrived. The starships from which they had been taken would remain for a few days in the harbor, and then depart.

Lydia was certain that her own clan had been detained and released. She was not at all certain that she would be. Every night she went down to the fence and gazed across the kilometers of water to the lights of the city. It was winter, and dark came early, and cold. There were far more lights than before, and they reached higher into the sky, but they were almost always veiled in murk. Overhead passed aircraft like she had never seen before, with bright lights at the wingtips and along the sides, and engines that roared. Surface vessels almost half the size of starships arrived, sitting low in the water, and left a day or two later riding high. Lydia was told that they delivered petroleum. It could be distilled and burned; hence the murk. She had seen this done on Croatan, but she had never thought that Nova Terra needed terraforming.

On clear nights, though, she could still see the stars. They now seemed forever beyond her reach. She could also see the moons, and the tiny new moons, the orbital forts and communications satellites in stately steady array. Beyond them, she could see the comets. Five in the one sky.

She talked to people in the evenings. Their stories were similar to her own, though none admitted, any more than she did, to having been changed by the aliens. Most of them had, like the Delibes, not encountered the aliens at all. Their kraken navigators had recoiled from the planets on which they landed, all of them fifty light-years or more away. Nobody had any idea what had happened here on Nova Terra.

After a month her interrogators either became convinced of her innocence or bored with her intransigence. They turned her over to the center's administrative office, who returned her suitcase and gave her ten thousand thalers. In Nova Babylonia this would have been a year's pay for a skilled worker. In New Babylon it was a month's. Lydia assumed this meant the standard of living had risen twelvefold in her absence. Every note and coin bore on its obverse the profile of Volkov, and on every one that image was defaced.

She climbed the ladder off the boat and found Esias waiting for her on the quay. They hugged each other and then stepped back. Other reunions went on noisily around them.

"How did you know to expect me?"

"I've been coming here every day."

"Oh."

They looked at each other warily.

"Are you all right?" Esias asked.

"How do you mean?"

"You don't suspect yourself of going mad?"

"Not at all," said Lydia. "Do you?"

Esias sighed. "No."

"Well then."

"Yes."

Esias insisted on carrying her suitcase. "Let's walk for a bit," he said. "See the sights." He grinned. "Welcome to New Babylon, by the way." He waved his free hand to encompass the banks of lights stacked in front of them in the gathering dusk. "And the glories of the Modern Regime!"

They walked from the docks to the Avenue of the Kings, on which the de Tenebre building had once stood. At the foot of the avenue, where Gilgamesh II had once stood in granite, rose a taller and grander statue in concrete. It showed a smiling and handsome young man in a space-suit, helmet under one arm, and a crushed octopod under one foot.

"When did this happen?"

"About thirty years after we left. The aliens came and New Babylon was ready for them. The battle was brief."

"I'll bet," said Lydia.

"They've just started calling that "the first invasion." What we left behind on Novakkad is the second. And they'll be ready for it, too."

The street name had been changed to Astronaut Avenue. Heavy metal vehicles filled it from end to end. Trucks and buses, mostly, which somehow despite all their noise and stink labored to carry or pull their loads. Bicycles wove perilously between them. The people who filled the pavements were drably dressed; even their better suits were modeled on work clothes: plain jacket, trousers, shirt. All the color had been leeched from the street and concentrated in tubes of neon, spelling out advertisements and assertions. The faces of some of the older people looked stretched and pitted, like copper beaten until it broke.

"Smallpox epidemic," said Esias. "It's a solved problem now."

The new buildings were higher and their sides more likely to be vertical. In other places new towers had been built on top of the existing buildings, extending them upward to double their original impressive enough height. What had been white marble was now black. The terraces had survived, but the gardens had not. Flying squirrels were few, and their variety diminished. Here and there the old cheerful erotic and ecstatic statuary clung on, like lovers and mystics hiding in corners, but most of the statues were heroic and earnest. Among them, on this corner and that traffic island, were occasional plinths empty except for jagged fragments of the feet or the boots. Lydia did not need to guess whose name they bore.

"What happened here?" she said. "What happened to Volkov?"

"He changed things less than you might think," Esias said. "The Senate and the Assembly, the guilds and associations—all these are still here. The main reform was that everybody became a Member of the Electorate. Many of the new Electors, and some of the old, joined the Modern Society. It became like the Party he used to talk about so proudly and so cynically. They harnessed everything to the space defense effort. They taxed everything that moved. They had the defenses built just in time. They destroyed the alien ships. And then they kept building more defenses. They had wars with neighboring provinces, and when these wars were being lost, Volkov was shot by his own security detail. The wars were lost anyway, the provinces broke away, but the space defense forces continued to be strengthened. We're told there's more freedom now. Reform. Liberalization. If this is freedom I'm glad we missed the tyranny."

"Yes," said Lydia. "But I'm sorry we missed Volkov. In his pride, in his power. A third Gilgamesh, one who really did find the secret of life."

"Except that he never did find it. It was in his body, but his scientists could never read it."

Lydia glanced sideways sharply at her father, but she could not read him.

The de Tenebre building was long gone, replaced by a concrete-and-glass tower. The headquarters of the Ninth still stood. Black-uniformed guards strutted and turned on its long steps. Close by was a much taller building, so tall in fact that Lydia had not registered it as a building, though she had seen its aircraft warning lights often enough from the island. It was like a wall of black glass, and was built with a twist, so that its top floor was at about thirty degrees to its lower. Set well back from the street, it overshadowed a plaza with fountains and lights. No name was indicated.

"Space Authority," said Esias. "It's supposed to represent the shape of a lightspeed engine." He smiled, relishing some well-worn joke. "It would have been more impressive if they'd actually built one."

Lydia shivered. She had seen a lightspeed engine. Its shape was nothing like this, but the architecture had indeed captured something of the spirit of that extraordinary machine: the feeling it had given her . . . of being watched.

"What did the saurs and the krakens think of all this?"

"They went away," said Esias. "Most of them. They are still going away, as ships come in and go. Of our ship, only Voronar has stayed." He smiled. "He calls himself a Salassoist."

"Where do they go?"

Esias shrugged, huddling deeper in his coat against a chill breeze off the wall of black glass. "Who knows?" he said.

" 'They all go up the line,' " she said, quoting an old and sinister space chantey.

"Perhaps." He caught her hand. "That reminds me. A truly great accomplishment which you are about to see."

He took her to the underground railway station, and they went up the line.

I'll die here, Lydia thought. All that had brought this on was that water had overlapped the welts of her shoes. It was not even as if they were good shoes. But the oil would do them no further good.

Oil on water. It was an indelible mark of industrialization. Lydia gazed gloomily at the puddle's rainbow hues and heaved another plastic sack of rubbish into the overflowing skip. Turning about, she made way for the invincibly cheerful Esias, who was lugging another sack. They did not exchange words or glances. As she picked her way to the foot of the block's outside stairwell Lydia heard her father's simian grunt as he disposed of his load, the brisk brush of his palms as he turned away, the squelch of his footsteps as he trudged back. Lydia hurried up the iron steps, looking up all the while. Behind her, Esias climbed more slowly, puffing and panting. At the landings Lydia could see the sky, blue after the rain, crisscrossed with contrails whose chalky scrawls marked another score on the progress chart.

Their flats were halfway up, on the eleventh level. Lydia stopped a few steps along the concrete balcony and leaned bare, dusty forearms on its black-painted iron rail. The adjacent block faced her across a ten-meter gulf. A line of washing, small garments that someone had neglected to take in from the recent shower, dripped and swayed. Music leaked from a hundred radios, up and down the shaft. A cleaning robot clambered, trailing hoses and cables, squirting and sudsing, sponging and rinsing. Here and there it had missed a window, and left behind a washed rectangle of wall.

Lydia heard Esias ascending the last flight. She straightened, turned away and strolled to the open door of the new flat. About half the clan had taken up residence along this balcony; the rest were scattered in ones and twos around the city's housing projects. New Babylon did not acknowledge polygamy; fortunately it recognized Claudia and Faustina as a couple in their own right. Their flat was between the one that had been kept for Lydia and the one rented in the names of Esias and Phoebe.

She still mourned Volkov. That must be why getting her socks wet made her miserable. Perhaps when she was as old as her father she would be as good a stoic. She had not loved the Cosmonaut but she had liked him and been fascinated with him, and over the past few eventful months of subjective time his capacity to change history had drawn her reluctant, even hostile respect. He had seemed as invincible as he was immortal, and now he was defeated and dead. And yet the regime perversely insisted on reminding people of him, every time money changed hands. Not all the coins and notes, surely, could have been in circulation at the time of his fall. Some of them at least must have been printed or minted since, and officially defaced. Unless people did that to new currency as soon as it was issued, as some kind of gesture of continuing hate. She wasn't sure which possibility was the more depressing to contemplate.

The flat was almost clear now of the rubbish from its recent refurbishment. The municipal authority workers had replaced some old walls and fittings with new ones, but had not cleared out the rubble. That was a job left for the new tenants. There was a kind of justice to it, a first few drops of sweat equity. Lydia picked up a brush and pushed some more brick and tile into a heap, then shoveled it into a sack. Esias came into the room and joined in.

While gathering up the last bits, he cut his hand on a piece of broken tile. He had always been careless about gloves. He hopped up and down, cursing. The cut was nasty and deep, blood was dripping everywhere. Lydia ran to the dusty new sink in the kitchen and ran cold water on a clean cloth. She caught his wrist and wiped the dirt and blood from his palm. The split skin sealed itself up as she watched, leaving nothing but a white line from which specks of dirt rose to the surface. She brushed a finger against the grubby flecks and looked at the palm again. The cut had left no trace.

Esias stared back at her. "It doesn't hurt any the less," he said.

"I know," she said.

"Perhaps we should not say any more."

She nodded. They lugged the last two sacks of rubbish down to the skip.

The clan had trade in their bones. They adapted to the new situation, and worked around the new restrictions, which to the rest of the city were the new relaxations: the post-Volkov reforms. Esias and his wives opened a stall at the docks. Lydia's cousins and siblings took up jobs or hustles; the distinction was obscure, as were the details.

Lydia applied and, to her surprise, was accepted, for a clerical job at the core of the Regime: the Space Authority. The twisted megalith of the building did not intimidate her. For her first day at work, she wore the best garment she had, her dress from old Nova Babylonia, and was amused to find in the days that followed that this was considered a gesture of defiance, but one for which—from sheer embarrassment— nobody in authority could reprove her or forbid. Other young women working on the statistical machines or the typewriters began to turn up in copies made from the artificial silk sold in the markets.

One day a message popped out of the pneumatic tube on her desk. She opened it expecting another report for her to abstract, and found it a summons to meet the President.

The President's office was in the top floor of the headquarters of the Ninth. Lydia's roll of paper took her past three sets of heavily armed guards to the reserved lift entrance on the ground floor. Inside it was a small burnished room, all carpet and mirror. The lift was so fast that Lydia felt the blood drain from her head, like it sometimes had on a ship when the field fluctuated.

The doors opened on more guards, and a metal detector, through which Lydia passed without a buzz or a challenge. The whole floor was open-plan, thickly carpeted. People bowed over rank upon rank of polished desks, scribbling and marking, ticking and signing in silence. Huge bouquets of fresh flowers stood in as many vases as there were desks. The fragrance was thick and the hush was thicker. Lydia was reminded of a crematorium.

A functionary in the strange archaic uniform of the breed—a suit of trousers, jacket, shirt, and necktie—looked at Lydia, peered at her summons, and guided her silently to a door at the back of the bureaucratic mausoleum. There was nothing special about the door. He opened it and bowed her in, then withdrew.

The room was an office. It had a tall high window behind the desk, stacked bookshelves around the walls, and doors that opened off to what a quick glance confirmed were living quarters. Tall vases of flowers filled this room with color and scent, even more overpowering than in the great antechamber.

Behind the big desk sat the most aged woman Lydia had ever seen. She seemed to have shrunk and shriveled within the black-silk kimono that swathed her. Her cheeks were sunken, her skin yellow, her teeth brown and long. The hand on the pommel of her ceremonial sword, and the hand on the open book on the desk, looked like some contraptions of thin leather and thick wire. This was not the swift dissolution that overtook people toward the end of their twelfth decade. This was something preserved, pushed through, carried forward beyond that by some desperate will, and doubtless by some corrupted application of saur or human medicine.

"Ah," breathed the President. She drooled slightly, and wiped her chin on her cuff. "Lydia de Tenebre. Thank you for coming." The eyes flashed, some life and humor shining through the yellowed sclera. "You may not think you had a choice, but you had. So I thank you. Sit down."

"Thank you, Madame President."

"I have been eager to see you since I heard of your return," the President went on. She leaned forward; Lydia caught a whiff of her terrible breath, and understood why there were so many flowers about. "Unfortunately it takes time for information to reach me, and even when it has, I have much to do."

Not much by the look of things, Lydia thought, but she nodded politely.

"It was your clan who brought us Volkov," said the President, closing her eyes. "Ah, how he charmed us all! We called him the Engineer. It was not like politics, you understand. It was like religion—no, it was like a mania, a bubble on the market, and we were all speculators. And when we had stopped believing, it was too late for us to turn back. He made us believe by force."

Another sigh, another stench. It was not from her mouth that this was coming—the teeth were dark but clean, the tongue was pink. It was coming from her lungs and her bowels.

"And years after we had stopped believing, and all feared to admit it to each other, the aliens came. They ran into the orbital defenses that Volkov had lashed us to build. They ran into them, smack! Their ships burst in the hellish light of the particle beams! Their outposts vaporized in the hellish heat of the nuclear bursts!"

Back and forth she swayed as she told the story, in a singsong voice like a crone of the pithkies reciting a tribal lay.

"Oh, how we all loved him again! Our Cosmonauts came back from the battles with his name on their lips! We built more forts and ships and waited for the next invasion. We built more rockets and waited for the gods to send down rocks in their wrath. We waited, and waited."

Her eyes snapped open. Her voice resumed a conversational cadence.

"They never came. And after a while, after a few more years, we stopped believing that they would ever come. Not for another million years, anyway. We grumbled at the taxes and the conscriptions and prescriptions. But that was not why I had him killed."

As the President's face had become more animated with her discourse, Lydia had gradually built up from glimpses an image of the face it once had been, and what now dawned on her was an awful recognition.

"Volkov not only promised us victory over the invaders. He promised us the long life, the long life like the saurs. Oh, the research, the institutes, the papers, the arguments. The labor of men and saurs, all of it sincere, all of it well-meant, some of it horrific, none of it successful. And for that failure to extend our lives and youth, I took his own."

Her gaze was distant, yet to Lydia it seemed like needles aimed at her eyes. The preternaturally old President sighed.

"He disappointed me," said Julia de Zama. "Severely."

2

The Human as Alien

8

New Earth (Political)

THE WINDOW WAS tiny and the glass was thick. Susan Harkness pressed her forehead against it, gasping, heart pounding, and stared out until all she could see was the stars. She imagined she stood in a field on a very dark night, looking up at the constellations. The Musketeer was there, and the jeweled pleiad of the Thrown Net, and the Hind. She imagined a cool breeze in her face, and that the sough of the ventilation was its sigh. Gradually her breathing eased, the bands around her chest loosened.

She had expected a price for her reckless light-century leap into the dark: regret, sorrow, homesickness. Fear. She had thought them all worth paying, for the chance of life at this intensity, and of being present at moments that could not but become history. She had not expected claustrophobia. It had sneaked up on her from behind. She felt betrayed by her own mind. They had spent two days lurking in the system's Oort cloud. It was absurd, but the thought of that cloud was actually making her sense of confinement worse, even though all it meant was a high probability that there was a piece of cometary matter within a few million kilometers.

Rolling in orbit around the selkies' world had been different. The beauty and variety of that terrestrial planet from space, and the alien fascination of its gas-giant primary and its red-giant sun, had made living in the narrow ships feel anything but confinement. One's attention was always turned to the outside. The skiffs had flitted from ship to ship, and she'd always been able to wangle a ride, always with a good reason: interviewing crew members, documenting discoveries. The only sense of confinement she had felt was the suffocating presence of her parents. That they were enlightened and meant well she knew, but they couldn't help casting long shadows. Anywhere in the Bright Star Cultures, she would always be the First Navigator's daughter, the Science Officer's girl. On cold reflection it seemed mad to move a hundred and three light-years to get away from her parents, but analyzing the moment of impulse that had made her do it revealed no other explanation. She felt obscurely insulted that her mother had automatically blamed it on Matt, as though Susan had no will of her own. She was certainly not besotted with Matt, nor he with her, though she suspected that without the ulterior motive of their irregular attachment he would never have connived at her escape, or escapade. In that sense he could be blamed, but she knew that if she ever blamed him she would never forgive herself.

She stepped back from the porthole and groped for the light switch. The cabin she shared with Ramona Garcia, a Cosmonaut mathematician slightly more ancient than Matt, seemed tinier than ever. She ducked out of it into the corridor before that thought could close in again.

The corridor was wider than the room. She could stretch out her arms and not touch the sides. But with the lights on, the windows showed nothing. She walked up to the cockpit. The viewscreens and windows in there gave the illusion of space, or would have done if the cabin hadn't been crammed with people: Matt, Salasso, and Delavar, the old Cosmonauts Mikhail Telesnikov and Ramona (who gave her a quick friendly smile), the Mingulayan captain Phil Johnson, and first mate Ann Derige, both of whom were an embarrassing year or two younger than she was and acted like they were about ten years older; and two of the Multis, the orange one and the blue one.

The Multipliers had spent the first day spinning a thirty-meter dish aerial and a complex receiving apparatus from a kilogram of scrap steel and some random bits of junk, and had detected a very faint microwave beam that swept across them every Nova Terran day. Just before her panic attack, Susan had heard an announcement that they'd extracted some information from it.

They were all staring at a rectangular patch on the viewscreen above the fore window. All except Matt looked delighted. Nobody told her what it was, and it took her a moment to recognize it as a map, a Mercator projection of Nova Terra. Maps in the Second Sphere were physical. The only imaginary lines on them were trade routes. This city, they told you, was linked with that. The map on the viewscreen was covered with imaginary lines separating patches of different colors, none of which looked as if they had anything to do with geography.

"What is that?" she asked.

"It's the first piece of information we've managed to crunch out of the microwave beam," said Ramona. "It's a world map, the logo of the official television station, New Babylon News. Presumably the beam's a daily news update aimed at deep-space missions. Almost certainly military missions, because it's encrypted. Matt doesn't know if it's worth the effort to crack—any news will be a year out of date anyway."

"I know it's a map, but—"

"What you're looking at," said Matt, "is the most obscene and disgusting thing I've seen for centuries. It's a map of the world that happens to be a rectangular sheet of chauvinist shit. Every one of those barbarously, artificially carved-up fragments of the world is tagged with a little rectangle of its own, a bloody badge of shame—a flag! They've got *nationalism* down there. If they had a virulent strain of bubonic plague instead, I'd be happy for them. I'm still red in the face from explaining all this to the Multipliers."

He was indeed red in the face, but he'd been looking flushed for the past day or so, and occasionally shivery. He'd brushed aside any enquiries. Just a cold or something. It hadn't spread.

The Multipliers quivered slightly, perhaps embarrassed themselves. Matt simmered down a little.

"The good thing, though," said Telesnikov, "is that we aren't picking up any deep-space radar beams. I expect there'll be some close in, but they're unlikely to be probing out farther than the asteroid belt."

"Nova Sol has an asteroid belt?" Matt asked.

"You don't know the system?" Telesnikov sounded incredulous.

Matt shrugged. "All the descriptions I ever saw of it were Ptolemaic. Couldn't get my head around the epicycles."

Ramona snorted. The saurs looked slightly abashed. Their species had not thought it necessary to inform the Nova Babylonians about the heliocentric hypothesis, knowledge of which had in the past few centuries spread inward from Croatan to shatter the most horrendously complicated arrangement of crystal spheres ever devised.

"All right," said Telesnikov. "Here it is in Copernican. Working in from here, and not counting contentious lumps of rock and ice which might be stray gods . . . we've got two gas giants, Juno and Zeus, about oh point seven and one point six Jupiter masses respectively. Both have a spectacular array of moons and rings—it's a fair bet these are garrisoned, if we assume Volkov has succeeded. Which we must, on the basis that pleasant surprises are not to be counted on. Next there's the asteroid belt, which is much richer than the Solar System's, probably the richest in the Second Sphere. There's nothing in the equivalent of Mars orbit, like our Raphael back home—probably never formed, hence the extent of the asteroid belt. Then there's Nova Terra itself, with its two satellites, Ea and Selene, each about two-thirds the size of Luna and resulting in diabolically complex tides. Finally, you have one which is kind of like a big Mercury or a close-orbit airless Venus, a thoroughly nasty ball of hot rock with a high albedo. Named Lucifer, aptly enough.

"Now, if I were applying the doctrine of system defense which I learned in Moscow Cosmotech—"

"You learned *Solar System defense*?" Matt interrupted.

"Asteroid detection and deflection was the practical side," said Telesnikov. He scratched the back of his neck. "The matter of repelling alien invasions was, ah, the speculative part. Anyway, I'm sure Volkov studied the same classified texts. The basics are the gas-giant moons, the asteroid belt—minimum of three armed and fortified mini-observatories cum missile or particle-beam stations, evenly spaced around it so you essentially have the inner system triangulated—and finally the home planet's moon—moons, in this case—and low orbit. All likewise fortified, and with harder armor and hotter weapons the closer in you are. Anything that gets through all of that is a matter for air and ground defense. Or disaster recovery."

"What about any inner planets?" Susan asked. "Didn't Volkov go to Venus?"

"He did," said Telesnikov. "But that was just a stunt. We never considered fortifying Venus! The great majority—I think historically, all—impact events come from the other direction, from outside Earth's orbit. As for intelligent threats—well, there was one theoretical case, a slingshot approach round the sun and out to Earth on the daylight side. Obviously a very smart manoeuvre if you could pull it off—observation would be difficult, interception an absolute nightmare. But that would come in so fast that frankly your lunar and low-orbit defenses would have a much better chance of catching it."

"Hmm," said Matt, tipping back the gimballed chair he'd appropriated and looking as if he wanted to light a cigarette, "it sounds like the dark side of Lucifer would be a good place to lurk. We could jump straight into its shadow cone and stay there—safe from Nova-Solar radiation, and within easy listening distance of Nova Terra."

"Provided it's not in opposition at the moment—I mean, when we get there."

The blue Multiplier jumped to the window and spread itself against it, like an expanding snowflake. Then it shrank its extensions back into its limbs and hopped back to its previous perch.

"It shall not," it said. "If we were to jump now we would encounter Lucifer at thirty-eight degrees from Nova Terra."

"Thank you," said Matt dryly. "The next thing we need to know is whether Volkov got any cooperation from the saurs, and therefore whether or not he has lightspeeders and skiffs." He looked hopefully at the alien. "I don't suppose you can tell us that?"

"Our skiffs have instruments for detecting other space-bending quantum manifold devices in operation," it said. "They can only be used when the skiff is in operation, which of course leaves them open to such detection themselves."

Everybody turned to look at the saurs.

"Ours do not have such devices," said Delavar.

"How do you avoid collisions?" asked the Multiplier.

"They just don't happen," said Delavar. "It's a question of skilled piloting."

"It is because of something called the Exclusion Principle," said Salasso stiffly.

"Ah," sighed the Multiplier, as though inhaling in order to say something, and then fell silent.

"Okay," said Matt, in a tone of heavy patience, "and have your skiffs detected any other ships or skiffs in the system?"

The two Multipliers touched hands, conferring.

"One starship arrived two days ago," said the orange Multiplier. "Another left yesterday. Some minor and local skiff activity accompanied them. That is all."

"How about rocket exhausts?" asked Ann Derige.

"We have no instruments to detect them," said the orange Multiplier. "Though doubtless," it added in a hopeful tone, waving its limbs excitedly, "such instruments could be improvised."

"Very difficult anyway," said Telesnikov. "Fusion torches and such apart, and even they'd be almost invisible at this distance."

"We seem to have arrived at a negative conclusion," said Delavar. "The deep-space communication suggests a deep-space presence, the absence of evidence of antigravity or nuclear drives suggests that this has been accomplished with conventional rockets. This is more or less what we would have anticipated, if we had done any anticipating."

Was this a dig at Matt? If it was, he laughed it off.
A day later, they jumped a year.

The dark side of Lucifer. Susan liked the idea; she knew that the Light-bearer was a dark power in some perverse mythologies. The interstellar flotilla, the *Investigator* and its five companions, hung in starlight a few hundred meters above the planet's cracked surface. This was lower than many of its mountains; their chances of detection equivalently small—

"We've been pinged," said Ann.

The two Multipliers pounced toward their apparatus. Their hands scrabbled over it and each other. Outside, the dish aerial moved, tracking.

"There appears to be a small artificial satellite in polar orbit."

"We can improvise a control system to send one of your missiles toward it."

"Within two of its orbits."

Phil Johnson looked over at Matt. It was Phil who gave orders to the crew, but it had been well established that it was Matt who was leading this expedition.

"Go for that?"

Matt rubbed his nose. "No," he said. "I have a better idea."

He turned to the Multipliers. "Could you ask one of the skiffs outside to go after the satellite, catch it, and reinsert it in equatorial orbit?"

Even he could hardly have expected the speed with which his suggestion was carried out. The orange Multiplier tapped at the apparatus. Within seconds one of the skiffs riding alongside disappeared. Two minutes later, it was back.

"We have picked up and redirected the satellite. It was approximately one meter in diameter."

"Fucking sputnik," said Matt. 'Now let's shift a thousand or so kilometers out of the way.'

"Why?" asked Johnson.

"We've been spotted by what is probably a scientific satellite mapping Lucifer," Matt said. "Within about one minute, the information will reach Nova Terra. If it's a purely scientific probe, the likely result is that it won't be processed for months. If it's not, if it's part of their space-defense network, we could be burned by a particle beam in about five or six minutes. So let's move."

They moved. It wasn't a lightspeed jump, just a very fast move. The landscape below didn't look any different.

"Right," said Matt, "now we set up a jump to Nova Terra. Make it somewhere on the surface with plenty of cover and far away from any settled areas. Ann, could you patch up that map again?"

Matt peered at the map for a moment, then pointed at a zigzag line marking the northern border of the Republic of New Babylon. "There," he said. "In the forests just north of the mountains, on the north side of the border. It looks pretty well uninhabited."

Everybody just stared at him.

"I was wrong about Lucifer," he said. "It's not a safe place to lurk. The safest place I can think of is Nova Terra itself. If you're watching for invaders from space, where's the last place you'd look?"

"They'll have spy satellites," Telesnikov pointed out. "They'll see *something*."

"Yup," said Matt. "I'm counting on it. I'm also guessing that the spy satellites are not likely to be those of"—he peered again at the map—"the Free Duchy of Illyria, and that it and New Babylon are not exactly friends."

"And if you're wrong?" said Phil.

Matt shrugged. "If I'm wrong, we'll move somewhere else."

Salasso stood up. "I am afraid," he said, "that that is not an adequate answer. I think I see what you are trying to do, Matt, and I very much look forward to finding out how the Nova Terran news media cover— or cover up—the anomalous event of a satellite suddenly orbiting at ninety degrees to its previous orbit. I agree entirely that Nova Terra is the best place to lurk, now that we have found that even Lucifer is under observation. However, I strongly suggest that we make our base somewhere much less accessible and much less noticeable than a border region, however wild it may appear."

He pointed to the map. "You will notice," he went on, "that the lines depicting political divisions are only present on one continent, Genea, the one inhabited mainly by the hominidae." He tapped a long finger on the other one. "The one inhabited mainly by saurs is still marked simply as Sauria."

It was something so obvious that none of them had noticed it. Every planet in their experience had at least an island continent reserved for saurs, and they had taken this one's for granted.

"I don't think blundering into a saur city or manufacturing plant is going to make us any less conspicuous," said Matt.

"Indeed not," said Salasso. "But as the Multipliers have told us, there are no skiffs operational except around the occasional starship, presumably in the harbor of New Babylon. That suggests strongly to me that there are no, or very few, saurs present on the planet. If for any reason we are detected there, what could be more natural than for our skiffs to be taken for those of returning or remaining saurs? Also, Sauria includes extensive areas of rainforest, mountain ranges, temperate forest, ruined cities. One in particular has ruins more than adequate to conceal our entire expedition."

"How do you know all this?" asked Susan.

The saur gave her his almost undetectable smile. "I remember it well," he said.

At that moment, Susan noticed Matt looking at his watch. A moment later, a bright flare filled the windows on one side, and the viewscreens went into an unstable cycle of failed adjustments. Several alarms went off. It was as though the ship had drifted out of the shadow cone into the savage sunlight; except it was the wrong window, and the light was fading, not increasing.

Matt looked from his watch to the window. "Plasma-cannon strike," he said. "Vaporized the ground just below where we were a few minutes ago. From lunar orbit, by my reckoning—shit, they must have something big up there, one hefty motherfucker of a death ray projector. Let's jump."

They jumped.

Rhododendrons and flying squirrels in a big square of blue. Susan staggered away from the foot of the *Investigator*'s stair ladder, mistiming her steps in the subtly different gravity, then found her feet and ran to the door of the hangar-sized megalithic structure within which the ship and the ships were parked. They'd come out of the lightspeed jump a thousand meters up and a few thousand meters away—the Multiplier navigators, and Salasso's memory, were that precise. Strangely, the flying squirrels avoided the structure, which might have seemed a suitable roost; Susan noticed as she ran that the floor was thick with dirt, but clear of any animal droppings.

Out in the open she stopped, and breathed deeply. She was ecstatic with relief. Only now that she was out of the ship could she realize how confined she had felt inside it; how tightly she had screwed a lid down on that feeling of confinement. The air was colder than she had expected, and better than she had hoped. It carried a sweet-sour smell of vegetation. She was facing northward, the mid-morning sun high to her right. Ahead of her was an area of ground covered with short grass and rhododendron overgrowth, riotous with rotten flowers. After about a hundred meters, the ground dropped away sharply to a rainforest valley many kilometers across, on the far side of which a range of mountains raised jagged white teeth to the sky. The cacophony of whoops and the symphony of chirps from the various species and sizes of flying squirrel, and the buzz and hum of insects, were the only sounds, and they were enough.

She turned to look back at the great door, fifty meters in width and height, whose lintel cast the black shadow from which the others were emerging. The two saurs first, and the other eight humans, and a dozen Multipliers. The aliens, to her surprise, suddenly rushed past everyone else, past her, and leapt onto the tops of the rhododendron bushes and then away down the slope into the trees, chasing the startled flying squirrels into flapping, screaming flocks.

"Are you all right?" Matt asked.

"Zeus! Wow! Am I all right!"

Nobody else seemed to be having quite the same reaction. They all stepped out into the glaring sunlight cautiously, sniffing the air like prey animals; turned around at once to check the sky and the skyline; the saurs wandered off to examine the side of the entrance. Matt stood beside her and looked about with more enthusiasm than the others, but without abandon.

"Plasma rifles," he said.

His high temperature seemed to have run its course; Susan noticed that she couldn't see the tracery of subcutaneous scar tissue he'd ruefully pointed out when they'd first met. It must be something about the light.

"What?"

"We should keep them handy. There are dinosaurs on Sauria." He laughed harshly. "Perhaps that's what's kept it from being colonized by humans. 'Here be dragons.' "

"Assuming it *has* kept it," said Telesnikov, coming up. "I can see a scramble for this continent as soon as the rival nation-states on the other one work themselves up to it."

"Yeah," said Matt vaguely. "The falling rate of profit, and all that."

"I hope not," said Susan. "Wow, it's beautiful!"

Matt's attention snapped back to her. "You're very high," he said.

"It's, um, just good to be off the ship," she said. "Uh, cabin fever, you know?"

"Oh, shit," said Matt. "*Now* I get it. You suffer from—"

"*Don't* fucking say it!"

The two Cosmonauts laughed unsympathetically.

"Just as well you didn't get the tests we went through—"

"You mean, the pipes we went—"

She grabbed his arm hard enough to hurt. "Don't. Fucking. Say it."

Matt gave her a warmer look. "All right," he said. "Sorry. Christ, I've been worried about you. You haven't cracked a smile since we jumped from Planet Selkie." Then he ruined it all by adding: "Thought you were missing your parents or having PMS or something."

She shrugged away from him. He looked at her helplessly for a moment, then turned away and called and beckoned everyone together.

"We have a couple of things to talk about," he said. "Let's get the first one out of the way while our friends are away enjoying themselves. Have any of you here taken up the Multipliers' offer?"

They all shook their heads. Including the saurs, Susan noticed, as if the question might be relevant to them. Maybe it was.

"I didn't know they could just do it, like, any time," said Obadiah Hynde, the rocketeer. "Didn't know we had the option, see."

"Well, we do," said Matt. "They don't need machines. It's like . . . an infection. They give it to you. I took it, when we were lurking out in the cometary cloud."

"How could you do something so crazy and irresponsible?" said Ramona. "Oh, what am I saying? I am talking to Matt after all. Well, Matt, tell us what it is like."

"That's the trouble," said Matt. "I don't know if I can, because one part of it didn't take. The orange Multiplier, the one who tried, said it was 'like biting fruit and finding stone.' They read your genes, then tweak them. I think that's what they do. They could read mine but they couldn't alter them, because they've been altered already by the process—whatever it was—that gave us longevity. But apart from that . . . yeah, I can tell you what it's like. It's like having an infection that doesn't make you ill, then an infestation that doesn't itch, and after that you remember things that never happened to you. That's the most disturbing thing about it, I'll give you that. But it's not delusional . . . I remember them happening, but I don't think they happened to me. I can remember doing things, without thinking that I did them."

"What kind of things?" asked Ramona.

"Budding," said Matt. "Seeing my hand break off and run away, and wishing it well. Sharing knowledge, knowledge of the world and knowledge of how my body was built. The pleasure of that." He laughed. "Our friends have more fun than we know. And now I know more. Strange things. So anyway—is anyone else willing to try it?"

"So you're telling us," said Ramona, "that the Multis can give us the long life. Except for those who already have it. For the rest of us, it's hardly an issue—I don't think there's one of us here who is over twenty-five, am I right? And besides that, they mess with your head. So what's the advantage in taking the risk?"

"Its one big advantage," said Matt, "apart from the long life, is that you do not fall sick, and that most injuries self-repair very fast. I do have that."

"How," asked Telesnikov, "if they could not alter your genes?"

"That part of it has nothing to do with genes," said Matt. "It has to do with . . . some of the very small offspring of the Multipliers continuing to live inside you."

"You stay infected?" Ramona Gracia took a couple of steps away from him. "No thanks."

Matt shrugged and spread his hands. "I see I haven't sold anyone on this. Well, you can all watch and see if I turn into something strange."

("You're there already," Ramona muttered.)

"The next thing we need to discuss is what we are doing. We didn't have any detailed plan before we came here, because we didn't know what we'd find. In a sense, we still don't. We know they have separate states, and that at least one of them, most likely Nova—New Babylon, as it calls itself now—has some pretty heavy space defense. Now I don't know about you, but I don't fancy our chances going up against that kind of hardware with our fireworks. I've considered stunts like, you know, jumping a skiff or even the *Investigator*, right inside one of the orbital forts, but, well, I'd rather not rely on dumb luck or brute force. So." He brushed imaginary dust off his palms. "Anyone got any bright ideas?"

"I had the impression," said Ann, "that Salasso thought you already had one."

"Well, kind of," said Matt evasively, "but I want to hear other suggestions first."

"I have one," said Ramona. "Let's brew up some goddam coffee and have something to fucking eat."

Susan had never before heard Ramona speak coarsely. The mathematician met her surprised look with a sullen flush.

"He has that effect," she said.

•   •   •

After the gunners and rocketeers had come back from the ship's galley with hot coffee and cold rations, people began to feel less fractious. One light-year lightspeed jump, one crack at turning a mapping satellite into a blatant anomalous phenomenon, a near miss from a plasma bolt, and another lightspeed jump to ruins so old there were fossils younger— all made for a tense morning.

"The first thing we should do," said Ramona, "is watch some television. Not as easy as it sounds—I doubt if even satellite broadcasting covers this continent."

"There's always radio," said Susan. She remembered that she had a radio in her pocket. "Hey! Wait a minute."

She switched the radio on and spun the dial slowly. Most of the stations played music. The scales were unfamiliar, the lyrics mostly in languages that had drifted from Trade Latin or never started from it, but the music was a reassurance of the planet's humanity. Other channels carried news or discussion—without context it was difficult to make sense of it, but context could be built up. One wavelength was pure bedlam: a welter of voices and sounds, fragmentary phrases, strange noises. It wasn't that she was picking up lots of stations at once; the more precisely she tuned it the weirder it got.

"Well," said Matt, "the radio is something to work on. Susan, could you look after that and try to compile a picture?"

"Sure."

"Okay. Anyone else?"

"I haven't finished," said Ramona. "I've been doing some back-of-the-envelope calculations. We have jumped from the selkies' world to here, more or less in the shortest possible time. It appears that the normal trade routes have been severely disrupted, if the number of starships in this system at any given moment is one or less! The obvious explanation is that our people are supplanting the kraken-saur-Trader partnership. Assuming that the Multipliers have indeed been assimilated to the Bright Star Cultures, and that they are spreading from star to star with only a small delay to build more ships and navigate the next jump, they cannot be far behind us. We have at the very most a few years, at the very least a few months, before the first Bright Star Culture ships arrive. In that time—short at best—we have to arrange matters so that they are not blasted out of the skies. We have one lightly armed starship, one human-built skiff with antigravity only, and five jump-capable Multiplier skiffs. The other side have an extensive space defense capability, built to all appearances with rocket technology. Evidently they have been unable or unwilling to persuade or coerce the other species into sharing antigravity and lightspeed tech."

She waved a hand at the dark interior of the enormous building. "All our advantage, such as it is, is right here. What we have to decide is how to use it."

"Exactly," said Mikhail Telesnikov. He stood up, incongruously gesturing with an empty coffee mug. "We have two basic options. One, and the most economical, is to make a direct approach to whoever is in power in New Babylon—presumably Volkov or his successors—and convince them that there is nothing to fear or fight. Considering that there are obviously no Multipliers here, and that some were on their way, it seems evident that the New Babylonians have already *won* such a fight and are unlikely to be persuaded that it was all a terrible mistake. I still say it should be our first option. The second—which the failure of the first might foreclose, so it's not the second in time—is to approach one or more of the rival powers, who are more likely to be convinced, and who must surely fear the power of New Babylon. It is at least possible that they would agree to a military strike against New Babylon, if they have the military capacity and the hope of winning. If they have the former, we can provide the latter."

"I don't see how we could," said Hynde. "Each of our missiles could take out a spy-sat. At close range. Maybe. That's about all we could do, and it don't sound like enough."

"I was thinking more," said Telesnikov, "that if the other powers have nuclear weapons, or even decent-sized conventional bombs, we could deliver them to the space battle stations very fast and unstoppably by lightspeed jump, then jump back out of the way."

"Problem with that," said Matt. "Do we want to destroy New Babylon's space defenses? If the gods get angry, we might shortly need them ourselves."

Susan jumped up. "We don't need to put bombs on them!" she said. "We can put troops on them!"

"You can't get many troops in a skiff," one of the gunners said.

She glared at him. "I know *that*," she said. "But you're thinking of one trip. Think lots. Every Multiplier skiff can zap back and forth lots of times—say it can carry six soldiers at a time, it could shift dozens in minutes, just pour them in. And at different places in the battle station, too."

Telesnikov was looking at her as though seeing her for the first time. "That's a very good point," he said.

By the time the Multipliers swarmed back from their cavort in the forest, the rest of the expedition was ready to explain their contingency plans. The Multipliers listened to Matt's enthusiastic outline and announced that they would not hear more of it. They squatted around the circle of humans like so many miserable balls of fur, twitching slightly and occasionally stroking each other's hands. At length Matt walked over to the orange Multiplier. Susan followed, discreetly recording.

"Do you have an ethical objection to taking life?" Matt asked.

The alien wrapped its limbs around its body and rolled away. After a tense minute it uncoiled and reached out to the nearest of its fellows. That one, magenta-furred, eventually stood up shakily and tottered into the center of the circle, near to the remains of lunch. It inspected spilled coffee grounds and bread crumbs and reconstructed a shrimp from a sliver of paste. The shrimp twitched and scrabbled, dying in the air. The Multiplier observed it with apparent curiosity, then ate it.

Then Mr. Magenta (a naming convention that Susan hit upon at that moment, and thereafter spread) waved a limb in a circle above itself and fixed, it seemed, its all-around gaze on everyone simultaneously.

"We are distressed," it announced, "by your plans. They are inelegant. We were under the impression from our reading of the Matt Cairns that you all understood how to survey a planet and neutralize its defenses. You have had such beautiful examples. Why do you not follow them?"

"What examples?" Matt asked.

"You are the Matt Cairns," said the alien. "You know. Please educate the others, and then we will be happy to make your invasion a wonder and delight for the ages, and give our descendants memories to warm them while they watch the stars turn to iron."

By the time Matt was five minutes into explaining his contingency plan he was beginning to scare people.

"Do you know how many Multiplier skiffs were in our system in the years before we left? Two! And you know what they did to us! They had us thinking we were under constant surveillance! Thinking we were about to be invaded! For every real incident there were ten unreal incidents! We made them up ourselves! That's what we have to do here! Make them doubt their concept of reality! Guerrilla ontology!"

He glared around like a lone gladiator facing a hostile colosseum.

"Fuck with their heads!" he shouted. *"Fuck with their heads!"*

•   •   •

That night Susan sat outside on a block around the side of the big building. The block was thirty meters long and five on a side. She had scrambled up the tough creeper that overgrew it. The air was cold and the sky was black. Fog lay over the forested valley, lit by the two small moons, both waxing gibbous, their surfaces so cratered that their terminators were visibly serrated even to the naked eye. Six comets were visible, low in the sky. She had never seen so much as one comet before. The Foamy Wake blazed a trail across the zenith. Every so often a meteor flared, and now and again what appeared to be a star would move steadily across the sky. These, she guessed, must be artificial satellites, like the spaceship yards that orbited around Mingulay.

After a while Salasso joined her. "That is a frightening sky," he said. "The gods' anger is written on it. Fortunately my anger is greater."

"You don't know what anger is," Susan said. "What Matt has, now that's anger."

"I am angry with the gods," said Salasso. "Matt is only angry with the saurs."

"I thought he liked you."

"He does," said Salasso. "It is not personal. All of the old Cosmonauts are like that."

"Ah!" Susan had a sudden insight. "It's because of what the saurs were doing back in the Solar System. All that stuff about Greys and flying saucers, it must have been like a bad dream."

"No," said Salasso. "At the time when Matt and the others lived on Earth, almost all of that was decades in the past. I have studied the literature, if you can call it that, and I found no reported sightings, abductions, or anything untoward for many years. The old stories were not taken seriously except by students of popular delusion, and the deluded, and a very few stubborn investigators."

"Oh! So it was the shock of finding that something they had dismissed was partly true after all—"

"Again, I fear not," said Salasso. "They had no emotional investment in its dismissal. It was not a live issue, either way."

Susan looked at the saur sitting beside her, gazing out over the valley in the double moonlight. His small shoulders were slumped, and his large head hung heavy.

"So why—"

Salasso turned to her. "Do you have your recording devices with you? Of course you do. I am telling you this because it is something I wish to be known after I . . . after all this is over. When the Bright Star

Cultures come here, and find a welcome, I want this to be known. Not before. Will you promise me this?"

Susan clamped her hands on her quivering knees. "Yes," she said. She fumbled, setting her apparatus, then turned to face the saur as though interviewing him.

"When the *Bright Star* arrived in orbit near Mingulay, three hundred—no, it is now four hundred—years ago, we were shocked and frightened. The crew claimed to have navigated here, and though we soon realized they were lying, that did little to allay our fears. We had no reason to think there might not be more ships. We knew that the Cosmonauts had received the instructions for the drive directly from a god. This suggested to us that the gods in the Solar System had lost patience with the saurs, and perhaps that the gods here had too.

"The saurs discovered how to manipulate genetic material many millions of years ago. With that discovery we built the manufacturing plant. This was an industry that did not disturb the planets, or displease the gods. With that knowledge we have been able to screen all the new arrivals from Earth, and to prevent the spread of diseases. We explained this to the Cosmonauts, and they agreed to be examined. They told us freely that they had taken life-extending drugs, and we soon found out why some of these drugs had worked. They modified a gene which is common to many species, including ours. In their case it was only somatic, not heritable, but it was still alarming. The effect of human longevity on the stability we had so carefully cultivated would be immensely disruptive—as indeed it is proving now, if Ramona is right, and I think she is.

"The effect of the knowledge in the ship's computer libraries, and the machinery it had to replicate the computers and disseminate the knowledge, would have been even more disruptive. At the same time it was not in our nature to deny or destroy that knowledge. So we later allowed the computer libraries to be transcribed to the manufacturing plant, and subsequently printed in books—a necessarily slow process, which made assimilating the knowledge the work of centuries, still incomplete. But we did not allow the Cosmonauts further access to their ship, and only allowed them to take from it such machinery and computers as they could carry.

"Before we even allowed them off the ship, we took one further precaution. We took them one by one and subjected them to a second medical examination. It was traumatic and intrusive, and not merely physically. We did everything to them that they had jokingly told us saurs were supposed to do." He looked away, then looked back. "We terrified the living shit out of them."

Susan's mouth was dry, her eyes wet. "Why are you telling me this, now?"

"Because I feel bad about it. And because as more and more people take up the Multipliers' offer, these memories will be shared and passed around like diseases. It is important that people are able to make sense of these frightening fragments of memory."

"You mean," she said, "that they don't find themselves fearing and hating the saurs for no reason they can understand."

"That too, yes."

"I don't know what to say," she said.

"Nor do I," said Salasso. He made a cutting gesture. She switched off her apparatus.

"Well, hell," she said, "I think you've made up for it since, Salasso."

"I wish you had recorded that," said Salasso.

"I will say it again."

They sat in silence for a while.

He took out his pipe. "Would you share a smoke?"

"Yes," she said.

The hemp knocked Salasso into a twenty-minute trance, and left Susan to gaze at the Foamy Wake and imagine the Solar System on the far side of it, and wonder what had befallen the saurs and humans there.

Salasso came to himself with a start. In silence the woman and the saur, one after the other, descended the precarious ladder of creeper.

"What is this building, anyway?" she asked, as they headed back.

"Before the saurs learned how to make the manufacturing plant," said Salasso, scuffing through the leaves beside her, "they constructed such buildings. This one, I believe, they used as a place to park their skiffs."

Susan glanced back at the megalith, one of many strewn around, evidently surplus to the requirements of the gargantuan structure, which was built from blocks of similar or greater size.

"And they used the skiffs to lift the blocks up here, and move them into position?"

"Oh, no," said Salasso. "That is physically impossible. They built enormous ramps of close-packed earth, and made ropes of the creeper vines, and tens of thousands of saurs dragged the blocks up." He spread his long hands and shrugged his small shoulders. "But when you tell people that, they don't believe you."

.   .   .

In stealth mode the skiff was visible only to the insane, the users of psychoactive chemicals, the very young, and dogs. To anyone else it was something that could be glimpsed, perhaps as an unfeasibly large meniscus of water, but not directly seen. It was certainly invisible to the sober agents of national defense, security, and law enforcement.

It had been highly visible earlier, during the day, when its sonic boom was breaking windows and its radar trace was scrambling jet fighters right across Genea. Over the New Babylon subcontinent it had appeared as a fleet above a small town in the Massif, making lightspeed jumps back and forth between five separate points so quickly that it was seen as five separate ships. It had been even more visible late in the afternoon, when it had loomed over the brows of nearby low hills like an early rising Lucifer and confronted and confounded a number of isolated farm laborers and one latifundia chairman. The skiff's occupants knew he was a latifundia chairman because they had followed him back to the biggest house in the village. He had kept looking back over his shoulder, unable to see the now stealth-mode skiff, but obviously feeling that he was being watched. His dog had dashed past him and barked at something outside the gate for a quarter of an hour.

Now it was barking again. Matt and Susan gave the dog a wide berth and walked up the short drive, their footsteps crunching in gravel. All the lights in the house were on. Under the lamp by the porch Matt gave Susan a critical look.

"Straighten your tie," he said.

She and Matt were identically dressed in black suits, white shirts, black ties, and black hats.

"I've always wanted to do this," Matt confided as he knocked on the door.

The latifundia chairman peered around it, holding a shotgun just in view. His expression went from suspicion to terror the moment he saw them.

"Good evening," Matt said, raising his hat. "There is no need to be alarmed. We're from the government."

9

The Hanging Libraries

THE MAN CAME into Gaius's office without knocking. Before Gaius could get up the stranger heeled the door shut behind him and sat down in the seat on the other side of the desk. He left his hat on. The plume fluttered slightly in the draft from the open window. None of this was good.

Gaius nodded at him, then at the door. "The sign says 'Gonatus Aerospace,'" he said. "Not 'Walk right it.'"

Ginger ringlets and a neat pointed beard, blue eyes behind eyelids like the slits in a shield. "My name's Attulus," he said, as though it wasn't. "Pleased to meet you, too."

He reached through one of the slashes in his blue padded jacket and withdrew a rolled piece of paper tied with a thin red ribbon. It made a hollow sound as it hit the desk.

"Read it."

The Ducal seal was enough, but Gaius read it anyway.

"The Department's number is in the book," the agent said. "Feel free."

"My export licenses are in that filing cabinet," Gaius said. "Feel free."

Attulus retrieved his commission and disappeared it. "That's not what this is about," he said. He pinched the bridge of his nose and gave his head a small shake, blinked and looked up. "We have reason to suspect that you, Ingenior Gonatus, are a loyal subject. Or a patriotic citizen, if you prefer."

So they knew about that. But of course they knew about that.

"I've done my service," Gaius said. "I understand that cancels out any youthful indiscretions."

"It does," Attulus said. "But—" He scratched his moustache. "There's another bargain, which applies to businessmen who make a habit of trading with the other side."

Again Gaius indicated the filing cabinet. "It's called an export license," he said. "On the other side, it's called a bribe. Either way, my accounts are in balance."

"Oh, but they're not, Ingenior. You owe your country a little more than a fee and a docket."

Gaius shrugged. "I've filed a report with the Department after every trip."

"Indeed you have, and I've read them. Observant, informative, complete. Quite useful, as these things go."

"Thank you."

"But, as I say, not enough. Not if you wish to continue trading."

"Continue trading with the other side?"

"Continue trading."

That, thought Gaius, is the trouble with the invisible hand. It leaves you wide open to the invisible fist.

"No need for that," he said. "Look, if you want me to spy for you, I'll do it gladly."

"That's what I like," Attulus said. "An enthusiastic volunteer. Sadly rare in the business community. And I didn't even have to ask."

And that was how it began.

Gaius Gonatus ran up a steep grassy bank and ducked through a rusted barrier to step onto the abandoned motorway. He walked onto the central lane and strolled up the intersection ramp for another hundred meters, until he was on the flyover. At its brow he looked around, remembered that the left-hand side afforded the better view—the other was cluttered by the small town and the striding pylons of the monorail—and crossed over to stand a pace or two back from the crumbled concrete of the parapet. It was at places like this that he felt most strongly the power and presence of the goddess. She alone had known how to call forth this mighty work, an overthrust of concrete implacable as rock. She alone had known to let it die, leaving it a twined green ribbon like the raffia knot on a wreath. Though the fancy pleased him, it struck him as too morbid, for the goddess had found a new use for the obsolete structure. Confined by the roadside crash barriers, flocks of sheep grazed along all the lanes, which formed strips of meadow through the forest and moorland. In the morning sun the smell of drying sheep droppings was faint above the smell of the grass and the trees. Far away a dog barked and a ewe bleated. At a further distance a sheep farmer's auto-gyro buzzed, quieter than a bee.

Where Gaius stood was above the tops of the tallest pines, and he gazed out across twenty miles of forested plain and foothill to the mountain range on the western horizon. Their tops, as on most days, were covered by clouds. Somewhere up there, on most days, small bands of people would be making their way through those clouds, on the high passes. The frozen faces of those who had failed in the same passage would grin at them from the side of the road. Tomorrow, Gaius thought, he would look down on those clouds, and not even see the mountains.

The sound of another autogyro rose to the south. Gaius turned, squinting against the sun. A nearby flock of sheep scattered as the small craft sank toward the long green strip. It touched down and bumped along to halt a few yards from him, its prop feathering, its rotor beating in slower and slower cycles. The pilot dismounted and strode over, pulling off goggles and leather helmet and running his finger through the bushy hair thus released. He was a slim, small man in his mid-twenties with red hair and a neatly trimmed beard. His flying-jacket was incongruous over his blue and distinctly urban suit; likewise the canvas satchel and the shiny, thin-soled shoes, already sheep-shat.

"Good morning, Attulus," said Gaius.

Attulus glowered. "Do you realize how inconvenient this is? And the cost to the Department?"

Gaius glanced over at the tiny flying machine and raised his eyebrows. "Lose it in the paperclip budget, why don't you?"

"Hah!" snorted Attulus. "Why don't you meet me in a café back in town?"

Gaius shrugged. "I like to keep our dealings out in the open."

Attulus snorted again. "All right," he said. "We don't have much time. At least *I* don't."

He lifted the satchel's flap and pulled out a thin sheaf of paper. Gaius folded it lengthways in half and stuck it in his inside jacket pocket, without looking.

"Don't take them with you," said Attulus, as though it didn't need saying but he had to say it anyway. "They give the background of a man we want you to see. He looks like a good prospect for your sales pitch, but he isn't. However, meeting him and stringing out the realization that he's a seat warmer and buck passer should give you the chance to talk to the person we really want you to meet, one of his assistants who do the actual work, who might turn out to be a useful business contact, but that's up to you. Full background on her, too. Her name is Lydia de Tenebre."

"Let me guess," said Gaius. "Old merchant family—"

"Fallen on hard times and working in the Space Authority. Yes. Also a malcontent, and part of a group."

"How long has she been back?"

"Ten years. Her previous landfall was a hundred years earlier, our time."

Gaius felt a chill. "She remembers old New Babylon."

"Nova Babylonia, yes, she does indeed. Which is more than most of the malcontents can claim. It carries a certain cachet, in these circles."

"How does she keep her job?"

Attulus grinned. "Competence counts. She has business skills the Modern Regime spent fifty years forgetting and another fifty trying to reinvent from first principles."

"Or pretending to," said Gaius. "They pirate our management textbooks, you know."

"The Department makes sure they pirate the right ones."

Gaius chuckled, under the misapprehension that Attulus was sharing a joke, then frowned. "Does she have access to any of their technical secrets?"

"Nothing like," said Attulus. "Her security clearance is two ticks above zilch, which is why she's stuck where she is."

Gaius took a deep breath. "So what," he said, "do you want me to talk to her about?"

Attulus stared away at the mountains for a moment, then asked abruptly: "Do you follow the litter press?"

"In an idle moment . . . the sports and television pages. The rest, well, I just look at the pictures."

"Look at them carefully, next time you get the chance."

"There's a connection?"

"If you don't see it," Attulus said, "then we'll have made a mistake, but apart from that, no harm will have been done. And if you do see it"—he smiled—"you'll let nothing stop you. You'll *want* to find out, and you'll *want* to tell us."

"You seem very sure of that."

"You'll do it," said Atullus, "or die trying."

He walked, then flew, swiftly away.

Gaius stared after the departing autogyro for a few minutes, until the dot was lost in the dazzle. Then he made his way back down the bank. He recognized rocks, now sinking into the grass, and trees, now reaching higher above it, that he'd used as handholds and footholds in boyhood scrambles. How well he had known that bank, known every tussock and hollow where a ball could come to rest or an ankle could twist. That intimate acquaintance and depth of detail had made it seem huge, even in his memory, and when he revisited it in dreams. How small it seemed now.

Gaius paid the visit to his mother that was the excuse for his trip, and took the monorail back to the city. He arrived at his office an hour before it was supposed to shut. He decided to call it a day. He put the phone on tape, locked up, and told Phyliss, the receptionist downstairs, to deflect any incoming calls until after the weekend. She looked up from her novel.

"You're going away for ten days after the weekend."

"So I am," Gaius said. He dropped the key on her desk. "Water my plant?"

"Of course, Gaius."

"Thanks. See you when I get back, then."

She waited for a beat. "You've forgotten something."

Gaius turned back, to see her holding out his airline tickets.

"As soon as I can afford a secretary . . ." he said, taking them. He almost meant it.

"You'll hire someone else," she said. "And you'll still rely on me. Happens all the time."

"Have a good weekend," he said.

Outside, the street was at the muggy end of autumn. Gaius slung his linen jacket over his shoulder and walked to the café on the corner. Inside, it was air-conditioned, which made it better than his office. In the old days it had *been* his office, and he sometimes regretted his move up in the world. Not that Gonatus Aerospace was much of a company. One office, one man, a lot of import-export deals. It looked like the sort of company a spy would set up as a front.

Gaius took a chilled coffee and cloves to a window table, scooping up abandoned newspapers as he went. Ten separate titles, all equally bad. Two glasses later he was cool, jumpy, and none the wiser. A dead kraken had washed up on a beach. The Duke's third son had a new boyfriend. The established cults had quarreled over their share of the god-tax. A forester claimed to have seen a gravity skiff. Scientists said the saurs had not come back. Cloud people had rioted in an overcrowded holding camp. Defense and electronics shares were up. His fingers were black with cheap ink.

He remembered what Attulus had said, just after Gaius had mentioned looking at the pictures. This time he ignored the text and looked at the pictures. The news and publicity pictures were less interesting than the erotica. Some of the sexual positions looked as though they might be spelling out some kind of message, but he put that down to fatigue. His, not theirs. The only photograph all of the papers had in common was one taken by the forester, of something that might have been a thrown ashtray. He stared at it for a while, letting the grainy dots blur together. Under this crude enhancement it looked almost realistic.

It was a connection of a sort. A merchant's daughter and a gravity skiff. Gaius had seen gravity skiffs, but only over the harbor of New Babylon, and then not for long. No one had seen a gravity skiff anywhere else in the past hundred years. If this was what Attulus had hoped would turn him into a fervent seeker after state secrets, it was a disappointment. All he felt was a tiny itch of curiosity.

There is this about that kind of a tiny itch, he thought. You do have to scratch.

Next he looked over the document Attulus had given him. It was a New Babylon Board of Trade handout. Not exactly deep background. David Daul sounded like a typical Modern Regime lower middle cadre. Son of a latifundia chairman. Farm school, military service, university, Society school, Space Agency. His current post was in technology procurement. He looked handsome in a spoiled way. Plenty of healthy sports, all with a military angle: skiing, martial arts, rifle shooting, hang gliding. He seemed exactly the man to approach with a sales pitch. Gaius almost regretted having not heard of him sooner.

The picture of Lydia de Tenebre had been taken at a long distance. She looked quite pretty. According to the briefing, she was about thirty years old. He'd have to allow for that. He scanned the background briefing, which was thin. Family large and conservative; former Traders usually were. No known political involvement, low profile, but she hung out with known malcontent artists and activists, and liked to mouth off about the good old days and the bad new ones. That was allowed. The Republic was a police state, but not totalitarian. You could think what you liked, and even say it. You just couldn't print or broadcast it. It saved the state a lot of trouble. Mere tolerance made that sort of dissidence inconsequential.

It was the rest of Lydia de Tenebre's background that was unusual. When he'd finished reading he could feel the hairs stand up on the back of his neck. The tiny itch of curiosity had become poison ivy.

He put the documents back in his briefcase, binned the papers, paid his tab, and left.

A bell chimed and Gaius refastened his seatbelt. Around him people stubbed out cigarettes. Uncollected litter rattled down the cabin floor as the airliner's nose dipped. Gaius pressed his temple to the small ellipse of window and peered out. Within seconds the uniform white of the cloud broke into racing strands, and the land came into view below. First a brown and green checkerboard of logged or growing forest; then, as the aircraft passed over the foothills and above the long undulations of the Massif, the similarly uniform rectangles of collective latifundia, gridded with irrigation trenches, dotted with villages built on a uniform circular plan. After a while the Massif dropped away to the coastal plain. Here the farms were much larger, the fields many hectares of wheat and barley, and each village the hub of a wider and more natural-looking small town.

As the airliner banked to sideslip into its steep final descent—New Babylon Airlines was officially part of the air force, and all its pilots were jet-fighter veterans—Gaius glimpsed in some of the fields a regular series of elaborate whorls, as though the crops had been flattened by a tornado as precise as a drill. Some strange folk art or public display, he guessed, as the circles slipped out of sight. Perhaps it had something to do with lithomancy, a fad or cult in New Babylon—a row of lithomancy pylons stood on a nearby hill. Lithomancy had been another of the Modern Regime's failures, a crackpot scheme of Volkov's to contact the mind that he had supposed inhabited the lithosphere, much as the gods inhabited the asteroids and comets. If there was a mind in the world it was mad. Gaius himself regarded the whole thing as an artefact of radio noise, spillover and echo from the communications networks.

He'd never tired of seeing the city from the air in the last moments of the flight. The river divided around the island, stapled to each shore by numerous bridges. The industrial and residential suburbs on either bank rose smoothly like lower slopes around the peak formed by the island. The buildings on the island itself looked like columnar basalt, a stepped ascent for giants. Built over ten millennia, further built upon and blackened by one century's industry. The tallest of the towers was the most recent. The Space Agency building was like an obsidian monolith that had been half-twisted while still hot. It was a bravura display of architectural skill, and an homage to the supposed shape of a lightspeed engine. It would have been more impressive if they'd actually built a lightspeed engine.

The city slid away under the wing and there was nothing but water below. The unmistakable shapes of oil tankers made him realize the aircraft was higher up than he'd thought—no matter how many times he'd seen New Babylon from the air, its scale didn't register. Another sharp bank and they were heading straight for the city at a fast-dropping height, over a lonely starship lost in the harbor's traffic, skimming masts, then above the long, projecting concrete finger of the airfield, and one wheel hit, then two, then with a jarring shudder the third, and they were down. He'd had more comfortable landings on carrier decks.

Gaius hauled his bag and briefcase from the overhead locker and joined the shuffling queue to the front. Half the passengers had lit up as soon as the seatbelt lights had gone off. After that landing, he couldn't blame them.

In the customs hall the officer thumbed through his passport as if it was subversive literature. With its gaudy variety of visa stamps, maybe it was. Gaius gave him more reactionary propaganda in body language.

"Point of departure?" the officer asked.

"Junopolis, Free Duchy of Illyria." *I would like to shout this in your streets.*

"Purpose of visit?"

"Business." *Who would come here for pleasure?*

"Duration of stay?"

"Ten days." *Too long.*

"Place of residence?"

"The Foreigners' Hotel, Messana District." *Where else?*

Lick, thumb, stamp. "Enjoy your stay."

"Thank you." *This is not your fault.*

At the Change Money, Gaius handed over a bag of Illyrian silver, and got in return a bale of paper and a fistful of nickel. Every note from the million up and every coin down to the hundred had been defaced— the paper with a pen, the base metal with a knife. The scribbles and scratches obscured the face of Volkov. Why the Regime had not simply replaced their worthless currency after the Great Engineer's fall Gaius had never discovered. Perhaps it was for the same reason that they'd left the plinths of his statues standing.

Gaius stuffed it all in his wallet—his actual business would be conducted in hard money—and headed for the underground station. He had
hand luggage only. The case of samples would go direct to the hotel.
Nothing would be missing, but everything would have been taken out,
shaken, turned over. And, no doubt, photographed for the Bureau of
Technology Procurement, where it would do them no good whatsoever.

Public transport was one of the things that New Babylon did well.
The stations were vaults of white tile. The trains had carriages of polished steel and seats of pale wood. Everything about it was good, and
modern, and cool, except the passengers. Their clothes didn't quite fit,
their skins were missing a vitamin, their bodies wanted to be somewhere
else, and their minds didn't know where it was. Gaius sat with his
briefcase on his knees and his bag between them, and stared straight
ahead like everybody else. The intersections afforded other opportunities, in the long curving corridors of bright tile. Before he'd made two
transfers he'd had three offers for his shirt. It wasn't a good shirt.

By the time he'd walked the hundred meters from Messana East to
the Foreigners' Hotel, the shirt might as well have been flannel. After
the hours in air-conditioning his pores opened to the street like storm
drains. His shadow looked cut off at the knees. The traffic was a slow
snarl of underpowered trucks and clanging bikes. The sidewalks were
crowded but quiet. Everybody was hurrying to some place they didn't
want to go. One person in fifty was a cop, and one in a hundred wore
a cop's uniform. The hotel was at the top of a small rise. At the step
Gaius paused and looked back, down the whole length of Astronaut
Avenue, a smooth sweep from the five-story tenements and office blocks
around him to the black canyon of the expensive end, and the blue slot
of sky and sea, and the dark speck of the starship.

If the concierge remembered him from six months earlier she gave
no indication of it. She took his passport and money and gave him a
key for Room 503. The lift was out of order and the stair carpet was
frayed, but for the air conditioning Gaius could forgive anything. He
dropped his baggage on the bed just to hear the springs creak and
opened a window. The room was nonsmoking, but not its most recent
occupant. Gaius showered in a rusty trickle, dried on scratchy nylon,
changed into a lighter shirt and thin trousers, and sat down on the bed.
There was a table with a mirror and a phone, and no chair. The boy
who brought up coffee stammered when Gaius tipped him ten million.
This was their good stuff, their best foot forward.

Gaius carried the phone over to the bed and worked down his list of contacts, setting up appointments. Some were previous clients, others new possibilities. All of them were departments of, or suppliers for, the Space Agency. Under the post-Volkov economic reforms, they were supposed to compete with each other. In practice they bought each other off. Under the Ten-Year Plans the Trusts' executives had competed fiercely, hitting each other with purges in the official system and hijackings and armed robberies in the unofficial system. Corruption was a step back toward civilization.

He put David Daul in about a third of the way down the list. The cadre was out but the woman who took the call made an appointment for the day after tomorrow. Gaius hoped the voice on the phone was that of Lydia de Tenebre, because it was a voice he wanted to hear again.

The thought kept him going for the rest of the afternoon and the rest of the list. By the end of it he had the next ten days blocked in. Most of the trusts had offices on Astronaut Avenue, and the Departments were of course in the Space Agency building. The few actual factories he had managed to arrange to visit were all close to the underground stations. His sample case arrived. Everything was there but in the wrong compartments.

He ate out in a local shop-front restaurant, another product of the economic reforms. There was a law about how many chairs it could have, so like most of the customers he ate standing up. Then he decided to go out and have a good time, so he went to the nearest public library.

The following day he made only one sale, but it was of one of his own inventions, a solid-state switching mechanism that would replace half a ton of diodes. It made the day a net plus but the trek around the offices left him drained. After dinner he just collapsed onto the bed and slept, and woke early and sticky. At this time in the morning the shower had enough heat and pressure to be refreshing. The underground railway journey undid all that, but Gaius still felt good as he strode in to the Space Agency building.

The guards were edgier than he'd expected. They ran his briefcase and samples through the scanner five times, patted him down thrice. He sweated calmly through it all, gazing at the murals around the reception area. Blow-up photos of rocket launches, orbital forts, plasma cannon, smiling astronauts. A blank space on the wall where once, he guessed, there had been a portrait of Volkov. The lift was shabby and its attendant had a pistol on his hip.

"Floor Twenty-seven, please." He showed his pass, dated and time-stamped under laminate.

The cage door rattled closed, the lift doors thudded. Gaius smiled at the attendant, who looked right back through him.

"Floor Twenty-seven." The attendant refused a tip, then took it in a deftly upturned palm as soon as his back was turned to the camera.

Daul's office door bore his name and the legend "Small Parts Procurement." Gaius let his smile at that carry over. The office was fairly large, with about a dozen people at small desks and one man at a large one in a glassed alcove at the back with a window. The rest of the walls were covered with trade advertisements and Agency or Regime posters. Typewriters and calculators clattered. It was a busy place; hardly anyone looked up as he came in. Most of the workers were in the modern suits favored by the Regime, a couple of the women wore old-fashioned wrap robes. With a jolt, he recognized one of them as the woman he'd come to meet. She seemed younger than he'd expected. The picture had done her less than justice. She didn't look up.

Gauis walked through to the alcove and tapped. David Daul, looking slightly older and grainier than his picture, nodded him in. They shook hands.

"Good morning, Citizen—" Daul broke of to correct himself, smiling—"*Mr.* Gonatus. Make yourself comfortable."

"Good morning, Citizen Daul. Thank you."

As he pulled a swivel chair into position, Gaius took the opportunity to glance over Daul's desk surface. It was cluttered with technical drawings and critical-path diagrams and work schedules, along with the predictable empty coffee mugs, full ashtrays, and chewed pencils, a pen holder, a small intricate mechanical calculator, and a slide rule. Daul rang out for coffee, which a brisk young man brought in; offered cigarettes.

"I've been looking forward to seeing you," Daul said, preliminaries over. "Frankly, getting decent kit on time out of some of the bastards I have to deal with is a pain in the arse. If the foreigners can give me better, on schedule and under budget, bring 'em on, I say." He cocked a grin at Gaius. "And don't think I'm giving too much away at the start. There are other foreign salesmen on our case, and not just Illyrian."

"Don't I know it," said Gaius. "However, I think you'll find us competitive."

"Great! Let's have a look at what you've got."

As Gaius worked through his well-researched and well-rehearsed pitch, Daul hit him with a succession of searching questions, not just on the technical side—which he'd expected—but costs and delivery dates, quality control, penalty clauses, and possibilities of undercutting or overperforming documented competing bids. Gaius found himself liking the man, and rapidly revising the assessment he'd been given by Attulus. In different circumstances, Gaius thought, Daul might have been the salesman, and he the bureaucrat.

Eventually they straightened their backs from leaning over the same diagram and looked at each other with a laugh that covered a certain mutual embarrassment—they'd been discussing a design problem as though they were on the same team.

"Well," said Daul, "I think I can make you an offer. Can't shake hands on it yet, I'm afraid—some paperwork has to be passed upstairs, forms in triplicate, you know the sort of thing. Call me back tomorrow and I can let you know if you've hit the mark."

Was this the buck-passing he'd been warned about, or was it genuinely a busy and competent man doing his best in a bureaucracy? Gaius couldn't be sure. Either way, Daul's swift proceeding was leaving him without the chance to meet Lydia de Tenebre. He tried to think fast.

"Excellent," he said. "I wish everyone I have to deal with were as prompt." He glanced at his watch. "You know, you've just cleared hours off my schedule—given me a bit of free time this evening. I'd quite like to wander around with someone who knows the city, maybe take in a beer and a meal."

Daul raised a hand. "Sorry, I can't help you there—strict rules about favors and all that. Kind of you to offer, though. Cuts both ways too, dammit, or I'd show you a good time myself."

"Oh, not at all, maybe another time." He feigned disappointment and let his gaze drift to the window. "Quite fascinating, the buildings that remain from the old city. Bit of a hobby of mine, to be honest."

"Ah," said Daul, "you're an old city man?" He punched his palm. "Of course, of course—you Illyrians. Bloody reactionaries to a man, eh? Well, you're in luck there, I know someone who isn't a buyer, so no rules bent, and who'll be delighted to tell you all about it, if she's free."

He poked his head around the door of the alcove. "Lydia? A moment please."

A young woman in an old-fashioned robe walked in. Gaius smiled, shook hands, and tried not to stare as Daul introduced him and explained his request.

"I'd be delighted," said Lydia. Her voice sounded even better than it had on the phone. "Where shall we meet?"

Gaius suddenly realized that he didn't know any good places. Well, maybe one. Call that two.

"What about the Library of Earth?" he said.

Lydia's smile was more than polite, it was complicit.

"Perfect," she said. "Seven after noon."

You could forget nuclear-power stations, orbital forts, plasma cannon, space rockets, interplanetary ballistic missiles, the public health service, education, irrigation, sanitation, the collectivization of the latifundia and the electrification of the proletariat. The greatest achievement of the Modern Regime was its libraries. Downtown stood two gigantic marble edifices: the Library of Earth, and next door to it, the Library of New Earth. The latter was by far the older. Its earliest texts were on clay tiles, in cuneiform. You could buy plastic replicas of them in the foyer. The former came originally from a machine smaller than a single book. You could buy plastic replicas of it too, as paperweights. A cosmonaut's pocket computer, it had the 2045 Library of Congress as a standard feature. It also had the libraries of the Vatican, the Kremlin, and the Academy of Sciences of Beijing. These were not standard. The manufacturer's marketing department had added them as a sales gimmick. The cosmonaut was Volkov. By the time he'd arrived on New Earth the computer was dead metal, a sentimental souvenir; but in the early years of his life on Mingulay the saurs had reproduced these millions of stored books on paper in their manufacturing plant; and via the merchant families, at least a million of them had reached New Earth.

Copies of books from both collections circulated endlessly through the system of public libraries. It was the one source of information in New Babylon that had never been censored. The Modern Regime allowed anyone to read books whose writing would have got them hanged. In its early years, it kept the old scholars of the Academy happily occupied in compiling a digest of human knowledge, the endlessly fascinating and dubiously reliable *Encyclopaedia Babylonica*. Gaius had a cheap, Illyrian-pirated edition of its thirty volumes on a shelf back home.

Lydia turned up a few minutes late with six thick books under her arm. She'd changed her antique robe for an aggressive outfit of leather jacket and trousers, rips and zips, but she still astonished his eyes.

"Sorry I'm late," she said. "The books slowed me down. Do you mind if we go in?"

"Not at all, this is one of my favorite places here."

She looked hard at him as they emerged from the revolving doors. "Surprised I haven't seen you before."

Gaius laughed. "I don't exactly come here often."

"Oh, I know, but—"

The library's vast hush silenced her.

She returned her books. He read their titles, side-on: *Capital* (three volumes); *Theories of Surplus Value* (two volumes); *The Accumulation of Capital* (one volume). He was impressed that she studied business methods in her spare time.

They went out. The street seemed loud, though it was far too quiet. "I love the library," she said, "but you can't talk. And you don't need me to show you around it. So—where would you like to go?"

To bed with you, he thought. Actually, no. Anywhere would do. "Are there still beer parlors in the old business district?"

"Yes," she said. "They're not as good as they were, of course. Bureaucrats don't drink like businessmen. At least not in public."

She ran down the steps and swung into an easy pace, as though not caring if he walked beside her or not.

"The bars around here are bugged," she said. "The staff are cops. So let's get this over out here. You're a spy, right?"

"What makes you think that?"

"Common sense and long experience. Any foreign businessmen who aren't spies are too stupid to be recruited, and you're not stupid."

"You're jumping to conclusions."

"You're not denying it."

He couldn't say anything to that.

"Let's get one thing clear," she went on. "I have my own opinions, but I'm a loyal citizen. More to the point, I'm a loyal employee. I like David Daul. If you're looking for some inside track on your sale or you're into industrial espionage, forget it."

"I'm not interested in any of that."

"Aha!" She stopped dead, throwing him a couple of steps forward. He turned back to face her.

"So what *are* you interested in?"

"You," he said, more forcefully than he'd meant. "I've been asked to contact you. That's all."

She started walking again, making him catch up. If she wanted them to look like lovers quarreling she was doing a good job of it.

"There must be some context," she said. "The name of the Free Duchy isn't enough to make me go weak at the knees. What do you want?"

"There is a context," he said. "Well, two."

"Uh-huh. Tell me the first one."

"Skiffs."

She broke her stride, recovered.

"There's the harbor." She pointed. "Go down and ask a saur, if you can find one."

"I'm talking about unidentified skiffs."

"Fuck off."

"What?"

"You heard me. Don't try to jerk me around. If you want to know about the Bright Star Cultures you can ask me right out. You don't need to pretend they're here."

"I don't know if they're here or not. All I know is that unidentified skiffs are being reported in our litter press."

She turned on him a look of withering scorn. "Oh, *that.*"

"I share your contempt for it," he said.

"Glad to hear it. What was the other context?"

"I was given to understand," Gaius said cautiously, "that you are known as a malcontent."

Lydia stopped again. When he'd turned back he saw her smiling, for the first time since the library. It had felt like a long time.

"Oh boy," she said, "have they ever sent you after the wrong girl."

"You're not a malcontent?"

"I am, just not the way you think." Her smile became a baring of teeth. "I'm a Volkovist."

They were standing outside a beer parlor. Gaius felt dizzy and slightly sick. He indicated the door.

"Shall we?" he said.

"I know somewhere better. Safer, anyway."

She led him down to the end of Astronaut Avenue and sharply right along the waterfront to an area where the lights were orange and the buildings were long and low, warehouses and offices long since turned to other purposes. Outside one of them, a beer parlor by the sign if nothing else, Lydia paused, then crossed the road to look across the quay and the water to the starship. By the time Gaius had caught up with her, she was looking up, at an orange sky through which a handful of stars were visible.

"I miss the stars," she said. "I miss traveling to them, but I miss seeing them even more. I'm a pantheist. Pollution is persecution."

"I'm an agorist," said Gaius. "Planning is sacrilege."

She gave him a tight smile. "Let's see you spend some money," she said.

They went back across the street to the drinking dive.

The bar had too much dust, smoke, verdegris. The roof beams were low and bare, with bare electrical bulbs hanging from them. The tables had benches that might have been recovered from a demolished temple. The clientele, thin at this time, looked unrespectable. The beer was still good.

"You knew Volkov," Gaius said "Is that safe to talk about?"

"Yes, and yes." She raised her glass. "To the Republic."

He moved a jug of water and lifted his glass above it. "The Republic."

He'd seen malcontents do this. On the other side of the Half Moon Sea, and not a dozen kilometers from where they sat, was the Republic of Lapithia—another breakaway province, of impressive size but largely desert, its coastal fishing devasted by New Babylon's industrial runoff. They exported mainly nurses, sailors, and mercenaries; imported exiles who sat in seafront bars and plotted till they died of drink.

She smiled. "Very good. The strait is patrolled. You have to go a long way up the coast to get past them, and by that point it's actually quicker and safer to go over the mountains."

"Cloud people."

"Yes. It's not illegal to emigrate, you know. Even the patrols are mainly to stop smuggling and raiding."

"So why do people—"

"Because your precious Duchy doesn't give visas. They'll take a trickle of cloud people, oh yes. Legal immigration would be too much to handle, and wouldn't supply sob stories for your litter press."

"It's a sore point," Gaius conceded. "You were saying about Volkov?"

Lydia shrugged. "I went to bed with him a few times. He was all right." She smiled. "Experienced."

Gaius felt himself go red in the face. "That's not what I was asking about."

"What is there to say? You must have read about him and my family. We met him on Mingulay, we brought him here, we went away and came back. He was dead. We found what he had left."

"Yes," said Gaius. "The greatest city in the known universe, turned into this heap of shit."

"It's a heap of shit all right," Lydia said. "But what he built was worth it."

"You can't truly believe that," said Gaius. "He fought off the aliens, I'll give you that."

"You don't need to," said Lydia. "The aliens aren't a threat anyway. I should know."

"I know you encountered them," said Gaius. "And the people who had been corrupted by them."

"Yes, and none of that is a threat. The Bright Star Cultures are out there, and coming closer, and no doubt when they do arrive the SDF will fight them off. Or maybe not." She chopped with her hand. "None of that matters."

"So what does? If you don't like the Modern Regime and you don't fear the aliens, what did Volkov do that was so great?"

"He gave us back our pride," she said. "He showed us we could be a great people, that we didn't need to limit ourselves to what the saurs would accept. All but a few of them cringe before the gods. Volkov said we can go out to space ourselves, face and fight the aliens, and deflect anything the gods care to throw at us. The saurs went away, they stopped sharing their skiffs and the krakens stopped sharing their ships. New Babylon built rockets. For the first time in ten thousand years, people stopped traveling to the stars—but for the first time, they actually visited the planets of this system. The saurs stopped healing us, and thousands upon thousands died in plagues. Maybe millions on the planet as a whole. The Modern Regime built hospitals, invented medicines, expanded health services to fill the gap. We lost the trade with the saurs, and everything they produced in their manufacturing plant. The Modern Regime built factories. The provinces broke away under the burden of Volkov's space defense taxes—and what are they now? They're nations, like yours, independent centers of development, with the capacity—if not yet the will—to build rockets of their own. You have no idea, Mr. Gonatus, no idea at all how much of a triumph it is for Volkov that I'm sitting here talking to you—gods above, an Illyrian, uh, businessman, of all things! Without Volkov Illyria would still be a sleepy agricultural province, with nothing to sell but sheep, and a dozy patrician on the

Senate of Nova Babylonia, who left every hard problem to his saur scribe!"

"We had to fight New Babylon to *get* independence!"

"Exactly," said Lydia. "And my friends here"—she waved vaguely at the now-growing crowd in the bar, a rabble of types who looked like artists or musicians or criminals—"who talk about the glories of old Nova Babylonia are right—I remember it, and I loved it too. But we can't go back to it, and we shouldn't want to. The Modern Regime will fall someday. Madame President will die, the gerontocratic camarilla around her will fall out with each other and with the security forces, the Society will split, and the crowd will pour through the gap. Competent people, like my boss, will move to the top floor. The crowd will pull down all that remains of Volkov's memorials, they'll demolish the bloody *plinths*. A century later, two centuries, it doesn't matter, their grandchildren will erect a modest statue of Volkov, the Engineer, maybe at the bottom of Astronaut Avenue, and nobody will think it strange."

Gaius covered his confusion by buying another couple of drinks. Somebody had started playing a zither. Others, even more misguidedly, were singing. Gaius was grateful that the malcontent musical ethos eschewed electrical amplification. He returned and set down the drinks and slid himself into the high-backed bench beside Lydia, who was sitting on a stool at the head of the table with her back to the wall. The matter of Volkov, he'd decided, was best dropped. He was not sure whether Lydia had been corrupted by adaptation to the Regime, or had acquired an inhumanly long view of history from her earlier life as an interstellar traveler. He leaned forward a little and spoke in a low voice.

"Your ideas deserve a better discussion," he said. "What concerns me at the moment is that the managers of my business back in Illyria clearly believe the unidentified skiff sightings are real, and that you know something which might explain them."

Lydia looked down into her drink. Her lips compressed, her fingers pressed on her temples.

"I can't begin to hope," she said, "that the ships have got through. Unless . . . oh, I remember now. We're such good navigators. Better than the kraken. Better than Gregor."

Gaius stared at her. "Who's 'we'? Who's Gregor?"

Her eyes were glazed. She wasn't really looking at him. Then she blinked and recovered. "Gregor Cairns," she said. "You know, the Mingulayan navigator."

Gaius had heard of the Mingulayan navigator. News of what went on in the Mingulayan-dominated sector of the Sphere—the Bright Star Cultures, as its inhabitants called it—had arrived in approximate reverse order over the past few years. Gregor Cairns had also been referred to in the information that had arrived more than a century earlier, with Volkov himself. That Lydia had had some acquaintance with him was briefly alluded to in Gaius's briefing.

"I know about Gregor," he said. "You haven't said who 'we' are."

"I'll show you," she said.

She took a dinky pen knife from her pocket and opened it, and very deliberately made a small cut in the tip of her ring finger (which bore no rings). She squeezed out a drop of blood and let it fall on the table.

"What are you doing?"

Lydia pointed at the red drop. "Watch," she said.

10

High Strangeness Incidents

T HIS WON'T HURT," said Mr. Magenta.

He puffed some spores over Susan. She inhaled them and immediately went into a spasm of coughing and sneezing.

"That is good," said Mr. Magenta. "It drives the small offspring into your sinuses."

Susan found herself breathing more calmly. She stepped away from the side of the hangar and looked around at the others, who stood at a safe distance.

"My mother said she was going to do it."

Even to her, it didn't sound like a good reason.

"And it hasn't harmed Matt."

"Hah!" said Ramona Garcia. "How could anyone tell?"

In truth there was a sort of fatalism to Susan's decision. Her own curiosity, if nothing else, would sooner or later drive her to it. The Multipliers would not force their infection on anyone, but sooner or later almost everyone was going to accept it. She might as well get there first.

It still didn't sound like a good reason.

The guerrilla ontology campaign, as Matt persisted in calling it, was into its second week. A sort of routine had become established. The *Investigator*, concealed in the hangar, remained the base camp and headquarters. The Multiplier skiffs were used to conduct operations. Apart from piloting the skiffs, the Multis foraged. They followed the saurs' advice about which fruits and seeds were nutritious and which were not, but they also—more or less at whim—synthesized new foods. They could make beef from a pile of grass, a process that as Matt pointed out was also regularly accomplished by cows, but that still seemed like a miracle.

The skiffs' missions varied from spectacular or subtle displays of their presence, to stealth missions for the sole purpose of information gathering. The latter sometimes shaded illicitly into shopping expeditions—not even the Multis could assure a supply of coffee and tobacco reliable enough for those addicted to them.

Gradually a picture of the world had been built up, from talking to people—whether in Matt's MIB stunts or more discreet contacts—and from books and newspapers, and from radio. The discovery that Volkov was dead—had been killed in a palace coup by his own security detail on the orders of his lover, the President—had left the Cosmonauts who'd known him shaken but, Susan thought, not altogether surprised. It didn't fundamentally alter the big picture.

Working inward:

The closest contact with the Bright Star Cultures had been from about fifty light-years away. These contacts reported an evidently stable and productive relationship between the Multipliers and at least the saurs and the hominidae. The most recently arrived information, ironically, came from farther away, as merchant ships jumped straight from the emerging Cultures on the home planets, Mingulay and Croatan, to Nova Babylonia, arriving shortly after others who had jumped fifty-odd years later but from fifty-odd light-years closer.

The Bright Star Culture wavefront was, of course, only intersecting the Second Sphere from one side. Traffic in the other sides of the great volume was becoming just as disrupted, as the majority of saurs and krakens broke off cooperation with New Babylon, or recoiled from the news of the new alien-human alliance. To an ever-increasing extent, New Earth—and, it would seem, all the other planets—were becoming isolated from interstellar trade.

The fortifications of the Nova Solar System were almost entirely the work of the Republic of New Babylon, and were much as Telesnikov had projected—his only mistake had been to assume that they extended to the gas-giant moons. There were three forts, as he'd supposed, in the asteroid belt, and orbital forts in the cislunar region to meet incoming starships. All of this cost money and resources, and some of the costs were met by the former provinces—when you have system defense, as the Cosmonauts pointed out, it wasn't that difficult to persuade other powers to contribute to the system defense budget. This was the cynical bottom line—there was genuine widespread support in the other states for the common defense, and although the supposed Multiplier invasion was fading from living memory, the suspicion of what was going on in the Bright Star Cultures was renewed with every panicking starship that arrived. The Cosmonauts, however, remained convinced that some of the other powers were approachable.

The Republic of New Babylon had expanded from its initial position as a hegemonic city-state to become a nation-state of the entire subcontinent. Its nearest neighbors, Illyria and Lapithia, were implacably hostile—Illyria as a richer power, Lapithia as a poorer. Beyond them lay a checkerboard of small states, really no more than the olden cities with their hinterlands, each with its own unique proportion of hominid species and its own fiercely local patriotism, somewhat mitigated by their economic union and defensive alliance as the grandly named Genean League. The diplomacy of the other powers consisted largely of manoeuvres designed to split the League or play its members off against each other. There was a sort of logarithmic relationship between the states—New Babylon outweighed Illyria and Lapithia together, and these three major powers about balanced the League as a whole, if not in wealth and firepower then in population and difficulty of conquest. The hominid population of Genea had increased from about a hundred million to about five hundred million in the last century.

This increase was more than balanced by a far steeper decline in the population of Sauria. If any saurs remained they hadn't been spotted by the Multis' stealth-mode overflights, which had returned with pictures and descriptions of invading jungle and of manufacturing plant gone to seed. A small fraction of this decline was attributable to the departure of those saurs who were willing to cooperate with the Modern Regime. The rest had fled to the stars.

Some few were left, though none had been seen—small bands that must be living in the forests, the only evidence of their presence some recently slaughtered dinosaurs, clearly deliberate forest fires, and traces of strange rituals—tree trunks piled into conical pyramids, dinosaur skulls mounted on hilltop poles like some magical early warning system. What this signified, the saurs with the expedition were unable or unwilling to divulge, and reluctant to discuss.

Susan felt the fever coming on her. She took a couple of tablets to bring down her temperature, and carried the bottle of water with which she had washed them down with her out of the hangar. The sun cast long shadows among the enigmatic ruins. Pushing through underbrush, jumping over long cables of creeper, she made her way to a part of the abandoned city that might once have been a public square. She sat down on one of the long, low steps that beveled the square's perimeter and sipped some more water. The blood moved in her veins like trickling sand.

As the sun set, the colors around her first became more vivid, the purple shadows seeming to have neon behind them, the greens and yellows of the foliage glossy like the skins of frogs; then they faded out to a silvery monochrome. The moons, now waning, became visible and as bright as the sun, though looking at them did not hurt. One by one, as if somewhere switches were being flicked, the planets and the brightest stars blinked on, then the steady procession of the satellites, and with a rush that made her gasp, the bright path of the Foamy Wake.

She leaned back against the steps behind her, the little steps of the saurs, so incongruous with the gigantism of the rest of their architecture, and gazed up at the crowded sky. After a while, one of the stars became a light that shone brighter and brighter until it was visibly growing bigger and then—in a sudden shocking shift of perspective and involvement—coming closer. Susan sat forward, and tried to stand, but her knees betrayed her. They would not, could not lock. She sat back heavily. The moving blood was a roar now, a rhythmic pulse that at first she mistook for the sound of her breathing, then realized that, slow as it was, her breath was slower still.

The light became the familiar lens shape of a skiff, picked out in the small lights at its top and bottom and around its rim. A few tens of meters above her it went into falling-leaf motion, and settled on the square in front of her on its tripod of landing legs. By this time the lights had disappeared, or been incorporated into the general glow of its surface. It was definitely a saur skiff—it didn't have the roughness of the ones humans built, nor yet the liquid-mercury gloss of the Multipliers' craft.

This was confirmed when the hatch opened, the ladder extended, and a saur descended. The way he walked across the overgrown ancient flagstones toward her was peculiar, as though he wasn't quite touching the ground—no, it was as though he was walking on a moon with a much lower gravity, rising too high and drifting down. But she only had seconds in which to form that impression, because by then he'd stopped and was standing about three meters away from her.

"Who are you?" he said in English.

The accent was Mingulayan, like Salasso's.

"Susan Cairns Harkness," she said.

"Why are you here?"

"We're here to stop a war," she said.

"That's good," he said.

The saur rose slightly off the ground and returned to the craft without further movement, like an image shrinking in a zoom lens. The hatch closed behind him, still looking straight at her; then all the gear retracted and the skiff rose into the sky—again, more like an image shrinking than something actually moving away. Within a minute it was once more an indistinguishable light among the stars.

She heard a footstep behind her and jumped up, stumbling and struggling to keep her balance as she went down the steps five at a time. Down in the square she stopped and whirled around.

A saur stood at the top of the steps, regarding her.

"It's all right, Susan," he said, in English with a Mingulayan accent, but she recognized the voice.

"Oh, Salasso!"

She bounded up the steps as fast as she'd fled down them and hugged the saur, holding his head to her midriff.

Then, slightly embarrassed, she released him and stepped back.

"Did you *see* that?" she cried.

"I saw a light through the trees," said Salasso.

The following morning she had a bad sunburn on her face and the backs of her hands. The Multipliers told her this was not a symptom of the infection. Neither were hallucinations. Their skiff-detecting instruments had detected nothing, and nobody but Salasso had seen any light. Susan dragged Matt to the square and pointed triumphantly to three indentations in the crushed vegetation. He was unusually quiet on the way back.

"For the next three days," Matt announced, "we're not going to make any manifestations. No daylight disks, no crop circles, no funny lights in the sky, no MIB. We've got to plan some trips, but all in stealth mode, and any EVA has to pass for local. In fact EVAs are going to be our main activity. We need to find out, on the streets, what effect we've been having."

Susan sat and shivered. She'd been tempted to give the early morning planning meeting in the hangar doorway a miss. The pain in her skin was easing off, the red was fading. She hadn't slept well, and she

716

couldn't even remember the dreams which had woken her, except one, which was of being tiny and being stepped on. She could remember the tread pattern on the sole of a descending boot.

"I have another suggestion," said Ann Derige. "If we're going to do stealth surveys, why not sneak up on some of the space installations?"

"Because we don't want to," said Matt, over a murmur of enthusiasm for Derige's idea—the gunners and rocketeers were getting impatient. "We don't want to give the slightest impression that we're interested in the space installations."

"We won't, if the stealth tech works," said Ann.

Mr. Orange waved a limb. "If I may," it said. "The stealth technology works against radar observation, and visual in most circumstances. It is not invisible to modes of detection outside the electromagnetic spectrum."

"Such as what? Telepathy? Smell?"

"Smell, yes, in the sense of ionized particles. Telepathy we know nothing about. More to the point, there are instruments for detecting minute variations in gravitational fields, instruments well within the capacity of this civilization's technology, and useful in space. The gravitational anomalies caused by the near presence of a skiff in stealth mode are more than minute."

"I'll take your word for it," said Ann, who clearly didn't.

"All right," said Matt, after they'd thrashed out a schedule for visiting various towns, timed for just before the dawn crept over the western continent. "Volunteers?"

Everyone stuck up a hand, or several.

"No saurs on EVA," said Matt dryly. "And nobody who's just taken the Multiplier treatment. Sorry, Susan."

"Didn't stop *you* making decisions," Ramona muttered.

Matt heard. "It was all right for me," he said. "I used to do drugs."

You get used to the weirdest things, Susan thought, as one by one the five Multiplier skiffs vanished from the hangar, leaving the *Investigator* alone in the middle, and her with Mr. Sort-of-Rainbow, Obadiah Hynde the rocketeer, Salasso, and Delavar.

"Drawn the short straw," said Obadiah, a cheerful young man with black hair and big hands. He peered at her over the flare as he lit a cigarette, a habit Susan was glad not to have. "Are you all right?"

"Yeah," said Susan. "I feel kind of weird. Light-headed."

"That is because of the very small offspring moving among your neurons," said Mr. Sort-of-Rainbow.

"Thanks," Susan glared. "That image is just what I need to calm me down."

"That was my intention," said the Multi, and scuttled off out to forage.

Obadiah looked down at the detritus of breakfast. "Might as well clean up," he said. "Give the old ship a good going over while I'm at it."

"We have decided," said Delavar, "to spend the day studying the information retrieved earlier."

Susan looked around. "I'm sorry," she said. "I'm just not up to anything right now. I'll just go and sit in the door."

"That is strongly recommended," said Salasso.

Susan dragged a log from the area in front of the hangar to the side of the entrance and sat down on it, leaning against the wall. She closed her eyes and watched the catherine wheels and rockets for a while. Then she opened her eyes and looked at the incredible intricacy of the lichens on the log, and contemplated the molecular machinery of the leaves on the trees. The insects moving about in the grass communicated by throwing little molecular machines at each other. She could almost understand what they were saying. She closed her eyes again. The sheer amount of information in front of her was too much to take in. She had to think about it.

When she opened her eyes again an inordinate amount of time had passed. The sun was a little higher in the sky. Mr. Sort-of-Rainbow emerged from the trees, jeweled with droplets of water, each of which refracted the light and reproduced the colors of his fur. He strolled up to her on four legs, the other four forming a mesh in which he held a great variety of fruit.

"Are you well?" he asked.

"Yes," she said. "All is well. God," she giggled helplessly, "is in *everything*."

"Yes," said the Multiplier. "Did you not know?"

Oh gods but this was a drag. People had come back, skiffs emerging inside the hangar as usual, and everybody was scurrying about and jabbering and ignoring her and she was tired like she had been working hard all day bloody hell she had been working hard all day she had gathered all this information and nobody was fucking interested and she had bloody spiders crawling out of her nostrils and nobody wanted to look at her and she just wanted to *die*. She heaved herself to her feet and trudged to the *Investigator* and climbed the ladder and crawled to her bunk and went out like a burnt filament.

"Good morning," said Matt, crouched over the electric heater and a coffeepot. "Welcome back."

Susan felt all bouncy and clean as though she had just had a shower, although she hadn't. Even her clothes felt clean, although she had slept in them.

"Oh, yeah, thanks." The previous day was a blur, but she distinctly remembered going away. "Everyone went away yesterday, didn't they?" She paused, puzzled. "Where did I go?"

He handed her a coffee. "Off on a little trip of your own."

Everything came crashing back. "Oh, God," she said.

"Well, quite," said Matt. "That was some sermon you gave us."

Susan felt like putting her head in her hands. "But it's still true," she said. She looked out through the wide doorway at the early morning landscape. Through the fog over the valley the sun was a red, coppery circle somewhat like a penny, and . . .

"Look at the *sun*!" she said.

"Yup," said Matt. " 'A great multitude of the heavenly host crying, "Glory, glory, glory to the Lord God Almighty." ' Well, something like that. You'll get used to it."

"It doesn't go away?"

"I'm afraid not," said Matt. "I understand it has something to do with an irreversibly increased awareness of the information density of reality. According to the Multis, anyway. Think about it. Your brain has been walked over by beasties that can *feel atoms*."

Susan snapped out of a contemplation of the steam rising from her cup. She examined the skin on her arms. "Speaking of beasties—where are they?"

"Crawled out of your bodily orifices, cleaned up your skin and clothes, and gone trooping back to Mr. Magenta."

"How embarrassing."

"Speaking of embarrassment . . ." said Matt. Elsewhere in the cavernous hangar, people were beginning to stir. "I think it might be best if we agree not to talk about, um . . ."

"All that infinity in a grain of sand shit?"

Matt grinned. "It's good to find someone whose mind is cruder than mine."

She smiled conspiratorially back, then very deliberately turned her attention to other things.

"Do you think I'm ready to go out on reconnaissance today?"

"Yeah," said Matt. "Just don't let your mouth hang open, and you'll pass for normal."

The inside of the Multiplier skiff was remarkably like the inside of every other skiff Susan had been in. She and Telesnikov sat side by side on the circular bench around the central engine fairing, and Mr. Blue squatted on a stool in front of the control panel. It was only when the Multiplier turned on the viewscreen that a major difference, or refinement, became apparent. The hull was all viewscreen. It was like sitting in midair. Susan grabbed the edge of the seat and smiled self-consciously at Telesnikov.

The view changed—the inside of the hangar was instantly replaced with dark-blue sky above and a wide stretch of Genea below. She looked down between her feet and saw greens and browns and the white of clouds, the fractal line of the coast, the semicircle of Half Moon Sea. After her first intake of breath her second emotion was a pang of nostalgia for Mingulay—she'd seen her home planet from space many times, on the way to or from her family's orbital factories where the saurs brought the exotic components—black hole atoms, unusual stable elements with atomic weights in the hundreds—for the engines and drives.

Instantly the view changed again. They sat a couple of hundred meters above the surface—they didn't want to leave crop circles—then descended to hover above damp grass in a field by a metaled road. A hundred or so meters away were low slope-roofed houses, which if Mr. Blue had got it right were on the edge of Junopolis, the capital of Illyria.

"Over by the hedge," said Telesnikov. The skiff glided to the bushes. Twelve eyes surveyed the surroundings. No eyes looked back. The hatch flowed open—the only way Susan could tell was by the air on her face—and the two humans jumped out. By the time they'd walked a dozen steps the skiff was nothing but an unease-inspiring shimmer in the air.

Their clothes would pass as Illyrian, though plain. Short hair was not so uncommon as to be noticed. Their pockets were stuffed with Multiplier-copied Illyrian money. Each of them had a legal weapon—

in the Duchy, wearing a knife was practically compulsory—and a small radio, of local manufacture but with Multiplier enhancements in its innards, most significantly an emergency alarm to call for a skiff and a tracking device to tell the skiff where to go.

They found a tram stop after walking a few hundred meters through the waking suburb—dogs barking, children running for buses—and rode into town accompanied by sleepy commuters. Several people left newspapers on their seats; Telesnikov and Susan each casually picked one up.

Their reading did not stay casual for long. The front pages of both papers—the sensational *New Morning* and the sober *The Day* alike—showed a clear photograph of a daylight disk over Junopolis. The captions agreed on the date and time of the sighting—the middle of the afternoon of the previous day. *The Day*'s headline was "Mystery Skiff Evades Fighters." The *New Morning*'s was "SPIDER SKIFF STUNS CITY!"

Susan turned over the rest of the pages. The sighting over Junopolis was only the biggest of many similar stories. Editorials screamed for action; when she silently swapped papers with Telesnikov, she read that the country's elected representatives were doing the same. Buried in the longer articles were references to earlier official denials of various odd events of the past fortnight, at some of which she had been present herself. The independent confirmation of the "Lucifer Probe anomaly" had resulted in a particularly embarrassing climb-down, it seemed.

Susan folded the paper glumly and looked out the windows. The day was heating up. Fall in this hemisphere, spring at the base in Sauria—the contrast was fierce. Junopolis looked like a town well adapted to seasonal change. From the depth of the recesses of windows she could see that most walls were thick, at least on the older buildings. Garish color washes were the fashion, or tradition—it was hard to say, because compared with her hometown even the new buildings looked old-fashioned, solid and ornate. Clothes were colorful, hair and beards generally long, with a sprinkling of clean-shaven cropheads who also tended to wear duller clothes.

At the tram's terminal in the center of town Susan bought copies of every paper on sale—all of which led with the same photo—and she and Telesnikov made their way to a big low-ceilinged café with lots of marble and mirrors and took their coffeepot and cups to the most isolated table they could find. They puzzled over the papers for a while.

"Is it possible," Susan asked, in careful Trade Latin, "that one of our teams made a big mistake yesterday?"

Telesnikov shook his head, almost angrily. "We're the first team into Junopolis," he said. "Last night I checked every report, every image brought back. There is no question about it—whatever this was, it wasn't us."

"Is it even thinkable that the . . . that our friends are lying to us? That they did this without our knowing?"

"I suppose it's thinkable," said Telesnikov. "But that way madness lies. If we can't trust them we should abandon the operation right now."

"If we don't know what's real and what's—" She stopped. "This is what Matt said would happen!"

" 'Guerrilla ontology,' " Telesnikov said heavily. " 'Make people question their concept of reality.' The trouble is, it's happening to *us*."

Susan sat back and watched the surrounding salarymen and women scoffing their breakfasts, reading the papers with expressions she could not read, talking animatedly in a dialect she could not quite follow at that volume and speed. She had missed crowds, she realized, and new faces.

"I'm not so worried about us," she said. "I saw something myself that we couldn't explain, and Salasso saw a light, and Matt saw the prints. Whatever it was it didn't seem hostile. But whatever is going on here seems hostile to them."

"To the people here? Yeah, you could say that. And no doubt to the security apparatuses as well. But what's even more worrying is how this appears to people in New Babylon, and *their* security apparatuses. This is much more blatant than anything we've done."

"So who's doing it?"

Telesnikov shrugged. "Relict saurs? Other Multipliers we don't know about? The—uh, our own folk? Arrived here without our knowing? Or even a local power that has developed or gotten hold of skiff technology? Or something altogether unknown? You can bet all of these possibilities are exercising some very bright minds right now."

"And the minds of very frightened people."

"Hell," said Telesnikov, "*I'm* very bright, and I'm very frightened." He swept his hand over the pile of newspapers. "What do you say we just head back?"

"No," said Susan. "I don't think the newspapers are enough. We have to talk to people."

"But how do we do that?"

"It's easy," Susan said. "I'm a journalist."

And with that she stood up and and wandered over to the other tables and started talking to people. It was easy. She was a journalist.

"Good morning," she said to a fat, anxious-looking middle-aged man with bags under his eyes and a cigarette between his knuckles, ash drifting on to a greasy plate. His greying hair was tied back in a ponytail and his coat and weskit were rumpled. "Mind if sit down?"

"Go ahead."

"Thanks. My name's Susan, I'm a journalist, from the—"

He held up his hand. "Don't tell me. The Dorian *Daily News*, right?"

"Yes," she said. Doria was one of the smallest and most remote of the lesser republics of the Genean League. It seemed a safe enough cover. "How did you guess?"

The fat man wagged a finger. "Your accent, young lady. Can't hide it. And I doubt if Doria can support more than one paper."

"True enough," she said, sounding regretful. She smiled brightly. "And your name, sir?"

"Horace Kamehan," he said, sticking out a hand. "And what can I do for you?"

She waved a battered black notebook. "I'd like to, uh, wire back a few comments from Junopolitans about the latest events."

Kamehan pushed his empty plate away and sipped his coffee. "Oh, right," he said. "Well, I don't think you'll find much disagreement. We should hit the bastards with everything we've got."

"How can we be certain that they *are* bastards?"

He blinked and frowned. "Maybe it's easy to be all evenhanded if you're sitting out there on your rocks in Doria, but from where I'm sitting it's not. It's quite clear who's making the threats, and frankly I don't think our government should stand for it. Which I don't think we will, I hasten to add. The Duke's got a bit of spine, thank the gods."

Susan struggled to hide her confusion by nodding, smiling, and scribbling a note of what the man had said.

"And if it comes to it," Kamehan went on, "I'm not too old to bloody sign up myself."

"Sign up?"

He gave her another puzzled look. "For the army—maybe you don't have that expression in Doria? Not surprising."

"But Mr. Kamehan," she said, "how do you expect to fight aliens?"

"Aliens?" He stared at her as though she'd just come from outer space. "Aliens? The Spiders? Who believes in this palpable nonsense? Not even you lot, I hope."

"But the papers—"

"The papers? Don't you listen to the bloody radio?"

"Of course, of course," said Susan desperately. "It's all very disturbing." She stood up. "Well, thank you, Mr. Kamehan, for your comments. All the best."

"Gods look after you," Kamehan said. "Because gods know, you need them to." He muttered something under his breath about fishermen and foreign correspondents.

"Thank you," she said, and retreated as fast as she could to the table where Telesnikov sat mulling over the papers. On her way she noticed something that the fashion for long hair had concealed—almost everyone was wearing earphones. She sat down, nodded to Mikhail, and worried her own earpieces in. She set the little radio on the table in front of her and thumbed the dial slowly. The fingers on a wall clock were climbing to third before noon—the café was not emptying, although it seemed a likely time for office hours to begin, and people were looking at the clock or at their watches, listening intently. Susan kept tuning, trying to identify the sound of a program coming to an end, or some hint that an hourly news bulletin was about to—ah, there it was.

She turned the radio toward Telesnikov and pointed to the spot on the dial, and to her ear. He took the hint.

There was a sound like a series of splashes, which puzzled Susan until she realized that it was the station's signature, intended to represent an archaic water clock. The announcer's voice was grave, his Trade Latin more formal than the spoken dialect or the fretful rancorous rant of the press.

"Junopolis Calls, third hour before noon, eleventh day of Frugora, Anno Civitas ten thousand three hundred and forty nine. Reports are coming in of serious damage and an unknown number of deaths and injuries in the coastal town of Palmir. Witnesses have described a 'bolt from the sky' followed by fires and explosions. The Duke's Minister of Defense has just stated that emergency assistance is being rushed to the stricken town. An urgent investigation is to begin immediately. He refused to comment when asked whether the disaster is linked to the warning issued earlier this morning by New Babylon. More information will be available from Palmira shortly.

"Meanwhile, in a further deterioration of relations with our southern neighbor, the Ducal Palace has made public a note delivered to the Consul of New Babylon. Junopolis Calls is authorized to read the note in its entirety:

> *"Your Exellency: The warning issued by the Senate of New Babylon, and reported on your country's radio stations at six before noon today, is viewed with great concern by Us, Our Ministers, and Our People's Representatives. We reject, in the strongest terms, any suggestion that hostile forces are operating in or above Our nation's territory, and will regard any action taken by your esteemed and respected country's forces on, around, or above that territory as an attack upon Our sovereignty and upon the sacred and inviolable territory of the Free Duchy of Illyria. In the presence of the indifferent gods and in the shadow of Our ancestors, We remain, your Excellency's humble correspondent, Duke Leonid the Second."*

The roar that followed from the customers in the café—and the passengers in the terminal—drowned out whatever was said next.

VEE—DOO! VEE—DOO!

"What are they shouting?"

"Long live the Duke, I think," said Telesnikov. "Doesn't matter. Whatever it is, it means war. Let's get out."

They gathered their armful of now-outdated but possibly still-useful papers and made their way through the standing, chanting crowd. Their path to the door was suddenly blocked by Kamehan. Two younger men stood shoulder to shoulder with him.

"Where do you think you're going?" Kamehan demanded.

"Excuse me," said Susan. "We have a story to file."

"I'll bet you do," said Kamehan. "With the Dorian *Daily News*, huh?"

"Yes," said Susan.

"Now ain't that odd?" said the young man at Kamehan's right. " 'Cause I'm the *News*'s Junopolis correspondent. Maybe you'd do better filing your story with my friend Mr. Kamehan, of the Junopolis—"

Telesnikov slugged him in the stomach, punched Kamehan in the face and shoved both of them hard against the third.

"Run!" he shouted.

Susan pushed through a sudden domino-effect of people flailing and stumbling and ran out the door onto the concourse. Telesnikov caught up with her a moment later. He had dropped the papers and was clutching his radio.

"Nearest open space," he gasped, and sprinted for the tram-line marshalling yard, which opened onto the two open sides of the terminal. Susan followed. Behind her she heard someone yelling "Spies!" and the cry being taken up. Diagonally across from her she saw a man in uniform running to head them off. Telesnikov saw him too and swerved. Susan took the opposite direction and the man dithered and lunged ineffectually. Then they were past him and in an area of metal grooves and overhead sparks and quietly gliding death that could come from any direction.

A tram loomed in front her, blue paint and polished brass, the startled face of a driver. She leapt across the parallel tracks and spun around on her next step, then grabbed a stanchion and swung onto the running board. The driver had just released the brake and hadn't seen anything beyond the fact that he hadn't run her down. She glanced back along the track. Telesnikov, with the uniformed man a few meters behind in hot pursuit, raced behind the tram and with a surge of speed caught up with it and jumped onto the rear platform.

The driver heard the thump and glanced in his mirror. The brakes squealed again. Susan felt a terrific wrench in her shoulders. She clung on, to see Telesnikov tumbling past as he was sent sprawling down the vehicle's aisle. As the tram slowed the policeman caught up and jumped aboard at the back. He ran forward just as Susan came through the open central door. She had time to see that he was not stopping—the deceleration pulled him forward—just before she ducked across his path. He tried to jump over her and succeeded only in kicking her in the ribs as he tripped over her back.

Telesnikov scrambled to his feet at the same moment as she did. The driver, almost thrown against the front of the cab, turned around and grabbed for him. Telesnikov caught his arm and slammed it on the half-door at the side of the driver's seat, then jumped down out of the door at the front, Susan following via the one she'd just come in by.

They both barely avoided stepping in front of another tram. When it had passed they saw they were outside the back of the terminal on a wide-open space of tarmac. Gleaming lines snaked to low sheds between rusty mounted wheels with coils of metal cable, like fishing reels for Leviathan, paired bare levers, buffered barriers. Telesnikov rounded the obstacles to the least-cluttered area, waving his arms above his head. Susan ran behind him, glanced back over her shoulder and saw the persistent policeman being helped to his feet by the driver. A few more uniforms ran in from various directions.

She turned her head forward again. Telesnikov had disappeared. Then she saw him, uncannily suspended a meter up in the air right in front of her, and Mr. Blue behind him. He was crouched down and reaching out. She jumped, they caught each other's forearms, and he hauled her into the skiff. They ended up sitting on the bench with their backs to the engine fairing. The sounds from outside abruptly ceased. The pursuers had stopped, and were looking at each other and at where they were. From the side of a wall about twenty meters away an old man in a bundle of rags staggered forward, pointing and shouting.

The scene changed to sky and the blue and white levels of air.

Telesnikov laughed harshly. "I'd like to see how they report *that* in tomorrow's papers."

Matt was indulging in one of his rants. For the Multipliers, he said at some length, speech was a distinctly secondary mode of communication. They shared knowledge through their fingertips. They tended to assume, he suggested, that more had been shared than had actually been said. As for the saurs, they volunteered so little about themselves that getting information out of them was like getting blood from a fucking stone.

The humans in the crew listened with embarrassment. The Multipliers formed a big circle and quivered and fingered each other. The two saurs stood together and shuffled occasionally. The day's missions had been hastily recalled. The sun was high and the hangar's interior was all in shadow. In the background a radio prattled away. Skiffs were still being sighted all over the place, and here and there were being chased by New Babylonian jet fighters or zapped by New Babylonian space-based plasma cannon, to the evident annoyance of every other power from Illyria to Doria. More details were coming through of extensive destruction in Palmir, apparently from a plasma-cannon bolt.

"So," said Matt in a chillingly reasonable voice, "do any of you have anything to tell us that you might not have thought worth mentioning?"

Salasso stepped forward and turned to face the others.

"There is something," he said, "which I hesitate to mention, but it may be relevant. Some of the very old legends of my people say that when they first came to the worlds of the Second Sphere, they met saurs who were *already here*. Saurs who flew in skiffs and behaved in . . . an enigmatic fashion, both intrusive and elusive. The rational explanation, which is usually given to the young of the species when they are told of these legends, is that different parties of saurs arrived on the various planets at different times, perhaps separated by centuries or millennia, and their first encounters were confusing on both sides. But I must admit that these stories . . . came to my mind when Susan described her encounter."

"Very good," said Matt. He laid a hand on Salasso's shoulder and looked down at the saur with a sort of troubled affection. "So you guys have Greys and flying saucers too, huh? Well, there's something nobody told me before. And, ah, just in case you've missed something out— have such stories been told about more recent events?"

"No," said Salasso. "These legends are of a time tens of millions of years ago. No such stories are of more recent date." He paused. "Other than literary pastiches, of course."

"Of course," said Matt. "Literature too, huh? We're advancing by leaps and bounds here."

"That is all I have to suggest," said Salasso.

"Thank you," said Matt. "Anyone else?"

Mr. Orange detached himself from a busy tangle of limbs and scuttled over.

"We do not understand and are distressed by the anger of the Matt Cairns. The invasion is proceeding according to plan. The mind of the world New Earth is responding as we expected it to. The humans of the world New Earth are misdirecting their defenses and in conflict with each other. Soon it will be possible to—"

"Excuse me," said Matt, waving a spread hand up and down. It was a way of getting the Multipliers' attention that often worked. "What was that about the mind of the world?"

II

Lithomancer

I N THE OLD days, the scientists of the Academy used to demonstrate the spontaneous generation of life: flies from rotting meat, mice from stored grain. What Gaius was seeing looked very like that: a tiny red spider forming out of a drop of blood. What shocked him was that Lydia snatched it up and swallowed it.

He grimaced. "Good trick," he said. "How did you do it?"

She picked up the knife and did it again. This time, she placed the spider—it was a different color, green—on his palm, and handed him a folding lens.

"Look at it carefully."

He peered through the magnifier. It wasn't a spider. *"That's a—"*

"Don't shout."

"Gods above." He held out his hand. It trembled a little. The minute Multiplier was turning around, as though looking for somewhere to run. He pushed his sleeve back from his wrist.

"Take it," he said. "Eat it, if you must."

"Swallow it yourself," said Lydia, daring him. Her eyes were bright. "Why don't you? It'll make you young forever, or so I was told. It's worked for me, so far."

He could believe her. "Take it," he pleaded.

She caught his bared wrist and kissed the bad thing away. "There," she said. "Well, not many people even have the chance to pass up a chance like that."

Gaius wiped his hands on his knees. "Is that how it works? How the Bright Star Cultures spread?"

"Yes," she said. "I suppose I'm a Bright Star Culture person, come to think of it."

"You haven't—?"

"Proselytized?" She leaned back and smiled. "I wouldn't tell you if I had, but . . . no."

"Why are you telling me this? Why did you show me that?"

"Because you needed evidence. These things, they live in my blood, small as cells. When it spills there's a sort of dog-eat-dog situation."

He nodded, understanding what he'd just seen, and why she'd told him. Telling him was no risk to her—he could not denounce her to the New Babylonian apparatus without giving them an intelligence coup that would strengthen them against his own country; her secret was now his, and, if she was thinking ahead as fast as he was, Illyria's. He had to get her out.

"Anyway," she went on, "they pass on bits and pieces of memories. All sorts of memories, of their progenitors and of the organisms they've been in. That's how I know that Multiplier navigation is precise enough to jump straight to a planet's surface."

"Why didn't they do that back in the first invasion?"

"Oh, I don't suppose they were expecting to be attacked. If it really is the Bright Star Cultures that are here now, they'll be expecting trouble." She smiled as if to herself. "The folks back on Mingulay and Croatan knew Volkov of old, and they knew he was coming here. They'll know what to expect."

"But what can they do?"

"With skiffs that can set up lightspeed jumps with an accuracy of a few meters? I can think of quite a lot they could do."

"When you put it that way," Gaius said, "so can I."

And all of them would tip the military balance against New Babylon. Whatever happened—and he was finding his assumptions about the long-feared arrival of the Bright Star Cultures shaken by Lydia's words and actions—it was surely better that Illyria should face it in a position of strength. If New Babylon's space defenses were knocked out, and the Regime itself tottering, the opportunities would be huge. He had to return to Junopolis, and take Lydia with him if he could. He was just turning this over in his mind when Lydia reached out and caught his arm.

"Don't move," she said. She was looking past his face. "A couple of cops just came into the bar. They're looking for somebody. Probably after one of the local loan sharks. Play it cool."

A moment later two men in dark suits came over. Gaius looked up at them with what he hoped was an expression of surprised but not alarmed query.

"Lydia de Tenebre?" one of them said. "We'd like you to accompany us to—"

Gaius didn't so much see as later reconstruct what happened next. Lydia heaved her end of the table upward, crouched down and grabbed the middle of both sides, and threw it straight at them. They both stumbled back and then fell over backwards as the table, which Lydia leaped on like a flying cat as it hit, crashed down on top of them. Arms and legs projected from beneath it. Broken glass slithered across the floor.

Gaius was still sitting on the bench, a glass halfway between his mouth and where the table had been.

Lydia turned on the upsided table like a dancer on a low stage, and reached out a hand. "I think we should leave," she said.

They ran to the door, past people who were carefully not stopping them—whether out of hostility to the police, or to maintain their cover, or fear of Lydia's suddenly revealed fighting prowess. Lydia looked both ways before going out.

"They'll have backup," she said.

A car parked a hundred meters down the road revved its engine and headed straight at them. Lydia led the way in a dash across the street. Gaius distinctly saw the car's fender a couple of meters away as he followed. Lydia vaulted the wall. Brakes squealed. Gaius hesitated at a drop of three meters onto slippery boulders, heard running footsteps, rolled onto the wall, swung down, clung and dropped. Lydia was already on her feet and steadied him as he landed and slipped.

The tide was out. The shore smelled like bad breath. Lydia ran alongside the bottom of the wall, surefooted. Gaius stumbled after her. He glanced up and saw two heads bobbing along above the top of the wall, keeping pace easily. This was hopeless. When he looked ahead again Lydia had vanished. A few steps more took him to the mouth of the tunnel she'd vanished into. He saw her face, pale in the light from the harbor. He ducked in after her. The tunnel's roof was low and its floor was a phosphorescent green stream. He tried not to stand in it.

"Industrial effluent," said Lydia. "You can walk in it. Just don't drink it. Come on."

Behind him, he heard a couple of crunching thuds, followed by yelled curses, then footsteps. He ran.

She had a pocket torch, and the faint glow from the effluent provided a path. It didn't last long. A few tens of meters in, Lydia turned off into a side tunnel just as voices echoed along from the entrance to the main one. There were other tunnels branching off, and Lydia led him through a maze of them. The voices and splashes of the pursuit faded after a couple more turns. Ten minutes later they reached a ladder up to a manhole and emerged in an alleyway off the lower end of Astronaut Avenue. Lydia rolled the heavy lid back into place, brushed her hands, and stood up.

"How the hells did you do that?"

"I'm not sure," said Lydia. "I may have seen the drainage system map in the Library."

"That's not an explanation."

"No," she said.

She strolled to a standpipe—it was not obvious, but she moved like she knew where to find it—and ran the tap over her boots. Gaius looked down at his shoes and trouser cuffs and decided to do the same. Better to be wet with water than with that gunk. It looked vaguely acidic and its smell, as it weakened in the open air, was becoming more nauseating, like cheap gin on the sinuses. He took off his shoes and rinsed them, then his socks and feet. Even wrung out, his socks felt horrible.

"Where now?"

"First thing I'm going to do," said Lydia, "is go to the nearest public phone booth and call home. See if the cops have come for them, too."

There was a phone around the corner. Lydia put down the receiver after trying a dozen numbers.

"Nobody home. Not good."

They walked on up Astronaut Avenue, pending some decision on what to do next. The streets were a bit livelier now, though not by the standards of Junopolis at this time of a fine night. No shops open, and few beer parlors or places of amusement. Three armored personnel carriers crossed a junction a few hundred meters ahead. Gaius desperately wanted to get off the street.

"Why did they come after you?"

"For the same reason as you did, I guess."

Gaius thought about that. "Let's get off the street," he said. He stopped outside a beer parlor. "In here."

"That's a bureaucrats' watering hole. One of the bugged bars I told you about."

"All the better," said Gaius. "We don't need to worry about that anymore. We need to worry about being bundled into a van."

The place was full of men and women in suits. Gaius was cynically unsurprised that nobody stared. He bought a brace of drastically over-priced stiff drinks and sat down with Lydia in an alcove. There was a menu on the table.

"Suddenly hungry?" said Gaius. Lydia nodded. They ordered grilled patties of minced beef, the main item.

"The seafood used to be wonderful," Lydia sighed. The waiter went away.

"What do you want to do?" Gaius asked.

"Walls have ears," said Lydia.

Gaius leaned back and sighed. "I know about surveillance here," he said. "Believe it or not, I know more than you do. It's used for evidence-gathering, not rapid response. Think about it. Unless there's a general alert out for us, or for you, all that's happening is that we're being taped, and sometime in the next few days some bored policeman is going to listen to us. And then only if they have reason to think this place's tapes are worth checking. Maybe a description of us has gone out to police patrol vehicles, but that's to cars, not bars. Besides, dragging people out of places like this is not their style. It tends to upset the lower middle cadre. So relax."

"All right," she said. "What I want to do is find out what's happened to my family."

"Have you ever been pulled in before?"

She shook her head. "They interrogate all the humans coming off Trader ships, release them, keep an eye on us but that's it."

"Any others like you?"

"Maybe one or two," she said, sounding evasive. She nibbled her lip. "I've checked this, I've asked around discreetly. The former Traders do sort of hang together, help each other out. It's only because of that that we haven't all ended up in a heap at the bottom."

"That's still a lot of people to check."

"It was," she said dryly. "But remember, most of the ships that come back haven't been in the Bright Star Culture's expanding sphere, and of those that have, very few have directly encountered the Mingulayans or the Spiders. We were one of the first to meet them, on Novakkad. Things were at a pretty early stage there. Mostly the krakens or the saurs pick up that something's going on within minutes of coming out of the jump, and they don't even land—they jump straight back. It's like a squid reflex."

Gaius was still smiling at this image when the waiter returned with two plates of food and three men with guns. Two of them looked bruised, and familiar. The third was a bit taller, older, and heavier, and acted like he'd had to take charge.

Lydia swallowed her drink and stood up. There could be no surprising them this time.

"Looks like there was a general alert out for me after all."

"It was the remark about the seafood," said the waiter.

Gaius held his hands out and stood up, sidling from the alcove.

"This lady is under the protection of the Free Duchy of Illyria," he said. "She has just asked me for asylum. I demand you let us go to the Consulate."

"The Consulate is closed," said the largest of the three men. "She's coming with us. And you, Mr. Gonatus, are *persona non* fucking *grata*. The only place *you*'re going is the train back to Illyria."

"I have an airline ticket—"

"The airport is closed."

"—and there are no trains back to Illyria."

"Oh yes, there are," said the big police agent. "Only they don't go quite all the way. Just to the foot of the mountains." He glanced at his watch and grinned nastily. "Consider yourself lucky. In a few hours you wouldn't be expelled for activities incompatible. You'd be fucking shot. So move it."

Gaius looked at Lydia. She was giving such a good impression of being unafraid that for a moment he wondered if she hadn't been setting him up. He dismissed it. She was brave and stoical, that was all. And probably difficult to kill or permanently damage. That must help.

"I'm sorry," he said.

"There's nothing more you can do," she said. She was shrugging into her jacket, which one of the men had returned to her after searching it. "Just go."

He thought about what the policeman had implied, and wondered if Lydia had picked up on it.

"See you after the war," he said.

The train left an hour before midnight. The one thing for which Gaius felt thankful was that his clothes had been left undamaged in his ransacked hotel room. He might not have his samples, but at least he had dry socks. He had filled the empty sample case with bottles of water and as much food as he could carry, bought in a hurry from the station's stalls and turning stale within hours. In every other respect he felt deeply ungrateful. The train was packed. He almost envied the people squeezed together on the wooden seats or sitting on the floor. The northwest train out of New Babylon was officially for latifundia peasants on their way to and from the official markets; and indeed there were quite a lot of peasants, mostly very old women, or men with faces red from sun and drink, snoring in cheap flashy suits. But unofficially, and blatantly, it was for emigrants. Tonight it carried far more than usual—refugees, he suspected, from the now widely rumored war. The cloud people carried more baggage than the peasants, and had better clothes, and before the week was out most of the baggage would be strewn along the passes, the clothes would be in rags, and some of the emigrants would be dead. Statistically, Gaius knew, he was looking at dead people, as surely as if he was riding a troop train heading for the front. Statistically, he also knew, he might be looking at a dead man reflected in the dark window.

The train rattled across the plain, labored up the long gradual slope, thundered across the Massif. Gaius, jammed upright by the press of bodies around him, jostled by the train's rhythm and the more annoying, random jolts as people made their way to and from the inadequate and increasingly foul-smelling toilets, dozed fitfully, now and again woken by a sudden shift in the balance of forces or by his forehead hitting the window. The train stopped every hour or so. At each stop some peasants got off and Gaius hoped the pressure would ease; but always, even more people got on. Mostly young men—draft dodgers, Gaius guessed and, patriotically, hoped. They drank a lot, smoked regardless of protests and talked loudly in a thick dialect. Gaius couldn't make out enough to gather any intelligence from them.

About three after midnight everyone on the train woke at once, as a shock and shouting ran through the packed carriages and all heads turned to the windows. Gaius found himself looking out through the yellow reflections then, as he managed to cup his hands between the glass and his face, directly, at a dozen slowly moving lights that suddenly changed color, loomed, flashed, and danced away. Minutes later, something fell from the sky and like lightning lit the rough land from horizon to horizon. Nobody slept much after that.

Dawn came up at five and a half after midnight. An hour later, the train halted at some crummy town: a water tower, a lithomancy pylon, a tractor depot, a straggle of houses. More peasants got off here, and mercifully few new passengers got on. Kids hawked papers along the platform: The morning edition of the Regime's official and only newspaper, wired from the capital and printed locally, with a local name.

THE ENGINES OF LIGHT

Gaius tugged the window down and exchanged a handful of Volkovs for the *Pergam Truth*. Lots of other hands stretched out to do the same. Gaius found a space to sit down and read it.

> ILLYRIA MUST ACT, SENATE WARNS
> In an emergency all-night session, the Senate of the Democratic Republic of New Babylon warned that the Illyrian aristocracy's criminal passivity in the face of recent incursions by Spider skiffs (see page 2) is a threat to the entire planet. The Defense Forces of the Republic stand ready to aid the Duchy's small military establishment at a moment's notice, but reserve the right to act unilaterally in defense of all the peoples of New Earth. Any rejection of this fraternal invitation to stand shoulder to shoulder against the alien menace will be regarded, by all reasonable people, as treachery to the species and collaboration with the enemy. The Senate strongly urged patriotic Illyrians, and in particular its brave though ill-equipped armed forces, to consider where their true loyalties lie.

A threat of war, and an incitement to treason. Gaius gritted his teeth and turned to page two, which gave—for the first time, as far as he knew—a quite sober account of the sightings and other strange events reported in his own country's litter press. A few incidents were recounted from within the Republic, all of them—unlike those reported from Illyria—described as having been swiftly countered by air or space forces. The implication here too was that Illyria was implicated in the Spider incursion—there were a lot of heavy hints about decadent aristocrats selling out to the enemy, though quite what they were selling and what they were getting in return was not stated.

Gaius turned over more pages as the train pulled out. Editorials, interviews, maps bristling with menacing arrows, vox-pop rants . . . the hostility to Illyria was so venomous that he felt very glad he wasn't instantly identifiable as Illyrian. Like most republicans in the Duchy, he followed the ancient fashion of short hair, and his clothes were by now as shoddy-looking as the locals'. One thing he'd expected to see in the paper, and that wasn't there, was any reference to enemies within—no incitement to spy mania, no warnings about foreigners or Traders. They seemed an obvious scapegoat. He doubted that the Regime was simply missing a trick. It didn't seem the sort of trick they would miss.

He opened his case, drank some tepid water and took out a curling sandwich. The very old woman sitting opposite him looked at it far more hungrily than he felt. He passed it over to her. She thanked him with a gap-toothed smile and munched it in a minute, wiped her hands on her already greasy black dress, and fiddled with something in her ear. Gaius noticed the wire that snaked to her clutched leather bag.

"You have a radio?" he asked. "Any further news?"

"Lithos is troubled," she said. "Lithos is afraid."

Gaius forced himself not to show his disdain. The old woman wasn't listening to the news, she was listening to the meaningless babble from the lithomancy pylons. The cult was seductive to the old, and to the bereaved who heard their loved ones' voices.

"She hears rumors of war, she sends her engines of light to meet the Spiders. She weeps at the lost blood filled with Spiders, the blood of life. The Spiders are close, they crawl over us, they hang in the spaces between the stars."

Gaius felt his skin go cold and his hair prickle. The old woman didn't notice his response. The lithomantic trance glazed her eyes, and the rest of what she said was gibberish, vocalized no doubt from the atmospheric howls and mutterings of the lithosphere. Then she fell asleep, drooling slightly. The man sitting beside her, an emigrant in a smart and sweaty shirt, shifted uncomfortably and gave Gaius an embarrassed look.

"The peasants go in for that sort of thing," he said. "Can't say I blame them, with the President setting such a bad example."

The man had recognized him as a foreigner, Gaius realized, hence the defensiveness. He smiled reassuringly and waved a hand, though his brain was buzzing so much that he could have done without a conversation.

"Oh, don't worry about it," he said. "Our own farmers are a lot of old pagans too, I must admit. They sacrifice mice to the new moons."

The man chuckled. "You're from—?" He nodded backwards, in the direction of travel.

"Yes," said Gaius. "Just had to cut short a business visit."

"You shouldn't have," the man said, defensive again. "You wouldn't have had anything to worry about."

"Hmm," said Gaius, raising his eyebrows.

The man sighed, and sat back and lit a cigarette, without apology, not that it made much difference by this stage in the journey.

"Yes, I'm a fine one to talk," he said. "I'm as patriotic as the next man, you understand, but when the Society's goons turned up last night and told me my workshop had just become part of the national defense, I thought, to the hells with them." He glanced affectionately at a woman and two teenage boys slumped in sleep on the adjacent seat. "And the lads, well, they're both conscription age . . ."

"I don't think," said Gaius gently, "that the passes are much safer. Or Illyria, for that matter."

The emigrant looked gloomy. "You may be right," he said. "But we've talked about it, and we'd rather die on the slopes than in this futile fratricide."

Gaius resisted the temptation to point out that these possibilities were not mutually exclusive. "What about the Spiders?" he said.

The man snorted. "I don't bloody believe it. If the Spiders were coming, do you think the Illyrians wouldn't join with us at once? Or that our government wouldn't ask them nicely? No, it's just an excuse."

"But last night we saw—"

"Some funny lights. Yes indeed. Let me tell you, my friend, funny lights over the Massif are not as uncommon as you may think. And in any case, who's to say these skiffs people claim to have seen aren't from Sauria—I'm sure there are a few saurs hanging on over there—or from a ship?"

"You may have a point there," said Gaius. He wondered how wide-spread this skepticism was, and decided to change the subject. "Ah, what was it you said about the President?"

The emigrant smiled and stubbed out his cigarette on the side of the seat. "It's a scandal, you know," he said, leaning forward and speaking in a low voice. "Madame President is kept alive with wires and transfusions and gods know what, all because of that leprous camarilla around her which fears more than anything else what happens when she dies. The poor old woman is capable of little more than clacking her false teeth and listening to that lithomancy gibberish. In her lucid moments she makes decisions. It's pathetic, it's shameful, to tell you the truth."

"How do you happen to know this?" asked Gaius. He thought himself well-informed on the Modern Regime's crepuscular politics—the tensions between the Society, internal security, and the Defense Forces were well known, and avidly followed by Illyrian intelligence—but this was news to him.

"Rumor," said the emigrant. He looked over his shoulder, then smiled as though at himself. "Malcontent scandal sheets circulate, you know."

"So I'm told," said Gaius, more dryly than he'd intended. Many of these sheets were, to his certain knowledge, drafted in Junopolis by the Department. Quite possibly this particular rumor had come from there in the first place. "Can't say I've come across them myself. Interesting."

"Yes," said the emigrant. "I say, my friend, you've gone rather pale. Are you unwell?"

Gaius forced a smile and stood up. "I think I need to stretch my legs and stick my head out of a window for a bit. Uh . . . would you mind keeping my place?"

"Not at all," said the emigrant, and put his feet up on Gaius's vacated seat. "Take your time."

Gaius made his way to the space at the end of the carriage by the door and wound the window down. He really did need fresh air. The lumpy landscape of the Massif crawled past, irrigated fields between outcrops and escarpments crested with olive groves and lemon trees, gnarled pines, windmill generators and lithomancy poles. What was really making his head swim was not the rocking motion and the smoky, fetid air of the carriage—though now that he thought about it, he wished he hadn't—but the connections he'd made. Lithomancy, Spiders, blood of life, transfusions . . . the rounding up of Lydia and her family, and the absence of any sign of a round-up of anyone else, even the mistrusted Traders. Thinking about what the old lithomancer had said still gave him chills. *The lost blood filled with Spiders, the blood of life*— where in the hells had that come from? And what if the other old woman, the one in the top of the tower of the Ninth, had picked up the same electric rumor?

He was torn between the desperate fantasy of going back to New Babylon and (somehow) rescuing Lydia, a more sober assessment that she'd likely just end up on a train after having had a blood sample taken (and the desperate fantasy of waiting for her at the end of the line) and the urgent and practical need to get back to Junopolis. If Madame President had let herself be infiltrated, literally, by the enemy in her frantic clinging to life and hope of rejuvenation, then the opportunities for Illyrian active measures were enticing indeed.

He wondered if there was a telephone still working at the station at the end of the line, and if he dared send his message through in clear.

Gaius wondered if the air was already noticeably thinner at this altitude. He stopped, leaned forward with his hands on his knees, and panted for a minute. Looking back, he could see the long straggle of emigrants behind him like a line of ants on the slope. Far below was the rail terminus and the cluster of houses around it, where a friendly peasant had taken his last money (real money) for enough water to fill his bottles and enough cheese and some kind of dubious-looking and worse-smelling wind-dried meat to fill his case, as well as (for a handful of Volkovs) the couple of meters of rope with which the unwieldy item of luggage was now lashed uncomfortably to his back. He had debated with himself whether to stick with the family he'd met on the train, and had decided against it—not that they seemed inviting. He had lost them while he'd been waiting in the queue for the telephone.

At this time of year the journey through the mountain pass was supposed to take two days, for a fit man, with only half of the second day above the snowline. For a fit man. Most of the emigrants he'd seen were, in one way or another, not fit men. They could count on three days, and a whole day going through last winter's snow. Or this autumn's, if the weather turned bad.

A pair of jet fighters from the southwest streaked across the Massif at five hundred meters, well below his vantage, flipped up and kept the same height as their bellies flashed by above him. They'd be over the mountains in seconds, above Junopolis in minutes. On the other hand, they might not come back.

A little while later the rough path took him along the bottom of a deep cleft, with a sharp upward slope. As he toiled up the slithering scree, he was aware, from the cliffs at either hand, of an inescapable sense of presence that made him look around, again and again, to see whether he was being followed, or watched. He was alone, and knew he was alone. There was no sound but the drip of water, no smell but the metallic scent of wet algae, no presence but the countless trillions of microorganisms and nanobacteria in all the crevices of the rockface; no communication but the radiation of their minute electrical potentials, and from the piezoelectric noise of the stresses in the rock itself. It was a natural and spontaneous lithomancy, and it carried no rumors to him.

12

Rocket Science

T HE MIND OF the world is a consciousness which emerges from the
interactions of the biosphere and the lithosphere of life-bearing
terrestrial-type planets such as this one. It is similar to that of the smaller
celestial bodies, the minds which some of you call the gods. Unlike
them it is incoherent. Unlike them it is capable of manipulating very
large energies, and of forming real images from plasma generated by
atmospheric or tectonic polarities and hallucinatory virtual images from
the effects of these electrical potentials on the nervous systems of animals. Its response to the intrusion of new and unfamiliar intelligent
species, especially those using quantum manifold devices, is to generate
real and virtual images of them. It is excitable, unpredictable, playful,
and violent. Its communications are confusing and in part subjective on
the part of the percipient. It is what produces phenomena such as the
'saurs who were here already,' of which the Salasso saur spoke, and it
is producing such phenomena now in response to the skiffs of our expedition. We thought you knew," said Mr. Orange.

"We didn't," said Matt. "None of us did." His glare focused on the
saurs. "Am I right?"

"We did not know that there was a god in the world," said Salasso.
"And we did not know what it was capable of."

"All right," said Matt. He turned again to the Multiplier. "What I
thought we were doing was surveying the planet and simultaneously
generating a degree of paranoia and mass hysteria which would at least
weaken the credibility and unity of the New Babylon regime, and thus
give us more possible points of contact and support. What did you think
we were doing?"

"Very much the same," said Mr. Orange. "With the addition that we knew that the mind of the world New Earth would generate many real and virtual images which would be quite unpredictable and uncontrollable and which could result in much military and political instability such as coups and wars and so forth, thus degrading the system's defenses to a point which would enable an easy assault by your and our main forces."

"*That* was your idea of an elegant invasion plan?"

"Yes," said the Multiplier. "It would have led to large numbers of deaths on the opposing side without great risk to our forces."

"We were kind of hoping," said Matt, "to accomplish our objectives without large numbers of deaths on any side."

"Ah," sighed Mr. Orange. "That makes a difference."

He scurried back to the other aliens and rapidly conferred by touch, then rotated to face the humans and saurs again.

"Death is different for us because our memories are distributed. It is not easy for us to bear in mind at all times that this is not so for you."

"Oh yes," said Ramona. "You'll have noticed how careful humans are to avoid killing each other in large numbers. Just out of idle curiosity—I had the impression you had picked up from Matt's memories some idea of something similar that happened on Earth—all kinds of strange phenomena that taunted and baffled the military forces and excited the populace. How did that not lead to wars and coups and so forth?"

"Did it not?" said Mr. Orange. "We had not formed from the Matt Cairns' memories an impression that the twentieth century was a period of political and military stability. However, as you have been told, the past is not of great interest to us. We may have misunderstood the probable causes of events."

A babble of speculative conversation ensued. Mikhail Telesnikov stood up and raised his fists to his forehead.

"Friends," he said, "let's agree with the Multipliers that the past is not a priority. The only history I'm interested in right now is the history that is happening right now, and that we can do something about." He waved a hand at the radio. "Armed clashes are beginning already. New Babylon and its neighbors could be at war within minutes or hours. We have to intervene right now to calm things down."

"Yes!" shouted Ramona. "Tell us a way to intervene that won't make things worse, why don't you!"

"I have an idea," said Susan. "We could just land somewhere real public, and tell them the truth. By the time the rest of the Bright Star Cultures arrive, we might well have convinced them it wasn't a threat."

"In principle that's a good idea," said Telesnikov, surprising her. "Unfortunately I don't see any of the major powers giving us mass media access to put our case, or even access to the political leaderships. We'd more likely just disappear instantly into the maw of the security apparatuses."

Matt slapped Mikhail's shoulder. "Brilliant!" he said. "That's exactly what we have to do."

"What?" asked Mikhail, voicing the general feeling.

" 'Disappear instantly into the maw of the security apparatuses,' " said Matt. "Now *that*'s a way of getting their undivided attention."

"It's not one I care to try," said Telesnikov. "We need to think this through very carefully. These plasma-cannon bolts are obviously—or at least ostensibly—aimed at what seem to be skiffs. Now there is no way I can think of that the forts in New Earth geostationary orbit—there are three, as far as I know—can be spotting them directly. They must be responding to information relayed from ground observation, probably radar. If we could take out these radar stations, we could blind the forts to anything happening in the atmosphere or on the surface. That's one vulnerability. Second, New Babylon has a launch facility on the coast of Genea, at the equator. If it's put out of action the orbital forts will eventually run out of supplies, and the farthest away—the ones out on the moons and asteroids—are likely to run out fastest."

"Other way round," said Matt. "They're likely to be more self-sufficient. Also, they'll have local resources, maybe even water ice."

The three Cosmonauts went into a brief technical bicker.

"All right," said Telesnikov, "we don't know. My point stands—the launch facility is a choke point. We should consider ways of taking it out."

"Before we do that, assuming we can," said Ramona dryly, "we'd do well to think through the politics. New Babylon's Space Defense may be aiming at skiffs, or what it thinks are skiffs, but it's actually hitting towns and villages and bits of random countryside in Illyria. It's risking war with Illyria. That strikes me as one hell of a big step to take in response to a few UFO phenomena, especially as Illyria seems quite ready to pick up the gauntlet."

Susan and Telesnikov nodded.

743

"They certainly are," Susan said. "And the guy I spoke to was pretty skeptical about the skiffs being from what they call the Spiders. I don't think he was in much of a minority. He sure didn't think he was."

"Okay," said Ramona. "So what else do we have to go on? New Babylon's Senate, no less, isn't afraid of antagonizing Illyria. That strongly suggests Illyria doesn't have nukes. But still, there's a sort of paranoid intensity about this reaction that strikes me as being about more than a few skiffs and so forth—ours or otherwise—seen over Illyria, and even over New Babylon's own territory. They're worried about something we don't—"

"Hey!" shouted Ann Derige, who was sitting closest to the radio, which had become unregarded background noise to everyone else. "Listen to this!"

She turned up the volume. It was the same news channel as Susan and Telesnikov had tuned into an hour or two earlier, in Junopolis.

"—Minister responded immediately to the news just in of a devastating explosion in downtown New Babylon with the following statement: 'We deplore the damage and loss of life in the capital of our neighbor and stand ready to offer all necessary humanitarian assistance on request. The present defensive mobilization of Illyrian armed forces is suspended by Ducal decree and with immediate effect. The Ministry of Defense strongly rebuts initial suggestions in New Babylonian reports that Illyrian forces are responsible for the explosion and repeats its longstanding categoric assurance that Illyria does not possess, and does not seek to acquire, nuclear weapons and supports the monopoly of such weapons by New Babylon's Space Defense Force. The Illyrian armed forces are hereby ordered to take no actions other than in immediate self-defense and to await further orders.' Now we go live to our correspondent in New Babylon, where—I'm sorry, the line appears to be down. Please stay tuned for further news flashes."

The voice was replaced by somber music.

"Fuck, fuck, fuck," said Matt. He looked utterly dismayed, his face pale and running with sweat.

Ann was already turning the dial.

"—small nuclear device aimed squarely between the HQ of the Ninth and the Space Authority building, both of which are now completely destroyed along with approximately two square kilometers of the eastern end of the island, which until half an hour ago was the administrative and business center of the entire Republic. So far, all known potential opponents have denied responsibility and—"

"—initial radioactivity readings confirm suspicions that—"

"—pointed out that the sole possessor of nuclear weapons is the Space Defense Force itself and strongly hinted that this may be related to an internal power struggle rather than current international tensions—"

"—possibility of a Spider attack has not been discounted, sources close to the Patriarch have averred—"

"—continuing emergency launches from the rocket base at Kairos—"

Telesnikov stalked over and turned the radio off. "Shut up, everyone!" he shouted above the chorus of protest. "We need a few minutes to think without all that speculation. Oh, all right, Ann—plug in your phones and tell us when any *news* comes in, okay?"

Ann glanced at Phil Johnson; the captain nodded.

"Suppose we believe the Illyrians," Telesnikov went on. "If it wasn't them, who was it? We can rule out the Lapithians and the lesser powers of the Genean League, they don't have the capability. I very much doubt that our own forces—unless the Bright Star Cultures have changed fundamentally in the past century—would do that even if they were here already, and I still think we would know if they were here already. They'd make some effort to contact us, and they could detect the presence of our skiffs. That leaves the only power we know for sure has nukes or equivalent—kinetic-energy weapons, heavy-duty plasma cannon or whatever—the New Babylon Space Defense Force itself. And there's only one reason I can see why they'd do something so drastic as to take out their own official headquarters—they believe that the enemy, the aliens, the Spiders—us—have somehow subverted it."

"There is another possibility," said Salasso. "You mentioned kinetic-energy weapons. It's possible that this was not a nuclear strike but a large meteor which was too fast for the orbital forts to stop, or too small for them to detect until it was too late."

"Yes," said Telesnikov heavily, "that's a possibility. But if it was a meteor strike the SDF would be saying so loud and clear. If they do, fine, in a sense. We can actually help if the gods are attacking, and it's help they'd be likely to accept. If it's the SDF itself that's attacking, we have to stop them before they do more damage, and stop them without destroying the orbital forts. That means jumping Illyrian troops into the forts."

"How do we let the Illyrians know about this offer?" Ramona asked.

"We do what Matt suggested," said Telesnikov. "We vanish into the maw of their security apparatus. Volunteers?"

Susan jumped up. "I'll go, in case they need convincing about the—about what happens when—"

Telesnikov nodded. "Understood. Matt? It was your idea."

Matt shook his head. "I'm sorry," he said. "I think this is all my fault, and I'm pretty useless for the moment."

"Okay," said Telesnikov. "Take it easy."

If Mikhail and Susan hadn't reported back by the end of the day, or if general war broke out, the others were to use their initiative; if all else failed, as Telesnikov pointed out, they could always navigate a jump to the nearest habitable system in the Bright Star Cultures' likely path, and warn them off. Some of the Multipliers took this as a hint to start constructing astronomical instruments from improbable materials.

Less than half an hour after the plan had been finalized, Susan found herself looking down at the garish rooftops of Junopolis.

"The building from which the greatest density of encrypted microwaves emanate is over here," said Mr. Blue, guiding the invisible machine toward a large yellow office block on whose roof—and, Susan guessed, unnoticeable from the street—dish antennae bristled.

"Are you sure it's not the television station?" she asked, half joking.

The Multiplier rattled some fingers like a bunch of twigs. "Television is not a major medium in Illyria. The population seem to have retained the traditional saur prejudice against it. In any case, the television tower is there."

She looked where it had pointed, to a tall building on whose roof meter-high neon letters spelled out "Television Tower."

"Oh, right," she said, somewhat abashed.

The rooftop stabilized a couple of meters below her feet. Her knees were knocking. She could see them. The plan was brutally simple. They were to gain access to the building from the top, find the most senior person they could, and tell him or her their story, producing their concealed weapons if necessary. They both had their tracking and comms devices rigged with hidden throat mikes, set up to maintain continuous contact on their own encrypted channel—if they called for help Mr. Blue would simply jump the skiff into the building right beside them. The skiff's emergence from a jump in a space occupied by other objects would damage the other objects, but not the skiff. It was, he assured them, something to do with the exclusion principle. Susan hoped he was as certain as he sounded, and also that any falling brickwork or whatever didn't fall on her skull, which as far as she knew, was not protected by the exclusion principle.

"Ready?" said Telesnikov.

They were both wearing the black suits—faked up from plant cellulose by the Multipliers—that they'd used earlier on what Matt had called MIB work. If they looked like intruders, at least they would look like respectable intruders, not Nova Babylonian commandos.

"Yes," said Susan, loosening her tie above the throat mike and patting her shoulder holster.

"Okay."

The hatch's opening was indicated by the inrush of hot city air. They jumped down. The skiff stayed where it was, like part of the mirage off the flat roof. Beneath it some gravel and grit on the tarpaper had been swirled into a complex circular pattern. Telesnikov cast about and led the way through the electronic shrubbery to a two-meter-high wooden box with a door in it.

"Not even locked," he said, and opened it. An alarm shrieked immediately.

"Dammit to hell!"

"Keep going," said Susan.

Telesnikov descended the ladder, looked around and beckoned. When she closed the door behind her, the alarm stopped.

"I don't think that's a good sign," said Telesnikov. "Shutting off when the intruders are inside strikes me as what Matt would call a *feature.*"

They were in a corridor dimly lit with caged electric lights and a red light at a metal door at the end. The door was thick and it was locked from the other side.

"There's a CCTV camera up there," Susan pointed out.

"Oh yes," said Telesnikov. "Well, let's see if anyone's watching."

They both stepped back from the door and stood waving their hands above their heads. After a minute they heard a lot of heavy steps coming up stairs. Something clunked against the other side of the door.

"Step back and put your hands on your heads," a voice boomed, amplified by the door as well as by whatever was behind it.

They complied. After some grating and clicking the door banged open to reveal two men with black visors and protective gear and rifles. The rest of the squad were literally backing them up, muzzles poking over the top of the stairwell.

"Who are you and how did you get in?"

"Cosmonaut Mikhail Telesnikov of the Cairns Fleet, Mingulay," said Mikhail. "And Susan Harkness, mission recorder. We're part of the advance party of the Bright Star Cultures. There's a Spider skiff above your roof. If has unlimited stealth and jump capability. If I ask—or if its pilot hears any sounds of violence—it can jump into the exact space where you're standing now, about two meters in front of me. I suggest you lower your weapons and take us to the most senior available officer of the Illyrian Defense Department."

Five blank visors and five black rifle muzzles glared back at them.

"All right," said the squad leader. "We'll have to search you first."

"We both have pistols in shoulder holsters," said Telesnikov.

Two of the men stepped forward and frisked them while a third and fourth kept everyone covered. They took the pistols and then tugged off the mikes and the adapted radios.

"Hey!" said Susan as the radio was pulled from her inside jacket pocket. "That wasn't—"

"Shut the fuck up."

The squad leader and his mate tossed the devices, then the pistols, back to the others.

"*Now* we take you—"

Susan heard an enormous crash behind her and hit the deck. Telesnikov's reflexes were just as fast. A split second later, the rifles opened up. Susan clasped her arms over her head and waited for it to stop. After a few seconds and a yelled command, it did. An implacable grinding noise, accompanied by more crashing, continued. Susan raised her head slightly. The two men who'd searched them were crouched at the top of the stairwell; one of them had an arm raised. He motioned to Susan and Telesnikov to get up. As they scrambled to their feet they glanced back and saw the skiff advancing down the corridor toward them. It was a lot wider than the corridor and on both sides its forward edge was cutting through plaster and lath, concrete and steel, like a plowshare through black earth. Telesnikov faced it and waved his hands above his head. The skiff stopped.

Glass tinkled somewhere.

"*Now* you take us," said Telesnikov.

"You may go," the Director of Military Intelligence told the two visored guards who'd escorted Susan and Mikhail to his office.

"But sir—"

An upraised hand and a mild querying look sent the two guards out. The Director sat back down. The office was modest, its only distinguishing feature what was undoubtedly the best view over Junopolis that the building afforded. An uncluttered desk, a leather office chair, a couple of smaller chairs and a few bookcases and a filing cabinet. The Director, a man in his thirties, was likewise modest in a dark suit with a minimum of slashes and padding. Only his ringletted red hair and luxuriant but neatly trimmed beard made him look vain, almost foppish.

"Please, please," he said. "Take a seat." He flicked his fingertips as though shaking off water. "And your weapons and radios." It was like he didn't want them spoiling the layout of his desk.

They sat down. "My name is Attulus," he said. "I have come here from a much busier and more crowded room, as you can imagine. So let's get down to business. The guard relayed what you claimed, and I'm willing to believe it. A Spider skiff on my top floor is . . . compelling. Tell me more. Fast."

He listened intently as they told him.

"This is fascinating," he said. "And your plan is feasible—if your alien allies can jump a skiff with this precision, they can jump right inside the orbital stations, whose location of course we know. But how can you ask us to trust you that"—he wiped a hand wearily across his face—"you're not as much of a menace to the rest of humanity as Volkov always warned?"

Susan stared at him with a feeling of angry helplessness, a sense that she had walked through a mirror into a world where truth was no argument. It was the world to which Matt had taken her, when they had walked through the door into the house of that frightened latifundia chairman and messed with the poor guy's head. He'd had a picture of Volkov among the family photographs on top of his television, and had squirmed when Matt had casually asked him about it. The older cadres were still loyal to the Engineer.

At that moment, Susan realized something that she wanted to blurt out right there, but it would have taken too long to explain her intuition and her reasoning. It would have to wait, and she had a more urgent point to make.

"We're not asking you to trust us," she said. "We're offering you a chance to get *your troops* inside the orbital forts. If by the time the Bright Star Cultures arrive we have not persuaded you, that's our problem. Besides, you must have information by now from Traders who have encountered the Bright Star Cultures."

Babylon, and been obeyed? Who is the one person who had more authority than the Senate and the President and all the rest of them put together?"

"Yes, informally, when he was alive, but—" said Matt.

"Come on Matt, Mikhail, you knew him, you've told me all about him. The consummate political Cosmonaut. He would never have fallen to a palace coup. Oh, the coup might have been carried out, the plotters might even have thought they'd succeeded, but Volkov would have been ahead of them. And I'll bet he's been up in one of these orbital forts for all the decades since. The SDF *must* have been Volkov's power base. So I think you and the brave lads there are going to face absolutely fanatical resistance in at least one of the forts."

"That or some very clever negotiation," said Mikhail, with a skeptical grin that partly humored her.

"You overestimate him," said Matt, half to Mikhail and half to Susan. "He had a way of setting things in motion that ran away from him. That's what happened with the Modern Regime, I don't doubt. But, yeah, I can see he could still be alive—hell, he still has supporters in the bureaucracy and the SDF, sure, if he was alive he could get them to do it if anyone could . . . but why should he attack New Babylon? Especially with a crisis like this. If he wanted to make his comeback he could do it without wiping out the people who ousted him. I mean, the old President was just about dead of—"

He stopped, and his hand jolted so hard he splashed hot coffee over it—Susan could just see the half-started gesture of slamming his fist on his palm.

"That's it!" he said. He was smiling for the first time in days, for the first time since it had all gone wrong, and now he was straightening up, a weight off his shoulders.

"Yes," said Susan. "I just thought of it when we were speaking to Attulus, and I mentioned the Traders who'd met our side already."

Mikhail and Phil frowned at them.

"You've lost us, you two," Phil said.

"Whoever hit New Babylon," she said, "wasn't just aiming to wipe out the central apparat. They were aiming to wipe out people in the apparat infected by the Multipliers. People right at the top."

She hardly had time to explain the rest—to the Marines as well as to her friends—before whistles sounded, and the run for the skiffs began.

• • •

Recording events from the hangar was a safe but uncanny and terrible way of being a war correspondent. The skiffs blurred into their jumps and returned for more troops about once every minute as they zipped back and forth at lightspeed between the geostationary and lunar forts, then in longer jumps as they took on the Trojan-orbit fort and, at even longer intervals, two of the three asteroid bases. It was from the Trojan fort that the first casualties from both sides came back, sliding in blood down from the skiffs' hatches. The dozen or so Multipliers who weren't piloting pounced on the wounded men and began repairing them without waiting for permission. Ramona and Susan rushed around explaining. All that the combat medics could do, and all they had to do, was hold down thrashing, screaming men while the Multipliers worked. After the first few terrifying miracles, soldiers who'd been mangled or dead minutes earlier could reassure the new arrivals that the Spiders were doing them good. Even some of these revenants were frightening—men with only a scaffolding of Multiplier offspring, a webwork of minute Spiders passing blood and bits along where parts of their bodies had been, visibly being repaired on the run. Some of the revived Marines went back into action, carried away by the fever of the benign infection, the ecstasy of the strange vision through their rebuilt eyes. There were still deaths—not even the Multipliers could do anything for a blasted-out brain. Corpses were laid out one by one, but they were not stacked up by the score, as without the Multipliers they certainly would have been.

After about half an hour of fighting, the first prisoners began to come back—initially the few armed men on the geostationary forts, then SDF cosmonauts and technicians, then a sudden flood from the Trojan fort and the two lunar stations. The space marines had fought hard, but the sheer surprise and the prisoners' shock as they arrived in the hangar after being thrown bodily aboard the skiffs made them compliant. As the nearer stations were secured forty-odd soldiers piled into four skiffs that were assigned to the first two asteroid forts, one only five light-minutes away, the other twenty-five. Matt traveled with one pair of skiffs, Telesnikov with the other. The departures were staggered by twenty minutes, so that they would hit each fort simultaneously.

A skiff from the first squad returned, with casualties and prisoners, after about half an hour. One of the prisoners, triumphantly collared by Matt, was Volkov.

The two Cosmonauts came off the skiff still screaming at each other. Blood ran from Volkov's mouth. Matt's pistol muzzle had been jammed against his upper lip, but despite that, he was still yelling. What they were saying was hard to make out but Matt's most oft-repeated epithet was "Murdering commie bastard" and Volkov's was "Spider-loving scumsucking traitor son of a bitch." Two Marines rushed up and parted them. Matt used his advantage as he was being dragged off to kick Volkov as hard as he could in the crotch. Volkov gasped and doubled up, almost wrenching himself away from the Marine, then shouted through a spray of vomit.

"You haven't won, you bastards! Give up while you still have a chance!"

"Jeez," said Matt, shrugging off his restraint, "I should kill him now."

"Do that if you want, you can't stop us!"

Then Volkov slumped, whether with delayed shock from the kick or in passive resistance it was hard to say, but at least he shut up. He was dragged off and snap-cuffed with the other prisoners.

"What happened?" Susan asked. One of the Marine officers rushed up.

"He got an appeal out before we got him," Matt said. "A call to the citizens and military of New Babylon to rise against the Spider-infiltrated remnants of the de Zama clique and resist their Illyrian pawns. Don't know how effective it'll be, but it may be taken up."

"Damn," said the officer. "Civil war and national resistance in the Republic is not what we need."

Matt jumped back on the skiff at the head of a fresh squad. Both skiffs returned shortly afterward, the station secure. The squad led by Telesnikov came back from the farther station in a bad way. They'd won, but they'd had a struggle getting back through howling, thinning air and then, briefly, vacuum as the defenders suited up and evacuated the air from the areas of fighting. The Multipliers had a lot of repairing and reviving to do.

"They got warnings off," said Telesnikov. "The third station will be ready for us, they'll have suited up and blown all the air out and they'll have armed men in every compartment."

"How many suits have you got?" the Marines' CO asked.

"Ten," said Johnson. "And our people aren't well-trained in them, let alone for fighting in them. Training up your guys would take too long."

"Could take the other sides' suits," said Susan, looking at some prisoners being taken off the *Investigator*, to which they'd been shuttled by a skiff on site.

Matt and Telesnikov were shaking their heads.

"Same problems, plus sabotage and creative misunderstanding," said Matt.

"Do we need to take the third station right away?" Ramona asked. "It's not like it can hit New Earth from the other side of the sun."

Matt glared at her. "You *know* this? I don't. It has onboard nukes which I don't want to see coming our way, even in a couple of months. And it can zap the other stations with its plasma cannon. No way are we going to leave it a minute longer than we have to. We'll have to nuke it from the outside."

"We don't have—" began the Marine commander. Then he grinned. "We do now."

"You'll need someone to arm it," said Ramona.

Matt and Telesnikov stalked off among the prisoners. After a few minutes in a clamor of raised voices, the two returned, to everyone's surprise, with Volkov. His arms were in their grip and his wrists were cuffed at his back, there was blood on his chin and bruises were swelling on his face, but he still looked defiant and dangerous.

"He has something to tell us," said Matt. "The others bear him out, for what that's worth."

"You've got all this wrong," Volkov said. "The strike on New Babylon did not come from us, I swear. When you have time you can check the stations' computers, check their arsenals, and you can verify what I say. All the nuclear weapons are there and accounted for. And none of them are small tactical nukes. They're all multimegaton asteroid-busters. What hit New Babylon today was a large meteor traveling very fast, punching vertically through the atmosphere. Unless it was a quite extraordinary accident, it came from the gods. They are capable of that, we know they are, they can line up orbital instabilities over decades ready to strike at will. There could be more at any moment, or worse. You know they have been preparing something, you've seen the comets!"

"Why should they strike now?" Matt asked. "It seems another extraordinary coincidence that they should finally get around to hitting New Babylon decades after you started annoying them and just when we happen to be—"

He stopped. "Oh, shit."

"Oh shit indeed," snarled Volkov. "They know you're here, and they're fighting on *your side*." He glared around. "Or you're fighting on theirs—that's what all my men concluded when you attacked the only defenses we have!"

"The defenses didn't work today," Susan said.

Volkov looked at her curiously. "They're not much use against something that small and fast. They're very useful indeed against something bigger and slower. Salasso can tell you all about major impact events."

The saur responded with a thin smile.

"All right," said Matt, "but if it wasn't you and it wasn't a nuke, why the hell didn't you say so?"

"I have to admit that we were still considering whether we could wring some political advantage from the misconception," said Volkov.

Matt let go of Volkov's arm and stood back. "You know," he said, "I can believe that. You haven't changed."

Volkov nodded. "Be that as it may, I can help you now. If you take me to any of the captured stations, I can use its comms to tell the remaining orbital station what is actually going on, and order them to accept your boarders without resistance."

"They'll do that?" said Telesnikov.

"Oh yes," said Volkov. "One thing you got right, they'll do what I tell them."

"Even if it means handing over the station to the enemy?"

Volkov snorted. "New Babylon's decapitated and in convulsions. Illyria is now the only power that can take charge of space defense— it's *our side*, not the enemy."

"Who is the enemy?" Susan asked. Quick, to record this, to get the history. . . .

Volkov's eyes narrowed. "The Spiders—the Bright Star Cultures may be the enemy. We'll see how that works out, and I would strongly recommend that these gentlemen"—he nodded at the Illyrian officers— "bear that in mind, whatever the tactical alliances of the moment. But the enemy of the moment and for the future, our certain and eternal enemies, are the gods. And we have good reason to think the gods have more of these strikes lined up. We have to hit back at them immediately and terribly, to make them aware that they cannot hit us with impunity."

"How can we do that?" Matt asked.

Volkov grinned suddenly. "You were looking for someone who could arm a nuke."

"This time I'm coming along," Susan said.

Volkov had been to the nearest orbital station and back, and a positive reply to his message had come back after over an hour's inevitable delay. They had used this time to mount an asteroid-buster warhead to

756

one of the *Investigator*'s ship-to-ship missiles, and to download the location of an asteroid that, according to Space Defense, had an indwelling god. The plan was for Mr. Orange to plot a jump to within a kilometer of the asteroid, fire off the missile with a hacked one-minute fuse, and jump back instantly to ten thousand kilometers, just ahead of the light.

"You're not coming," said Matt.

"It's not up to you," said Susan.

Phil Johnson, with some reluctance, was persuaded. Susan followed him, Ann, and Matt aboard. The rest of the crew consisted only of Salasso, Volkov, Mr. Orange, and Obadiah Hynde the rocketeer.

Crouched in the cockpit, videoing through the window, Susan fought the sense of panic and strangeness at jumping from the ground in a human-built ship. The scene in the hangar, with soldiers and revenants and prisoners milling about in the dusk and skiffs blurring in and out of jump, was bizarre enough to make her queasy even without this. The cabin lights were out, so that they could see the asteroid's night side.

"Coordinates set," said Mr. Orange.

"Coordinates entered and checked," said Matt.

"Missile primed and deployed," came Obadiah's voice on the speaker.

"Comms open and clear," said Salasso.

"Jump," said Phil.

The next thing that appeared in Susan's viewfinder was a dim-lit wall of rock. The impression that it was falling on them was overpowering.

"Fuse set to one minute and counting down," said Volkov.

"Release missile grapple," said Phil.

"Missile released," said Obadiah. "Holding fire."

Phil and Ann looked at each other. The first ten seconds of countdown ticked away.

"I can't make this decision," said Phil. "Handing over command to First Contact Convener."

"Nuke the fucker," said Matt.

"Mr. Hynde," said Salasso gently, "fire the missile on my responsibility, and on my mark. Is this entirely understood?"

"The missile trigger," said Obadiah shakily, "is the red-handled knife switch on the left of the control panel."

Susan was never able to tell from her recording whether it was Matt's hand, or Salasso's, or Volkov's, that reached the switch first.

13

Blood of Spiders

T HE MIST THINNED. Gaius Gonatus walked a few more steps down
the rough trail and found that he was below the cloud, and looking
over forested foothills to the moors of southeastern Illyria. The wire of
the refugee camp glinted in the valley just a couple of kilometers below.
It seemed farther away than the entire journey behind him. He wondered
if the perception of distance to be traveled was logarithmic. He wondered if "logarithmic" was the appropriate analogy. Pondering this
thought kept him going until he reached "asymptopic" and the gate.

The guard had the green helmet of the Civil Corps. He had watched
Gaius's slow approach without moving to help.

"Welcome to Illyria," he said, without moving his eyes.

"Fuck you," said Gaius. "I'm Illyrian."

He lurched through the open gate and into the reception area. His
feet had just been examined for frostbite and treated with disinfectant
for blisters and cuts when the Department's man in the camp found him
and loaded him onto a big military autogyro reeking of paraffin and full
of North Genean mercenaries. He was back in New Babylon in two
hours. The autogyro landed between craters at the main airport. The
sound of distant small arms fire came from several directions. The mercenaries deployed to the perimeter. Gaius limped to the terminal building. Illyrian, Lapithian, and Genean League soldiers were everywhere.
Attulus met him in the lounge. The window was broken but the bar was
open.

"What the hells happened downtown?" asked Gaius, as soon as the
first brandy was inside him and the next was in front of him.

"Tactical nuke," said Attulus. "Volkov is alive, apparently. He ordered the strike from orbit."

Gaius felt the back of his neck tighten, hunching his shoulders against a blow from above. He straightened up.

"It's all right," said Attulus. "Volkov's safe in our hands. So are the space stations."

"How?"

"Mingulayan advance guard. It was their skiffs we saw. They came in on our side. They and their furry alien friends."

Atullus scuttled his fingers across the tabletop. Gaius closed his eyes and opened them again.

"Why did Volkov nuke his own capital?"

"He made an impassioned television broadcast just before he was captured, calling on all good Volkovists to rise." Attulus waved at the window. "Which they have. He claimed that the central apparat was riddled with people who had sold out to the Spiders, starting at the top. The very top."

"Good gods above. Where did he get that idea from?"

"You should know, old chap," said Attulus.

Gaius took a gulp of brandy to stop the hot rise of his gorge. "They tapped my call?"

Attulus grinned thinly. "Nothing so melodramatic. As soon as we got your call we passed every juicy detail, garbled rumor, and reckless speculation to our contacts in the Volkovist old guard in the SDF. I must admit, we didn't expect to get quite so much detonation for a dinar, but there you go."

Gaius said nothing. His mouth had dried up completely. A burst of small arms fire echoed from beyond the perimeter.

"The same with Volkov's call to his supporters to attack the Regime's degenerate apparatus. Very convenient for us. That's exactly what we want them to do. With the Regime's air force in disarray and the space stations in our hands, we've been able to just walk in. Unopposed air and sea landings, mostly. Of course he also called on patriots to attack the aristocratic reactionary invaders, but our boys are giving them something of an education in confining their attention to easier targets. It's not just the old guard, of course. We've won, but there's no one left to surrender to us. Various units of the Regime's forces and local militias are running around shooting at each other for tediously obscure reasons. All sorts of scores are being settled out there. Lampposts and petrol, you know the sort of thing. Very messy. But it means we're the only force which can maintain order, so we'll end up on top of the heap."

"Some heap," said Gaius. "And what about the Bright Star Cultures?"

Attulus shrugged. "The Mingulayans and the Multipliers—I gather that's what the Spiders call themselves—are presently firmly under the guns of the Ducal Marines, though they may not realize it yet. They can't move against us, that's the main thing."

"I was thinking of their main force," said Gaius.

"Well," said Attulus, "they evidently thought New Babylon's Space Defense was a threat to that main force. It's now *Illyria*'s Space Defense—which rather suggests we can handle them when they do turn up."

"We're not going to *fight* them?"

"Not for me to say, old chap. Political decision. Point is, we have the option." Attulus frowned. "Same applies here, of course. Until we're quite certain that the Spiders aren't going to eat our brains and turn us into drooling zombies, we need to keep a very firm grip on people with baby Spiders swimming around in their blood. Without going quite as far as Volkov and his brave band of renegades, one can understand his concern about the ex-Traders and de Zama's camarilla. Potential enemy within, and all that."

"I don't know about the ex-Traders," said Gaius, "but surely de Zama and her lot are all dead under the rubble."

"I rather think not," said Attulus. "If they are, they'd be the first ruling clique in history to stay in their top-floor offices while expecting war within hours. We may hope so, of course, but it would be foolish to count on it." He smiled. "Which is where you come in, Gonatus. You know your way around the city—what's left of it. Find the de Tenebre woman and her sept. Find any Traders or senior Modern Society members that you can. Find them, and pull them in."

"I may possibly need a revolver," said Gaius. He looked at his feet. "A decent pair of boots would not go amiss."

Attulus snorted. "We're not asking you to do it on your own. We're rounding up both categories as part of the peacemaking operation—protective custody, detention centers, fair trials, health inspections—you know the score. All you have to do is winkle out the Spider people. Plenty of backup on call, and a couple of good assistants."

He stood up and beckoned. Gaius turned to see two junior officers of the Illyrian Army bestir themselves from a nearby table and head toward where he sat.

"John Terence and Matthew Scipion," said Attulus, introducing them. "Sound chaps. They'll look after you." He stuck out his hand. "Must be off. See you around."

The low-slung, open-topped Army vehicle careened down Astronaut Avenue, swerving in and out between abandoned cars and fallen masonry. After a certain point all the windows were shattered, their glass covering the street like ice on a refrozen lake, shards crunching under the thick tires. A few hundred meters further, and everything was covered with dust. There was black dust and there was white dust, and here and there a flash of color from something—the side of a car, a scrap of clothing, a sign—that had been momentarily sheltered from the monochrome hurricane. A little further on, the ruins started. All the buildings of the Volkov era and the Modern Regime had been blown away, leaving the granite and marble and sandstone blocks of the ancient city merely damaged.

Closer now, and everything was down. Rubble blocked the streets. People with and without equipment were already—or had been all night—hauling it off chunk by chunk, shovelful by shovelful. Black-furred flying squirrels pawed through it like demonic rescue workers. At the sound of the car, they glanced over their caped shoulders and resumed their sinister rummaging and occasional exultant caw.

Terence pulled up and turned off the engine. They got out. It was the first morning of Gaius's new job—he had collapsed with exhaustion the previous afternoon and slept all night—and he had felt obliged to see the destruction before he settled into any kind of routine. Terence and Scipion had not queried his motive.

They ascended the rubble barrier—it was like going up a very unreliable staircase—and paused at the top. The sun was in their eyes.

"Gods above," said Gaius.

For about a kilometer, there was not even rubble. The very stones had been pulverized to jagged lumps, fist-sized and smaller. Faint traces of radial lines indicated the direction of the blast, outward from a central crater several meters deep. A dozen or so yellow-painted ground vehicles and two green autogyros stood about at random points within the blast radius, as though they had miraculously survived it. Whatever initial impulse had taken them there had ebbed at the sight, leaving them stranded. There was simply no possibility of anything's being alive here. Not even the carrion-eating flying squirrels were looking into it.

Gaius crunched and slithered forward down the atomic scree, occasionally stopping to peer and poke at the ground. Terence and Scipion came after him.

"What are you looking for?" Terence asked.

Gaius straightened and put the heels of his hands on the small of his back. "Spiders."

There were no Spiders. The three men traversed the blast area in two directions and returned to the vehicle in a couple of hours. A stench had risen with the sun, but it didn't come from the blast area. It came from the wider area around it, the next circle of hell.

"Boss," said Scipion, after draining a water bottle, "shouldn't we get to work?"

"That was work," Gaius said. His back ached and his eyes stung. He was beginning to worry, belatedly, about radioactivity. He brushed his palms together briskly. "But you're right. Let's go and look for Spiders somewhere else."

What constituted a safe route through the streets changed by the minute. Scipion crouched on the back seat yelling instructions with a radio-telephone at his ear and a street map in front of him, penciling updated locations of allied occupation troops, Regime loyalists, Regime defectors, Volkovist partisan bands, and gangs of youths who had gone immediately and utterly feral.

For all that, the streets outside the bomb-damaged area and the immediate rescue or recovery operations were busy and, Gaius thought, livelier than they had been before the war. Stalls had sprung up everywhere, selling food, Illyrian goods, and loot. Most businesses were open. Above all people were talking to each other, in ones and twos or in larger groups, in a way he hadn't seen before. They talked to the troops and to the members of the less belligerent, or just temporarily inactive, militias on the corner. Every so often a flurry of shots would clear a street, and then the firefight would continue until superior forces arrived, or would die down of themselves, and people would drift back and resume their activities. Here and there Terence had to swerve or reverse rapidly out of such incidents, or away from scuffles as Illyrian soldiers broke up lynchings, or arrived too late to do more than cut down the bodies of the victims and shoot at the likely—because fleeing—perpetrators.

Eventually the car managed to fall in with a convoy of New Babylonian trucks driven by Illyrian troops and escorted by Lapithian motorcycle outriders and a clattering autogyro high overhead. The convoy took them to a newly built camp on the outskirts. Hundreds of meters square, it was surrounded by four-meter posts with barbed wire still being strung around the outside. Existing buildings had become part of the camp, and soldiers and prisoners were busy erecting prefabricated huts.

Gaius and his men showed their passes and drove in. They parked the car in a big pound and headed for the admin block. The Ducal raptor-claw crest on a sky-blue flag fluttered above it. There was a long list of names to look through, and it was extending with every courier who came in from the screening sheds. The clerks were far too busy to help, and the names they'd typed out had not gone into their long-term memories. They did not put it quite like that.

"Look for de Tenebre," Gaius said. "Any other Trader names you recognize, sure—Rodriguez, Delibes, Bronterre. But de Tenebre is the goods."

Scipion found a cluster of names within half an hour. "De Tenebre, P, F, C, and E," he announced.

Gaius hid his disappointment with a pleased smile.

A clerk was able to tell them, by a quick flip through a card index, that the three people mentioned had been screened and had not yet had their health check, so they were probably in the—

"Oh, and thank *you*, gentlemen," he said to the banging door.

A burly man with ginger hair and a stubborn scowl stood in front of a long table behind which sat medics in white coats.

"Why?" he was saying.

"There's a big demand for blood products," the technician said. "A lot of burns and lacerations and major trauma. Suspected radiation sickness. We need every contribution we can get."

"Ah, I understand that," the man said. "Unfortunately I can't help." He glanced around at three women on the front bench a few steps behind him. "Nor can my w . . . my wife and her friends. We're all Traders, and we've all picked up some nasty bugs on our travels. Always been told not to donate."

"I know that's been the policy," said the technician patiently. She glanced at the impassive Illyrian military policeman at her shoulder. "Nevertheless. This is an emergency and frankly the people down at the hospitals are not worried about malaria or odd tropical diseases. They're *dying* down there for lack of platelets and plasma." She licked her lips.

"Come on, this is just a test. If there's anything really nasty, we'll pick it up. Stick out your hand. It's just a prick in your finger."

The man folded his arms.

"No."

Gaius tapped his shoulder. "Esias de Tenebre?"

"Who the hells are you?"

"Gaius Gonatus, Allied Civil Assistance," Gaius improvised smoothly. "I believe I can help you to find Lydia."

De Tenebre's face convulsed with consternation and rage. "I *know* where Lydia is," he said. "She's in the hospital. Emergency Field Hospital Two, Ward Five. The serious burns unit." He looked away. "You can tell who she is by the name on the end of the bed."

Gaius met his eyes. They were distressed, but calmer than his voice had sounded. "You know she's going to be all right," Gaius said. "And I know that's why you don't want to cooperate here."

Esias tensed and looked around but it was too late. Five military policemen had already surrounded the three women, and Terence and Scipion were closing on his arms.

"Now please come with us," said Gaius. "There's nothing to be afraid of. Only a little prick in your finger."

The building to which Gaius took the four prisoners had been some kind of cattle shed. It stank of herbivore shit, and the electric lamps were few and dim. Gaius dismissed the military policemen with thanks and asked the prisoners to line up against a stack of bales of hay. Under the guns of Terence and Scipion they complied. Gaius shoved a barrel against the door with his foot and sat down on it, cradling a revolver. The polygamist and his three wives were, according to their particulars in the admin files, in their early fifties, but they looked a lot younger. Gaius was not surprised.

"I and these gentlemen," said Gaius, "have been asked by Illyrian Military Intelligence to detain people who are suspected of being infected by the Spiders. What I know, and what these gentlemen don't, is what Spider infection does to people. Citizen Esias de Tenebre, I am about to toss a small knife on the ground in front of you. I strongly urge you not to do anything foolish with it. Instead, I would like you to demonstrate to my colleagues some of the more, ah, spectacular effects of Spider infection."

"Sure," said Esias, picking up the knife. He opened it and tested the blade on his thumb. Then he held up his hand and made a quick, deep slash across the palm. The welling of blood was dark and clear in the yellow light. He clenched his fingers over it, laid the knife back on the trampled straw, and walked over to the two soldiers.

"Boo!" he said, opening his hand.

Childish though the gesture was, it made them jump.

"Five little Spiders," said Esias. He clapped his hand to his mouth, then held it out again, palm upward. "And then there were none."

"He never cut himself," said Terence.

"Good gods," said Gaius. "Please repeat the demonstration, slowly."

"Do I have to?" said Esias. "It bloody hurts."

"Your own fault for leaving open the possibility of a trick," said Gaius. "Do it again."

Esias retrieved the knife and did so, right in front of Scipion and Terence. This time he didn't close his hand.

"Satisfied?" said Gaius.

The soldiers nodded. Esias strolled back to his wives.

"How long have you had this infection?" asked Gaius.

"Ten years," said Esias. He glanced sidelong at his wives. "The ladies, a bit less."

"Now, if—purely hypothetically you understand—I and these gentlemen were to shoot you down where you stand, what would happen?"

Esias paled. "If you were to blow our brains out," he said, "we'd be dead. Otherwise, we'd, well, recover. Not that I would like to try it." His voice became more cheerful as he added, "Blood would get everywhere, you know."

"Oh, I know," said Gaius. "I've seen what happens when people are shot. Blood gets, as you say, everywhere. Especially when brains are, as you say, blown out. And we've seen what happens when your blood is spilt, and starts to dry. How easy would it be, do you reckon, to retrieve or confine or destroy the little Spiders that would swarm from your blood?"

"Not easy at all," said Esias. "They come in all sizes, down to the size of germs, and when they have to survive independently they can be very hard to deal with. You'd have to catch or kill every last one, and I don't know if even burning the barn around us would do the trick. You'd have to, I don't know—"

"Nuke the place," said Gaius. "I know."

He looked over at Terence and Scipion. "As we saw this morning, that seems to do the trick."

"What's all this in aid of?" said Scipion. "I mean, it's very interesting, but where's it getting us?"

"Ah," said Gaius. "In a moment, gentlemen."

He gestured to the de Tenebres. "Please, citizens. Haul yourselves down some bales to sit on, and heave a couple over for my friends here. This may take some time."

It took some time. At the end of it, Gaius and the soldiers returned with the de Tenebres to the medical shed. He led them over to the blood transfusion technicians.

"We've checked them over," he said. "Unfortunate misunderstanding earlier. There's nothing wrong with their blood. In fact, you can put them down as universal donors."

The technician looked at him suspiciously. "Are you certain of that?"

"Absolutely," said Gaius. "We've tested them thoroughly. Take as much as they can spare out of each of them. There's no time to waste. People are dying as we speak. In fact, I can take their donations directly to the hospital—and any others you have ready, of course."

"That would be helpful. Thank you."

"You're welcome," said Gaius. "We're going there anyway."

He had thought the center of the nuclear blast was the most appalling place in the city, but the emergency field hospital was worse. It was a town of tents in a park, and it was full of people who had been pulled from the rubble or who had staggered in or been carried from the flash radius. The serious burns unit was the worst of all. Perhaps not quite. There was a closed ward beyond it, where great efforts had been made to maintain a sterile atmosphere, and to which there was no admittance. Gaius had a horrible suspicion that there was nothing much on offer there but palliative care and opiate euthanasia.

He and his two guardians were stopped by a teenage soldier at the positive-pressure plastic flap of the burns unit. Gaius showed him the chit from the transfusion service.

"Go ahead."

Gaius had three liters of the de Tenebres' blood in sterile plastic bags with valves at the top. The other two had larger quantities of other blood donations from the detainees. They walked over to the harried nurse at the admissions desk, averting their eyes from the scores of beds. The place smelled of disinfectant and of cooked meat. Gaius realized that transfusions would not do the job, would not begin to do the job. He felt sick and feverish, and a little light-headed. He smiled at the nurse and walked on past the desk and up the ward. He took out his knife and slit the bags one by one and squirted and sprayed blood over every patient he passed, aiming at what areas of exposed flesh were visible. He got all the way to the end of the ward before a man in a white coat rushed up.

"*What are you doing?*" he shouted.

"Excuse me," said Gaius, and straight-armed the medic hard as he walked past him, faster now. There was a lot of screaming going on, not all of it from the patients.

"Soldier!" yelled the medic, staggering as he rebounded off the end of a bed. "Guard!"

The young soldier ducked through the flap.

"Stop that man!"

Gaius slashed the remaining bag and whirled it around as the soldier raised his rifle. Blood spattered everywhere, like in the ceremonies of a primitive cult. The bag was empty, and the room was still not bloody enough. He threw the bag against a wall.

"Careful, soldier," said the medic. "He's got a knife."

Terence and Scipion had slipped out. Good. They would do their bit too, in other wards.

"Drop that knife! Sir."

"Please don't shoot," said Gaius. "I'm about to drop the knife."

And he did, but not before he'd managed to slash his left forearm. Down, not across, wasn't that the way? The blood spurted with shocking speed and abundance. The knife clattered. Gaius clawed his arm, trying to keep the wound open as long as possible. There was a loud bang and something hit him very hard in the chest. The last thing he saw before the floor hit his face was a reddish mist.

Gaius awoke from strange dreams that, unlike most dreams, didn't fade from his mind. It hurt to breathe. His left arm throbbed dully. From the woolly feeling in his head he knew that he would be hurting a lot more if he weren't soused in opiates. His eyes opened stickily to focus on Attulus. He found himself suddenly and acutely aware of the man, of his uniqueness and of the universality of the divine spark that blazed behind his eyes, the consciousness that—

"Ah, there you are," said the Director, without enthusiasm.

"Where am I?"

"Illyrian military hospital," said Attulus. "You have been unconscious for two days, from the infection and from your bullet wound."

"Ah." A military hospital. That would explain the green walls and the scratchy sheets. "How much trouble am I in?"

"You really have been very foolish," said Attulus. "Because of your bizarre actions in the burns unit, seven of the patients there have died, in considerable pain. The fever of the infection raised their body temperature to the point where they went into hyperthermic shock. The other patients are making . . . remarkable progress. Similar outcomes are reported from the other major trauma units where Terence and Scipion made their own dramatic blood donations." He sighed. "I suppose it's my fault. I didn't realize you would consider yourself responsible for the New Babylon blast."

"If I hadn't—" Gaius began miserably.

Attulus raised his hand. "Your action was a link in a chain of causes. Even if it had led to the attack, that still would not make you morally responsible. As it happens, it didn't. There was no nuclear attack."

"What?"

"It was a meteor strike. Volkov has said so, and we've confirmed it. The raised levels of radioactivity in the immediate area and in the fallout plume came from pulverized granite. All that your action triggered off was Volkov's call for an uprising."

"Oh, gods," said Gaius. He felt immensely relieved, and at the same time guilty all over again.

"And don't start a whole new round of beating yourself up over the patients who died," said Attulus. "Those who wouldn't have died anyway would have wished they had. Well, perhaps not, if the Spiders' healing powers are as great as your friends claim. Still. You have other problems."

"What—"

"Oh, what you might expect. I'm spending a lot of political capital holding back people who regard you as a menace to the human race."

"To hell with the human race," said Gaius. He tried to raise himself on his elbows, failed and settled for raising his head off the pillow. "What has happened to Lydia de Tenebre?"

"She is one of those who are recovering. She already was, as I'm sure you know."

"I would like to see her."

"You would not," said Attulus. "Not for some time. I assure you of that."

"Where was she?"

"In de Zama's private clinic, somewhat to the west of the blast area. So was de Zama, who had decided, on the brink of death, to accept the Multiplier infection—which she already had heard rumors of, and which her agents were alert to evidence for. Evidence which, one way or another, you or your contact may have inadvertently provided."

Gaius winced, remembering how quickly the agents had come for Lydia after her demonstration of the infection. Or had it been lithomancy that had done it, after all? It no longer mattered. Attulus was still talking.

"Madame President poses something of a problem, as I'm sure you can imagine." Attulus smirked. "One solution that's being floated is to affect not to recognize her. Not diplomatically—physically, we would literally not recognize her when she completes her recovery. The healthy and younger woman who then claims to be de Zama is obviously deluded or an impostor."

Gaius laughed painfully. "It's too late for that."

Attulus fingered his beard. "You're right, of course. Rumors are spreading faster than the infection. People are actively *demanding* the infection, for themselves or for people who are seriously injured. Particularly in New Babylon, there is a huge wish to believe that the Bright Star Cultures are not a threat. In a sense they are throwing off the defensive part of Volkov's legacy, and embracing the part which he used to attract initial support—the quest for longevity and other benefits of biological engineering. One or two Traders who've escaped the dragnet have popped up with wild tales of what the Bright Star Cultures have achieved in symbiosis with the Multipliers—not just in biological matters, but in terms of wealth. I reserve judgment on that, but for the moment we have to accept that it is unstoppably becoming the popular view. Unfortunately it undermines the rationale for space defense, which we now need more urgently than ever."

"Ah, yes," said Gaius. "The meteor."

Attulus nodded. "Precisely. More where that came from, as they say." He twined a ringlet of hair around a finger. "And, ah, this may come as a shock. Volkov and the Mingulayans—with the cooperation of some officers in the Ducal Marines, I'm astonished to tell you—have already taken some preemptive action in that respect."

"They've stopped another meteor attack?"

"No," said Attulus uncomfortably. "They have destroyed a god."

Gaius fell back to the pillow and stared at the ceiling for a while. The knowledge that he, like every educated person, had in the back of his mind suddenly became vivid and visual. He could see, he could imagine, the ring of asteroids and outside it and the farthest planets, the light-year-wide sphere of cometary bodies around the sun. An unknown but large proportion of them, he knew, harbored the strange slow life of the extremophile nanobacteria, and the innumerable fast minds that that life sustained. Trillions of intelligent beings, megayears of civilization, lay within each one, and over all the sum of the minds of each a wider consciousness, a god. To strike at and destroy such a thing, even in self-defense, was blasphemous in its disproportionality, appalling in its hubris. To exterminate all life on a planet to avert a sting— even a fatal sting—from one of that planet's insects would be only the faintest analogy to the shocking scale of the offense.

His hands were clutching the sheets, regardless of the pain in his arm. He wanted to pull the sheets over his head.

"Gods above," he said. "Do the people know this?"

"Not yet," said Attulus.

"Good." Gaius was beginning to calm down, and beginning to think through the ramifications. "There's a serious danger of the returned Volkov—in our hands or otherwise—becoming a popular hero. From our point of view, he was the tyrant, and the Regime since his departure is an improvement. From the point of view of a lot of people in New Babylon, he's a much more ambiguous figure, to say the least. The camarilla and the bureaucracy are hated much more than his memory. The fact that Volkov can still raise a small army of insurgents while many people suspect his supporters in Space Defense of having struck at the heart—or the head—of New Babylon just shows how dangerous things are. The one thing that could shock people out of their deluded fascination with the Engineer is if we can nail the charge of theicide to his forehead." He lay back and thought some more. "The same applies, of course, to the Mingulayans and the Multipliers—also implicated, and also potential contenders for popular influence."

Attulus frowned. "Very astute, Gonatus. But I thought you were sympathetic to the Multipliers—given your propensity for spreading their infection about!"

"You misunderstand," said Gaius. "The Bright Star Cultures are founded on mutual adaptation between the Multipliers and the Mingulayans. There is no reason why there should not be a new culture, based on Multipliers adapting to us." He smiled. "The way the Multipliers reproduce, after all, is to *divide*."

"As I said, I'll reserve judgment on that. The question is, what do we do now?"

Gaius wasn't sure whether the Director really was asking him for advice, or brainstorming for ideas to which he would apply his own judgment. He decided not to flatter himself too much.

"What I would suggest," he said, trying to sit up again and succeeding in propping himself on his right elbow this time, "is that we return Julia de Zama to power as soon as she is fit to be seen in public. New Babylon is unlikely to accept Illyrian occupation for long, memory and gratitude being what they are. She is unpopular, but she is likely to be more popular than us, and an element of stability. And who knows, if she has visibly become rejuvenated she should make a very different impression than when she was a living corpse on a drip. Meanwhile, we make quite clear to her that she is in power on our sufferance, and get as many concessions as possible with regard to internal reforms, trade, and peace. We talk individually to the members of the Bright Star Culture expedition—not all of whom, I am sure, will have gone along with the theicide, and even fewer of whom will be willing to stand by it in the cold light of day. We isolate Volkov and his Mingulayan accomplices, and then we make the evidence of what they have done public. The resulting howl of execration should demoralize the Volkovists, including those in the Space Defense apparatus."

"Hmm," said Attulus, rising from his bedside seat. "This has been a very useful conversation, old chap. You have, as they say, given me something to lay before the Duke. There is one problem. If we expose Volkov and his accomplices as theicides, we shall have no choice but to shoot them."

"Is that a problem?"

Attulus chuckled darkly and went out.

14

The New Moon's Arms

S O THIS IS how it ends," Matt said. "Up against a fucking wall."
He sat warming his feet in front of a fire in a hut in the detention camp on the island in the sound off New Babylon's harbor, smoking a cigarette and drinking whiskey. Susan had brought a good supply of both. Matt's fellow prisoners, Salasso and Volkov, sat with him and her around the fire, variously soothing their angst and ennui with hemp and whiskey. They both nodded philosophically. Their attitude annoyed Susan intensely.

"You shouldn't just give up," she said.

"I've had a long life," Matt said, "and I'm not too bothered by the prospect of not having more of it. I'm after immortality."

Volkov snorted. "Immortality doesn't last, my friend. I've outlived mine already. All it takes is a good hammer."

Salasso, who was evidently turning his last weeks or months to good account by testing the limits of his species' capacity to smoke hemp and stay conscious, turned a loll of the head into a nod. This irritated Susan even more.

"Your crewmates are doing everything they can for you. You could at least pretend you appreciate their efforts."

"We do," said Matt. "But we know they're not going to get anywhere. And so do you."

Susan nodded glumly. She had spoken often enough to Phil, Ann, and the others, who had not been indicted and seemed to feel obscurely guilty about that. They had petitioned and agitated with a sort of Mingulayan Scoffer militancy and naivete, and had almost been lynched themselves. It was like defending child murderers.

"Your appeals might get through the Senate," she said. "And then there's the Assembly of Notables."

The two men guffawed. Salasso's shoulders shook a little. The winter wind rattled the windows; even now, in mid-morning, the place felt like night. Farther up the fuggy hut sat other men, Volkovist prisoners and a few criminals, around other fireplaces and around tables of dominoes and checkers. A few of them read. There was nothing much else to do. All of them kept a respectful distance from the dead men on leave, and had even refrained from overt primate displays when she had walked in. They knew who she was, and who she was with. It was far from her first visit.

She had arrived by a Prison Department launch across the choppy water of the sound, through rain and sleet. New Babylon's winters were cold and pervasively damp, the converse of its hot and pervasively humid summer. She had found a niche there—a politically savvy and, at the same time, inquisitive and naive journalist, especially one from off-world, was just what the newly liberated media wanted—but she hated the place. There was too much of the prehuman in New Babylon, and not only in its architecture. Something in the culture of the place looked back to an age of giants. Too much antiquity, too much continuity, had accumulated here for it to be a place where something new could begin. No wonder Volkov had failed; as, in a different way, de Zama was failing. Susan wanted to get away, to do things that had never been done before, to see new worlds like that of the selkies, outside the Second Sphere altogether and away. At the same time she wanted to stay here, to be with Matt and the others to the bitter end, or to help them avert that end. She wanted her experiences, her very self, to be multiple. She realized she was thinking like a Multiplier.

Matt wasn't, instead contemplating his end with a gloomy relish. He pointed out of the nearest window, which overlooked the sound and afforded through the rain and mist a view of the city's mutilated skyline.

"Look at that," he said. "No matter what the gods do that should make people angry, it only makes them more afraid. Cringing bastards. They're as bad as the fucking saurs, no offense, Salasso."

"No offense is taken," said Salasso. "I despise them myself. Even millions of years after something much worse than genocide was committed against my people, they still regard the gods as good and theicide as the ultimate sin."

"The Multis don't," said Susan. "They would be quite delighted to help you escape. To help *us*. The migration will continue after the Bright Star Cultures arrive, you know. There are people—humans and saurs—who are interested in going with it. Hundreds of light-years, thousands, right across to the next spiral arm. They could take you off the island at a word, and hide you in the forest until—"

"No," said Salasso.

"Not a chance," said Matt. "I'm not running away. I'm not giving these people the satisfaction. Fuck 'em. They either accept self-defense and retaliation as a justification for theicide, or not. If they don't, then nothing we've done means anything anyway. I don't want to live another few hundred years, or whatever I've got left, with the gods behind the back of my neck."

Susan wanted to shake him. "Look, when the Bright Star Cultures arrive, this'll all change. The Illyrians, the Postmodern Regime, whatever—they'll all be overwhelmed by people like us, people who have the Multiplier outlook, not just the infection but the attitudes. Besides, the Cairns Fleet sent us to do a job, and we did it. They can't let you be shot for doing what you had to do."

"Well, yes," said Matt, more cheerfully. "There is that."

They came in the spring, on the eighth day of the month Florida, A.C. 10,350. A swarm of ships like enormous flies—multilegged, wide-bellied, stubby-winged—appeared suddenly in the sky above New Babylon. Susan, walking down Astronaut Avenue in the green fresh post-rainshower morning to cover a story—for Junopolis Calls, ironically enough—about the rebuilding of the Ninth HQ, saw them and saw the city stop around her. She started running. The ships came down so fast they had disappeared behind buildings before she could see where they were landing, but she made a guess that they would head for parks, and so she turned at a corner and ran along a side street of apartment houses and there it was squatting on the grass among the trees like a piece of play equipment for giant children.

Around her other people approached more cautiously. Among them a couple of members of the militia, the Ninth, had unslung their plasma rifles and were talking fast into their radios as they jogged forward, bravely in the circumstances. Susan outran them all, vaulted a low fence and padded across damp trampled grass. The only children in the park this early were quite young. They bawled and clutched at their mothers or stared, thumb in mouth, at the ship. Flying squirrels fled to the trees and chattered abuse.

A curved segment of the side of the ship slid back and a ladder rattled down. Susan was by now close enough to see and hear it. The mechanism was reassuringly clunky and creaky, not like the seamless refinement of the Multiplier or even saur skiffs. It wanted oiling somewhere. A young man in loose green fatigues came down the ladder and stood at the foot of it, blinking in the sunlight and gazing at the buildings and the slowly gathering crowd. From the dark of the hatch at the top other faces, including children's, peered out. The man shaded his eyes with one hand and waved with the other.

"Trade Latin still spoken here?" he called out.

"Yes," said Susan, walking up to him and holding out a hand. She had the camera and the mike on the side of her head. "You should really try to say something more historic. Anyway, welcome to New Babylon."

"Thank you," said the man, shaking hands. "Are you a Mingulayan?"

"Yes," said Susan. "I came here with Matt Cairns."

"Oh my God," the man said, in English. "You're the one who's fucking historic." He waved vaguely in the direction of the harbor. "The First Navigator's ship is coming down over there. You should probably go and report to him."

"Yes," said Susan, stepping back to let the militiamen check the guy out. "I probably should."

The people from the neighborhood were still hanging back about fifty meters away, as if that would make them any safer. The arrival of the ships, and even their appearance, was not unexpected. But it was only when a purple and a red Multiplier descended the ladder, stepping down after a few more adults and children had emerged and stood around on the grass talking to the militiamen and a few other bold locals, that the crowd surged forward, children in the lead. The new arrivals were almost bowled over, and the Multipliers had to move their limbs smartly and skitter about in a slightly threatening manner to clear some space around themselves.

"Make things!" the children were shouting. "Make things for us! Please!"

In the past half-year, since the Crisis (as it was now called, or the Events) the Multipliers who had arrived with the *Investigator* had themselves multiplied by the thousands. They had begun to integrate and educate the numerous free-living small offspring that had resulted from the mass infections that had spread from the recovering casualties of the attack. They had taken up residence in old warehouses and under piers and bridges. They roamed the streets and conjured things out of air and grass and dirt. They talked on the radio and on television, wheezing and waving their limbs like mad old scientists. It was all strange and unsettling, but also in a way reassuring to the people of New Babylon. The whimsical frivolity of their conjurings—here a piece of jewelery, there a machine for making shoes—and their enthusiasm and curiosity as they scuttled around factories and fingered all the pages of all the volumes of the great libraries, all this could not help but charm. The decades of preparing to fight off the dreaded Spiders only increased the relief at the arrival of these engaging octopods. Eight-limbed fuzzy shapes of many different colors had become the most popular type of soft toy.

Susan made her way out of the park and back to the avenue, where she headed for the nearest underground station. Street-level traffic looked like it would remain snarled up for hours. The trains were unaffected. She emerged from the underground at Port Station One and immediately found another crowd surrounding several of the Bright Star Culture ships. Multipliers swarmed in the trees, displacing complaining flocks of flying squirrels. Multiplier skiffs flitted, autogyros hovered overhead, microphones and cameras dangling—she was not filing the story of the century, and she didn't care. The search took a while, during which she ruthlessly used her journalist's card and her elbows. Eventually she found the ship of the First Navigator, and her parents.

They were in a small inner ring of people: the President and her entourage and bodyguards, who had arrived, grandly enough, by skiff. Susan saw Elizabeth and Gregor through the surrounding heads and almost did not recognize them. She had thought of their parting as being over a century long, which of course was irrational—they had traveled the hundred-odd light-years in not much more time than she had, with stops of a few days or weeks while the next course was plotted and new ships were built. Somehow this brought home to her for the first time the sheer force of the Multiplier migration, its quality of being a cascading explosion of thistledown birling through and filling and abhorring the vacuum. Her parents had been changed in those months, perhaps more than she had; they looked younger, almost as young as herself. It was weirder than seeing Matt naked and remembering he was centuries old. She had a shocking premonition that a world in which the senior generation did not grow older would have its disadvantages that could only be overcome by endless expansion, if the hominidae were not to become a second version of the saurs. Almost she started her own trajectory in that expansion right then; almost, she fled. But Elizabeth saw her and smiled, and Susan pushed through and rushed forward. She hugged Elizabeth and Gregor, everyone babbled for a bit, and then became serious again. The conversation with the President resumed, slightly out of Susan's earshot.

Susan slid a finger under her hair and switched on her recording equipment. Her channel might as well get some benefit from her proximity. As Susan watched her parents talking to Julia de Zama and to the President's new security adviser, a memorably forgettable-looking man called Gaius Gonatus, she found herself standing beside another of the President's entourage, Lydia de Tenebre. She'd met the Trader woman at some diplomatic banquet whose afterglow had been open to the press, and had interviewed her briefly. Lydia was now some kind of high official in the Space Authority, and spent much of her time, as far as Susan could make out, trying to reassure the saurs and krakens on newly arrived Trader ships, without much success so far, other than to persuade one or two saurs to remain with their skiffs. Hence, no doubt, the President's prestige vehicle.

Susan smiled sideways at Lydia, who looked as though she too had been pushed to one side.

"It's like a conspiracy," Lydia said quietly. "A conspiracy of the old against the young. Except they now have the advantage of experience, and we don't have the advantage of vigor."

Susan nodded, craning to catch what was being said, upping the gain on her mike. The voices became clearer. As she leaned closer she suddenly realized they were talking about the theicides.

"No question," her mother was saying, "it's a hard one, but we can't intervene. It's a capital crime in our code too, one of the few—"

"No!" Susan's outcry was involuntary, turning heads, raising eyebrows. She broke into the charmed circle and confronted her mother.

"You can't let them carry out the executions!" she said. "You can't let them kill Salasso!"

Elizabeth looked at her sadly. "I can and will," she said. "Look, I'm sorry, Susan. I loved that saur, and Matt I liked and Volkov I could, well, I could stand, but it's out of my hands, it's out of the President's hands. We can't let theicide go unpunished. The precedent is too dangerous. There are some crimes that can't be forgiven. That's why we have the category of heinous crimes, and theicide is one of them—in the Bright Star Cultures too."

"But everything else is changing around us," Susan protested. "The

Multipliers, they're changing everything, they're changing us. They've changed you. Why can't we change the law, or at least recognize that this time it was justified?"

"That's exactly why we can't change it," said Elizabeth. "It's very difficult to maintain our humanity. The Multiplier outlook literally infiltrates us. We have their worldview in our blood. There is a continuous option to simply dissolve into Spiders, if not physically then culturally. For that reason we maintain our own laws with scrupulous severity. And we are not going to interfere with New Babylon's."

Susan's vision of Elizabeth blurred. She felt as though she had been punched in the stomach by this stranger who could have been her sister. Her father's face was more concerned but, with its tracery of smoothed-out creases, too frighteningly reminiscent of Matt's to be of any comfort.

"*What* bloody humanity?" Susan shouted. "Just because *you're* the Science Officer doesn't make you—"

"Don't lose it with me," Elizabeth said, in a flat, calm voice. It was an order Susan had last heard at the age of nine. It infuriated her to hear it now, but it had its effect, a cold blade in the belly.

Susan blinked hard, clenching her fists at her sides. "You've lost it already," she said. "Your humanity."

She knew this was not true. It was a stone to hand, and she threw it, and she could see the hurt and she didn't care. She could see right through her mother to the omnipresent deity infinitely greater than the gods, and she could not see why Elizabeth couldn't see it too, in her and in the condemned. Or did she, she thought wildly, and did it make no difference?

Susan whirled on de Zama. The young-old President was a very strange-looking person, her smooth skin thin and shining, like the paper of a lantern over her bones.

"Can't you at least use your gods-damned prerogative, Madame? Can't you give clemency? Surely you still feel something for Volkov, he was your partner"—*in crime*, she almost said—"for fifty years or longer, and you have already killed him once! Isn't that enough?"

"For that very reason I cannot give clemency," said de Zama, quite unperturbed by Susan's flaming disrespect. "People would say it was personal. And I cannot give clemency to the other two without giving it to Grigory Andreievich. In any case, when the people have spoken, and the Senate has spoken, and all the world knows what the Notables will say, it would be a foolish President who cast the prerogative in their teeth. There would be a constitutional crisis, which with things as they are we cannot afford." She spread her hands. "With the best will in the world I could not do it."

And you do not have the best will in the world!

Susan turned and walked away, out through the inner circle and the growing crowd. She had just reached the area of devastation at the bottom of Astronaut Avenue when Lydia caught up with her.

"I can't stand it either," Lydia said. "Come on—we can't stand for this, we can do something."

She seemed furious and determined, standing there in the grey dust, incongruous in a fluttery, flower-printed silk trouser-suit and platform shoes.

"What *can* we do?" Susan asked.

"We have experienced the Multiplier enlightenment," said Lydia. "We can think of something."

"So have they!" said Susan. "Much good it does them!"

Lydia laid a hand on her arm. "That's no reason for us not to use our heads. Come on."

"Where? Where is there to go?"

Susan sniffed noisily and wiped her nose on her sleeve. She felt disgusted with herself. She switched the recording gear off. Lydia put an arm around her shoulders, and that made them start to shake. Susan willed their shaking to stop, but it didn't. Lydia said nothing for a while. When Susan opened her eyes again, Lydia was regarding her soberly. Susan blinked away the rainbow effects on her eyelashes, sniffled noisily again, smiled weakly.

"I don't know about me," said Lydia, "but you could use a drink."

Susan took a deep breath. "Oh, yes."

Lydia led Susan around a corner into one of the relatively undamaged shorefront streets, to a drinking den called The New Moon's Arms. The sign that swung above the door was a stylized orbital fort, petaled with solar power panels, bristling with weaponry.

"Old malcontent hangout," Lydia said as she held the door open. "I suppose it's still bugged." She laughed suddenly. "This time it'll be Gonatus who will be listening."

It was almost empty, and the barman was watching television, agog at the landings, begrudging the attention it took to pour them drinks. The pictures flickered silently; he was listening in with earphones.

"Amazing," he kept saying. "Amazing. A great day."

"A great day," Lydia agreed. She bought a clinking double handful of bottles. Susan turned away to sit down. Lydia caught her elbow.

"Outside," she said.

They returned to Astronaut Avenue and sat down with their backs against one of the Volkov plinths. A selkie, walking past, glanced down at them from its swaying height, then strolled on, rubbernecking. Lydia wrenched the tops off two of the bottles. The drinks were sugarcane spirit diluted with a bittersweet juice. It tasted rough.

"What was that about Gonatus?" Susan asked. She had to talk about something else for a while. They would get back to what they had to talk about soon enough. From here, the prison island was visible on the horizon.

"I first met him last year," Lydia said, "about the time you people showed up. I took him to that bar back there for what I thought was a secure enough chat. I was a malcontent and he was an Illyrian spy. Still is, I suppose."

"Perhaps I should file that story with Junopolis Calls," said Susan, with a shaky laugh. "Give them one scoop at least, having missed today's big news."

"Oh, they'll know," said Lydia. "They'll spike it."

"You know my employers better than I do?"

"Yes," said Lydia, unabashed. "I've lived here longer than you have. A hell of a lot longer. It's not like good old free-wheeling, free-thinking Mingulay. They have security apparats here that go back to deep antiquity. And the Illyrian one, remember, is just a chunk of the old Nova Babylonian one that broke away."

"And Gonatus has just changed departments?"

Lydia smiled sourly. "Yes, you could see it like that. He's an interesting guy, in his way. Very intense, very sincere, strange though it is to say about a spy."

"What was his interest in you?"

"Well, I worked in the Space Authority, I had been in the Bright Star Cultures, and I had known Volkov."

They looked at each other. Susan put her drink down. The bottle drummed momentarily as it touched the pavement. "I think you have some explaining to do," she said.

After a while she interrupted and said: "You were once in love with Gregor? My *father*?"

"Yes," said Lydia. "Well, maybe, but . . . anyway, that's why it was so weird just now, seeing him just as he was when I knew him twelve years ago."

"Twelve—oh, right. I see. I think."

Susan pulled out a notebook—it was a local one, made from paper, which, as Matt had once said, sure cracked the screen-resolution problem—and started writing names and drawing lines.

"Fuck," she said. "It's lucky none of you had a sexually transmissible disease."

Susan opened another bottle. The pain of her parents' refusal to intervene was still like a coiled snake in her belly. The alcohol was stunning it, but it would come back. She would vomit it out.

"So is this why you want to save them?"

"No," said Lydia, bleakly. "I want to save them because they were right. They don't deserve to end up against a wall."

"A wall is what all this feels like," said Susan. She knocked the back of her head on the plinth. It hurt a little. "And I'm bashing my head against it."

"Every wall has its weak points."

"The weakest point I can see," Susan said, "and the only one we can work on directly, is their bloody-minded refusal to escape." She clenched her fist in front of her. Her knuckles were grazed, she noticed from a distance. She looked out past the docks and the harbor to the island. "They could do it, you know. I could raise enough Multis to lift them off within minutes. But they'd have to be dragged, because they think they'd lose the argument by fleeing."

"Fuck them and their fucking arguments," said Lydia vehemently. "They'd rather die than lose, and they can't win. It's not a political argument, it's not even a cultural one, it's a . . . I don't know, a superstition. How is it that we can see past that, and the Multis can, and our friends themselves can, and most people can't? When did we lose our respect for the gods? How did we lose our fear?" She nibbled at her lower lip. "I don't remember, myself. I haven't feared the gods since I was a little girl. Not since after my first journey."

Susan frowned. "Space travel?" she said. "Lightspeed jumps? That's what we all have in common. Even the Marines who went along with our attack on the god."

Lydia shook her head. "Doesn't work. Your parents—"

"My parents don't fear the gods! They're just committed to the law taking its course for political reasons, cultural reasons. They think there's a line to hold—damn them."

"You're right," said Lydia. "And Esias and Faustina and all my family, even Voronar, an old saur who stuck around with us, they don't have that horror either, and they're pretty conservative. I mean, apart

from Faustina"—she waved a finger at Susan's scribbled diagram—
"they'd be happy to see Volkov shot, they detested what he did to this
city, and Salasso and Matt mean nothing to them, but they don't *exe-
crate* them like everyone seems to be assuming everyone does."

Susan thought over all the buzz and mutter she'd heard in the past
months, weeks, hours. "Well, about everybody else, they're right."

"*Vox populi, vox Dei*, huh?" Lydia said bitterly.

The voice of the people is the voice of God. Which people, and
which god?

"That's it," said Susan, with a cold feeling like water down her
back. "That is it."

"What is?"

"The answer. It is space travel. I mean, I can see how it might be."

She felt a sudden surge of relief, perhaps no more than a rebound
from her earlier dismay and despair, but it was something to feel hope
again. She jumped up and drained her bottle and hurled it to crash on
the rubble, and reached down to grab Lydia by the hand. "Come on,
get up. We have to talk to some of the Bright Star Culture people. If
I'm right, they'll feel the same as we do."

She fell over. Lydia helped her up and made to go back to the area
around Port Station One.

"Not back there," Susan said. "One of the small parks."

Taking a complex route through side alleys to circle around the area
of destruction and reconstruction, Lydia led the way unerringly to the
nearest park. A Bright Star Culture ship squatted there, and around it
stalls had been set up, by the humans and saurs and Multipliers on board
and by those of the locals whose entrepreneurial talents had emerged
from under the overturned bushel of the Modern Regime.

Lydia said: "This is just like something I saw before, on Novakkad.
We're becoming a Bright Star Culture already."

"How long do you think trade will last, when the Multis can reproduce anything?"

Lydia looked at her sideways. "Good question. What the ships end
up selling is space travel, and the access to space to gather the exotica
to make more ships."

Susan grinned. "Good."

"Why?"

"I'll tell you later."

They walked over and started talking to the Traders. Almost every
one of the new arrivals were shocked at what was being done to people

whom they regarded—once the background had been quickly filled in—as heroes. Many of them hadn't even known about the advance expedition, and how it had saved them from being blasted from the skies as soon as they emerged from the jump. With the locals it was a different story entirely.

"These three?" The man they bought coffee from drew a finger across his throat. "They should have been shot months ago." He leaned closer. "You know, it's safe to say now, I always admired old Volkov, got that from my own old man, real old Modernist he was. But now, gods above—" He caught himself and chuckled nervously. "So to speak. Volkov and the others *killed a god*. The sooner they're rotting in Traitors' Pit, the better for all of us."

With that, quite unselfconsciously, he looked up and shivered.

"Hmm," said Susan. "Thanks for sharing your thoughts."

They wandered on. The coffee didn't really sober Susan, and she became less discreet in her questions. After one particularly awkward moment, the two women had to flee the park.

"Are we satisfied?" said Lydia, as they emerged halfway up Astronaut Avenue after running a kilometer through a warren of apartment blocks. Traffic was getting back to normal, but people were still hanging around and talking a lot. The early edition newspapers were being so eagerly snatched up that Susan felt vaguely in dereliction of duty.

Susan ducked her head around the corner. No signs of pursuit. "I don't know," she said, a little short of breath, heart pounding, "but I think we're safe."

"Good," said Lydia, putting her shoes back on as the cuts in her feet cleaned themselves. "Now, can you tell me what difference this is going to make?"

Susan told her. "It's Lithos," she said. "It's the god in the world, the god under our feet." She looked down and swayed. Lydia steadied her. "The gods in all the worlds. They fuck with our heads. It's only by space travel that we break the bond. You see?"

Lydia shook her head. "I don't see what difference it makes, except to make things worse. Nothing we do can make people who've never traveled through space change their minds about theicide."

Susan looked at her. Gods, the woman could be so stupid sometimes.

"Exactly," she said, straightening up and letting go of Lydia's arm and walking on very steadily. "So there's no need for our friends to die if it won't change anything."

"I think we can sell them that," Lydia said. "That one will fly." Her expression became distant, calculating. "Or if not that, something else. Do you have a phone number for any of the *Investigator* crew?"

"Oh, sure, I have them all."

Lydia jerked a thumb toward a newly repaired public phone stall. "Call them now."

"You aren't thinking of—"

"Maybe," said Lydia, "but the first thing we have to do is check this out with your friend Mr. Orange. Come to think of it," she added, "a lift to the island by skiff would not go amiss."

The Prison Department guards might have challenged and surrounded an autogyro, and impounded an unauthorized boat. They had a healthy respect for a Multiplier skiff. They let it land between the huts and didn't so much as give a dirty look to Susan, Lydia, and Mr. Orange. Matt, Volkov, and Salasso were easily enough spotted, strolling by the cliff at the far end of the small island.

Susan's heart sank a little at their eager expressions. They had affected fatalism, but they must have placed a lot of hope in the arrival of the Bright Star Cultures. She gave them the news of Elizabeth's unwavering decision.

"I'm sorry," she said.

"Bitch," said Matt.

"Bourgeois," said Volkov. He made it sound a nastier epithet than Matt's.

Salasso took it more stoically. "People change," he said.

"Let's find somewhere to sit down," Susan said. "Mr. Orange has something to tell you. There's a way out of this."

There was a windbreak shelter with benches and a table, built by prisoners, a hundred meters away. As they headed for it Matt rushed off to the hut. He came back with a pot of coffee and some mugs. The Multiplier draped itself across the supports like a gibbon and leaned down, its speaking mouth forward, and delivered its usual wheezy breathless ramble. People, saurs, everybody who lived on planets, it explained, were influenced by the minds in those planets and formed attachments to them. Only space travel could break those attachments. In the long run many more people would travel in space and would lose their fear of the gods. To die for the sake of not fearing the gods was both superfluous and futile.

"We thought you knew," said Mr. Orange.

The two men and the saur stared at Mr. Orange for a few moments.

"Fuck off," said Matt at last. "What difference does it make, if the space-going people have a rational attitude and the others don't? It's the others who have decided to kill us, and I am not going to let them off that hook. Let them see the consequences of their actions and their beliefs. That's what a public stoning is *for*! It's not to deter the wicked, it's to deter the righteous. You should know that, Susan. You were raised a gods-dammed Scoffer."

'Well, I was not!' said Lydia. She slammed a fist on the table. "I was raised a good Stoic, and I *became* a Volkovist. No thanks to you, Grigory, but behind all your Communist claptrap there was something great. And there is still something great there, in the Space Defense cadre who still look up to you. And in the new traders, the Bright Star people, and the Multipliers. Between them they have the power to rescue you, not to run away and hide but to defy the world and all the superstitious gods-fearing bastards that live on it like nits in its hair."

Volkov folded his arms. "And then what? Another revolution from above? I've lived through three already, two of them my fault. I'm not doing it again. Enough people have died here, and not only here. Enough."

"Adding three more deaths won't help," said Susan.

Volkov snorted. "It's not a question of what *helps*."

Susan turned to Salasso. "You can see it, can't you?" she pleaded. "You've tried to change minds, and now you know why you couldn't. It's not political, it's not cultural, it's a physical influence. You could—"

The saur's sneer was thinner than the men's, but no less scornful.

"Take my people on day trips to space?" His mouth stretched sideways a few millimeters. "Most of them are already in space, and no doubt on their way to fight the gods' battles somewhere else."

Susan felt herself shaking inside again, and tears escaping through that treacherous instability. She turned it to anger, and the anger away from herself.

"You can't just sit here and wait to die!" she said. "What honor or defiance is there in that? It's just the same wretched passivity you say you're fighting against. Go away—*come* away! Join the Multiplier migration, join *us*. There's no need to hide now, we're here, and we're going away."

She did not know if she meant that. She was too various. It was the small offspring within her talking, just as her mother had feared. It was what her mother was fighting. She could almost sympathize; or rather, she could, and she could not.

"You might have a point," said Matt, reluctantly. His voice sounded as if it was being dragged out with hooks. "I mean, why push it, if these people can't change no matter what—"

The skiff came out of nowhere—not out of a jump, but out of an aerial manouevre so fast that its hull glowed red as it halted right beside them. The shock wave was still rocking the gazebo as a dozen heavily-armed men jumped out and surrounded them, plasma rifles leveled.

One of the men removed his helmet to reveal a pair of earphones, which he likewise removed.

"You were right, Lydia," said Gaius Gonatus. "We're still listening."

The sun was in their eyes and they had disdained the offer of blindfolds. Susan was at the front of the crowd, with the other reporters. She could zoom her camera, zoom the mike, and watch and hear them all. It was only her concentration on this, her fierce determination that her draft of history would be the one to get through all the edits and be in all the books and tapes about the event, that kept her from weeping. That and the thought that weeping would be self-indulgent, because she was not mourning the two men and the saur. She would be weeping for the loss of her mother, who in clinging to her humanity had become inhumane.

The officer with three black cloths over his wrist was holding out two packets. "Hemp or tobacco?"

"I'll go for a joint," said Volkov.

"Let's share it and a cigarette," said Matt.

"All right."

"I think I wish to die consciously," said Salasso. "Hemp would tend to prevent that. Therefore, I will take a cigarette. I have on occasion wondered what their attraction is."

"They're bad for your health," said Matt, predictably.

They accepted the officer's offer of a light, and he returned to the squad. "You may address the public while you smoke," he said.

Volkov and Matt glanced at each other. Matt shrugged and waved his cigarette. They swapped their smokes around.

"I wish I respected you all enough to despise you," Volkov said to the outstretched microphones and to the world. "But you aren't worth it. You have chosen to become part of an alien culture. That is your

Coda: State of Play

T HERE IS NO meanwhile. But, across a hundred thousand years and light-years, the events of A.C. 10,350 and the Seasonally Adjusted Year of Our Lord 2360 were approximately in step with the year A.D. 2362.

In the year A.D. 2357 the god in the asteroid 10049 Lora made one of its regular close approaches to Earth; and, as had become customary, a delegation from the Military Subcommittee of the Executive Committee of the Solar Commonwealth came out to visit and consult. Their skiffs hovered above its pitted surface, gently docking with the vast web of the interface that gave them access to the wealth of information in its many minds.

Greetings were exchanged, something that the humans managed through the combined actions of a myriad quantum computers and the god with the equivalent of the twitch of a toe. With some slightly higher-level processing it conveyed its thanks and congratulations on the defeat of the octopod invasion. The humans acknowledged that the war against the Spiders had been long and terrible, but that driving the alien invaders from the Solar System had been worth the cost. They mentioned the cost with a certain urgency. The long-term damage to Earth's atmosphere and biosphere, and the losses to the many habitats across the system, had been substantial and painful.

The god thought they were taking a very short-term view, given that habitats could be replaced within decades and the atmosphere and biosphere restored to something like equilibrium within a million years. It did not, however, convey this thought to the delegation. Much as it appreciated their defense, and much as it appreciated their cooperation in maintaining a blessed radio silence throughout the system—their

choice. What will you do when the next alien culture comes along, one which may be less easily adapted to? You will have to fight, as I taught you to fight. I hope I taught you well."

He looked as though he was about to throw the diminished cigarette on the ground, but Matt reached out for it and passed him the hemp.

"Ah," said Matt, exhaling gratefully, "there's nothing like a butt for a roach. If you're looking for words of wisdom from me, you can fucking forget it. I've had a good run and I have no complaints. Volkov was defending the human race according to his lights, and so was I. Come on, man, give Salasso that roach."

"Thank you," said Salasso, taking it and sucking hard. "The small quantity remaining should not affect my lucidity. Tell Bishlayan I love her, and tell Delavar I quite liked him, on the whole. As for most of the rest of my species, they have feared the gods, they feared the hominidae, and now they fear the Multipliers. I have shown that I feared none of them. I have killed a god, I have had friends among the hominidae, including Matt and including Elizabeth and Gregor, and when my blood runs out it will be full of Spiders."

"Gods above, Salasso," said Matt, "you never told—"

The rifles, as ever, had the last word.